The Complete Works of
WASHINGTON
IRVING

Richard Dilworth Rust

General Editor

TALES OF A TRAVELLER
BY GEOFFREY CRAYON, GENT.

Washington Irving in 1824, Paris

WASHINGTON IRVING

TALES OF A TRAVELLER

BY GEOFFREY CRAYON, GENT.

Edited by
Judith Giblin Haig

(With the Cooperation of
Brom Weber and David S. Wilson)

Twayne Publishers

Boston

1987

Published by Twayne Publishers
A Division of G.K. Hall & Co.

Copyright © 1987 by
G.K. Hall & Co.

The Complete Works of Washington Irving
Volume X

CENTER FOR EDITIONS OF
AMERICAN AUTHORS

AN APPROVED TEXT

MODERN LANGUAGE
ASSOCIATION OF AMERICA

®

Library of Congress Cataloging-in-Publication Data

Irving, Washington, 1783–1859.
    Tales of a traveller / by Geoffrey Crayon, Gent. ; edited by Judith Giblin Haig ; with
the cooperation of Brom Weber and David S. Wilson.
        p.   cm. — (The Complete works of Washington Irving ; v. 10)
    ISBN 0-8057-8515-9
    I. Haig, Judith Giblin. II. Title. III. Series: Irving, Washington, 1783–1859.
Works. 1969 ; v. 10
PS2070.A2H35 1987
818'.207—dc19   87-20888
                                                                                                                CIP

Manufactured in the United States of America

For Robert Haig

ACKNOWLEDGMENTS

Work toward a critical edition of *Tales of a Traveller* began eighteen years ago at the University of Wisconsin at Madison, first home of *The Complete Works of Washington Irving*. From 1970–1978 it proceeded at the University of California at Davis under the direction of Brom Weber and David S. Wilson, who graciously supplied photocopies, microfilm, and their collations when the project was moved to the University of North Carolina at Chapel Hill. Relevant texts were entirely recollated there, largely through the efforts of students in the graduate course in bibliography and textual criticism. Their contribution has been invaluable. My efforts as editor began in 1981 and have been aided by a Faculty Summer Research Grant from the University of South Carolina and a National Endowment for the Humanities grant to *The Complete Works*. Many institutions have contributed their resources: Houghton Library of Harvard University, New York Public Library, the Bodleian Library, the Library of Congress, and the libraries of the University of Wisconsin at Madison, the University of Chicago, the University of Illinois, Duke University, and Wesleyan University. Particular thanks are due Holly Hall, Head of Special Collections at Washington University in St. Louis; Edmund Berkeley, Jr., Curator, and Gregory A. Johnson, Senior Public Services Assistant, of the Manuscripts Department at Alderman Library, University of Virginia; Sue Hodson, Curator of Manuscripts, Henry E. Huntington Library; and Hollee Haswell, Librarian of Sleepy Hollow Restorations. I am also grateful for the assistance of Professors Laurence G. Avery, Robert A. Bain, Edwin T. Bowden, Jo Ann Boydston, Harold I. Shapiro, Joseph S. Wittig, Paul M. Zall, and, especially, of Richard D. Rust, General Editor and generous friend.

J. G. H.

University of South Carolina, Columbia

CONTENTS

ACKNOWLEDGMENTS viii
INTRODUCTION xiii

TALES OF A TRAVELLER

To the Reader 2

PART I, STRANGE STORIES BY A NERVOUS GENTLEMAN

The Great Unknown 9
The Hunting Dinner 10
The Adventure of My Uncle 13
The Adventure of My Aunt 22
The Bold Dragoon, or the Adventure of My Grandfather . . . 25
The Adventure of the German Student 32
The Adventure of the Mysterious Picture 36
The Adventure of the Mysterious Stranger 42
The Adventure of the Young Italian 48

PART II, BUCKTHORNE AND HIS FRIENDS

Literary Life 71
A Literary Dinner 72
The Club of Queer Fellows 75
The Poor Devil Author 79
Notoriety 92
A Practical Philosopher 94
Buckthorne, or the Young Man of Great Expectations . . . 95
Grave Reflections of a Disappointed Man 128
The Booby Squire 131
The Strolling Manager 135

PART III, THE ITALIAN BANDITTI

The Inn at Terracina 149
The Adventure of the Little Antiquary 158
The Belated Travellers 164
The Adventure of the Popkins Family 176
The Painter's Adventure 179
The Story of the Bandit Chieftain 186
The Story of the Young Robber 194
The Adventure of the Englishman 202

PART IV, THE MONEY DIGGERS

Hell Gate 211
Kidd the Pirate 213

THE DEVIL AND TOM WALKER 217
WOLFERT WEBBER, OR GOLDEN DREAMS 227
THE ADVENTURE OF THE BLACK FISHERMAN 243

EDITORIAL APPENDIX

LIST OF ABBREVIATIONS 267
EXPLANATORY NOTES 268
TEXTUAL COMMENTARY 281
DISCUSSIONS OF ADOPTED READINGS 318
LIST OF EMENDATIONS 330
LIST OF REJECTED SUBSTANTIVES 397
LIST OF COMPOUND WORDS HYPHENATED AT ENDS OF LINES 430

FRONTISPIECE

Anonymous engraving reproduced from the Bibliophile Society's edition of
The Journals of Washington Irving (Boston, 1919).

INTRODUCTION

Tales of a Traveller is a pivotal work in the career of America's first literary celebrity. "[I]t is written in a different mood from my late works," Irving noted shortly after its publication. "For my own part," he added, "I think there are in it some of the best things I have ever written. They may not be so highly finished as some of my former writings, but they are touched off with a freer spirit, and are more true to life. . . ."[1] The differences that Irving construed as strengths, his immediate critical audience would see as weaknesses. Acutely sensitive to unenthusiastic, occasionally hostile reviews of *Tales*, he would turn from experiments with fiction to history and biography—the work of the final phase of his career.

Irving's confidence that the collection contained some of his "best things" has been borne out in the high regard accorded the most often reprinted of the tales: "The Bold Dragoon," "The Adventure of the German Student," and "The Devil and Tom Walker." In most respects, though, *Tales* was destined to disappoint. Irving's public expected a sketch book based on his year-long odyssey in Germany; he gave them instead a four-part miscellany of short fiction, his most extensive specimen of the genre in which American literary historians would regard him as a pioneer.[2] Unlike *The Sketch Book* (1820) and *Bracebridge Hall* (1822), which seemed largely products of leisurely inquiry into the literature and legends of the past, *Tales* was written rapidly and under great pressure, assembled from anecdotes in common circulation or derived from friends.

Irving acknowledged the haste and "freer spirit" in his preface, using the metaphor that a traveller's tales resemble "odds and ends" of "heterogeneous matters" jumbled together "as the articles are apt to be in an ill packed travelling trunk."[3] To the extent that the "freer spirit" included elements of comedy and melodrama not previously associated with the genteel Geoffrey Crayon, Irving provoked censorship from his English publisher and censure from critics. The pressures which attended the composition, publication, and reception of *Tales* produced a crisis that indelibly marked Irving's life and career.

---

1. Washington Irving, *Letters*, vol. 2, *1823–1838*, ed. Ralph M. Aderman, Herbert L. Kleinfield, and Jenifer S. Banks (Boston: Twayne, 1979), p. 76. This portion of the letter to his sister is dated September 20, 1824. *Tales* was published in August 1824.

2. See, particularly, Fred Lewis Pattee, *The Development of the American Short Story* (New York: Harper & Brothers, 1923).

3. Below, p. 4.

Tales was not the collection Irving had planned to write or that his publisher and public anticipated. Always fearful of raising expectations too high, Irving was careful to restrict news of his projects until publication had begun. He was, however, an acclaimed author whose activities and movements were newsworthy. His tour of Germany, which included eight months in Dresden as a favorite of the court of Frederick Augustus, King of Saxony (December 1822 to July 1823), encouraged the expectation in both the United States and England of a collection of German sketches and tales.

Irving was himself committed to such a project. As early as 1818, he had begun to study German with an eye toward its utility: "It is a severe task, and has required hard study; but the rich mine of German Literature holds forth abundant reward," he wrote his friend Henry Brevoort.[4] Just setting out on his journey in 1822, Irving wrote Thomas W. Storrow of his plan "to get into the confidence of every old woman I meet with in Germany and get from her, her budget of wonderful stories."[5] His notebooks for the early months of his tour show him stockpiling accounts of landscapes, legends, and characters discovered en route.

Once established in Dresden, he began taking lessons in German but did little or no writing toward the proposed sketch book. That he was still committed to the project a year later seems clear from his remarks to his brother Peter after returning to Paris in the fall of 1823: "I have been thinking over the German subjects. It will take me a little time to get hold of them properly, as I must read a little and digest the plan and nature of them in my mind. There are such quantities of these legendary and romantic tales now littering from the press both in England and Germany, that one must take care not to fall into the commonplace of the day."[6] More than a reluctance to follow fashion, Irving's temporizing, he confided, was caused by "an affair of the nerves, a kind of reaction in consequence of coming to a state of repose after so long moving about, and produced also by the anxious feeling on resuming literary pursuits."[7]

Irving apparently abandoned the plan in mid-December 1823 after a frustrating period of trying to "commence work on Germany,"[8] which resulted only in a sketch of Heidelberg Castle, later discarded, and troubled nights out of which he awoke "full of doubts as to literary prospects."[9] "Woke ear-

4. Washington Irving, *Letters*, vol. 1, *1802–1823*, ed. Ralph M. Aderman, Herbert L. Kleinfield, and Jenifer S. Banks (Boston: Twayne, 1978), p. 526.

5. Ibid., I, 692.

6. *Letters*, II, 5.

7. Ibid., II, 4.

8. Washington Irving, *Journals and Notebooks*, vol. 3, *1819–1827*, ed. Walter A. Reichart (Madison: Univ. of Wisconsin Press, 1970), p. 254.

9. Ibid., III, 257.

ly—felt depressed & desponding—suddenly a thot struck me how to arrange the Mss. on hand so as to make 2 vols of Sketch Book—that quite enlivened me. . . ."[10] Even though he wrote his English publisher John Murray II just before Christmas 1823 promising the work for the spring, Irving had not yet struck upon the plan or type of work which would become *Tales of a Traveller*.[11] He had, in fact, very little confidence in the material "on hand." Temporarily, he set to work on a series of sketches about French and English character eventually published as "Sketches in Paris in 1825" in *The Knickerbocker; or, New-York Monthly Magazine* (1840) and collected in *Wolfert's Roost* (1855).

What caused him to abandon the German work we cannot know with certainty. The belief long prevailed that despondency over a failed romance crippled Irving's literary prospects in Paris in 1823–1824. Evidence that came to light in 1863 suggests that Irving's intimacy with the family of Mrs. John Foster, an Englishwoman residing in Dresden for the education of her children, culminated when he proposed marriage to one of the daughters, eighteen-year-old Emily Foster, and was refused. Though Irving's emotional attachment to the family and to the lively Emily in particular seems clear, he confided no hint of a proposal, its rejection, or subsequent depression to his journals or in surviving letters. Biographer Stanley T. Williams believes that frustrated affection for Emily Foster was only a contributing factor in the agitation and melancholy that delayed Irving's work.[12] Williams, always less than adulatory, assigns the cause of Irving's troubles to a failure of nerve and self-discipline: "[H]e could not overcome the dread of not matching his earlier achievements. In 1819 he had everything to gain, and nothing to lose; now, so he thought, the reverse was true."[13]

The planned sketch book was thwarted in one instance not so much by fear of failure as by the prospects of success on another front. Spurred by

10. Ibid., III, 258.

11 *Letters*, II, 26. At least one idea appears to have died for lack of Murray's cooperation. Irving, in this letter and two others, asked for manuscripts of Arabian tales" Murray had once shown him. "I have always felt an inclination towards those Mss: and a persuasion that I could make something out of them worth your publishing," Irving wrote on his first request (*Letters*, II, 16). Ben Harris McClary speculates the manuscripts might have comprised a translation of *The Arabian Nights* Murray could have acquired when he purchased the bookseller William Miller's stock at 50 Albemarle Street. See McClary, ed., *Washington Irving and the House of Murray: Geoffrey Crayon Charms the British, 1817–1856* (Knoxville: Univ. of Tennessee Press, 1969), p. 48n.

12. Stanley T. Williams, *The Life of Washington Irving*, 2 vols. (New York: Oxford Univ. Press, 1935), I, 236–54.

13. Ibid., I, 265. For a qualification of this view, see Judith G. Haig, "Washington Irving and the Romance of Travel," *The Old and New World Romanticism of Washington Irving*, ed. Stanley Brodwin (Westport, CT: Greenwood, 1986), pp. 61–68.

his own deep interest in the stage and the success of small private entertainments throughout his stay in Dresden, Irving was drawn into a series of theatrical experiments. He collaborated with Colonel Barham Livius in spring and early summer of 1823 on translating the German operas *Abu Hassan* and *Der Freischütz* into English. By the time he reached Paris, both projects were nearly complete. There, his interest persisting, he began to assist John Howard Payne in revising and adapting French plays for the London stage. In both collaborations, Irving wished to remain an anonymous partner.[14]

Only his recognition of financial need turned him from playwriting to his sketches and tales. Four days after having written John Murray a second letter promising two volumes in the spring, Irving wrote Payne, "I am sorry to say I cannot afford to write any more for the theatres. The experiment has satisfied me that I never should in any wise be compensated for my time & trouble. I speak not with any reference to my talents; but to the market prices my productions will command in other departments of literature. . . . My long interval of travelling, and the time expended in these dramatic experiments have thrown me quite behind hand, both as to pecuniary & literary affairs & I am now applying myself to make up for it; but I shall run low in purse before I can get a work ready for publication. . . ."[15]

Resolution did not yield results. He complained in a letter to the painter Charles R. Leslie on February 8, 1824, of a month-long "fit of sterility . . . that throws me all aback, and discourages me as to the hope of getting ready for a Spring appearance." The letter reveals that a plan for *Tales* had begun to suggest itself, though its form was not yet clear. His primary stock of material, he told Leslie, consisted of "a Dutch story" and "my history of an author," which he planned to divide into separate sections and distribute "through the two volumes."[16] The Dutch story, a draft of "Wolfert Webber," became the centerpiece of Part IV of *Tales*. "History of an Author" was Irving's title for a lengthy manuscript about Buckthorne, the central character in Part II. Irving had, at Leslie's suggestion, kept the manuscript back during the publication of *Bracebridge Hall* with the design of expanding it into a novel but had barely touched it.[17] He admitted to Leslie that he was at an impasse: "I am at this moment in a sad heartless mood and nothing seems

14. *Letters*, II, 25, 27–28. Walter A. Reichart's chapter "The Aspiring Dramatist" (in *Washington Irving and Germany* [Ann Arbor: Univ. of Michigan Press, 1957], pp. 121–36) provides a thorough account of this phase of Irving's career.

15. Ibid., II, 34–36.

16. Ibid., II, 37.

17. For the early history of the "Buckthorne" manuscript, see Williams, I, 204, or Pierre Munro Irving, *The Life and Letters of Washington Irving*, 4 vols. (New York: Putnam, 1862–1864), II, 55.

to present to rouse me out of it."[18] A week later, quite by accident, the tide turned.

On February 15, Irving's friend Thomas Medwin, the cousin and biographer of Shelley, read from the "journal of a painter" who had been imprisoned by "robbers near Rome."[19] The next morning, Irving heard anecdotes that further ignited his interest from William Foy, himself a painter recently returned from Italy. He went home and began to write. What he appears to have gleaned from these two encounters was inspiration for Parts I and III of *Tales*. The "Italian story" Irving seems to have had in mind as he recorded his progress in his journal became the trio of stories in Part I called "The Adventure of the Mysterious Picture," "The Adventure of the Mysterious Stranger," and "The Story of the Young Italian."[20] Within the week, he had a fair start on these as well as four other stories in Part I. The next week, beginning February 23, he sketched the "robber tales" of Part III, including "The Painter's Adventure," translated from Medwin's source.[21] In the days ahead, Irving wrote steadily and continued to mine the memories of his friends for anecdotes and descriptions of Italy.[22]

A considerable number of the stories benefited from just this kind of adventitious or hastily assimilated material. A long footnote in "The Adventure of the Little Antiquary" may owe its inception to a conversation with his friend Frank Mills about the legendary Pelasgian cities.[23] An encounter with a "cursed bore" of an Italian improvisatore at a party may have provided Irving the model for the would-be Roman tale teller at "The Inn at Terracina."[24] An account of a bandit attack on the consul at Naples supplied by Count Grégoire Vladimirovich Orlov also found its way into Part III of *Tales*.[25] In a similar manner he would embellish his story of "Kidd the Pirate" in Part IV with information supplied by Colonel Thomas Aspinwall, American consul-general in London.[26] Irving had in addition to these conversa-

18. *Lettera*, II, 38.

19. *Journals*, III, 289.

20. Ibid., III, 290–92.

21. Ibid., III, 296. Although Irving says in his preface to *Tales* (p. 4, below) that he took the story from "an authentic narrative in manuscript," Walter A. Reichart has identified Medwin's source as a published account: "Die Schicksale des Malers Salathe unter den Räuberbanden in den Appenninen, von ihm selbst erzählt." See *Washington Irving and Germany*, p. 155.

22. Nathalia Wright proposes that Irving drew as well from his own early journal of travel in Italy, 1804–1805: "Irving's Use of His Italian Experience in *Tales of a Traveller*: The Beginning of an American Tradition," *American Literature*, 31 (May 1959), 191–96.

23. *Journals*, III, 290.

24. Ibid., III, 328.

25. Ibid., III, 316.

26. Ibid., III, 326.

tional sources access to the Bibliothèque Nationale, a five-minute walk from
his lodgings at 89 Rue Richelieu, from which he withdrew books to provide
background material about Italy and to add touches of French history in
"The Adventure of My Uncle."

When he first offered Murray a "brace more of Volumes of the Sketch
Book in the course of the spring," Irving claimed, "I am already far advanced
in them."[27] At that time his statement was more wish than fact. Three
months later, replying to Murray's offer of 1200 guineas for the new work,
Irving's confidence derived from six weeks' steady effort and a clear design:
"I do not regret having turned aside from my idea of preparing two more
volumes of the Sketch Book as I think I have run into a plan & thrown off
writings which will be more novel & attractive. . . . I think the title will be
'Tales of a Traveller, by Geoffrey Crayon, Gent[.]' Your offer of twelve
hundred guineas without seeing the Mss: is I confess a liberal one and made
in your own gentlemanlike manner, but I would rather you would see the
Mss: and make it *fifteen hundred*—Dont think me greedy after money—but
in fact I have need of all I can get just now. . . ."[28]

During the next two months Irving worked fitfully to finish and revise the
stories that would comprise the work's four parts. His progress was sporad-
ic—a half page of "Wolfert Webber" one day, a full morning's work on "The
Devil and Tom Walker" another.[29] Meanwhile, as he had from the start,
Irving suffered a host of distractions and interruptions. He stopped briefly
to "correct" *Salmagundi* and *A History of New York* for the French bookseller A. and W. Galignani,[30] and, during a particularly hectic period from
the middle of March to early May, he worked concurrently on "adapting" a
biography of Oliver Goldsmith as a preface in Galignani's series of British
Classics he had contracted to edit.[31]

His time was further encumbered by family responsibilities and social
engagements. He spent several sleepless nights and most of the first two
weeks in March nursing his nephew Irving Van Wart through smallpox. Irving had general supervision of two Van Wart youngsters then in boarding
school in Paris. Even in the period of his nephew's illness, Irving's social
diversions were unabated. Between February 15 and May 24, when his
work on *Tales* was at its steadiest, the journal shows only two days without

27. *Letters*, II, 26.
28. Ibid., II, 41.
29. *Journals*, III, 324, 328.
30. See Bruce I. Granger and Martha Hartzog, ed., *Letters of Jonathan Oldstyle,
Gent. / Salmagundi* (Boston: Twayne, 1977), pp. 402–405; also, Michael L. Black and Nancy
B. Black, ed., *A History of New York* (Boston: Twayne, 1984), pp. xxxvi–xxxviii.
31. See Elsie Lee West, ed., *Oliver Goldsmith: A Biography* (Boston: Twayne, 1978), pp.
xvii–xviii.

social engagements, days when he was not visiting or visited, or attending concerts, the opera, or other entertainments. Of course, a considerable portion of Irving's social life during the spring directly served his artistic purposes, providing in addition to seminal anecdotes necessary doses of reassurance. A journal entry for April 8—"Out of Spirits—distrustful of my work—particularly Robber Stories"—is followed by an entry recording Frank Mills's visit the next day and his advice "to touch up the Frenchman tale."[32]

Personal and social obligations continued to intermingle with his professional responsibilities when Irving reached London on May 28, his first visit to that city in nearly two years. On the evening of his arrival, he barely stopped to store his luggage before setting off for Covent Garden theatre to attend a performance of *Charles II; or, The Merry Monarch*, on which he had collaborated with Payne. The next afternoon, following a round of visits and a stop at the Royal Academy to view new paintings by Charles Leslie and Gilbert Stuart Newton, Irving called on Murray, who agreed to pay 1500 guineas for *Tales*, sight unseen. "In a word," Irving wrote his brother Peter, "every thing went as smoothly and pleasantly as heart could wish."[33] His exhilaration was temporary.

Not until he could escape London for the countryside was he able to concentrate on the final phase of preparing *Tales*. He spent most of June outside the city, in Southampton, Bath, and later Birmingham, preparing, revising, copying his manuscripts, and juggling the demands of transatlantic publication, sending separate parcels to London and to New York, where his brother Ebenezer acted as agent for the American edition. In this month he finished an elaboration of "Kidd the Pirate" based on additional information from Colonel Aspinwall and turned an anecdote told him by the poet Thomas Moore into "The Adventure of the German Student."[34] Meanwhile he still performed odds and ends of revision for Payne.

Returning to London early in July, Irving confronted the first of several setbacks that dogged the English edition—news that Murray intended to postpone publication until November.[35] The "danger of being anticipated by an American edition" was obviated by Murray's quick agreement to return to an August publication date. Murray "set the press hard at work," Irving reported to Peter; "I now receive proof sheets daily and can push the pub-

32. *Journals*, III, 317, 318.

33. *Letters*, II, 50.

34. *Journals*, III, 340, 353. The source of the anecdote, which Irving alludes to in his preface (p. 4, below), was Horace Smith, according to Moore: *Memoirs, Journals, and Correspondence of Thomas Moore*, 8 vols., ed. Lord John Russell (London: Longmans, 1853–1856), IV, 207–208.

35. *Journals*, III, 356.

lication as briskly as I please. . . ."[36] Irving had no fear of losing the American copyright but did not want to risk an English piracy appearing before Murray's volumes could be published. The other problems that beset the publication of *Tales* were not so readily or happily resolved.

Late in July, though he must have suspected it earlier, Irving learned that the work lacked the number of pages needed for two octavo volumes. In the space of a week he expanded the "Buckthorne" section and added two sketches, "Notoriety" and "A Practical Philosopher"; he wrote "The Belated Travellers," a rambling robber tale for Part III, and supplied a preface "To the Reader."[37] The final frustration came at a point when Irving might otherwise have considered himself finished with the "vile Book work."[38]

At the suggestion of William Gifford, editor of the *Quarterly Review* and his respected editorial adviser, John Murray asked Irving for extensive changes designed to blunt the edge of his satire on the English upper classes in Parts II and III.[39] Privately resentful of the criticism, Irving replied that his portraits were drawn from life but not designed to give offense. In a letter that bristles as it capitulates, he pronounced himself "honoured by [Gifford's] censorship."[40] With but a week remaining before his planned departure for Paris, he threw himself into the work of excising and rewriting to suit Gifford and Murray, believing he was damaging *Tales* with his final labors.

Fatigued, pursued even to the edge of the Channel by last-minute proof sheets sent from London, Irving wrote from Brighton the morning of his departure for France, "I have dragged myself out of London as a horse drags himself out of the slough or a fly out of a honey pot, almost leaving a limb behind him at every tug. Not that I have been immersed in pleasure and surrounded by sweets, but rather up to the ears in ink and harassed by printers' devils. . . . From the time I first started pen in hand on this work, it has been nothing but hard driving with me."[41]

A cryptic journal entry may refer to the prepublication history of *Tales of a Traveller* by a different metaphor: "Writers who write as fast as they travel can only throw off the frothy risings of sudden and turbid thought[.]"[42] Its composition had been forced and hectic, and Irving was rightly concerned about public reaction to the work. In taking leave of his friend Thomas

---

36. *Letters*, II, 63.
37. *Journals*, III, 374–77.
38. Ibid., III, 374.
39. Gifford's letter is quoted by McClary, pp. 58–59n.
40. *Letters*, II, 67. The letter is quoted extensively in the Textual Commentary, pp. 309–11, below.
41. Ibid., II, 71.
42. *Journals*, III, 381.

Moore, he revealed his anxiety: "Let me hear from you, if but a line; particularly if my work pleases you, but don't say a word against it. I am easily
put out of humor with what I do."[43]

"Take my word for it, the only happy author in this world is he who is
below the care of reputation," concludes Irving's own Poor Devil Author.[44]
Irving's customary sensitivity to and dread of criticism were to be sorely
tried by the response to *Tales of a Traveller*. It received little critical approbation on either side of the Atlantic. One of the earliest and most prominent
reviews, "Letters of Timothy Tickler, Esq." in *Blackwood's Edinburgh Magazine*, may have set the pattern of disparagement. "I have been miserably
disappointed in the 'Tales of a Traveller,'" the character Tickler asserts.
"There is nothing German here at all, except that the preface is dated *Mentz*,
and that the author has cribbed from the German books he has been dab-
bling in, some fables which have not the merit either of being originally or
characteristically German. . . . Why a man of education and talent should
have ventured to put forth such poor secondhand, second-rate manufactures, at this time of day, it entirely passes my imagination to conceive.—
Good Heavens! are we come to this, that men of this rank cannot even make
a robbery terrific, or a love-story tolerable?"[45] Tickler labels hackneyed all
but the fourth section, Diedrich Knickerbocker's account of the Dutch money diggers. That he calls "not only worth the bulk of it five hundred times
over, but really, and in every respect, worthy of himself and his fame. This
will live, the rest will die in three months."[46]

Critics condemned as tedious or trite stories which frustrated their expectations. The *United States Literary Gazette* concluded, "On the whole, we
are not satisfied with these Tales. Some of them, indeed, are quite respectable as productions of a light kind of literature; but . . . the public have been
led to expect better things as the result of . . . Irving's travels."[47] A more

43. *Letters*, II, 72.
44. Below, p. 92.
45. "Letters of Timothy Tickler, Esq.," *Blackwood's Edinburgh Magazine*, 16 (September
1824), 294–95. Modern scholars, too, have regretted that the tales contain "nothing German," or at least very little of it. Henry A. Pochmann, in "Irving's German Tour and Its
Influence on His Tales," *PMLA*, 45 (December 1930), 1150–87, stretches to find German
influence in the "Buckthorne" section and in three other stories. Walter A. Reichart finds
even less—and entirely different—evidence of German influence in *Tales* and sensibly re-
futes Pochmann's argument for direct descent of "Buckthorne" from Goethe's *Wilhelm Meis-
ters Lehrjahre* (see *Washington Irving and Germany*, pp. 146–56).
46. "Letters of Timothy Tickler, Esq.," p. 296.
47. The *United States Literary Gazette*, vol. 1, reviewed *Tales* in three installments: on
September 15, 1824, pp. 161–63; October 1, pp. 177–78; and November 15, pp. 228–29.
The judgment quoted appears in the final notice, p. 228.

vehement denunciation appeared in the *European Magazine and London Review*, which complained of disappointment not only in the subject matter but also in the author's manner. In abandoning the familiar essay and the sketch for the story, Irving "betrays a precocity of decay, which, whether of tact or of intellect, is truly disappointing and deplorable. The 'Tales of a Traveller' have been for some time expected, and to so high a pitch had risen the public curiosity, that, when they appeared, the trade, as a witty periodical has expressed it, 'nearly *swallowed* them.' And readers too, will do well to *swallow* them likewise. An oyster-eating kind of perusal, without 'chewing,' and especially without *ruminating* on them, is all they will bear without being found nauseous."[48]

Irving was blamed for not having fulfilled the expectation of a German sketch book and derided for not having produced a sketch book at all. A review quoted by the *New-York Mirror, and Ladies' Literary Gazette* pronounced *Tales* "a mere shadow of the previous works of the same writer, without their spirit, humour, or interest; being a dull imitation of himself, by a writer who was never remarkable for originality of genius, richness of invention, or vivacity of fancy. No man in the republic of Letters has been more overrated than Mr. Washington Irving."[49]

He was of course not without his defenders. The *Atlantic* was among the first to condemn the easy and invidious denigrations: "There is nothing so disgusting, we think, as the perpetual cant of tea-table critics about an author's 'falling off,' as they call it." The reviewer, striving for a balanced assessment, argued that Irving's tales failed to please "[n]ot because they are not excellent of their kind, but because they are not of the kind we anticipated."[50] The London *Eclectic Review* cautioned readers against unfairly judging *Tales* "by the standard of our own expectations, rather than by the plan and the intention which [Irving] himself had in view when he undertook it."[51] Open minded readers "who have not sate down to the perusal with unreasonable expectations, which it is no sin in [Irving] not to have gratified," will be rewarded by "an agreeable accession to the stock of light reading."[52]

Such pallid and indulgent approval is typical of the positive notices *Tales* received. In the United States, Irving occasionally benefited from chauvinistic applause: "Let us read then, and let us venture to admire, before we have seen the last English reviews, the productions of our scientific and literary countrymen, not only because they are often inherently excellent,

48. *European Magazine and London Review*, 86 (September 1824), 251.
49. *New-York Mirror, and Ladies' Literary Gazette*, 2 (September 25, 1824), 70.
50. In the second of sequential reviews, *Atlantic*, 2 (December 1824), 85.
51. *Eclectic Review*, 42, NS 24 (July 1825), 65.
52. Ibid., p. 74.

but (we say it believing that there exists such a national obligation,) because they are American."[53] Likewise, he received his share of the stock compliments to "the amiable and gentle spirit which pervades all his writings [and] the polished sweetness and elegance of his style" which had characterized his most favorable notices since the publication of the *Sketch Book*.[54] One autoretractive compliment appears in an otherwise caustic review in the London *Examiner*: "Mr. Irving is a pleasant, imitative writer, whose chief merit lies in a light and evanescent vein of humour on the surface, a gentle ripple of the mind, and a highly polished style. The latter, indeed, is probably his principal distinction, and, we may almost assert, typical of the mind which it conveys,—always smooth and elegant, without the exhibition of any of those distinctive forms of expression and peculiar collocations with which originality of conception will invariably clothe itself. The man of ardent imagination and vigorous conception uniformly arrays his thoughts in a language of his own; the style of Mr. Irving is a highly-wrought general style."[55]

More galling than the faint praise or extravagant disappointment must have been the charges of toadying and indecency, which frequently resorted to ad hominem attack. He was accused of catering to popular tastes, writing not for the sake of literature but for profit. "He knew Ghost merchandise would sell to the best advantage, and contracted with his bookseller accordingly," said an American reviewer.[56] An English review made him a scapegoat for its political biases, calling Irving "indisputably feeble . . . a mere adjective of a man," groveling before fashionable society: he "would strike out his best passage, dilute his best argument, or recant his sincerest opinion, in the fear of losing the next invitation to dinner he may expect from Grosvenor-square."[57] Another called him "a sort of American mockbird" cozying up to polite society "without startling them by any fatiguing originality of thought, or offending them with the intrusion of a sentiment which can disturb the self-complacency, which is their elysium."[58]

Other reviewers found much to offend genteel society in what they perceived as a new "coarseness" in Irving's writing. "[I]n the present volumes, he displays a levity, and sometimes stoops to a vulgarity, which must pain a serious, and disgust a delicate mind," said the *Eclectic*.[59] A Boston paper, remarking that "the standard of delicacy is higher in our country than in England," charged Irving with "the vulgarism of indelicacy. This is a fault

---

53. *Atlantic*, 2 (November 1824), 62.
54. Ibid., p. 63.
55. *Examiner*, No. 866 (September 5, 1824), 564–65.
56. Quoted by *New-York Mirror, and Ladies' Literary Gazette*, p. 71.
57. *Westminster Review*, 2 (October 1824), 340, 346.
58. *Examiner*, p. 563.
59. *Eclectic Review*, p. 74.

which seems peculiarly out of place in him; for he must owe any rank he may hereafter hold in our literature, to his refinement rather than to his strength." The American reviewer singled out among the instances most likely to offend, "the indecency drowned in the crack! crack! of the postillion's whip at Terracina; the innuendoes in the 'Bold Dragoon;' . . . and finally, the shocking story of the 'Young Robber,' where a scene the most revolting to humanity is twice unnecessarily forced on the reader's imagination."[60] Even the *Quarterly Review* of Irving's English publisher, setting out to offer "friendly criticism" some six months after the publication of *Tales*, objected strenuously to the rape of Rosetta: "the story of the Young Robber—it ought not to have been written—it ought not to be read—the feelings which it excites are not tragic horror or pity, but pure unmingled disgust: it is simply shocking to the feelings of our nature . . . . and if the book should ever reach a second edition, we trust Mr. Irving will expunge it."[61]

One of the strongest voices to come to Irving's defense was that of his countryman John Neal in a survey of American writers for *Blackwood's Edinburgh Magazine*. He set out to rescue Irving from the harsh judgments that followed inflated expectations: "Irving has been foolishly praised; cruelly, wickedly abused. He went up too high; he has fallen too low." The critics "anointed him wickedly: they are now dishonouring him, far more wickedly."[62] Yet Neal himself pronounced *Tales* a "sad affair" and echoed in palliated form what others had stated more stridently—that the work was derivative and "quite unpardonable, for two or three droll indecencies."[63] Finally, Neal admonished Irving directly: "We rejoice in your failure, now, because we believe that it will drive you into a style of original composition, far more worthy of yourself.—Go to work. Lose no time. Your foundations, will be the stronger for this uproar."[64]

The intensity of the attacks on *Tales* ought perhaps, as Neal suggests, to be regarded as the measure of, or proportionate to, Irving's considerable celebrity. The critical failure of *Tales* did little damage to Irving's eminence as a man of letters. However, his perception of and reaction to that failure constituted a personal crisis which altered the direction of his career.

60. *United States Literary Gazette*, 1 (November 15, 1824), 229.

61. *Quarterly Review*, 31 (March 1825), 474, 483.

62. "American Writers. No. IV.," *Blackwood's Edinburgh Magazine*, 17 (January 1825), 59.

63. Ibid., p. 67.

64. Ibid., p. 67. Additional contemporary reviews are mentioned by Williams, II, 294–96, and briefly annotated in Haskell Springer, *Washington Irving: A Reference Guide* (Boston: G.K. Hall, 1976), pp. 13–20.

Before his family and friends, Irving affected a balanced perspective and portrayed himself as untouched by the reviews. To Henry Brevoort he wrote, "The fact is I have kept myself so aloof from all clan ship in literature, that I have no allies among the scribblers for the periodical press; and some of them have taken a pique against me for having treated them a little cavalierly in my writings—However, as I do not read criticism good or bad, I am out of the reach of attack—If my writings are worth any thing they will out live temporary criticism; if not they are not worth caring about."[65] He was, however, deeply wounded. From the first news of "unfavorable" notices early in September and for the remainder of 1824 and well into 1825, Irving recorded bitterly in his journals his dejection over the harsh reviews.[66] Often the reviews were sent him or called to his attention by "friends," as in the case of an anonymous letter from New York received December 14, 1824, "containing a scurrilous newspaper tirade against me."[67] His diary entry for New Year's Eve 1824 reveals the magnitude of the damage: "This has been a dismal day of depression &c and closes a year part of which has been full of sanguine hope; of social enjoyment; peace of mind, and health of body—and the latter part saddened by disappointments & distrust of the world & of myself; by sleepless nights & joyless days—May the coming year prove more thoroughly propitious[.]"[68]

But he was to find little relief in the months ahead. And, in fact, almost a year after the publication of *Tales*, the reviews still rankled. "Read illnatured fling at me in Am: papers," he wrote in his journal in April 1825. "*It is hard to be stabbd in the back by ones own kin when attacked in front by strangers. No matter—my countrymen may regret some day or other that they turnd from me with such caprice, the moment foes abroad assailed me*[.]"[69] In this season of his forty-second birthday, Irving's record of his moods shows him "extremely depressed—incapable of exertion," unable to "summon force & spirit" to write.[70]

The frustration he experienced both before and after its publication made *Tales* an emotional and professional watershed. It ended the major phase of Irving's contribution to the short story, and almost four years were to elapse before the publication of his next substantial work, *The Life and Voyages of Christopher Columbus* (1828).

Irving may have been the more damaged by the reviews because he never lost faith in the worth of *Tales of a Traveller*. A letter to his friend Brevoort

65. *Letters*, II, 90.
66. *Journals*, III, 392 ff.
67. Ibid., III, 436.
68. Ibid., III, 442.
69. Ibid., III, 480.
70. Ibid., III, 480, 479.

asserts his confidence in the work and in his method. The passage in defense of *Tales* has come to be regarded as one of Irving's major aesthetic pronouncements. "There was more of an artist like touch about it—though this is not a thing to be appreciated by the many," he said. "I fancy much of what I value myself upon in writing, escapes the observation of the great mass of my readers: who are intent more upon the story than the way in which it is told. For my part I consider a story merely as a frame on which to stretch my materials. It is the play of thought, and sentiment and language; the weaving in of characters, lightly yet expressively delineated; the familiar and faithful exhibition of scenes in common life; and the half concealed vein of humour that is often playing through the whole—these are among what I aim at, and upon which I felicitate myself in proportion as I think I succeed."[71]

Though readers for almost two centuries have acknowledged the unevenness of his achievement in *Tales*, most would be inclined, selectively, to agree with Irving that the collection contains "some of the best things I have ever written."[72]

71. *Letters*, II, 90.
72. Ibid., II, 76.

TALES OF A TRAVELLER
BY
GEOFFREY CRAYON, GENT.

I am neither your minotaure, nor your centaure, nor your satyr, nor your hyæna, nor your babion, but your meer traveller, believe me.

BEN JONSON

TO THE READER

WORTHY AND DEAR READER!
Hast thou ever been waylaid in the midst of a pleasant tour by some treacherous malady; thy heels tripped up, and thou left to count the tedious minutes as they passed, in the solitude of an inn chamber? If thou hast, thou
wilt be able to pity me. Behold me, interrupted in the course of my jour-
neying up the fair banks of the Rhine, and laid up by indisposition in this
old frontier town of Mentz. I have worn out every source of amusement. I
know the sound of every clock that strikes, and bell that rings, in the place.
I know to a second when to listen for the first tap of the Prussian drum, as
it summons the garrison to parade; or at what hour to expect the distant
sound of the Austrian military band. All these have grown wearisome to me,
and even the well known step of my doctor, as he slowly paces the corridor,
with healing in the creak of his shoes, no longer affords an agreeable interruption to the monotony of my apartment.

For a time I attempted to beguile the weary hours by studying German
under the tuition of mine host's pretty little daughter, Katrine; but I soon
found even German had not power to charm a languid ear, and that the
conjugating of *ich liebe* might be powerless, however rosy the lips which
uttered it.

I tried to read, but my mind would not fix itself; I turned over volume
after volume, but threw them by with distaste: "Well, then," said I at length
in despair, "if I cannot read a book, I will write one." Never was there a
more lucky idea; it at once gave me occupation and amusement.

The writing of a book was considered, in old times, as an enterprise of toil
and difficulty, insomuch that the most trifling lucubration was denominated
a "work," and the world talked with awe and reverence of "the labours of
the learned." These matters are better understood now adays. Thanks to the
improvements in all kind of manufactures, the art of book making has been
made familiar to the meanest capacity. Every body is an author. The scribbling of a quarto is the mere pastime of the idle; the young gentleman throws
off his brace of duodecimos in the intervals of the sporting season, and the
young lady produces her set of volumes with the same facility that her great
grandmother worked a set of chair bottoms.

The idea having struck me, therefore, to write a book, the reader will
easily perceive that the execution of it was no difficult matter. I rummaged
my portfolio, and cast about, in my recollection, for those floating materials
which a man naturally collects in travelling; and here I have arranged them
in this little work.

As I know this to be a story telling and a story reading age, and that the

world is fond of being taught by apologue, I have digested the instruction I
would convey into a number of tales. They may not possess the power of
amusement which the tales told by many of my contemporaries possess; but
then I value myself on the sound moral which each of them contains. This
may not be apparent at first, but the reader will be sure to find it out in the
end. I am for curing the world by gentle alteratives, not by violent doses;
indeed the patient should never be conscious that he is taking a dose. I have
learnt this much from my experience under the hands of the worthy Hip-
pocrates of Mentz.

I am not, therefore, for those barefaced tales which carry their moral on
the surface, staring one in the face; they are enough to deter the squeamish
reader. On the contrary, I have often hid my moral from sight, and disguised
it as much as possible by sweets and spices, so that while the simple reader
is listening with open mouth to a ghost or a love story, he may have a bolus
of sound morality popped down his throat, and be never the wiser for the
fraud.

As the public is apt to be curious about the sources whence an author
draws his stories, doubtless that it may know how far to put faith in them, I
would observe, that the Adventure of the German Student, or rather the
latter part of it, is founded on an anecdote related to me as existing somewhere in French; and, indeed, I have been told, since writing it, that an
ingenious tale has been founded on it by an English writer; but I have never
met with either the former or the latter in print. Some of the circumstances
in the Adventure of the Mysterious Picture, and in the Story of the Young
Italian, are vague recollections of anecdotes related to me some years since;
but from what source derived I do not know. The Adventure of the Young
Painter among the banditti is taken almost entirely from an authentic narrative in manuscript.

As to the other tales contained in this work, and, indeed, to my tales
generally, I can make but one observation. I am an old traveller. I have read
somewhat, heard and seen more, and dreamt more than all. My brain is
filled, therefore, with all kinds of odds and ends. In travelling, these heterogeneous matters have become shaken up in my mind, as the articles are
apt to be in an ill packed travelling trunk; so that when I attempt to draw
forth a fact, I cannot determine whether I have read, heard, or dreamt
it; and I am always at a loss to know how much to believe of my own
stories.

These matters being premised, fall to, worthy reader, with good appetite,
and, above all, with good humour, to what is here set before thee. If the
tales I have furnished should prove to be bad, they will at least be found
short; so that no one will be wearied long on the same theme. "Variety is
charming," as some poet observes. There is a certain relief in change, even

though it be from bad to worse; as I have found in travelling in a stage coach, that it is often a comfort to shift one's position and be bruised in a new place.

Ever thine,
GEOFFREY CRAYON
Dated from the HOTEL DE DARMSTADT,
ci-devant HOTEL DE PARIS,
MENTZ, *otherwise called* MAYENCE.

PART I
STRANGE STORIES

BY A NERVOUS GENTLEMAN

I'll tell you more; there was a fish taken,
A monstrous fish, with a sword by's side, a long sword,
A pike in's neck, and a gun in's nose, a huge gun.
And letters of mart in's mouth, from the Duke of Florence.
   Cleanthes. This is a monstrous lie.
   Tony. I do confess it.
Do you think I'd tell you truths?

FLETCHER'S WIFE FOR A MONTH

THE GREAT UNKNOWN

The following adventures were related to me by the same nervous gentleman who told me the romantic tale of THE STOUT GENTLEMAN, published in Bracebridge Hall.

It is very singular, that although I expressly stated that story to have been told to me, and described the very person who told it, still it has been received as an adventure that happened to myself. Now, I protest I never met with any adventure of the kind. I should not have grieved at this, had it not been intimated by the author of Waverley, in an introduction to his novel of Peveril of the Peak, that he was himself the Stout Gentleman alluded to. I have ever since been importuned by questions and letters from gentlemen, and particularly from ladies without number, touching what I had seen of the great unknown.

Now, all this is extremely tantalizing. It is like being congratulated on the high prize when one has drawn a blank; for I have just as great a desire as any one of the public to penetrate the mystery of that very singular personage, whose voice fills every corner of the world, without any one being able to tell whence it comes.

My friend, the nervous gentleman, also, who is a man of very shy retired habits, complains that he has been excessively annoyed in consequence of its getting about in his neighbourhood that he is the fortunate personage. Insomuch, that he has become a character of considerable notoriety in two or three country towns; and has been repeatedly teased to exhibit himself at blue stocking parties, for no other reason than that of being "the gentleman who has had a glimpse of the author of Waverley."

Indeed, the poor man has grown ten times as nervous as ever, since he has discovered, on such good authority, who the stout gentleman was; and will never forgive himself for not having made a more resolute effort to get a full sight of him. He has anxiously endeavoured to call up a recollection of what he saw of that portly personage; and has ever since kept a curious eye on all gentlemen of more than ordinary dimensions, whom he has seen getting into stage coaches. All in vain! The features he had caught a glimpse of seem common to the whole race of stout gentlemen; and the great unknown remains as great an unknown as ever.

Having premised these circumstances, I will now let the nervous gentleman proceed with his stories.

THE HUNTING DINNER

I was once at a hunting dinner, given by a worthy fox-hunting old Baronet, who kept Bachelor's Hall in jovial style, in an ancient rook-haunted family mansion, in one of the middle counties. He had been a devoted admirer of the fair sex in his young days; but having travelled much, studied the sex in various countries with distinguished success, and returned home profoundly instructed, as he supposed, in the ways of woman, and a perfect master of the art of pleasing, he had the mortification of being jilted by a little boarding school girl, who was scarcely versed in the accidence of love.

The Baronet was completely overcome by such an incredible defeat; retired from the world in disgust, put himself under the government of his housekeeper, and took to fox hunting like a perfect Nimrod. Whatever poets may say to the contrary, a man will grow out of love as he grows old; and a pack of fox hounds may chase out of his heart even the memory of a boarding school goddess. The Baronet was when I saw him as merry and mellow an old bachelor as ever followed a hound; and the love he had once felt for one woman had spread itself over the whole sex; so that there was not a pretty face in the whole country round, but came in for a share.

The dinner was prolonged till a late hour; for our host having no ladies in his household to summon us to the drawing room, the bottle maintained its true bachelor sway, unrivalled by its potent enemy the tea kettle. The old hall in which we dined echoed to bursts of robustious fox hunting merriment, that made the ancient antlers shake on the walls. By degrees, however, the wine and wassail of mine host began to operate upon bodies already a little jaded by the chase. The choice spirits which flashed up at the beginning of the dinner, sparkled for a time, then gradually went out one after another, or only emitted now and then a faint gleam from the socket. Some of the briskest talkers, who had given tongue so bravely at the first burst, fell fast asleep; and none kept on their way but certain of those long winded prosers, who, like short legged hounds, worry on unnoticed at the bottom of conversation, but are sure to be in at the death. Even these at length subsided into silence; and scarcely any thing was heard but the nasal communications of two or three veteran masticators, who, having been silent while awake, were indemnifying the company in their sleep.

At length the announcement of tea and coffee in the cedar parlour roused all hands from this temporary torpor. Every one awoke marvellously renovated, and while sipping the refreshing beverage out of the Baronet's old fashioned hereditary china, began to think of departing for their several homes. But here a sudden difficulty arose. While we had been prolonging our repast, a heavy winter storm had set in, with snow, rain, and sleet, driven by such bitter blasts of wind, that they threatened to penetrate to the very bone.

"It's all in vain," said our hospitable host, "to think of putting one's head out of doors in such weather. So, gentlemen, I hold you my guests for this night at least, and will have your quarters prepared accordingly."

The unruly weather, which became more and more tempestuous, rendered the hospitable suggestion unanswerable. The only question was, whether such an unexpected accession of company, to an already crowded house, would not put the housekeeper to her trumps to accommodate them.

"Pshaw," cried mine host, "did you ever know of a Bachelor's Hall that was not elastic, and able to accommodate twice as many as it could hold?" So out of a good humoured pique the housekeeper was summoned to consultation before us all. The old lady appeared, in her gala suit of faded brocade, which rustled with flurry and agitation, for in spite of our host's bravado, she was a little perplexed. But in a bachelor's house, and with bachelor guests, these matters are readily managed. There is no lady of the house to stand upon squeamish points about lodging gentlemen in odd holes and corners, and exposing the shabby parts of the establishment. A bachelor's housekeeper is used to shifts and emergencies; so, after much worrying to and fro; and divers consultations about the red room, and the blue room, and the chintz room, and the damask room, and the little room with the bow window, the matter was finally arranged.

When all this was done, we were once more summoned to the standing rural amusement of eating. The time that had been consumed in dozing after dinner, and in the refreshment and consultation of the cedar parlour, was sufficient, in the opinion of the rosy faced butler, to engender a reasonable appetite for supper. A slight repast had therefore been tricked up from the residue of dinner, consisting of a cold sirloin of beef; hashed venison; a devilled leg of a turkey or so, and a few other of those light articles taken by country gentlemen to ensure sound sleep and heavy snoring.

The nap after dinner had brightened up every one's wit; and a great deal of excellent humour was expended upon the perplexities of mine host and his housekeeper, by certain married gentlemen of the company, who considered themselves privileged in joking with a bachelor's establishment. From this the banter turned as to what quarters each would find, on being thus suddenly billeted in so antiquated a mansion.

"By my soul," said an Irish captain of dragoons, one of the most merry and boisterous of the party—"by my soul, but I should not be surprised if some of those good looking gentlefolks that hang along the walls, should walk about the rooms of this stormy night; or if I should find the ghost of one of these long waisted ladies turning into my bed in mistake for her grave in the church yard."

"Do you believe in ghosts, then?" said a thin hatchet-faced gentleman, with projecting eyes like a lobster.

I had remarked this last personage during dinner time for one of those incessant questioners, who have a craving, unhealthy, appetite in conversation. He never seemed satisfied with the whole of a story; never laughed when others laughed; but always put the joke to the question. He could never enjoy the kernel of the nut, but pestered himself to get more out of the shell.

"Do you believe in ghosts, then?" said the inquisitive gentleman.

"Faith, but I do," replied the jovial Irishman; "I was brought up in the fear and belief of them: we had a Benshee in our own family, honey."

"A Benshee—and what's that?" cried the questioner.

"Why an old lady ghost that tends upon your real Milesian families, and wails at their window to let them know when some of them are to die."

"A mighty pleasant piece of information," cried an elderly gentleman, with a knowing look and a flexible nose, to which he could give a whimsical twist when he wished to be waggish.

"By my soul, but I'd have you to know it's a piece of distinction to be waited on by a Benshee. It's a proof that one has pure blood in one's veins. But i'faith, now we are talking of ghosts, there never was a house or a night better fitted than the present for a ghost adventure. Pray, Sir John, haven't you such a thing as a haunted chamber to put a guest in?"

"Perhaps," said the Baronet smiling, "I might accommodate you even on that point."

"Oh, I should like it of all things, my jewel. Some dark oaken room, with ugly wobegone portraits that stare dismally at one, and about which the housekeeper has a power of delightful stories of love and murder. And then a dim lamp, a table with a rusty sword across it, and a spectre all in white to draw aside one's curtains at midnight"——

"In truth," said an old gentleman at one end of the table, "you put me in mind of an anecdote"——

"Oh, a ghost story! a ghost story!" was vociferated round the board, every one edging his chair a little nearer.

The attention of the whole company was now turned upon the speaker. He was an old gentleman, one side of whose face was no match for the other. The eyelid drooped and hung down like an unhinged window shutter. Indeed, the whole side of his head was dilapidated, and seemed like the wing of a house shut up and haunted. I'll warrant that side was well stuffed with ghost stories.

There was a universal demand for the tale.

"Nay," said the old gentleman, "it's a mere anecdote—and a very commonplace one; but such as it is you shall have it. It is a story that I once heard my uncle tell as having happened to himself. He was a man very apt to meet with strange adventures. I have heard him tell of others much more singular."

"What kind of man was your uncle?" said the questioning gentleman.

"Why, he was rather a dry, shrewd kind of body; a great traveller, and fond of telling his adventures."

"Pray, how old might he have been when this happened?"

"When what happened?" cried the gentleman with the flexible nose, impatiently—"Egad, you have not given any thing a chance to happen—come, never mind our uncle's age; let us have his adventures."

The inquisitive gentleman being for the moment silenced, the old gentleman with the haunted head proceeded.

THE ADVENTURE OF MY UNCLE

Many years since, some time before the French revolution, my uncle passed several months at Paris. The English and French were on better terms, in those days, than at present, and mingled cordially in society. The English went abroad to spend money then, and the French were always ready to help them: they go abroad to save money at present, and that they can do without French assistance. Perhaps the travelling English were fewer and choicer than at present, when the whole nation has broke loose, and inundated the continent At any rate, they circulated more readily and currently in foreign society, and my uncle, during his residence at Paris, made many very intimate acquaintances among the French noblesse.

Some time afterwards, he was making a journey in the winter time, in that part of Normandy called the Pays de Caux, when, as evening was closing in, he perceived the turrets of an ancient chateau rising out of the trees of its walled park, each turret with its high conical roof of grey slate, like a candle with an extinguisher on it.

"To whom does that chateau belong, friend?" cried my uncle to a meagre but fiery postillion, who, with tremendous jack boots and cocked hat, was floundering on before him.

"To Monseigneur the Marquis de ——," said the postillion, touching his hat, partly out of respect to my uncle, and partly out of reverence to the noble name pronounced. My uncle recollected the Marquis for a particular friend in Paris, who had often expressed a wish to see him at his paternal chateau. My uncle was an old traveller, one who knew how to turn things to account. He revolved for a few moments in his mind how agreeable it would be to his friend the Marquis to be surprised in this sociable way by a pop visit; and how much more agreeable to himself to get into snug quarters in a chateau, and have a relish of the Marquis's well known kitchen, and a smack of his superior champagne and burgundy; rather than put up with the

miserable lodgement, and miserable fare of a provincial inn. In a few minutes, therefore, the meagre postillion was cracking his whip like a very devil,
or like a true Frenchman, up the long straight avenue that led to the
chateau.

You have no doubt all seen French chateaus, as every body travels in
France now adays. This was one of the oldest; standing naked and alone, in
the midst of a desert of gravel walks and cold stone terraces; with a cold
looking formal garden, cut into angles and rhomboids; and a cold leafless
park, divided geometrically by straight alleys; and two or three cold looking
noseless statues; and fountains spouting cold water enough to make one's
teeth chatter. At least, such was the feeling they imparted on the wintry day
of my uncle's visit; though, in hot summer weather, I'll warrant there was
glare enough to scorch one's eyes out.

The smacking of the postillion's whip, which grew more and more intense
the nearer they approached, frightened a flight of pigeons out of the dove
cote, and rooks out of the roofs; and finally a crew of servants out of the
chateau, with the Marquis at their head. He was enchanted to see my uncle;
for his chateau, like the house of our worthy host, had not many more guests
at the time than it could accommodate. So he kissed my uncle on each
cheek, after the French fashion, and ushered him into the castle.

The Marquis did the honours of the house with the urbanity of his country. In fact, he was proud of his old family chateau; for part of it was extremely old. There was a tower and chapel which had been built almost before
the memory of man; but the rest was more modern; the castle having been
nearly demolished during the wars of the League. The Marquis dwelt upon
this event with great satisfaction, and seemed really to entertain a grateful
feeling towards Henry the Fourth, for having thought his paternal mansion
worth battering down. He had many stories to tell of the prowess of his
ancestors, and several skull caps, helmets and cross bows, and divers huge
boots and buff jerkins, to show, which had been worn by the Leaguers.
Above all, there was a two handled sword, which he could hardly wield; but
which he displayed as a proof that there had been giants in his family.

In truth, he was but a small descendant from such great warriors. When
you looked at their bluff visages and brawny limbs, as depicted in their portraits, and then at the little Marquis, with his spindle shanks, and his sallow
lanthern visage, flanked with a pair of powdered ear locks, or *ailes de pigeon*,
that seemed ready to fly away with it; you could hardly believe him to be of
the same race. But when you looked at the eyes that sparkled out like a
beetle's from each side of his hooked nose, you saw at once that he inherited
all the fiery spirit of his forefathers. In fact, a Frenchman's spirit never ex-
hales, however his body may dwindle. It rather rarifies, and grows more
inflammable, as the earthy particles diminish; and I have seen valour enough
in a little fiery hearted French dwarf, to have furnished out a tolerable giant.

When once the Marquis, as he was wont, put on one of the old helmets stuck up in his hall; though his head no more filled it than a dry pea its pease cod; yet his eyes flashed from the bottom of the iron cavern with the brilliancy of carbuncles; and when he poised the ponderous two handled sword of his ancestors, you would have thought you saw the doughty little David wielding the sword of Goliath, which was unto him like a weaver's beam.

However, gentlemen, I am dwelling too long on this description of the Marquis and his chateau; but you must excuse me; he was an old friend of my uncle's, and whenever my uncle told the story, he was always fond of talking a great deal about his host.—Poor little Marquis! He was one of that handful of gallant courtiers, who made such a devoted, but hopeless stand in the cause of their sovereign, in the chateau of the Tuilleries, against the irruption of the mob, on the sad tenth of August. He displayed the valour of a preux French chevalier to the last; flourished feebly his little court sword with a sa-sa! in face of a whole legion of *sans culottes*, but was pinned to the wall like a butterfly, by the pike of a poissarde, and his heroic soul was borne up to heaven on his *ailes de pigeon*.

But all this has nothing to do with my story: to the point then:—When the hour arrived for retiring for the night, my uncle was shown to his room, in a venerable old tower. It was the oldest part of the chateau, and had in ancient times been the Donjon or strong hold; of course the chamber was none of the best. The Marquis had put him there, however, because he knew him to be a traveller of taste, and fond of antiquities; and also because the better apartments were already occupied. Indeed, he perfectly reconciled my uncle to his quarters by mentioning the great personages who had once inhabited them, all of whom were in some way or other connected with the family. If you would take his word for it, John Baliol, or as he called him Jean de Bailleul had died of chagrin in this very chamber on hearing of the success of his rival, Robert the Bruce, at the battle of Bannockburn; and when he added that the Duke de Guise had slept in it, my uncle was fain to felicitate himself upon being honoured with such distinguished quarters.

The night was shrewd and windy, and the chamber none of the warmest. An old long faced, long bodied servant in quaint livery, who attended upon my uncle, threw down an armful of wood beside the fire place, gave a queer look about the room, and then wished him *bon repos*, with a grimace and a shrug that would have been suspicious from any other than an old French servant. The chamber had indeed a wild crazy look, enough to strike any one who had read romances with apprehension and foreboding. The windows were high and narrow, and had once been loop holes, but had been rudely enlarged, as well as the extreme thickness of the walls would permit; and the ill fitted casements rattled to every breeze. You would have thought, on a windy night, some of the old Leaguers were tramping and clanking about the apartment in their huge boots and rattling spurs. A door which stood ajar, and like a true French door would stand ajar, in spite of every reason and effort to the contrary, opened upon a long dark corridor, that led the Lord knows whither, and seemed just made for ghosts to air themselves in, when they turned out of their graves at midnight. The wind would spring up into a hoarse murmur through this passage, and creak the door to and fro, as if some dubious ghost were balancing in its mind whether to come in or not. In a word, it was precisely the kind of comfortless apartment that a ghost, if ghost there were in the chateau, would single out for its favourite lounge.

My uncle, however, though a man accustomed to meet with strange adventures, apprehended none at the time. He made several attempts to shut the door, but in vain. Not that he apprehended any thing, for he was too old a traveller to be daunted by a wild looking apartment; but the night, as I have said, was cold and gusty, and the wind howled about the old turret, pretty much as it does round this old mansion at this moment; and the breeze from the long dark corridor came in as damp and chilly as if from a dungeon. My uncle, therefore, since he could not close the door threw a quantity of wood on the fire, which soon sent up a flame in the great wide mouthed chimney that illumined the whole chamber, and made the shadow of the tongs, on the opposite wall, look like a long legged giant. My uncle now clambered on top of the half score of mattresses which form a French bed, and which stood in a deep recess; then tucking himself snugly in, and burying himself up to the chin in the bed clothes, he lay looking at the fire, and listening to the wind, and thinking how knowingly he had come over his friend the Marquis for a night's lodging: and so he fell asleep.

He had not taken above half of his first nap, when he was awakened by the clock of the chateau, in the turret over his chamber, which struck midnight. It was just such an old clock as ghosts are fond of. It had a deep, dismal tone, and struck so slowly and tediously that my uncle thought it would never have done. He counted and counted till he was confident he counted thirteen, and then it stopped.

The fire had burnt low, and the blaze of the last faggot was almost expiring, burning in small blue flames, which now and then lengthened up into little white gleams. My uncle lay with his eyes half closed, and his nightcap drawn almost down to his nose. His fancy was already wandering, and began to mingle up the present scene with the crater of Vesuvius, the French opera, the Coliseum at Rome, Dolly's chop house in London, and all the farrago of noted places with which the brain of a traveller is crammed—in a word, he was just falling asleep.

Suddenly he was roused by the sound of footsteps slowly pacing along the corridor. My uncle, as I have often heard him say himself, was a man not easily frightened; so he lay quiet, supposing this some other guest, or some servant on his way to bed. The footsteps, however, approached the door;

the door gently opened; whether of its own accord, or whether pushed open, my uncle could not distinguish:—a figure all in white glided in. It was a female, tall and stately, and of a commanding air. Her dress was of an ancient fashion, ample in volume and sweeping the floor. She walked up to the fire place without regarding my uncle; who raised his nightcap with one hand, and stared earnestly at her. She remained for some time standing by the fire, which flashing up at intervals cast blue and white gleams of light that enabled my uncle to remark her appearance minutely.

Her face was ghastly pale, and perhaps rendered still more so by the blueish light of the fire. It possessed beauty, but its beauty was saddened by care and anxiety. There was the look of one accustomed to trouble, but of one whom trouble could not cast down nor subdue; for there was still the predominating air of proud, unconquerable resolution. Such at least was the opinion formed by my uncle, and he considered himself a great physiognomist.

The figure remained, as I said, for some time by the fire, putting out first one hand, then the other, then each foot alternately, as if warming itself; for your ghosts, if ghost it really was, are apt to be cold. My uncle furthermore remarked that it wore high heeled shoes, after an ancient fashion, with paste or diamond buckles, that sparkled as though they were alive. At length the figure turned gently round, casting a glassy look about the apartment, which, as it passed over my uncle, made his blood run cold, and chilled the very marrow in his bones. It then stretched its arms towards heaven, clasped its hands, and wringing them in a supplicating manner, glided slowly out of the room.

My uncle lay for some time meditating on this visitation, for (as he remarked when he told me the story) though a man of firmness, he was also a man of reflection, and did not reject a thing because it was out of the regular course of events. However, being as I have before said, a great traveller, and accustomed to strange adventures, he drew his nightcap resolutely over his eyes, turned his back to the door, hoisted the bed clothes high over his shoulders, and gradually fell asleep.

How long he slept he could not say, when he was awakened by the voice of some one at his bed side. He turned round and beheld the old French servant, with his ear locks in tight buckles on each side of a long, lanthorn face, on which habit had deeply wrinkled an everlasting smile. He made a thousand grimaces and asked a thousand pardons for disturbing Monsieur, but the morning was considerably advanced. While my uncle was dressing, he called vaguely to mind the visitor of the preceding night. He asked the ancient domestic what lady was in the habit of rambling about this part of the chateau at night. The old valet shrugged his shoulders as high as his head, laid one hand on his bosom, threw open the other with every finger extended; made a most whimsical grimace, which he meant to be complimentary, and replied, that it was not for him to know any thing of *les bonnes fortunes* of Monsieur.

My uncle saw there was nothing satisfactory to be learnt in this quarter.— After breakfast he was walking with the Marquis through the modern apartments of the chateau; sliding over the well waxed floors of silken saloons, amidst furniture rich in gilding and brocade; until they came to a long picture gallery, containing many portraits, some in oil and some in chalks.

Here was an ample field for the eloquence of his host, who had all the family pride of a nobleman of the *ancien regime*. There was not a grand name in Normandy, and hardly one in France, which was not, in some way or other, connected with his house. My uncle stood listening with inward impatience, resting sometimes on one leg, sometimes on the other, as the little Marquis descanted, with his usual fire and vivacity, on the achievements of his ancestors, whose portraits hung along the wall; from the martial deeds of the stern warriors in steel, to the gallantries and intrigues of the blue eyed gentlemen, with fair smiling faces, powdered ear locks, laced ruffles, and pink and blue silk coats and breeches; not forgetting the conquests of the lovely shepherdesses, with hoop petticoats and waists no thicker than an hour glass, who appeared ruling over their sheep and their swains with dainty crooks decorated with fluttering ribbands.

In the midst of his friend's discourse my uncle was startled on beholding a full length portrait, the very counterpart of his visitor of the preceding night.

"Methinks," said he, pointing to it, "I have seen the original of this portrait."

"*Pardonnez moi,*" replied the Marquis politely, "that can hardly be, as the lady has been dead more than a hundred years. That was the beautiful Duchess de Longueville, who figured during the minority of Louis the Fourteenth."

"And was there any thing remarkable in her history?"

Never was question more unlucky. The little Marquis immediately threw himself into the attitude of a man about to tell a long story. In fact, my uncle had pulled upon himself the whole history of the civil war of the Fronde, in which the beautiful Duchess had played so distinguished a part. Turenne, Coligni, Mazarin, were called up from their graves to grace his narration; nor were the affairs of the Barricadoes, nor the chivalry of the Port Cocheres forgotten. My uncle began to wish himself a thousand leagues off from the Marquis and his merciless memory, when suddenly the little man's recollections took a more interesting turn. He was relating the imprisonment of the Duke de Longueville, with the Princes Condé and Conti, in the chateau of Vincennes, and the ineffectual efforts of the Duchess to rouse the sturdy Normans to their rescue. He had come to that part where she was invested by the royal forces in the Castle of Dieppe.

"The spirit of the Duchess," proceeded the Marquis, "rose with her trials. It was astonishing to see so delicate and beautiful a being buffet so resolutely with hardships. She determined on a desperate means of escape. You may have seen the chateau in which she was mewed up; an old ragged wart of an edifice, standing on the knuckle of a hill, just above the rusty little town of Dieppe. One dark unruly night, she issued secretly out of a small postern gate of the castle, which the enemy had neglected to guard. The postern gate is there to this very day; opening upon a narrow bridge over a deep fosse between the castle and the brow of the hill. She was followed by her female attendants, a few domestics, and some gallant cavaliers who still remained faithful to her fortunes. Her object was to gain a small port about two leagues distant, where she had privately provided a vessel for her escape in case of emergency.

"The little band of fugitives were obliged to perform the distance on foot. When they arrived at the port the wind was high and stormy, the tide contrary, the vessel anchored far off in the road, and no means of getting on board, but by a fishing shallop which lay tossing like a cockle shell on the edge of the surf. The Duchess determined to risk the attempt. The seamen endeavoured to dissuade her, but the imminence of her danger on shore, and the magnanimity of her spirit urged her on. She had to be borne to the shallop in the arms of a mariner. Such was the violence of the wind and waves, that he faltered, lost his foothold, and let his precious burthen fall into the sea.

"The Duchess was nearly drowned; but partly through her own struggles, partly by the exertions of the seamen, she got to land. As soon as she had a little recovered strength, she insisted on renewing the attempt. The storm, however, had by this time become so violent as to set all efforts at defiance. To delay, was to be discovered and taken prisoner. As the only resource left, she procured horses; mounted with her female attendants *en croupe* behind the gallant gentlemen who accompanied her; and scoured the country to seek some temporary asylum.

"While the Duchess," continued the Marquis, laying his forefinger on my uncle's breast to arouse his flagging attention, "while the Duchess, poor lady, was wandering amid the tempest in this disconsolate manner, she arrived at this chateau. Her approach caused some uneasiness; for the clattering of a troop of horse, at dead of night, up the avenue of a lonely chateau, in those unsettled times, and in a troubled part of the country, was enough to occasion alarm.

"A tall, broad shouldered chasseur, armed to the teeth, gallopped ahead, and announced the name of the visitor. All uneasiness was dispelled. The household turned out with flambeaux to receive her, and never did torches gleam on a more weather beaten, travel stained band than came tramping into the court. Such pale, careworn faces, such bedraggled dresses, as the poor Duchess and her females presented, each seated behind her cavalier; while half drenched, half drowsy pages and attendants, seemed ready to fall from their horses with sleep and fatigue.

"The Duchess was received with a hearty welcome by my ancestor. She was ushered into the Hall of the chateau, and the fires soon crackled and blazed to cheer herself and her train; and every spit and stewpan was put in requisition to prepare ample refreshments for the wayfarers.

"She had a right to our hospitalities," continued the little Marquis, drawing himself up with a slight degree of stateliness, "for she was related to our family. I'll tell you how it was: Her father, Henry de Bourbon, Prince of Condé"——

"But did the Duchess pass the night in the chateau?" said my uncle rather abruptly, terrified at the idea of getting involved in one of the Marquis's genealogical discussions.

"Oh, as to the Duchess, she was put into the very apartment you occupied last night; which, at that time, was a kind of state apartment. Her followers were quartered in the chambers opening upon the neighbouring corridor, and her favourite page slept in an adjoining closet. Up and down the corridor walked the great chasseur, who had announced her arrival, and who acted as a kind of sentinel or guard. He was a dark, stern, powerful looking fellow, and as the light of a lamp in the corridor fell upon his deeply marked face and sinewy form, he seemed capable of defending the castle with his single arm.

"It was a rough, rude night; about this time of the year.—*Apropos*—now I think of it, last night was the anniversary of her visit. I may well remember the precise date, for it was a night not to be forgotten by our house. There is a singular tradition concerning it in our family." Here the Marquis hesitated, and a cloud seemed to gather about his bushy eyebrows. "There is a tradition—that a strange occurrence took place that night—a strange, mysterious, inexplicable occurrence."

Here he checked himself and paused.

"Did it relate to that Lady?" inquired my uncle, eagerly.

"It was past the hour of midnight," resumed the Marquis—"when the whole chateau——"

Here he paused again—my uncle made a movement of anxious curiosity.

"Excuse me," said the Marquis—a slight blush streaking his sallow visage. "There are some circumstances connected with our family history which I do not like to relate. That was a rude period. A time of great crimes among great men: for you know high blood, when it runs wrong, will not run tamely like blood of the *canaille*—poor lady!—But I have a little family pride, that— excuse me—we will change the subject if you please."—

My uncle's curiosity was piqued. The pompous and magnificent introduction had led him to expect something wonderful in the story to which it served as a kind of avenue. He had no idea of being cheated out of it by a sudden fit of unreasonable squeamishness. Besides, being a traveller, in quest of information, he considered it his duty to inquire into every thing.

The Marquis, however, evaded every question.

"Well," said my uncle, a little petulantly, "whatever you may think of it, I saw that lady last night."

The Marquis stepped back and gazed at him with surprise.

"She paid me a visit in my bed chamber."

The Marquis pulled out his snuff box with a shrug and a smile; taking this no doubt for an awkward piece of English pleasantry, which politeness required him to be charmed with. My uncle went on gravely, however, and related the whole circumstance. The Marquis heard him through with profound attention, holding his snuff box unopened in his hand. When the story was finished he tapped on the lid of his box deliberately; took a long sonorous pinch of snuff—

"Bah!" said the Marquis, and walked towards the other end of the gallery.——

———

Here the narrator paused. The company waited for some time for him to resume his narration; but he continued silent.

"Well," said the inquisitive gentleman, "and what did your uncle say then?"

"Nothing," replied the other.

"And what did the Marquis say further?"

"Nothing."

"And is that all?"

"That is all," said the narrator filling a glass of wine.

"I surmise," said the shrewd old gentleman with the waggish nose—"I surmise the ghost must have been the old housekeeper walking her rounds to see that all was right."

"Bah!" said the narrator, "my uncle was too much accustomed to strange sights not to know a ghost from a housekeeper!"

There was a murmur round the table half of merriment half of disappointment. I was inclined to think the old gentleman had really an afterpart of his story in reserve; but he sipped his wine and said nothing more; and there was an odd expression about his dilapidated countenance which left me in doubt whether he were in drollery or earnest.

"Egad," said the knowing gentleman with the flexible nose, "this story of your uncle puts me in mind of one that used to be told of an aunt of mine, by the mother's side; though I don't know that it will bear a comparison; as the good lady was not so prone to meet with strange adventures. But at any rate, you shall have it."

THE ADVENTURE OF MY AUNT

My aunt was a lady of large frame, strong mind, and great resolution; she was what might be termed a very manly woman. My uncle was a thin, puny little man, very meek and acquiescent, and no match for my aunt. It was observed that he dwindled and dwindled gradually away, from the day of his marriage. His wife's powerful mind was too much for him; it wore him out. My aunt, however, took all possible care of him, had half the doctors in town to prescribe for him, made him take all their prescriptions, and dosed him with physic enough to cure a whole hospital. All was in vain. My uncle grew worse and worse the more dosing and nursing he underwent, until in the end he added another to the long list of matrimonial victims, who have been killed with kindness.

"And was it his ghost that appeared to her?" asked the inquisitive gentleman, who had questioned the former story teller.

"You shall hear," replied the narrator:—My aunt took on mightily for the death of her poor dear husband! Perhaps she felt some compunction at having given him so much physic, and nursed him into his grave. At any rate, she did all that a widow could do to honour his memory. She spared no expense in either the quantity or quality of her mourning weeds; wore a miniature of him about her neck, as large as a little sun dial; and had a full length portrait of him always hanging in her bed chamber. All the world extolled her conduct to the skies; and it was determined, that a woman who behaved so well to the memory of one husband, deserved soon to get another.

It was not long after this that she went to take up her residence in an old country seat in Derbyshire, which had long been in the care of merely a steward and housekeeper. She took most of her servants with her, intending to make it her principal abode. The house stood in a lonely, wild part of the country, among the grey Derbyshire hills; with a murderer hanging in chains on a bleak height in full view.

The servants from town were half frightened out of their wits, at the idea of living in such a dismal, pagan looking place; especially when they got together in the servants' hall in the evening, and compared notes on all the hobgoblin stories picked up in the course of the day. They were afraid to venture alone about the gloomy, black looking chambers. My lady's maid, who was troubled with nerves, declared she could never sleep alone in such a "gashly, rummaging old building;" and the footman, who was a kind hearted young fellow, did all in his power to cheer her up.

My aunt was struck with the lonely appearance of the house. Before going to bed, therefore, she examined well the fastenings of the doors and windows, locked up the plate with her own hands, and carried the keys, together with a little box of money and jewels, to her own room; for she was a notable woman, and always saw to all things herself. Having put the keys under her pillow, and dismissed her maid, she sat by her toilet arranging her hair; for, being, in spite of her grief for my uncle, rather a buxom widow, she was somewhat particular about her person. She sat for a little while looking at her face in the glass, first on one side, then on the other, as ladies are apt to do, when they would ascertain whether they have been in good looks; for a roystering country squire of the neighbourhood, with whom she had flirted when a girl, had called that day to welcome her to the country.

All of a sudden she thought she heard something move behind her. She looked hastily round, but there was nothing to be seen. Nothing but the grimly painted portrait of her poor dear man, hanging against the wall. She gave a heavy sigh to his memory, as she was accustomed to do, whenever she spoke of him in company; and then went on adjusting her night dress, and thinking of the squire. Her sigh was re-echoed; or answered by a long drawn breath. She looked round again, but no one was to be seen. She ascribed these sounds to the wind, oozing through the rat holes of the old mansion; and proceeded leisurely to put her hair in papers, when, all at once, she thought she perceived one of the eyes of the portrait move.

"The back of her head being towards it!" said the story teller with the ruined head, "good!"

"Yes sir!" replied drily the narrator, "her back being towards the portrait, but her eye fixed on its reflection in the glass."

Well, as I was saying, she perceived one of the eyes of the portrait move. So strange a circumstance, as you may well suppose, gave her a sudden shock. To assure herself of the fact, she put one hand to her forehead, as if rubbing it; peeped through her fingers, and moved the candle with the other hand. The light of the taper gleamed on the eye, and was reflected from it. She was sure it moved. Nay, more, it seemed to give her a wink, as she had sometimes known her husband to do when living! It struck a momentary chill to her heart; for she was a lone woman, and felt herself fearfully situated.

The chill was but transient. My aunt, who was almost as resolute a personage as your uncle, sir, (turning to the old story teller,) became instantly calm and collected. She went on adjusting her dress. She even hummed an air, and did not make a single false note. She casually overturned a dressing box; took a candle and picked up the articles, one by one, from the floor; pursued a rolling pin cushion that was making the best of its way under the bed; then opened the door; looked for an instant into the corridor, as if in doubt whether to go; and then walked quietly out.

She hastened down stairs, ordered the servants to arm themselves with the weapons first at hand, placed herself at their head, and returned almost immediately.

Her hastily levied army presented a formidable force. The steward had a rusty blunderbuss; the coachman a loaded whip; the footman a pair of horse pistols; the cook a huge chopping knife, and the butler a bottle in each hand. My aunt led the van with a red hot poker; and, in my opinion, she was the most formidable of the party. The waiting maid, who dreaded to stay alone in the servants' hall, brought up the rear, smelling to a broken bottle of volatile salts, and expressing her terror of the ghostesses.

"Ghosts!" said my aunt resolutely, "I'll singe their whiskers for them!"

They entered the chamber. All was still and undisturbed as when she left it. They approached the portrait of my uncle.

"Pull me down that picture!" cried my aunt.

A heavy groan, and a sound like the chattering of teeth, issued from the portrait. The servants shrunk back. The maid uttered a faint shriek, and clung to the footman for support.

"Instantly!" added my aunt, with a stamp of the foot.

The picture was pulled down, and from a recess behind it, in which had formerly stood a clock, they hauled forth a round shouldered, black bearded varlet, with a knife as long as my arm, but trembling all over like an aspen leaf.

"Well, and who was he? No ghost, I suppose!" said the inquisitive gentleman.

"A Knight of the Post," replied the narrator, "who had been smitten with the worth of the wealthy widow; or rather a marauding Tarquin, who had stolen into her chamber to violate her purse and rifle her strong box when all the house should be asleep. In plain terms," continued he, "the vagabond was a loose idle fellow of the neighbourhood, who had once been a servant in the house, and had been employed to assist in arranging it for the reception of its mistress. He confessed that he had contrived this hiding place for his nefarious purposes, and had borrowed an eye from the portrait by way of a reconnoitering hole."

"And what did they do with him—did they hang him?" resumed the questioner.

"Hang him?—how could they?" exclaimed a beetle browed barrister, with a hawk's nose—"the offence was not capital—no robbery, nor assault had been committed—no forcible entry or breaking into the premises"——

"My aunt," said the narrator, "was a woman of spirit, and apt to take the law into her own hands. She had her own notions of cleanliness also. She ordered the fellow to be drawn through the horsepond to cleanse away all offences, and then to be well rubbed down with an oaken towel."

"And what became of him afterwards?" said the inquisitive gentleman.

"I do not exactly know—I believe he was sent on a voyage of improvement to Botany Bay."

"And your aunt"—said the inquisitive gentleman—"I'll warrant she took care to make her maid sleep in the room with her after that."

"No, sir, she did better—she gave her hand shortly after to the roystering squire; for she used to observe it was a dismal thing for a woman to sleep alone in the country."

"She was right," observed the inquisitive gentleman, nodding sagaciously—"but I am sorry they did not hang that fellow."

It was agreed on all hands that the last narrator had brought his tale to the most satisfactory conclusion; though a country clergyman present regretted that the uncle and aunt, who figured in the different stories, had not been married together. They certainly would have been well matched.

"But I don't see, after all," said the inquisitive gentleman, "that there was any ghost in this last story."

"Oh, if it's ghosts you want, honey," cried the Irish captain of dragoons, "if it's ghosts you want, you shall have a whole regiment of them. And since these gentlemen have given the adventures of their uncles and aunts, faith and I'll e'en give you a chapter out of my own family history."

THE BOLD DRAGOON, OR
THE ADVENTURE OF MY GRANDFATHER

My grandfather was a bold dragoon, for its a profession, d'ye see, that has run in the family. All my forefathers have been dragoons and died upon the field of honour except myself, and I hope my posterity may be able to say the same; however, I don't mean to be vainglorious. Well, my grandfather, as I said, was a bold dragoon, and had served in the Low Countries. In fact, he was one of that very army, which, according to my uncle Toby, "swore so terribly in Flanders." He could swear a good stick himself; and, moreover, was the very man that introduced the doctrine Corporal Trim mentions, of radical heat and radical moisture; or in other words, the mode of keeping out the damps of ditch water by burnt brandy. Be that as it may, it's nothing to the purport of my story. I only tell it to show you that my grandfather was a man not easily to be humbugged. He had seen service; or, according to his own phrase, "he had seen the divil"—and that's saying every thing.

Well, gentlemen, my grandfather was on his way to England, for which he intended to embark at Ostend;—bad luck to the place for one where I was kept by storms and head winds for three long days, and the divil of a jolly companion or pretty face to comfort me. Well, as I was saying, my grandfather was on his way to England, or rather to Ostend—no matter which, it's all the same. So one evening, towards nightfall, he rode jollily into Bruges. Very like you all know Bruges, gentlemen, a queer, old fashioned Flemish town, once they say a great place for trade and money making, in old times, when the Mynheers were in their glory; but almost as large and as empty as an Irishman's pocket at the present day. Well, gentlemen, it was the time of the annual fair. All Bruges was crowded; and the canals swarmed with Dutch boats, and the streets swarmed with Dutch merchants; and there was hardly any getting along for goods, wares, and merchandises, and peasants in big breeches, and women in half a score of petticoats.

My grandfather rode jollily along, in his easy slashing way, for he was a saucy, sunshiny fellow—staring about him at the motley crowd, and the old houses with gabel ends to the street and storks' nests on the chimneys; winking at the ya vrouws who showed their faces at the windows, and joking the women right and left in the street; all of whom laughed and took it in amazing good part; for though he did not know a word of their language, yet he had always a knack of making himself understood among the women.

Well, gentlemen, it being the time of the annual fair, all the town was crowded; every inn and tavern full, and my grandfather applied in vain from one to the other for admittance. At length he rode up to an old rackety inn that looked ready to fall to pieces, and which all the rats would have run away from, if they could have found room in any other house to put their heads. It was just such a queer building as you see in Dutch pictures, with a tall roof that reached up into the clouds; and as many garrets, one over the other, as the seven heavens of Mahomet.—Nothing had saved it from tumbling down but a stork's nest on the chimney, which always brings good luck to a house in the Low Countries; and at the very time of my grandfather's arrival, there were two of these long legged birds of grace, standing like ghosts on the chimney top. Faith, but they've kept the house on its legs to this very day; for you may see it any time you pass through Bruges, as it stands there yet; only it is turned into a brewery—a brewery of strong Flemish beer; at least it was so when I came that way after the battle of Waterloo.

My grandfather eyed the house curiously as he approached. It might not altogether have struck his fancy, had he not seen in large letters over the door,

HEER VERKOOPT MAN GOEDEN DRANK.

My grandfather had learnt enough of the language to know that the sign promised good liquor. "This is the house for me," said he, stopping short before the door.

The sudden appearance of a dashing dragoon was an event in an old inn, frequented only by the peaceful sons of traffick. A rich burgher of Antwerp, a stately ample man, in a broad Flemish hat, and who was the great man and great patron of the establishment, sat smoking a clean long pipe on one side of the door; a fat little distiller of Geneva from Schiedam, sat smoking on the other, and the bottle nosed host stood in the door, and the comely hostess, in crimped cap, beside him; and the hostess' daughter, a plump Flanders lass, with long gold pendants in her ears, was at a side window.

"Humph!" said the rich burgher of Antwerp, with a sulky glance at the stranger.

"Die duyvel!" said the fat little distiller of Schiedam.

The landlord saw with the quick glance of a publican that the new guest was not at all to the taste of the old ones; and to tell the truth, he did not like my grandfather's saucy eye. He shook his head—"Not a garret in the house but was full."

"Not a garret!" echoed the landlady.

"Not a garret!" echoed the daughter.

The burgher of Antwerp and the little distiller of Schiedam continued to smoke their pipes sullenly, eyed the enemy askance from under their broad hats, but said nothing.

My grandfather was not a man to be browbeaten. He threw the reins on his horse's neck, cocked his hat on one side, stuck one arm akimbo—

"Faith and troth!" said he, "but I'll sleep in this house this very night!"

As he said this he gave a slap on his thigh, by way of emphasis—the slap went to the landlady's heart.

He followed up the vow by jumping off his horse, and making his way past the staring Mynheers into the public room.—May be you've been in the bar room of an old Flemish inn—faith, but a handsome chamber it was as you'd wish to see; with a brick floor, and a great fire place, with the whole bible history in glazed tiles; and then the mantle piece, pitching itself head foremost out of the wall, with a whole regiment of cracked tea pots and earthen jugs paraded on it; not to mention half a dozen great Delft platters hung about the room by way of pictures; and the little bar in one corner, and the bouncing bar maid inside of it with a red calico cap and yellow ear drops.

My grandfather snapped his fingers over his head, as he cast an eye round the room: "Faith, this is the very house I've been looking after," said he.

There was some further show of resistance on the part of the garrison, but my grandfather was an old soldier, and an Irishman to boot, and not easily repulsed, especially after he had got into the fortress. So he blarney'd the landlord, kissed the landlord's wife, tickled the landlord's daughter, chucked the bar maid under the chin; and it was agreed on all hands that it would be a thousand pities, and a burning shame into the bargain, to turn such a bold dragoon into the streets. So they laid their heads together, that is to say, my grandfather and the landlady, and it was at length agreed to accommodate him with an old chamber that had for some time been shut up.

"Some say it's haunted!" whispered the landlord's daughter, "but you're a bold dragoon, and I dare say don't fear ghosts."

"The divil a bit!" said my grandfather, pinching her plump cheek; "but if I should be troubled by ghosts, I've been to the Red Sea in my time, and have a pleasant way of laying them, my darling!"

And then he whispered something to the girl which made her laugh, and give him a good humoured box on the ear. In short, there was nobody knew better how to make his way among the petticoats than my grandfather.

In a little while, as was his usual way, he took complete possession of the house; swaggering all over it:—into the stable to look after his horse; into the kitchen to look after his supper. He had something to say or do with every one; smoked with the Dutchmen; drank with the Germans; slapped the landlord on the shoulder, romped with his daughter and the bar maid:— never since the days of Ally Croaker had such a rattling blade been seen. The landlord stared at him with astonishment; the landlord's daughter hung her head and giggled whenever he came near; and as he swaggered along the corridor, with his sword trailing by his side, the maids looked after him, and whispered to one another—"What a proper man!"

At supper my grandfather took command of the table d'hôte as though he had been at home; helped every body, not forgetting himself; talked with every one, whether he understood their language or not; and made his way into the intimacy of the rich burgher of Antwerp, who had never been known to be sociable with any one during his life. In fact, he revolutionized the whole establishment, and gave it such a rouse, that the very house reeled with it. He outsat every one at table excepting the little fat distiller of Schiedam, who sat soaking a long time before he broke forth; but when he did, he was a very devil incarnate. He took a violent affection for my grandfather; so they sat drinking, and smoking, and telling stories, and sing- ing Dutch and Irish songs, without understanding a word each other said, until the little Hollander was fairly swampt with his own gin and water, and carried off to bed, whooping and hiccuping, and trolling the burthen of a Low Dutch love song.

Well, gentlemen, my grandfather was shown to his quarters, up a large staircase composed of loads of hewn timber; and through long rigmarole passages, hung with blackened paintings of fruit, and fish, and game, and country frolicks, and huge kitchens, and portly burgomasters, such as you see about old fashioned Flemish inns, till at length he arrived at his room.

An old times chamber it was, sure enough, and crowded with all kinds of trumpery. It looked like an infirmary for decayed and superannuated furniture; where every thing diseased and disabled was sent to nurse, or to be forgotten. Or rather, it might have been taken for a general congress of old legitimate moveables, where every kind and country had a representative. No two chairs were alike: such high backs and low backs, and leather bottoms and worsted bottoms, and straw bottoms, and no bottoms; and cracked marble tables with curiously carved legs, holding balls in their claws, as though they were going to play at ninepins.

My grandfather made a bow to the motley assemblage as he entered, and having undressed himself, placed his light in the fire place, asking pardon of the tongs, which seemed to be making love to the shovel in the chimney corner, and whispering soft nonsense in its ear.

The rest of the guests were by this time sound asleep; for your Mynheers are huge sleepers. The house maids, one by one, crept up yawning to their atticks, and not a female head in the inn was laid on a pillow that night without dreaming of the Bold Dragoon.

My grandfather, for his part, got into bed, and drew over him one of those great bags of down, under which they smother a man in the Low Countries; and there he lay, melting between two feather beds, like an anchovy sandwich between two slices of toast and butter. He was a warm complexioned man, and this smothering played the very deuce with him. So, sure enough, in a little time it seemed as if a legion of imps were twitching at him, and all the blood in his veins was in fever heat.

He lay still, however, until all the house was quiet, excepting the snoring of the Mynheers from the different chambers; who answered one another in all kinds of tones and cadences, like so many bull frogs in a swamp. The quieter the house became, the more unquiet became my grandfather. He waxed warmer and warmer, until at length the bed became too hot to hold him.

"May be the maid had warmed it too much?" said the curious gentleman inquiringly.

"I rather think the contrary," replied the Irishman. "But be that as it may, it grew too hot for my grandfather."

"Faith there's no standing this any longer," says he; so he jumped out of bed and went strolling about the house.

"What for?" said the inquisitive gentleman.

"Why, to cool himself to be sure—or perhaps to find a more comfortable bed—or perhaps——but no matter what he went for—he never mentioned; and there's no use in taking up our time in conjecturing."

Well, my grandfather had been for some time absent from his room, and was returning, perfectly cool, when just as he reached the door he heard a strange noise within. He paused and listened. It seemed as if some one were trying to hum a tune in defiance of the asthma. He recollected the report of the room's being haunted; but he was no believer in ghosts. So he pushed the door gently open, and peeped in.

Egad, gentlemen, there was a gambol carrying on within enough to have astonished St. Anthony himself.

By the light of the fire he saw a pale weazen-faced fellow in a long flannel gown and a tall white nightcap with a tassel to it, who sat by the fire, with a bellows under his arm by way of bagpipe, from which he forced the asthmatical music that had bothered my grandfather. As he played, too, he kept twitching about with a thousand queer contortions; nodding his head and bobbing about his tasselled nightcap.

My grandfather thought this very odd, and mighty presumptuous, and was about to demand what business he had to play his wind instrument in another gentleman's quarters, when a new cause of astonishment met his eye. From the opposite side of the room a long backed, bandy legged chair, covered with leather, and studded all over in a coxcomical fashion with little brass nails, got suddenly into motion; thrust out first a claw foot, then a crooked arm, and at length, making a leg, slided gracefully up to an easy chair, of tarnished brocade, with a hole in its bottom, and led it gallantly out in a ghostly minuet about the floor.

The musician now played fiercer and fiercer, and bobbed his head and his nightcap about like mad. By degrees the dancing mania seemed to seize upon all the other pieces of furniture. The antique, long bodied chairs paired off in couples and led down a country dance; a three legged stool danced a hornpipe, though horribly puzzled by its supernumerary limb; while the amorous tongs seized the shovel round the waist, and whirled it about the room in a German waltz. In short, all the moveables got in motion; pirouetting, hands across, right and left, like so many devils, all except a great clothes press, which kept curtseying and curtseying in one corner, like a dowager, in exquisite time to the music;—being either too corpulent to dance, or perhaps at a loss for a partner.

My grandfather concluded the latter to be the reason; so, being, like a true Irishman, devoted to the sex, and at all times ready for a frolick, he bounced into the room, calling to the musician to strike up "Paddy O'Rafferty," capered up to the clothes press and seized upon two handles to lead her out:—When, whirr!—the whole revel was at an end. The chairs, tables, tongs, and shovel slunk in an instant as quietly into their places as if nothing had happened; and the musician vanished up the chimney, leaving the bellows behind him in his hurry. My grandfather found himself seated in the middle of the floor, with the clothes press sprawling before him, and the two handles jerked off and in his hands.

"Then after all, this was a mere dream!" said the inquisitive gentleman.

"The divil a bit of a dream!" replied the Irishman: "there never was a truer fact in this world. Faith, I should have liked to see any man tell my grandfather it was a dream."

Well, gentlemen, as the clothes press was a mighty heavy body, and my grandfather likewise, particularly in rear, you may easily suppose two such heavy bodies coming to the ground would make a bit of a noise. Faith, the old mansion shook as though it had mistaken it for an earthquake. The whole garrison was alarmed. The landlord, who slept below, hurried up with a candle to inquire the cause, but with all his haste his daughter had arrived at the scene of uproar before him. The landlord was followed by the land-lady, who was followed by the bouncing bar maid, who was followed by the simpering chambermaids all holding together, as well as they could, such garments as they had first laid hands on; but all in a terrible hurry to see what the deuce was to pay in the chamber of the bold dragoon.

My grandfather related the marvellous scene he had witnessed, and the broken handles of the prostrate clothes press bore testimony to the fact. There was no contesting such evidence; particularly with a lad of my grandfather's complexion, who seemed able to make good every word either with sword or shillelah. So the landlord scratched his head and looked silly, as he was apt to do when puzzled. The landlady scratched—no, she did not scratch her head,—but she knit her brow, and did not seem half pleased with the explanation. But the landlady's daughter corroborated it, by recollecting that the last person who had dwelt in that chamber was a famous juggler who had died of St. Vitus's dance, and no doubt had infected all the furniture.

This set all things to rights, particularly when the chambermaids declared that they had all witnessed strange carryings on in that room;—and as they declared this "upon their honours," there could not remain a doubt upon the subject.

"And did your grandfather go to bed again in that room?" said the inquisitive gentleman.

"That's more than I can tell. Where he passed the rest of the night was a secret he never disclosed. In fact, though he had seen much service, he was but indifferently acquainted with geography, and apt to make blunders in his travels about inns at night, which it would have puzzled him sadly to account for in the morning."

"Was he ever apt to walk in his sleep?" said the knowing old gentleman.

"Never that I heard of."

There was a little pause after this rigmarole Irish romance, when the old gentleman with the haunted head observed, that the stories hitherto related had rather a burlesque tendency. "I recollect an adventure, however," added he, "which I heard of during a residence at Paris, for the truth of which I can undertake to vouch, and which is of a very grave and singular nature."

THE ADVENTURE OF THE GERMAN STUDENT

On a stormy night, in the tempestuous times of the French revolution, a young German was returning to his lodgings, at a late hour, across the old part of Paris. The lightning gleamed, and the loud claps of thunder rattled through the lofty, narrow streets—but I should first tell you something about this young German.

Gottfried Wolfgang was a young man of good family. He had studied for some time at Göttingen, but being of a visionary and enthusiastic character, he had wandered into those wild and speculative doctrines which have so often bewildered German students. His secluded life, his intense application, and the singular nature of his studies, had an effect on both mind and body. His health was impaired; his imagination diseased. He had been indulging in fanciful speculations on spiritual essences until, like Swedenborg, he had an ideal world of his own around him. He took up a notion, I do not know from what cause, that there was an evil influence hanging over him; an evil genius or spirit seeking to ensnare him and ensure his perdition. Such an idea working on his melancholy temperament produced the most gloomy effects. He became haggard and desponding. His friends discovered the mental malady preying upon him, and determined that the best cure was a change of scene; he was sent, therefore, to finish his studies amidst the splendours and gaieties of Paris.

Wolfgang arrived at Paris at the breaking out of the revolution. The popular delirium at first caught his enthusiastic mind, and he was captivated by the political and philosophical theories of the day: but the scenes of blood which followed shocked his sensitive nature; disgusted him with society and the world, and made him more than ever a recluse. He shut himself up in a solitary apartment in the *Pays Latin*, the quarter of students. There in a gloomy street not far from the monastic walls of the Sorbonne, he pursued his favourite speculations. Sometimes he spent hours together in the great libraries of Paris, those catacombs of departed authors, rummaging among their hoards of dusty and obsolete works in quest of food for his unhealthy appetite. He was, in a manner, a literary goul, feeding in the charnel house of decayed literature.

Wolfgang, though solitary and recluse, was of an ardent temperament, but for a time it operated merely upon his imagination. He was too shy and ignorant of the world to make any advances to the fair, but he was a passionate admirer of female beauty, and in his lonely chamber would often lose himself in reveries on forms and faces which he had seen, and his fancy would deck out images of loveliness far surpassing the reality.

While his mind was in this excited and sublimated state, a dream produced an extraordinary effect upon him. It was of a female face of transcendent beauty. So strong was the impression made, that he dreamt of it again and again. It haunted his thoughts by day, his slumbers by night; in fine, he became passionately enamoured of this shadow of a dream. This lasted so long, that it became one of those fixed ideas which haunt the minds of melancholy men, and are at times mistaken for madness.

Such was Gottfried Wolfgang, and such his situation at the time I mentioned. He was returning home late one stormy night, through some of the old and gloomy streets of the *Marais*, the ancient part of Paris. The loud claps of thunder rattled among the high houses of the narrow streets. He came to the Place de Grève, the square where public executions are performed. The lightning quivered about the pinnacles of the ancient Hôtel de Ville, and shed flickering gleams over the open space in front. As Wolfgang was crossing the square, he shrank back with horror at finding himself close by the guillotine. It was the height of the reign of terror, when this dreadful instrument of death stood ever ready, and its scaffold was continually running with the blood of the virtuous and the brave. It had that very day been actively employed in the work of carnage, and there it stood in grim array amidst a silent and sleeping city, waiting for fresh victims.

Wolfgang's heart sickened within him, and he was turning shuddering from the horrible engine, when he beheld a shadowy form cowering as it were at the foot of the steps which led up to the scaffold. A succession of vivid flashes of lightning revealed it more distinctly. It was a female figure, dressed in black. She was seated on one of the lower steps of the scaffold, leaning forward, her face hid in her lap, and her long dishevelled tresses hanging to the ground, streaming with the rain which fell in torrents. Wolfgang paused. There was something awful in this solitary monument of wo. The female had the appearance of being above the common order. He knew the times to be full of vicissitude, and that many a fair head, which had once been pillowed on down, now wandered houseless. Perhaps this was some poor mourner whom the dreadful axe had rendered desolate, and who sat here heartbroken on the strand of existence, from which all that was dear to her had been launched into eternity.

He approached, and addressed her in the accents of sympathy. She raised her head and gazed wildly at him. What was his astonishment at beholding, by the bright glare of the lightning, the very face which had haunted him in his dreams. It was pale and disconsolate, but ravishingly beautiful.

Trembling with violent and conflicting emotions, Wolfgang again accosted her. He spoke something of her being exposed at such an hour of the night, and to the fury of such a storm, and offered to conduct her to her friends. She pointed to the guillotine with a gesture of dreadful signification.

"I have no friend on earth!" said she.

"But you have a home," said Wolfgang.

"Yes—in the grave!"

The heart of the student melted at the words.

"If a stranger dare make an offer," said he, "without danger of being misunderstood, I would offer my humble dwelling as a shelter; myself as a devoted friend. I am friendless myself in Paris, and a stranger in the land; but if my life could be of service, it is at your disposal, and should be sacrificed before harm or indignity should come to you."

There was an honest earnestness in the young man's manner that had its effect. His foreign accent, too, was in his favour; it showed him not to be a hackneyed inhabitant of Paris. Indeed there is an eloquence in true enthusiasm that is not to be doubted. The homeless stranger confided herself implicitly to the protection of the student.

He supported her faltering steps across the Pont Neuf, and by the place where the statue of Henry the Fourth had been overthrown by the populace. The storm had abated, and the thunder rumbled at a distance. All Paris was quiet; that great volcano of human passion slumbered for a while, to gather fresh strength for the next day's eruption. The student conducted his charge through the ancient streets of the *Pays Latin*, and by the dusky walls of the Sorbonne to the great, dingy hotel which he inhabited. The old portress who admitted them stared with surprise at the unusual sight of the melancholy Wolfgang with a female companion.

On entering his apartment, the student, for the first time, blushed at the scantiness and indifference of his dwelling. He had but one chamber—an old fashioned saloon—heavily carved and fantastically furnished with the remains of former magnificence, for it was one of those hotels in the quarter of the Luxembourg palace which had once belonged to nobility. It was lumbered with books and papers, and all the usual apparatus of a student, and his bed stood in a recess at one end.

When lights were brought, and Wolfgang had a better opportunity of contemplating the stranger, he was more than ever intoxicated by her beauty. Her face was pale, but of a dazzling fairness, set off by a profusion of raven hair that hung clustering about it. Her eyes were large and brilliant, with a singular expression approaching almost to wildness. As far as her black dress permitted her shape to be seen, it was of perfect symmetry. Her whole appearance was highly striking, though she was dressed in the simplest style. The only thing approaching to an ornament which she wore was a broad, black band round her neck, clasped by diamonds.

The perplexity now commenced with the student how to dispose of the helpless being thus thrown upon his protection. He thought of abandoning his chamber to her, and seeking shelter for himself elsewhere. Still he was so fascinated by her charms, there seemed to be such a spell upon his thoughts and senses, that he could not tear himself from her presence. Her manner, too, was singular and unaccountable. She spoke no more of the guillotine. Her grief had abated. The attentions of the student had first won her confidence, and then, apparently, her heart. She was evidently an enthusiast like himself, and enthusiasts soon understand each other.

In the infatuation of the moment Wolfgang avowed his passion for her. He told her the story of his mysterious dream, and how she had possessed his heart before he had even seen her. She was strangely affected by his recital, and acknowledged to have felt an impulse towards him equally unaccountable. It was the time for wild theory and wild actions. Old prejudices and superstitions were done away; every thing was under the sway of the "God dess of Reason." Among other rubbish of the old times, the forms and ceremonies of marriage began to be considered superfluous bonds for honourable minds. Social compacts were the vogue. Wolfgang was too much of a theorist not to be tainted by the liberal doctrines of the day.

"Why should we separate?" said he: "our hearts are united; in the eye of reason and honour we are as one. What need is there of sordid forms to bind high souls together?"

The stranger listened with emotion: she had evidently received illumination at the same school.

"You have no home nor family," continued he; "let me be every thing to you, or rather let us be every thing to one another. If form is necessary, form shall be observed—there is my hand. I pledge myself to you for ever."

"For ever?" said the stranger, solemnly.

"For ever!" repeated Wolfgang.

The stranger clasped the hand extended to her: "Then I am yours," murmured she, and sank upon his bosom.

The next morning the student left his bride sleeping, and sallied forth at an early hour to seek more spacious apartments, suitable to the change in his situation. When he returned, he found the stranger lying with her head hanging over the bed, and one arm thrown over it. He spoke to her, but received no reply. He advanced to awaken her from her uneasy posture. On taking her hand, it was cold—there was no pulsation—her face was pallid and ghastly.—In a word—she was a corpse.

Horrified and frantic, he alarmed the house. A scene of confusion ensued. The police was summoned. As the officer of police entered the room, he started back on beholding the corpse.

"Great heaven!" cried he, "how did this woman come here?"

"Do you know any thing about her?" said Wolfgang, eagerly.

"Do I?" exclaimed the police officer: "she was guillotined yesterday!"

He stepped forward; undid the black collar round the neck of the corpse, and the head rolled on the floor!

The student burst into a frenzy. "The fiend! the fiend has gained possession of me!" shrieked he: "I am lost for ever!"

They tried to soothe him, but in vain. He was possessed with the frightful belief that an evil spirit had reanimated the dead body to ensnare him. He went distracted, and died in a madhouse.

––––––––

Here the old gentleman with the haunted head finished his narrative.

"And is this really a fact?" said the inquisitive gentleman.

"A fact not to be doubted," replied the other. "I had it from the best authority. The student told it me himself. I saw him in a madhouse at Paris."

THE ADVENTURE OF THE MYSTERIOUS PICTURE

As one story of the kind produces another, and as all the company seemed fully engrossed by the subject, and disposed to bring their relatives and ancestors upon the scene, there is no knowing how many more strange adventures we might have heard, had not a corpulent old fox hunter, who had slept soundly through the whole, now suddenly awakened, with a loud and long drawn yawn. The sound broke the charm; the ghosts took to flight as though it had been cock-crowing, and there was a universal move for bed.

"And now for the haunted chamber," said the Irish captain, taking his candle.

"Aye, who's to be the hero of the night?" said the gentleman with the ruined head.

"That we shall see in the morning," said the old gentleman with the nose: "whoever looks pale and grizzly will have seen the ghost."

"Well, gentlemen," said the Baronet, "there's many a true thing said in jest. In fact, one of you will sleep in a room tonight"——

"What—a haunted room? a haunted room? I claim the adventure—and I—and I—and I," cried a dozen guests, talking and laughing at the same time.

"No—no," said mine host, "there is a secret about one of my rooms on which I feel disposed to try an experiment. So, gentlemen, none of you shall know who has the haunted chamber, until circumstances reveal it. I will not even know it myself, but will leave it to chance and the allotment of the housekeeper. At the same time, if it will be any satisfaction to you, I will observe, for the honour of my paternal mansion, that there's scarcely a chamber in it but is well worthy of being haunted."

We now separated for the night, and each went to his allotted room. Mine was in one wing of the building, and I could not but smile at its resemblance in style to those eventful apartments described in the tales of the supper table. It was spacious and gloomy, decorated with lamp black portraits, a bed of ancient damask, with a tester sufficiently lofty to grace a couch of state, and a number of massive pieces of old fashioned furniture. I drew a great claw-footed arm chair before the wide fire place, stirred up the fire; sat looking into it, and musing upon the odd stories I had heard; until, partly overcome by the fatigue of the day's hunting, and partly by the wine and wassail of mine host, I fell asleep in my chair.

The uneasiness of my position made my slumber troubled, and laid me at the mercy of all kinds of wild and fearful dreams; now it was that my perfidi ous dinner and supper rose in rebellion against my peace. I was hag-ridden by a fat saddle of mutton; a plum pudding weighed like lead upon my con science; the merry thought of a capon filled me with horrible suggestions; and a devilled leg of a turkey stalked in all kinds of diabolical shapes through my imagination. In short, I had a violent fit of the nightmare. Some strange indefinite evil seemed hanging over me which I could not avert; something terrible and loathsome oppressed me which I could not shake off. I was conscious of being asleep, and strove to rouse myself, but every effort re doubled the evil; until gasping, struggling, almost strangling, I suddenly sprang bolt upright in my chair, and awoke.

The light on the mantle piece had burnt low, and the wick was divided; there was a great winding sheet made by the dripping wax, on the side towards me. The disordered taper emitted a broad flaring flame, and threw a strong light on a painting over the fire place, which I had not hitherto observed.

It consisted merely of a head, or rather a face, staring full upon me, with an expression that was startling. It was without a frame, and at the first glance I could hardly persuade myself that it was not a real face, thrusting itself out of the dark oaken pannel. I sat in my chair gazing at it, and the more I gazed the more it disquieted me. I had never before been affected in the same way by any painting. The emotions it caused were strange and indefinite. They were something like what I have heard ascribed to the eyes of the basilisk; or like that mysterious influence in reptiles termed fascina tion. I passed my hand over my eyes several times, as if seeking instinctively to brush away the illusion—in vain—they instantly reverted to the picture, and its chilling, creeping influence over my flesh and blood was redoubled.

I looked round the room on other pictures, either to divert my attention,

or to see whether the same effect would be produced by them. Some of
them were grim enough to produce the effect, if the mere grimness of the
painting produced it—no such thing. My eye passed over them all with perfect indifference, but the moment it reverted to this visage over the fire
place, it was as if an electric shock darted through me. The other pictures
were dim and faded; but this one protruded from a plain black ground in
the strongest relief, and with wonderful truth of colouring. The expression
was that of agony—the agony of intense bodily pain; but a menace scowled
upon the brow, and a few sprinklings of blood added to its ghastliness. Yet
it was not all these characteristics—it was some horror of the mind, some
inscrutable antipathy awakened by this picture, which harrowed up my
feelings.

I tried to persuade myself that this was chimerical; that my brain was
confused by the fumes of mine host's good cheer, and, in some measure, by
the odd stories about paintings which had been told at supper. I determined
to shake off these vapours of the mind; rose from my chair, and walked about
the room; snapped my fingers; rallied myself; laughed aloud. It was a forced
laugh, and the echo of it in the old chamber jarred upon my ear. I walked
to the window; tried to discern the landscape through the glass. It was pitch
darkness, and howling storm without; and as I heard the wind moan among
the trees, I caught a reflection of this accursed visage in the pane of glass,
as though it were staring through the window at me. Even the reflection of
it was thrilling.

How was this vile nervous fit, for such I now persuaded myself it was, to
be conquered? I determined to force myself not to look at the painting, but
to undress quickly and get into bed. I began to undress, but in spite of every
effort I could not keep myself from stealing a glance every now and then at
the picture; and a glance was now sufficient to distress me. Even when my
back was turned to it, the idea of this strange face behind me, peering over
my shoulder, was insufferable. I threw off my clothes and hurried into bed;
but still this visage gazed upon me. I had a full view of it in my bed, and for
some time could not take my eyes from it. I had grown nervous to a dismal
degree.

I put out the light, and tried to force myself to sleep;—all in vain! The fire
gleaming up a little, threw an uncertain light about the room, leaving, however, the region of the picture in deep shadow. What, thought I, if this be
the chamber about which mine host spoke as having a mystery reigning over
it?—I had taken his words merely as spoken in jest; might they have a real
import? I looked around. The faintly lighted apartment had all the qualifications requisite for a haunted chamber. It began in my infected imagination
to assume strange appearances. The old portraits turned paler and paler,
and blacker and blacker; the streaks of light and shadow thrown among the
quaint articles of furniture, gave them more singular shapes and characters.

There was a huge dark clothes press of antique form, gorgeous in brass and lustrous with wax, that began to grow oppressive to me.

Am I then, thought I, indeed, the hero of the haunted room? Is there really a spell laid upon me, or is this all some contrivance of mine host, to raise a laugh at my expense? The idea of being hag-ridden by my own fancy all night, and then bantered on my haggard looks the next day was intolerable; but the very idea was sufficient to produce the effect, and to render me still more nervous. Pish, said I, it can be no such thing. How could my worthy host imagine that I, or any man would be so worried by a mere picture? It is my own diseased imagination that torments me. I turned in bed, and shifted from side to side, to try to fall asleep; but all in vain. When one cannot get asleep by lying quiet, it is seldom that tossing about will effect the purpose. The fire gradually went out and left the room in darkness. Still I had the idea of that inexplicable countenance gazing and keeping watch upon me through the gloom. Nay, what was worse, the very darkness seemed to magnify its terrors. It was like having an unseen enemy hanging about one in the night. Instead of having one picture now to worry me, I had a hundred. I fancied it in every direction. There it is, thought I,   and there, and there,—with its horrible and mysterious expression, still gazing and gazing on me. No—if I must suffer this strange and dismal influence, it were better face a single foe, than thus be haunted by a thousand images of it.

Whoever has been in a state of nervous agitation, must know that the longer it continues, the more uncontroulable it grows; the very air of the chamber seemed at length infected by the baleful presence of this picture. I fancied it hovering over me. I almost felt the fearful visage from the wall approaching my face,—it seemed breathing upon me. This is not to be borne, said I, at length, springing out of bed. I can stand this no longer. I shall only tumble and toss about here all night; make a very spectre of myself, and become the hero of the haunted chamber in good earnest. Whatever be the ill consequence, I'll quit this cursed room, and seek a night's rest elsewhere. They can but laugh at me at all events, and they'll be sure to have the laugh upon me if I pass a sleepless night and show them a haggard and wobegone visage in the morning.

All this was half muttered to myself, as I hastily slipped on my clothes; which having done, I groped my way out of the room, and down stairs to the drawing room. Here, after tumbling over two or three pieces of furniture, I made out to reach a sopha, and stretching myself upon it determined to bivouack there for the night.

The moment I found myself out of the neighbourhood of that strange picture, it seemed as if the charm were broken. All its influence was at an end. I felt assured that it was confined to its own dreary chamber, for I had, with a sort of instinctive caution, turned the key when I closed the door. I soon calmed down, therefore, into a state of tranquillity; from that into a drowsiness, and finally into a deep sleep; out of which I did not awake, until the housemaid, with her besom and her matin song, came to put the room in order. She stared at finding me stretched upon the sofa; but I presume circumstances of the kind were not uncommon after hunting dinners, in her master's bachelor establishment; for she went on with her song and her work, and took no further heed of me.

I had an unconquerable repugnance to return to my chamber; so I found my way to the butler's quarters, made my toilette in the best way circumstances would permit, and was among the first to appear at the breakfast table. Our breakfast was a substantial fox-hunter's repast, and the company were generally assembled at it. When ample justice had been done to the tea, coffee, cold meats, and humming ale, for all these were furnished in abundance, according to the tastes of the different guests, the conversation began to break out, with all the liveliness and freshness of morning mirth.

"But who is the hero of the haunted chamber?—Who has seen the ghost last night?" said the inquisitive gentleman, rolling his lobster eyes about the table.

The question set every tongue in motion; a vast deal of bantering; criticizing of countenances; of mutual accusation and retort took place. Some had drunk deep, and some were unshaven, so that there were suspicious faces enough in the assembly. I alone could not enter with ease and vivacity into the joke. I felt tongue-tied—embarrassed. A recollection of what I had seen and felt the preceding night still haunted my mind. It seemed as if the mysterious picture still held a thrall upon me. I thought also that our host's eye was turned on me with an air of curiosity. In short, I was conscious that I was the hero of the night, and felt as if every one might read it in my looks.

The joke, however, passed over, and no suspicion seemed to attach to me. I was just congratulating myself on my escape, when a servant came in, saying, that the gentleman who had slept on the sofa in the drawing room, had left his watch under one of the pillows. My repeater was in his hand.

"What!" said the inquisitive gentleman, "did any gentleman sleep on the sofa?"

"Soho! soho! a hare—a hare!" cried the old gentleman with the flexible nose.

I could not avoid acknowledging the watch, and was rising in great confusion, when a boisterous old squire who sat beside me, exclaimed, slapping me on the shoulder, "'Sblood, lad! thou'rt the man as has seen the ghost!"

The attention of the company was immediately turned to me; if my face had been pale the moment before, it now glowed almost to burning. I tried to laugh, but could only make a grimace; and found the muscles of my face twitching at sixes and sevens, and totally out of all controul.

It takes but little to raise a laugh among a set of fox hunters. There was a world of merriment and joking on the subject; and as I never relished a joke overmuch when it was at my own expense, I began to feel a little nettled. I tried to look cool and calm and to restrain my pique; but the coolness and calmness of a man in a passion are confounded treacherous.

Gentlemen, said I, with a slight cocking of the chin, and a bad attempt at a smile, this is all very pleasant—ha! ha!—very pleasant—but I'd have you know I am as little superstitious as any of you—ha! ha!—and as to any thing like timidity—you may smile, gentlemen—but I trust there's no one here means to insinuate that.——As to a room's being haunted, I repeat, gentlemen—(growing a little warm at seeing a cursed grin breaking out round me)—as to a room's being haunted, I have as little faith in such silly stories as any one. But, since you put the matter home to me, I will say that I have met with something in my room strange and inexplicable to me—(a shout of laughter.) Gentlemen, I am serious—I know well what I am saying—I am calm, gentlemen, (striking my fist upon the table)—by heaven I am calm. I am neither trifling, nor do I wish to be trifled with—(the laughter of the company suppressed with ludicrous attempts at gravity.) There is a picture in the room in which I was put last night, that has had an effect upon me the most singular and incomprehensible.

"A picture!" said the old gentleman with the haunted head. "A picture!" cried the narrator with the nose. "A picture! a picture!" echoed several voices. Here there was an ungovernable peal of laughter.

I could not contain myself. I started up from my seat—looked round on the company with fiery indignation—thrust both my hands into my pockets, and strode up to one of the windows, as though I would have walked through it. I stopped short; looked out upon the landscape without distinguishing a feature of it; and felt my gorge rising almost to suffocation.

Mine host saw it was time to interfere. He had maintained an air of gravity through the whole of the scene, and now stepped forth as if to shelter me from the overwhelming merriment of my companions.

"Gentlemen," said he, "I dislike to spoil sport, but you have had your laugh, and the joke of the haunted chamber has been enjoyed. I must now take the part of my guest. I must not only vindicate him from your pleasantries, but I must reconcile him to himself, for I suspect he is a little out of humour with his own feelings; and above all, I must crave his pardon for having made him the subject of a kind of experiment.

"Yes, gentlemen, there is something strange and peculiar in the chamber to which our friend was shown last night. There is a picture in my house which possesses a singular and mysterious influence; and with which there is connected a very curious story. It is a picture to which I attach a value from a variety of circumstances; and though I have often been tempted to destroy it, from the odd and uncomfortable sensations it produces in every one that beholds it; yet I have never been able to prevail upon myself to make the sacrifice. It is a picture I never like to look upon myself; and which is held in awe by all my servants. I have therefore banished it to a room but rarely used; and should have had it covered last night, had not the nature of our conversation, and the whimsical talk about a haunted chamber tempted me to let it remain, by way of experiment, to see whether a stranger, totally unacquainted with its story, would be affected by it."

The words of the Baronet had turned every thought into a different channel; all were anxious to hear the story of the mysterious picture; and for myself, so strongly were my feelings interested, that I forgot to feel piqued at the experiment which my host had made upon my nerves, and joined eagerly in the general entreaty.

As the morning was stormy, and denied all egress, my host was glad of any means of entertaining his company; so drawing his arm chair towards the fire, he began—

THE ADVENTURE OF THE MYSTERIOUS STRANGER

Many years since, when I was a young man, and had just left Oxford, I was sent on the grand tour to finish my education. I believe my parents had tried in vain to inoculate me with wisdom; so they sent me to mingle with society, in hopes I might take it the natural way. Such, at least, appears the reason for which nine tenths of our youngsters are sent abroad.

In the course of my tour I remained some time at Venice. The romantic character of the place delighted me; I was very much amused by the air of adventure and intrigue prevalent in this region of masks and gondolas; and I was exceedingly smitten by a pair of languishing black eyes, that played upon my heart from under an Italian mantle. So I persuaded myself that I was lingering at Venice to study men and manners. At least I persuaded my friends so, and that answered all my purpose. Indeed, I was a little prone to be struck by peculiarities in character and conduct, and my imagination was so full of romantic associations with Italy, that I was always on the look out for adventure.

Every thing chimed in with such a humour in this old mermaid of a city. My suite of apartments were in a proud, melancholy palace on the grand canal, formerly the residence of a Magnifico, and sumptuous with the traces of decayed grandeur. My gondolier was one of the shrewdest of his class, active, merry, intelligent, and, like his brethren, secret as the grave; that is to say, secret to all the world except his master. I had not had him a week before he put me behind all the curtains in Venice. I liked the silence and mystery of the place, and when I sometimes saw from my window a black gondola gliding mysteriously along in the dusk of the evening, with nothing visible but its little glimmering lantern, I would jump into my own zenda-letto, and give a signal for pursuit. But I am running away from my subject with the recollection of youthful follies, said the Baronet, checking himself, "let us come to the point."

Among my familiar resorts was a Cassino under the Arcades on one side of the grand square of St. Mark. Here I used frequently to lounge and take my ice on those warm summer nights when in Italy every body lives abroad until morning. I was seated here one evening, when a groupe of Italians took seats at a table on the opposite side of the saloon. Their conversation was gay and animated, and carried on with Italian vivacity and gesticulation.

I remarked among them one young man, however, who appeared to take no share, and find no enjoyment in the conversation; though he seemed to force himself to attend to it. He was tall and slender, and of extremely pre possessing appearance. His features were fine, though emaciated. He had a profusion of black glossy hair that curled lightly about his head, and con-trasted with the extreme paleness of his countenance. His brow was haggard; deep furrows seemed to have been ploughed into his visage by care, not by age, for he was evidently in the prime of youth. His eye was full of expres-sion and fire, but wild and unsteady. He seemed to be tormented by some strange fancy or apprehension. In spite of every effort to fix his attention on the conversation of his companions, I noticed that every now and then he would turn his head slowly round, give a glance over his shoulder, and then withdraw it with a sudden jerk, as if something painful met his eye. This was repeated at intervals of about a minute; and he appeared hardly to have recovered from one shock, before I saw him slowly preparing to encounter another.

After sitting some time in the Cassino, the party paid for the refreshments they had taken, and departed. The young man was the last to leave the saloon, and I remarked him glancing behind him in the same way, just as he passed out of the door. I could not resist the impulse to rise and follow him; for I was at an age when a romantic feeling of curiosity is easily awakened. The party walked slowly down the Arcades, talking and laughing as they went. They crossed the Piazzetta, but paused in the middle of it to enjoy the scene. It was one of those moonlight nights so brilliant and clear in the pure atmosphere of Italy. The moon beams streamed on the tall tower of St. Mark, and lighted up the magnificent front and swelling domes of the Ca-thedral. The party expressed their delight in animated terms. I kept my eye upon the young man. He alone seemed abstracted and self occupied. I no-ticed the same singular, and as it were, furtive glance over the shoulder which had attracted my attention in the Cassino. The party moved on, and I followed; they passed along the walk called the Broglio; turned the corner of the Ducal palace, and getting into a gondola, glided swiftly away.

The countenance and conduct of this young man dwelt upon my mind, and interested me exceedingly. I met him a day or two afterwards in a gallery of paintings. He was evidently a connoisseur, for he always singled out the most masterly productions, and the few remarks drawn from him by his companions showed an intimate acquaintance with the art. His own taste, however, ran on singular extremes. On Salvator Rosa in his most savage and solitary scenes; on Raphael, Titian and Correggio in their softest delineations of female beauty. On these he would occasionally gaze with transient enthusiasm. But this seemed only a momentary forgetfulness. Still would recur that cautious glance behind, and always quickly withdrawn, as though something terrible met his view.

I encountered him frequently afterwards. At the theatre, at balls, at concerts; at the promenades in the gardens of San Georgio; at the grotesque exhibitions in the square of St. Mark; among the throng of merchants on the Exchange by the Rialto. He seemed, in fact, to seek crowds; to hunt after bustle and amusement; yet never to take any interest in either the business or gaiety of the scene. Ever an air of painful thought, of wretched abstraction; and ever that strange and recurring movement, of glancing fearfully over the shoulder. I did not know at first but this might be caused by apprehension of arrest; or perhaps from dread of assassination. But, if so, why should he go thus continually abroad; why expose himself at all times and in all places?

I became anxious to know this stranger. I was drawn to him by that romantic sympathy which sometimes draws young men towards each other. His melancholy threw a charm about him, no doubt heightened by the touching expression of his countenance, and the manly graces of his person; for manly beauty has its effect even upon men. I had an Englishman's habitual diffidence and awkwardness to contend with; but from frequently meeting him in the Cassino, I gradually edged myself into his acquaintance. I had no reserve on his part to contend with. He seemed on the contrary to court society; and in fact to seek any thing rather than be alone.

When he found I really took an interest in him he threw himself entirely upon my friendship. He clung to me like a drowning man. He would walk with me for hours up and down the place of St. Mark—or would sit until night was far advanced in my apartments; he took rooms under the same roof with me; and his constant request was, that I would permit him, when it did not incommode me, to sit by me in my saloon. It was not that he seemed to take a particular delight in my conversation; but rather that he craved the vicinity of a human being; and above all, of a being that sympathized with him. "I have often heard," said he, "of the sincerity of English-men—thank God I have one at length for a friend!"

Yet he never seemed disposed to avail himself of my sympathy other than by mere companionship. He never sought to unbosom himself to me; there appeared to be a settled corroding anguish in his bosom that neither could be soothed "by silence nor by speaking." A devouring melancholy preyed upon his heart, and seemed to be drying up the very blood in his veins. It was not a soft melancholy—the disease of the affections; but a parching with-ering agony. I could see at times that his mouth was dry and feverish; he panted rather than breathed; his eyes were bloodshot; his cheeks pale and livid; with now and then faint streaks of red athwart them—baleful gleams of the fire that was consuming his heart. As my arm was within his, I felt him press it at times with a convulsive motion to his side; his hands would clinch themselves involuntarily, and a kind of shudder would run through his frame. I reasoned with him about his melancholy, and sought to draw from him the cause—he shrunk from all confiding. "Do not seek to know it," said he, "you could not relieve it if you knew it; you would not even seek to relieve it—on the contrary, I should lose your sympathy; and that," said he, pressing my hand convulsively, "that I feel has become too dear to me to risk."

I endeavoured to awaken hope within him. He was young; life had a thou-sand pleasures in store for him; there is a healthy reaction in the youthful heart; it medicines all its own wounds—"Come, come," said I, "there is no grief so great that youth cannot outgrow it."—"No! no!" said he, clinching his teeth, and striking repeatedly, with the energy of despair, upon his bos-om—"It is here—here—deep rooted; draining my heart's blood. It grows and grows, while my heart withers and withers! I have a dreadful monitor that gives me no repose—that follows me step by step; and will follow me step by step, until it pushes me into my grave!"

As he said this he gave involuntarily one of those fearful glances over his shoulder, and shrunk back with more than usual horror. I could not resist the temptation, to allude to this movement, which I supposed to be some mere malady of the nerves. The moment I mentioned it his face became crimsoned and convulsed—he grasped me by both hands: "For God's sake," exclaimed he, with a piercing voice—"never allude to that again—let us avoid this subject, my friend: you cannot relieve me, indeed you cannot relieve me; but you may add to the torments I suffer;—at some future day you shall know all."

I never resumed the subject; for however much my curiosity might be roused, I felt too true a compassion for his sufferings to increase them by my intrusion. I sought various ways to divert his mind, and to arouse him from the constant meditations in which he was plunged. He saw my efforts, and seconded them as far as in his power, for there was nothing moody or wayward in his nature; on the contrary, there was something frank, generous, unassuming, in his whole deportment. All the sentiments he uttered were noble and lofty. He claimed no indulgence, asked no toleration, but seemed content to carry his load of misery in silence, and only sought to carry it by my side. There was a mute beseeching manner about him, as if he craved companionship as a charitable boon; and a tacit thankfulness in his looks, as if he felt grateful to me for not repulsing him.

I felt this melancholy to be infectious. It stole over my spirits; interfered with all my gay pursuits, and gradually saddened my life; yet I could not prevail upon myself to shake off a being who seemed to hang upon me for support. In truth, the generous traits of character which beamed through all this gloom penetrated to my heart. His bounty was lavish and open handed. His charity melting and spontaneous. Not confined to mere donations, which humiliate as much as they relieve. The tone of his voice, the beam of his eye, enhanced every gift, and surprised the poor suppliant with that rarest and sweetest of charities, the charity not merely of the hand but of the heart. Indeed, his liberality seemed to have something in it of self abasement and expiation. He, in a manner, humbled himself before the mendicant. "What right have I to ease and affluence," would he murmur to himself, "when innocence wanders in misery and rags?"

The Carnival time arrived. I hoped the gay scenes then presented might have some cheering effect. I mingled with him in the motley throng that crowded the place of St. Mark. We frequented operas, masquerades, balls. All in vain. The evil kept growing on him; he became more and more haggard and agitated. Often, after we had returned from one of these scenes of revelry, I have entered his room, and found him lying on his face on the sofa: his hands clinched in his fine hair, and his whole countenance bearing traces of the convulsions of his mind.

The Carnival passed away; the time of Lent succeeded; Passion week arrived. We attended one evening a solemn service in one of the churches; in the course of which, a grand piece of vocal and instrumental music was performed relating to the death of our Saviour.

I had remarked that he was always powerfully affected by music; on this occasion he was so in an extraordinary degree. As the pealing notes swelled through the lofty aisles, he seemed to kindle with fervour. His eyes rolled upwards, until nothing but the whites were visible; his hands were clasped together, until the fingers were deeply imprinted in the flesh. When the music expressed the dying agony, his face gradually sank upon his knees; and at the touching words resounding through the church "*Jesu mori*," sobs burst from him uncontrouled. I had never seen him weep before; his had always been agony rather than sorrow. I augured well from the circumstance, and let him weep on uninterrupted. When the service was ended, we left the church. He hung on my arm as we walked homewards, with something of a softer and more subdued manner; instead of that nervous agitation I had been accustomed to witness. He alluded to the service we had heard. "Music," said he, "is indeed the voice of heaven; never before have I felt more impressed by the story of the atonement of our Saviour. Yes, my friend," said he, clasping his hands with a kind of transport, "I know that my Redeemer liveth."

We parted for the night. His room was not far from mine, and I heard him for some time busied in it. I fell asleep, but was awakened before daylight. The young man stood by my bed side, dressed for travelling. He held a sealed pacquet and a large parcel in his hand, which he laid on the table. "Farewell, my friend," said he, "I am about to set forth on a long journey; but, before I go, I leave with you these remembrances. In this pacquet you will find the particulars of my story. When you read them, I shall be far away; do not remember me with aversion. You have been, indeed, a friend to me. You have poured oil into a broken heart,—but you could not heal it —Farewell—let me kiss your hand—I am unworthy to embrace you." He sank on his knees, seized my hand in despite of my efforts to the contrary, and covered it with kisses. I was so surprised by all this scene that I had not been able to say a word.

"But we shall meet again," said I, hastily, as I saw him hurrying towards the door.

"Never—never in this world!" said he solemnly. He sprang once more to my bed side—seized my hand, pressed it to his heart and to his lips, and rushed out of the room.

Here the Baronet paused. He seemed lost in thought, and sat looking upon the floor and drumming with his fingers on the arm of his chair.

"And did this mysterious personage return?" said the inquisitive gentleman. "Never!" replied the Baronet, with a pensive shake of the head: "I never saw him again." "And pray what has all this to do with the picture?" inquired the old gentleman with the nose —"True!" said the questioner—"Is it the portrait of that crack brained Italian?" "No!" said the Baronet, drily, not half liking the appellation given to his hero; "but this picture was inclosed in the parcel he left with me. The sealed pacquet contained its explanation. There was a request on the outside that I would not open it until six months had elapsed. I kept my promise, in spite of my curiosity. I have a translation of it by me, and had meant to read it, by way of accounting for the mystery of the chamber, but I fear I have already detained the company too long."

Here there was a general wish expressed to have the manuscript read; particularly on the part of the inquisitive gentleman. So the worthy Baronet drew out a fairly written manuscript, and wiping his spectacles, read aloud the following story:—

THE STORY OF THE YOUNG ITALIAN

I was born at Naples. My parents, though of noble rank, were limited in fortune, or rather my father was ostentatious beyond his means, and expended so much on his palace, his equipage, and his retinue, that he was continually straightened in his pecuniary circumstances. I was a younger son, and looked upon with indifference by my father, who, from a principle of family pride, wished to leave all his property to my elder brother.

I showed, when quite a child, an extreme sensibility. Every thing affected me violently. While yet an infant in my mother's arms, and before I had learnt to talk, I could be wrought upon to a wonderful degree of anguish or delight by the power of music. As I grew older my feelings remained equally acute, and I was easily transported into paroxysms of pleasure or rage. It was the amusement of my relatives and of the domestics to play upon this irritable temperament. I was moved to tears, tickled to laughter, provoked to fury, for the entertainment of company, who were amused by such a tempest of mighty passion in a pigmy frame. They little thought, or perhaps little heeded the dangerous sensibilities they were fostering. I thus became a little creature of passion, before reason was developed. In a short time I grew too old to be a plaything, and then I became a torment. The tricks and passions I had been teased into became irksome, and I was disliked by my teachers for the very lessons they had taught me.

My mother died; and my power as a spoiled child was at an end. There was no longer any necessity to humour or tolerate me, for there was nothing to be gained by it, as I was no favourite of my father. I therefore experienced the fate of a spoiled child in such a situation, and was neglected, or noticed only to be crossed and contradicted. Such was the early treatment of a heart, which, if I can judge of it at all, was naturally disposed to the extremes of tenderness and affection.

My father, as I have already said, never liked me—in fact he never understood me; he looked upon me as wilful and wayward, as deficient in natural affection:—it was the stateliness of his own manner; the loftiness and grandeur of his own look which had repelled me from his arms. I always pictured him to myself as I had seen him clad in his senatorial robes, rustling with pomp and pride. The magnificence of his person daunted my young imagination. I could never approach him with the confiding affection of a child.

My father's feelings were wrapped up in my elder brother. He was to be the inheritor of the family title and the family dignity, and every thing was sacrificed to him—I, as well as every thing else. It was determined to devote me to the church, that so my humours and myself might be removed out of the way, either of tasking my father's time and trouble, or interfering with the interests of my brother. At an early age, therefore, before my mind had dawned upon the world and its delights, or known any thing of it beyond the precincts of my father's palace, I was sent to a convent, the superior of which was my uncle, and was confided entirely to his care.

My uncle was a man totally estranged from the world; he had never relished, for he had never tasted its pleasures; and he regarded rigid self denial as the great basis of Christian virtue. He considered every one's temperament like his own; or at least he made them conform to it. His character and habits had an influence over the fraternity of which he was superior. A more gloomy saturnine set of beings were never assembled together. The convent, too, was calculated to awaken sad and solitary thoughts. It was situated in a gloomy gorge of those mountains away south of Vesuvius. All distant views were shut out by sterile volcanic heights. A mountain stream raved beneath its walls, and eagles screamed about its turrets.

I had been sent to this place at so tender an age as soon to lose all distinct recollection of the scenes I had left behind. As my mind expanded, therefore, it formed its idea of the world from the convent and its vicinity, and a dreary world it appeared to me. An early tinge of melancholy was thus infused into my character; and the dismal stories of the monks, about devils and evil spirits, with which they affrighted my young imagination, gave me a tendency to superstition, which I could never effectually shake off. They took the same delight to work upon my ardent feelings that had been so mischievously executed by my father's household.

I can recollect the horrors with which they fed my heated fancy during an eruption of Vesuvius. We were distant from that volcano, with mountains between us; but its convulsive throes shook the solid foundations of nature. Earthquakes threatened to topple down our convent towers. A lurid, baleful light hung in the heavens at night, and showers of ashes, borne by the wind, fell in our narrow valley. The monks talked of the earth being honey-combed beneath us; of streams of molten lava raging through its veins; of caverns of sulphurous flames roaring in the centre, the abodes of demons and the damned; of fiery gulfs ready to yawn beneath our feet. All these tales were told to the doleful accompaniment of the mountain's thunders, whose low bellowing made the walls of our convent vibrate.

One of the monks had been a painter, but had retired from the world, and embraced this dismal life in expiation of some crime. He was a melancholy man, who pursued his art in the solitude of his cell, but made it a source of penance to him. His employment was to portray, either on canvass or in waxen models, the human face and human form, in the agonies of death, and in all the stages of dissolution and decay. The fearful mysteries of the charnel house were unfolded in his labours—the loathsome banquet of the beetle and the worm.——I turn with shuddering even from the recollection of his works. Yet, at the time, my strong but ill directed imagination seized with ardour upon his instructions in his art. Any thing was a variety from the dry studies and monotonous duties of the cloister. In a little while I became expert with my pencil, and my gloomy productions were thought worthy of decorating some of the altars of the chapel.

In this dismal way was a creature of feeling and fancy brought up. Every thing genial and amiable in my nature was repressed, and nothing brought out but what was unprofitable and ungracious. I was ardent in my temperament; quick, mercurial, impetuous, formed to be a creature all love and adoration; but a leaden hand was laid on all my finer qualities. I was taught nothing but fear and hatred. I hated my uncle, I hated the monks, I hated the convent in which I was immured. I hated the world, and I almost hated myself, for being, as I supposed, so hating and hateful an animal.

When I had nearly attained the age of sixteen, I was suffered, on one occasion, to accompany one of the brethren on a mission to a distant part of the country. We soon left behind us the gloomy valley in which I had been pent up for so many years, and after a short journey among the mountains, emerged upon the voluptuous landscape that spreads itself about the Bay of Naples. Heavens! how transported was I, when I stretched my gaze over a vast reach of delicious sunny country, gay with groves and vineyards; with Vesuvius rearing its forked summit to my right; the blue Mediterranean to my left, with its enchanting coast, studded with shining towns and sumptuous villas; and Naples, my native Naples, gleaming far, far in the distance.

Good God! was this the lovely world from which I had been excluded! I had reached that age when the sensibilities are in all their bloom and freshness. Mine had been checked and chilled. They now burst forth with the suddenness of a retarded spring time. My heart, hitherto unnaturally shrunk up, expanded into a riot of vague but delicious emotions. The beauty of nature intoxicated, bewildered me. The song of the peasants; their cheerful looks; their happy avocations; the picturesque gaiety of their dresses; their rustic music; their dances; all broke upon me like witchcraft. My soul responded to the music; my heart danced in my bosom. All the men appeared amiable, all the women lovely.

I returned to the convent, that is to say, my body returned, but my heart and soul never entered there again. I could not forget this glimpse of a beautiful and a happy world; a world so suited to my natural character. I had felt so happy while in it; so different a being from what I felt myself when in the convent—that tomb of the living. I contrasted the countenances of the beings I had seen, full of fire and freshness and enjoyment, with the pallid, leaden, lack lustre visages of the monks; the music of the dance, with the droning chant of the chapel. I had before found the exercises of the cloister wearisome; they now became intolerable. The dull round of duties wore away my spirit; my nerves became irritated by the fretful tinkling of the convent bell; evermore dinging among the mountain echoes; evermore calling me from my repose at night, my pencil by day, to attend to some tedious and mechanical ceremony of devotion.

I was not of a nature to meditate long, without putting my thoughts into action. My spirit had been suddenly aroused, and was now all awake within me. I watched an opportunity, fled from the convent, and made my way on foot to Naples. As I entered its gay and crowded streets, and beheld the variety and stir of life around me, the luxury of palaces, the splendour of equipages, and the pantomimic animation of the motley populace, I seemed as if awakened to a world of enchantment, and solemnly vowed that nothing should force me back to the monotony of the cloister.

I had to inquire my way to my father's palace, for I had been so young on leaving it, that I knew not its situation. I found some difficulty in getting admitted to my father's presence, for the domestics scarcely knew that there was such a being as myself in existence, and my monastic dress did not operate in my favour. Even my father entertained no recollection of my person. I told him my name, threw myself at his feet, implored his forgiveness, and entreated that I might not be sent back to the convent.

He received me with the condescension of a patron rather than the fondness of a parent; listened patiently, but coldly to my tale of monastic grievances and disgusts, and promised to think what else could be done for me. This coldness blighted and drove back all the frank affection of my nature that was ready to spring forth at the least warmth of parental kindness. All my early feelings towards my father revived; I again looked up to him as the stately magnificent being that had daunted my childish imagination, and felt as if I had no pretensions to his sympathies. My brother engrossed all his care and love; he inherited his nature, and carried himself towards me with a protecting rather than a fraternal air. It wounded my pride, which was great. I could brook condescension from my father, for I looked up to him with awe as a superior being; but I could not brook patronage from a brother, who, I felt, was intellectually my inferior. The servants perceived that I was an unwelcome intruder in the paternal mansion, and, menial-like, they treated me with neglect. Thus baffled at every point; my affections outraged wherever they would attach themselves, I became sullen, silent and desponding. My feelings driven back upon myself, entered and preyed upon my own heart. I remained for some days an unwelcome guest rather than a restored son in my father's house. I was doomed never to be properly known there. I was made, by wrong treatment, strange even to myself; and they judged of me from my strangeness.

I was startled one day at the sight of one of the monks of my convent, gliding out of my father's room. He saw me, but pretended not to notice me; and this very hypocrisy made me suspect something. I had become sore and susceptible in my feelings; every thing inflicted a wound on them. In this state of mind I was treated with marked disrespect by a pampered minion, the favourite servant of my father. All the pride and passion of my nature rose in an instant, and I struck him to the earth.

My father was passing by; he stopped not to inquire the reason, nor indeed could he read the long course of mental sufferings which were the real cause. He rebuked me with anger and scorn; summoning all the haughtiness of his nature, and grandeur of his look, to give weight to the contumely with which he treated me. I felt I had not deserved it—I felt that I was not appreciated—I felt that I had that within me which merited better treatment; my heart swelled against a father's injustice. I broke through my habitual awe of him. I replied to him with impatience; my hot spirit flushed in my cheek and kindled in my eye, but my sensitive heart swelled as quickly, and before I had half vented my passion I felt it suffocated and quenched in my tears. My father was astonished and incensed at this turning of the worm, and ordered me to my chamber. I retired in silence, choaking with contending emotions.

I had not been long there when I overheard voices in an adjoining apartment. It was a consultation between my father and the monk, about the means of getting me back quietly to the convent. My resolution was taken. I had no longer a home nor a father. That very night I left the paternal roof. I got on board a vessel about making sail from the harbour, and abandoned myself to the wide world. No matter to what port she steered; any part of so beautiful a world was better than my convent. No matter where I was cast by fortune; any place would be more a home to me than the home I had left behind. The vessel was bound to Genoa. We arrived there after a voyage of a few days.

As I entered the harbour, between the moles which embrace it, and beheld the amphitheatre of palaces and churches and splendid gardens, rising one above another, I felt at once its title to the appellation of Genoa the Superb. I landed on the mole an utter stranger, without knowing what to do, or whither to direct my steps. No matter; I was released from the thraldom of the convent and the humiliations of home! When I traversed the Strada Balbi and the Strada Nuova, those streets of palaces, and gazed at the wonders of architecture around me; when I wandered at close of day, amid a gay throng of the brilliant and the beautiful, through the green alleys of the Aqua Verde, or among the colonnades and terraces of the magnificent Doria Gardens; I thought it impossible to be ever otherwise than happy in Genoa.

A few days sufficed to show me my mistake. My scanty purse was exhausted, and for the first time in my life I experienced the sordid distress of penury. I had never known the want of money, and had never adverted to the possibility of such an evil. I was ignorant of the world and all its ways; and when first the idea of destitution came over my mind its effect was withering. I was wandering pensively through the streets which no longer delighted my eyes, when chance led my steps into the magnificent church of the Annunciata.

A celebrated painter of the day was at that moment superintending the placing of one of his pictures over an altar. The proficiency which I had acquired in his art during my residence in the convent had made me an enthusiastic amateur. I was struck, at the first glance, with the painting. It was the face of a Madonna. So innocent, so lovely, such a divine expression of maternal tenderness! I lost for the moment all recollection of myself in the enthusiasm of my art. I clasped my hands together, and uttered an ejaculation of delight. The painter perceived my emotion. He was flattered and gratified by it. My air and manner pleased him, and he accosted me. I felt too much the want of friendship to repel the advances of a stranger, and there was something in this one so benevolent and winning that in a moment he gained my confidence.

I told him my story and my situation, concealing only my name and rank. He appeared strongly interested by my recital; invited me to his house, and from that time I became his favourite pupil. He thought he perceived in me extraordinary talents for the art, and his encomiums awakened all my ardour. What a blissful period of my existence was it that I passed beneath his roof. Another being seemed created within me, or rather, all that was amiable and excellent was drawn out. I was as recluse as ever I had been at the convent, but how different was my seclusion. My time was spent in storing my mind with lofty and poetical ideas; in meditating on all that was striking and noble in history and fiction; in studying and tracing all that was sublime and beautiful in nature. I was always a visionary imaginative being, but now my reveries and imaginings all elevated me to rapture.

I looked up to my master as to a benevolent genius that had opened to me a region of enchantment. He was not a native of Genoa, but had been drawn thither by the solicitations of several of the nobility, and had resided there but a few years, for the completion of certain works. His health was delicate, and he had to confide much of the filling up of his designs to the pencils of his scholars. He considered me as particularly happy in delineating the human countenance; in seizing upon characteristic, though fleeting expressions, and fixing them powerfully upon my canvas. I was employed continually, therefore, in sketching faces, and often when some particular grace or beauty of expression was wanted in a countenance, it was entrusted to my pencil. My benefactor was fond of bringing me forward; and partly, perhaps, through my actual skill, and partly through his partial praises, I began to be noted for the expressions of my countenances.

Among the various works which he had undertaken, was an historical piece for one of the palaces of Genoa, in which were to be introduced the likenesses of several of the family. Among these was one entrusted to my pencil. It was that of a young girl, as yet in a convent for her education. She came out for the purpose of sitting for the picture. I first saw her in an apartment of one of the sumptuous palaces of Genoa. She stood before a

casement that looked out upon the bay: a stream of vernal sunshine fell upon
her, and shed a kind of glory round her as it lit up the rich crimson chamber.
She was but sixteen years of age—and oh how lovely! The scene broke upon
me like a mere vision of spring, and youth, and beauty. I could have fallen
down and worshipped her. She was like one of those fictions of poets and
painters, when they would express the *beau ideal* that haunts their minds
with shapes of indescribable perfection.

I was permitted to sketch her countenance in various positions, and I
fondly protracted the study that was undoing me. The more I gazed on her
the more I became enamoured; there was something almost painful in my
intense admiration. I was but nineteen years of age; shy, diffident, and inexperienced. I was treated with attention by her mother; for my youth and
my enthusiasm in my art had won favour for me; and I am inclined to think
something in my air and manner inspired interest and respect. Still the kindness with which I was treated could not dispel the embarrassment into which
my own imagination threw me when in presence of this lovely being. It
elevated her into something almost more than mortal. She seemed too exquisite for earthly use; too delicate and exalted for human attainment. As I
sat tracing her charms on my canvas, with my eyes occasionally riveted on
her features, I drank in delicious poison that made me giddy. My heart alternately gushed with tenderness, and ached with despair. Now I became
more than ever sensible of the violent fires that had lain dormant at the
bottom of my soul. You who are born in a more temperate climate and under
a cooler sky, have little idea of the violence of passion in our southern
bosoms.

A few days finished my task; Bianca returned to her convent, but her
image remained indelibly impressed upon my heart. It dwelt in my imagination; it became my pervading idea of beauty. It had an effect even upon
my pencil; I became noted for my felicity in depicting female loveliness; it
was but because I multiplied the image of Bianca. I soothed, and yet fed my
fancy, by introducing her in all the productions of my master. I have stood
with delight in one of the chapels of the Annunciata, and heard the crowd
extol the seraphic beauty of a saint which I had painted; I have seen them
bow down in adoration before the painting: they were bowing before the
loveliness of Bianca.

I existed in this kind of dream, I might almost say delirium, for upwards
of a year. Such is the tenacity of my imagination that the image which was
formed in it continued in all its power and freshness. I was a solitary, med-
itative being, much given to reverie, and apt to foster ideas which had once
taken strong possession of me. I was roused from this fond, melancholy,
delicious dream by the death of my worthy benefactor. I cannot describe
the pangs his death occasioned me. It left me alone and almost broken hearted. He bequeathed to me his little property; which, from the liberality of

his disposition and his expensive style of living, was indeed but small; and he most particularly recommended me, in dying, to the protection of a nobleman who had been his patron.

The latter was a man who passed for munificent. He was a lover and an encourager of the arts, and evidently wished to be thought so. He fancied he saw in me indications of future excellence; my pencil had already attracted attention; he took me at once under his protection; seeing that I was overwhelmed with grief, and incapable of exerting myself in the mansion of my late benefactor, he invited me to sojourn for a time at a villa which he possessed on the border of the sea, in the picturesque neighbourhood of Sestri di Ponente.

I found at the villa the Count's only son Filippo: he was nearly of my age, prepossessing in his appearance, and fascinating in his manners; he attached himself to me, and seemed to court my good opinion. I thought there was something of profession in his kindness, and of caprice in his disposition; but I had nothing else near me to attach myself to, and my heart felt the need of something to repose upon. His education had been neglected; he looked upon me as his superior in mental powers and acquirements, and tacitly acknowledged my superiority. I felt that I was his equal in birth, and that gave an independence to my manner, which had its effect. The caprice and tyranny I saw sometimes exercised on others, over whom he had power, were never manifested towards me. We became intimate friends, and frequent companions. Still I loved to be alone, and to indulge in the reveries of my own imagination, among the scenery by which I was surrounded.

The villa commanded a wide view of the Mediterranean, and the picturesque Ligurian coast. It stood alone in the midst of ornamented grounds, finely decorated with statues and fountains, and laid out into groves and alleys, and shady lawns. Every thing was assembled here that could gratify the taste or agreeably occupy the mind. Soothed by the tranquillity of this elegant retreat, the turbulence of my feelings gradually subsided, and, blending with the romantic spell which still reigned over my imagination, produced a soft voluptuous melancholy.

I had not been long under the roof of the Count, when our solitude was enlivened by another inhabitant. It was the daughter of a relative of the Count, who had lately died in reduced circumstances, bequeathing this only child to his protection. I had heard much of her beauty from Filippo, but my fancy had become so engrossed by one idea of beauty as not to admit of any other. We were in the central saloon of the villa when she arrived. She was still in mourning, and approached, leaning on the Count's arm. As they ascended the marble portico, I was struck by the elegance of her figure and movement, by the grace with which the *mezzaro*, the bewitching veil of Genoa, was folded about her slender form. They entered. Heavens! what was my surprise when I beheld Bianca before me. It was herself; pale with grief; but still more matured in loveliness than when I had last beheld her. The time that had elapsed had developed the graces of her person; and the sorrow she had undergone had diffused over her countenance an irresistible tenderness.

She blushed and trembled at seeing me, and tears rushed into her eyes, for she remembered in whose company she had been accustomed to behold me. For my part, I cannot express what were my emotions. By degrees I overcame the extreme shyness that had formerly paralyzed me in her presence. We were drawn together by sympathy of situation. We had each lost our best friend in the world; we were each, in some measure, thrown upon the kindness of others. When I came to know her intellectually, all my ideal picturings of her were confirmed. Her newness to the world, her delightful susceptibility to every thing beautiful and agreeable in nature, reminded me of my own emotions when first I escaped from the convent. Her rectitude of thinking delighted my judgment; the sweetness of her nature wrapped itself round my heart; and then her young and tender and budding loveliness, sent a delicious madness to my brain.

I gazed upon her with a kind of idolatry, as something more than mortal; and I felt humiliated at the idea of my comparative unworthiness. Yet she was mortal; and one of mortality's most susceptible and loving compounds; for she loved me!

How first I discovered the transporting truth I cannot recollect; I believe it stole upon me by degrees, as a wonder past hope or belief. We were both at such a tender and loving age; in constant intercourse with each other; mingling in the same elegant pursuits; for music, poetry and painting were our mutual delights, and we were almost separated from society, among lovely and romantic scenery! Is it strange that two young hearts thus brought together should readily twine round each other?

Oh gods! what a dream—a transient dream! of unalloyed delight then passed over my soul! Then it was that the world around me was indeed a paradise, for I had woman—lovely, delicious woman, to share it with me. How often have I rambled along the picturesque shores of Sestri, or climbed its wild mountains, with the coast gemmed with villas, and the blue sea far below me, and the slender Pharo of Genoa on its romantic promontory in the distance; and as I sustained the faltering steps of Bianca, have thought there could no unhappiness enter into so beautiful a world. How often have we listened together to the nightingale, as it poured forth its rich notes among the moonlight bowers of the garden, and have wondered that poets could ever have fancied any thing melancholy in its song! Why, oh why is this budding season of life and tenderness so transient—why is this rosy cloud of love that sheds such a glow over the morning of our days so prone to brew up into the whirlwind and the storm!

I was the first to awaken from this blissful delirium of the affections. I had gained Bianca's heart; what was I to do with it? I had no wealth nor prospects to entitle me to her hand. Was I to take advantage of her ignorance of the world, of her confiding affection, and draw her down to my own poverty? Was this requiting the hospitality of the Count?—was this requiting the love of Bianca?

Now first I began to feel that even successful love may have its bitterness. A corroding care gathered about my heart. I moved about the palace like a guilty being. I felt as if I had abused its hospitality—as if I were a thief within its walls. I could no longer look with unembarrassed mien in the countenance of the Count. I accused myself of perfidy to him, and I thought he read it in my looks, and began to distrust and despise me. His manner had always been ostentatious and condescending, it now appeared cold and haughty. Filippo, too, became reserved and distant; or at least I suspected him to be so. Heavens!—was this mere coinage of my brain: was I to become suspicious of all the world?—a poor surmising wretch; watching looks and gestures; and torturing myself with misconstructions. Or if true—was I to remain beneath a roof where I was merely tolerated, and linger there on sufferance? "This is not to be endured!" exclaimed I, "I will tear myself from this state of self abasement; I will break through this fascination and fly—— Fly?—whither?—from the world?—for where is the world when I leave Bianca behind me!"

My spirit was naturally proud, and swelled within me at the idea of being looked upon with contumely. Many times I was on the point of declaring my family and rank, and asserting my equality, in the presence of Bianca, when I thought her relatives assumed an air of superiority. But the feeling was transient. I considered myself discarded and contemned by my family; and had solemnly vowed never to own relationship to them, until they themselves should claim it.

The struggle of my mind preyed upon my happiness and my health. It seemed as if the uncertainty of being loved would be less intolerable than thus to be assured of it, and yet not dare to enjoy the conviction. I was no longer the enraptured admirer of Bianca; I no longer hung in ecstacy on the tones of her voice, nor drank in with insatiate gaze the beauty of her countenance. Her very smiles ceased to delight me, for I felt culpable in having won them.

She could not but be sensible of the change in me, and inquired the cause with her usual frankness and simplicity. I could not evade the inquiry, for my heart was full to aching. I told her all the conflict of my soul; my devouring passion, my bitter self upbraiding. "Yes!" said I, "I am unworthy of you. I am an offcast from my family—a wanderer—a nameless, homeless wanderer, with nothing but poverty for my portion, and yet I have dared to love you—have dared to aspire to your love!"

My agitation moved her to tears; but she saw nothing in my situation so hopeless as I had depicted it. Brought up in a convent, she knew nothing of the world, its wants, its cares;—and indeed, what woman is a worldly casuist in matters of the heart!—Nay, more—she kindled into a sweet enthusiasm when she spoke of my fortunes and myself. We had dwelt together on the works of the famous masters. I had related to her their histories; the high reputation, the influence, the magnificence to which they had attained;— the companions of princes, the favourites of kings, the pride and boast of nations. All this she applied to me. Her love saw nothing in all their great productions that I was not able to achieve; and when I beheld the lovely creature glow with fervour, and her whole countenance radiant with visions of my glory, I was snatched up for the moment into the heaven of her own imagination.

I am dwelling too long upon this part of my story; yet I cannot help lingering over a period of my life, on which, with all its cares and conflicts, I look back with fondness; for as yet my soul was unstained by a crime. I do not know what might have been the result of this struggle between pride, delicacy, and passion, had I not read in a Neapolitan gazette an account of the sudden death of my brother. It was accompanied by an earnest inquiry for intelligence concerning me, and a prayer, should this notice meet my eye, that I would hasten to Naples, to comfort an infirm and afflicted father.

I was naturally of an affectionate disposition; but my brother had never been as a brother to me; I had long considered myself as disconnected from him, and his death caused me but little emotion. The thoughts of my father, infirm and suffering, touched me, however, to the quick; and when I thought of him, that lofty magnificent being, now bowed down and desolate, and suing to me for comfort, all my resentment for past neglect was subdued, and a glow of filial affection was awakened within me.

The predominant feeling, however, that overpowered all others was transport at the sudden change in my whole fortunes. A home—a name—rank— wealth awaited me; and love painted a still more rapturous prospect in the distance. I hastened to Bianca, and threw myself at her feet. "Oh, Bianca," exclaimed I, "at length I can claim you for my own. I am no longer a nameless adventurer, a neglected, rejected outcast. Look—read, behold the tidings that restore me to my name and to myself!"

I will not dwell on the scene that ensued. Bianca rejoiced in the reverse of my situation, because she saw it lightened my heart of a load of care; for her own part she had loved me for myself, and had never doubted that my own merits would command both fame and fortune.

I now felt all my native pride buoyant within me. I no longer walked with my eyes bent to the dust; hope elevated them to the skies; my soul was lit up with fresh fires, and beamed from my countenance.

I wished to impart the change in my circumstances to the Count; to let him know who and what I was, and to make formal proposals for the hand of Bianca; but he was absent on a distant estate. I opened my whole soul to Filippo. Now first I told him of my passion; of the doubts and fears that had distracted me, and of the tidings that had suddenly dispelled them. He overwhelmed me with congratulations and with the warmest expressions of sympathy. I embraced him in the fullness of my heart. I felt compunctious for having suspected him of coldness, and asked him forgiveness for having ever doubted his friendship.

Nothing is so warm and enthusiastic as a sudden expansion of the heart between young men. Filippo entered into our concerns with the most eager interest. He was our confidant and counsellor. It was determined that I should hasten at once to Naples to re-establish myself in my father's affections and my paternal home, and the moment the reconciliation was effected and my father's consent insured, I should return and demand Bianca of the Count. Filippo engaged to secure his father's acquiescence; indeed, he undertook to watch over our interests, and was to be the channel through which we might correspond.

My parting with Bianca was tender—delicious—agonizing. It was in a little pavilion of the garden which had been one of our favourite resorts. How often and often did I return to have one more adieu—to have her look once more on me in speechless emotion—to enjoy once more the rapturous sight of those tears streaming down her lovely cheeks—to seize once more on that delicate hand, the frankly accorded pledge of love, and cover it with tears and kisses! Heavens! There is a delight even in the parting agony of two lovers worth a thousand tame pleasures of the world. I have her at this moment before my eyes—at the window of the pavilion, putting aside the vines which clustered about the casement   her light form beaming forth in virgin white—her countenance all tears and smiles—sending a thousand and a thousand adieus after me, as, hesitating, in a delirium of fondness and agitation, I faltered my way down the avenue.

As the bark bore me out of the harbour of Genoa, how eagerly my eye stretched along the coast of Sestri, till it discovered the villa gleaming from among trees at the foot of the mountain. As long as day lasted, I gazed and gazed upon it, till it lessened and lessened to a mere white speck in the distance; and still my intense and fixed gaze discerned it, when all other objects of the coast had blended into indistinct confusion, or were lost in the evening gloom.

On arriving at Naples, I hastened to my paternal home. My heart yearned for the long withheld blessing of a father's love. As I entered the proud portal of the ancestral palace, my emotions were so great that I could not speak. No one knew me. The servants gazed at me with curiosity and surprise. A few years of intellectual elevation and development had made a prodigious change in the poor fugitive stripling from the convent. Still that no one should know me in my rightful home was overpowering. I felt like the prodigal son returned. I was a stranger in the house of my father. I burst into tears, and wept aloud. When I made myself known, however, all was changed. I, who had once been almost repulsed from its walls, and forced to fly as an exile, was welcomed back with acclamation, with servility. One of the servants hastened to prepare my father for my reception; my eagerness to receive the paternal embrace was so great that I could not await his return; but hurried after him.

What a spectacle met my eyes as I entered the chamber. My father, whom I had left in the pride of vigourous age, whose noble and majestic bearing had so awed my young imagination, was bowed down and withered into decrepitude. A paralysis had ravaged his stately form, and left it a shaking ruin. He sat propped up in his chair, with pale relaxed visage and glassy wandering eye. His intellects had evidently shared in the ravage of his frame. The servant was endeavouring to make him comprehend the visitor that was at hand. I tottered up to him and sank at his feet. All his past coldness and neglect were forgotten in his present sufferings. I remembered only that he was my parent, and that I had deserted him. I clasped his knees; my voice was almost stifled with convulsive sobs. "Pardon—pardon—oh my father!" was all that I could utter. His apprehension seemed slowly to return to him. He gazed at me for some moments with a vague, inquiring look; a convulsive tremor quivered about his lips; he feebly extended a shaking hand, laid it upon my head, and burst into an infantine flow of tears.

From that moment he would scarcely spare me from his sight. I appeared the only object that his heart responded to in the world: all else was as a blank to him. He had almost lost the powers of speech, and the reasoning faculty seemed at an end. He was mute and passive; excepting that fits of childlike weeping would sometimes come over him without any immediate cause. If I left the room at any time, his eye was incessantly fixed on the door till my return, and on my entrance there was another gush of tears.

To talk with him of my concerns, in this ruined state of mind, would have been worse than useless: to have left him, for ever so short a time, would have been cruel, unnatural. Here then was a new trial for my affections. I wrote to Bianca an account of my return and of my actual situation; painting in colours vivid, for they were true, the torments I suffered at our being thus separated; for to the youthful lover every day of absence is an age of love lost. I enclosed the letter in one to Filippo who was the channel of our correspondence. I received a reply from him full of friendship and sympathy; from Bianca full of assurances of affection and constancy.

Week after week; month after month elapsed, without making any change in my circumstances. The vital flame, which had seemed nearly extinct when first I met my father, kept fluttering on without any apparent diminution. I watched him constantly, faithfully—I had almost said patiently. I knew that his death alone would set me free; yet I never at any moment wished it. I felt too glad to be able to make any atonement for past disobedience; and, denied as I had been all endearments of relationship in my early days, my heart yearned towards a father, who, in his age and helplessness, had thrown himself entirely on me for comfort. My passion for Bianca gained daily more force from absence; by constant meditation it wore itself a deeper and deeper channel. I made no new friends nor acquaintances; sought none of the pleasures of Naples which my rank and fortune threw open to me. Mine was a heart that confined itself to few objects, but dwelt upon them with the intenser passion. To sit by my father, administer to his wants, and to meditate on Bianca in the silence of his chamber, was my constant habit. Sometimes I amused myself with my pencil in portraying the image ever present to my imagination. I transferred to canvas every look and smile of hers that dwelt in my heart. I showed them to my father in hopes of awakening an interest in his bosom for the mere shadow of my love; but he was too far sunk in intellect to take any notice of them.

When I received a letter from Bianca it was a new source of solitary luxury. Her letters, it is true, were less and less frequent, but they were always full of assurances of unabated affection. They breathed not the frank and innocent warmth, with which she expressed herself in conversation, but I accounted for it from the embarrassment which inexperienced minds have often to express themselves upon paper. Filippo assured me of her unaltered constancy. They both lamented in the strongest terms our continued separation, though they did justice to the filial piety that kept me by my father's side.

Nearly two years elapsed in this protracted exile. To me they were so many ages. Ardent and impetuous by nature, I scarcely know how I should have supported so long an absence, had I not felt assured that the faith of Bianca was equal to my own. At length my father died. Life went from him almost imperceptibly. I hung over him in mute affliction, and watched the expiring spasms of nature. His last faltering accents whispered repeatedly a blessing on me— alas! how has it been fulfilled!

When I had paid due honours to his remains, and laid them in the tomb of our ancestors, I arranged briefly my affairs; put them in a posture to be easily at my command from a distance, and embarked once more, with a bounding heart for Genoa.

Our voyage was propitious, and oh! what was my rapture when first, in the dawn of morning, I saw the shadowy summits of the Apennines rising almost like clouds above the horizon. The sweet breath of summer just moved us over the long wavering billows that were rolling us on towards Genoa. By degrees the coast of Sestri rose like a creation of enchantment from the silver bosom of the deep. I beheld the line of villages and palaces studding its borders. My eye reverted to a well known point, and at length, from the confusion of distant objects, it singled out the villa which contained

Bianca. It was a mere speck in the landscape, but glimmering from afar, the polar star of my heart.

Again I gazed at it for a livelong summer's day; but oh how different the emotions between departure and return. It now kept growing and growing, instead of lessening and lessening on my sight. My heart seemed to dilate with it. I looked at it through a telescope. I gradually defined one feature after another. The balconies of the central saloon where first I met Bianca beneath its roof; the terrace where we so often had passed the delightful summer evenings; the awning which shaded her chamber window—I almost fancied I saw her form beneath it. Could she but know her lover was in the bark whose white sail now gleamed on the sunny bosom of the sea! My fond impatience increased as we neared the coast. The ship seemed to lag lazily over the billows; I could almost have sprung into the sea and swam to the desired shore.

The shadows of evening gradually shrouded the scene, but the moon arose in all her fullness and beauty, and shed the tender light so dear to lovers, over the romantic coast of Sestri. My soul was bathed in unutterable tenderness. I anticipated the heavenly evenings I should pass in once more wandering with Bianca by the light of that blessed moon.

It was late at night before we entered the harbour. As early next morning as I could get released from the formalities of landing I threw myself on horseback and hastened to the villa. As I galloped round the rocky promontory on which stands the Faro, and saw the coast of Sestri opening upon me, a thousand anxieties and doubts suddenly sprang up in my bosom. There is something fearful in returning to those we love, while yet uncertain what ills or changes absence may have effected. The turbulence of my agitation shook my very frame. I spurred my horse to redoubled speed; he was covered with foam when we both arrived panting at the gateway that opened to the grounds around the villa. I left my horse at a cottage and walked through the grounds that I might regain tranquillity for the approaching interview. I chid myself for having suffered mere doubts and surmises thus suddenly to overcome me; but I was always prone to be carried away by gusts of the feelings.

On entering the garden every thing bore the same look as when I had left it; and this unchanged aspect of things reassured me. There were the alleys in which I had so often walked with Bianca as we listened to the song of the nightingale; the same shades under which we had so often sat during the noontide heat. There were the same flowers of which she was fond; and which appeared still to be under the ministry of her hand. Every thing looked and breathed of Bianca; hope and joy flushed in my bosom at every step. I passed a little arbour in which we had often sat and read together. A book and a glove lay on the bench. It was Bianca's glove; it was a volume of the Metastasio I had given her. The glove lay in my favourite passage. I clasped them to my heart with rapture. "All is safe!" exclaimed I, "she loves me! she is still my own!"

I bounded lightly along the avenue down which I had faltered so slowly at my departure. I beheld her favourite pavilion which had witnessed our parting scene. The window was open, with the same vine clambering about it, precisely as when she waved and wept me an adieu. Oh! how transporting was the contrast in my situation. As I passed near the pavilion, I heard the tones of a female voice. They thrilled through me with an appeal to my heart not to be mistaken. Before I could think, I *felt* they were Bianca's. For an instant I paused, overpowered with agitation. I feared to break in so suddenly upon her. I softly ascended the steps of the pavilion. The door was open. I saw Bianca seated at a table; her back was towards me; she was warbling a soft melancholy air, and was occupied in drawing. A glance sufficed to show me that she was copying one of my own paintings. I gazed on her for a moment in a delicious tumult of emotions. She paused in her singing; a heavy sigh, almost a sob followed. I could no longer contain myself. "Bianca!" exclaimed I, in a half smothered voice. She started at the sound; brushed back the ringlets that hung clustering about her face; darted a glance at me; uttered a piercing shriek, and would have fallen to the earth, had I not caught her in my arms.

"Bianca! my own Bianca!" exclaimed I, folding her to my bosom; my voice stifled in sobs of convulsive joy. She lay in my arms without sense or motion. Alarmed at the effects of my precipitation, I scarce knew what to do. I tried by a thousand endearing words to call her back to consciousness. She slowly recovered, and half opening her eyes—"where am I?" murmured she faintly. "Here," exclaimed I, pressing her to my bosom, "Here! close to the heart that adores you; in the arms of your faithful Ottavio!"

"Oh no! no! no!" shrieked she, starting into sudden life and terror—"away! away! leave me! leave me!"

She tore herself from my arms; rushed to a corner of the saloon, and covered her face with her hands, as if the very sight of me were baleful. I was thunderstruck—I could not believe my senses. I followed her, trembling, confounded. I endeavoured to take her hand, but she shrunk from my very touch with horror.

"Good heavens, Bianca," exclaimed I, "what is the meaning of this? Is this my reception after so long an absence? Is this the love you professed for me?"

At the mention of love, a shuddering ran through her. She turned to me a face wild with anguish. "No more of that! no more of that!" gasped she— "talk not to me of love—I—I—am married!"

I reeled as if I had received a mortal blow. A sickness struck to my very heart. I caught at a window frame for support. For a moment or two, every thing was chaos around me. When I recovered, I beheld Bianca lying on a sofa; her face buried in the pillow, and sobbing convulsively. Indignation at her fickleness for a moment overpowered every other feeling.

"Faithless—perjured—" cried I, striding across the room. But another glance at that beautiful being in distress, checked all my wrath. Anger could not dwell together with her idea in my soul.

"Oh Bianca," exclaimed I, in anguish, "could I have dreamt of this; could I have suspected you would have been false to me?"

She raised her face all streaming with tears, all disordered with emotion, and gave me one appealing look—"False to you!——they told me you were dead!"

"What," said I, "in spite of our constant correspondence?"

She gazed wildly at me—"correspondence!—what correspondence?"

"Have you not repeatedly received and replied to my letters?"

She clasped her hands with solemnity and fervour—"As I hope for mercy, never!"

A horrible surmise shot through my brain—"Who told you I was dead?"

"It was reported that the ship in which you embarked for Naples perished at sea."

"But who told you the report?"

She paused for an instant, and trembled—

"Filippo!"

"May the God of heaven curse him!" cried I, extending my clinched fists aloft.

"Oh do not curse him—do not curse him!" exclaimed she—"He is—he is—my husband!"

This was all that was wanting to unfold the perfidy that had been practised upon me. My blood boiled like liquid fire in my veins. I gasped with rage too great for utterance. I remained for a time bewildered by the whirl of horrible thoughts that rushed through my mind. The poor victim of deception before me thought it was with her I was incensed. She faintly murmured forth her exculpation. I will not dwell upon it. I saw in it more than she meant to reveal. I saw with a glance how both of us had been betrayed. "'Tis well!" muttered I to myself in smothered accents of concentrated fury. "He shall render an account of all this!"

Bianca overheard me. New terror flashed in her countenance. "For mercy's sake do not meet him—say nothing of what has passed—for my sake say nothing to him—I only shall be the sufferer!"

A new suspicion darted across my mind—"what!" exclaimed I—"do you then *fear* him—is he *unkind* to you—tell me," reiterated I, grasping her hand and looking her eagerly in the face—"tell me—*dares* he to use you harshly!"

"No! no! no!" cried she faltering and embarrassed; but the glance at her face had told me volumes. I saw in her pallid and wasted features; in the

prompt terror and subdued agony of her eye a whole history of a mind broken down by tyranny. Great God! and was this beauteous flower snatched
from me to be thus trampled upon. The idea roused me to madness. I
clinched my teeth and my hands; I foamed at the mouth; every passion
seemed to have resolved itself into the fury that like a lava boiled within my
heart. Bianca shrunk from me in speechless affright. As I strode by the window my eye darted down the alley. Fatal moment! I beheld Filippo at a
distance! My brain was in delirium—I sprang from the pavilion, and was
before him with the quickness of lightning. He saw me as I came rushing
upon him —he turned pale, looked wildly to right and left, as if he would
have fled, and trembling drew his sword:—

"Wretch!" cried I, "well may you draw your weapon!"

I spoke not another word—I snatched forth a stiletto, put by the sword
which trembled in his hand, and buried my poniard in his bosom. He fell
with the blow, but my rage was unsated. I sprang upon him with the blood
thirsty feeling of a tiger; redoubled my blows; mangled him in my frenzy,
grasped him by the throat, until with reiterated wounds and strangling convulsions he expired in my grasp. I remained glaring on the countenance,
horrible in death, that seemed to stare back with its protruded eyes upon
me. Piercing shrieks roused me from my delirium. I looked round and beheld Bianca flying distractedly towards us. My brain whirled. I waited not
to meet her, but fled from the scene of horror. I fled forth from the garden
like another Cain, a hell within my bosom, and a curse upon my head. I fled
without knowing whither—almost without knowing why—my only idea was
to get farther and farther from the horrors I had left behind; as if I could
throw space between myself and my conscience. I fled to the Apennines,
and wandered for days and days among their savage heights. How I existed
I cannot tell—what rocks and precipices I braved, and how I braved them,
I know not. I kept on and on—trying to outtravel the curse that clung to
me. Alas, the shrieks of Bianca rung for ever in my ears. The horrible countenance of my victim was for ever before my eyes. "The blood of Filippo
cried to me from the ground." Rocks, trees, and torrents all resounded with
my crime.

Then it was I felt how much more insupportable is the anguish of remorse
than every other mental pang. Oh! could I but have cast off this crime that
festered in my heart; could I but have regained the innocence that reigned
in my breast as I entered the garden at Sestri; could I but have restored my
victim to life, I felt as if I could look on with transport even though Bianca
were in his arms.

By degrees this frenzied fever of remorse settled into a permanent malady
of the mind. Into one of the most horrible that ever poor wretch was cursed
with. Wherever I went the countenance of him I had slain appeared to follow
me. Whenever I turned my head I beheld it behind me, hideous with the

contortions of the dying moment. I have tried in every way to escape from this horrible phantom; but in vain. I know not whether it be an illusion of the mind, the consequence of my dismal education at the convent, or whether a phantom really sent by heaven to punish me; but there it ever is—at all times—in all places—nor has time nor habit had any effect in familiarizing me with its terrors. I have travelled from place to place, plunged into amusements—tried dissipation and distraction of every kind—all—all in vain.

I once had recourse to my pencil as a desperate experiment. I painted an exact resemblance of this phantom face. I placed it before me in hopes that by constantly contemplating the copy I might diminish the effect of the original. But I only doubled instead of diminishing the misery.

Such is the curse that has clung to my footsteps—that has made my life a burthen—but the thought of death, terrible. God knows what I have suffered. What days and days, and nights and nights, of sleepless torment. What a never dying worm has preyed upon my heart; what an unquenchable fire has burned within my brain. He knows the wrongs that wrought upon my poor weak nature; that converted the tenderest of affections into the deadliest of fury. He knows best whether a frail erring creature has expiated by long enduring torture and measureless remorse, the crime of a moment of madness. Often, often have I prostrated myself in the dust, and implored that he would give me a sign of his forgiveness, and let me die.——

Thus far had I written some time since. I had meant to leave this record of misery and crime with you, to be read when I should be no more. My prayer to heaven has at length been heard. You were witness to my emotions last evening at the church, when the vaulted temple resounded with the words of atonement and redemption. I heard a voice speaking to me from the midst of the music; I heard it rising above the pealing of the organ and the voices of the choir: it spoke to me in tones of celestial melody; it promised mercy and forgiveness, but demanded from me full expiation. I go to make it. Tomorrow I shall be on my way to Genoa to surrender myself to justice. You who have pitied my sufferings; who have poured the balm of sympathy into my wounds, do not shrink from my memory with abhorrence now that you know my story. Recollect, when you read of my crime I shall have atoned for it with my blood!

———

When the Baronet had finished, there was a universal desire expressed to see the painting of this frightful visage. After much entreaty the Baronet consented, on condition that they should only visit it one by one. He called his housekeeper and gave her charge to conduct the gentlemen singly to the chamber. They all returned varying in their stories: some affected in one way, some in another; some more, some less; but all agreeing that there was a certain something about the painting that had a very odd effect upon the feelings.

I stood in a deep bow window with the Baronet, and could not help expressing my wonder. "After all," said I, "there are certain mysteries in our nature, certain inscrutable impulses and influences, which warrant one in being superstitious. Who can account for so many persons of different characters being thus strangely affected by a mere painting?"

"And especially when not one of them has seen it!" said the Baronet with a smile.

"How?" exclaimed I, "not seen it?"

"Not one of them!" replied he, laying his finger on his lips in sign of secrecy. "I saw that some of them were in a bantering vein, and I did not choose that the memento of the poor Italian should be made a jest of. So I gave the housekeeper a hint to show them all to a different chamber!"

———————

Thus end the Stories of the Nervous Gentleman.

PART II
BUCKTHORNE AND HIS FRIENDS

This world is the best that we live in,
To lend, or to spend, or to give in;
But to beg, or to borrow, or get a man's own,
'Tis the very worst world, sir, that ever was known.
LINES FROM AN INN WINDOW

Among other subjects of a traveller's curiosity, I had at one time a great craving after anecdotes of literary life; and being at London, one of the most noted places for the production of books, I was excessively anxious to know something of the animals which produced them. Chance fortunately threw me in the way of a literary man by the name of Buckthorne, an eccentric personage, who had lived much in the metropolis, and could give me the natural history of every odd animal to be met with in that wilderness of men. He readily imparted to me some useful hints upon the subject of my inquiry.

"The literary world," said he, "is made up of little confederacies, each looking upon its own members as the lights of the universe; and considering all others as mere transient meteors, doomed soon to fall and be forgotten, while its own luminaries are to shine steadily on to immortality."

"And pray," said I, "how is a man to get a peep into those confederacies you speak of? I presume an intercourse with authors is a kind of intellectual exchange, where one must bring his commodities to barter, and always give a quid pro quo."

"Pooh, pooh—how you mistake," said Buckthorne, smiling: "you must never think to become popular among wits by shining. They go into society to shine themselves, not to admire the brilliancy of others. I once thought as you do, and never went into literary society without studying my part before hand. The consequence was, I soon got the name of an intolerable proser, and should in a little while have been completely excommunicated had I not changed my plan of operations. No, sir, no character succeeds so well among wits as that of a good listener, or if ever you are eloquent, let it be when tête-à-tête with an author, and then in praise of his own works, or what is nearly as acceptable, in disparagement of the works of his contemporaries. If ever he speaks favourably of the productions of a particular friend, dissent boldly from him; pronounce his friend to be a blockhead; never fear his being vexed; much as people speak of the irritability of authors, I never found one to take offense at such contradictions. No-no sir, authors are particularly candid in admitting the faults of their friends.

"Indeed I would advise you to be extremely sparing of remarks on all modern works, excepting to make sarcastic observations on the most distinguished writers of the day."

"Faith," said I, "I'll praise none that have not been dead for at least half a century."

"Even then," observed Mr. Buckthorne, "I would advise you to be rather cautious; for you must know that many old writers have been enlisted under the banners of different sects, and their merits have become as complete topics of party discussion as the merits of living statesmen and politicians. Nay, there have been whole periods of literature absolutely *taboo'd*, to use a South Sea phraze. It is, for example, as much as a man's critical reputation is worth, in some circles, to say a word in praise of any writers of the reign of Charles the Second, or even of Queen Anne; they being all declared Frenchmen in disguise."

"And pray then," said I, "when am I to know that I am on safe grounds; being totally unacquainted with the literary landmarks and the boundary lines of fashionable taste?"

"Oh," replied he, "there is fortunately one tract of literature which forms a kind of neutral ground, on which all the literary meet amicably, and run riot in the excess of their good humour. And this is, the reigns of Elizabeth and James. Here you may praise away at random; here it is 'cut and come again,' and the more obscure the author, and the more quaint and crabbed his style; the more your admiration will smack of the real relish of the Connoisseur; whose taste, like that of an Epicure, is always for game that has an antiquated flavour.

"But," continued he, "as you seem anxious to know something of literary society I will take an opportunity to introduce you to some coterie, where the talents of the day are assembled. I cannot promise you, however, that they will all be of the first order. Some how or other, our great geniuses are not gregarious, they do not go in flocks; but fly singly in general society. They prefer mingling, like common men, with the multitude; and are apt to carry nothing of the author about them but the reputation. It is only the inferior orders that herd together, acquire strength and importance by their confederacies, and bear all the distinctive characteristics of their species."

A LITERARY DINNER

A few days after this conversation with Mr. Buckthorne, he called upon me, and took me with him to a regular literary dinner. It was given by a great Bookseller, or rather a company of Booksellers, whose firm surpassed in length even that of Shadrach, Meshach and Abed-nego.

I was surprised to find between twenty and thirty guests assembled, most of whom I had never seen before. Buckthorne explained this to me, by informing me that this was a "business dinner," or kind of field day which the house gave about twice a year to its authors. It is true they did occasionally give snug dinners to three or four literary men at a time; but then these were generally select authors; favourites of the public; such as had arrived at their sixth or seventh editions. "There are," said he, "certain geographical boundaries in the land of literature, and you may judge tolerably well of an author's popularity, by the wine his bookseller gives him. An author crosses the port line about the third edition and gets into claret, but when he has reached the sixth and seventh, he may revel in champagne and burgundy."

"And pray," said I, "how far may these gentlemen have reached that I see around me; are any of these claret drinkers?"

"Not exactly, not exactly. You find at these great dinners the common steady run of authors, one, two-edition men; or if any others are invited they are aware that it is a kind of republican meeting.—You understand me—a meeting of the republic of letters, and that they must expect nothing but plain substantial fare."

These hints enabled me to comprehend more fully the arrangement of the table. The two ends were occupied by two partners of the House—and the host seemed to have adopted Addison's idea as to the literary precedence of his guests. A popular poet had the post of honour, opposite to whom was a hotpressed traveller in Quarto with plates. A grave looking antiquarian, who had produced several solid works, which were much quoted and little read, was treated with great respect, and scated next to a neat dressy gentleman in black, who had written a thin, genteel, hotpressed octavo on political economy that was getting into fashion. Several three volume duodecimo men of fair currency were placed about the centre of the table; while the lower end was taken up with small poets, translators and authors who had not as yet risen into much notoriety.

The conversation during dinner was by fits and starts; breaking out here and there in various parts of the table in small flashes, and ending in smoke. The poet who had the confidence of a man on good terms with the world and independent of his bookseller, was very gay and brilliant, and said many clever things, which set the partner next him in a roar, and delighted all the company. The other partner, however, maintained his sedateness and kept carving on, with the air of a thorough man of business, intent upon the occupation of the moment. His gravity was explained to me by my friend Buckthorne. He informed me that the concerns of the house were admirably distributed among the partners. "Thus, for instance," said he, "The grave gentleman is the carving partner who attends to the joints, and the other is the laughing partner who attends to the jokes."

The general conversation was chiefly carried on at the upper end of the table; as the authors there seemed to possess the greatest courage of the tongue. As to the crew at the lower end, if they did not make much figure in talking they did in eating. Never was there a more determined, inveterate, thoroughly sustained attack on the trencher, than by this phalanx of masticators. When the cloth was removed, and the wine began to circulate, they grew very merry and jocose among themselves. Their jokes, however, if by chance any of them reached the upper end of the table, seldom produced much effect. Even the laughing partner did not think it necessary to honour them with a smile; which my neighbour Buckthorne accounted for, by informing me that there was a certain degree of popularity to be obtained, before a bookseller could afford to laugh at an author's jokes.

Among this crew of questionable gentlemen thus seated below the salt, my eye singled out one in particular. He was rather shabbily dressed; though he had evidently made the most of a rusty black coat, and wore his shirt frill plaited and puffed out voluminously at the bosom. His face was dusky, but florid, perhaps a little too florid, particularly about the nose; though the rosy hue gave the greater lustre to a twinkling black eye. He had a little the look of a boon companion, with that dash of the poor devil in it which gives an inexpressibly mellow tone to a man's humour. I had seldom seen a face of richer promise; but never was promise so ill kept. He said nothing; ate and drank with the keen appetite of a Garretteer, and scarcely stopped to laugh even at the good jokes from the upper end of the table. I inquired who he was. Buckthorne looked at him attentively; "Gad," said he, "I have seen that face before but where I cannot recollect. He cannot be an author of any note. I suppose some writer of sermons or grinder of foreign travels."

After dinner we retired to another room to take tea and coffee, where we were reinforced by a cloud of inferior guests. Authors of small volumes in boards, and pamphlets stitched in blue paper. These had not as yet arrived to the importance of a dinner invitation, but were invited occasionally to pass the evening "in a friendly way." They were very respectful to the partners, and indeed seemed to stand a little in awe of them; but they paid devoted court to the Lady of the house, and were extravagantly fond of the children. Some few, who did not feel confidence enough to make such advances, stood shyly off in corners, talking to one another; or turned over the portfolios of prints, which they had not seen above five thousand times, or moused over the music on the forte-piano.

The poet and the thin octavo gentleman were the persons most current and at their ease in the drawing room; being men evidently of circulation in the west end. They got on each side of the lady of the house, and paid her a thousand compliments and civilities, at some of which I thought she would have expired with delight. Every thing they said and did had the odour of fashionable life. I looked round in vain for the poor devil author in the rusty black coat; he had disappeared immediately after leaving the table; having a dread, no doubt, of the glaring light of a drawing room. Finding nothing further to interest my attention, I took my departure soon after coffee had been served, leaving the poet and the thin, genteel, hotpressed, octavo gentleman, masters of the field.

THE CLUB OF QUEER FELLOWS

I think it was but the very next evening that in coming out of Covent Garden theatre with my excentric friend Buckthorne, he proposed to give me another peep at life and character. Finding me willing for any research of the kind, he took me through a variety of the narrow courts and lanes about Covent Garden until we stopped before a tavern from which we heard the bursts of merriment of a jovial party. There would be a loud peal of laughter, then an interval, then another peal, as if a prime wag were telling a story. After a little while there was a song, and at the close of each stanza a hearty roar and a vehement thumping on the table.

"This is the place," whispered Buckthorne. "It is the 'club of queer fellows,' a great resort of the small wits, third rate actors, and newspaper critics of the theatres. Any one can go in, on paying a sixpence at the bar for the use of the club."

We entered, therefore, without ceremony and took our seats at a lone table in a dusky corner of the room. The club was assembled round a table, on which stood beverages of various kinds, according to the taste of the individual. The members were a set of queer fellows indeed; but what was my surprize on recognizing in the prime wit of the meeting the poor devil author, whom I had remarked at the Booksellers' dinner for his promising face and his complete taciturnity. Matters, however, were entirely changed with him. There he was a mere cypher: here he was lord of the ascendant; the choice spirit, the dominant genius. He sat at the head of the table with his hat on, and an eye beaming even more luminously than his nose. He had a quip and a fillip for every one, and a good thing on every occasion. Nothing could be said or done without eliciting a spark from him; and I solemnly declare I have heard much worse wit even from noblemen. His jokes it must be confessed, were rather wet, but they suited the circle in which he presided. The company were in that maudlin mood when a little wit goes a great way. Every time he opened his lips there was sure to be a roar, and even sometimes before he had time to speak.

We were fortunate enough to enter in time for a glee composed by him expressly for the club, and which he sang with two boon companions who would have been worthy subjects for Hogarth's pencil. As they were each provided with a written copy; I was enabled to procure the reading of it.

> Merrily, merrily push round the glass,
> And merrily troll the glee,
> For he who won't drink till he wink is an ass,
> So neighbour I drink to thee.
>
> Merrily, merrily fiddle thy nose,
> Until it right rosy shall be;

> For a jolly red nose, I speak under the rose,
> Is a sign of good company.

We waited until the party broke up, and no one but the wit remained. He sat at the table with his legs stretched under it, and wide apart; his hands in his breeches pockets; his head drooped upon his breast; and gazing with lack lustre countenance on an empty tankard. His gaiety was gone, his fire completely quenched.

My companion approached and startled him from his fit of brown study, introducing himself on the strength of their having dined together at the Booksellers'.

"By the way," said he, "it seems to me I have seen you before; your face is surely that of an old acquaintance, though for the life of me I cannot tell where I have known you."

"Very likely," replied he with a smile; "many of my old friends have forgotten me. Though, to tell the truth my memory in this instance is as bad as your own. If however it will assist your recollection in any way, my name is Thomas Dribble, at your service."

"What. Tom Dribble, who was at old Birchell's school in Warwickshire—"

"The same," said the other, coolly. "Why then we are old schoolmates, though it's no wonder you don't recollect me. I was your junior by several years; don't you recollect little Jack Buckthorne?"

Here then ensued a scene of school fellow recognition—and a world of talk about old school times and school pranks. Mr. Dribble ended by observing with a heavy sigh "that times were sadly changed since those days."

"Faith, Mr. Dribble," said I, "you seem quite a different man here from what you were at dinner. I had no idea that you had so much stuff in you. There you were all silence; but here you absolutely keep the table in a roar."

"Ah my dear sir," replied he, with a shake of the head and a shrug of the shoulder, "I'm a mere glow worm. I never shine by daylight. Besides, it's a hard thing for a poor devil of an author to shine at the table of a rich bookseller. Who, do you think, would laugh at any thing I could say, when I had some of the current wits of the day about me? But, here, though a poor devil, I am among still poorer devils than myself: men who look up to me as a man of letters and a bel esprit, and all my jokes pass as sterling gold from the mint."

"You surely do yourself injustice, sir," said I. "I have certainly heard more good things from you this evening, than from any of those beaux esprits by whom you appear to have been so daunted."

"Ah, sir! but they have luck on their side; they are in the fashion—there's nothing like being in fashion. A man that has once got his character up for a wit, is always sure of a laugh, say what he may. He may utter as much nonsense as he pleases, and all will pass current. No one stops to question the coin of a rich man; but a poor devil cannot pass off either a joke or a guinea, without its being examined on both sides. Wit and coin are always doubted with a threadbare coat.

"For my part," continued he, giving his hat a twitch a little more on one side, "for my part, I hate your fine dinners; there's nothing, sir, like the freedom of a chop house. I'd rather, any time, have my steak and tankard among my own set, than drink claret and eat venison with your cursed civil, elegant company who never laugh at a good joke from a poor devil for fear of its being vulgar. A good joke grows in a wet soil; it flourishes in low places, but withers on your d——d high, dry grounds. I once kept high company, sir, until I nearly ruined myself, I grew so dull, and vapid and genteel. Nothing saved me but being arrested by my Landlady and thrown into prison; where a course of catch clubs, eightpenny ale and poor devil company, manured my mind and brought it back to itself again."

As it was now growing late we parted for the evening; though I felt anxious to know more of this practical philosopher. I was glad therefore when Buckthorne proposed to have another meeting to talk over old school times, and inquired his schoolmate's address. The latter seemed at first a little shy of naming his lodgings; but suddenly assuming an air of hardihood—"Green Arbour Court Sir," exclaimed he—"number —— in Green Arbour Court. You must know the place. Classic ground, sir! classic ground! It was there Goldsmith wrote his Vicar of Wakefield—I always like to live in literary haunts—"

I was amused with this whimsical apology for shabby quarters. On our way homewards Buckthorne assured me that this Dribble had been the prime wit and great wag of the school in their boyish days and one of those unlucky urchins denominated bright geniuses. As he perceived me curious respecting his old schoolmate he promised to take me with him in his proposed visit to Green Arbour Court.

A few mornings afterwards he called upon me and we set forth on our Expedition. He led me through a variety of singular alleys, and courts, and blind passages; for he appeared to be profoundly versed in all the intricate geography of the metropolis. At length we came out upon Fleet Market and traversing it turned up a narrow street to the bottom of a long steep flight of stone steps called Break neck Stairs. These he told me led up to Green Arbour Court, and that, down them poor Goldsmith might many a time have risked his neck. When we entered the court, I could not but smile to think in what out of the way corners genius produces her bantlings! And the muses, those capricious dames, who forsooth, so often refuse to visit palaces, and deny a single smile to votaries in splendid studies and gilded drawing rooms,—what holes and burrows will they frequent to lavish their favours on some ragged disciple!

This Green Arbour Court I found to be a small square surrounded by tall miserable houses, the very intestines of which seemed turned inside out, to judge from the old garments and frippery fluttering from every window. It appeared to be a region of washerwomen, and lines were stretched about the little square, on which clothes were dangling to dry. Just as we entered the square, a scuffle took place between two viragos about a disputed right to a washtub, and immediately the whole community was in a hubbub. Heads in mob caps popped out of every window, and such a clamour of tongues ensued that I was fain to stop my ears. Every Amazon took part with one or other of the disputants, and brandished her arms dripping with soap-suds, and fired away from her window as from the embrazure of a fortress; while the swarms of children nestled and cradled in every procreant chamber of this hive, waking with the noise, set up their shrill pipes to swell the general concert.

Poor Goldsmith! what a time must he have had of it, with his quiet disposition and nervous habits, penned up in this den of noise and vulgarity. How strange that while every sight and sound was sufficient to embitter the heart and fill it with misanthropy, his pen should be dropping the honey of Hybla. Yet it is more than probable that he drew many of his inimitable pictures of low life from the scenes which surrounded him in this abode. The circumstance of Mrs. Tibbs being obliged to wash her husband's two shirts in a neighbour's house, who refused to lend her washtub, may have been no sport of fancy, but a fact passing under his own eye. His landlady may have sat for the picture, and Beau Tibbs' scanty wardrobe have been a fac simile of his own.

It was with some difficulty that we found our way to Dribble's lodgings. They were up two pair of stairs, in a room that looked upon the Court, and when we entered he was seated on the edge of his bed, writing at a broken table. He received us, however, with a free, open, poor devil air, that was irresistible. It is true he did at first appear slightly confused; buttoned up his waistcoat a little higher and tucked in a stray frill of linen. But he recollected himself in an instant; gave a half swagger, half leer as he stepped forth to receive us; drew a three legged stool for Mr. Buckthorne; pointed me to a lumbering old Damask chair that looked like a dethroned monarch in exile, and bade us welcome to his garret.

We soon got engaged in conversation. Buckthorne and he had much to say about early school scenes, and as nothing opens a man's heart more than recollections of the kind we soon drew from him a brief outline of his literary career.

THE POOR DEVIL AUTHOR

I began life unluckily by being the wag and bright fellow at school; and I had the further misfortune of becoming the great genius of my native village. My father was a country attorney, and intended I should succeed him in business; but I had too much genius to study, and he was too fond of my genius to force it into the traces. So I fell into bad company and took to bad habits. Do not mistake me. I mean that I fell into the company of village literati and village blues, and took to writing village poetry.

It was quite the fashion in the village to be literary. There was a little knot of choice spirits of us who assembled frequently together, formed ourselves into a Literary, Scientific and Philosophical Society, and fancied ourselves the most learned philos in existence. Every one had a great character assigned him, suggested by some casual habit or affectation. One heavy fellow drank an enormous quantity of tea; rolled in his arm chair, talked sententiously, pronounced dogmatically, and was considered a second Dr. Johnson; another who happened to be a curate uttered coarse jokes, wrote doggerel rhymes, and was the Swift of our association. Thus we had also our Popes, and Goldsmiths and Addisons, and a blue stocking lady whose drawing room we frequented, who corresponded about nothing, with all the world, and wrote letters with the stiffness and formality of a printed book, was cried up as another Mrs. Montagu. I was, by common consent, the juvenile prodigy, the poetical youth, the great genius, the pride and hope of the village, through whom it was to become one day as celebrated as Stratford on Avon.

My father died and left me his blessing and his business. His blessing brought no money into my pocket; and as to his business it soon deserted me: for I was busy writing poetry, and could not attend to law; and my clients, though they had great respect for my talents, had no faith in a poetical attorney.

I lost my business, therefore, spent my money and finished my poem. It was the Pleasures of Melancholy, and was cried up to the skies by the whole circle. The Pleasures of Imagination, the Pleasures of Hope and the Pleasures of Memory though each had placed its author in the first rank of poets, were blank prose in comparison. Our Mrs. Montagu would cry over it from beginning to end. It was pronounced by all the members of the Literary, Scientific and Philosophical Society, the greatest poem of the age, and all anticipated the noise it would make in the great world. There was not a doubt but the London booksellers would be mad after it, and the only fear of my friends was, that I would make a sacrifice by selling it too cheap. Every time they talked the matter over they encreased the price. They reckoned up the great sums given for the poems of certain popular writers, and determined that mine was worth more than all put together, and ought to be paid for accordingly. For my part, I was modest in my expectations, and determined that I would be satisfied with a thousand guineas. So I put my poem in my pocket and set off for London.

My journey was joyous. My heart was light as my purse, and my head full of anticipations of fame and fortune. With what swelling pride did I cast my eyes upon old London from the heights of Highgate. I was like a general looking down upon a place he expects to conquer. The great metropolis lay stretched before me, buried under a home made cloud of murky smoke, that wrapped it from the brightness of a sunny day, and formed for it a kind of artificial bad weather. At the outskirts of the city, away to the west, the smoke gradually decreased until all was clear and sunny, and the view stretched uninterrupted to the blue line of the Kentish Hills.

My eye turned fondly to where the mighty cupola of St. Paul's swelled dimly through this misty chaos, and I pictured to myself the solemn realm of learning that lies about its base. How soon should the Pleasures of Melancholy throw this world of Booksellers and printers into a bustle of business and delight! How soon should I hear my name repeated by printers' devils throughout Paternoster Row, and Angel Court, and Ave Maria Lane, until Amen Corner should echo back the sound!

Arrived in town, I repaired at once to the most fashionable publisher. Every new author patronizes him of course. In fact, it had been determined in the village circle that he should be the fortunate man. I cannot tell you how vaingloriously I walked the streets; my head was in the clouds. I felt the airs of heaven playing about it, and fancied it already encircled by a halo of literary glory. As I passed by the windows of bookshops, I anticipated the time when my work would be shining among the hotpressed wonders of the day; and my face, scratched on copper, or cut in wood, figuring in fellowship with those of Scott and Byron and Moore.

When I applied at the publisher's house there was something in the loftiness of my air, and the dinginess of my dress, that struck the clerks with reverence. They doubtless took me for some person of consequence, probably a digger of Greek roots or a penetrater of pyramids. A proud man in a dirty shirt is always an imposing character in the world of letters; one must feel intellectually secure before he can venture to dress shabbily; none but a great scholar or a great genius dares to be dirty; so I was ushered at once, to the sanctum sanctorum of this high priest of Minerva.

The publishing of books is a very different affair now adays, from what it was in the time of Bernard Lintot. I found the publisher a fashionably dressed man, in an elegant drawing room, furnished with sophas; and portraits of celebrated authors, and cases of splendidly bound books. He was writing letters at an elegant table. This was transacting business in style. The place seemed suited to the magnificent publications that issued from it. I rejoiced at the choice I had made of a publisher, for I always liked to encourage men of taste and spirit.

I stepped up to the table with the lofty poetical port I had been accustomed to maintain in our village circle; though I threw in it something of a patronizing air, such as one feels when about to make a man's fortune. The publisher paused with his pen in hand, and seemed waiting in mute suspense to know what was to be announced by so singular an apparition.

I put him at his ease in a moment, for I felt that I had but to come, see and conquer. I made known my name, and the name of my poem; produced my precious roll of blotted manuscript, laid it on the table with an emphasis, and told him at once, to save time and come directly to the point, the price was one thousand guineas.

I had given him no time to speak, nor did he seem so inclined. He continued looking at me for a moment with an air of whimsical perplexity; scanned me from head to foot; looked down at the manuscript; then up again at me, then pointed to a chair; and whistling softly to himself, went on writing his letter.

I sat for some time waiting his reply; supposing he was making up his mind; but he only paused occasionally to take a fresh dip of ink; to stroke his chin or the tip of his nose and then resumed his writing. It was evident his mind was intently occupied upon some other subject; but I had no idea that any other subject should be attended to and my poem lie unnoticed on the table. I had supposed that every thing would make way for the Pleasures of Melancholy.

My gorge at length rose within me. I took up my manuscript; thrust it into my pocket, and walked out of the room; making some noise as I went, to let my departure be heard. The publisher, however, was too much buried in minor concerns to notice it. I was suffered to walk down stairs without being called back. I sallied forth into the street, but no clerk was sent after me; nor did the publisher call after me from the drawing room window. I have been told since, that he considered me either a madman or a fool. I leave you to judge how much he was in the wrong in his opinion.

When I turned the corner my crest fell. I cooled down in my pride and my expectations, and reduced my terms with the next bookseller to whom I applied. I had no better success: nor with a third; nor with a fourth. I then desired the booksellers to make an offer themselves; but the deuce an offer would they make. They told me poetry was a mere drug; every body wrote poetry; the market was overstocked with it. And then, they said, the title of my poem was not taking: that pleasures of all kinds were worn threadbare, nothing but horrors did now adays, and even those were almost worn out. Tales of Pirates, Robbers and bloody Turks might answer tolerably well; but then they must come from some established well known name, or the public would not look at them.

At last I offered to leave my poem with a bookseller to read it and judge for himself. "Why really, my dear Mr.——a—a —I forget your name," said he, cutting an eye at my rusty coat and shabby gaiters, "really, sir, we are so pressed with business just now, and have so many manuscripts on hand to read, that we have not time to look at any new production, but if you can call again in a week or two, or say the middle of next month, we may be able to look over your writings and give you an answer. Don't forget, the month after next——good morning, sir—happy to see you any time you are passing this way—"; so saying he bowed me out in the civilest way imaginable.—In short, sir, instead of an eager competition to secure my poem, I could not even get it read! In the meantime I was harrassed by letters from my friends, wanting to know when the work was to appear; who was to be my publisher; but above all things warning me not to let it go too cheap.

There was but one alternative left. I determined to publish the poem myself; and to have my triumph over the booksellers, when it should become the fashion of the day. I accordingly published the Pleasures of Melancholy and ruined myself. Excepting the copies sent to the reviews, and to my friends in the country, not one I believe ever left the bookseller's ware house. The printer's bill drained my purse, and the only notice that was taken of my work was contained in the advertisements paid for by myself.

I could have borne all this, and have attributed it as usual to the mismanagement of the publisher; or the want of taste in the public; and could have made the usual appeal to posterity; but my village friends would not let me rest in quiet. They were picturing me to themselves feasting with the great, communing with the literary, and in the high career of fortune and renown. Every little while, some one would call on me with a letter of introduction from the village circle, recommending him to my attentions, and requesting that I would make him known in society: with a hint that an introduction to a celebrated literary nobleman would be extremely agreeable.

I determined, therefore, to change my lodgings, drop my correspondence, and disappear altogether from the view of my village admirers. Besides, I was anxious to make one more poetic attempt. I was by no means disheartened by the failure of my first. My poem was evidently too didactic. The public was wise enough. It no longer read for instruction. "They want horrors, do they?" said I, "I'faith then they shall have enough of them." So I looked out for some quiet retired place, where I might be out of reach of my friends, and have leisure to cook up some delectable dish of poetical "hell-broth."

I had some difficulty in finding a place to my mind, when chance threw me in the way of Canonbury Castle. It is an ancient brick tower, hard by "merry Islington;" the remains of a hunting seat of Queen Elizabeth, where she took the pleasures of the country, when the neighbourhood was all woodland. What gave it particular interest in my eyes was the circumstance that it had been the residence of a Poet. It was here Goldsmith resided when he wrote his Deserted Village. I was shown the very apartment. It was a

relique of the original style of the castle, with pannelled wainscots and Gothic windows. I was pleased with its air of antiquity, and with its having been
the residence of poor Goldy. "Goldsmith was a pretty poet," said I to myself,
"a very pretty poet; though rather of the old school. He did not think and
feel so strongly as is the fashion now adays; but had he lived in these times
of hot hearts and hot heads, he would no doubt have written quite
differently."

In a few days I was quietly established in my new quarters; my books all
arranged, my writing desk placed by a window looking out into the fields;
and I felt as snug as Robinson Crusoe, when he had finished his bower. For
several days I enjoyed all the novelty of change and the charms which grace
new lodgings before one has found out their defects. I rambled about the
fields where I fancied Goldsmith had rambled. I explored merry Islington;
ate my solitary dinner at the Black Bull, which according to tradition was a
country seat of Sir Walter Raleigh, and would sit and sip my wine and muse
on old times in a quaint old room, where many a council had been held.

All this did very well for a few days; I was stimulated by novelty; inspired
by the associations awakened in my mind by these curious haunts; and began
to think I felt the spirit of composition stirring within me; but Sunday came,
and with it the whole city world, swarming about Canonbury Castle. I could
not open my window but I was stunned with shouts and noises from the
cricket ground. The late quiet road beneath my window, was alive with the
tread of feet and clack of tongues, and to complete my misery, I found that
my quiet retreat was absolutely a "show house!" the tower and its contents
being shewn to strangers at sixpence a head.

There was a perpetual tramping up stairs of citizens and their families, to
look about the country from the top of the tower, and to take a peep at the
city through the telescope, to try if they could discern their own chimnies.
And then, in the midst of a vein of thought, or a moment of inspiration, I
was interrupted and all my ideas put to flight, by my intolerable landlady's
tapping at the door, and asking me, if I would "jist please to let a lady and
gentleman come in to take a look at Mr. Goldsmith's room."

If you know any thing what an author's study is, and what an author is
himself, you must know that there was no standing this. I put a positive
interdict on my room's being exhibited; but then it was shewn when I was
absent and my papers put in confusion; and on returning home one day, I
absolutely found a cursed tradesman and his daughters gaping over my manuscripts; and my landlady in a panic at my appearance. I tried to make out
a little longer by taking the key in my pocket, but it would not do. I overheard mine hostess one day telling some of her customers on the stairs that
the room was occupied by an author, who was always in a tantrum if interrupted; and I immediately perceived, by a slight noise at the door, that they
were peeping at me through the keyhole. By the head of Apollo, but this

was quite too much! With all my eagerness for fame, and my ambition of the stare of the million, I had no idea of being exhibited by retail at sixpence a head, and that through a Key hole. So I bade adieu to Canonbury Castle, Merry Islington, and the haunts of poor Goldsmith, without having advanced a single line in my labours.

My next quarters were at a small white washed cottage, which stands not far from Hampstead, just on the brow of a hill; looking over Chalk Farm, and Camden Town, remarkable for the rival houses of Mother Red Cap and Mother Black Cap; and so across Crackscull Common to the distant city.

The cottage was in no wise remarkable in itself; but I regarded it with reverence, for it had been the asylum of a persecuted author. Hither poor Steele had retreated and lain perdu, when persecuted by creditors and bailiffs; those immemorial plagues of authors and free spirited gentlemen; and here he had written many numbers of the Spectator. It was hence, too, that he had dispatched those little notes to his lady, so full of affection and whimsicality; in which the fond husband, the careless gentleman, and the shifting spendthrift, were so oddly blended. I thought, as I first eyed the window of his apartment, that I could sit within it, and write volumes.

No such thing! It was Haymaking season, and, as ill luck would have it, immediately opposite the cottage was a little ale house with the sign of the Load of Hay. Whether it was there in Steele's time I cannot say; but it set all attempts at conception or inspiration at defiance. It was the resort of all the Irish Haymakers who mow the broad fields in the neighbourhood; and of drovers and teamsters who travel that road. Here would they gather in the endless summer twilight, or by the light of the harvest moon, and sit round a table at the door; and tipple, and laugh, and quarrel, and fight, and sing drowsy songs, and dawdle away the hours until the deep solemn notes of St. Paul's clock would warn the varlets home.

In the day time I was still less able to write. It was broad summer. The haymakers were at work in the fields, and the perfume of the new mown hay brought with it the recollection of my native fields. So instead of remaining in my room to write, I went wandering about Primrose Hill and Hampstead Heights and Shepherd's Fields; and all those Arcadian scenes so celebrated by London Bards. I cannot tell you how many delicious hours I have passed lying on the cocks of new mown hay, on the pleasant slopes of some of those hills, inhaling the fragrance of the fields; while the summer fly buzzed about me, or the grasshopper leaped into my bosom; and how I have gazed with half shut eye upon the smoky mass of London, and listened to the distant sound of its population; and pitied the poor sons of earth, toiling in its bowels, like Gnomes in the "dark gold mine."

People may say what they please about Cockney pastorals; but after all, there is a vast deal of rural beauty about the western vicinity of London; and any one that has looked down upon the valley of West End, with its soft bosom of green pasturage, lying open to the south and dotted with cattle; the steeple of Hampstead rising among rich groves on the brow of the hill; and the learned height of Harrow in the distance; will confess that never has he seen a more absolutely rural landscape in the vicinity of a great metropolis.

Still, however, I found myself not a whit the better off for my frequent change of lodgings; and I began to discover that in literature, as in trade, the old proverb holds good, "a rolling stone gathers no moss."

The tranquil beauty of the country played the very vengeance with me. I could not mount my fancy into the termagant vein. I could not conceive, amidst the smiling landscape, a scene of blood and murder; and the smug citizens in breeches and gaiters, put all ideas of heroes and Bandits out of my brain. I could think of nothing but dulcet subjects—"the pleasures of spring" "the pleasures of solitude"—"the pleasures of tranquility"—"the pleasures of sentiment"—nothing but pleasures; and I had the painful experience of "the pleasures of melancholy" too strongly in my recollection to be beguiled by them

Chance at length befriended me. I had frequently in my ramblings loitered about Hampstead Hill; which is a kind of Parnassus of the metropolis. At such times I occasionally took my dinner at Jack Straw's Castle. It is a country Inn so named. The very spot where that notorious rebel and his followers held their council of war. It is a favourite resort of citizens when rurally inclined, as it commands fine fresh air and a good view of the city.

I sat one day in the public room of this Inn, ruminating over a beefsteak and a pint of port, when my imagination kindled up with ancient and heroic images. I had long wanted a theme and a hero; both suddenly broke upon my mind; I determined to write a poem on the history of Jack Straw. I was so full of my subject that I was fearful of being anticipated; I wondered that none of the poets of the day, in their search after ruffian heroes, had ever thought of Jack Straw. I went to work pell mell, blotted several sheets of paper with choice floating thoughts, and battles and descriptions, to be ready at a moment's warning. In a few days' time I sketched out the skeleton of my poem, and nothing was wanting but to give it flesh and blood. I used to take my manuscript and stroll about Caen Wood, and read aloud; and would dine at the castle, by way of keeping up the vein of thought.

I was there one day, at rather a late hour, in the public room. There was no other company but one man, who sat enjoying his pint of port at a window, and noticing the passers by. He was dressed in a green shooting coat. His countenance was strongly marked. He had a hooked nose, a romantic eye, excepting that it had something of a squint, and altogether, as I thought, a poetical style of head. I was quite taken with the man, for you must know I am a little of a physiognomist; I set him down at once for either a poet or a philosopher.

As I like to make new acquaintances, considering every man a volume of human nature, I soon fell into conversation with the stranger, who, I was pleased to find, was by no means difficult of access. After I had dined, I joined him at the window, and we became so sociable that I proposed a bottle of wine together, to which he most cheerfully assented.

I was too full of my poem to keep long quiet on the subject, and began to talk about the origin of the tavern and the history of Jack Straw. I found my new acquaintance to be perfectly at home on the topic, and to jump exactly with my humour in every respect. I became elevated by the wine and the conversation. In the fullness of an author's feelings, I told him of my projected poem, and repeated some passages, and he was in raptures. He was evidently of a strong poetical turn.

"Sir," said he, filling my glass at the same time, "our poets don't look at home. I don't see why we need go out of old England for robbers and rebels to write about. I like your Jack Straw, sir. He's a home made hero. I like him, sir. I like him exceedingly. He's English to the back bone—damme— Give me honest old England after all; them's my sentiments, sir!"

"I honour your sentiment," cried I zealously, "it is exactly my own. An English ruffian is as good a ruffian for poetry as any in Italy, or Germany, or the Archipelago; but it is hard to make our poets think so."

"More shame for them!" replied the man in green. "What a plague would they have? What have we to do with their Archipelagos of Italy and Germany? Haven't we heaths and commons and high ways on our own little island?—Aye and stout fellows to pad the hoof over them too? Stick to home, I say—them's my sentiments.—Come sir, my service to you—I agree with you perfectly."

"Poets in old times had right notions on this subject," continued I; "witness the fine old ballads about Robin Hood, Allan a'Dale and other staunch blades of yore." "Right, sir, right," interrupted he. "Robin Hood! He was the lad to cry stand! to a man, and never flinch."

"Ah sir!" said I, "they had famous bands of robbers in the good old times. Those were glorious poetical days. The merry crew of Sherwood Forest, who led such a roving picturesque life, 'under the greenwood tree.' I have often wished to visit their haunts, and tread the scenes of the exploits of Friar Tuck, and Clym of the Clough, and Sir William of Cloudeslie."

"Nay sir," said the gentleman in green, "we have had several very pretty gangs since their day. Those gallant dogs that kept about the great heaths in the neighbourhood of London; about Bagshot, and Hounslow, and Blackheath, for instance. Come sir, my service to you. You don't drink."

"I suppose," said I, emptying my glass, "I suppose you have heard of the famous Turpin who was born in this very village of Hampstead, and who used to lurk with his gang in Epping Forest, about a hundred years since."

"Have I?" cried he. "To be sure I have! A hearty old blade that, sound as pitch. Old Turpentine!—as we used to call him. A famous fine fellow, sir."

"Well sir," continued I, "I have visited Waltham Abbey, and Chingford Church merely from the stories I heard when a boy of his exploits there, and I have searched Epping Forest for the cavern where he used to conceal himself. You must know," added I, "that I am a sort of amateur of Highwaymen. They were dashing, daring fellows; the last apologies that we had for the Knights errants of yore. Ah sir! the country has been sinking gradually into tameness and common place. We are losing the old English spirit. The bold Knights of the Post have all dwindled down into lurking footpads and sneaking pickpockets. There's no such thing as a dashing gentlemanlike robbery committed now adays on the King's high way. A man may roll from one end of England to the other, in a drowsy coach or jingling postchaise without any other adventure than that of being occasionally overturned, sleeping in damp sheets, or having an ill cooked dinner.

"We hear no more of public coaches being stopped and robbed by a well mounted gang of resolute fellows with pistols in their hands and crapes over their faces. What a pretty poetical incident was it for example, in domestic life, for a family carriage, on its way to a country seat, to be attacked about dusk, the old gentleman eased of his purse and watch, the ladies of their necklaces and ear rings, by a politely spoken Highwayman on a blood mare, who afterwards leaped the hedge and gallopped across the country, to the admiration of Miss Carolina the daughter, who would write a long and romantic account of the adventure to her friend Miss Juliana in town. Ah sir! we meet with nothing of such incidents now adays!"

"That, sir, " said my companion, taking advantage of a pause, when I stopped to recover breath and to take a glass of wine, which he had just poured out—"that, sir, craving your pardon, is not owing to any want of old English pluck. It is the effect of this cursed system of banking. People do not travel with bags of gold, as they did formerly. They have post notes and drafts on Bankers. To rob a coach is like catching a crow; where you have nothing but carrion flesh and feathers for your pains. But a coach in old times, sir, was as rich as a Spanish Galloon. It turned out the yellow boys bravely. And a private carriage was a cool hundred or two at least."

I cannot express how much I was delighted with the sallies of my new acquaintance. He told me that he often frequented the castle, and would be glad to know more of me; and I promised myself many a pleasant afternoon with him, when I should read him my poem, as it proceeded, and benefit by his remarks; for it was evident he had the true poetical feeling.

"Come, sir!" said he, pushing the bottle, "Damme I like you!—You're a man after my own heart; I'm cursed slow in making new acquaintances. One must be on the reserve, you know. But when I meet with a man of your kidney, damme my heart jumps at once to him—Them's my sentiments, sir—Come, sir, here's Jack Straw's health! I presume one can drink it now adays without treason!"

"With all my heart," said I gaily, "and Dick Turpin's into the bargain!"

"Ah, sir!" said the man in green, "those are the kind of men for poetry. The Newgate Kalender, sir! the Newgate Kalender is your only reading! There's the place to look for bold deeds and dashing fellows."

We were so much pleased with each other that we sat until a late hour. I insisted on paying the bill, for both my purse and my heart were full, and I agreed that he should pay the score at our next meeting. As the coaches had all gone that run between Hampstead and London he had to return on foot. He was so delighted with the idea of my poem that he could talk of nothing else. He made me repeat such passages as I could remember, and though I did it in a very mangled manner, having a wretched memory, yet he was in raptures.

Every now and then he would break out with some scrap which he would misquote most terribly, but would rub his hands and exclaim, "By Jupiter that's fine! that's noble! Damme, sir, if I can conceive how you hit upon such ideas!"

I must confess I did not always relish his misquotations, which sometimes made absolute nonsense of the passages; but what author stands upon trifles when he is praised?

Never had I spent a more delightful evening. I did not perceive how the time flew. I could not bear to separate but continued walking on, arm in arm, with him, past my lodgings, through Camden Town, and across Crack-scull Common talking the whole way about my poem.

When we were half way across the common he interrupted me in the midst of a quotation by telling me that this had been a famous place for footpads, and was still occasionally infested by them; and that a man had recently been shot there in attempting to defend himself.

"The more fool he!" cried I. "A man is an ideot to risk life, or even limb, to save a paltry purse of money. It's quite a different case from that of a duel, where one's honour is concerned. For my part," added I, "I should never think of making resistance against one of those desperadoes."

"Say you so?" cried my friend in green, turning suddenly upon me, and putting a pistol to my breast, "Why then have at you my lad!—come—disburse! empty! unsack!"

In a word, I found that the muse had played me another of her tricks, and had betrayed me into the hands of a footpad. There was no time to parley; he made me turn my pockets inside out; and hearing the sound of distant footsteps, he made one fell swoop upon purse, watch and all, gave me a thwack over my unlucky pate that laid me sprawling on the ground; and scampered away with his booty.

I saw no more of my friend in green until a year or two afterwards; when I caught a sight of his poetical countenance among a crew of scapegraces, heavily ironed, who were on the way for transportation. He recognized me at once, tipped me an impudent wink, and asked me how I came on with the history of Jack Straw's Castle.

The catastrophe at Crackscull Common put an end to my summer's campaign. I was cured of my poetical enthusiasm for rebels, robbers and highwaymen. I was put out of conceit of my subject, and what was worse I was lightened of my purse, in which was almost every farthing I had in the world. So I abandoned Sir Richard Steele's cottage in despair, and crept into less celebrated, though no less poetical and airy lodgings in a garret in town.

I now determined to cultivate the society of the literary, and to enrol myself in the fraternity of authorship. It is by the constant collision of mind, thought I, that authors strike out the sparks of genius, and kindle up with glorious conceptions. Poetry is evidently a contagious complaint: I will keep company with poets; who knows but I may catch it as others have done?

I found no difficulty in making a circle of literary acquaintances, not having the sin of success lying at my door; indeed, the failure of my poem was a kind of recommendation to their favour. It is true my new friends were not of the most brilliant names in literature; but then, if you would take their words for it, they were like the prophets of old, men of whom the world was not worthy; and who were to live in future ages, when the ephemeral favourites of the day should be forgotten.

I soon discovered, however, that the more I mingled in literary society, the less I felt capacitated to write; that poetry was not so catching as I imagined; and that in familiar life there was often nothing less poetical than a poet. Besides, I wanted the *esprit du corps* to turn these literary fellowships to any account. I could not bring myself to enlist in any particular sect: I saw something to like in them all, but found that would never do, for that the tacit condition on which a man enters into one of these sects is, that he abuses all the rest.

I perceived that there were little knots of authors who lived with, and for, and by one another. They considered themselves the salt of the earth. They fostered and kept up a conventional vein of thinking and talking, and joking on all subjects; and they cried each other up to the skies. Each sect had its particular creed; and set up certain authors as divinities, and fell down and worshipped them; and considered every one who did not worship them, or who worshipped any other, as a heretic and an infidel.

In quoting the writers of the day, I generally found them extolling names of which I had scarcely heard, and talking slightingly of others who were the favourites of the public. If I mentioned any recent work from the pen of a first rate author, they had not read it; they had not time to read all that was spawned from the press; he wrote too much to write well;—and then they would break out into raptures about some Mr. Timson, or Tomson, or Jackson, whose works were neglected at the present day, but who was to be the wonder and delight of posterity. Alas! what heavy debts is this neglectful world daily accumulating on the shoulders of poor posterity!

But above all, it was edifying to hear with what contempt they would talk of the great. Ye gods! how immeasurably the great are despised by the small fry of literature! It is true, an exception was now and then made of some nobleman, with whom, perhaps, they had casually shaken hands at an election, or hob or nobbed at a public dinner, and who was pronounced a "devilish good fellow," and "no humbug;" but, in general, it was enough for a man to have a title to be the object of their sovereign disdain: you have no idea how poetically and philosophically they would talk of nobility.

For my part, this affected me but little; for though I had no bitterness against the great, and did not think the worse of a man for having innocently been born to a title, yet I did not feel myself at present called upon to resent the indignities poured upon them by the little. But the hostility to the great writers of the day went sorely against the grain with me. I could not enter into such feuds, nor participate in such animosities. I had not become author sufficiently to hate other authors. I could still find pleasure in the novelties of the press, and could find it in my heart to praise a contemporary, even though he were successful. Indeed, I was miscellaneous in my taste, and could not confine it to any age or growth of writers. I could turn with delight from the glowing pages of Byron to the cool and polished raillery of Pope; and, after wandering among the sacred groves of Paradise Lost, I could give myself up to voluptuous abandonment in the enchanted bowers of Lalla Rookh.

"I would have my authors," said I, "as various as my wines, and, in relishing the strong and the racy, would never decry the sparkling and exhilarating. Port and sherry are excellent stand-by's, and so is Madeira; but claret and Burgundy may be drunk now and then without disparagement to one's palate; and Champagne is a beverage by no means to be despised."

Such was the tirade I uttered one day, when a little flushed with ale, at a literary club. I uttered it, too, with something of a flourish, for I thought my simile a clever one. Unluckily, my auditors were men who drank beer and hated Pope; so my figure about wines went for nothing, and my critical toleration was looked upon as downright heterodoxy. In a word, I soon became like a freethinker in religion, an outlaw from every sect, and fair game for all. Such are the melancholy consequences of not hating in literature.

I see you are growing weary, so I will be brief with the residue of my literary career. I will not detain you with a detail of my various attempts to get astride of Pegasus; of the poems I have written which were never printed, the plays I have presented which were never performed, and the tracts I have published which were never purchased.—It seemed as if booksellers, managers, and the very public, had entered into a conspiracy to starve me. Still I could not prevail upon myself to give up the trial nor abandon those dreams of renown in which I had indulged. How should I ever be able to look the literary circle of my native village in the face, if I were so completely to falsify their predictions. For some time longer therefore I continued to write for fame, and of course was the most miserable dog in existence, besides being in continual risk of starvation. I accumulated loads of literary treasure on my shelves—loads which were to be treasures to posterity; but, alas! they put not a penny into my purse. What was all this wealth to my present necessities? I could not patch my elbows with an ode; nor satisfy my hunger with blank verse. "Shall a man fill his belly with the east wind?" says the proverb. He may as well do so as with poetry.

I have many a time strolled sorrowfully along, with a sad heart and an empty stomach, about five o'clock, and looked wistfully down the areas in the west end of the town; and seen through the kitchen windows the fires gleaming, and the joints of meat turning on the spits and dripping with gravy; and the cook maids beating up puddings, or trussing turkeys, and felt for the moment that if I could but have the run of one of those kitchens, Apollo and the muses might have the hungry heights of Parnassus for me. Oh sir! talk of meditations among the tombs—they are nothing so melancholy as the meditations of a poor devil without penny in pouch, along a line of kitchen windows towards dinner time.

At length, when almost reduced to famine and despair, the idea all at once entered my head, that perhaps I was not so clever a fellow as the village and myself had supposed It was the salvation of me. The moment the idea popped into my brain it brought conviction and comfort with it. I awoke as from a dream. I gave up immortal fame to those who could live on air; took to writing for mere bread; and have ever since led a very tolerable life of it. There is no man of letters so much at his ease, sir, as he who has no character to gain or lose. I had to train myself to it a little, and to clip my wings short at first, or they would have carried me up into poetry in spite of myself. So I determined to begin by the opposite extreme, and abandoning the higher regions of the craft I came plump down to the lowest, and turned Creeper.

"Creeper! and pray what is that?" said I. "Oh sir! I see you are ignorant of the language of the craft; a creeper is one who furnishes the newspapers with paragraphs at so much a line: one who goes about in quest of misfortunes; attends the Bow Street Office; the courts of justice and every other den of mischief and iniquity. We are paid at the rate of a penny a line, and as we can sell the same paragraph to almost every paper, we sometimes pick up a very decent day's work. Now and then the muse is unkind, or the day uncommonly quiet, and then we rather starve; and sometimes the unconscionable editors will clip our paragraphs when they are a little too rhetorical, and snip off twopence or threepence at a go. I have many a time had my pot of porter snipped off of my dinner in this way; and have had to dine with dry lips. However I cannot complain. I rose gradually in the lower ranks of the craft, and am now I think in the most comfortable region of literature."

"And pray," said I, "what may you be at present?"

"At present," said he, "I am a regular job writer and turn my hand to any thing. I work up the writings of others at so much a sheet; turn off translations; write second rate articles to fill up reviews and magazines; compile travels and voyages, and furnish theatrical criticisms for the newspapers. All this authorship, you perceive, is anonymous; it gives no reputation, except among the trade, where I am considered an author of all work, and am always sure of employ. That's the only reputation I want. I sleep soundly, without dread of duns or critics, and leave immortal fame to those that choose to fret and fight about it. Take my word for it, the only happy author in this world is he who is below the care of reputation."

NOTORIETY

When we had emerged from the literary nest of honest Dribble, and had passed safely through the dangers of Break neck Stairs, and the labyrinths of Fleet Market, Buckthorne indulged in many comments upon the peep into literary life which he had furnished me.

I expressed my surprise at finding it so different a world from what I had imagined. "It is always so," said he, "with strangers. The land of literature is a fairy land to those who view it from a distance, but like all other landscapes, the charm fades on a nearer approach, and the thorns and briars become visible. The republic of letters is the most factious and discordant of all republics, ancient or modern."

"Yet," said I, smiling, "you would not have me take honest Dribble's experience as a view of the land. He is but a mousing owl; a mere groundling. We should have quite a different strain from one of those fortunate authors whom we see sporting about the empyreal heights of fashion, like swallows in the blue sky of a summer's day."

"Perhaps we might," replied he, "but I doubt it. I doubt whether if any one, even of the most successful, were to tell his actual feelings, you would not find the truth of friend Dribble's philosophy with respect to reputation. One you would find carrying a gay face to the world, while some vulture critic was preying upon his very liver. Another, who was simple enough to mistake fashion for fame, you would find watching countenances, and cultivating invitations, more ambitious to figure in the *beau monde* than the world of letters, and apt to be rendered wretched by the neglect of an illiterate peer, or a dissipated duchess. Those who were rising to fame, you would find tormented with anxiety to get higher; and those who had gained the summit, in constant apprehension of a decline.

"Even those who are indifferent to the buzz of notoriety, and the farce of fashion, are not much better off, being incessantly harassed by intrusions on their leisure, and interruptions of their pursuits; for, whatever may be his feelings, when once an author is launched into notoriety, he must go the rounds until the idle curiosity of the day is satisfied, and he is thrown aside to make way for some new caprice. Upon the whole, I do not know but he is most fortunate who engages in the whirl through ambition, however tormenting; as it is doubly irksome to be obliged to join in the game without being interested in the stake.

"There is a constant demand in the fashionable world for novelty, every nine days must have its wonder, no matter of what kind. At one time it is an author; at another a fire eater; at another a composer, an Indian juggler, or an Indian chief; a man from the North Pole or the Pyramids: each figures through his brief term of notoriety, and then makes way for the succeeding wonder. You must know that we have oddity fanciers among our ladies of rank, who collect about them all kinds of remarkable beings: fiddlers, statesmen, singers, warriors, artists, philosophers, actors, and poets; every kind of personage, in short, who is noted for something peculiar: so that their routs are like fancy balls, where every one comes 'in character.'

"I have had infinite amusement at these parties in noticing how industriously every one was playing a part, and acting out of his natural line. There is not a more complete game at cross purposes than the intercourse of the literary and the great. The fine gentleman is always anxious to be thought a wit, and the wit a fine gentleman.

"I have noticed a lord endeavouring to look wise and to talk learnedly with a man of letters, who was aiming at a fashionable air, and the tone of a man who had lived about town. The peer quoted a score or two of learned authors, with whom he would fain be thought intimate, while the author talked of Sir John this, and Sir Harry that, and extolled the Burgundy he had drank at Lord Such-a-one's.—Each seemed to forget that he could only be interesting to the other in his proper character. Had the peer been merely a man of erudition, the author would never have listened to his prosing; and had the author known all the nobility in the Court Calendar, it would have given him no interest in the eyes of the peer.

"In the same way I have seen a fine lady, remarkable for beauty, weary a philosopher with flimsy metaphysics, while the philosopher put on an awkward air of gallantry, played with her fan, and prattled about the Opera. I have heard a sentimental poet talk very stupidly with a statesman about the national debt; and on joining a knot of scientific old gentlemen conversing in a corner, expecting to hear the discussion of some valuable discovery, I found they were only amusing themselves with a fat story."

A PRACTICAL PHILOSOPHER

The anecdotes I had heard of Buckthorne's early schoolmate, together with a variety of peculiarities which I had remarked in himself, gave me a strong curiosity to know something of his own history. I am a traveller of the good old school, and am fond of the custom laid down in books, according to which, whenever travellers met, they sat down forthwith, and gave a history of themselves and their adventures. This Buckthorne, too, was a man much to my taste; he had seen the world, and mingled with society, yet retained the strong eccentricities of a man who had lived much alone. There was a careless dash of good humour about him which pleased me exceedingly, and at times an odd tinge of melancholy mingled with his humour and gave it an additional zest. He was apt to run into long speculations upon society and manners, and to indulge in whimsical views of human nature; yet there was nothing ill tempered in his satire. It ran more upon the follies than the vices of mankind; and even the follies of his fellow man were treated with the leniency of one who felt himself to be but frail. He had evidently been a little chilled and buffetted by fortune, without being soured thereby; as some fruits become mellower and more generous in their flavour from having been bruised and frostbitten.

I have always had a great relish for the conversation of practical philosophers of this stamp, who have profited by the "sweet uses" of adversity without imbibing its bitterness; who have learnt to estimate the world rightly, yet good humouredly; and who, while they perceive the truth of the saying, that "all is vanity," are yet able to do so without vexation of spirit.

Such a man was Buckthorne. In general a laughing philosopher; and if at any time a shade of sadness stole across his brow, it was but transient; like a summer cloud, which soon goes by, and freshens and revives the fields over which it passes.

I was walking with him one day in Kensington Gardens—for he was a knowing epicure in all the cheap pleasures and rural haunts within reach of the metropolis. It was a delightful warm morning in spring; and he was in the happy mood of a pastoral citizen, when just turned loose into grass and sunshine. He had been watching a lark which, rising from a bed of daisies and yellow cups, had sung his way up to a bright snowy cloud floating in the deep blue sky.

"Of all birds," said he, "I should like to be a lark. He revels in the brightest time of the day, in the happiest season of the year, among fresh meadows and opening flowers; and when he has sated himself with the sweetness of earth, he wings his flight up to Heaven as if he would drink in the melody of the morning stars. Hark to that note! How it comes trilling down upon the ear! What a stream of music, note falling over note in delicious cadence! Who would trouble his head about operas and concerts when he could walk in the fields and hear such music for nothing? These are the enjoyments which set riches at scorn, and make even a poor man independent:

> I care not, Fortune, what you do deny:—
>   You cannot rob me of free nature's grace;
> You cannot shut the windows of the sky,
>   Through which Aurora shows her bright'ning face;
>   You cannot bar my constant feet to trace
> The woods and lawns by living streams at eve——

"Sir, there are homilies in nature's works worth all the wisdom of the schools, if we could but read them rightly; and one of the pleasantest lessons I ever received in a time of trouble, was from hearing the notes of a lark."

I profited by this communicative vein to intimate to Buckthorne a wish to know something of the events of his life, which I fancied must have been an eventful one.

He smiled when I expressed my desire. "I have no great story," said he, "to relate. A mere tissue of errors and follies. But, such as it is, you shall have one epoch of it, by which you may judge of the rest." And so, without any further prelude, he gave me the following anecdotes of his early adventures.

BUCKTHORNE, OR THE YOUNG MAN OF GREAT EXPECTATIONS

I was born to very little property, but to great expectations; which is perhaps one of the most unlucky fortunes a man can be born to. My father was a country gentleman, the last of a very ancient and honourable but decayed family, and resided in an old hunting lodge in Warwickshire. He was a keen sportsman and lived to the extent of his moderate income, so that I had little to expect from that quarter; but then I had a rich uncle by the mother's side, a penurious, accumulating curmudgeon, who it was confidently expected would make me his heir; because he was an old Bachelor; because I was named after him, and because he hated all the world except myself.

He was, in fact, an inveterate hater; a miser even in misanthropy, and hoarded up a grudge as he did a guinea. Thus, though my mother was an only sister, he had never forgiven her marriage with my father, against whom he had a cold, still, immoveable pique, which had lain at the bottom of his heart, like a stone in a well, ever since they had been school boys together. My mother, however, considered me as the intermediate being that was to bring every thing again into harmony, for she looked upon me as a prodigy— God bless her! My heart overflows whenever I recall her tenderness. She was the most excellent, the most indulgent of mothers. I was her only child; it was a pity she had no more, for she had fondness of heart enough to have spoiled a dozen!

I was sent at an early age to a public school sorely against my mother's wishes; but my father insisted that it was the only way to make boys hardy. The school was kept by a conscientious prig of the ancient system who did his duty by the boys entrusted to his care; that is to say we were flogged soundly when we did not get our lessons. We were put into classes and thus flogged on in droves along the highways of knowledge, in much the same manner as cattle are driven to market, where those that are heavy in gait or short in leg have to suffer for the superior alertness or longer limbs of their companions.

For my part, I confess it with shame, I was an incorrigible laggard. I have always had the poetical feeling, that is to say I have always been an idle fellow and prone to play the vagabond. I used to get away from my books and school whenever I could and ramble about the fields. I was surrounded by seductions for such a temperament. The school house was an old fashioned whitewashed mansion of wood and plaister, standing on the skirts of a beautiful village. Close by it was the venerable church with a tall Gothic spire. Before it spread a lovely green valley, with a little stream glistening along through willow groves; while a line of blue hills bounding the landscape gave rise to many a summer day dream as to the fairy land that lay beyond.

In spite of all the scourgings I suffered at that school to make me love my book I cannot but look back upon the place with fondness. Indeed I considered this frequent flagellation as the common lot of humanity and the regular mode in which scholars were made. My kind mother used to lament over my details of the sore trials I underwent in the cause of learning; but my father turned a deaf ear to her expostulations. He had been flogged through school himself and swore there was no other way of making a man of parts; though, let me speak it with all due reverence, my father was but an indifferent illustration of his theory, for he was considered a grievous blockhead.

My poetical temperament evinced itself at a very early period. The village church was attended every Sunday by a neighbouring squire; the lord of the manor, whose park stretched quite to the village and whose spacious country seat seemed to take the church under its protection. Indeed you would have thought the church had been consecrated to him instead of to the Deity. The parish clerk bowed low before him and the vergers humbled themselves unto the dust in his presence. He always entered a little late and with some stir, striking his cane emphatically on the ground; swaying his hat in his hand, and looking loftily to the right and left as he walked slowly up the aisle, and the parson, who always ate his Sunday dinner with him, never commenced service until he appeared. He sat with his family in a large pew gorgeously lined, humbling himself devoutly on velvet cushions and reading lessons of meekness and lowliness of spirit out of splendid gold and morocco prayer books. Whenever the parson spoke of the difficulty of a rich man's entering the kingdom of heaven, the eyes of the congregation would turn towards the "grand pew," and I thought the squire seemed pleased with the application.

The pomp of this pew and the aristocratical air of the family struck my imagination wonderfully and I fell desperately in love with a little daughter of the squire's, about twelve years of age. This freak of fancy made me more truant from my studies than ever. I used to stroll about the squire's park, and lurk near the house: to catch glimpses of this little damsel at the windows, or playing about the lawns; or walking out with her governess.

I had not enterprize, nor impudence enough to venture from my concealment; indeed I felt like an arrant poacher, until I read one or two of Ovid's Metamorphoses, when I pictured myself as some sylvan deity and she a coy wood nymph of whom I was in pursuit. There is something extremely delicious in these early awakenings of the tender passion. I can feel, even at this moment, the thrilling of my boyish bosom, whenever by chance I caught a glimpse of her white frock fluttering among the shrubbery. I carried about in my bosom a volume of Waller, which I had purloined from my mother's library; and I applied to my little fair one all the compliments lavished upon Sacharissa.

At length I danced with her at a school ball. I was so awkward a booby that I dared scarcely speak to her; I was filled with awe and embarrassment in her presence; but I was so inspired that my poetical temperament for the first time broke out in verse and I fabricated some glowing lines, in which I berhymed the little lady under the favourite name of Sacharissa. I slipped the verses, trembling and blushing, into her hand the next Sunday as she came out of church. The little prude handed them to her mamma; the mamma handed them to the squire; the squire, who had no soul for poetry, sent them in dudgeon to the schoolmaster; and the schoolmaster, with a barbarity worthy of the dark ages, gave me a sound and peculiarly humiliating flogging for thus trespassing upon Parnassus.

This was a sad outset for a votary of the muse. It ought to have cured me of my passion for poetry; but it only confirmed it, for I felt the spirit of a martyr rising within me. What was as well, perhaps, it cured me of my passion for the young lady, for I felt so indignant at the ignominious horsing I had incurred in celebrating her charms, that I could not hold up my head in church.

Fortunately for my wounded sensibility the midsummer holydays came on, and I returned home. My mother, as usual, enquired into all my school concerns, my little pleasures, and cares, and sorrows; for boyhood has its share of the one as well as of the others. I told her all, and she was indignant at the treatment I had experienced. She fired up at the arrogance of the squire, and the prudery of the daughter; and as to the schoolmaster, she wondered where was the use of having schoolmasters, and why boys could not remain at home and be educated by tutors, under the eye of their mothers. She asked to see the verses I had written, and she was delighted with them, for to confess the truth, she had a pretty taste in poetry. She even shewed them to the parson's wife, who protested they were charming, and the parson's three daughters insisted on each having a copy of them.

All this was exceedingly balsamic, and I was still more consoled and encouraged when the young ladies, who were the blue stockings of the neighbourhood, and had read Dr. Johnson's Lives quite through, assured my mother that great geniuses never studied, but were always idle; upon which I began to surmise that I was myself something out of the common run. My father, however, was of a very different opinion, for when my mother, in the pride of her heart, shewed him my copy of verses, he threw them out of the window, asking her "if she meant to make a ballad monger of the boy." But he was a careless, common thinking man, and I cannot say that I ever loved him much; my mother absorbed all my filial affection.

I used occasionally during holydays to be sent on short visits to the uncle, who was to make me his heir; they thought it would keep me in his mind and render him fond of me. He was a withered, anxious looking old fellow, and lived in a desolate old country seat, which he suffered to go to ruin from absolute niggardliness. He kept but one man servant who had lived, or rather starved with him for years. No woman was allowed to sleep in the house. A daughter of the old servant lived by the gate in what had been a porter's lodge, and was permitted to come into the house about an hour each day, to make the beds, and cook a morsel of provisions.

The park that surrounded the house was all run wild; the trees grown out of shape; the fish ponds stagnant; the urns and statues fallen from their pedestals and buried among the rank grass. The hares and pheasants were so little molested, except by poachers, that they bred in great abundance, and sported about the rough lawns and weedy avenues. To guard the premises and frighten off robbers, of whom he was somewhat apprehensive, and visitors, whom he held in almost equal awe, my uncle kept two or three blood hounds, who were always prowling round the house, and were the dread of the neighbouring peasantry. They were gaunt and half starved, seemed ready to devour one from mere hunger, and were an effectual check on any stranger's approach to this wizard castle.

Such was my uncle's house, which I used to visit now and then during the holydays. I was, as I before said, the old man's favourite; that is to say he did not hate me so much as he did the rest of the world. I had been apprised of his character and cautioned to cultivate his good will; but I was too young and careless to be a courtier; and indeed have never been sufficiently studious of my interests, to let them govern my feelings. However, we jogged on very well together, and as my visits cost him almost nothing, they did not seem to be very unwelcome. I brought with me my fishing rod and half supplied the table from the fish ponds.

Our meals were solitary and unsocial. My uncle rarely spoke; he pointed for whatever he wanted and the servant perfectly understood him. Indeed his man John, or Iron John as he was called in the neighbourhood, was a counterpart of his master. He was a tall bony old fellow, with a dry wig that seemed made of cow's tail and a face as tough as though it had been made of bull's hide. He was generally clad in a long, patched livery coat, taken out of the wardrobe of the house; and which bagged loosely about him, having evidently belonged to some corpulent predecessor, in the more plenteous days of the mansion. From long habits of taciturnity the hinges of his jaws seemed to have grown absolutely rusty; and it cost him as much effort to set them ajar, and to let out a tolerable sentence, as it would have done to set open the iron gates of the park and let out the old family carriage that was dropping to pieces in the coach house.

I cannot say, however, but that I was for some time amused with my uncle's peculiarities. Even the very desolateness of the establishment had something in it that hit my fancy. When the weather was fine I used to amuse myself, in a solitary way, by rambling about the park, and coursing like a colt across its lawns. The hares and pheasants seemed to stare with surprize to see a human being walking these forbidden grounds by day light. Sometimes I amused myself by jerking stones, or shooting at birds with a bow and arrows; for to have used a gun would have been treason. Now and then my path was crossed by a little red-headed ragged-tailed urchin, the son of the woman at the lodge, who ran wild about the premises. I tried to draw him into familiarity and to make a companion of him; but he seemed to have imbibed the strange, unsocial character of every thing around him;

and always kept aloof; so I considered him as another Orson, and amused myself with shooting at him with my bow and arrows, and he would hold up his breeches with one hand and scamper away like a deer.

There was something in all this loneliness and wildness strangely pleasing to me. The great stables, empty and weather broken, with the names of favourite horses over the vacant stalls; the windows bricked and boarded up; the broken roofs, garrisoned by Rooks and Jackdaws; all had a singularly forlorn appearance: One would have concluded the house to be totally un-inhabited, were it not for a little thread of blue smoke, which now and then curled up like a corkscrew, from the center of one of the wide chimneys, when my uncle's starveling meal was cooking.

My uncle's room was in a remote corner of the building, strongly secured and generally locked; I was never admitted into this strong hold; where the old man would remain for the greater part of the time, drawn up like a veteran spider, in the citadel of his web. The rest of the mansion, however, was open to me, and I wandered about it, unconstrained. The damp and rain which beat in through the broken windows, crumbled the paper from the walls; mouldered the pictures and gradually destroyed the furniture. I loved to rove about the wide waste chambers in bad weather, and listen to the howling of the wind, and the banging about of the doors and window shutters. I pleased myself with the idea how completely, when I came to the estate, I would renovate all things, and make the old building ring with merriment, till it was astonished at its own jocundity.

The chamber which I occupied on these visits had been my mother's, when a girl. There was still the toilet table of her own adorning; the land-scapes of her own drawing. She had never seen it since her marriage, but would often ask me if every thing was still the same. All was just the same, for I loved that chamber on her account, and had taken pains to put every thing in order, and to mend all the flaws in the windows with my own hands. I anticipated the time when I should once more welcome her to the house of her fathers, and restore her to this little nestling place of her childhood.

At length my evil genius, or, what perhaps is the same thing, the muse, inspired me with the notion of rhyming again. My uncle, who never went to church, used on Sundays to read chapters out of the bible, and Iron John, the woman from the lodge and myself were his congregation. It seemed to be all one to him what he read, so long as it was something from the bible; sometimes therefore it would be the Song of Solomon, and this withered anatomy would read about being "stayed with flaggons and comforted with apples, for he was sick of love." Sometimes he would hobble with spectacles on nose, through whole chapters of hard Hebrew names in Deuteronomy; at which the poor woman would sigh and groan as if wonderfully moved. His favourite book however was "The Pilgrim's Progress," and when he came to that part which treats of Doubting Castle and Giant Despair, I thought invariably of him and his desolate old country seat. So much did the idea amuse me, that I took to scribbling about it under the trees in the park; and in a few days had made some progress in a poem, in which I had given a description of the place, under the name of Doubting Castle, and personified my uncle as Giant Despair.

I lost my poem somewhere about the house, and I soon suspected that my uncle had found it; as he harshly intimated to me that I could return home, and that I need not come and see him again until he should send for me.

Just about this time my mother died.—I cannot dwell upon the circumstance; my heart, careless and wayworn as it is, gushes with the recollection. Her death was an event that perhaps gave a turn to all my after fortunes. With her died all that made home attractive. I had no longer any body whom I was ambitious to please, or fearful to offend. My father was a good kind of man in his way, but he had bad maxims in education, and we differed on material points. It makes a vast difference in opinion about the utility of the rod, which end happens to fall to one's share. I never could be brought into my father's way of thinking on the subject.

I now, therefore, began to grow very impatient of remaining at school to be flogged for things that I did not like. I longed for variety, especially now that I had not my uncle's to resort to, by way of diversifying the dullness of school with the dreariness of his country seat. I was now almost seventeen, tall for my age and full of idle fancies. I had a roving, inextinguishable desire to see different kinds of life, and different orders of society; and this vagrant humour had been fostered in me by Tom Dribble, the prime wag and great genius of the school, who had all the rambling propensities of a poet.

I used to sit at my desk in the school, on a fine summer's day, and instead of studying the book which lay open before me, my eye was gazing through the window on the green fields and blue hills. How I envied the happy groups seated on the tops of stage coaches chatting, and joking, and laughing, as they were whirled by the school house, on their way to the metropolis. Even the Waggoners trudging along beside their ponderous teams, and traversing the Kingdom, from one end to the other, were objects of envy to me. I fancied to myself what adventures they must experience, and what odd scenes of life they must witness. All this was, doubtless, the poetical temperament working within me and tempting me forth into a world of its own creation, which I mistook for the world of real life.

While my mother lived this strong propensity to rove was counteracted by the stronger attractions of home and by the powerful ties of affection which drew me to her side; but now that she was gone, the attractions had ceased; the ties were severed. I had no longer an anchorage ground for my heart; but was at the mercy of every vagrant impulse. Nothing but the narrow allowance on which my father kept me, and the consequent penury of my purse, prevented me from mounting the top of a stage coach and launching myself adrift on the great ocean of life.

Just about this time the village was agitated for a day or two, by the passing through of several caravans, containing wild beasts, and other spectacles for a great fair annually held at a neighbouring town.

I had never seen a fair of any consequence, and my curiosity was powerfully awakened by this bustle of preparation. I gazed with respect and wonder at the vagrant personages who accompanied these caravans. I loitered about the village inn, listening with curiosity and delight to the slang talk and cant jokes of the showmen and their followers; and I felt an eager desire to witness this fair, which my fancy decked out as something wonderfully fine.

A holyday afternoon presented, when I could be absent from noon until evening. A waggon was going from the village to the fair. I could not resist the temptation, nor the eloquence of Tom Dribble, who was a truant to the very heart's core. We hired seats, and set off full of boyish expectation. I promised myself that I would but take a peep at the land of promise, and hasten back again before my absence should be noticed.

Heavens! how happy I was on arriving at the fair! How I was enchanted with the world of fun and pageantry around me! The humours of Punch, the feats of the Equestrians, the magical tricks of the Conjurors! But what principally caught my attention was—an itinerant theatre; where a tragedy, pantomime and farce were all acted in the course of half an hour, and more of the Dramatis personæ murdered, than at either Drury Lane or Covent Garden in the course of a whole evening. I have since seen many a play performed by the best actors in the world, but never have I derived half the delight from any, that I did from this first representation.

There was a ferocious tyrant in a skull cap, like an inverted porringer, and a dress of red baize, magnificently embroidered with gilt leather; with his face so be-whiskered and his eyebrows so knit and expanded with burnt cork, that he made my heart quake within me as he stamped about the little stage. I was enraptured too with the surpassing beauty of a distressed damsel, in faded pink silk, and dirty white muslin, whom he held in cruel captivity by way of gaining her affections; and who wept and wrung her hands and flourished a ragged white handkerchief from the top of an impregnable tower, of the size of a band box.

Even after I had come out from the play, I could not tear myself from the vicinity of the theatre; but lingered, gazing and wondering, and laughing at the dramatis personæ, as they performed their antics, or danced upon a stage in front of the booth, to decoy a new set of spectators.

I was so bewildered by the scene, and so lost in the crowd of sensations that kept swarming upon me, that I was like one entranced. I lost my companion Tom Dribble in a tumult and scuffle that took place near one of the shows, but I was too much occupied in mind to think long about him. I strolled about until dark, when the fair was lighted up, and a new scene of magic opened upon me. The illumination of the tents and booths; the brilliant effect of the stages decorated with lamps, with dramatic groups flaunting about them in gaudy dresses, contrasted splendidly with the surrounding darkness; while the uproar of drums, trumpets, fiddles, hautboys and cymbals, mingled with the harangues of the showmen, the squeaking of Punch, and the shouts and laughter of the crowd, all united to complete my giddy distraction.

Time flew without my perceiving it. When I came to myself and thought of the school, I hastened to return. I enquired for the waggon in which I had come: it had been gone for hours. I asked the time. It was almost midnight! A sudden quaking seized me. How was I to get back to school? I was too weary to make the journey on foot, and I knew not where to apply for a conveyance. Even if I should find one, could I venture to disturb the school house long after midnight?—to arouse that sleeping lion the usher, in the very midst of his night's rest? The idea was too dreadful for a delinquent schoolboy. All the horrors of return rushed upon me—my absence must long before this have been remarked—and absent for a whole night!—a deed of darkness not easily to be expiated. The rod of the pedagogue budded forth into tenfold terrors before my affrighted fancy. I pictured to myself punishment and humiliation in every variety of form; and my heart sickened at the picture. Alas! how often are the petty ills of boyhood as painful to our tender natures, as are the sterner evils of manhood to our robuster minds.

I wandered about among the booths, and I might have derived a lesson from my actual feelings, how much the charms of this world depend upon ourselves; for I no longer saw any thing gay or delightful in the revelry around me. At length I lay down, wearied and perplexed, behind one of the large tents, and, covering myself with the margin of the tent cloth, to keep off the night chill, I soon fell asleep.

I had not slept long when I was awakened by the noise of merriment within an adjoining booth. It was the itinerant theatre, rudely constructed of boards and canvass. I peeped through an aperture and saw the whole dramatis personæ, tragedy, comedy and pantomime all refreshing themselves after the final dismissal of their auditors. They were merry and gamesome and made the flimsy theatre ring with their laughter. I was astonished to see the Tragedy tyrant in red baize and fierce whiskers who had made my heart quake as he strutted about the boards; now transformed into a fat, good humoured fellow; the beaming porringer laid aside from his brow, and his jolly face washed from all the terrors of burnt cork. I was delighted, too, to see the distressed damsel, in faded silk and dirty muslin, who had trembled under his tyranny, and afflicted me so much by her sorrows; now seated familiarly on his knee, and quaffing from the same tankard. Harlequin lay asleep on one of the benches; and monks, satyrs and vestal virgins were grouped together, laughing outrageously at a broad story, told by an unhappy count who had been barbarously murdered in the tragedy.

This was, indeed, novelty to me. It was a peep into another planet. I gazed and listened with intense curiosity and enjoyment. They had a thousand odd stories and jokes about the events of the day; and burlesque descriptions and mimickings of the spectators, who had been admiring them. Their conversation was full of allusions to their adventures at different places where they had exhibited; the characters they had met with in different villages; and the ludicrous difficulties in which they had occasionally been involved. All past cares and troubles were now turned by these thoughtless beings into matter of merriment; and made to contribute to the gaiety of the moment. They had been moving from fair to fair about the kingdom, and were the next morning, to set out on their way to London.

My resolution was taken. I stole from my nest; and crept through a hedge into a neighbouring field, where I went to work to make a tatterdemalion of myself. I tore my clothes; soiled them with dirt; begrimed my face and hands; and, crawling near one of the booths, purloined an old hat, and left my new one in its place. It was an honest theft, and I hope may not hereafter rise up in judgment against me.

I now ventured to the scene of merrymaking, and, presenting myself before the Dramatic corps, offered myself as a volunteer. I felt terribly agitated and abashed, for—"never before stood I in such a presence." I had addressed myself to the manager of the company. He was a fat man dressed in dirty white; with a red sash fringed with tinsel, swathed round his body. His face was smeared with paint, and a majestic plume towered from an old spangled black bonnet. He was the Jupiter Tonans of this Olympus, and was surrounded by the inferior gods and goddesses of his court. He sat on the end of a bench, by a table, with one arm akimbo and the other extended to the handle of a tankard, which he had slowly set down from his lips, as he surveyed me from head to foot. It was a moment of awful scrutiny, and I fancied the groupes around, all watching us in silent suspence, and waiting for the imperial nod.

He questioned me as to who I was; what were my qualifications; and what terms I expected. I passed myself off for a discharged servant from a gentleman's family; and as, happily, one does not require a special recommendation to get admitted into bad company, the questions on that head were easily satisfied. As to my accomplishments, I could spout a little poetry, and knew several scenes of plays, which I had learnt at school exhibitions. I could dance——that was enough; no further questions were asked me as to accomplishments; it was the very thing they wanted; and, as I asked no wages, but merely meat and drink, and safe conduct about the world, a bargain was struck in a moment.

Behold me, therefore, transformed of a sudden, from a gentleman student, to a dancing buffoon; for such, in fact, was the character in which I made my debut. I was one of those who formed the groupes in the dramas, and were principally employed on the stage in front of the booth, to attract company. I was equipped as a Satyr, in a dress of drab frize that fitted to my shape; with a great laughing mask, ornamented with huge ears and short horns. I was pleased with the disguise, because it kept me from the danger of being discovered, whilst we were in that part of the country; and, as I had merely to dance and make antics, the character was favourable to a debutant; being almost on a par with Simon Snug's part of the Lion, which required nothing but roaring.

I cannot tell you how happy I was at this sudden change in my situation. I felt no degradation, for I had seen too little of society to be thoughtful about the differences of rank; and a boy of sixteen is seldom aristocratical. I had given up no friend; for there seemed to be no one in the world that cared for me, now my poor mother was dead. I had given up no pleasure; for my pleasure was to ramble about and indulge the flow of a poetical imagination; and I now enjoyed it in perfection. There is no life so truly poetical as that of a dancing buffoon.

It may be said that all this argued grovelling inclinations. I do not think so. Not that I mean to vindicate myself in any great degree; I know too well what a whimsical compound I am. But in this instance I was seduced by no love of low company, nor disposition to indulge in low vices. I have always despised the brutally vulgar, and had a disgust at vice, whether in high or low life. I was governed merely by a sudden and thoughtless impulse. I had no idea of resorting to this profession as a mode of life; or of attaching myself to these people, as my future class of society. I thought merely of a temporary gratification of my curiosity, and an indulgence of my humours. I had already a strong relish for the peculiarities of character and the varieties of situation, and I have always been fond of the comedy of life and desirous of seeing it through all its shifting scenes.

In mingling, therefore, among mountebanks and buffoons I was protected by the very vivacity of imagination which had led me among them. I moved about envelloped, as it were, in a protecting delusion, which my fancy spread around me. I assimilated to these people only as they struck me poetically; their whimsical ways and a certain picturesqueness in their mode of life entertained me; but I was neither amused nor corrupted by their vices. In short, I mingled among them, as Prince Hal did among his graceless associates, merely to gratify my humour.

I did not investigate my motives in this manner, at the time, for I was too careless and thoughtless to reason about the matter; but I do so now, when I look back with trembling to think of the ordeal to which I unthinkingly exposed myself and the manner in which I passed through it. Nothing, I am convinced, but the poetical temperament, that hurried me into the scrape; brought me out of it without my becoming an arrant vagabond.

Full of the enjoyment of the moment, giddy with the wildness of animal spirits, so rapturous in a boy; I capered, I danced, I played a thousand fantastic tricks about the stage, in the villages in which we exhibited; and I was universally pronounced the most agreeable monster that had ever been seen in those parts. My disappearance from school had awakened my father's anxiety; for I one day heard a description of myself cried before the very booth in which I was exhibiting; with the offer of a reward for any intelligence of me. I had no great scruple about letting my father suffer a little uneasiness on my account; it would punish him for past indifference, and would make him value me the more when he found me again. I have wondered that some of my comrades did not recognize in me the stray sheep that was cried; but they were all, no doubt, occupied by their own concerns. They were all labouring seriously in their antic vocation; for folly was a mere trade with most of them, and they often grinned and capered with heavy hearts. With me, on the contrary, it was all real. I acted *con amore*, and rattled and laughed from the irrepressible gaiety of my spirits. It is true that, now and then, I started and looked grave on receiving a sudden thwack from the wooden sword of Harlequin, in the course of my gambols; as it brought to mind the birch of my schoolmaster. But I soon got accustomed to it; and bore all the cuffing, and kicking, and tumbling about, which form the practical wit of your itinerant pantomime, with a good humour that made me a prodigious favourite.

The country campaign of the troop was soon at an end, and we set off for the metropolis, to perform at the fairs which are held in its vicinity. The greater part of our theatrical property was sent on direct, to be in a state of preparation for the opening of the fairs; while a detachment of the company travelled slowly on, foraging among the villages. I was amused with the desultory, hap hazard kind of life we led; here today and gone tomorrow. Sometimes revelling in ale houses, sometimes feasting under hedges in the green fields. When audiences were crowded and business profitable we fared well, and when otherwise, we fared scantily, and consoled ourselves with anticipations of the next day's success.

At length the increasing frequency of coaches hurrying past us, covered with passengers; the increasing number of carriages, carts, waggons, gigs, droves of cattle and flocks of sheep, all thronging the road; the snug country boxes with trim flower gardens twelve feet square, and their trees twelve feet high, all powdered with dust; and the innumerable seminaries for young ladies and gentlemen, situated along the road for the benefit of country air and rural retirement; all these insignia announced that the mighty London was at hand. The hurry, and the crowd and the bustle and the noise, and the dust, increased as we proceeded, until I saw the great cloud of smoke hanging in the air, like a canopy of state, over this queen of cities.

In this way, then, did I enter the metropolis; a strolling vagabond; on the top of a caravan with a crew of vagabonds about me; but I was as happy as a prince, for, like Prince Hal, I felt myself superior to my situation, and knew that I could at any time cast it off and emerge into my proper sphere.

How my eyes sparkled as we passed Hyde Park Corner, and I saw splendid equipages rolling by, with powdered footmen behind, in rich liveries; and fine nosegays and gold headed canes; and with lovely women within, so sumptuously dressed and so surpassingly fair. I was always extremely sensible to female beauty; and here I saw it in all its fascination, for, whatever may be said of "beauty unadorned," there is something almost awful in female loveliness decked out in jewelled state. The swanlike neck encircled with diamonds; the raven locks, clustered with pearls; the ruby glowing on the snowy bosom are objects which I could never contemplate without emotion; and a dazzling white arm clasped with bracelets, and taper transparent fingers laden with sparkling rings are to me irresistible. My very eyes ached as I gazed at the high and courtly beauty before me. It surpassed all that my imagination had conceived of the sex. I shrank, for a moment, into shame at the company in which I was placed, and repined at the vast distance that seemed to intervene between me and these magnificent beings.

I forbear to give a detail of the happy life I led about the skirts of the metropolis, playing at the various fairs held there during the latter part of spring and the beginning of summer. This continual change from place to place, and scene to scene, fed my imagination with novelties, and kept my spirits in a perpetual state of excitement.

As I was tall of my age I aspired, at one time, to play heroes in tragedy; but after two or three trials, I was pronounced, by the manager, totally unfit for the line; and our first tragic actress, who was a large woman, and held a small hero in abhorrence, confirmed his decision.

The fact is I had attempted to give point to language which had no point, and nature to scenes which had no nature. They said I did not fill out my characters; and they were right. The characters had all been prepared for a different sort of man. Our Tragedy hero was a round robustious fellow, with an amazing voice; who stamped, and slapped his breast until his wig shook again; and who roared and bellowed out his bombast, until every phraze swelled upon the ear like the sound of a Kettle drum. I might as well have attempted to fill out his clothes as his characters. When we had a dialogue together I was nothing before him, with my slender voice and discriminating manner. I might as well have attempted to parry a cudgel with a small sword. If he found me in any way gaining ground upon him, he would take refuge in his mighty voice and throw his tones like peals of thunder at me. until they were drowned in the still louder thunders of applause from the audience.

To tell the truth, I suspect that I was not shewn fair play, and that there was management at the bottom; for without vanity, I think I was a better actor than he. As I had not embarked in the vagabond line through ambition I did not repine at lack of preferment; but I was grieved to find that a vagrant life was not without its cares and anxieties, and that jealousies, intrigues and mad ambition were to be found even among vagabonds.

Indeed, as I became more familiar with my situation, and the delusions of fancy gradually faded away, I began to find that my associates were not the happy careless creatures I had at first imagined them. They were jealous of each other's talents; they quarrelled about parts, the same as the actors on the grand theatres; they quarrelled about dresses; and there was one robe of yellow silk, trimmed with red, and a headdress of three rumpled ostrich feathers, which were continually setting the ladies of the Company by the ears. Even those who had attained the highest honours, were not more happy than the rest; for Mr. Flimsey himself, our first tragedian, and apparently a jovial good humoured fellow, confessed to me one day, in the fullness of his heart, that he was a miserable man. He had a brother in law—a relative by marriage, though not by blood; who was manager of a theatre in a small country town. And this same Brother ("a little more than kin but less than kind") looked down upon him, and treated him with contumely, because forsooth he was but a strolling player. I tried to console him with the thoughts of the vast applause he daily received, but it was all in vain. He declared that it gave him no delight, and that he should never be a happy man until the name of Flimsey rivalled the name of Crimp.

How little do those before the scenes know of what passes behind; how little can they judge, from the countenances of actors, of what is passing in their hearts. I have known two lovers quarrel like cats behind the scenes, who were, the moment after, to fly into each other's embraces. And I have dreaded, when our Belvidera was to take her farewell kiss of her Jaffier, lest she should bite a piece out of his cheek. Our tragedian was a rough joker off the stage; our prime clown the most peevish mortal living. The latter used to go about snapping and snarling, with a broad laugh painted on his countenance; and I can assure you that, whatever may be said of the gravity of a monkey; or the melancholy of a gibed cat; there is no more melancholy creature in existence than a mountebank off duty.

The only thing in which all parties agreed, was to back bite the manager, and cabal against his regulations. This, however, I have since discovered to be a common trait of human nature, and to take place in all communities. It would seem to be the main business of man to repine at government. In all situations of life into which I have looked, I have found mankind divided into two grand parties; those who ride, and those who are ridden. The great struggle of life seems to be which shall keep in the saddle. This it appears to me is the fundamental principle of politics, whether in great or little life.—However, I do not mean to moralize; but one cannot always sink the philosopher.

Well then, to return to myself. It was determined, as I said, that I was not fit for tragedy; and, unluckily, as my study was bad, having a very poor memory, I was pronounced unfit for comedy also; besides, the line of young gentlemen was already engrossed by an actor with whom I could not pretend to enter into competition, he having filled it for almost half a century. I came down again therefore to pantomime. In consequence, however, of the good offices of the manager's lady, who had taken a liking to me, I was promoted from the part of the satyr to that of the Lover; and with my face patched and painted; a huge cravat of paper; a steeple crowned hat, and dangling long skirted, sky blue coat, was metamorphosed into the lover of Columbine. My part did not call for much of the tender and sentimental. I had merely to pursue the fugitive fair one; to have a door now and then slammed in my face; to run my head occasionally against a post; to tumble and roll about with Pantaloon and the Clown; and to endure the hearty thwacks of Harlequin's wooden sword.

As ill luck would have it, my poetical temperament began to ferment within me, and to work out new troubles. The inflammatory air of a great metropolis; added to the rural scenes in which the fairs were held; such as Greenwich Park; Epping Forest; and the lovely valley of West End, had a powerful effect upon me. While in Greenwich Park I was witness to the old holyday games of running down hill; and kissing in the ring; and then the firmament of blooming faces and blue eyes that would be turned towards me, as I was playing antics on the stage; all these set my young blood, and my poetical vein, in full flow. In short, I played my character to the life and became desperately enamoured of Columbine. She was a trim, well made, tempting girl; with a roguish dimpling face, and fine chesnut hair clustering all about it. The moment I got fairly smitten, there was an end to all playing. I was such a creature of fancy and feeling, that I could not put on a pretended, when I was powerfully affected by a real emotion. I could not sport with a fiction that came so near to the fact. I became too natural in my acting to succeed. And then; what a situation for a lover! I was a mere stripling, and she played with my passion; for girls soon grow more adroit and knowing in these matters than your awkward youngsters. What agonies had I to suffer. Every time that she danced in front of the booth, and made such liberal displays of her charms, I was in torment. To complete my misery, I had a real rival in Harlequin; an active, vigorous, knowing varlet of six and twenty. What had a raw inexperienced youngster like me to hope from such a competition.

I had still, however, some advantages in my favour. In spite of my change of life, I retained that indescribable something which always distinguishes the gentleman; that something which dwells in a man's air and deportment, and not in his clothes; and which is as difficult for a gentleman to put off, as for a vulgar fellow to put on. The company generally felt it, and used to call me little gentleman Jack. The girl felt it too; and in spite of her predilection for my powerful rival; she liked to flirt with me. This only aggravated my troubles, by encreasing my passion, and awakening the jealousy of her particoloured Lover.

Alas! think what I suffered, at being obliged to keep up an ineffectual chase after my Columbine through whole pantomimes; to see her carried off in the vigorous arms of the happy Harlequin; and to be obliged instead of snatching her from him to tumble sprawling with Pantaloon and the clown; and bear the infernal and degrading thwacks of my rival's weapon of lath; which, may heaven confound him! (excuse my passion) the villain laid on with a malicious good will; nay I could absolutely hear him chuckle and laugh beneath his accursed mask.—I beg pardon for growing a little warm in my narration. I wish to be cool, but these recollections will sometimes agitate me. I have heard and read of many desperate and deplorable situations of lovers; but none I think in which true love was ever exposed to so severe and peculiar a trial.

This could not last long! Flesh and blood, at least such flesh and blood as mine, could not bear it. I had repeated heartburnings and quarrels with my rival, in which he treated me with the mortifying forbearance of a man towards a child. Had he quarrelled outright with me I could have stomached it; at least I should have known what part to take; but to be humoured and treated as a child in the presence of my mistress; when I felt all the bantam spirit of a little man swelling within me—gods, it was insufferable!

At length we were exhibiting one day at West End fair, which was at that time a very fashionable resort, and often beleaguered by gay equipages from town. Among the spectators that filled the front row of our little canvas theatre one afternoon, when I had to figure in a pantomime, was a party of young ladies from a boarding school, with their governess. Guess my confusion, when, in the midst of my antics, I beheld among the number my quondam flame; her whom I had berhymed at school; her for whose charms I had smarted so severely; the cruel Sacharissa! What was worse, I fancied she recollected me; and was repeating the story of my humiliating flagellation, for I saw her whispering her companions and her governess. I lost all consciousness of the part I was acting, and of the place where I was. I felt shrunk to nothing, and could have crept into a rat hole—unluckily, none was open to receive me. Before I could recover from my confusion I was tumbled over by Pantaloon and the clown; and I felt the sword of Harlequin making vigorous assaults in a manner most degrading to my dignity.

Heaven and earth! was I again to suffer martyrdom in this ignominious

manner, in the knowledge, and even before the very eyes, of this most beautiful, but most disdainful of fair ones? All my long smothered wrath broke
out at once; the dormant feelings of the gentleman arose within me; stung
to the quick by intolerable mortification. I sprang on my feet in an instant;
leaped upon Harlequin like a young tiger; tore off his mask; buffetted him
in the face, and soon shed more blood on the stage, than had been spilt upon
it during a whole tragic campaign of battles and murders.

As soon as Harlequin recovered from his surprize he returned my assault
with interest. I was nothing in his hands. I was game to be sure, for I was a
gentleman; but he had the clownish advantages of bone and muscle. I felt
as if I could have fought even unto the death; and I was likely to do so; for
he was, according to the boxing phraze, "putting my head into Chancery,"
when the gentle Columbine flew to my assistance. God bless the women!
they are always on the side of the weak and the oppressed!

The battle now became general; the dramatis personæ ranged on either
side. The manager interposed in vain. In vain were his spangled black bonnet and towering white feathers seen whisking about, and nodding, and bobbing, in the thickest of the fight. Warriors, Ladies, Priests, Satyrs, Kings,
Queens, gods and goddesses all joined pell mell in the fray. Never, since the
conflict under the walls of Troy, had there been such a chance medley warfare of combatants, human and divine. The audience applauded; the ladies
shrieked and fled from the theatre, and a scene of discord ensued that baffles
all description.

Nothing but the interference of the peace officers restored some degree
of order. The havoc, however, among dresses and decorations put an end to
all further acting for that day. The battle over, the next thing was to enquire
why it was begun; a common question among politicians, after a bloody and
unprofitable war; and one not always easy to be answered. It was soon traced
to me, and my unaccountable transport of passion, which they could only
attribute to my having *run a muck*. The manager was judge, and jury, and
plaintiff into the bargain, and in such cases justice is always speedily admin-
istered. He came out of the fight as sublime a wreck as the Santissima Trin-
idada. His gallant plumes which once towered aloft, were drooping about
his ears. His robe of state hung in ribbands from his back, and but ill concealed the ravages he had suffered in the rear. He had received kicks and
cuffs from all sides, during the tumult; for every one took the opportunity
of slyly gratifying some lurking grudge on his fat carcass. He was a discreet
man and did not choose to declare war with all his company; so he swore all
those kicks and cuffs had been given by me, and I let him enjoy the opinion.
Some wounds he bore, however, which were the incontestable traces of a
woman's warfare. His sleek rosy cheek was scored by trickling furrows which
were ascribed to the nails of my intrepid and devoted Columbine. The ire
of the monarch was not to be appeased. He had suffered in his person, and

he had suffered in his purse; his dignity too had been insulted, and that went for something; for dignity is always more irascible, the more petty the potentate. He wreaked his wrath upon the beginners of the affray, and Columbine and myself were discharged, at once, from the Company.

Figure me, then, to yourself, a stripling of little more than sixteen; a gentleman by birth; a vagabond by trade; turned adrift upon the world; making the best of my way through the crowd of West End fair; my mountebank dress fluttering in rags about me; the weeping Columbine hanging upon my arm, in splendid, but tattered finery; the tears coursing one by one down her face; carrying off the red paint in torrents, and literally "preying upon her damask cheek."

The crowd made way for us as we passed and hooted in our rear. I felt the ridicule of my situation, but had too much gallantry to desert this fair one, who had sacrificed every thing for me. Having wandered through the fair, we emerged, like another Adam and Eve, into unknown regions, and "had the world before us, where to choose." Never was a more disconsolate pair seen in the soft valley of West End. The luckless Columbine cast back many a lingering look at the fair, which seemed to put on a more than usual splendour; its tents, and booths, and party coloured groups, all brightening in the sunshine, and gleaming among the trees; and its gay flags and streamers playing and fluttering in the light summer airs. With a heavy sigh she would lean on my arm and proceed. I had no hope nor consolation to give her; but she had linked herself to my fortunes; and she was too much of a woman to desert me.

Pensive and silent, then, we traversed the beautiful fields which lie behind Hampstead, and wandered on, until the fiddle, and the hautboy, and the shout, and the laugh, were swallowed up in the deep sound of the big bass drum, and even that died away into a distant rumble. We passed along the pleasant sequestered walk of Nightingale Lane. For a pair of lovers what scene could be more propitious?—But such a pair of lovers! Not a nightingale sang to soothe us; the very gipsies who were encamped there during the fair made no offer to tell the fortunes of such an ill omened couple, whose fortunes, I suppose, they thought too legibly written to need an interpreter; and the gipsey children crawled into their cabins and peeped out fearfully at us as we went by. For a moment I paused, and was almost tempted to turn gipsey, but the poetical feeling for the present was fully satisfied, and I passed on. Thus we travelled, and travelled, like a prince and princess in Nursery Tale, until we had traversed a part of Hampstead Heath and arrived in the vicinity of Jack Straw's Castle.

Here, wearied and dispirited we seated ourselves on the margin of the hill, hard by the very mile stone where Whittington of yore heard the Bow bells ring out the presage of his future greatness. Alas! no Bell rung an invitation to us, as we looked disconsolately upon the distant city. Old London seemed to wrap itself unsociably in its mantle of brown smoke; and to offer no encouragement to such a couple of tatterdemalions.

For once at least the usual course of the pantomime was reversed. Harlequin was jilted and the lover had carried off Columbine in good earnest. But what was I to do with her? I could not take her in my hand, return to my father, throw myself on my knees, and crave his forgiveness and his blessing according to dramatic usage. The very dogs would have chased such a draggletailed beauty from the grounds.

In the midst of my doleful dumps, some one tapped me on the shoulder, and looking up I saw a couple of rough sturdy fellows standing behind me. Not knowing what to expect I jumped on my legs and was preparing again to make battle; but I was tripped up and secured in a twinkling.

"Come, come, young master," said one of the fellows in a gruff, but good humoured tone, "don't let's have any of your tantrums. One would have thought you had had swing enough for this bout. Come, it's high time to leave off harlequinading, and go home to your father."

In fact I had fallen into the hands of remorseless men. The cruel Sacharissa had proclaimed who I was, and that a reward had been offered throughout the country for any tidings of me; and they had seen a description of me which had been inserted in the public papers. Those harpies, therefore, for the mere sake of filthy lucre, were resolved to deliver me over into the hands of my father and the clutches of my Pedagogue.

In vain I swore I would not leave my faithful and afflicted Columbine. In vain I tore myself from their grasp, and flew to her; and vowed to protect her; and wiped the tears from her cheek, and with them a whole blush that might have vied with the Carnation for brilliancy. My persecutors were inflexible: they even seemed to exult in our distress; and to enjoy this theatrical display of dirt, and finery, and tribulation. I was carried off in despair, leaving my Columbine destitute in the wide world; but many a look of agony did I cast back at her, as she stood gazing piteously after me from the brink of Hampstead Hill; so forlorn, so fine, so ragged, so bedraggled, yet so beautiful.

Thus ended my first peep into the world. I returned home, rich in good-for-nothing experience, and dreading the reward I was to receive for my improvement. My reception, however, was quite different from what I had expected. My father had a spice of the devil in him, and did not seem to like me the worse for my freak, which he termed "sewing my wild oats." He happened to have several of his sporting friends to dine the very day of my return; they made me tell some of my adventures; and laughed heartily at them. One old fellow with an outrageously red nose took to me hugely. I heard him whisper to my father that I was a lad of mettle and might make something clever, to which my father replied that "I had good points, but was an ill broken whelp and required a great deal of the whip." Perhaps this very conversation raised me a little in his esteem, for I found the red nosed old gentleman was a veteran fox hunter of the neighbourhood, for whose opinion my father had vast deference. Indeed I believe he would have pardoned any thing in me more readily than poetry; which he called a cursed sneaking, puling, housekeeping employment, the bane of all true manhood. He swore it was unworthy of a youngster of my expectations, who was one day to have so great an estate, and would be able to keep horses and hounds and hire poets to write songs for him into the bargain.

I had now satisfied, for a time, my roving propensity. I had exhausted the poetical feeling. I had been heartily buffetted out of my love for theatrical display. I felt humiliated by my exposure and willing to hide my head any where for a season; so that I might be out of the way of the ridicule of the world; for I found folks not altogether so indulgent abroad, as they were at my father's table. I could not stay at home; the house was intolerably doleful now that my mother was no longer there to cherish me. Every thing around spoke mournfully of her. The little flower garden in which she delighted, was all in disorder and overrun with weeds. I attempted, for a day or two, to arrange it, but my heart grew heavier and heavier as I laboured. Every little broken down flower, that I had seen her rear so tenderly, seemed to plead in mute eloquence to my feelings. There was a favourite honeysuckle which I had seen her often training with assiduity and had heard her say it should be the pride of her garden. I found it grovelling along the ground, tangled and wild, and twining round every worthless weed, and it struck me as an emblem of myself, a mere scatterling, running to waste and uselessness. I could work no longer in the garden.

My father sent me to pay a visit to my uncle, by way of keeping the old gentleman in mind of me. I was received, as usual, without any expression of discontent; which we always considered equivalent to a hearty welcome. Whether he had ever heard of my strolling freak or not I could not discover; he and his man were both so taciturn. I spent a day or two roaming about the dreary mansion and neglected park; and felt at one time, I believe, a touch of poetry, for I was tempted to drown myself in a fish pond; I rebuked the evil spirit, however, and it left me. I found the same redheaded boy running wild about the park, but I felt in no humour to hunt him at present. On the contrary I tried to coax him to me, and to make friends with him, but the young savage was untameable.

When I returned from my uncle's I remained at home for some time, for my father was disposed, he said, to make a man of me. He took me out hunting with him, and I became a great favourite of the red nosed squire, because I rode at every thing, never refused the boldest leap, and was always sure to be in at the death. I used often however to offend my father at hunting dinners, by taking the wrong side in politics. My father was amazingly ignorant, so ignorant in fact as not to know, that he knew nothing. He was staunch, however, to church and King, and full of old fashioned prejudices. Now I had picked up a little knowledge in politics and religion, during my rambles with the strollers, and found myself capable of setting him right as to many of his antiquated notions. I felt it my duty to do so; we were apt therefore to differ occasionally in the political discussions which sometimes arose at these hunting dinners.

I was at that age when a man knows least and is most vain of his knowledge; and when he is extremely tenacious in defending his opinion upon subjects about which he knows nothing. My father was a hard man for any one to argue with, for he never knew when he was refuted. I sometimes posed him a little, but then he had one argument that always settled the question; he would threaten to knock me down. I believe he at last grew tired of me, because I both outtalked and outrode him. The red nosed squire too got out of conceit of me, because in the heat of the chace, I rode over him one day as he and his horse lay sprawling in the dirt. My father, therefore, thought it high time to send me to college—and accordingly to Trinity College at Oxford was I sent.

I had lost my habits of study while at home; and I was not likely to find them again at college. I found that study was not the fashion at college, and that a lad of spirit only ate his terms, and grew wise by dint of knife and fork. I was always prone to follow the fashions of the company into which I fell; so I threw by my books, and became a man of spirit. As my father made me a tolerable allowance, notwithstanding the narrowness of his income, having an eye always to my great expectations, I was enabled to appear to advantage among my fellow students. I cultivated all kinds of sports and exercises. I was one of the most expert oarsmen that rowed on the Isis. I boxed, fenced, angled, shot, and hunted, and my rooms in college were always decorated with whips of all kinds, spurs, fowling pieces, fishing rods, foils and boxing gloves. A pair of leather breeches would seem to be throwing one leg out of the half open drawers, and empty bottles lumbered the bottom of every closet.

I soon grew tired of this; and relapsed into my vein of mere poetical indulgence. I was charmed with Oxford for it was full of poetry to me. I thought I should never grow tired of wandering about its courts and cloisters; and visiting the different college halls. I used to love to get in places surrounded by the colleges, where all modern buildings were screened from the sight; and to walk about them in twilight, and see the professors and students sweeping along in the dusk in their caps and gowns. There was complete delusion in the scene. It seemed to transport me among the edifices and the people of old times. It was a great luxury, too, for me to attend the evening service, in the New College Chapel; and to hear the fine organ and the choir swelling an anthem in that solemn building; where painting and music and architecture seem to combine their grandest effects.

I became a loiterer, also, about the Bodleian library, and a great dipper into books; but too idle to follow any course of study or vein of research. One of my favourite haunts was the beautiful walk, bordered by lofty elms, along the Isis, under the old grey walls of Magdalen College, which goes by the name of Addison's Walk; and was his resort when a student at the college. I used to take a volume of poetry in my hand and stroll up and down this walk for hours.

My father came to see me at college. He asked me how I came on with my studies; and what kind of hunting there was in the neighbourhood. He examined my sporting apparatus; wanted to know if any of the professors were fox hunters; and whether they were generally good shots; for he suspected this reading so much was rather hurtful to the sight. Such was the only person to whom I was responsible for my improvement: is it matter of wonder therefore that I became a confirmed idler?

I do not know how it is, but I cannot be idle long without getting in love. I became deeply enamoured of a shopkeeper's daughter in the High Street; who in fact was the admiration of many of the students. I wrote several sonnets in praise of her, and spent half of my pocket money at the shop, in buying articles which I did not want, that I might have an opportunity of speaking to her. Her father, a severe looking old gentleman, with bright silver buckles and a crisp curled wig, kept a strict guard on her; as the fathers generally do upon their daughters in Oxford; and well they may. I tried to get into his good graces, and to be sociable with him, but all in vain. I said several good things in his shop, but he never laughed; he had no relish for wit and humour. He was one of those dry old gentlemen who keep youngsters at bay. He had already brought up two or three daughters, and was experienced in the ways of students. He was as knowing and wary as a grey old badger that has often been hunted. To see him on Sunday, so stiff and starched in his demeanour; so precise in his dress; with his daughter under his arm, was enough to deter all graceless youngsters from approaching.

I managed, however, in spite of his vigilance, to have several conversations with the daughter, as I cheapened articles in the shop. I made terrible long bargains, and examined the articles over and over, before I purchased. In the mean time, I would convey a sonnet or an acrostic under cover of a piece of cambric, or slipped into a pair of stockings; I would whisper soft nonsense into her ear as I haggled about the price; and would squeeze her hand tenderly as I received my halfpence of change, in a bit of whity-brown paper. Let this serve as a hint to all haberdashers, who have pretty daughters for shop girls, and young students for customers. I do not know whether my words and looks were very eloquent; but my poetry was irresistible; for, to tell the truth, the girl had some literary taste, and was seldom without a book from the circulating library.

By the divine power of poetry, therefore, which is so potent with the lovely sex, did I subdue the heart of this fair little Haberdasher. We carried on a sentimental correspondence for a time across the counter, and I supplied her with rhyme by the stocking full. At length I prevailed on her to grant an assignation. But how was this to be effected? Her father kept her always under his eye; she never walked out alone; and the house was locked up the moment that the shop was shut. All these difficulties served but to give zest to the adventure. I proposed that the assignation should be in her own chamber, into which I would climb at night. The plan was irresistible. A cruel father, a secret lover, and a clandestine meeting! All the little girl's studies from the circulating library seemed about to be realized.

But what had I in view in making this assignation? Indeed I know not. I had no evil intentions; nor can I say that I had any good ones. I liked the girl, and wanted to have an opportunity of seeing more of her; and the assignation was made, as I have done many things else, heedlessly and without fore thought. I asked myself a few questions of the kind, after all my arrangements were made; but the answers were very unsatisfactory. "Am I to ruin this poor thoughtless girl?" said I to myself. "No!" was the prompt and indignant answer. "Am I to run away with her?"—"Whither—and to what purpose?"—"Well then, am I to marry her?"—"Pah! a man of my expectations marry a shopkeeper's daughter!"—"What then am I to do with her?"— "Hum—Why—Let me get into her chamber first, and then consider,"—and so the self examination ended.

Well sir, "come what come might," I stole under cover of the darkness to the dwelling of my dulcinea. All was quiet. At the concerted signal her window was gently opened. It was just above the projecting bow window of her father's shop, which assisted me in mounting. The house was low, and I was enabled to scale the fortress with tolerable ease. I clambered with a beating heart; I reached the casement; I hoisted my body half into the chamber and was welcomed, not by the embraces of my expecting fair one, but by the grasp of the crabbed looking old father in the crisp curled wig.

I extricated myself from his clutches and endeavoured to make my retreat; but I was confounded by his cries of thieves! and robbers! I was bothered too by his Sunday cane; which was amazingly busy about my head as I descended; and against which my hat was but a poor protection. Never before had I an idea of the activity of an old man's arm, and hardness of the knob of an Ivory headed cane. In my hurry and confusion I missed my footing, and fell sprawling on the pavement. I was immediately surrounded by myrmidons, who I doubt not were on the watch for me. Indeed I was in no situation to escape, for I had sprained my ancle in the fall, and could not stand. I was seized as a housebreaker; and to exonerate myself from a greater crime I had to accuse myself of a less—I made known who I was, and why I came there. Alas! the varlets knew it already, and were only amusing themselves at my expense. My perfidious muse had been playing me one of her slippery tricks. The old curmudgeon of a father had found my sonnets and acrostics hid away in holes and corners of his shop; he had no taste for poetry like his daughter, and had instituted a rigorous though silent observation. He had moused upon our letters; detected our plans, and prepared every thing for my reception. Thus was I ever doomed to be led into scrapes by the muse. Let no man henceforth carry on a secret amour in poetry!

The old man's ire was in some measure appeased by the pummelling of my head, and the anguish of my sprain; so he did not put me to death on the spot. He was even humane enough to furnish a shutter, on which I was carried back to college like a wounded warrior. The porter was roused to admit me; the college gate was thrown open for my entry; the affair was blazed abroad the next morning, and became the joke of the college from the Buttry to the Hall.

I had leisure to repent during several weeks' confinement by my sprain, which I passed in translating Boethius' Consolations of Philosophy. I received a most tender and ill spelled letter from my mistress, who had been sent to a relation in Coventry. She protested her innocence of my misfortunes and vowed to be true to me "till deth." I took no notice of the letter, for I was cured, for the present, both of love and poetry. Women, however, are more constant in their attachments than men, whatever philosophers may say to the contrary. I am assured that she actually remained faithful to her vow for several months; but she had to deal with a cruel father whose heart was as hard as the knob of his cane. He was not to be touched by tears or poetry; but absolutely compelled her to marry a reputable young tradesman; who made her a happy woman in spite of herself, and of all the rules of romance; and what is more, the mother of several children. They are at this very day a thriving couple, and keep a snug corner shop, just opposite the figure of Peeping Tom at Coventry.

I will not fatigue you by any more details of my studies at Oxford, though they were not always as severe as these; nor did I always pay as dear for my lessons. People may say what they please, a studious life has its charms and there are many places more gloomy than the cloisters of a university.

To be brief then, I lived on in my usual miscellaneous manner, gradually getting a knowledge of good and evil until I had attained my twenty first year. I had scarcely come of age when I heard of the sudden death of my father. The shock was severe, for though he had never treated me with much kindness, still he was my father, and at his death I felt alone in the world.

I returned home, and found myself the solitary master of the paternal mansion. A crowd of gloomy feelings came thronging upon me. It was a place that always sobered me, and brought me to reflection. Now especially, it looked so deserted and melancholy. I entered the little breakfasting room. There were my father's whip and spurs hanging by the fire place; the Stud Book, Sporting Magazine, and Racing Calendar, his only reading. His favourite spaniel lay on the hearth rug. The poor animal, who had never before noticed me, now came fondling about me, licked my hand, then looked round the room, whined, wagged his tail slightly, and gazed wistfully in my face. I felt the full force of the appeal. "Poor Dash!" said I, "we are both alone in the world, with no body to care for us, and we'll take care of one another."—The dog never quitted me afterwards.

I could not go into my mother's room: my heart swelled when I passed within sight of the door. Her portrait hung in the parlour just over the place where she used to sit. As I cast my eyes on it I thought it looked at me with tenderness, and I burst into tears. My heart had long been seared by living in public schools, and buffetting about among strangers who cared nothing for me; but the recollection of a mother's tenderness was overcoming.

I was not of an age or a temperament to be long depressed. There was a reaction in my system that always brought me up again after every pressure; and indeed my spirits were most buoyant after a temporary prostration. I settled the concerns of the estate as soon as possible; realized my property, which was not very considerable; but which appeared a vast deal to me, having a poetical eye that magnified every thing; and finding myself at the end of a few months, free of all further business or restraint, I determined to go to London and enjoy myself. Why should not I?—I was young, animated, joyous; had plenty of funds for present pleasures, and my uncle's estate in the perspective. Let those mope at college and pore over books, thought I, who have their way to make in the world; it would be ridiculous drudgery in a youth of my expectations.

Away to London, therefore, I rattled in a tandem, determined to take the town gaily. I passed through several of the villages where I had played the jack pudding a few years before; and I visited the scenes of many of my adventures and follies, merely from that feeling of melancholy pleasure which we have in stepping again in the footprints of foregone existence, even when they have passed among weeds and briars. I made a circuit in the latter part of my journey, so as to take in West End and Hampstead, the scenes of my last dramatic exploit, and of the battle royal of the Booth. As I drove along the ridge of Hampstead Hill, by Jack Straw's Castle, I paused at the spot where Columbine and I had sat down so disconsolately in our ragged finery, and had looked dubiously upon London. I almost expected to see her again, standing on the hill's brink, "like Niobe all tears;"—mournful as Babylon in ruins!

"Poor Columbine!" said I, with a heavy sigh, "thou wert a gallant, generous girl—a true woman; faithful to the distressed, and ready to sacrifice thyself in the cause of worthless man!"

I tried to whistle off the recollection of her, for there was always something of self reproach with it. I drove gaily along the road, enjoying the stare of Hostlers and stable boys as I managed my horses knowingly down the steep

street of Hampstead; when, just at the skirts of the village, one of the traces
of my leader came loose. I pulled up, and, as the animal was restive, and
my servant a bungler, I called for assistance to the robustious master of a
snug ale house, who stood at his door with a tankard in his hand. He came
readily to assist me, followed by his wife with her bosom half open, a child
in her arms, and two more at her heels. I stared for a moment as if doubting
my eyes. I could not be mistaken: in the fat beerblown landlord of the ale
house I recollected my old rival Harlequin, and in his slattern spouse, the
once trim and dimpling Columbine.

The change of my looks, from youth to manhood, and the change of my
circumstances, prevented them from recognizing me. They could not suspect, in the dashing young buck, fashionably dressed, and driving his own
equipage, the painted beau, with old peaked hat and long, flimsy, sky blue
coat. My heart yearned with kindness towards Columbine, and I was glad
to see her establishment a thriving one. As soon as the harness was adjusted
I tossed a small purse of gold into her ample bosom; and then, pretending
to give my horses a hearty cut of the whip, I made the lash curl with a
whistling about the sleek sides of ancient Harlequin. The horses dashed off
like lightning, and I was whirled out of sight, before either of the parties
could get over their surprize at my liberal donations. I have always considered this as one of the greatest proofs of my poetical genius. It was distrib-
uting poetical justice in perfection.

I now entered London *en cavalier*, and became a blood upon town. I took
fashionable lodgings in the west end; employed the first Taylor; frequented
the regular lounges; gambled a little; lost my money good humouredly, and
gained a number of fashionable, good for nothing acquaintances. I gained
some reputation, also, for a man of science, having become an expert boxer
in the course of my studies at Oxford. I was distinguished, therefore, among
the gentlemen of the fancy; became hand and glove with certain boxing
noblemen, and was the admiration of the Fives Court. A gentleman's science, however, is apt to get him into sad scrapes: he is too prone to play the
knight errant, and to pick up quarrels which less scientific gentlemen would
quietly avoid. I undertook one day to punish the insolence of a porter; he
was a Hercules of a fellow, but then I was so secure in my science! I gained
the victory of course. The porter pocketed his humiliation, bound up his
broken head, and went about his business as unconcernedly as though nothing had happened; while I went to bed with my victory, and did not dare to
show my battered face for a fortnight, by which I discovered that a gentleman may have the worst of the battle even when victorious.

I am naturally a philosopher, and no one can moralize better after a misfortune has taken place: so I lay on my bed and moralized on this sorry
ambition, which levels the gentleman with the clown. I know it is the opinion of many sages, who have thought deeply on these matters, that the noble

science of boxing keeps up the bull dog courage of the nation; and far be it from me to decry the advantage of becoming a nation of bull dogs; but I now saw clearly that it was calculated to keep up the breed of English ruffians. "What is the Fives Court," said I to myself, as I turned uncomfortably in bed, "but a college of scoundrelism, where every bully ruffian in the land may gain a fellowship? What is the slang language of 'The Fancy' but a jargon by which fools and knaves commune and understand each other, and enjoy a kind of superiority over the uninitiated? What is a boxing match but an arena, where the noble and the illustrious are jostled into familiarity with the infamous and the vulgar? What, in fact, is The Fancy itself, but a chain of easy communication, extending from the peer down to the pickpocket, through the medium of which, a man of rank may find, he has shaken hands, at three removes, with the murderer on the gibbet?—

"Enough!" ejaculated I, thoroughly convinced through the force of my philosophy, and the pain of my bruises—"I'll have nothing more to do with The Fancy." So when I had recovered from my victory, I turned my attention to softer themes, and became a devoted admirer of the ladies. Had I had more industry and ambition in my nature, I might have worked my way to the very height of fashion; as I saw many laborious gentlemen doing around me. But it is a toilsome, an anxious, and an unhappy life; there are few beings so sleepless and miserable as your cultivators of fashionable smiles.

I was quite content with that kind of society which forms the frontiers of fashion, and may be easily taken possession of. I found it a light, easy, pro ductive soil. I had but to go about and sow visiting cards, and I reaped a whole harvest of invitations. Indeed my figure and address were by no means against me. It was whispered, too, among the young ladies, that I was prodigiously clever, and wrote poetry; and the old ladies had ascertained that I was a young gentleman of good family, handsome fortune, and "great expectations."

I now was carried away by the hurry of gay life; so intoxicating to a young man; and which a man of poetical temperament enjoys so highly on his first tasting of it. That rapid variety of sensations; that whirl of brilliant objects; that succession of pungent pleasures! I had no time for thought, I only felt. I never attempted to write poetry; my poetry seemed all to go off by transpiration. I lived poetry; it was all a poetical dream to me. A mere sensualist knows nothing of the delights of a splendid metropolis. He lives in a round of animal gratifications and heartless habits. But to a young man of poetical feelings it is an ideal world; a scene of enchantment and delusion; his imagination is in perpetual excitement, and gives a spiritual zest to every pleasure.

A season of town life, however, somewhat sobered me of my intoxication; or rather I was rendered more serious by one of my old complaints—I fell in love. It was with a very pretty, though a very haughty fair one; who had come to London under the care of an old maiden aunt, to enjoy the pleasures of a winter in town, and to get married. There was not a doubt of her commanding a choice of lovers; for she had long been the belle of a little cathedral town; and one of the prebendaries had absolutely celebrated her beauty in a copy of Latin verses. The most extravagant anticipations were formed by her friends of the sensation she would produce. It was feared by some that she might be precipitate in her choice, and take up with some inferior title. The aunt was determined nothing should gain her under a lord.

Alas! with all her charms, the young lady lacked the one thing needful— she had no money. So she waited in vain for duke, marquis, or earl, to throw himself at her feet. As the season waned, so did the lady's expectations; when, just towards the close, I made my advances.

I was most favourably received by both the young lady and her aunt. It is true, I had no title; but then such great expectations! A marked preference was immediately shewn me, over two rivals, the younger son of a needy Baronet, and a captain of Dragoons on half pay. I did not absolutely take the field in form, for I was determined not to be precipitate; but I drove my equipage frequently through the street in which she lived, and was always sure to see her at the window, generally with a book in her hand. I resumed my knack at rhyming, and sent her a long copy of verses; anonymously to be sure; but she knew my hand writing. Both aunt and niece, however, displayed the most delightful ignorance on the subject. The young lady shewed them to me; wondered who they could be written by; and declared there was nothing in this world she loved so much as poetry: while the maiden aunt would put her pinching spectacles on her nose, and read them, with blunders in sense and sound, excruciating to an author's ears; protesting there was nothing equal to them in the whole Elegant Extracts.

The fashionable season closed without my adventuring to make a declaration, though I certainly had encouragement. I was not perfectly sure that I had effected a lodgement in the young lady's heart; and, to tell the truth the aunt overdid her part, and was a little too extravagant in her liking of me. I knew that maiden aunts were not apt to be captivated by the mere personal merits of their nieces' admirers, and I wanted to ascertain how much of all this favour I owed to driving an equipage and having great expectations.

I had received many hints how charming their native town was during the summer months; what pleasant society they had; and what beautiful drives about the neighbourhood. They had not, therefore, returned home long before I made my appearance in dashing style, driving down the principal street. It is an easy thing to put a little quiet cathedral town in a buzz. The very next morning, I was seen at prayers, seated in the pew of the reigning belle. All the congregation was in a flutter. The prebends eyed me from their stalls; questions were whispered about the aisles after service, "who is he?"

and "what is he?" and the replies were as usual—"a young gentleman of good family and fortune, and great expectations."

I was pleased with the peculiarities of a cathedral town, where I found I was a personage of some consequence. I was quite a brilliant acquisition to the young ladies of the cathedral circle, who were glad to have a beau that was not in a black coat and clerical wig. You must know that there was a vast distinction between the classes of society of the town. As it was a place of some trade, there were many wealthy inhabitants among the commercial and manufacturing classes, who lived in style and gave many entertainments. Nothing of trade, however, was admitted into the cathedral circle— faugh! the thing could not be thought of. The cathedral circle, therefore, was apt to be very select, very dignified, and very dull. They had evening parties, at which the old ladies played cards with the Prebends and the young ladies sat and looked on, and shifted from one chair to another about the room, until it was time to go home.

It was difficult to get up a ball from the want of partners, the cathedral circle being very deficient in dancers; and on those occasions, there was an occasional drafting among the dancing men of the other circle, who, however, were generally regarded with great reserve and condescension by the gentlemen in powdered wigs. Several of the young ladies, assured me, in confidence, that they had often looked with a wistful eye at the gaiety of the other circle, where there was such plenty of young beaux, and where they all seemed to enjoy themselves so merrily; but that it would be degradation to think of descending from their sphere.

I admired the degree of old fashioned ceremony, and superannuated courtesy that prevailed in this little place. The bowings and curtseyings that would take place about the cathedral porch after morning service; where knots of old gentlemen and ladies would collect together to ask after each other's health, and settle the card party for the evening. The little presents of fruit and delicacies, and the thousand petty messages that would pass from house to house; for in a tranquil community like this, living entirely at ease and having little to do, little duties and little civilities and little amusements, fill up the day. I have smiled, as I looked from my window on a quiet street near the cathedral, in the middle of a warm summer day, to see a corpulent powdered footman in rich livery, carrying a small tart on a large silver salver. A dainty tit bit, sent, no doubt, by some worthy old dowager, to top off the dinner of her favourite Prebend.

Nothing could be more delectable, also, than the breaking up of one of their evening card parties. Such shakings of hands; such mobbing up in cloaks and tippets! There were two or three old sedan chairs that did the duty of the whole place; though the greater part made their exit in clogs or pattens, with a footman or waiting maid carrying a lanthorn in advance; and at a certain hour of the night the clank of pattens and the gleam of these jack lanthorns, here and there, about the quiet little town, gave notice, that the cathedral card party had dissolved, and the luminaries were severally seeking their homes.

To such a community therefore, or at least to the female part of it, the accession of a gay dashing young beau was a matter of some importance. The old ladies eyed me with complacency through their spectacles, and the young ladies pronounced me divine. Every body received me favourably, excepting the gentleman who had written the Latin verses on the Belle.— Not that he was jealous of my success with the Lady, for he had no pretensions to her; but he heard my verses praised wherever he went, and he could not endure a rival with the muse.

I was thus carrying every thing before me, I was the Adonis of the cathedral circle; when one evening there was a public ball which was attended likewise by the gentry of the neighbourhood. I took great pains with my toilet on the occasion and I had never looked better. I had determined that night to make my grand assault on the heart of the young lady, to batter it with all my forces, and the next morning to demand a surrender in due form.

I entered the ball room amidst a buzz and flutter, which generally took place among the young ladies on my appearance. I was in fine spirits, for to tell the truth I had exhilarated myself by a cheerful glass of wine on the occasion. I talked, and rattled, and said a thousand silly things, slap dash, with all the confidence of a man sure of his auditors; and every thing had its effect.

In the midst of my triumph I observed a little knot gathering together in the upper part of the room. By degrees it encreased. A tittering broke out there; and glances were cast round at me, and then there would be fresh tittering. Some of the young ladies would hurry away to distant parts of the room, and whisper to their friends; wherever they went there was still this tittering and glancing at me. I did not know what to make of all this: I looked at myself from head to foot; and peeped at my back in a glass, to see if any thing was odd about my person; any awkward exposure; any whimsical tag hanging out—no—every thing was right. I was a perfect picture. I determined that it must be some choice saying of mine, that was bandied about in this knot of merry beauties, and I determined to enjoy one of my good things in the rebound.

I stepped gently, therefore, up the room, smiling at every one as I passed, who I must say all smiled and tittered in return. I approached the group, smirking and perking my chin, like a man who is full of pleasant feeling, and sure of being well received. The cluster of little belles opened as I advanced.

Heavens and earth! whom should I perceive in the midst of them, but my early and tormenting flame, the everlasting Sacharissa! She was grown, it is true, into the full beauty of Womanhood, but shewed by the provoking merriment of her countenance, that she perfectly recollected me, and the ridiculous flagellations of which she had twice been the cause.

I saw at once the exterminating cloud of ridicule bursting over me. My crest fell. The flame of love went suddenly out, or was extinguished by overwhelming shame. How I got down the room I know not; I fancied every one tittering at me. Just as I reached the door I caught a glance of my mistress and her aunt listening to the whispers of my poetic rival; the old lady raising her hands and eyes, and the face of the young one lighted up with scorn ineffable. I paused to see no more; but made two steps from the top of the stairs to the bottom. The next morning, before sunrise, I beat a retreat; and did not feel the blushes cool from my tingling cheeks, until I had lost sight of the old towers of the Cathedral.

I now returned to town thoughtful and crestfallen. My money was nearly spent, for I had lived freely and without calculation. The dream of love was over, and the reign of pleasure at an end. I determined to retrench while I had yet a trifle left; so, selling my equipage and horses for half their value, I quietly put the money in my pocket, and turned pedestrian. I had not a doubt that, with my great expectations, I could at any time raise funds, either on usury or by borrowing; but I was principled against both, and resolved, by strict economy, to make my slender purse hold out, until my uncle should give up the ghost; or rather, the estate.

I staid at home, therefore, and read, and would have written; but I had already suffered too much from my poetical productions, which had generally involved me in some ridiculous scrape. I gradually acquired a rusty look, and had a straightened, money borrowing air, upon which the world began to shy me. I have never felt disposed to quarrel with the world for its conduct. It has always used me well. When I have been flush, and gay, and disposed for society, it has caressed me, and when I have been pinched, and reduced, and wished to be alone, why, it has left me alone; and what more could a man desire?—Take my word for it, this world is a more obliging world than people generally represent it.

Well sir—In the midst of my retrenchment, my retirement, and my studiousness, I received news that my uncle was dangerously ill. I hastened on the wings of an heir's affections to receive his dying breath and his last testament. I found him attended by his faithful valet old Iron John; by the woman who occasionally worked about the house; and by the foxy headed boy young Orson, whom I had occasionally hunted about the park. Iron John gasped a kind of asthmatical salutation as I entered the room, and received me with something almost like a smile of welcome. The woman sat blubbering at the foot of the bed; and the foxy headed Orson, who had now grown up to be a lubberly lout, stood gazing in stupid vacancy at a distance.

My uncle lay stretched upon his back. The chamber was without fire, or any of the comforts of a sick room. The cobwebs flaunted from the ceiling. The tester was covered with dust and the curtains were tattered. From underneath the bed peeped out one end of his strong box. Against the wainscot were suspended rusty blunderbusses; horse pistols and a cut and thrust sword, with which he had fortified his room to defend his life and treasure. He had employed no physician during his illness, and from the scanty relics lying on the table, seemed almost to have denied himself the assistance of a cook.

When I entered the room he was lying motionless; his eyes fixed and his mouth open; at the first look I thought him a corpse. The noise of my entrance made him turn his head. At the sight of me a ghastly smile came over his face, and his glazing eye gleamed with satisfaction. It was the only smile he had ever given me, and it went to my heart. "Poor old man!" thought I, "why would you force me to leave you thus desolate; when I see that my presence has the power to cheer you?"

"Nephew," said he, after several efforts and in a low gasping voice—"I am glad you are come. I shall now die with satisfaction. Look—" said he, raising his withered hand and pointing—"look—in that box on the table you will find that I have not forgotten you."

I pressed his hand to my heart, and the tears stood in my eyes. I sat down by his bed side, and watched him, but he never spoke again. My presence, however, gave him evident satisfaction—for every now and then as he looked at me a vague smile would come over his visage, and he would feebly point to the sealed box on the table. As the day wore away his life appeared to wear away with it. Towards sun set, his hand sank on the bed and lay motionless; his eyes grew glazed; his mouth remained open and thus he gradually died.

I could not but feel shocked at this absolute extinction of my kindred. I dropped a tear of real sorrow over this strange old man, who had thus reserved his smile of kindness, to his death bed; like an evening sun after a gloomy day, just shining out to set in darkness. Leaving the corpse in charge of the domestics I retired for the night.

It was a rough night. The winds seemed as if singing my uncle's requiem about the mansion; and the bloodhounds howled without as if they knew of the death of their old master. Iron John almost grudged me the tallow candle to burn in my apartment and light up its dreariness; so accustomed had he been to starveling economy. I could not sleep. The recollection of my uncle's dying scene and the dreary sounds about the house, affected my mind. These however were succeeded by plans for the future, and I lay awake the greater part of the night indulging the poetical anticipation, how soon I should make these old walls ring with cheerful life, and restore the hospitality of my mother's ancestors.

My uncle's funeral was decent but private. I knew that no body respected his memory; and I was determined none should be summoned to sneer over his funeral, and make merry at his grave. He was buried in the church of the neighbouring village, though it was not the burying place of his race; but he had expressly injoined that he should not be buried with his family; he had quarrelled with most of them when living, and he carried his resentments even into the grave.

I defrayed the expenses of the funeral out of my own purse, that I might have done with the undertakers at once, and clear the ill omened birds from the premises. I invited the parson of the parish, and the lawyer from the village to attend at the house the next morning and hear the reading of the will. I treated them to an excellent breakfast, a profusion that had not been seen at the house for many a year. As soon as the breakfast things were removed, I summoned Iron John, the woman and the boy, for I was particular in having every one present and proceeding regularly. The box was placed on the table. All was silence. I broke the seal; raised the lid; and beheld—not the will; but my accursed poem of Doubting Castle and Giant Despair!

Could any mortal have conceived that this old withered man; so taciturn, and apparently lost to feeling, could have treasured up for years the thoughtless pleasantry of a boy, to punish him with such cruel ingenuity? I now could account for his dying smile, the only one he had ever given me. He had been a grave man all his life; it was strange that he should die in the enjoyment of a joke; and it was hard that that joke should be at my expense.

The Lawyer and the Parson seemed at a loss to comprehend the matter. "Here must be some mistake," said the Lawyer, "there is no will here."

"Oh," said Iron John, creaking forth his rusty jaws, "if it is a will you are looking for, I believe I can find one."

He retired with the same singular smile with which he had greeted me on my arrival and which I now apprehended, boded me no good. In a little while he returned with a will, perfect at all points, properly signed and sealed and witnessed and worded with horrible correctness, in which he left large legacies to Iron John and his daughter, and the residue of his fortune to the foxy headed boy; who, to my utter astonishment, was his son by this very woman; he having married her privately, and, as I verily believe, for no other purpose than to have an heir and so baulk my father and his issue of the inheritance. There was one little proviso, in which he mentioned that having discovered his nephew to have a pretty turn for poetry, he presumed he had no occasion for wealth: he recommended him, however, to the patronage of his heir; and requested that he might have a garret, rent free, in Doubting Castle.

GRAVE REFLECTIONS OF A DISAPPOINTED MAN

Mr. Buckthorne had paused at the death of his uncle, and the downfall of his great expectations, which formed, as he said, an epoch in his history; and it was not until some little time afterwards, and in a very sober mood, that he resumed his particoloured narrative.

After leaving the domains of my defunct uncle, said he, when the gate closed between me and what was once to have been mine, I felt thrust out naked into the world, and completely abandoned to fortune. What was to become of me? I had been brought up to nothing but expectations, and they had all been disappointed. I had no relations to look to for counsel or assistance. The world seemed all to have died away from me. Wave after wave of relationship had ebbed off, and I was left a mere hulk upon the strand. I am not apt to be greatly cast down, but at this time I felt sadly disheartened. I could not realize my situation, nor form a conjecture how I was to get forward.

I was now to endeavour to make money. The idea was new and strange to me. It was like being asked to discover the philosophers' stone. I had never thought about money, other than to put my hand into my pocket and find it, or if there were none there, to wait until a new supply came from home. I had considered life as a mere space of time to be filled up with enjoyments; but to have it portioned out into long hours and days of toil, merely that I might gain bread to give me strength to toil on; to labour but for the purpose of perpetuating a life of labour was new and appalling to me. This may appear a very simple matter to some, but it will be understood by every unlucky wight in my predicament, who has had the misfortune of being born to great expectations.

I passed several days in rambling about the scenes of my boyhood; partly because I absolutely did not know what to do with myself, and partly because I did not know that I should ever see them again. I clung to them as one clings to a wreck, though he knows he must eventually cast himself loose and swim for his life. I sat down on a little hill within sight of my paternal home, but I did not venture to approach it, for I felt compunction at the thoughtlessness with which I had dissipated my patrimony. But was I to blame, when I had the rich possessions of my curmudgeon of an uncle in expectation?

The new possessor of the place was making great alterations. The house was almost rebuilt. The trees which stood about it were cut down; my mother's flower garden was thrown into a lawn; all was undergoing a change. I turned my back upon it with a sigh, and rambled to another part of the country.

How thoughtful a little adversity makes one. As I came within sight of the school house where I had so often been flogged in the cause of wisdom, you would hardly have recognized the truant boy who but a few years since had eloped so heedlessly from its walls. I leaned over the paling of the play ground and watched the scholars at their games and looked to see if there might not be some urchin among them, like I was once, full of gay dreams about life and the world. The play ground seemed smaller than when I used to sport about it. The house and park too of the neighbouring squire, the father of the cruel Sacharissa, had shrunk in size and diminished in magnificence. The distant hills no longer appeared so far off, and, alas! no longer awakened ideas of a fairy land beyond.

As I was rambling pensively through a neighbouring meadow, in which I had many a time gathered primroses, I met the very pedagogue who had been the tyrant and dread of my boyhood. I had sometimes vowed to myself, when suffering under his rod, that I would have my revenge if ever I met him when I had grown to be a man. The time had come; but I had no disposition to keep my vow. The few years which had matured me into a vigorous man had shrunk him into decrepitude. He appeared to have had a paralytic stroke. I looked at him, and wondered that this poor helpless mortal could have been an object of terror to me! That I should have watched with anxiety the glance of that failing eye, or dreaded the power of that trembling hand! He tottered feebly along the path and had some difficulty getting over a style. I ran and assisted him. He looked at me with surprize but did not recognize me and made a low bow of humility and thanks. I had no disposition to make myself known for I felt that I had nothing to boast of. The pains he had taken and the pains he had inflicted had been equally useless. His repeated predictions were fully verified, and I felt that little Jack Buckthorne the idle boy had grown up to be a very good for nothing man.

This is all very comfortless detail, but as I have told you of my follies, it is meet that I shew you how for once I was schooled for them. The most thoughtless of mortals will some time or other have this day of gloom when he will be compelled to reflect. I felt on this occasion as if I had a kind of penance to perform, and I made a pilgrimage in expiation of my past levity.

Having passed a night at Leamington, I set off by a private path which leads up a hill, through a grove, and across quiet fields, until I came to the small village, or rather hamlet of Lenington. I sought the village church. It is an old low edifice of grey stone on the brow of a small hill, looking over fertile fields towards where the proud towers of Warwick Castle lift themselves against the distant horizon. A part of the church yard is shaded by large trees. Under one of these my mother lay buried. You have no doubt thought me a light, heartless being. I thought myself so; but there are moments of adversity which let us into some feelings of our nature, to which we might otherwise remain perpetual strangers.

I sought my mother's grave. The weeds were already matted over it, and the tombstone was half hid among nettles. I cleared them away and they stung my hands; but I was heedless of the pain, for my heart ached too severely. I sat down on the grave, and read over and over again the epitaph on the stone.

It was simple, but it was true. I had written it myself. I had tried to write a poetical epitaph but in vain; my feelings refused to utter themselves in rhyme. My heart had gradually been filling during my lonely wanderings; it was now charged to the brim and overflowed. I sank upon the grave and buried my face in the tall grass and wept like a child. Yes, I wept in manhood upon the grave, as I had in infancy upon the bosom of my mother. Alas! how little do we appreciate a mother's tenderness while living! How heedless are we, in youth, of all her anxieties and kindness. But when she is dead and gone, when the cares and coldness of the world come withering to our hearts; when we find how hard it is to meet with true sympathy; how few love us for ourselves; how few will befriend us in our misfortunes; then it is we think of the mother we have lost. It is true I had always loved my mother, even in my most heedless days; but I felt how inconsiderate and ineffectual had been my love. My heart melted as I retraced the days of infancy, when I was led by a mother's hand, and rocked to sleep in a mother's arms, and was without care or sorrow. "Oh my mother!" exclaimed I, burying my face again in the grass of the grave. "Oh that I were once more by your side; sleeping never to wake again on the cares and troubles of this world!"

I am not naturally of a morbid temperament, and the violence of my emotion gradually exhausted itself. It was a hearty, honest, natural discharge of griefs which had been slowly accumulating, and gave me wonderful relief. I rose from the grave as if I had been offering up a sacrifice, and I felt as if that sacrifice had been accepted.

I sat down again on the grass and plucked, one by one, the weeds from her grave; the tears trickled more slowly down my cheeks, and ceased to be bitter. It was a comfort to think that she had died before sorrow and poverty came upon her child, and that all his great expectations were blasted.

I leaned my cheek upon my hand and looked upon the landscape. Its quiet beauty soothed me. The whistle of a peasant from an adjoining field came cheerily to my ear. I seemed to respire hope and comfort with the free air that whispered through the leaves and played lightly with my hair, and dried the tears upon my cheek. A lark, rising from the field before me, and leaving, as it were, a stream of song behind him as he rose, lifted my fancy with him. He hovered in the air just above the place where the towers of Warwick Castle marked the horizon; and seemed as if fluttering with delight at his own melody. "Surely," thought I, "if there were such a thing as transmigration of souls, this might be taken for some poet, let loose from earth, but still revelling in song, and carrolling about fair fields and lordly towers."

At this moment the long forgotten feeling of poetry rose within me. A thought sprang at once into my mind. "I will become an author!" said I. "I have hitherto indulged in poetry as a pleasure and it has brought me nothing but pain. Let me try what it will do, when I cultivate it with devotion as a pursuit."

The resolution, thus suddenly aroused within me, heaved a load from off my heart. I felt a confidence in it from the very place where it was formed. It seemed as though my mother's spirit whispered it to me from her grave. "I will henceforth," said I, "endeavour to be all that she fondly imagined me. I will endeavour to act as if she were witness of my actions. I will endeavour to acquit myself in such manner, that when I revisit her grave there may, at least, be no compunctious bitterness in my tears."

I bowed down and kissed the turf in solemn attestation of my vow. I plucked some primroses that were growing there and laid them next my heart. I left the church yard with my spirits once more lifted up, and set out a third time for London, in the character of an author.

Here my companion made a pause, and I waited in anxious suspence; hoping to have a whole volume of literary life unfolded to me. He seemed however to have sunk into a fit of pensive musing; and when after some time I gently roused him by a question or two as to his literary career—

"No," said he smiling, "over that part of my story I wish to leave a cloud. Let the mysteries of the craft rest sacred for me. Let those who have never adventured into the republic of letters still look upon it as a fairy land. Let them suppose the author the very being they picture him from his works. I am not the man to mar their illusion. I am not the man to hint, while one is admiring the silken web of Persia, that it has been spun from the entrails of a miserable worm."

"Well," said I, "if you will tell me nothing of your literary history, let me know at least if you have had any further intelligence from Doubting Castle."

"Willingly," replied he, "though I have but little to communicate."

THE BOOBY SQUIRE

A long time elapsed, said Buckthorne, without my receiving any accounts of my cousin and his estate. Indeed I felt so much soreness on the subject, that I wished, if possible, to shut it from my thoughts. At length chance took me into that part of the country, and I could not refrain from making some enquiries.

I learnt that my cousin had grown up ignorant, self willed, and clownish. His ignorance and clownishness had prevented his mingling with the neighbouring gentry. In spite of his great fortune he had been unsuccessful in an attempt to gain the hand of the daughter of the Parson, and had at length shrunk into the limits of such society, as a mere man of wealth can gather in a country neighbourhood.

He kept horses and hounds and a roaring table, at which were collected the loose livers of the country round, and the shabby gentlemen of a village in the vicinity. When he could get no other company he would smoke and drink with his own servants, who in their turns fleeced and despised him. Still, with all this apparent prodigality, he had a leaven of the old man in him, which shewed that he was his true born son. He lived far within his income, was vulgar in his expenses, and penurious on many points on which a gentleman would be extravagant. His house servants were obliged occasionally to work on the estate, and part of the pleasure grounds were ploughed up and devoted to husbandry.

His table though plentiful was coarse; his liquors strong and bad; and more ale and whiskey were expended in his establishment than generous wine. He was loud and arrogant at his own table, and exacted a rich man's homage from his vulgar and obsequious guests.

As to Iron John, his old grandfather, he had grown impatient of the tight hand his own grandson kept over him and quarrelled with him soon after he came to the estate. The old man had retired to a neighbouring village where he lived on the legacy of his late master, in a small cottage, and was as seldom seen out of it as a rat out of his hole in day light.

The Cub, like Caliban, seemed to have an instinctive attachment to his mother. She resided with him; but from long habit she acted more as servant than as mistress of the mansion; for she toiled in all the domestic drudgery and was oftener in the kitchen than the parlour. Such was the information which I collected of my rival cousin who had so unexpectedly elbowed me out of all my expectations.

I now felt an irresistible hankering to pay a visit to this scene of my boyhood; and to get a peep at the odd kind of life that was passing within the mansion of my maternal ancestors. I determined to do so in disguise. My booby cousin had never seen enough of me to be very familiar with my countenance, and a few years make great difference between youth and manhood. I understood he was a breeder of cattle and proud of his stock. I dressed myself therefore as a substantial farmer, and with the assistance of a red scratch that came low down on my forehead, made a complete change in my physiognomy.

It was past three o'clock when I arrived at the gate of the park, and was admitted by an old woman, who was washing in a dilapidated building which had once been a porter's lodge. I advanced up the remains of a noble avenue, many of the trees of which had been cut down and sold for timber. The grounds were in scarcely better keeping than during my uncle's life time.

The grass was overgrown with weeds, and the trees wanted pruning and clearing of dead branches. Cattle were grazing about the lawns and ducks and geese swimming in the fishponds.

The road to the house bore very few traces of carriage wheels as my Cousin received few visitors but such as came on foot or horseback, and never used a carriage himself. Once indeed, as I was told, he had had the old family carriage drawn out from among the dust and cobwebs of the coach house and furbished up, and had driven, with his mother, to the village church, to take formal possession of the family pew; but there was such hooting and laughing after them as they passed through the village, and such giggling and bantering about the church door, that the pageant had never made a reappearance.

As I approached the house a legion of whelps sallied out barking at me, accompanied by the low howling rather than barking of two old worn out bloodhounds, which I recognized for the ancient life guards of my uncle. The house had still a neglected, random appearance, though much altered for the better since my last visit. Several of the windows were broken and patched up with boards; and others had been bricked up, to save taxes. I observed smoke, however, rising from the chimnies; a phenomenon rarely witnessed in the ancient establishment. On passing that part of the house where the dining room was situated I heard the sound of boisterous merriment; where three or four voices were talking at once, and oaths and laughter were horribly mingled.

The uproar of the dogs had brought a servant to the door, a tall hardfisted country clown, with a livery coat put over the undergarments of a plowman. I requested to see the master of the house, but was told he was at dinner with some "gemmen" of the neighbourhood. I made known my business and sent in to know if I might talk with the master about his cattle; for I felt a great desire to have a peep at him at his orgies. Word was returned that he was engaged with company and could not attend to business, but that if I would "step in and take a drink of something, I was heartily welcome." I accordingly entered the hall, where whips and hats of all kinds and shapes were lying on an oaken table; two or three clownish servants were lounging about; every thing had a look of confusion and carelessness.

The apartments through which I passed had the same air of departed gentility and sluttish housekeeping. The once rich curtains were faded and dusty, the furniture greased and tarnished. On entering the dining room I found a number of odd vulgar looking rustic gentlemen seated round a table on which were bottles, decanters, tankards, pipes and tobacco. Several dogs were lying about the room, or sitting and watching their masters, and one was gnawing a bone under a side table.

The master of the feast sat at the head of the board. He was greatly altered. He had grown thick set and rather gummy, with a fiery foxy head of hair. There was a singular mixture of foolishness, arrogance and conceit in his countenance. He was dressed in a vulgarly fine style, with leather breeches, a red waistcoat and green coat, and was evidently, like his guests, a little flushed with drinking. The whole company stared at me with a whimsical muzzy look; like men whose senses were a little obfuscated by beer rather than wine.

My Cousin, (God forgive me! the appellation sticks in my throat) my cousin invited me with awkward civility, or, as he intended it, condescension, to sit to the table and drink. We talked as usual, about the weather, the crops, politics, and hard times. My Cousin was a loud politician, and evidently accustomed to talk without contradiction at his own table. He was amazingly loyal, and talked of standing by the throne to the last guinea, "as every gentleman of fortune should do." The village Exciseman, who was half asleep, could just ejaculate "very true" to every thing he said.

The conversation turned upon cattle; he boasted of his breed, his mode of crossing it, and of the general management of his estate. This unluckily drew on a history of the place and of the family. He spoke of my late uncle with the greatest irreverence, which I could easily forgive. He mentioned my name, and my blood began to boil. He described my frequent visits to my uncle when I was a lad, and I found the varlet, even at that time, imp as he was, had known that he was to inherit the estate.

He described the scene of my uncle's death and the opening of the will, with a degree of coarse humour that I had not expected from him; and, vexed as I was, I could not help joining in the laugh; for I have always relished a joke, even though made at my own expense. He went on to speak of my various pursuits; my strolling freak, and that somewhat nettled me; at length he talked of my parents. He ridiculed my father; I stomached even that, though with great difficulty. He mentioned my mother with a sneer—and in an instant he lay sprawling at my feet.

Here a tumult succeeded. The table was nearly overturned. Bottles, glasses and tankards rolled crashing and clattering about the floor. The company seized hold of both of us to keep us from doing any further mischief. I struggled to get loose, for I was boiling with fury. My cousin defied me to strip and fight him on the lawn. I agreed, for I felt the strength of a giant in me, and I longed to pummel him soundly.

Away then we were borne. A ring was formed. I had a second assigned me in true boxing style. My cousin, as he advanced to fight, said something about his generosity in shewing me such fair play, when I had made such an unprovoked attack upon him at his own table—

"Stop there!" cried I, in a rage.—"Unprovoked!—know that I am John Buckthorne, and you have insulted the memory of my mother."

The lout was suddenly struck by what I said. He drew back and thought for a moment.

"Nay, damn it," said he, "that's too much—that's clean another thing—
I've a mother myself, and no one shall speak ill of her, bad as she is."—

He paused again: nature seemed to have a rough struggle in his rude
bosom.

"Damn it cousin," cried he, "I'm sorry for what I said. Thou'st served me
right in knocking me down, and I like thee the better for it. Here's my hand.
Come and live with me, and damme but the best room in the house, and
the best horse in the stable, shall be at thy service."

I declare to you I was strongly moved at this instance of nature, breaking
her way through such a lump of flesh. I forgave the fellow in a moment his
two heinous crimes of having been born in wedlock and inheriting my estate. I shook the hand he offered me, to convince him that I bore him no ill-
will; and then making my way through the gaping crowd of toad eaters, bade
adieu to my uncle's domains forever. This is the last I have seen or heard of
my cousin or of the domestic concerns of Doubting Castle.

THE STROLLING MANAGER

As I was walking one morning with Buckthorne, near one of the principal
theatres, he directed my attention to a groupe of those equivocal beings that
may often be seen hovering about the stage doors of theatres. They were
marvellously ill favoured in their attire, their coats buttoned up to their
chins, yet they wore their hats smartly on one side, and had a certain know
ing, dirty-gentlemanlike air, which is common to the subalterns of the drama. Buckthorne knew them well by early experience.

"These," said he, "are the ghosts of departed Kings and heroes; fellows
who sway sceptres and truncheons; command kingdoms and armies; and
after giving away realms and treasures over night, have scarce a shilling to
pay for a breakfast in the morning. Yet they have the true vagabond abhorrence of all useful and industrious employment; and they have their pleasures too: one of which is to lounge in this way in the sunshine, at the stage
door, during rehearsals, and make hackneyed theatrical jokes on all passers
by.

"Nothing is more traditional and legitimate than the stage. Old scenery,
old clothes, old sentiments, old ranting, and old jokes, are handed down
from generation to generation; and will probably continue to be so until time
shall be no more. Every hanger on of a theatre becomes a wag by inheritance, and flourishes about at tap rooms and sixpenny clubs with the property jokes of the green room."

While amusing ourselves with reconnoitering this groupe, we noticed one in particular who appeared to be the oracle. He was a weather beaten veteran, a little bronzed by time and beer, who had no doubt grown grey in the parts of robbers, cardinals, Roman senators, and walking noblemen.

"There's something in the set of that hat, and the turn of that physiognomy, extremely familiar to me," said Buckthorne. He looked a little closer. "I cannot be mistaken, that must be my old brother of the truncheon, Flimsey, the tragic hero of the Strolling Company."

It was he in fact. The poor fellow shewed evident signs that times went hard with him: he was so finely and shabbily dressed. His coat was some what threadbare, and of the Lord Townly cut; single breasted, and scarcely capable of meeting in front of his body; which, from long intimacy, had acquired the symmetry and robustness of a beer barrel. He wore a pair of dingy white stockinet pantaloons, which had much ado to reach his waistcoat; a great quantity of dirty cravat; and a pair of old russet coloured tragedy boots.

When his companions had dispersed, Buckthorne drew him aside and made himself known to him. The tragic veteran could scarcely recognize him, or believe that he was really his quondam associate "little gentleman Jack." Buckthorne invited him to a neighbouring coffee house to talk over old times; and in the course of a little while we were put in possession of his history in brief.

He had continued to act the heroes in the Strolling Company for some time after Buckthorne had left it, or rather had been driven from it, so abruptly. At length the manager died and the troop was thrown into confusion. Every one aspired to the crown, every one was for taking the lead; and the manager's widow, although a tragedy queen, and a brimstone to boot, pronounced it utterly impossible for a woman to keep any controul over such a set of tempestuous rascallions.

"Upon this hint, I spake"—said Flimsey. I stepped forward, and offered my services in the most effectual way. They were accepted. In a week's time I married the widow and succeeded to the throne. "The funeral baked meats did coldly furnish forth the marriage table," as Hamlet says. But the ghost of my predecessor never haunted me; and I inherited crowns, sceptres, bowls, daggers, and all the stage trappings and trumpery, not omitting the widow, without the least molestation.

I now led a flourishing life of it; for our company was pretty strong and attractive, and as my wife and I took the heavy parts of tragedy, it was a great saving to the treasury. We carried off the palm from all the rival shows at country fairs; and I assure you we have even drawn full houses, and been applauded by the critics at Bartlemy Fair itself, though we had Astley's Troop, the Irish giant and "the death of Nelson" in wax work to contend against.

I soon began to experience, however, the cares of command. I discovered that there were cabals breaking out in the company, headed by the clown, who you may recollect was a terribly peevish, fractious fellow, and always in ill humour. I had a great mind to turn him off at once, but I could not do without him, for there was not a droller scoundrel on the stage. His very shape was comic, for he had but to turn his back upon the audience and all the ladies were ready to die with laughing. He felt his importance, and took advantage of it. He would keep the audience in a continual roar, and then come behind the scenes and fret and fume and play the very devil. I excused a great deal in him, however, knowing that comic actors are a little prone to this infirmity of temper.

I had another trouble of a nearer and dearer nature to struggle with; which was, the affection of my wife. As ill luck would have it she took it into her head to be very fond of me, and became intolerably jealous. I could not keep a pretty girl in the company, and hardly dared embrace an ugly one, even when my part required it. I have known her reduce a fine lady to tatters, "to very rags" as Hamlet says, in an instant, and destroy one of the very best dresses in the wardrobe; merely because she saw me kiss her at the side scenes;—though I give you my honour it was done merely by way of rehearsal.

This was doubly annoying, because I have a natural liking to pretty faces and wish to have them about me; and because they are indispensible to the success of a company at a fair, where one has to vie with so many rival theatres. But when once a jealous wife gets a freak in her head, there's no use in talking of interest or any thing else. Egad, sirs, I have more than once trembled when during a fit of her tantrums, she was playing high tragedy and flourishing her tin dagger on the stage, lest she should give way to her humour and stab some fancied rival in good earnest.

I went on better, however, than could be expected, considering the weakness of my flesh and the violence of my rib. I had not a much worse time of it than old Jupiter, whose spouse was continually ferretting out some new intrigue, and making the heavens almost too hot to hold him.

At length, as luck would have it, we were performing at a country fair, when I understood the theatre of a neighbouring town to be vacant. I had always been desirous to be enrolled in a settled company, and the height of my desire was to get on a par with a brother in law, who was manager of a regular theatre, and who had looked down upon me. Here was an opportunity not to be neglected. I concluded an agreement with the proprietors, and in a few days opened the theatre with great eclat.

Behold me now at the summit of my ambition, "the high top gallant of my joy," as Romeo says. No longer a chieftain of a wandering tribe, but the monarch of a legitimate throne; and entitled to call even the great potentates of Covent Garden and Drury Lane cousin. You no doubt think my happiness complete. Alas, sir! I was one of the most uncomfortable dogs living. No one knows, who has not tried, the miseries of a manager; but above all, of a country manager.—No one can conceive the contentions and quarrels within doors, the oppressions and vexations from without.

I was pestered with the bloods and loungers of a country town, who infested my green room, and played the mischief among my actresses. But there was no shaking them off. It would have been ruin to affront them; for, though troublesome friends, they would have been dangerous enemies. Then there were the village critics and village amateurs, who were continually tormenting me with advice, and getting into a passion if I would not take it:—especially the village doctor and the village attorney; who had both been to London occasionally, and knew what acting should be.

I had also to manage as arrant a crew of scape graces as were ever collected together within the walls of a theatre. I had been obliged to combine my original troop, with some of the former troop of the theatre, who were favourites with the public. Here was a mixture that produced perpetual ferment. They were all the time either fighting or frolicking with each other, and I scarcely know which mood was least troublesome. If they quarrelled every thing went wrong; and if they were friends they were continually playing off some confounded prank upon each other, or upon me; for I had unhappily acquired among them the character of an easy good natured fellow, the worst character that a manager can possess.

Their waggery at times drove me almost crazy; for there is nothing so vexatious as the hackneyed tricks and hoaxes and pleasantries of a veteran band of theatrical vagabonds. I relished them well enough, it is true, while I was merely one of the company, but as manager I found them detestable. They were incessantly bringing some disgrace upon the theatre by their tavern frolicks, and their pranks about the country town. All my lectures upon the importance of keeping up the dignity of the profession, and the respectability of the company, were in vain. The villains could not sympathize with the delicate feelings of a man in station. They even trifled with the seriousness of stage business. I have had the whole piece interrupted and a crowded audience of at least twenty five pounds kept waiting, because the actors had hid away the breeches of Rosalind; and have known Hamlet stalk solemnly on to deliver his soliloquy, with a dish clout pinned to his skirts. Such are the baleful consequences of a manager's getting a character for good nature.

I was intolerably annoyed, too, by the great actors who came down *Starring*, as it is called, from London. Of all baneful influences, keep me from that of a London Star. A first rate actress, going the rounds of the country theatres, is as bad as a blazing comet, whisking about the heavens, and shaking fire, and plagues, and discords from its tail.

The moment one of these "heavenly bodies" appeared on my horizon, I was sure to be in hot water. My theatre was overrun by provincial dandies, copper-washed counterfeits of Bond Street loungers; who are always proud to be in the train of an actress from town, and anxious to be thought on exceeding good terms with her. It was really a relief to me when some random young nobleman would come in pursuit of the bait, and awe all this small fry to a distance. I have always felt myself more at ease with a nobleman, than with the dandy of a country town.

And then the injuries I suffered in my personal dignity and my managerial authority from the visits of these great London actors. 'Sblood, sir, I was no longer master of myself or my throne. I was hectored and lectured in my own green room, and made an absolute nincompoop on my own stage. There is no tyrant so absolute and capricious as a London Star at a country theatre.

I dreaded the sight of all of them; and yet if I did not engage them, I was sure of having the public clamourous against me. They drew full houses and appeared to be making my fortune, but they swallowed up all the profits by their insatiable demands. They were absolute tape worms to my little theatre; the more it took in, the poorer it grew. They were sure to leave me with an exhausted public, empty benches, and a score or two of affronts to settle among the town's folk, in consequence of misunderstandings about the taking of places.

But the worst thing I had to undergo in my managerial career was patronage. Oh sir, of all things deliver me from the patronage of the great people of a country town. It was my ruin. You must know that this town, though small, was filled with feuds, and parties, and great folks; being a busy little trading and manufacturing town. The mischief was that their greatness was of a kind not to be settled by reference to the court calender, or college of heraldry. It was therefore the most quarrelsome kind of greatness in existence. You smile sir, but let me tell you there are no feuds more furious than the frontier feuds, which take place on these "debateable lands" of gentility. The most violent dispute that I ever knew in high life, was one which occurred at a country town, on a question of precedence between the ladies of a manufacturer of pins, and a manufacturer of needles.

At the town where I was situated there were perpetual altercations of the kind. The head manufacturer's lady, for instance, was at daggers drawings with the head shopkeeper's, and both were too rich, and had too many friends to be treated lightly. The Doctor's and Lawyer's ladies held their heads still higher; but they in their turn were kept in check by the wife of a country banker, who kept her own carriage; while a masculine widow of cracked character, and second hand fashion, who lived in a large house, and claimed to be, in some way, related to nobility, looked down upon them all. To be sure her manners were not over elegant, nor her fortune over large, but then, sir, her blood—oh her blood carried it all hollow; there was no withstanding a woman with such blood in her veins.

After all, her claims to high connexion were questioned, and she had frequent battles for precedence at balls and assemblies; with some of the sturdy dames of the neighbourhood, who stood upon their wealth and their virtue; but then she had two dashing daughters, who dressed as fine as dragons, had as high blood as their mother, and seconded her in every thing. So they carried their point with high heads, and every body hated, abused, and stood in awe of the Fantadlins.

Such was the state of the fashionable world in this self important little town. Unluckily I was not as well acquainted with its politics as I should have been. I had found myself a stranger and in great perplexities during my first season; I determined, therefore, to put myself under the patronage of some powerful name, and thus to take the field with the prejudices of the public in my favour. I cast round my thoughts for the purpose, and, in an evil hour they fell upon Mrs. Fantadlin. No one seemed to me to have a more absolute sway in the world of fashion. I had always noticed that her party slammed the box door the loudest at the theatre; had most beaux attending on them; and talked and laughed loudest during the performance; and then the Miss Fantadlins wore always more feathers and flowers than any other ladies; and used quizzing glasses incessantly. The first evening of my theatre's re-opening, therefore, was announced, in flaring capitals on the play bills, "under the patronage of The Honourable Mrs. Fantadlin."

Sir, the whole community flew to arms! The Banker's wife felt her dignity grievously insulted, at not having the preference; her husband being high bailiff, and the richest man in the place. She immediately issued invitations for a large party for the night of the performance, and asked many a lady to it whom she never had noticed before. Presume to patronize the theatre! Insufferable! And then for me to dare to term her "The Honourable!" What claim had she to the title, forsooth! The fashionable world had long groaned under the tyranny of the Fantadlins, and were glad to make a common cause against this new instance of assumption. Those, too, who had never before been noticed by the banker's lady, were ready to enlist in any quarrel, for the honour of her acquaintance. All minor feuds were forgotten. The Doctor's lady and the Lawyer's lady met together; and the Manufacturer's lady and the Shopkeeper's lady kissed each other; and all, headed by the Banker's lady, voted the theatre a *bore*, and determined to encourage nothing but the Indian Jugglers, and Mr. Walker's Eidouranion.

Alas for poor Pillgarlick! I little knew the mischief that was brewing against me. My box book remained blank. The evening arrived; but no audience. The musick struck up to a tolerable pit and gallery, but no fashionables! I peeped anxiously from behind the curtain, but the time passed away; the play was retarded until pit and gallery became furious; and I had to raise the curtain, and play my greatest part in tragedy to "a beggarly account of empty boxes."

It is true the Fantadlins came late, as was their custom, and entered like a tempest, with a flutter of feathers and red shawls; but they were evidently disconcerted at finding they had no one to admire and envy them; and were enraged at this glaring defection of their fashionable followers. All the beau monde were engaged at the Banker's lady's rout. They remained for some time in solitary and uncomfortable state, and though they had the theatre almost to themselves, yet, for the first time they talked in whispers. They left the house at the end of the first piece, and I never saw them afterwards.

Such was the rock on which I split. I never got over the patronage of the Fantadlin family. My house was deserted; my actors grew discontented because they were ill paid; my door became a hammering place for every bailiff in the county; and my wife became more and more shrewish and tormenting, the more I wanted comfort.

I tried for a time the usual consolation of a harassed and henpecked man: I took to the bottle, and tried to tipple away my cares, but in vain. I don't mean to decry the bottle; it is no doubt an excellent remedy in many cases, but it did not answer in mine. It cracked my voice, coppered my nose, but neither improved my wife nor my affairs.

My establishment became a scene of confusion and peculation. I was considered a ruined man, and of course fair game for every one to pluck at, as every one plunders a sinking ship. Day after day some of the troop deserted, and like deserting soldiers, carried off their arms and accoutrements with them. In this manner my wardrobe took legs and walked away; my finery strolled all over the country; my swords and daggers glittered in every barn; until at last my taylor made "one fell swoop," and carried off three dress coats, half a dozen doublets, and nineteen pair of flesh coloured pantaloons.

This was the "be all and the end all" of my fortune. I no longer hesitated what to do. Egad, thought I, since stealing is the order of the day I'll steal too. So I secretly gathered together the jewels of my wardrobe; packed up a hero's dress in a handkerchief, slung it on the end of a tragedy sword, and quietly stole off at dead of night,—"the bell then beating one,"—leaving my queen and Kingdom to the mercy of my rebellious subjects, and my merciless foes the bumbailiffs.

Such, sir, was the "end of all my greatness." I was heartily cured of all passion for governing, and returned once more into the ranks. I had for some time the usual run of an actor's life. I played in various country theatres, at fairs and in barns; sometimes hard pushed, sometimes flush, until on one occasion I came within an ace of making my fortune, and becoming one of the wonders of the age.

I was playing the part of Richard the Third in a country barn and in my best style, for, to tell the truth, I was a little in liquor, and the critics of the company always observed that I played with most effect when I had a glass too much. There was a thunder of applause when I came to that part where

Richard cries for "a horse! a horse!" My cracked voice had always a wonderful effect here; it was like two voices run into one; you would have thought two men had been calling for a horse, or that Richard had called for two horses. And when I flung the taunt at Richmond, "Richard is *hoarse* with calling thee to arms," I thought the barn would have come down about my ears with the raptures of the audience.

The very next morning a person waited upon me at my lodgings; I saw at once he was a gentleman by his dress, for he had a large brooch in his bosom, thick rings on his fingers, and used a quizzing glass. And a gentleman he proved to be, for I soon ascertained that he was a kept author, or kind of literary tailor to one of the great London theatres; one who worked under the manager's directions, and cut up and cut down plays, and patched and pieced, and new faced, and turned them inside out; in short, he was one of the readiest and greatest writers of the day.

He was now on a foraging excursion in quest of something that might be got up as a prodigy. The theatre it seems was in desperate condition—nothing but a miracle could save it. He had seen me act Richard the night before and had pitched upon me for that miracle. I had a remarkable bluster in my style and swagger in my gait; I certainly differed from all other heroes of the barn; so the thought struck the agent to bring me out as a theatrical wonder; as the restorer of natural and legitimate acting; as the only one who could understand and act Shakespeare rightly. When he opened his plan I shrunk from it with becoming modesty, for, well as I thought of myself, I doubted my competency to such an undertaking.

I hinted at my imperfect knowledge of Shakespeare, having played his characters only after mutilated copies, interlarded with a great deal of my own talk by way of helping memory or heightening the effect.

"So much the better," cried the gentleman with rings on his fingers; "so much the better. New readings, sir!—new readings! Don't study a line—let us have Shakespeare after your own fashion."

"But then my voice was cracked; it could not fill a London theatre."

"So much the better! so much the better! The public is tired of intonation—the *ore rotundo* has had its day. No, sir, your cracked voice is the very thing—spit and splutter, and snap and snarl, and 'play the very dog' about the stage, and you'll be the making of us."

"But then,"—I could not help blushing to the end of my very nose as I said it, but I was determined to be candid;—"but then," added I, "there is one awkward circumstance; I have an unlucky habit—my misfortunes, and the exposures to which one is subjected in country barns, have obliged me now and then to—to—take a drop of something comfortable—and so—and so——"

"What! you drink?" cried the agent eagerly.

I bowed my head in blushing acknowledgment.

"So much the better! so much the better! The irregularities of genius! A sober fellow is common place. The public like an actor that drinks.—Give me your hand, sir. You're the very man to make a dash with."

I still hung back with lingering diffidence, declaring myself unworthy of such praise.

"'Sblood man!" cried he, "no praise at all. You don't imagine I think you a wonder. I only want the public to think so. Nothing so easy as gulling the public if you only set up a prodigy. Common talent any body can measure by common rule; but a prodigy sets all rule and measurement at defiance."

These words opened my eyes in an instant: we now came to a proper understanding; less flattering, it is true, to my vanity, but much more satisfactory to my judgment.

It was agreed that I should make my appearance before a London audience, as a dramatic sun just bursting from behind the clouds: one that was to banish all the lesser lights and false fires of the stage. Every precaution was to be taken to possess the public mind at every avenue. The pit was to be packed with sturdy clappers; the newspapers secured by vehement puffers; every theatrical resort to be haunted by hireling talkers. In a word, every engine of theatrical humbug was to be put in action. Wherever I differed from former actors, it was to be maintained that I was right and they were wrong. If I ranted, it was to be pure passion; if I were vulgar, it was to be pronounced a familiar touch of nature; if I made any queer blunder, it was to be a new reading. If my voice cracked, or I got out in my part, I was only to bounce, and grin, and snarl at the audience, and make any horrible grimace that came into my head, and my admirers were to call it "a great point," and to fall back and shout and yell with rapture.

"In short," said the gentleman with the quizzing glass, "strike out boldly and bravely: no matter how or what you do, so that it be but odd and strange. If you do but escape pelting the first night, your fortune and the fortune of the theatre is made."

I set off for London, therefore, in company with the kept author, full of new plans and new hopes. I was to be restorer of Shakespeare and nature, and the legitimate drama; my very swagger was to be heroic, and my cracked voice the standard of elocution. Alas sir! my usual luck attended me. Before I arrived at the metropolis a rival wonder had appeared. A woman who could dance the slack rope, and run up a cord from the stage to the gallery with fire works all round her. She was seized on by the manager with avidity; she was the saving of the great national theatre for the season. Nothing was talked of but Madame Saqui's fire works and flame coloured pantaloons; and nature, Shakespeare, the legitimate drama and poor Pillgarlic were completely left in the lurch.

When Madame Saqui's performance grew stale, other wonders succeeded; horses, and harlequinades, and mummery of all kinds; until another dramatic prodigy was brought forward to play the very game for which I had been intended. I called upon the kept author for an explanation, but he was deeply engaged in writing a melo-drame or a pantomime, and was extremely testy on being interrupted in his studies.

However, as the theatre was in some measure pledged to provide for me, the manager acted, according to the usual phrase, "like a man of honour," and I received an appointment in the corps. It had been a turn up of a die whether I should be Alexander the Great or Alexander the Coppersmith: the latter carried it. I could not be put at the head of the drama so I was put at the tail. In other words I was enrolled among the number of what are called *useful men*; those who enact soldiers, senators, and Banquo's shadowy line. I was perfectly satisfied with my lot; for I have always been a bit of a philosopher. If my situation was not splendid, it at least was secure; and in fact I have seen half a dozen prodigies appear, dazzle, burst like bubbles and pass away, and yet here I am, snug, unenvied and unmolested at the foot of the profession.

You may smile; but let me tell you, we "useful men" are the only comfortable actors on the stage. We are safe from hisses and below the hope of applause. We fear not the success of rivals, nor dread the critic's pen. So long as we get the words of our parts, and they are not often many, it is all we care for. We have our own merriment, our own friends, and our own admirers; for every actor has his friends and admirers, from the highest to the lowest. The first rate actor dines with the noble amateur, and entertains a fashionable table with scraps and songs and theatrical slip-slop. The second rate actors have their second rate friends and admirers, with whom they likewise spout tragedy and talk slip-slop; and so down even to us; who have our friends and admirers among spruce clerks and aspiring apprentices, who treat us to a dinner now and then, and enjoy at tenth hand the same scraps, and songs, and slip-slop, that have been served up by our more fortunate brethren at the tables of the great.

I now for the first time in my theatrical life experience what true pleasure is. I have known enough of notoriety to pity the poor devils who are called favourites of the public. I would rather be a Kitten in the arms of a spoiled child to be one moment petted and pampered, and the next moment thumped over the head with the spoon. I smile to see our leading actors, fretting themselves with envy and jealousy about a trumpery renown, questionable in its quality and uncertain in its duration. I laugh too, though of course in my sleeve, at the bustle and importance and trouble and perplexities of our manager, who is harrassing himself to death in the hopeless effort to please every body.

I have found among my fellow subalterns two or three quondam managers, who like myself, have wielded the sceptres of country theatres; and we have many a sly joke together at the expense of the manager and the public. Sometimes too we meet like deposed and exiled Kings, talk over the events of our respective reigns, moralize over a tankard of ale, and laugh at the humbug of the great and little world; which, I take it, is the essence of practical philosophy.

———

Thus end the anecdotes of Buckthorne and his friends. It grieves me much that I could not procure from him further particulars of his history, and especially of that part of it which passed in town. He had evidently seen much of literary life; and, as he had never risen to eminence in letters, and yet was free from the gall of disappointment, I had hoped to gain some candid intelligence concerning his contemporaries. The testimony of such an honest chronicler would have been particularly valuable at the present time; when, owing to the extreme fecundity of the press, and the thousand anecdotes, criticisms, and biographical sketches that are daily poured forth concerning public characters, it is extremely difficult to get at any truth concerning them.

He was always, however, excessively reserved and fastidious on this point, at which I very much wondered, authors in general appearing to think each other fair game, and being ready to serve each other up for the amusement of the public.

A few mornings after hearing the history of the ex manager, I was surprised by a visit from Buckthorne before I was out of bed. He was dressed for travelling.

"Give me joy! give me joy!" said he, rubbing his hands with the utmost glee; "my great expectations are realized!"

I gazed at him with a look of wonder and inquiry.

"My booby cousin is dead!" cried he, "may he rest in peace! He nearly broke his neck in a fall from his horse in a fox chace. By good luck he lived long enough to make his will. He has made me his heir, partly out of an odd feeling of retributive justice, and partly because, as he says, none of his own family or friends know how to enjoy such an estate. I'm off to the country to take possession. I've done with authorship.—That for the critics!" said he, snapping his fingers. "Come down to Doubting Castle when I get settled, and egad I'll give you a rouse." So saying he shook me heartily by the hand and bounded off in high spirits.

A long time elapsed before I heard from him again. Indeed it was but lately that I received a letter written in the happiest of moods. He was getting the estate into fine order; every thing went to his wishes, and what was more, he was married to Sacharissa; who it seems had always entertained an ardent though secret attachment for him, which he fortunately discovered just after coming to his estate.

"I find," said he, "you are a little given to the sin of authorship, which I renounce. If the anecdotes I have given you of my story are of any interest, you may make use of them; but come down to Doubting Castle and see how we live, and I'll give you my whole London life over a social glass; and a rattling history it shall be about authors and reviewers."

If ever I visit Doubting Castle, and get the history he promises, the public shall be sure to hear of it.

PART III
THE ITALIAN BANDITTI

THE INN AT TERRACINA

Crack! crack! crack! crack! crack!

"Here comes the estafette from Naples," said mine host of the inn at Terracina, "bring out the relay."

The estafette came galloping up the road according to custom, brandishing over his head a short handled whip, with a long knotted lash; every smack of which made a report like a pistol. He was a tight square-set young fellow, in the usual uniform—a smart blue coat, ornamented with facings and gold lace, but so short behind as to reach scarcely below his waistband, and cocked up not unlike the tail of a wren. A cocked hat, edged with gold lace; a pair of stiff riding boots; but instead of the usual leathern breeches he had a fragment of a pair of drawers that scarcely furnished an apology for modesty to hide behind.

The estafette galloped up to the door and jumped from his horse.

"A glass of rosolio, a fresh horse, and a pair of breeches," said he, "and quickly—*per l'amor di Dio,* I am behind my time, and must be off."

"San Gennaro!" replied the host, "why, where hast thou left thy garment?"

"Among the robbers between this and Fondi."

"What! rob an estafette! I never heard of such folly. What could they hope to get from thee?"

"My leather breeches!" replied the estafette. "They were bran new, and shone like gold, and hit the fancy of the captain."

"Well, these fellows grow worse and worse. To meddle with an estafette! And that merely for the sake of a pair of leather breeches!"

The robbing of a government messenger seemed to strike the host with more astonishment than any other enormity that had taken place on the road; and indeed it was the first time so wanton an outrage had been committed; the robbers generally taking care not to meddle with any thing belonging to government.

The estafette was by this time equipped; for he had not lost an instant in making his preparations while talking. The relay was ready: the rosolio tossed off. He grasped the reins and the stirrup.

"Were there many robbers in the band?" said a handsome, dark young man, stepping forward from the door of the inn.

"As formidable a band as ever I saw," said the estafette, springing into the saddle.

"Are they cruel to travellers?" said a beautiful young Venetian lady, who had been hanging on the gentleman's arm.

"Cruel, signora!" echoed the estafette, giving a glance at the lady as he put spurs to his horse. "*Corpo di Bacco!* they stiletto all the men, and as to the women——"

Crack! crack! crack! crack! crack!—the last words were drowned in the smacking of the whip, and away galloped the estafette along the road to the Pontine marshes.

"Holy Virgin!" ejaculated the fair Venetian, "what will become of us!"

The inn of which we are speaking stands just outside of the walls of Terracina, under a vast precipitous height of rocks, crowned with the ruins of the castle of Theodoric the Goth. The situation of Terracina is remarkable. It is a little, ancient, lazy Italian town, on the frontiers of the Roman territory. There seems to be an idle pause in every thing about the place. The Mediterranean spreads before it—that sea without flux or reflux. The port is without a sail, excepting that once in a while a solitary felucca may be seen, disgorging its holy cargo of baccala, or codfish, the meagre provision for the Quaresima or Lent. The inhabitants are apparently a listless, heedless race, as people of soft, sunny climates are apt to be; but under this passive, indolent exterior are said to lurk dangerous qualities. They are supposed by many to be little better than the banditti of the neighbouring mountains, and indeed to hold a secret correspondence with them. The solitary watch towers, erected here and there along the coast, speak of pirates and corsairs which hover about these shores: while the low huts, as stations for soldiers, which dot the distant road, as it winds up through an olive grove, intimate that in the ascent there is danger for the traveller and facility for the bandit.

Indeed, it is between this town and Fondi, that the road to Naples is most infested by banditti. It has several winding and solitary places, where the robbers are enabled to see the traveller from a distance, from the brows of hills or impending precipices, and to lie in wait for him, at lonely and difficult passes.

The Italian robbers are a desperate class of men that have almost formed themselves into an order of society. They wear a kind of uniform, or rather costume, which openly designates their profession. This is probably done to diminish its sculking, lawless character, and to give it something of a military air in the eyes of the common people; or, perhaps, to catch by outward show and finery the fancies of the young men of the villages, and thus to gain recruits. Their dresses are often very rich and picturesque. They wear jackets and breeches of bright colours, sometimes gaily embroidered; their breasts are covered with medals and relics; their hats are broad brimmed, with conical crowns, decorated with feathers, or variously coloured ribbands; their hair is sometimes gathered in silk nets; they wear a kind of sandal of cloth or leather, bound round the legs with thongs, and extremely flexible, to enable them to scramble with ease and celerity among the mountain precipices; a broad belt of cloth, or a sash of silk net, is stuck full of pistols and stilettos; a carbine is slung at the back, while about them is generally thrown, in a negligent manner, a great dingy mantle, which serves as a protection in storms, or a bed in their bivouacs among the mountains.

They range over a great extent of wild country, along the chain of Apennines bordering on different states; they know all the difficult passes, the short cuts for retreat, and the impracticable forests of the mountain summits, where no force dare follow them. They are secure of the good will of the inhabitants of those regions, a poor and semi-barbarous race, whom they never disturb and often enrich. Indeed, they are considered as a sort of illegitimate heroes among the mountain villages, and in certain frontier towns, where they dispose of their plunder. Thus countenanced, and sheltered and secure in the fastnesses of their mountains, the robbers have set the weak police of the Italian states at defiance. It is in vain that their names and descriptions are posted on the doors of country churches, and rewards offered for them alive or dead; the villagers are either too much awed by the terrible instances of vengeance inflicted by the Brigands, or have too good an understanding with them to be their betrayers. It is true they are now and then hunted and shot down like beasts of prey by the *gens d'armes*, their heads put in iron cages and stuck upon posts by the road side, or their limbs hung up to blacken in the trees near the places where they have committed their atrocities; but these ghastly spectacles only serve to make some dreary pass of the road still more dreary, and to dismay the traveller without deterring the bandit.

At the time that the estafette made this sudden appearance, almost *in cuerpo*, as has been mentioned, the audacity of the robbers had risen to an unparalleled height. They had laid villas under contribution, they had sent messages into country towns, to tradesmen and rich burghers, demanding supplies of money, of clothing, or even of luxuries, with menaces of vengeance in case of refusal; they had their spies and emissaries in every town, village and inn, along the principal roads, to give them notice of the quality and movements of travellers. They had plundered carriages; carried people of rank and fortune into the mountains and obliged them to write for heavy ransoms; and had committed outrages on females who had fallen into their hands.

Such was briefly the state of the robbers, or rather such was the amount of the rumours prevalent concerning them, when the scene took place at the inn of Terracina. The dark, handsome, young man, and the Venetian lady, incidentally mentioned, had arrived early that afternoon in a private carriage, drawn by mules and attended by a single servant. They had been recently married, were spending the honey moon in travelling through these delicious countries, and were on their way to visit a rich aunt of the bride's at Naples.

The lady was young, and tender and timid. The stories she had heard along the road had filled her with apprehension, not more for herself than for her husband; for though she had been married almost a month, she still loved him almost to idolatry. When she reached Terracina the rumours of

the road had increased to an alarming magnitude; and the sight of two robbers' skulls grinning in iron cages on each side of the old gateway of the town
brought her to a pause. Her husband had tried in vain to reassure her. They
had lingered all the afternoon at the inn, until it was too late to think of
starting that evening, and the parting words of the estafette completed her
affright.

"Let us return to Rome," said she, putting her arm within her husband's,
and drawing towards him as if for protection—"let us return to Rome and
give up this visit to Naples."

"And give up the visit to your aunt, too," said the husband.

"Nay—what is my aunt in comparison with your safety," said she, looking
up tenderly in his face.

There was something in her tone and manner that showed she really was
thinking more of her husband's safety at that moment than of her own; and
being so recently married, and a match of pure affection, too, it is very
possible that she was. At least her husband thought so. Indeed, any one who
has heard the sweet, musical tone of a Venetian voice, and the melting tenderness of a Venetian phrase, and felt the soft witchery of a Venetian eye,
would not wonder at the husband's believing whatever they professed.

He clasped the white hand that had been laid within his, put his arm
round her slender waist, and drawing her fondly to his bosom—"This night
at least," said he, "we will pass at Terracina."

Crack! crack! crack! crack! crack!

Another apparition of the road attracted the attention of mine host and his
guests. From the direction of the Pontine marshes, a carriage drawn by half
a dozen horses, came driving at a furious rate—the postillions smacking their
whips like mad, as is the case when conscious of the greatness or the mu-
nificence of their fare. It was a landaulet, with a servant mounted on the
dickey. The compact, highly finished, yet proudly simple construction of the
carriage; the quantity of neat, well arranged trunks and conveniencies; the
loads of box coats and upper benjamins on the dickey—and the fresh, burly,
gruff looking face at the window, proclaimed at once that it was the equipage
of an Englishman.

"Horses to Fondi," said the Englishman, as the landlord came bowing to
the carriage door.

"Would not his Eccellenza alight and take some refreshment?"

"No—he did not mean to eat until he got to Fondi!"

"But the horses will be some time in getting ready—"

"Ah—that's always the case—nothing but delay in this cursed country."

"If his Eccellenza would only walk into the house——"

"No, no, no!—I tell you no!—I want nothing but horses, and as quick as
possible. John! see that the horses are got ready, and don't let us be kept

here an hour or two. Tell him if we're delayed over the time, I'll lodge a complaint with the postmaster."

John touched his hat, and set off to obey his master's orders, with the taciturn obedience of an English servant. He was a ruddy, round faced fellow, with hair cropped close; a short coat, drab breeches, and long gaiters; and appeared to have almost as much contempt as his master for every thing around him.

In the mean time the Englishman got out of the carriage and walked up and down before the inn, with his hands in his pockets: taking no notice of the crowd of idlers who were gazing at him and his equipage. He was tall, stout, and well made; dressed with neatness and precision, wore a travelling cap of the colour of gingerbread, and had rather an unhappy expression about the corners of his mouth; partly from not having yet made his dinner, and partly from not having been able to get on at a greater rate than seven miles an hour. Not that he had any other cause for haste than an Englishman's usual hurry to get to the end of a journey; or, to use the regular phrase, "to get on."

After some time the servant returned from the stable with as sour a look as his master.

"Are the horses ready, John?"

"No, sir—I never saw such a place. There's no getting any thing done. I think your honour had better step into the house and get something to eat; it will be a long while before we get to Fundy."

"D—n the house—it's a mere trick—I'll not eat any thing, just to spite them," said the Englishman, still more crusty at the prospect of being so long without his dinner.

"They say your honour's very wrong," said John, "to set off at this late hour. The road's full of highwaymen."

"Mere tales to get custom."

"The estafette which passed us was stopped by a whole gang," said John, increasing his emphasis with each additional piece of information.

"I don't believe a word of it."

"They robbed him of his breeches," said John, giving at the same time a hitch to his own waistband.

"All humbug!"

Here the dark, handsome young man stepped forward and addressing the Englishman very politely in broken English, invited him to partake of a repast he was about to make. "Thank'ee," said the Englishman, thrusting his hands deeper into his pockets, and casting a slight side glance of suspicion at the young man, as if he thought from his civility he must have a design upon his purse.

"We shall be most happy if you will do us that favour," said the lady, in her soft Venetian dialect. There was a sweetness in her accents that was most persuasive. The Englishman cast a look upon her countenance; her beauty was still more eloquent. His features instantly relaxed. He made an attempt at a civil bow. "With great pleasure, signora," said he.

In short, the eagerness to "get on" was suddenly slackened; the determination to famish himself as far as Fondi by way of punishing the landlord was abandoned; John chose the best apartment in the inn for his master's reception, and preparations were made to remain there until morning.

The carriage was unpacked of such of its contents as were indispensable for the night. There was the usual parade of trunks, and writing desks, and portfolios, and dressing boxes, and those other oppressive conveniencies which burthen a comfortable man. The observant loiterers about the inn door, wrapped up in great dirt coloured cloaks, with only a hawk's eye uncovered, made many remarks to each other on this quantity of luggage that seemed enough for an army. And the domestics of the inn talked with wonder of the splendid dressing case, with its gold and silver furniture that was spread out on the toilette table, and the bag of gold that chinked as it was taken out of the trunk. The strange "Milor's" wealth, and the treasures he carried about him, were the talk, that evening, over all Terracina.

The Englishman took some time to make his ablutions and arrange his dress for table, and after considerable labour and effort in putting himself at his ease, made his appearance, with stiff white cravat, his clothes free from the least speck of dust, and adjusted with precision. He made a formal bow on entering, which no doubt he meant to be cordial, but which any one else would have considered cool, and took his seat.

The supper, as it was termed by the Italian, or dinner, as the Englishman called it, was now served. Heaven and earth, and the waters under the earth, had been moved to furnish it, for there were birds of the air and beasts of the field and fish of the sea. The Englishman's servant, too, had turned the kitchen topsy turvy in his zeal to cook his master a beefsteak; and made his appearance loaded with ketchup, and soy, and Cayenne pepper, and Harvey sauce, and a bottle of port wine, from that warehouse, the carriage, in which his master seemed desirous of carrying England about the world with him. Every thing, however, according to the Englishman, was execrable. The tureen of soup was a black sea, with livers and limbs and fragments of all kinds of birds and beasts, floating like wrecks about it. A meagre winged animal, which my host called a delicate chicken, was too delicate for his stomach, for it had evidently died of a consumption. The macaroni was smoked. The beefsteak was tough buffalo's flesh, and the countenance of mine host confirmed the assertion. Nothing seemed to hit his palate but a dish of stewed eels, of which he ate with great relish, but had nearly refunded them when told that they were vipers, caught among the rocks of Terracina, and esteemed a great delicacy.

In short, the Englishman ate and growled, and ate and growled, like a cat eating in company, pronouncing himself poisoned by every dish, yet eating on in defiance of death and the doctor. The Venetian lady, not accustomed to English travellers, almost repented having persuaded him to the meal; for though very gracious to her, he was so crusty to all the world beside, that she stood in awe of him. Nothing, however, conquers John Bull's crustiness sooner than eating, whatever may be the cookery; and nothing brings him into good humour with his company sooner than eating together; the Englishman, therefore, had not half finished his repast and his bottle, before he began to think the Venetian a very tolerable fellow for a foreigner, and his wife almost handsome enough to be an Englishwoman.

In the course of the repast the usual topics of travellers were discussed, and among others, the reports of robbers which harassed the mind of the fair Venetian. The landlord and the waiter dipped into the conversation with that familiarity permitted on the continent, and served up so many bloody tales as they served up the dishes, that they almost frightened away the poor lady's appetite. The Englishman, who had a national antipathy to every thing technically called "humbug," listened to them all with a certain screw of the mouth, expressive of incredulity. There was the well known story of the school of Terracina, captured by the robbers; and one of the scholars coolly massacred, in order to bring the parents to terms for the ransom of the rest. And another, of a gentleman of Rome, who received his son's ear in a letter, with information, that his son would be remitted to him in this way, by instalments, until he paid the required ransom.

The fair Venetian shuddered as she heard these tales. The landlord, like a true narrator of the terrible, doubled the dose when he saw how it operated. He was just proceeding to relate the misfortunes of a great English lord and his family, when the Englishman, tired of his volubility, testily interrupted him, and pronounced these accounts mere travellers' tales, or the exaggerations of ignorant peasants and designing innkeepers. The landlord was indignant at the doubt levelled at his stories, and the innuendo levelled at his cloth; he cited, in corroboration, half a dozen tales still more terrible.

"I don't believe a word of them," said the Englishman.

"But the robbers have been tried and executed."

"All a farce!"

"But their heads are stuck up along the road."

"Old skulls accumulated during a century."

The landlord muttered to himself as he went out at the door, "San Gennaro, quanto sono singolari questi Inglesi."

A fresh hubbub outside of the inn announced the arrival of more travellers; and from the variety of voices, or rather clamours, the clattering of hoofs, the rattling of wheels, and the general uproar both within and without, the arrival seemed to be numerous. It was in fact the procaccio, and its convoy—a kind of caravan which sets out on certain days for the transportation of merchandise, with an escort of soldiery to protect it from the robbers. Travellers avail themselves of its protection, and a long file of carriages generally accompany it. A considerable time elapsed before either landlord or waiter returned, being hurried hither and thither by that tempest of noise and bustle which takes place in an Italian inn on the arrival of any considerable accession of custom. When mine host reappeared, there was a smile of triumph on his countenance.—"Perhaps," said he, as he cleared the table, "perhaps the signor has not heard of what has happened."

"What?" said the Englishman, drily.

"Why, the procaccio has brought accounts of fresh exploits of the robbers, signor."

"Pish!"

"There's more news of the English Milor and his family," said the host, exultingly.

"An English lord—What English lord?"

"Milor Popkin."

"Lord Popkins? I never heard of such a title!"

"*O Sicuro*—a great nobleman who passed through here lately with his mi ladi and her daughters—a magnifico—one of the grand councillors of London—un almanno."

"Almanno—almanno?—tut! he means alderman."

"Sicuro, aldermanno Popkin, and the principessa Popkin, and the signorine Popkin!" said mine host, triumphantly. He now put himself into an attitude, and would have launched into a full detail, had he not been thwarted by the Englishman, who seemed determined neither to credit nor indulge him in his stories, but drily motioned for him to clear away the table. An Italian tongue, however, is not easily checked: that of mine host continued to wag with increasing volubility as he conveyed the reliques of the repast out of the room, and the last that could be distinguished of his voice, as it died away along the corridor, was the iteration of the favourite word Popkin—Popkin—Popkin—pop—pop—pop.

The arrival of the procaccio had indeed filled the house with stories as it had with guests. The Englishman and his companions walked after supper up and down the large hall, or common room of the inn, which ran through the centre of the building. It was spacious, and somewhat dirty, with tables placed in various parts, at which groups of travellers were seated; while others strolled about, waiting in famished impatience for their evening's meal.

It was a heterogeneous assemblage of people of all ranks and countries, who had arrived in all kinds of vehicles. Though distinct knots of travellers, yet the travelling together under one common escort had jumbled them into a certain degree of companionship on the road: besides, on the continent travellers are always familiar, and nothing is more motley than the groups which gather casually together in sociable conversation in the public rooms of inns. Their formidable number and the formidable guard of the procaccio had prevented any molestation from banditti; but every party of travellers had its tale of wonder, and one carriage vied with another in its budget of assertions and surmises. Fierce, whiskered faces had been seen peering over the rocks; carbines and stilettos gleaming from among the bushes; suspicious looking fellows, with flapped hats, and scowling eyes, had occasionally reconnoitred a straggling carriage, but had disappeared on seeing the guard.

The fair Venetian listened to all these stories with that avidity with which we always pamper any feeling of alarm. Even the Englishman began to feel interested in the common topic, and desirous of gaining more correct information than mere flying reports. He mingled in one of the groups which appeared to be the most respectable, and which was assembled round a tall thin Italian, with long aquiline nose, a high forehead, and lively prominent eye, beaming from under a green velvet travelling cap, with gold tassel. He was of Rome; a surgeon by profession, a poet by choice, and something of an improvvisatore.

In the present instance, however, he was talking in plain prose, but holding forth with the fluency of one who talks well and likes to exert his talent. A question or two from the Englishman drew copious replies; for an Englishman sociable among strangers is regarded as a phenomenon on the continent, and always treated with attention for the rarity's sake. The improvvisatore gave much the same account of the banditti that I have already furnished.

"But why does not the police exert itself and root them out?" demanded the Englishman.

"Because the police is too weak and the banditti are too strong," replied the other. "To root them out would be a more difficult task than you imagine. They are connected and almost identified with the mountain peasantry and the people of the villages. The numerous bands have an understanding with each other, and with the country round. A *gens d'armes* cannot stir without their being aware of it. They have their scouts every where, who lurk about towns, villages, and inns,—mingle in every crowd, and pervade every place of resort. I should not be surprised if some one should be supervising us at this moment."

The fair Venetian looked round fearfully and turned pale.

Here the improvvisatore was interrupted by a lively Neapolitan lawyer. "By the way," said he, "I recollect a little adventure of a learned doctor, a friend of mine, which happened in this very neighbourhood; not far from the ruins of Theodoric's Castle, which are on the top of those great, rocky heights above the town."

A wish was of course expressed to hear the adventure of the doctor by all excepting the improvvisatore, who being fond of talking and of hearing himself talk, and accustomed moreover to harangue without interruption, looked rather annoyed at being checked when in full career.

The Neapolitan, however, took no notice of his chagrin, but related the following anecdote.

THE ADVENTURE OF THE LITTLE ANTIQUARY

My friend the doctor was a thorough antiquary: a little rusty, musty old fellow, always groping among ruins. He relished a building as you Englishmen relish a cheese,—the more mouldy and crumbling it was, the more it suited his taste. A shell of an old nameless temple, or the cracked walls of a broken down amphitheatre, would throw him into raptures; and he took more delight in these crusts and cheese parings of antiquity than in the best conditioned modern palaces.

He was a curious collector of coins also, and had just gained an accession of wealth that almost turned his brain. He had picked up, for instance, several Roman Consulars, half a Roman As, two Punics, which had doubtless belonged to the soldiers of Hannibal, having been found on the very spot where they had encamped among the Apennines. He had, moreover, one Samnite, struck after the Social War, and a Philistis, a queen that never existed; but above all, he valued himself upon a coin, indescribable to any but the initiated in these matters, bearing a cross on one side, and a pegasus on the other, and which, by some antiquarian logic, the little man adduced as an historical document, illustrating the progress of christianity.

All these precious coins he carried about him in a leathern purse, buried deep in a pocket of his little black breeches.

The last maggot he had taken into his brain was to hunt after the ancient cities of the Pelasgi which are said to exist to this day among the mountains of the Abruzzi; but about which a singular degree of obscurity prevails.* He

---

*Among the many fond speculations of antiquaries is that of the existence of traces of the ancient Pelasgian cities in the Apennines; and many a wistful eye is cast by the traveller, versed in antiquarian lore, at the richly wooded mountains of the Abruzzi, as a forbidden fairy land of research. These spots, so beautiful yet so inaccessible, from the rudeness of their inhabitants and the hordes of banditti which infest them, are a region of fable to the learned. Sometimes a wealthy virtuoso, whose purse and whose consequence could command a military escort, has penetrated to some individual point among the mountains; and sometimes a wandering artist or student, under protection of poverty or insignificance, has

had made many discoveries concerning them, and had recorded a great many valuable notes and memorandums on the subject, in a voluminous book, which he always carried about with him, either for the purpose of frequent reference, or through fear lest the precious document should fall into the hands of brother antiquaries. He had therefore a large pocket in the skirt of his coat, where he bore about this inestimable tome, banging against his rear as he walked.

Thus heavily laden with the spoils of antiquity, the good little man, during a sojourn at Terracina, mounted one day the rocky cliffs which overhang the town, to visit the castle of Theodoric. He was groping about these ruins, towards the hour of sunset, buried in his reflections,—his wits no doubt wool gathering among the Goths and Romans, when he heard footsteps behind him.

He turned and beheld five or six young fellows, of rough, saucy demeanour, clad in a singular manner, half peasant, half huntsman, with carbines in their hands. Their whole appearance and carriage left him no doubt into what company he had fallen.

The doctor was a feeble little man, poor in look and poorer in purse. He had but little gold or silver to be robbed of; but then he had his curious ancient coin in his breeches pocket. He had, moreover, certain other valuables, such as an old silver watch, thick as a turnip, with figures on it large enough for a clock, and a set of seals at the end of a steel chain, dangling half way down to his knees. All these were of precious esteem, being family reliques. He had also a seal ring, a veritable antique intaglio, that covered

---

brought away some vague account, only calculated to give a keener edge to curiosity and conjecture.

By those who maintain the existence of the Pelasgian cities, it is affirmed, that the formation of the different kingdoms in the Peloponnesus gradually caused the expulsion thence of the Pelasgi; but that their great migration may be dated from the finishing the wall round Acropolis, and that at this period they came into Italy. To these, in the spirit of theory, they would ascribe the introduction of the elegant arts into the country. It is evident, however, that, as barbarians flying before the first dawn of civilization, they could bring little with them superior to the inventions of the aborigines, and nothing that would have survived to the antiquarian through such a lapse of ages. It would appear more probable, that these cities, improperly termed Pelasgian, were coeval with many that have been discovered. The romantic Aricia, built by Hippolytus before the siege of Troy, and the poetic Tibur, Æsculate and Proenes, built by Telegonus after the dispersion of the Greeks. These, lying contiguous to inhabited and cultivated spots, have been discovered. There are others, too, on the ruins of which the later and more civilized Grecian colonists have engrafted themselves, and which have become known by their merits or their medals. But that there are many still undiscovered, imbedded in the Abruzzi, it is the delight of the antiquarians to fancy. Strange that such a virgin soil for research, such an unknown realm of knowledge, should at this day remain in the very centre of hackneyed Italy!

half his knuckles. It was a Venus, which the old man almost worshipped with the zeal of a voluptuary. But what he most valued was, his inestimable collection of hints relative to the Pelasgian cities, which he would gladly have given all the money in his pocket to have had safe at the bottom of his trunk in Terracina.

However, he plucked up a stout heart; at least as stout a heart as he could, seeing that he was but a puny little man at the best of times. So, he wished the hunters a "buon giorno." They returned his salutation, giving the old gentleman a sociable slap on the back that made his heart leap into his throat.

They fell into conversation, and walked for some time together among the heights, the doctor wishing them all the while at the bottom of the crater of Vesuvius. At length they came to a small osteria on the mountain, where they proposed to enter and have a cup of wine together. The doctor consented; though he would as soon have been invited to drink hemlock.

One of the gang remained sentinel at the door; the others swaggered into the house; stood their guns in a corner of the room; and each drawing a pistol or stiletto out of his belt, laid it upon the table. They now drew benches round the board, called lustily for wine, and hailing the doctor as though he had been a boon companion of long standing, insisted upon his sitting down and making merry. The worthy man complied with forced grimace, but with fear and trembling; sitting uneasily on the edge of his chair; eyeing ruefully the black muzzled pistols, and cold, naked stilettos; and supping down heartburn with every drop of liquor. His new comrades, however, pushed the bottle bravely, and plied him vigorously; they sang, they laughed, told excellent stories of their robberies and combats, mingled with many ruffian jokes; and the little doctor was fain to laugh at all their cut-throat pleasantries, though his heart was dying away at the very bottom of his bosom.

By their own account they were young men from the villages, who had recently taken up this line of life out of the wild caprice of youth. They talked of their murderous exploits as a sportsman talks of his amusements. To shoot down a traveller seemed of little more consequence to them than to shoot a hare. They spoke with rapture of the glorious roving life they led; free as birds; here today, gone tomorrow; ranging the forests, climbing the rocks, scouring the valleys; the world their own wherever they could lay hold of it; full purses, merry companions; pretty women.——The little antiquary got fuddled with their talk and their wine, for they did not spare bumpers. He half forgot his fears, his seal ring and his family watch; even the treatise on the Pelasgian cities which was warming under him, for a time faded from his memory, in the glowing picture which they drew. He declares that he no longer wonders at the prevalence of this robber mania among the mountains; for he felt at the time, that had he been a young man and a strong man, and had there been no danger of the galleys in the back ground, he should have been half tempted himself to turn bandit.

At length the hour of separating arrived. The doctor was suddenly called to himself and his fears, by seeing the robbers resume their weapons. He now quaked for his valuables, and above all for his antiquarian treatise. He endeavoured, however, to look cool and unconcerned; and drew from out of his deep pocket a long, lank, leathern purse, far gone in consumption, at the bottom of which a few coin chinked with the trembling of his hand.

The chief of the party observed this movement; and laying his hand upon the antiquary's shoulder—"Harkee! Signor Dottore!" said he, "we have drunk together as friends and comrades, let us part as such. We understand you; we know who and what you are; for we know who every body is that sleeps at Terracina, or that puts foot upon the road. You are a rich man, but you carry all your wealth in your head. We cannot get at it, and we should not know what to do with it, if we could. I see you are uneasy about your ring; but don't worry yourself; it is not worth taking; you think it an antique, but it's a counterfeit—a mere sham."

Here the ire of the antiquary arose: the doctor forgot himself in his zeal for the character of his ring. Heaven and earth! his Venus a sham! Had they pronounced the wife of his bosom "no better than she should be," he could not have been more indignant. He fired up in vindication of his intaglio.

"Nay, nay," continued the robber, "we have no time to dispute about it. Value it as you please. Come, you're a brave little old signor—one more cup of wine and we'll pay the reckoning. No compliments—You shall not pay a grain—You are our guest—I insist upon it. So—now make the best of your way back to Terracina; it's growing late—buono viaggio!—and hark'ee, take care how you wander among these mountains,—you may not always fall into such good company."

They shouldered their guns, sprang gaily up the rocks, and the little doctor hobbled back to Terracina, rejoicing that the robbers had left his watch, his coins, and his treatise unmolested, but still indignant that they should have pronounced his Venus an imposter

---

The improvvisatore had shown many symptoms of impatience during this recital. He saw his theme in danger of being taken out of his hands, which to an able talker is always a grievance; but to an improvvisatore is an absolute calamity: and then for it to be taken away by a Neapolitan was still more vexatious; the inhabitants of the different Italian states having an implacable jealousy of each other in all things, great and small. He took advantage of the first pause of the Neapolitan to catch hold again of the thread of the conversation.

"As I observed before," said he, "the prowlings of the banditti are so extensive; they are so much in league with one another, and so interwoven with various ranks of society"——

"For that matter," said the Neapolitan, "I have heard that your government has had some understanding with these gentry, or at least has winked at their misdeeds."

"My government?" said the Roman, impatiently.

"Aye—they say that Cardinal Gonsalvi"——

"Hush!" said the Roman, holding up his finger, and rolling his large eyes about the room.

"Nay—I only repeat what I heard commonly rumoured in Rome," replied the Neapolitan, sturdily. "It was openly said that the Cardinal had been up to the mountains, and had an interview with some of the chiefs. And I have been told, moreover, that while honest people have been kicking their heels in the Cardinal's anti-chamber, waiting by the hour for admittance, one of these stiletto looking fellows has elbowed his way through the crowd, and entered without ceremony into the Cardinal's presence."

"I know," observed the improvvisatore, "that there have been such reports; and it is not impossible that government may have made use of these men at particular periods, such as at the time of your late abortive revolution, when your carbonari were so busy with their machinations all over the country. The information which such men could collect, who were familiar, not merely with the recesses and secret places of the mountains, but also with the dark and dangerous recesses of society, who knew every suspicious character, and all his movements and all his lurkings; in a word, who knew all that was plotting in the world of mischief; the utility of such men as instruments in the hands of government was too obvious to be overlooked, and Cardinal Gonsalvi as a politic statesman may perhaps have made use of them. Besides, he knew that with all their atrocities the robbers were always respectful towards the church, and devout in their religion."

"Religion!—religion?" echoed the Englishman.

"Yes—religion!" repeated the Roman. "They have each their patron saint. They will cross themselves and say their prayers, whenever, in their mountain haunts, they hear the matin or the *ave maria* bells sounding from the valleys; and will often descend from their retreats, and run imminent risks to visit some favourite shrine. I recollect an instance in point: I was one evening in the village of Frascati, which stands on the beautiful brow of hills rising from the Campagna, just below the Abruzzi mountains. The people, as is usual in fine evenings in our Italian towns and villages, were recreating themselves in the open air, and chatting in groups in the public square. While I was conversing with a knot of friends, I noticed a tall fellow, wrapped in a great mantle, passing across the square, but skulking along in the dusk, as if anxious to avoid observation. The people drew back as he passed. It was whispered to me that he was a notorious bandit."

"But why was he not immediately siezed?" said the Englishman.

"Because it was nobody's business; because nobody wished to incur the vengeance of his comrades; because there were not sufficient *gens d'armes* near to insure security against the numbers of desperadoes he might have at hand; because the *gens d'armes* might not have received particular instructions with respect to him, and might not feel disposed to engage in a hazardous conflict without compulsion. In short, I might give you a thousand reasons, rising out of the state of our government and manners, not one of which after all might appear satisfactory."

The Englishman shrugged his shoulders, with an air of contempt.

"I have been told," added the Roman, rather quickly, "that even in your metropolis of London, notorious thieves, well known to the police as such, walk the streets at noon day, in search of their prey, and are not molested unless caught in the very act of robbery."

The Englishman gave another shrug, but with a different expression.

"Well, sir, I fixed my eye on this daring wolf thus prowling through the fold, and saw him enter a church. I was curious to witness his devotions. You know our spacious, magnificent churches. The one in which he entered was vast and shrouded in the dusk of evening. At the extremity of the long aisles a couple of tapers feebly glimmered on the grand altar. In one of the side chapels was a votive candle placed before the image of a saint. Before this image the robber had prostrated himself. His mantle partly falling off from his shoulders as he knelt, revealed a form of Herculean strength; a stiletto and pistol glittered in his belt, and the light falling on his countenance showed features not unhandsome, but strongly and fiercely charactered. As he prayed he became vehemently agitated; his lips quivered; sighs and murmurs, almost groans burst from him; he beat his breast with violence, then clasped his hands and wrung them convulsively as he extended them towards the image. Never had I seen such a terrific picture of remorse. I felt fearful of being discovered watching him, and withdrew. Shortly afterwards I saw him issue from the church, wrapped in his mantle; he recrossed the square, and no doubt returned to his mountain with disburthened conscience, ready to incur a fresh arrear of crime."

Here the Neapolitan was about to get hold of the conversation, and had just preluded with the ominous remark, "That puts me in mind of a circumstance," when the improvvisatore, too adroit to suffer himself to be again superseded, went on, pretending not to hear the interruption.

"Among the many circumstances connected with the banditti which serve to render the traveller uneasy and insecure, is the understanding which they sometimes have with innkeepers. Many an isolated inn among the lonely parts of the Roman territories, and especially about the mountains, are of a dangerous and perfidious character. They are places where the banditti gather information, and where the unwary traveller, remote from hearing or assistance, is betrayed to the midnight dagger. The robberies committed at such inns are often accompanied by the most atrocious murders; for it is only by the complete extermination of their victims that the assassins can escape detection. I recollect an adventure," added he, "which occurred at one of these solitary mountain inns, which, as you all seem in a mood for robber anecdotes, may not be uninteresting."

Having secured the attention and awakened the curiosity of the bystanders, he paused for a moment, rolled up his large eyes as improvvisatori are apt to do when they would recollect an impromptu, and then related with great dramatic effect the following story, which had, doubtless, been well prepared and digested beforehand.

THE BELATED TRAVELLERS

It was late one evening that a carriage, drawn by mules, slowly toiled its way up one of the passes of the Apennines. It was through one of the wildest defiles, where a hamlet occurred only at distant intervals, perched on the summit of some rocky height, or the white towers of a convent peeped out from among the thick mountain foliage. The carriage was of ancient and ponderous construction. Its faded embellishments spoke of former splendor, but its crazy springs and axletrees creaked out the tale of present decline. Within was seated a tall, thin old gentleman, in a kind of military travelling dress, and a foraging cap trimmed with fur, though the grey locks which stole from under it hinted that his fighting days were over. Beside him was a pale, beautiful girl of eighteen, dressed in something of a northern or Polish costume. One servant was seated in front, a rusty, crusty looking fellow, with a scar across his face; an orange-tawny *schnur-bart,* or pair of mustachios, bristling from under his nose, and altogether the air of an old soldier.

It was, in fact, the equipage of a Polish nobleman; a wreck of one of those princely families once of almost oriental magnificence, but broken down and impoverished by the disasters of Poland. The Count, like many other generous spirits, had been found guilty of the crime of patriotism, and was, in a manner, an exile from his country. He had resided for some time in the first cities of Italy for the education of his daughter, in whom all his cares and pleasures were now centred. He had taken her into society, where her beauty and her accomplishments gained her many admirers; and had she not been the daughter of a poor broken down Polish nobleman, it is more than probable many would have contended for her hand. Suddenly, however, her health became delicate and drooping; her gaiety fled with the roses of her cheek, and she sank into silence and debility. The old Count saw the change with the solicitude of a parent. "We must try a change of air and scene," said he; and in a few days the old family carriage was rumbling among the Apennines.

Their only attendant was the veteran Caspar, who had been born in the family, and grown rusty in its service. He had followed his master in all his fortunes; had fought by his side; had stood over him when fallen in battle; and had received, in his defence, the sabre cut which added such grimness to his countenance. He was now his valet, his steward, his butler, his factotum. The only being that rivalled his master in his affections was his youthful mistress; she had grown up under his eye. He had led her by the hand when she was a child, and he now looked upon her with the fondness of a parent; nay, he even took the freedom of a parent in giving his blunt opinion on all matters which he thought were for her good; and felt a parent's vanity in seeing her gazed at and admired.

The evening was thickening: they had been for some time passing through narrow gorges of the mountains, along the edge of a tumbling stream. The scenery was lonely and savage. The rocks often beetled over the road, with flocks of white goats browsing on their brinks, and gazing down upon the travellers. They had between two and three leagues yet to go before they could reach any village; yet the muleteer, Pietro, a tippling old fellow, who had refreshed himself at the last halting place with a more than ordinary quantity of wine, sat singing and talking alternately to his mules, and suffering them to lag on at a snail's pace, in spite of the frequent entreaties of the Count and maledictions of Caspar.

The clouds began to roll in heavy masses among the mountains, shrouding their summits from view. The air was damp and chilly. The Count's solicitude on his daughter's account overcame his usual patience. He leaned from the carriage, and called to old Pietro in an angry tone.

"Forward!" said he. "It will be midnight before we arrive at our inn."

"Yonder it is, Signor," said the muleteer.

"Where?" demanded the Count.

"Yonder," said Pietro, pointing to a desolate pile about a quarter of a league distant.

"That the place?—why, it looks more like a ruin than an inn. I thought we were to put up for the night at a comfortable village."

Here Pietro uttered a string of piteous exclamations and ejaculations, such as are ever at the tip of the tongue of a delinquent muleteer. "Such roads! and such mountains! and then his poor animals were wayworn, and leg weary; they would fall lame; they would never be able to reach the village. And then what could his Eccellenza wish for better than the inn; a perfect castello—a palazza—and such people!—and such a larder!—and such beds!—His Eccellenza might fare as sumptuously and sleep as soundly there as a prince!"

The Count was easily persuaded, for he was anxious to get his daughter out of the night air; so in a little while the old carriage rattled and jingled into the great gateway of the inn.

The building did certainly in some measure answer to the muleteer's description. It was large enough for either castle or palazza; built in a strong, but simple and almost rude style; with a great quantity of waste room. It had, in fact, been, in former times, a hunting seat for one of the Italian princes. There was space enough within its walls and outbuildings to have accommodated a little army.

A scanty household seemed now to people this dreary mansion. The faces that presented themselves on the arrival of the travellers were begrimed with dirt, and scowling in their expression. They all knew old Pietro, however, and gave him a welcome as he entered, singing and talking, and almost whooping, into the gateway.

The hostess of the inn waited herself on the Count and his daughter, to show them the apartments. They were conducted through a long gloomy corridor, and then through a suite of chambers opening into each other, with lofty ceilings, and great beams extending across them. Every thing, however, had a wretched, squalid look. The walls were damp and bare, excepting that here and there hung some great painting, large enough for a chapel, and blackened out of all distinctness.

They chose two bedrooms, one within another; the inner one for the daughter. The bedsteads were massive and misshapen; but on examining the beds, so vaunted by old Pietro, they found them stuffed with fibres of hemp, knotted in great lumps. The Count shrugged his shoulders, but there was no choice left.

The chilliness of the apartments crept to their bones; and they were glad to return to a common chamber, or kind of hall, where there was a fire burning in a huge cavern, miscalled a chimney. A quantity of green wood, just thrown on, puffed out volumes of smoke. The room corresponded to the rest of the mansion. The floor was paved and dirty. A great oaken table stood in the centre, immoveable from its size and weight.

The only thing that contradicted this prevalent air of indigence was the dress of the hostess. She was a slattern of course; yet her garments, though dirty and negligent, were of costly materials. She wore several rings of great value on her fingers, and jewels in her ears, and round her neck was a string of large pearls, to which was attached a sparkling crucifix. She had the re-

mains of beauty; yet there was something in the expression of her countenance that inspired the young lady with singular aversion. She was officious
and obsequious in her attentions, and both the Count and his daughter were
relieved when she consigned them to the care of a dark, sullen looking servant maid, and went off to superintend the supper.

Caspar was indignant at the muleteer for having, either through negli-
gence or design, subjected his master and mistress to such quarters; and
vowed by his mustachios to have revenge on the old varlet the moment they
were safe out from among the mountains. He kept up a continual quarrel
with the sulky servant maid, which only served to increase the sinister
expression with which she regarded the travellers, from under her strong
dark eyebrows.

As to the Count, he was a good humoured, passive traveller. Perhaps real
misfortunes had subdued his spirit, and rendered him tolerant of many of
those petty evils which make prosperous men miserable. He drew a large,
broken arm chair to the fireside for his daughter, and another for himself,
and seizing an enormous pair of tongs, endeavoured to rearrange the wood
so as to produce a blaze. His efforts, however, were only repaid by thicker
puffs of smoke, which almost overcame the good gentleman's patience. He
would draw back, cast a look upon his delicate daughter, then upon the
cheerless, squalid apartment, and shrugging his shoulders, would give a
fresh stir to the fire.

Of all the miseries of a comfortless inn, however, there is none greater
than sulky attendance: the good Count for some time bore the smoke in
silence, rather than address himself to the scowling servant maid. At length
he was compelled to beg for drier firewood. The woman retired muttering.
On re-entering the room hastily, with an armful of faggots, her foot slipped;
she fell, and striking her head against the corner of a chair, cut her temple
severely. The blow stunned her for a time, and the wound bled profusely.
When she recovered, she found the Count's daughter administering to her
wound, and binding it up with her own handkerchief. It was such an attention as any woman of ordinary feeling would have yielded; but perhaps there
was something in the appearance of the lovely being who bent over her, or
in the tones of her voice, that touched the heart of the woman, unused to
be ministered to by such hands. Certain it is, she was strongly affected. She
caught the delicate hand of the Polonaise, and pressed it fervently to her
lips:

"May San Francesco watch over you, Signora!" exclaimed she.

A new arrival broke the stillness of the inn. It was a Spanish princess with
a numerous retinue. The court yard was in an uproar; the house in a bustle;
the landlady hurried to attend such distinguished guests; and the poor Count
and his daughter, and their supper, were for the moment forgotten. The

veteran Caspar muttered Polish maledictions enough to agonize an Italian ear; but it was impossible to convince the hostess of the superiority of his old master and young mistress to the whole nobility of Spain.

The noise of the arrival had attracted the daughter to the window just as the new comers had alighted. A young cavalier sprang out of the carriage, and handed out the princess. The latter was a little shrivelled old lady, with a face of parchment, and a sparkling black eye; she was richly and gaily dressed, and walked with the assistance of a gold headed cane as high as herself. The young man was tall and elegantly formed. The Count's daughter shrunk back at sight of him, though the deep frame of the window screened her from observation. She gave a heavy sigh as she closed the casement. What that sigh meant I cannot say. Perhaps it was at the contrast between the splendid equipage of the princess, and the crazy, rheumatic looking old vehicle of her father, which stood hard by. Whatever might be the reason, the young lady closed the casement with a sigh. She returned to her chair;— a slight shivering passed over her delicate frame; she leaned her elbow on the arm of the chair; rested her pale cheek in the palm of her hand, and looked mournfully into the fire.

The Count thought she appeared paler than usual.—

"Does any thing ail thee, my child?" said he.

"Nothing, dear father!" replied she, laying her hand within his, and looking up smiling in his face; but as she said so, a treacherous tear rose suddenly to her eye, and she turned away her head.

"The air of the window has chilled thee," said the Count, fondly, "but a good night's rest will make all well again."

The supper table was at length laid, and the supper about to be served, when the hostess appeared, with her usual obsequiousness, apologizing for showing in the new comers; but the night air was cold, and there was no other chamber in the inn with a fire in it.—She had scarcely made the apology when the Princess entered, leaning on the arm of the elegant young man.

The Count immediately recognized her for a lady whom he had met frequently in society both at Rome and Naples; and at whose conversaziones, in fact, he had constantly been invited. The cavalier, too, was her nephew and heir, who had been greatly admired in the gay circles both for his merits and prospects, and who had once been on a visit at the same time with his daughter and himself at the villa of a nobleman near Naples. Report had recently affianced him to a rich Spanish heiress.

The meeting was agreeable to both the Count and the Princess. The former was a gentleman of the old school, courteous in the extreme; the Princess had been a belle in her youth, and a woman of fashion all her life, and liked to be attended to.

The young man approached the daughter, and began something of a complimentary observation; but his manner was embarrassed, and his compliment ended in an indistinct murmur, while the daughter bowed without looking up, moved her lips without articulating a word, and sank again into her chair, where she sat gazing into the fire, with a thousand varying expressions passing over her countenance.

This singular greeting of the young people was not perceived by the old ones, who were occupied at the time with their own courteous salutations. It was arranged that they should sup together; and as the Princess travelled with her own cook, a very tolerable supper soon smoked upon the board; this, too, was assisted by choice wines, and liqueurs, and delicate confitures brought from one of her carriages; for she was a veteran epicure, and curious in her relish for the good things of this world. She was, in fact, a vivacious little old lady, who mingled the woman of dissipation with the devotee. She was actually on her way to Loretto to expiate a long life of gallantries and peccadilloes by a rich offering at the holy shrine. She was, to be sure, rather a luxurious penitent, and a contrast to the primitive pilgrims, with scrip, and staff, and cockleshell; but then it would be unreasonable to expect such self denial from people of fashion; and there was not a doubt of the ample efficacy of the rich crucifixes, and golden vessels, and jewelled ornaments, which she was bearing to the treasury of the blessed Virgin.

The Princess and the Count chatted much during supper about the scenes and society in which they had mingled, and did not notice that they had all the conversation to themselves: the young people were silent and con strained. The daughter ate nothing, in spite of the politeness of the Princess, who continually pressed her to taste one or other of the delicacies. The Count shook his head:

"She is not well this evening," said he. "I thought she would have fainted just now as she was looking out of the window at your carriage on its arrival."

A crimson glow flushed to the very temples of the daughter; but she leaned over her plate, and her tresses cast a shade over her countenance.

When supper was over, they drew their chairs about the great fireplace. The flame and smoke had subsided, and a heap of glowing embers diffused a grateful warmth. A guitar, which had been brought from the Count's carriage, leaned against the wall; the Princess perceived it: "Can we not have a little music before parting for the night?" demanded she.

The Count was proud of his daughter's accomplishment, and joined in the request. The young man made an effort of politeness, and taking up the guitar presented it, though in an embarrassed manner, to the fair musician. She would have declined it, but was too much confused to do so; indeed, she was so nervous and agitated, that she dared not trust her voice to make an excuse. She touched the instrument with a faltering hand, and, after preluding a little, accompanied herself in several Polish airs. Her father's eyes glistened as he sat gazing on her. Even the crusty Caspar lingered in the room, partly through a fondness for the music of his native country, but chiefly through his pride in the musician. Indeed, the melody of the voice, and the delicacy of the touch, were enough to have charmed more fastidious ears. The little Princess nodded her head and tapped her hand to the music, though exceedingly out of time; while the nephew sat buried in profound contemplation of a black picture on the opposite wall.

"And now," said the Count, patting her cheek fondly, "one more favour. Let the princess hear that little Spanish air you were so fond of. You can't think," added he, "what a proficiency she made in your language; though she has been a sad girl and neglected it of late."

The colour flushed the pale cheek of the daughter; she hesitated, murmured something; but with sudden effort collected herself, struck the guitar boldly, and began. It was a Spanish romance, with something of love and melancholy in it. She gave the first stanza with great expression, for the tremulous, melting tones of her voice went to the heart; but her articulation failed, her lip quivered, the song died away, and she burst into tears.

The Count folded her tenderly in his arms. "Thou art not well, my child," said he, "and I am tasking thee cruelly. Retire to thy chamber, and God bless thee!" She bowed to the company without raising her eyes, and glided out of the room.

The Count shook his head as the door closed. "Something is the matter with that child," said he, "which I cannot divine. She has lost all health and spirits lately. She was always a tender flower, and I had much pains to rear her. Excuse a father's foolishness," continued he, "but I have seen much trouble in my family; and this poor girl is all that is now left to me; and she used to be so lively—"

"May be she's in love!" said the little Princess, with a shrewd nod of the head.

"Impossible!" replied the good Count artlessly. "She has never mentioned a word of such a thing to me."

How little did the worthy gentleman dream of the thousand cares, and griefs, and mighty love concerns which agitate a virgin heart, and which a timid girl scarce breathes unto herself.

The nephew of the Princess rose abruptly and walked about the room.

When she found herself alone in her chamber, the feelings of the young lady, so long restrained, broke forth with violence. She opened the casement, that the cool air might blow upon her throbbing temples. Perhaps there was some little pride or pique mingled with her emotions; though her gentle nature did not seem calculated to harbour any such angry inmate.

"He saw me weep!" said she, with a sudden mantling of the cheek, and a swelling of the throat,—"but no matter!—no matter!"

And so saying, she threw her white arms across the window frame, buried her face in them, and abandoned herself to an agony of tears. She remained lost in a reverie, until the sound of her father's and Caspar's voices in the adjoining room gave token that the party had retired for the night. The lights gleaming from window to window, showed that they were conducting the Princess to her apartments, which were in the opposite wing of the inn; and she distinctly saw the figure of the nephew as he passed one of the casements.

She heaved a deep heart-drawn sigh, and was about to close the lattice, when her attention was caught by words spoken below her window by two persons who had just turned an angle of the building.

"But what will become of the poor young lady?" said a voice, which she recognized for that of the servant woman.

"Pooh! she must take her chance," was the reply from old Pietro.

"But cannot she be spared?" asked the other entreatingly; "she's so kind hearted!"

"Cospetto! what has got into thee?" replied the other petulantly: "would you mar the whole business for the sake of a silly girl?" By this time they had got so far from the window that the Polonaise could hear nothing further.

There was something in this fragment of conversation calculated to alarm. Did it relate to herself?—and if so, what was this impending danger from which it was entreated that she might be spared? She was several times on the point of tapping at her father's door, to tell him what she had heard; but she might have been mistaken; she might have heard indistinctly; the conversation might have alluded to some one else; at any rate it was too indefinite to lead to any conclusion. While in this state of irresolution, she was startled by a low knocking against the wainscot in a remote part of her gloomy chamber. On holding up the light, she beheld a small door there, which she had not before remarked. It was bolted on the inside. She advanced, and demanded who knocked, and was answered in the voice of the female domestic. On opening the door, the woman stood before it pale and agitated. She entered softly, laying her finger on her lips in sign of caution and secrecy.

"Fly!" said she: "leave this house instantly, or you are lost!"

The young lady, trembling with alarm, demanded an explanation.

"I have no time," replied the woman, "I dare not—I shall be missed if I linger here—but fly instantly, or you are lost."

"And leave my father?"

"Where is he?"

"In the adjoining chamber."

"Call him, then, but lose no time."

The young lady knocked at her father's door. He was not yet retired to bed. She hurried into his room, and told him of the fearful warning she had received. The Count returned with her into her chamber, followed by Caspar. His questions soon drew the truth out of the embarrassed answers of the woman. The inn was beset by robbers. They were to be introduced after midnight, when the attendants of the Princess and the rest of the travellers were sleeping, and would be an easy prey.

"But we can barricado the inn, we can defend ourselves," said the Count.

"What! when the people of the inn were in league with the banditti?"

"How then are we to escape? Can we not order out the carriage and depart?"

"San Francesco! for what? To give the alarm that the plot is discovered? That would make the robbers desperate, and bring them on you at once. They have had notice of the rich booty in the inn, and will not easily let it escape them."

"But how else are we to get off?"

"There is a horse behind the inn," said the woman, "from which the man has just dismounted who has been to summon the aid of a part of the band at a distance."

"One horse! and there are three of us!" said the Count.

"And the Spanish Princess!" cried the daughter anxiously—"How can she be extricated from the danger?"

"Diavolo! what is she to me?" said the woman in sudden passion. "It is *you* I come to save, and you will betray me, and we shall all be lost! Hark!" continued she, "I am called—I shall be discovered—one word more. This door leads by a staircase to the court yard. Under the shed, in the rear of the yard, is a small door leading out to the fields. You will find a horse there; mount it; make a circuit under the shadow of a ridge of rocks that you will see; proceed cautiously and quietly until you cross a brook, and find yourself on the road just where there are three white crosses nailed against a tree; then put your horse to his speed, and make the best of your way to the village—but recollect, my life is in your hands—say nothing of what you have heard or seen, whatever may happen at this inn."

The woman hurried away. A short and agitated consultation took place between the Count, his daughter, and the veteran Caspar. The young lady seemed to have lost all apprehension for herself in her solicitude for the safety of the Princess. "To fly in selfish silence, and leave her to be massacred!"—A shuddering seized her at the very thought. The gallantry of the Count, too, revolted at the idea. He could not consent to turn his back upon a party of helpless travellers, and leave them in ignorance of the danger which hung over them.

"But what is to become of the young lady," said Caspar, "if the alarm is given, and the inn thrown in a tumult? What may happen to her in a chance medley affray?"

Here the feelings of the father were roused: he looked upon his lovely, helpless child, and trembled at the chance of her falling into the hands of ruffians.

The daughter, however, thought nothing of herself. "The Princess! the Princess!—only let the Princess know her danger."—She was willing to share it with her.

At length Caspar interfered with the zeal of a faithful old servant. No time was to be lost—the first thing was to get the young lady out of danger. "Mount the horse," said he to the Count, "take her behind you, and fly! Make for the village, rouse the inhabitants, and send assistance. Leave me here to give the alarm to the Princess and her people. I am an old soldier, and I think we shall be able to stand siege until you send us aid."

The daughter would again have insisted on staying with the Princess—

"For what?" said old Caspar, bluntly, "You could do no good—You would be in the way—We should have to take care of you instead of ourselves."

There was no answering these objections: the Count seized his pistols, and taking his daughter under his arm, moved towards the staircase. The young lady paused, stepped back, and said, faltering with agitation—"There is a young cavalier with the Princess—her nephew—perhaps he may—"

"I understand you, Mademoiselle," replied old Caspar with a significant nod; "not a hair of his head shall suffer harm if I can help it!"

The young lady blushed deeper than ever: she had not anticipated being so thoroughly understood by the blunt old servant.

"That is not what I mean," said she, hesitating. She would have added something, or made some explanation, but the moments were precious, and her father hurried her away.

They found their way through the court yard to the small postern gate, where the horse stood, fastened to a ring in the wall. The Count mounted, took his daughter behind him, and they proceeded as quietly as possible in the direction which the woman had pointed out. Many a fearful and an anxious look did the daughter cast back upon the gloomy pile: the lights which had feebly twinkled through the dusty casements were one by one disappearing, a sign that the inmates were gradually sinking to repose; and she trembled with impatience, lest succour should not arrive until that repose had been fatally interrupted.

They passed silently and safely along the skirts of the rocks, protected from observation by their overhanging shadows. They crossed the brook, and reached the place where three white crosses nailed against a tree told of some murder that had been committed there. Just as they had reached this ill omened spot they beheld several men in the gloom coming down a craggy defile among the rocks.

"Who goes there?" exclaimed a voice. The Count put spurs to his horse, but one of the men sprang forward and seized the bridle. The horse started back, and reared, and had not the young lady clung to her father, she would have been thrown off. The Count leaned forward, put a pistol to the very head of the ruffian, and fired. The latter fell dead. The horse sprang forward. Two or three shots were fired which whistled by the fugitives, but only served to augment their speed. They reached the village in safety.

The whole place was soon roused: but such was the awe in which the banditti were held, that the inhabitants shrunk at the idea of encountering them. A desperate band had for some time infested that pass through the mountains, and the inn had long been suspected of being one of those horrible places where the unsuspicious wayfarer is entrapped and silently disposed of. The rich ornaments worn by the slattern hostess of the inn had excited heavy suspicions. Several instances had occurred of small parties of travellers disappearing mysteriously on that road, who it was supposed, at first, had been carried off by the robbers for the purpose of ransom, but who had never been heard of more. Such were the tales buzzed in the ears of the Count by the villagers as he endeavoured to rouse them to the rescue of the princess and her train from their perilous situation. The daughter seconded the exertions of her father with all the eloquence of prayers, and tears, and beauty. Every moment that elapsed increased her anxiety until it became agonizing. Fortunately, there was a body of gens d'armes resting at the village. A number of the young villagers volunteered to accompany them, and the little army was put in motion. The Count having deposited his daughter in a place of safety, was too much of the old soldier not to hasten to the scene of danger. It would be difficult to paint the anxious agitation of the young lady while awaiting the result.

The party arrived at the inn just in time. The robbers, finding their plans discovered, and the travellers prepared for their reception, had become open and furious in their attack. The Princess's party had barricadoed themselves in one suite of apartments, and repulsed the robbers from the doors and windows. Caspar had shown the generalship of a veteran, and the nephew of the Princess the dashing valour of a young soldier. Their ammunition, however, was nearly exhausted, and they would have found it difficult to hold out much longer, when a discharge from the musketry of the gens d'armes gave them the joyful tidings of succour.

A fierce fight ensued, for part of the robbers were surprised in the inn, and had to stand siege in their turn; while their comrades made desperate attempts to relieve them from under cover of the neighbouring rocks and thickets.

I cannot pretend to give a minute account of the fight, as I have heard it related in a variety of ways. Suffice it to say, the robbers were defeated; several of them killed, and several taken prisoners; which last, together with the people of the inn, were either executed or sent to the galleys.

I picked up these particulars in the course of a journey which I made some time after the event had taken place. I passed by the very inn. It was then dismantled, excepting one wing, in which a body of gens d'armes was stationed. They pointed out to me the shot holes in the window frames, the walls, and the pannels of the doors. There were a number of withered limbs dangling from the branches of a neighbouring tree, and blackening in the air, which I was told were the limbs of the robbers who had been slain, and the culprits who had been executed. The whole place had a dismal, wild, forlorn look.

"Were any of the Princess's party killed?" inquired the Englishman.

"As far as I can recollect, there were two or three."

"Not the nephew, I trust?" said the fair Venetian.

"Oh no: he hastened with the Count to relieve the anxiety of the daughter by the assurances of victory. The young lady had been sustained throughout the interval of suspense by the very intensity of her feelings. The moment she saw her father returning in safety, accompanied by the nephew of the Princess, she uttered a cry of rapture and fainted. Happily, however, she soon recovered, and what is more, was married shortly afterwards to the young cavalier, and the whole party accompanied the old Princess in her pilgrimage to Loretto, where her votive offerings may still be seen in the treasury of the Santa Casa."

It would be tedious to follow the devious course of the conversation as it wound through a maze of stories of the kind, until it was taken up by two other travellers who had come under convoy of the Procaccio: Mr. Hobbs and Mr. Dobbs, a linen draper and a green grocer, just returning from a hasty tour in Greece and the Holy Land. They were full of the story of Alderman Popkins. They were astonished that the robbers should dare to molest a man of his importance on 'Change, he being an eminent dry salter of Throgmorton Street, and a magistrate to boot.

In fact, the story of the Popkins family was but too true. It was attested by too many present to be for a moment doubted; and from the contradictory and concordant testimony of half a score, all eager to relate it, and all talking at the same time, the Englishman was enabled to gather the following particulars.

THE ADVENTURE OF THE POPKINS FAMILY

It was but a few days before that the carriage of Alderman Popkins had driven up to the inn of Terracina. Those who have seen an English family carriage on the continent, must have remarked the sensation it produces. It is an epitome of England; a little morsel of the old island rolling about the world—every thing about it compact, snug, finished and fitting. The wheels turning on patent axles without rattling; the body hanging so well on its springs, yielding to every motion, yet protecting from every shock. The ruddy faces gaping from the windows; sometimes, of a portly old citizen, sometimes of a voluminous dowager, and sometimes of a fine fresh hoyden, just from boarding school. And then the dickeys loaded with well dressed servants, beef fed and bluff; looking down from their heights with contempt on all the world around; profoundly ignorant of the country and the people, and devoutly certain that every thing not English must be wrong.

Such was the carriage of Alderman Popkins, as it made its appearance at Terracina. The courier who had preceded it, to order horses, and who was a Neapolitan, had given a magnificent account of the riches and greatness of his master, blundering with an Italian's splendour of imagination about the alderman's titles and dignities; the host had added his usual share of exaggeration, so that by the time the alderman drove up to the door, he was a Milor—Magnifico—Principe——the Lord knows what!

The alderman was advised to take an escort to Fondi and Itri, but he refused. It was as much as a man's life was worth, he said, to stop him on the king's highway; he would complain of it to the ambassador at Naples; he would make a national affair of it. The principessa Popkins, a fresh, motherly dame, seemed perfectly secure in the protection of her husband, so omnipotent a man in the city. The signorine Popkins, two fine bouncing girls looked to their brother Tom, who had taken lessons in boxing; and as to the dandy himself, he swore no scaramouch of an Italian robber would dare to meddle with an Englishman. The landlord shrugged his shoulders and turned out the palms of his hands with a true Italian grimace, and the carriage of Milor Popkins rolled on.

They passed through several very suspicious places without any molestation. The Misses Popkins, who were very romantic, and had learnt to draw in water colours, were enchanted with the savage scenery around; it was so like what they had read in Mrs. Radcliffe's romances, they should like of all things to make sketches. At length, the carriage arrived at a place where the road wound up a long hill. Mrs. Popkins had sunk into a sleep; the young ladies were lost in the "Loves of the Angels;" and the dandy was hectoring the postilions from the coach box. The alderman got out, as he said, to stretch his legs up the hill. It was a long winding ascent, and obliged him every now and then to stop and blow and wipe his forehead with many a pish! and phew! being rather pursy and short of wind. As the carriage, however, was far behind him, and moved slowly under the weight of so many well stuffed trunks and well stuffed travellers, he had plenty of time to walk at leisure.

On a jutting point of rock that overhung the road nearly at the summit of the hill, just where the route began again to descend, he saw a solitary man seated, who appeared to be tending goats. Alderman Popkins was one of your shrewd travellers who always like to be picking up small information along the road, so he thought he'd just scramble up to the honest man, and have a little talk with him by way of learning the news and getting a lesson in Italian. As he drew near to the peasant he did not half like his looks. He was partly reclining on the rocks wrapped in the usual long mantle, which, with his slouched hat, only left a part of a swarthy visage, with a keen black eye, a beetle brow and a fierce moustache to be seen. He had whistled several times to his dog which was roving about the side of the hill. As the alderman approached he rose and greeted him. When standing erect he seemed almost gigantic, at least in the eyes of Alderman Popkins; who, however, being a short man, might be deceived.

The latter would gladly now have been back in the carriage, or even on 'change in London, for he was by no means well pleased with his company. However, he determined to put the best face on matters, and was beginning a conversation about the state of the weather, the baddishness of the crops and the price of goats in that part of the country, when he heard a violent screaming. He ran to the edge of the rock, and, looking over, beheld his carriage surrounded by robbers. One held down the fat footman, another had the dandy by his starched cravat, with a pistol to his head; one was rummaging a portmanteau, another rummaging the principessa's pockets, while the two Misses Popkins were screaming from each window of the carriage, and their waiting maid squalling from the dickey.

Alderman Popkins felt all the ire of the parent and the magistrate roused within him. He grasped his cane and was on the point of scrambling down the rocks, either to assault the robbers or to read the riot act, when he was suddenly seized by the arm. It was by his friend the goatherd, whose cloak, falling open, discovered a belt stuck full of pistols and stilettos. In short, he found himself in the clutches of the captain of the band, who had stationed himself on the rock to look out for travellers and to give notice to his men.

A sad ransacking took place. Trunks were turned inside out, and all the finery and frippery of the Popkins family scattered about the road. Such a chaos of Venice beads and Roman mosaics; and Paris bonnets of the young ladies, mingled with the alderman's night caps and lamb's wool stockings, and the dandy's hair brushes, stays, and starched cravats.

The gentlemen were eased of their purses and their watches; the ladies of their jewels, and the whole party were on the point of being carried up into the mountain, when fortunately the appearance of soldiery at a distance obliged the robbers to make off with the spoils they had secured, and leave the Popkins family to gather together the remnants of their effects, and make the best of their way to Fondi.

When safe arrived, the alderman made a terrible blustering at the inn; threatened to complain to the ambassador at Naples, and was ready to shake his cane at the whole country. The dandy had many stories to tell of his scuffles with the brigands, who overpowered him merely by numbers. As to the Misses Popkins, they were quite delighted with the adventure, and were occupied the whole evening in writing it in their journals. They declared the captain of the band to be a most romantic looking man; they dared to say some unfortunate lover, or exiled nobleman: and several of the band to be very handsome young men—"quite picturesque!"

"In verity," said mine host of Terracina, "they say the captain of the band is *un galant uomo.*"

"A gallant man!" said the Englishman indignantly. "I'd have your gallant man hang'd like a dog!"

"To dare to meddle with Englishmen!" said Mr. Hobbs.

"And such a family as the Popkinses!" said Mr. Dobbs.

"They ought to come upon the county for damages!" said Mr. Hobbs.

"Our ambassador should make a complaint to the government of Naples," said Mr. Dobbs.

"They should be obliged to drive these rascals out of the country," said Hobbs.

"And if they did not, we should declare war against them!" said Dobbs.

"Pish!—humbug!" muttered the Englishman to himself, and walked away.

The Englishman had been a little wearied by this story, and by the ultra zeal of his countrymen, and was glad when a summons to their supper relieved him from the crowd of travellers. He walked out with his Venetian friends and a young Frenchman of an interesting demeanour, who had become sociable with them in the course of the conversation. They directed their steps toward the sea, which was lit up by the rising moon. The Venetian, out of politeness, left his beautiful wife to be escorted by the Englishman. The latter, however, either from shyness or reserve, did not avail himself of the civility, but walked on without offering his arm. The fair Venetian, with all her devotion to her husband, was a little nettled at a want of gallantry to which her charms had rendered her unaccustomed, and took the proffered arm of the Frenchman with a pretty air of pique, which, however, was entirely lost upon the phlegmatic delinquent.

As they strolled along the beach they came to where a body of soldiers were stationed in a circle. They were guarding a number of galley slaves, who were permitted to refresh themselves in the evening breeze, and sport and roll upon the sand.

The Frenchman paused, and pointed to the group of wretches at their sports. "It is difficult," said he, "to conceive a more frightful mass of crime than is here collected. Many of these have probably been robbers, such as you have heard described. Such is, too often, the career of crime in this country. The parricide, the fratricide, the infanticide, the miscreant of every kind first flies from justice and turns mountain bandit, and then, when wearied of a life of danger, becomes traitor to his brother desperadoes, betrays them to punishment, and thus buys a commutation of his own sentence from death to the galleys: happy in the privilege of wallowing on the shore an hour a day, in this mere state of animal enjoyment."

The fair Venetian shuddered as she cast a look at the horde of wretches at their evening amusement. "They seemed," she said, "like so many serpents writhing together." And yet the idea that some of them had been robbers, those formidable beings that haunted her imagination, made her still cast another fearful glance, as we contemplate some terrible beast of prey, with a degree of awe and horror, even though caged and chained.

The conversation reverted to the tales of banditti which they had heard at the inn. The Englishman condemned some of them as fabrications, others as exaggerations. As to the story of the improvvisatore, he pronounced it a mere piece of romance, originating in the heated brain of the narrator.

"And yet," said the Frenchman, "there is so much romance about the real life of those beings, and about the singular country they infest, that it is hard to tell what to reject on the ground of improbability. I have had an adventure happen to myself which gave me an opportunity of getting some insight into their manners and habits, which I found altogether out of the common run of existence."

There was an air of mingled frankness and modesty about the Frenchman which had gained the good will of the whole party, not even excepting the Englishman. They all eagerly inquired after the particulars of the circumstance he alluded to, and as they strolled slowly up and down the sea shore, he related the following adventure.

THE PAINTER'S ADVENTURE

I am an historical painter by profession, and resided for some time in the family of a foreign prince, at his villa, about fifteen miles from Rome, among some of the most interesting scenery of Italy. It is situated on the heights of ancient Tusculum. In its neighbourhood are the ruins of the villas of Cicero, Sylla, Lucullus, Rufinus, and other illustrious Romans, who sought refuge

here occasionally, from their toils, in the bosom of a soft and luxurious repose. From the midst of delightful bowers, refreshed by the pure mountain
breeze, the eye looks over a romantic landscape full of poetical and historical
associations. The Albanian mountains, Tivoli, once the favourite residence
of Horace and Mæcenas; the vast, deserted, melancholy Campagna with the
Tiber winding through it, and St. Peter's dome swelling in the midst, the
monument—as it were, over the grave of ancient Rome.

I assisted the prince in researches which he was making among the classic
ruins of his vicinity. His exertions were highly successful. Many wrecks of
admirable statues and fragments of exquisite sculpture were dug up; mon-
uments of the taste and magnificence that reigned in the ancient Tusculan
abodes. He had studded his villa and its grounds with statues, relievos, vases
and sarcophagi, thus retrieved from the bosom of the earth.

The mode of life pursued at the villa was delightfully serene, diversified
by interesting occupations and elegant leisure. Every one passed the day
according to his pleasure or pursuits; and we all assembled in a cheerful
dinner party at sunset. It was on the fourth of November, a beautiful serene
day, that we had assembled in the saloon at the sound of the first dinner
bell. The family were surprised at the absence of the prince's confessor. They
waited for him in vain, and at length placed themselves at table. They first
attributed his absence to his having prolonged his customary walk; and the
early part of the dinner passed without any uneasiness. When the desart was
served, however, without his making his appearance, they began to feel anxious. They feared he might have been taken ill in some alley of the woods;
or, might have fallen into the hands of robbers. Not far from the villa, with
the interval of a small valley, rose the mountains of the Abruzzi, the strong
hold of banditti. Indeed, the neighbourhood had, for some time past, been
infested by them; and Barbone, a notorious bandit chief, had often been met
prowling about the solitudes of Tusculum. The daring enterprises of these
ruffians were well known; the objects of their cupidity or vengeance were
insecure even in palaces. As yet they had respected the possessions of the
prince; but the idea of such dangerous spirits hovering about the neighbourhood was sufficient to occasion alarm.

The fears of the company increased as evening closed in. The prince ordered out forest guards, and domestics with flambeaux to search for the
confessor. They had not departed long, when a slight noise was heard in the
corridor of the ground floor. The family were dining on the first floor, and
the remaining domestics were occupied in attendance. There was no one on
the ground floor at this moment but the housekeeper, the laundress, and
three field labourers, who were resting themselves, and conversing with the
women.

I heard the noise from below, and presuming it to be occasioned by the
return of the absentee, I left the table, and hastened down stairs, eager to

gain intelligence that might relieve the anxiety of the prince and princess. I
had scarcely reached the last step, when I beheld before me a man dressed
as a bandit; a carbine in his hand, and a stiletto and pistols in his belt. His
countenance had a mingled expression of ferocity and trepidation. He sprang
upon me, and exclaimed exultingly, "Ecco il principe!"

I saw at once into what hands I had fallen, but endeavoured to summon
up coolness and presence of mind. A glance towards the lower end of the
corridor, showed me several ruffians, clothed and armed in the same manner
with the one who had seized me. They were guarding the two females and
the field labourers. The robber, who held me firmly by the collar, demanded
repeatedly whether or not I were the prince. His object evidently was to
carry off the prince, and extort an immense ransom. He was enraged at
receiving none but vague replies; for I felt the importance of misleading
him.

A sudden thought struck me how I might extricate myself from his clutches. I was unarmed, it is true, but I was vigorous. His companions were at a
distance. By a sudden exertion I might wrest myself from him, and spring
up the staircase, whither he would not dare to follow me singly. The idea
was put in practice as soon as conceived. The ruffian's throat was bare: with
my right hand I seized him by it, with my left hand I grasped the arm which
held the carbine. The suddenness of my attack took him completely unawares; and the strangling nature of my grasp paralized him. He choked and
faltered. I felt his hand relaxing its hold, and was on the point of jerking
myself away, and darting up the staircase before he could recover himself,
when I was suddenly seized by some one from behind.

I had to let go my grasp. The bandit, once more released, fell upon me
with fury, and gave me several blows with the butt end of his carbine, one
of which wounded me severely in the forehead, and covered me with blood.
He took advantage of my being stunned, to rifle me of my watch, and whatever valuables I had about my person.

When I recovered from the effects of the blow, I heard the voice of the
chief of the banditti, who exclaimed, "Quello e il principe, siamo contente,
andiamo!" (It is the prince, enough, let us be off.) The band immediately
closed round me, and dragged me out of the palace, bearing off the three
labourers likewise.

I had no hat on, and the blood flowed from my wound; I managed to
staunch it, however, with my pocket handkerchief, which I bound round my
forehead. The captain of the band conducted me in triumph, supposing me
to be the prince. We had gone some distance, before he learnt his mistake
from one of the labourers. His rage was terrible. It was too late to return to
the villa, and endeavour to retrieve his error, for by this time the alarm must
have been given, and every one in arms. He darted at me a ferocious look;
swore I had deceived him, and caused him to miss his fortune; and told me

to prepare for death. The rest of the robbers were equally furious. I saw their hands upon their poniards; and I knew that death was seldom an empty threat with these ruffians.

The labourers saw the peril into which their information had betrayed me, and eagerly assured the captain that I was a man for whom the prince would pay a great ransom. This produced a pause. For my part, I cannot say that I had been much dismayed by their menaces. I mean not to make any boast of courage; but I have been so schooled to hardship during the late revolutions, and have beheld death around me in so many perilous and disastrous scenes, that I have become, in some measure, callous to its terrors. The frequent hazard of life makes a man at length as reckless of it, as a gambler of his money. To their threat of death I replied, "that the sooner it was executed the better." This reply seemed to astonish the captain, and the prospect of ransom held out by the labourers had, no doubt, a still greater effect on him. He considered for a moment; assumed a calmer manner, and made a sign to his companions, who had remained waiting for my death warrant. *"Forward,"* said he, "we will see about this matter by and bye."

We descended rapidly towards the road of La Molara, which leads to Rocca Priori. In the midst of this road is a solitary inn. The captain ordered the troop to halt at the distance of a pistol shot from it; and enjoined profound silence. He approached the threshold alone, with noiseless steps. He examined the outside of the door very narrowly, and then returning precipitately, made a sign for the troop to continue its march in silence. It has since been ascertained, that this was one of those infamous inns which are the secret resorts of banditti. The innkeeper had an understanding with the captain, as he most probably had with the chiefs of the different bands. When any of the patroles and gens d'armes were quartered at his house, the brigands were warned of it by a preconcerted signal on the door; when there was no such signal, they might enter with safety, and be sure of welcome.

After pursuing our road a little further, we struck off towards the woody mountains, which envelope Rocca Priori. Our march was long and painful, with many circuits and windings; at length we clambered a steep ascent, covered with a thick forest, and when we had reached the centre, I was told to seat myself on the ground. No sooner had I done so, than at a sign from their chief, the robbers surrounded me, and spreading their great cloaks from one to the other, formed a kind of pavilion of mantles, to which their bodies might be said to serve as columns. The captain then struck a light, and a flambeau was lit immediately. The mantles were extended to prevent the light of the flambeau from being seen through the forest. Anxious as was my situation, I could not look round upon this screen of dusky drapery, relieved by the bright colours of the robbers' garments, the gleaming of their weapons, and the variety of strong marked countenances, lit up by the flambeau, without admiring the picturesque effect of the scene. It was quite theatrical.

The captain now held an inkhorn, and giving me pen and paper, ordered me to write what he should dictate. I obeyed.—It was a demand, couched in the style of robber eloquence, "that the prince should send three thousand dollars for my ransom, or that my death should be the consequence of a refusal."

I knew enough of the desperate character of these beings to feel assured this was not an idle menace. Their only mode of insuring attention to their demands, is to make the infliction of the penalty inevitable. I saw at once, however, that the demand was preposterous, and made in improper language.

I told the captain so, and assured him, that so extravagant a sum would never be granted; "that I was neither a friend nor relative of the prince, but a mere artist, employed to execute certain paintings. That I had nothing to offer as a ransom but the price of my labours; if this were not sufficient, my life was at their disposal: it was a thing on which I set but little value."

I was the more hardy in my reply, because I saw that coolness and hardihood had an effect upon the robbers. It is true, as I finished speaking the captain laid his hand upon his stiletto, but he restrained himself, and snatching the letter, folded it, and ordered me, in a peremptory tone, to address it to the prince. He then despatched one of the labourers with it to Tusculum, who promised to return with all possible speed.

The robbers now prepared themselves for sleep, and I was told that I might do the same. They spread their great cloaks on the ground, and lay down around me. One was stationed at a little distance to keep watch, and was relieved every two hours. The strangeness and wildness of this mountain bivouac, among lawless beings whose hands seemed ever ready to grasp the stiletto, and with whom life was so trivial and insecure, was enough to banish repose. The coldness of the earth and of the dew, however, had a still greater effect than mental causes in disturbing my rest. The airs wafted to these mountains from the distant Mediterranean diffused a great chilliness as the night advanced. An expedient suggested itself. I called one of my fellow prisoners, the labourers, and made him lie down beside me. Whenever one of my limbs became chilled I approached it to the robust limb of my neighbour, and borrowed some of his warmth. In this way I was able to obtain a little sleep.

Day at length dawned, and I was roused from my slumber by the voice of the chieftain. He desired me to rise and follow him. I obeyed. On considering his physiognomy attentively, it appeared a little softened. He even assisted me in scrambling up the steep forest among rocks and brambles. Habit had made him a vigorous mountaineer; but I found it excessively toilsome to climb those rugged heights. We arrived at length at the summit of the mountain.

Here it was that I felt all the enthusiasm of my art suddenly awakened; and I forgot, in an instant, all my perils and fatigues at this magnificent view of the sunrise in the midst of the mountains of the Abruzzi. It was on these heights that Hannibal first pitched his camp, and pointed out Rome to his followers. The eye embraces a vast extent of country. The minor height of Tusculum, with its villas, and its sacred ruins, lie below; the Sabine hills and the Albanian mountains stretch on either hand, and beyond Tusculum and Frascati spreads out the immense Campagna, with its lines of tombs, and here and there a broken aqueduct stretching across it, and the towers and domes of the eternal city in the midst.

Fancy this scene lit up by the glories of a rising sun, and bursting upon my sight, as I looked forth from among the majestic forests of the Abruzzi. Fancy, too, the savage foreground, made still more savage by groups of banditti, armed and dressed in their wild picturesque manner, and you will not wonder that the enthusiasm of a painter for a moment overpowered all his other feelings.

The banditti were astonished at my admiration of a scene which familiarity had made so common in their eyes. I took advantage of their halting at this spot, drew forth a quire of drawing paper, and began to sketch the features of the landscape. The height, on which I was seated, was wild and solitary, separated from the ridge of Tusculum by a valley nearly three miles wide; though the distance appeared less from the purity of the atmosphere. This height was one of the favourite retreats of the banditti, commanding a look out over the country; while, at the same time, it was covered with forests, and distant from the populous haunts of men.

While I was sketching, my attention was called off for a moment by the cries of birds and the bleatings of sheep. I looked around, but could see nothing of the animals which uttered them. They were repeated, and appeared to come from the summits of the trees. On looking more narrowly, I perceived six of the robbers perched in the tops of oaks, which grew on the breezy crest of the mountain, and commanded an uninterrupted prospect. They were keeping a look out, like so many vultures; casting their eyes into the depths of the valley below us; communicating with each other by signs, or holding discourse in sounds, which might be mistaken by the wayfarer, for the cries of hawks and crows, or the bleating of the mountain flocks. After they had reconnoitred the neighbourhood, and finished their singular discourse, they descended from their airy perch, and returned to their prisoners. The captain posted three of them at three naked sides of the mountain, while he remained to guard us with what appeared his most trusty companion.

I had my book of sketches in my hand; he requested to see it, and after having run his eye over it, expressed himself convinced of the truth of my assertion, that I was a painter. I thought I saw a gleam of good feeling dawning in him, and determined to avail myself of it. I knew that the worst of men have their good points and their accessible sides, if one would but study them carefully. Indeed, there is a singular mixture in the character of the Italian robber. With reckless ferocity, he often mingles traits of kindness and good humour. He is not always radically bad, but driven to his course of life by some unpremeditated crime, the effect of those sudden bursts of passion to which the Italian temperament is prone. This has compelled him to take to the mountains, or, as it is technically termed among them, "andare in Campagna." He has become a robber by profession; but like a soldier, when not in action, he can lay aside his weapon and his fierceness, and become like other men.

I took occasion from the observations of the captain on my sketchings, to fall into conversation with him and found him sociable and communicative. By degrees I became completely at my ease with him. I had fancied I perceived about him a degree of self love, which I determined to make use of. I assumed an air of careless frankness, and told him that, as an artist, I pretended to the power of judging of the physiognomy; that I thought I perceived something in his features and demeanour, which announced him worthy of higher fortunes. That he was not formed to exercise the profession to which he had abandoned himself; that he had talents and qualities fitted for a nobler sphere of action; that he had but to change his course of life, and in a legitimate career, the same courage and endowments which now made him an object of terror, would ensure him the applause and admiration of society.

I had not mistaken my man. My discourse both touched and excited him. He seized my hand, pressed it, and replied with strong emotion, "You have guessed the truth; you have judged of me rightly." He remained for a moment silent; then with a kind of effort he resumed. "I will tell you some particulars of my life, and you will perceive that it was the oppression of others, rather than my own crimes, which drove me to the mountains. I sought to serve my fellow men, and they have persecuted me from among them." We seated ourselves on the grass, and the robber gave me the following anecdotes of his history.

THE STORY OF THE BANDIT CHIEFTAIN

I am a native of the village of Prossedi. My father was easy enough in circumstances, and we lived peaceably and independently, cultivating our fields. All went on well with us until a new chief of the Sbirri was sent to our village to take command of the police. He was an arbitrary fellow, prying into every thing, and practising all sorts of vexations and oppressions in the discharge of his office.

I was at that time eighteen years of age, and had a natural love of justice and good neighbourhood. I had also a little education, and knew something of history, so as to be able to judge a little of men and their actions. All this inspired me with hatred for this paltry despot. My own family, also, became the object of his suspicion or dislike, and felt more than once the arbitrary abuse of his power. These things worked together on my mind, and I gasped after vengeance. My character was always ardent and energetic; and acted upon by my love of justice, determined me by one blow to rid the country of the tyrant.

Full of my project I rose one morning before peep of day, and concealing a stiletto under my waistcoat—here you see it!—(and he drew forth a long keen poniard)—I lay in wait for him in the outskirts of the village. I knew all his haunts, and his habit of making his rounds and prowling about like a wolf, in the grey of the morning; at length I met him and attacked him with fury. He was armed, but I took him unawares, and was full of youth and vigour. I gave him repeated blows to make sure work, and laid him lifeless at my feet.

When I was satisfied that I had done for him, I returned with all haste to the village, but had the ill luck to meet two of the Sbirri as I entered it. They accosted me and asked if I had seen their chief. I assumed an air of tranquillity, and told them I had not. They continued on their way, and, within a few hours, brought back the dead body to Prossedi. Their suspicions of me being already awakened, I was arrested and thrown into prison. Here I lay several weeks, when the prince who was Seigneur of Prossedi directed judicial proceedings against me. I was brought to trial, and a witness was produced who pretended to have seen me flying with precipitation not far from the bleeding body, and so I was condemned to the galleys for thirty years.

"Curse on such laws," vociferated the bandit, foaming with rage; "curse on such a government, and ten thousand curses on the prince who caused me to be adjudged so rigorously, while so many other Roman princes harbour and protect assassins a thousand times more culpable. What had I done but what was inspired by a love of justice and my country? Why was my act more culpable than that of Brutus, when he sacrificed Cæsar to the cause of liberty and justice!"

There was something at once both lofty and ludicrous in the rhapsody of this robber chief, thus associating himself with one of the great names of antiquity. It showed, however, that he had at least the merit of knowing the remarkable facts in the history of his country. He became more calm, and resumed his narrative.

I was conducted to Civita Vecchia in fetters. My heart was burning with rage. I had been married scarce six months to a woman whom I passionately loved, and who was pregnant. My family was in despair. For a long time I made unsuccessful efforts to break my chain. At length I found a morsel of iron which I hid carefully, and endeavoured with a pointed flint to fashion it into a kind of file. I occupied myself in this work during the night time, and when it was finished, I made out, after a long time, to sever one of the rings of my chain. My flight was successful.

I wandered for several weeks in the mountains which surround Prossedi, and found means to inform my wife of the place where I was concealed. She came often to see me. I had determined to put myself at the head of an armed band. She endeavoured for a long time to dissuade me; but finding my resolution fixed, she at length united in my project of vengeance, and brought me, herself, my poniard.

By her means I communicated with several brave fellows of the neighbouring villages, who I knew to be ready to take to the mountains, and only panting for an opportunity to exercise their daring spirits. We soon formed a combination, procured arms, and we have had ample opportunities of revenging ourselves for the wrongs and injuries which most of us have suffered. Every thing has succeeded with us until now, and had it not been for our blunder in mistaking you for the prince, our fortunes would have been made.

———

Here the robber concluded his story. He had talked himself into complete companionship, and assured me he no longer bore me any grudge for the error of which I had been the innocent cause. He even professed a kindness for me, and wished me to remain some time with them. He promised to give me a sight of certain grottos which they occupied beyond Villetri, and whither they resorted during the intervals of their expeditions. He assured me that they led a jovial life there; had plenty of good cheer; slept on beds of moss, and were waited upon by young and beautiful females, whom I might take for models.

I confess I felt my curiosity roused by his descriptions of these grottos and their inhabitants: they realized those scenes in robber story which I had always looked upon as mere creations of the fancy. I should gladly have accepted his invitation, and paid a visit to those caverns, could I have felt more secure in my company.

I began to find my situation less painful. I had evidently propitiated the good will of the chieftain, and hoped that he might release me for a moderate ransom. A new alarm, however, awaited me. While the captain was looking out with impatience for the return of the messenger who had been sent to the prince, the sentinel posted on the side of the mountain facing the plain of La Molara, came running towards us. "We are betrayed!" exclaimed he. "The police of Frascati are after us. A party of carabiniers have just stopped at the inn below the mountain." Then laying his hand on his stiletto, he swore, with a terrible oath, that if they made the least movement towards the mountain, my life and the lives of my fellow prisoners should answer for it.

The chieftain resumed all his ferocity of demeanour, and approved of what his companion said; but when the latter had returned to his post, he turned to me with a softened air: "I must act as chief," said he, "and humour my dangerous subalterns. It is a law with us to kill our prisoners rather than suffer them to be rescued; but do not be alarmed. In case we are surprised keep by me; fly with us, and I will consider myself responsible for your life."

There was nothing very consolatory in this arrangement, which would have placed me between two dangers; I scarcely knew in case of flight, which I should have most to apprehend from, the carbines of the pursuers, or the stilettos of the pursued. I remained silent, however, and endeavoured to maintain a look of tranquillity.

For an hour was I kept in this state of peril and anxiety. The robbers, crouching among their leafy coverts, kept an eagle watch upon the carabiniers below, as they loitered about the inn; sometimes lolling about the portal; sometimes disappearing for several minutes, then sallying out, examining their weapons, pointing in different directions and apparently asking questions about the neighbourhood; not a movement or gesture was lost upon the keen eyes of the brigands. At length we were relieved from our apprehensions. The carabiniers having finished their refreshment, seized their arms, continued along the valley towards the great road, and gradually left the mountain behind them. "I felt almost certain," said the chief, "that they could not be sent after us. They know too well how prisoners have fared in our hands on similar occasions. Our laws in this respect are inflexible, and are necessary for our safety. If we once flinched from them, there would no longer be such thing as a ransom to be procured."

There were no signs yet of the messenger's return. I was preparing to resume my sketching, when the captain drew a quire of paper from his knapsack—"Come," said he, laughing, "you are a painter; take my likeness. The leaves of your portfolio are small; draw it on this." I gladly consented, for it was a study that seldom presents itself to a painter. I recollected that Salvator Rosa in his youth had voluntarily sojourned for a time among the banditti of Calabria, and had filled his mind with the savage scenery and savage associates by which he was surrounded. I seized my pencil with enthusiasm at the thought. I found the captain the most docile of subjects, and after various shiftings of position, I placed him in an attitude to my mind.

Picture to yourself a stern muscular figure, in fanciful bandit costume, with pistols and poniards in belt, his brawny neck bare, a handkerchief loosely thrown round it, and the two ends in front strung with rings of all kinds, the spoils of travellers; reliques and medals hung on his breast; his hat decorated with various coloured ribbands; his vest and short breeches of bright colours and finely embroidered; his legs in buskins or leggins. Fancy him on a mountain height, among wild rocks and rugged oaks, leaning on his carbine as if meditating some exploit, while far below are beheld villages and villas, the scenes of his maraudings, with the wide Campagna dimly extending in the distance.

The robber was pleased with the sketch, and seemed to admire himself upon paper. I had scarcely finished, when the labourer arrived who had been sent for my ransom. He had reached Tusculum two hours after midnight. He brought me a letter from the prince, who was in bed at the time of his arrival. As I had predicted, he treated the demand as extravagant, but offered five hundred dollars for my ransom. Having no money by him at the moment, he had sent a note for the amount, payable to whomever should conduct me safe and sound to Rome. I presented the note of hand to the chieftain, he received it with a shrug. "Of what use are notes of hand to us?" said he, "who can we send with you to Rome to receive it? We are all marked men, known and described at every gate and military post, and village church door. No, we must have gold and silver; let the sum be paid in cash and you shall be restored to liberty."

The captain again placed a sheet of paper before me to communicate his determination to the prince. When I had finished the letter and took the sheet from the quire, I found on the opposite side of it the portrait which I had just been tracing. I was about to tear it off and give it to the chief.

"Hold," said he, "let it go to Rome; let them see what kind of looking fellow I am. Perhaps the prince and his friends may form as good an opinion of me from my face as you have done."

This was said sportively, yet it was evident there was vanity lurking at the bottom. Even this wary, distrustful chief of banditti forgot for a moment his usual foresight and precaution in the common wish to be admired. He never reflected what use might be made of this portrait in his pursuit and conviction.

The letter was folded and directed, and the messenger departed again for Tusculum. It was now eleven o'clock in the morning, and as yet we had eaten nothing. In spite of all my anxiety, I began to feel a craving appetite. I was glad therefore to hear the captain talk something of eating. He observed that for three days and nights they had been lurking about among rocks and woods, meditating their expedition to Tusculum, during which time all their provisions had been exhausted. He should now take measures to procure a supply. Leaving me therefore in the charge of his comrade, in whom he appeared to have implicit confidence, he departed, assuring me that in less than two hours we should make a good dinner. Where it was to come from was an enigma to me, though it was evident these beings had their secret friends and agents throughout the country.

Indeed, the inhabitants of these mountains and of the valleys which they embosom are a rude, half civilized set. The towns and villages among the forests of the Abruzzi, shut up from the rest of the world, are almost like savage dens. It is wonderful that such rude abodes, so little known and visited, should be embosomed in the midst of one of the most travelled and civilized countries of Europe. Among these regions the robber prowls unmolested, not a mountaineer hesitates to give him secret harbour and assistance. The shepherds, however, who tend their flocks among the mountains, are the favourite emissaries of the robbers, when they would send messages down to the valleys either for ransom or supplies. The shepherds of the Abruzzi are as wild as the scenes they frequent. They are clad in a rude garb of black or brown sheep skin, they have high conical hats, and coarse sandals of cloth bound round their legs with thongs, similar to those worn by the robbers. They carry long staffs, on which as they lean they form picturesque objects in the lonely landscape, and they are followed by their ever constant companion the dog. They are a curious questioning set, glad at any time to relieve the monotony of their solitude by the conversation of the passer by, and the dog will lend an attentive ear, and put on as sagacious and inquisitive a look as his master.

But I am wandering from my story. I was now left alone with one of the robbers, the confidential companion of the chief. He was the youngest and most vigorous of the band, and though his countenance had something of that dissolute fierceness which seems natural to this desperate, lawless mode of life, yet there were traits of manly beauty about it. As an artist I could not but admire it. I had remarked in him an air of abstraction and reverie, and at times a movement of inward suffering and impatience. He now sat on the ground; his elbows on his knees, his head resting between his clenched fists, and his eyes fixed on the earth with an expression of sad and bitter rumination. I had grown familiar with him from repeated conversations, and had found him superior in mind to the rest of the band. I was anxious to seize every opportunity of sounding the feelings of these singular beings. I fancied I read in the countenance of this one traces of self condemnation and remorse; and the ease with which I had drawn forth the confidence of the chieftain, encouraged me to hope the same with his follower.

After a little preliminary conversation I ventured to ask him if he did not feel regret at having abandoned his family, and taken to this dangerous profession. "I feel," replied he, "but one regret, and that will end only with my life." As he said this he pressed his clenched fists upon his bosom, drew his breath through his set teeth, and added with deep emotion, "I have something within here that stifles me; it is like a burning iron consuming my very heart. I could tell you a miserable story, but not now—another time."—He relapsed into his former position, and sat with his head between his hands, muttering to himself in broken ejaculations; and what appeared at times to be curses and maledictions. I saw he was not in a mood to be disturbed, so I left him to himself. In a little while the exhaustion of his feelings, and probably the fatigues he had undergone in this expedition, began to produce drowsiness. He struggled with it for a time, but the warmth and stillness of midday made it irresistible, and he at length stretched himself upon the herbage and fell asleep.

I now beheld a chance of escape within my reach. My guard lay before me at my mercy. His vigorous limbs relaxed by sleep; his bosom open for the blow; his carbine slipped from his nerveless grasp, and lying by his side; his stiletto half out of the pocket in which it was usually carried. But two of his comrades were in sight, and those at a considerable distance, on the edge of the mountain; their backs turned to us, and their attention occupied in keeping a look out upon the plain. Through a strip of intervening forest, and at the foot of a steep descent, I beheld the village of Rocca Priori. To have secured the carbine of the sleeping brigand, to have seized upon his poniard and have plunged it in his heart, would have been the work of an instant. Should he die without noise, I might dart through the forest and down to Rocca Priori before my flight might be discovered. In case of alarm, I should still have a fair start of the robbers, and a chance of getting beyond the reach of their shot.

Here then was an opportunity for both escape and vengeance; perilous, indeed, but powerfully tempting. Had my situation been more critical I could not have resisted it. I reflected, however, for a moment. The attempt, if successful, would be followed by the sacrifice of my two fellow prisoners, who were sleeping profoundly, and could not be awakened in time to escape. The labourer who had gone after the ransom might also fall a victim to the rage of the robbers, without the money which he brought being saved. Besides, the conduct of the chief towards me made me feel certain of speedy deliverance. These reflections overcame the first powerful impulse, and I calmed the turbulent agitation which it had awakened.

I again took out my materials for drawing, and amused myself with sketching the magnificent prospect. It was now about noon, and every thing had sunk into repose, like the sleeping bandit before me. The noontide stillness that reigned over these mountains, the vast landscape below, gleaming with distant towns and dotted with various habitations and signs of life, yet all so silent, had a powerful effect upon my mind. The intermediate valleys, too, which lie among the mountains have a peculiar air of solitude. Few sounds are heard at midday to break the quiet of the scene. Sometimes the whistle of a solitary muleteer, lagging with his lazy animal along the road which winds through the centre of the valley; sometimes the faint piping of a shepherd's reed from the side of the mountain, or sometimes the bell of an ass slowly pacing along, followed by a monk with bare feet and bare shining head; and carrying provisions to the convent.

I had continued to sketch for some time among my sleeping companions, when at length I saw the captain of the band approaching, followed by a peasant leading a mule, on which was a well filled sack. I at first apprehended that this was some new prey fallen into the hands of the robbers, but the contented look of the peasant soon relieved me, and I was rejoiced to hear that it was our promised repast. The brigands now came running from the three sides of the mountain, having the quick scent of vultures. Every one busied himself in unloading the mule and relieving the sack of its contents.

The first thing that made its appearance was an enormous ham of a colour and plumpness that would have inspired the pencil of Teniers. It was followed by a large cheese, a bag of boiled chesnuts, a little barrel of wine, and a quantity of good household bread. Every thing was arranged on the grass with a degree of symmetry, and the captain presenting me his knife, requested me to help myself. We all seated ourselves round the viands, and nothing was heard for a time but the sound of vigorous mastication, or the gurgling of the barrel of wine as it revolved briskly about the circle. My long fasting and the mountain air and exercise had given me a keen appetite, and never did repast appear to me more excellent or picturesque.

From time to time one of the band was despatched to keep a look out upon the plain: no enemy was at hand, and the dinner was undisturbed.

The peasant received nearly three times the value of his provisions, and set off down the mountain highly satisfied with his bargain. I felt invigorated by the hearty meal I had made, and notwithstanding that the wound I had received the evening before was painful, yet I could not but feel extremely interested and gratified by the singular scenes continually presented to me. Every thing was picturesque about these wild beings and their haunts. Their bivouacs, their groups on guard, their indolent noontide repose on the mountain brow, their rude repast on the herbage among rocks and trees, every thing presented a study for a painter. But it was towards the approach of evening that I felt the highest enthusiasm awakened.

The setting sun, declining beyond the vast Campagna, shed its rich yellow beams on the woody summits of the Abruzzi. Several mountains crowned with snow shone brilliantly in the distance, contrasting their brightness with others, which thrown into shade, assumed deep tints of purple and violet. As the evening advanced, the landscape darkened into a sterner character. The immense solitude around; the wild mountains broken into rocks and precipices, intermingled with vast oaks, corks and chesnuts; and the groups of banditti in the foreground, reminded me of the savage scenes of Salvator Rosa.

To beguile the time the captain proposed to his comrades to spread before me their jewels and cameos, as I must doubtless be a judge of such articles, and able to form an estimate of their value. He set the example, the others followed it, and in a few moments I saw the grass before me sparkling with jewels and gems that would have delighted the eyes of an antiquary or a fine lady. Among them were several precious jewels and antique intaglios and cameos of great value, the spoils doubtless of travellers of distinction. I found that they were in the habit of selling their booty in the frontier towns; but as these in general were thinly and poorly peopled, and little frequented by travellers, they could offer no market for such valuable articles of taste and luxury. I suggested to them the certainty of their readily obtaining great prices for these gems among the rich strangers with which Rome was thronged.

The impression made upon their greedy minds was immediately apparent. One of the band, a young man, and the least known, requested permission of the captain to depart the following day in disguise for Rome, for the purpose of traffick; promising on the faith of a bandit (a sacred pledge amongst them) to return in two days to any place he might appoint. The captain consented, and a curious scene took place. The robbers crowded round him eagerly, confiding to him such of their jewels as they wished to dispose of, and giving him instructions what to demand. There was much bargaining and exchanging and selling of trinkets among them, and I beheld my watch which had a chain and valuable seals, purchased by the young robber merchant of the ruffian who had plundered me, for sixty dollars. I now conceived a faint hope that if it went to Rome, I might somehow or other regain possession of it.*

---

*The hopes of the artist were not disappointed—the robber was stopped at one of the gates of Rome. Something in his looks or deportment had excited suspicion. He was searched, and the valuable trinkets found on him sufficiently evinced his character. On applying to the police, the artist's watch was returned to him.

In the mean time day declined, and no messenger returned from Tusculum.

The idea of passing another night in the woods was extremely disheartening; for I began to be satisfied with what I had seen of robber life. The chieftain now ordered his men to follow him that he might station them at their posts, adding, that if the messenger did not return before night they must shift their quarters to some other place.

I was again left alone with the young bandit who had before guarded me: he had the same gloomy air and haggard eye, with now and then a bitter sardonic smile. I was determined to probe this ulcerated heart, and reminded him of a kind of promise he had given me to tell me the cause of his suffering.

It seemed to me as if these troubled spirits were glad of an opportunity to disburthen themselves; and of having some fresh undiseased mind with which they could communicate. I had hardly made the request but he seated himself by my side, and gave me his story in, as nearly as I can recollect, the following words.

THE STORY OF THE YOUNG ROBBER

I was born at the little town of Frosinone, which lies at the skirts of the Abruzzi. My father had made a little property in trade, and gave me some education, as he intended me for the church, but I had kept gay company too much to relish the cowl, so I grew up a loiterer about the place. I was a heedless fellow, a little quarrelsome on occasions, but good humoured in the main, so I made my way very well for a time, until I fell in love. There lived in our town a surveyor, or land bailiff, of the prince's, who had a young daughter, a beautiful girl of sixteen. She was looked upon as something better than the common run of our townsfolk, and was kept almost entirely at home. I saw her occasionally, and became madly in love with her, she looked so fresh and tender, and so different from the sunburnt females to whom I had been accustomed.

As my father kept me in money, I always dressed well, and took all opportunities of showing myself off to advantage in the eyes of the little beauty. I used to see her at church; and as I could play a little upon the guitar, I gave a tune sometimes under her window of an evening; and I tried to have interviews with her in her father's vineyard, not far from the town, where she sometimes walked. She was evidently pleased with me, but she was young and shy, and her father kept a strict eye upon her, and took alarm at my attentions, for he had a bad opinion of me, and looked for a better match for his daughter. I became furious at the difficulties thrown in my way, having been accustomed always to easy success among the women, being considered one of the smartest young fellows of the place.

Her father brought home a suitor for her; a rich farmer from a neighbouring town. The wedding day was appointed, and preparations were making. I got sight of her at her window, and I thought she looked sadly at me. I determined the match should not take place, cost what it might. I met her intended bridegroom in the market place, and could not restrain the expression of my rage. A few hot words passed between us, when I drew my stiletto, and stabbed him to the heart. I fled to a neighbouring church for refuge; and with a little money I obtained absolution; but I did not dare to venture from my asylum.

At that time our captain was forming his troop. He had known me from boyhood, and hearing of my situation, came to me in secret, and made such offers, that I agreed to enrol myself among his followers. Indeed, I had more than once thought of taking to this mode of life, having known several brave fellows of the mountains, who used to spend their money freely among us youngsters of the town. I accordingly left my asylum late one night, repaired to the appointed place of meeting; took the oaths prescribed, and became one of the troop. We were for some time in a distant part of the mountains, and our wild adventurous kind of life hit my fancy wonderfully, and diverted my thoughts. At length they returned with all their violence to the recollection of Rosetta. The solitude in which I often found myself, gave me time to brood over her image, and as I have kept watch at night over our sleeping camp in the mountains, my feelings have been roused almost to a fever.

At length we shifted our ground, and determined to make a descent upon the road between Terracina and Naples. In the course of our expedition, we passed a day or two in the woody mountains which rise above Frosinone. I cannot tell you how I felt when I looked down upon the place, and distinguished the residence of Rosetta. I determined to have an interview with her; but to what purpose? I could not expect that she would quit her home, and accompany me in my hazardous life among the mountains. She had been brought up too tenderly for that; and when I looked upon the women who were associated with some of our troop, I could not have borne the thoughts of her being their companion. All return to my former life was likewise hopeless; for a price was set upon my head. Still I determined to see her; the very hazard and fruitlessness of the thing made me furious to accomplish it.

It is about three weeks since I persuaded our captain to draw down to the vicinity of Frosinone, in hopes of entrapping some of its principal inhabitants, and compelling them to a ransom. We were lying in ambush towards evening, not far from the vineyard of Rosetta's father. I stole quietly from my companions, and drew near to reconnoitre the place of her frequent walks.

How my heart beat when among the vines, I beheld the gleaming of a white dress! I knew it must be Rosetta's; it being rare for any female of the place to dress in white. I advanced secretly and without noise, until putting aside the vines, I stood suddenly before her. She uttered a piercing shriek, but I seized her in my arms, put my hand upon her mouth and conjured her to be silent. I poured out all the frenzy of my passion; offered to renounce my mode of life, to put my fate in her hands, to fly with her where we might live in safety together. All that I could say, or do, would not pacify her. Instead of love, horror and affright seemed to have taken possession of her breast.—She struggled partly from my grasp, and filled the air with her cries. In an instant the captain and the rest of my companions were around us. I would have given any thing at that moment had she been safe out of our hands, and in her father's house. It was too late. The captain pronounced her a prize, and ordered that she should be borne to the mountains. I represented to him that she was my prize, that I had a previous claim to her; and I mentioned my former attachment. He sneered bitterly in reply; observed that brigands had no business with village intrigues, and that, according to the laws of the troop, all spoils of the kind were determined by lot. Love and jealousy were raging in my heart, but I had to choose between obedience and death. I surrendered her to the captain, and we made for the mountains.

She was overcome by affright, and her steps were so feeble and faltering, that it was necessary to support her. I could not endure the idea that my comrades should touch her, and assuming a forced tranquillity, begged she might be confided to me, as one to whom she was more accustomed. The captain regarded me for a moment with a searching look, but I bore it without flinching, and he consented. I took her in my arms: she was almost senseless. Her head rested on my shoulder; I felt her breath on my face, and it seemed to fan the flame which devoured me. Oh God! to have this glowing treasure in my arms, and yet to think it was not mine!

We arrived at the foot of the mountain. I ascended it with difficulty, particularly where the woods were thick; but I would not relinquish my delicious burthen. I reflected with rage, however, that I must soon do so. The thoughts that so delicate a creature must be abandoned to my rude companions, maddened me. I felt tempted, the stiletto in my hand, to cut my way through them all, and bear her off in triumph. I scarcely conceived the idea, before I saw its rashness; but my brain was fevered with the thought that any but myself should enjoy her charms. I endeavoured to outstrip my companions by the quickness of my movements; and to get a little distance a head, in case any favourable opportunity of escape should present. Vain ef-

fort! The voice of the captain suddenly ordered a halt. I trembled, but had
to obey. The poor girl partly opened a languid eye, but was without strength
or motion. I laid her upon the grass. The captain darted on me a terrible
look of suspicion, and ordered me to scour the woods with my companions,
in search of some shepherd who might be sent to her father's to demand a
ransom.

I saw at once the peril. To resist with violence was certain death; but to
leave her alone, in the power of the captain!—I spoke out then with a fervour, inspired by my passion and my despair. I reminded the captain that I
was the first to seize her; that she was my prize, and that my previous attachment for her ought to make her sacred among my companions. I insisted, therefore, that he should pledge me his word to respect her; otherwise
I should refuse obedience to his orders. His only reply was, to cock his
carbine; and at the signal my comrades did the same. They laughed with
cruelty at my impotent rage. What could I do? I felt the madness of resistance. I was menaced on all hands, and my companions obliged me to
follow them. She remained alone with the chief—yes, alone—and almost
lifeless!——

Here the robber paused in his recital, overpowered by his emotions.
Great drops of sweat stood on his forehead; he panted rather than breathed;
his brawny bosom rose and fell like the waves of a troubled sea. When he
had become a little calm, he continued his recital.

I was not long in finding a shepherd, said he. I ran with the rapidity of a
deer, eager, if possible, to get back before what I dreaded might take place.
I had left my companions far behind, and I rejoined them before they had
reached one half the distance I had made. I hurried them back to the place
where we had left the captain. As we approached, I beheld him seated by
the side of Rosetta. His triumphant look, and the desolate condition of the
unfortunate girl, left me no doubt of her fate. I know not how I restrained
my fury.

It was with extreme difficulty, and by guiding her hand, that she was made
to trace a few characters, requesting her father to send three hundred dollars
as her ransom. The letter was despatched by the shepherd. When he was
gone, the chief turned sternly to me: "You have set an example," said he,
"of mutiny and self will, which if indulged would be ruinous to the troop.
Had I treated you as our laws require, this bullet would have been driven
through your brain. But you are an old friend: I have borne patiently with
your fury and your folly; I have even protected you from a foolish passion
that would have unmanned you. As to this girl, the laws of our association
must have their course." So saying, he gave his commands, lots were drawn,
and the helpless girl was abandoned to the troop.

Here the robber paused again, panting with fury, and it was some moments before he could resume his story.

Hell, said he, was raging in my heart. I beheld the impossibility of avenging myself, and I felt that, according to the articles in which we stood bound to one another, the captain was in the right. I rushed with frenzy from the place. I threw myself upon the earth; tore up the grass with my hands, and beat my head, and gnashed my teeth in agony and rage. When at length I returned, I beheld the wretched victim, pale, dishevelled; her dress torn and disordered. An emotion of pity for a moment subdued my fiercer feelings. I bore her to the foot of a tree, and leaned her gently against it. I took my gourd, which was filled with wine, and applying it to her lips, endeavoured to make her swallow a little. To what a condition was she reduced! She, whom I had once seen the pride of Frosinone, who but a short time before I had beheld sporting in her father's vineyard, so fresh and beautiful and happy! Her teeth were clenched; her eyes fixed on the ground; her form without motion, and in a state of absolute insensibility. I hung over her in an agony of recollection of all that she had been, and of anguish at what I now beheld her. I darted round a look of horror at my companions, who seemed like so many fiends exulting in the downfall of an angel, and I felt a horror at myself for being their accomplice.

The captain, always suspicious, saw with his usual penetration what was passing within me, and ordered me to go upon the ridge of the woods to keep a look out over the neighbourhood and await the return of the shepherd. I obeyed, of course, stifling the fury that raged within me, though I felt for the moment that he was my most deadly foe.

On my way, however, a ray of reflection came across my mind. I perceived that the captain was but following with strictness the terrible laws to which we had sworn fidelity. That the passion by which I had been blinded might with justice have been fatal to me but for his forbearance; that he had penetrated my soul, and had taken precautions, by sending me out of the way, to prevent my committing any excess in my anger. From that instant I felt that I was capable of pardoning him.

Occupied with these thoughts, I arrived at the foot of the mountain. The country was solitary and secure; and in a short time I beheld the shepherd at a distance crossing the plain. I hastened to meet him. He had obtained nothing. He had found the father plunged in the deepest distress. He had read the letter with violent emotion, and then calming himself with a sudden exertion, he had replied coldly, "My daughter has been dishonoured by those wretches; let her be returned without ransom, or let her die!"

I shuddered at this reply. I knew, according to the laws of our troop, her death was inevitable. Our oaths required it. I felt, nevertheless, that, not having been able to have her to myself, I could be her executioner!

The robber again paused with agitation. I sat musing upon his last frightful words, which proved to what excess the passions may be carried when escaped from all moral restraint. There was a horrible verity in this story that reminded me of some of the tragic fictions of Dante.

We now come to a fatal moment, resumed the bandit. After the report of the shepherd, I returned with him, and the chieftain received from his lips the refusal of the father. At a signal, which we all understood, we followed him some distance from the victim. He there pronounced her sentence of death. Every one stood ready to execute his order; but I interfered. I observed that there was something due to pity, as well as to justice. That I was as ready as any one to approve the implacable law which was to serve as a warning to all those who hesitated to pay the ransoms demanded for our prisoners, but that, though the sacrifice was proper, it ought to be made without cruelty. The night is approaching, continued I; she will soon be wrapped in sleep: let her then be despatched. All I now claim on the score of former kindness is, let me strike the blow. I will do it as surely, though more tenderly than another.

Several raised their voices against my proposition, but the captain imposed silence on them. He told me I might conduct her into a thicket at some distance, and he relied upon my promise.

I hastened to seize my prey. There was a forlorn kind of triumph at having at length become her exclusive possessor. I bore her off into the thickness of the forest. She remained in the same state of insensibility or stupor. I was thankful that she did not recollect me; for had she once murmured my name, I should have been overcome. She slept at length in the arms of him who was to poniard her. Many were the conflicts I underwent before I could bring myself to strike the blow. But my heart had become sore by the recent conflicts it had undergone, and I dreaded lest, by procrastination, some other should become her executioner. When her repose had continued for some time, I separated myself gently from her, that I might not disturb her sleep, and seizing suddenly my poniard, plunged it into her bosom. A painful and concentrated murmur, but without any convulsive movement, accompanied her last sigh. So perished this unfortunate.

He ceased to speak. I sat horror struck, covering my face with my hands, seeking, as it were, to hide from myself the frightful images he had presented to my mind. I was roused from this silence, by the voice of the captain. "You sleep," said he, "and it is time to be off. Come, we must abandon this height, as night is setting in, and the messenger is not returned. I will post some one on the mountain edge, to conduct him to the place where we shall pass the night."

This was no agreeable news to me. I was sick at heart with the dismal story I had heard. I was harassed and fatigued, and the sight of the banditti began to grow insupportable to me.

The captain assembled his comrades. We rapidly descended the forest which we had mounted with so much difficulty in the morning, and soon arrived in what appeared to be a frequented road. The robbers proceeded with great caution, carrying their guns cocked, and looking on every side with wary and suspicious eyes. They were apprehensive of encountering the civic patrole. We left Rocca Priori behind us. There was a fountain near by, and as I was excessively thirsty, I begged permission to stop and drink. The captain himself went, and brought me water in his hat. We pursued our route, when, at the extremity of an alley which crossed the road, I perceived a female on horseback, dressed in white. She was alone. I recollected the fate of the poor girl in the story, and trembled for her safety.

One of the brigands saw her at the same instant, and plunging into the bushes, he ran precipitately in the direction towards her. Stopping on the border of the alley, he put one knee to the ground, presented his carbine ready to menace her, or to shoot her horse if she attempted to fly, and in this way awaited her approach. I kept my eyes fixed on her with intense anxiety. I felt tempted to shout, and warn her of her danger, though my own destruction would have been the consequence. It was awful to see this tiger crouching ready for a bound, and the poor innocent victim wandering unconsciously near him. Nothing but a mere chance could save her. To my joy, the chance turned in her favour. She seemed almost accidentally to take an opposite path, which led outside of the wood, where the robber dared not venture. To this casual deviation, she owed her safety.

I could not imagine why the captain of the band had ventured to such a distance from the height, on which he had placed the sentinel to watch the return of the messenger. He seemed himself anxious at the risk to which he exposed himself. His movements were rapid and uneasy; I could scarce keep pace with him. At length, after three hours of what might be termed a forced march, we mounted the extremity of the same woods, the summit of which we had occupied during the day; and I learnt, with satisfaction, that we had reached our quarters for the night. "You must be fatigued," said the chieftain; "but it was necessary to survey the environs, so as not to be surprised during the night. Had we met with the famous civic guard of Rocca Priori you would have seen fine sport." Such was the indefatigable precaution and forethought of this robber chief, who really gave continual evidences of military talent.

The night was magnificent. The moon rising above the horizon in a cloudless sky, faintly lit up the grand features of the mountains, while lights twinkling here and there, like terrestrial stars, in the wide, dusky expanse of the landscape, betrayed the lonely cabins of the shepherds. Exhausted by fatigue, and by the many agitations I had experienced, I prepared to sleep, soothed by the hope of approaching deliverance. The captain ordered his companions to collect some dry moss; he arranged with his own hands a kind of mattress and pillow of it, and gave me his ample mantle as a covering. I could not but feel both surprised and gratified by such unexpected attentions on the part of this benevolent cut-throat: for there is nothing more striking than to find the ordinary charities, which are matters of course in common life, flourishing by the side of such stern and sterile crime. It is like finding the tender flowers and fresh herbage of the valley growing among the rocks and cinders of the volcano.

Before I fell asleep, I had some further discourse with the captain, who seemed to feel great confidence in me. He referred to our previous conversation of the morning, told me he was weary of his hazardous profession; that he had acquired sufficient property, and was anxious to return to the world and lead a peaceful life in the bosom of his family. He wished to know whether it was not in my power to procure him a passport for the United States of America. I applauded his good intentions, and promised to do every thing in my power to promote its success. We then parted for the night. I stretched myself upon my couch of moss, which, after my fatigues, felt like a bed of down, and sheltered by the robber's mantle from all humidity, I slept soundly without waking, until the signal to arise.

It was nearly six o'clock, and the day was just dawning. As the place where we had passed the night was too much exposed, we moved up into the thickness of the woods. A fire was kindled. While there was any flame, the mantles were again extended round it; but when nothing remained but glowing cinders, they were lowered, and the robbers seated themselves in a circle.

The scene before me reminded me of some of those described by Homer. There wanted only the victim on the coals, and the sacred knife, to cut off the succulent parts, and distribute them around. My companions might have rivaled the grim warriors of Greece. In place of the noble repasts, however, of Achilles and Agamemnon, I beheld displayed on the grass the remains of the ham which had sustained so vigorous an attack on the preceding evening, accompanied by the reliques of the bread, cheese and wine.

We had scarcely commenced our frugal breakfast, when I heard again an imitation of the bleating of sheep, similar to what I had heard the day before. The captain answered it in the same tone. Two men were soon after seen descending from the woody height, where we had passed the preceding evening. On nearer approach, they proved to be the sentinel and the messenger. The captain rose and went to meet them. He made a signal for his comrades to join him. They had a short conference, and then returning to me with great eagerness, "Your ransom is paid," said he; "you are free!"

Though I had anticipated deliverance, I cannot tell you what a rush of delight these tidings gave me. I cared not to finish my repast, but prepared to depart. The captain took me by the hand; requested permission to write

to me, and begged me not to forget the passport. I replied, that I hoped to
be of effectual service to him, and that I relied on his honour to return the
prince's note for five hundred dollars, now that the cash was paid. He regarded me for a moment with surprise; then, seeming to recollect himself,
"E giusto," said he, "eccolo—adio!"* He delivered me the note, pressed my
hand once more, and we separated. The labourers were permitted to follow
me, and we resumed with joy our road towards Tusculum.

————

The Frenchman ceased to speak; the party continued for a few moments
to pace the shore in silence. The story had made a deep impression, particularly on the Venetian lady. At that part which related to the young girl of
Frosinone, she was violently affected; sobs broke from her; she clung closer
to her husband, and as she looked up to him as if for protection, the moon
beams shining on her beautifully fair countenance showed it paler than usual, while tears glittered in her fine dark eyes.

"Corragio, mia vita!" said he, as he gently and fondly tapped the white
hand that lay upon his arm.

The Englishman alone preserved his usual phlegm, and the fair Venetian
was piqued at it.

She had pardoned him a want of gallantry towards herself, though a sin of
omission seldom met with in the gallant climate of Italy, but the quiet coolness which he maintained in matters which so much affected her; and the
slow credence which he had given to the stories which had filled her with
alarm, were quite vexatious.

"Santa Maria!" said she to her husband as they retired for the night, "what
insensible beings these English are!"

THE ADVENTURE OF THE ENGLISHMAN

In the morning all was bustle in the inn at Terracina.

The procaccio had departed at day break, on its route towards Rome, but
the Englishman was yet to start, and the departure of an English equipage
is always enough to keep an inn in a bustle. On this occasion there was more
than usual stir; for the Englishman having much property about him, and
having been convinced of the real danger of the road, had applied to the

*It is just—there it is—adieu!

police and obtained, by dint of liberal pay, an escort of eight dragoons and twelve foot soldiers, as far as Fondi.

Perhaps, too, there might have been a little ostentation at bottom, from which, with great delicacy be it spoken, English travellers are not always exempt; though to say the truth, he had nothing of it in his manner. He moved about taciturn and reserved as usual, among the gaping crowd, in his gingerbread coloured travelling cap, with his hands in his pockets. He gave laconic orders to John as he packed away the thousand and one indispensable conveniencies of the night, double loaded his pistols with great *sang froid*, and deposited them in the pockets of the carriage, taking no notice of a pair of keen eyes gazing on him from among the herd of loitering idlers. The fair Venetian now came up with a request made in her dulcet tones, that he would permit their carriage to proceed under protection of his escort. The Englishman, who was busy loading another pair of pistols for his servant, and held the ramrod between his teeth, nodded assent as a matter of course, but without lifting up his eyes. The fair Venetian was not accustomed to such indifference. "O Dio!" ejaculated she softly as she retired, "Quanto sono insensibili questi Inglesi." At length off they set in gallant style, the eight dragoons prancing in front, the twelve foot soldiers marching in rear, and the carriages moving slowly in the centre to enable the infantry to keep pace with them. They had proceeded but a few hundred yards when it was discovered that some indispensable article had been left behind.

In fact the Englishman's purse was missing, and John was despatched to the inn to search for it.

This occasioned a little delay, and the carriage of the Venetians drove slowly on. John came back out of breath and out of humour, the purse was not to be found, his master was irritated, he recollected the very place where it lay: the cursed Italian servant had pocketed it. John was again sent back. He returned once more, without the purse, but with the landlord and the whole household at his heels. A thousand ejaculations and protestations, accompanied by all sorts of grimaces and contortions. "No purse had been seen— his eccellenza must be mistaken."

No—his eccellenza was not mistaken; the purse lay on the marble table, under the mirror, a green purse, half full of gold and silver. Again a thousand grimaces and contortions, and vows by San Gennaro, that no purse of the kind had been seen.

The Englishman became furious. "The waiter had pocketed it. The landlord was a knave. The inn a den of thieves—it was a d——d country—he had been cheated and plundered from one end of it to the other—but he'd have satisfaction—he'd drive right off to the police."

He was on the point of ordering the postillions to turn back, when, on rising, he displaced the cushion of the carriage, and the purse of money fell chinking to the floor.

All the blood in his body seemed to rush into his face. "D—n the purse," said he, as he snatched it up. He dashed a handfull of money on the ground before the pale cringing waiter. "There—be off," cried he: "John, order the postillions to drive on."

Above half an hour had been exhausted in this altercation. The Venetian carriage had loitered along; its passengers looking out from time to time, and expecting the escort every moment to follow. They had gradually turned an angle of the road that shut them out of sight. The little army was again in motion, and made a very picturesque appearance as it wound along at the bottom of the rocks; the morning sunshine beaming upon the weapons of the soldiery.

The Englishman lolled back in his carriage, vexed with himself at what had passed, and consequently out of humour with all the world. As this, however, is no uncommon case with gentlemen who travel for their pleasure, it is hardly worthy of remark.

They had wound up from the coast among the hills, and came to a part of the road that admitted of some prospect ahead.

"I see nothing of the lady's carriage, sir," said John, leaning down from the coach box.

"Hang the lady's carriage!" said the Englishman, crustily; "don't plague me about the lady's carriage; must I be continually pestered with strangers?"

John said not another word, for he understood his master's mood. The road grew more wild and lonely; they were slowly proceeding in a foot pace up a hill; the dragoons were some distance ahead, and had just reached the summit of the hill, when they uttered an exclamation, or rather shout, and galloped forward. The Englishman was roused from his sulky reverie. He stretched his head from the carriage which had attained the brow of the hill. Before him extended a long hollow defile, commanded on one side by rugged precipitous heights, covered with bushes and scanty forest. At some distance, he beheld the carriage of the Venetians overturned; a numerous gang of desperadoes were rifling it; the young man and his servant were overpowered and partly stripped, and the lady was in the hands of two of the ruffians. The Englishman seized his pistols, sprang from the carriage, and called upon John to follow him. In the mean time as the dragoons came forward, the robbers who were busy with the carriage quitted their spoil, formed themselves in the middle of the road, and taking deliberate aim, fired. One of the dragoons fell, another was wounded, and the whole were for a moment checked and thrown in confusion. The robbers loaded again in an instant. The dragoons discharged their carbines, but without apparent effect; they received another volley, which, though none fell, threw them again into confusion. The robbers were loading a second time, when they saw the foot soldiers at hand.—"Scampa via!" was the word. They abandoned their prey, and retreated up the rocks; the soldiers after them. They fought from cliff to cliff and bush to bush, the robbers turning every now and then to fire upon their pursuers; the soldiers scrambling after them, and discharging their muskets whenever they could get a chance. Sometimes a soldier or a robber was shot down, and came tumbling among the cliffs. The dragoons kept firing from below, whenever a robber came in sight.

The Englishman had hastened to the scene of action, and the balls discharged at the dragoons had whistled past him as he advanced. One object, however, engrossed his attention. It was the beautiful Venetian lady in the hands of two of the robbers, who during the confusion of the fight, carried her shrieking up the mountain. He saw her dress gleaming among the bushes, and he sprang up the rocks to intercept the robbers as they bore off their prey. The ruggedness of the steep and the entanglements of the bushes, delayed and impeded him. He lost sight of the lady, but was still guided by her cries, which grew fainter and fainter. They were off to the left, while the reports of muskets showed that the battle was raging to the right.

At length he came upon what appeared to be a rugged footpath, faintly worn in a gully of the rocks, and beheld the ruffians at some distance hurrying the lady up the defile. One of them hearing his approach let go his prey, advanced towards him, and levelling the carbine which had been slung on his back, fired. The ball whizzed through the Englishman's hat, and carried with it some of his hair. He returned the fire with one of his pistols; and the robber fell. The other brigand now dropped the lady, and drawing a long pistol from his belt, fired on his adversary with deliberate aim; the ball passed between his left arm and his side, slightly wounding the arm. The Englishman advanced and discharged his remaining pistol, which wounded the robber, but not severely. The brigand drew a stiletto, and rushed upon his adversary, who eluded the blow, receiving merely a slight wound, and defended himself with his pistol, which had a spring bayonet. They closed with one another, and a desperate struggle ensued. The robber was a square built, thick set man, powerful, muscular and active. The Englishman though of larger frame and greater strength, was less active and less accustomed to athletic exercises and feats of hardihood, but he showed himself practised and skilled in the art of defence. They were on a craggy height, and the Englishman perceived that his antagonist was striving to press him to the edge.

A side glance showed him also the robber whom he had first wounded, scrambling up to the assistance of his comrade, stiletto in hand. He had, in fact, attained the summit of the cliff, he was within a few steps, and the Englishman felt that his case was desperate, when he heard suddenly the report of a pistol and the ruffian fell. The shot came from John, who had arrived just in time to save his master.

The remaining robber, exhausted by loss of blood and the violence of the contest, showed signs of faltering. The Englishman pursued his advantage;

pressed on him, and as his strength relaxed, dashed him headlong from the precipice. He looked after him and saw him lying motionless among the rocks below.

The Englishman now sought the fair Venetian. He found her senseless on the ground. With his servant's assistance he bore her down to the road, where her husband was raving like one distracted. He had sought her in vain, and had given her over for lost; and when he beheld her thus brought back in safety, his joy was equally wild and ungovernable. He would have caught her insensible form to his bosom had not the Englishman restrained him. The latter, now really aroused, displayed a true tenderness and manly gallantry which one would not have expected from his habitual phlegm. His kindness, however, was practical, not wasted in words. He despatched John to the carriage for restoratives of all kinds, and, totally thoughtless of himself, was anxious only about his lovely charge.

The occasional discharge of fire arms along the height showed that a re-treating fight was still kept up by the robbers. The lady gave signs of reviving animation. The Englishman, eager to get her from this place of danger, conveyed her to his own carriage, and, committing her to the care of her husband, ordered the dragoons to escort them to Fondi. The Venetian would have insisted on the Englishman's getting into the carriage; but the latter refused. He poured forth a torrent of thanks and benedictions; but the Englishman beckoned to the postillions to drive on.

John now dressed his master's wounds, which were found not to be serious, though he was faint with loss of blood. The Venetian carriage had been righted, and the baggage replaced; and, getting into it, they set out on their way towards Fondi, leaving the foot soldiers still engaged in ferreting out the banditti.

Before arriving at Fondi the fair Venetian had completely recovered from her swoon. She made the usual question—

"Where was she?"

"In the Englishman's carriage."

"How had she escaped from the robbers?"

"The Englishman had rescued her."

Her transports were unbounded; and mingled with them were enthusiastic ejaculations of gratitude to her deliverer. A thousand times did she reproach herself for having accused him of coldness and insensibility. The moment she saw him she rushed into his arms with the vivacity of her nation, and hung about his neck in a speechless transport of gratitude.

Never was man more embarrassed by the embraces of a fine woman.

"Tut! tut!" said the Englishman.

"You are wounded!" shrieked the fair Venetian, as she saw blood upon his clothes.

"Pooh—nothing at all!"

"My deliverer!—my angel!" exclaimed she, clasping him again round the neck and sobbing on his bosom.

"Pooh!" said the Englishman, looking somewhat foolish, "this is all nonsense."

PART IV
THE MONEY DIGGERS

FOUND AMONG THE PAPERS OF
THE LATE DIEDRICH KNICKERBOCKER

Now I remember those old women's words
Who in my youth would tell me winter's tales;
And speak of spirits and ghosts that glide by night
About the place where treasure hath been hid.
                    MARLOW'S JEW OF MALTA

HELL GATE

About six miles from the renowned city of the Manhattoes, in that Sound, or arm of the sea, which passes between the main land and Nassau or Long Island, there is a narrow strait, where the current is violently compressed between shouldering promontories, and horribly perplexed by rocks and shoals. Being at the best of times a very violent, impetuous current, it takes these impediments in mighty dudgeon; boiling in whirlpools; brawling and fretting in ripples; raging and roaring in rapids and breakers; and, in short, indulging in all kinds of wrong headed paroxysms. At such times, wo to any unlucky vessel that ventures within its clutches.

This termagant humour, however, prevails only at certain times of tide. At low water, for instance, it is as pacific a stream as you would wish to see; but as the tide rises, it begins to fret; at half tide it roars with might and main, like a bully bellowing for more drink; but when the tide is full it relapses into quiet, and for a time sleeps as soundly as an alderman after dinner. In fact, it may be compared to a quarrelsome toper, who is a peaceable fellow enough when he has no liquor at all, or when he has a skin full, but who, when half seas over, plays the very devil.

This mighty blustering, bullying, hard drinking little strait was a place of great danger and perplexity to the Dutch navigators of ancient days; hectoring their tub built barks in a most unruly style; whirling them about, in a manner to make any but a Dutchman giddy, and not unfrequently stranding them upon rocks and reefs, as it did the famous squadron of Oloffe the Dreamer, when seeking a place to found the city of the Manhattoes. Whereupon out of sheer spleen they denominated it Hellegat and solemnly gave it over to the devil. This appellation has since been aptly rendered into English by the name of Hell Gate; and into nonsense by the name of Hurl Gate, according to certain foreign intruders who neither understood Dutch nor English.—May St. Nicholas confound them!

This strait of Hell Gate was a place of great awe and perilous enterprise to me in my boyhood; having been much of a navigator on those small seas, and having more than once run the risk of shipwreck and drowning in the course of certain holyday voyages, to which in common with other Dutch urchins I was rather prone. Indeed, partly from the name, and partly from various strange circumstances connected with it, this place had far more terrors in the eyes of my truant companions and myself than had Scylla and Charybdis for the navigators of yore.

In the midst of this strait, and hard by a group of rocks called "the Hen and Chickens," there lay the wreck of a vessel which had been entangled in the whirlpools and stranded during a storm. There was a wild story told to us of this being the wreck of a pirate, and some tale of bloody murder which I cannot now recollect, but which made us regard it with great awe, and keep far from it in our cruisings. Indeed, the desolate look of this forlorn hulk, and the fearful place where it lay rotting, were enough to awaken strange notions. A row of timber heads, blackened by time, just peered above the surface at high water; but at low tide a considerable part of the hull was bare, and its great ribs or timbers, partly stripped of their planks and dripping with sea weeds, looked like the huge skeleton of some sea monster. There was also the stump of a mast, with a few ropes and blocks swinging about and whistling in the wind, while the sea gull wheeled and screamed around the melancholy carcass. I have a faint recollection of some hobgoblin tale of sailors' ghosts being seen about this wreck at night, with bare sculls, and blue lights in their sockets instead of eyes, but I have forgotten all the particulars.

In fact, the whole of this neighbourhood was, like the straits of Pylorus of yore, a region of fable and romance to me. From the strait to the Manhattoes the borders of the Sound are greatly diversified, being broken and indented by rocky nooks overhung with trees, which give them a wild and romantic look. In the time of my boyhood they abounded with traditions about pirates, ghosts, smugglers, and buried money; which had a wonderful effect upon the young minds of my companions and myself.

As I grew to more mature years I made diligent research after the truth of these strange traditions; for I have always been a curious investigator of the valuable but obscure branches of the history of my native province. I found infinite difficulty, however, in arriving at any precise information. In seeking to dig up one fact it is incredible the number of fables which I unearthed. I will say nothing of the Devil's Stepping Stones, by which that arch fiend made his retreat from Connecticut to Long Island, across the Sound; seeing the subject is likely to be learnedly treated by a worthy friend and contemporary historian whom I have furnished with particulars thereof.* Neither will I say any thing of the black man in a three cornered hat, seated in the stern of a jolly boat who used to be seen about Hell Gate in stormy weather; and who went by the name of the Pirate's Spuke (i.e. Pirate's Ghost), and whom, it is said, old Governor Stuyvesant once shot with a silver bullet; because I never could meet with any person of stanch credibility who professed to have seen this spectrum; unless it were the widow of Manus Conklin the blacksmith of Frogs Neck; but then, poor woman, she was a little purblind, and might have been mistaken; though they say she saw farther than other folks in the dark.

All this, however, was but little satisfactory in regard to the tales of pirates and their buried money about which I was most curious; and the following

---

*For a very interesting and authentic account of the Devil and his Stepping Stones, see the valuable memoir read before the New-York Historical Society since the death of Mr. Knickerbocker, by his friend, an eminent jurist of the place.

is all that I could for a long time collect that had any thing like an air of authenticity.

KIDD THE PIRATE

In old times, just after the territory of the New Netherlands had been wrested from the hands of their High Mightinesses the Lords States General of Holland, by King Charles the Second, and while it was as yet in an unquiet state, the province was a great resort of random adventurers, loose livers, and all that class of haphazard fellows who live by their wits, and dislike the old fashioned restraint of law and gospel. Among these, the foremost were the Buccaneers. These were rovers of the deep, who, perhaps, in time of war had been educated in those schools of piracy, the privateers; but having once tasted the sweets of plunder, had ever retained a hankering after it. There is but a slight step from the privateersman to the pirate; both fight for the love of plunder; only that the latter is the bravest, as he dares both the enemy and the gallows.

But in whatever school they had been taught, the Buccaneers who kept about the English colonies were daring fellows, and made sad work in times of peace among the Spanish settlements and Spanish merchantmen. The easy access to the harbour of the Manhattoes, the number of hiding places about its waters, and the laxity of its scarcely organized government, made it a great rendezvous of the pirates, where they might dispose of their booty, and concert new depredations. As they brought home with them wealthy lading of all kinds, the luxuries of the tropics, and the sumptuous spoils of the Spanish provinces, and disposed of them with the proverbial carelessness of freebooters, they were welcome visitors to the thrifty traders of the Manhattoes. Crews of these desperadoes, therefore, the runagates of every country and every clime, might be seen swaggering, in open day, about the streets of the little burgh; elbowing its quiet Mynheers; trafficking away their rich outlandish plunder, at half or quarter price, to the wary merchant, and then squandering their prize money in taverns; drinking, gambling, singing, swearing, shouting, and astounding the neighbourhood with midnight brawl and ruffian revelry.

At length these excesses rose to such a height as to become a scandal to the provinces, and to call loudly for the interposition of government. Measures were accordingly taken to put a stop to the widely extended evil, and to ferret this vermin brood out of the colonies.

Among the agents employed to execute this purpose was the notorious Captain Kidd. He had long been an equivocal character; one of those nondescript animals of the ocean that are neither fish, flesh, nor fowl. He was somewhat of a trader, something more of a smuggler, with a considerable dash of the pickaroon. He had traded for many years among the pirates, in a little rakish, musquito built vessel, that could run into all kinds of waters. He knew all their haunts and lurking places; was always hooking about on mysterious voyages; and as busy as a Mother Cary's chicken in a storm.

This nondescript personage was pitched upon by government as the very man to hunt the pirates by sea, upon the good old maxim of "setting a rogue to catch a rogue;" or as otters are sometimes used to catch their cousins german, the fish. Kidd accordingly sailed for New York, in 1695, in a gallant vessel called the Adventure Galley, well armed and duly commissioned. On arriving at his old haunts, however, he shipped his crew on new terms; enlisted a number of his old comrades, lads of the knife and the pistol, and then set sail for the East. Instead of cruising against pirates he turned pirate himself: steered to the Madeiras, to Bonavista, and Madagascar, and cruised about the entrance of the Red Sea. Here, among other maritime robberies, he captured a rich Quedah merchantman, manned by Moors, though commanded by an Englishman. Kidd would fain have passed this off for a worthy exploit, as being a kind of crusade against the infidels; but government had long since lost all relish for such Christian triumphs.

After roaming the seas, trafficking his prizes, and changing from ship to ship, Kidd had the hardihood to return to Boston, laden with booty, with a crew of swaggering companions at his heels.

Times, however, had changed. The buccaneers could no longer show a whisker in the colonies with impunity. The new governor, Lord Bellamont, had signalized himself by his zeal in extirpating these offenders; and was doubly exasperated against Kidd, having been instrumental in appointing him to the trust which he had betrayed. No sooner, therefore, did he show himself in Boston, than the alarm was given of his reappearance, and measures were taken to arrest this cut-purse of the ocean. The daring character which Kidd had acquired, however, and the desperate fellows who followed like bull dogs at his heels, caused a little delay in his arrest. He took advantage of this, it is said, to bury the greater part of his treasures, and then carried a high head about the streets of Boston. He even attempted to defend himself when arrested; but was secured and thrown into prison, with his followers. Such was the formidable character of this pirate and his crew, that it was thought advisable to despatch a frigate to bring them to England. Great exertions were made to screen him from justice, but in vain; he and his comrades were tried, condemned, and hanged at Execution Dock in London. Kidd died hard, for the rope with which he was first tied up broke with his weight, and he tumbled to the ground; he was tied up a second time, and more effectually; hence came, doubtless, the story of Kidd's having a charmed life, and that he had to be twice hanged.

Such is the main outline of Kidd's history; but it has given birth to an innumerable progeny of traditions. The report of his having buried great treasures of gold and jewels before his arrest set the brains of all the good people along the coast in a ferment. There were rumours on rumours of great sums of money found here and there; sometimes in one part of the country, sometimes in another; of coins with Moorish inscriptions, doubtless the spoils of his eastern prizes, but which the common people looked upon with superstitious awe, regarding the Moorish letters as diabolical or magical characters.

Some reported the treasure to have been buried in solitary unsettled places, about Plymouth and Cape Cod; but by degrees various other parts, not only on the eastern coast, but along the shores of the Sound, and even of Manhattan and Long Island, were gilded by these rumours. In fact, the rigorous measures of Lord Bellamont spread sudden consternation among the buccaneers in every part of the provinces: they secreted their money and jewels in lonely out of the way places, about the wild shores of the rivers and sea coast, and dispersed themselves over the face of the country. The hand of justice prevented many of them from ever returning to regain their buried treasures, which remained, and remain probably to this day, objects of enterprise for the money digger.

This is the cause of those frequent reports of trees and rocks bearing mysterious marks, supposed to indicate the spots where treasure lay hidden; and many have been the ransackings after the pirates' booty.

In all the stories which once abounded of these enterprizes the devil played a conspicuous part. Either he was conciliated by ceremonies and invocations, or some solemn compact was made with him. Still he was ever prone to play the money diggers some slippery trick. Some would dig so far as to come to an iron chest, when some baffling circumstance was sure to take place. Either the earth would fall in and fill up the pit, or some direful noise or apparition would frighten the party from the place; and sometimes the devil himself would appear and bear off the prize when within their very grasp; and if they revisited the place the next day not a trace would be found of their labours of the preceding night.

All these rumours, however, were extremely vague, and for a long time tantalized without gratifying my curiosity. There is nothing in this world so hard to get at as truth, and there is nothing in this world but truth that I care for. I sought among all my favourite sources of authentic information, the oldest inhabitants, and particularly the old Dutch wives of the province; but though I flatter myself I am better versed than most men in the curious history of my native province, yet for a long time my inquiries were unattended with any substantial result.

At length it happened that, one calm day in the latter part of summer, I was relaxing myself from the toils of severe study by a day's amusement in fishing in those waters which had been the favourite resort of my boyhood. I was in company with several worthy burghers of my native city, among whom were more than one illustrious member of the corporation, whose names, did I dare to mention them, would do honour to my humble page. Our sport was indifferent; the fish did not bite freely; and we frequently changed our fishing ground, without bettering our luck. We were at length anchored close under a ledge of rocky coast, on the eastern side of the island of Mannahata. It was a still, warm day. The stream whirled and dimpled by us without a wave or even a ripple, and every thing was so calm and quiet, that it was almost startling when the kingfisher would pitch himself from the branch of some dry tree, and after suspending himself for a moment in the air to take his aim, would souse into the smooth water after his prey. While we were lolling in our boat, half drowsy with the warm stillness of the day and the dullness of our sport, one of our party, a worthy alderman, was overtaken by a slumber, and as he dozed suffered the sinker of his drop line to lie upon the bottom of the river. On waking he found he had caught something of importance, from the weight; on drawing it to the surface, we were much surprised to find a long pistol of very curious and outlandish fashion, which from its rusted condition, and its stock being worm eaten, and covered with barnacles, appeared to have lain a long time under water. The unexpected appearance of this document of warfare occasioned much speculation among my pacific companions. One supposed it to have fallen there during the revolutionary war. Another, from the peculiarity of its fashion, attributed it to the voyagers in the earliest days of the settlement; perchance to the renowned Adrian Block who explored the Sound and discovered Block Island, since so noted for its cheese. But a third, after regarding it for some time, pronounced it to be of veritable Spanish workmanship.

"I'll warrant," said he, "if this pistol could talk it would tell strange stories of hard fights among the Spanish Dons. I've no doubt but it is a relique of the buccaneers of old times—who knows but it belonged to Kidd himself?"

"Ah, that Kidd was a resolute fellow," cried an iron faced Cape Cod whaler. "There's a fine old song about him, all to the tune of

'My name is Robert Kidd,
As I sailed, as I sailed.'

And then it tells all about how he gained the devil's good graces by burying the bible;

'I had the bible in my hand,
As I sailed, as I sailed,

> And I buried it in the sand,
>   As I sailed.'

Odsfish, if I thought this pistol had belonged to Kidd I should set great store by it for curiosity's sake. By the way, I recollect a story about a fellow who once dug up Kidd's buried money, which was written by a neighbour of mine, and which I learnt by heart. As the fish don't bite just now, I'll tell it to you, by way of passing away the time."—And so saying, he gave us the following narration.

THE DEVIL AND TOM WALKER

A few miles from Boston, in Massachusetts, there is a deep inlet winding several miles into the interior of the country from Charles Bay, and terminating in a thickly wooded swamp, or morass. On one side of this inlet is a beautiful dark grove; on the opposite side the land rises abruptly from the water's edge, into a high ridge on which grow a few scattered oaks of great age and immense size. Under one of these gigantic trees, according to old stories, there was a great amount of treasure buried by Kidd the pirate. The inlet allowed a facility to bring the money in a boat secretly and at night to the very foot of the hill. The elevation of the place permitted a good look out to be kept that no one was at hand, while the remarkable trees formed good landmarks by which the place might easily be found again. The old stories add, moreover, that the devil presided at the hiding of the money, and took it under his guardianship; but this, it is well known, he always does with buried treasure, particularly when it has been ill gotten. Be that as it may, Kidd never returned to recover his wealth; being shortly after seized at Boston, sent out to England, and there hanged for a pirate.

About the year 1727, just at the time when earthquakes were prevalent in New England, and shook many tall sinners down upon their knees, there lived near this place a meagre miserly fellow of the name of Tom Walker. He had a wife as miserly as himself; they were so miserly that they even conspired to cheat each other. Whatever the woman could lay hands on she hid away: a hen could not cackle but she was on the alert to secure the new laid egg. Her husband was continually prying about to detect her secret hoards, and many and fierce were the conflicts that took place about what ought to have been common property. They lived in a forlorn looking house, that stood alone and had an air of starvation. A few straggling savin trees, emblems of sterility, grew near it; no smoke ever curled from its chimney;

no traveller stopped at its door. A miserable horse, whose ribs were as articulate as the bars of a gridiron, stalked about a field where a thin carpet of
moss, scarcely covering the ragged beds of pudding stone, tantalized and
balked his hunger; and sometimes he would lean his head over the fence,
look piteously at the passer by, and seem to petition deliverance from this
land of famine. The house and its inmates had altogether a bad name. Tom's
wife was a tall termagant, fierce of temper, loud of tongue, and strong of
arm. Her voice was often heard in wordy warfare with her husband; and his
face sometimes showed signs that their conflicts were not confined to words.
No one ventured, however, to interfere between them; the lonely wayfarer
shrank within himself at the horrid clamour and clapper clawing; eyed the
den of discord askance, and hurried on his way, rejoicing, if a bachelor, in
his celibacy.

One day that Tom Walker had been to a distant part of the neighbourhood, he took what he considered a short cut homewards through the
swamp. Like most short cuts, it was an ill chosen route. The swamp was
thickly grown with great gloomy pines and hemlocks, some of them ninety
feet high; which made it dark at noonday, and a retreat for all the owls of
the neighbourhood. It was full of pits and quagmires, partly covered with
weeds and mosses; where the green surface often betrayed the traveller into
a gulf of black smothering mud; there were also dark and stagnant pools, the
abodes of the tadpole, the bull frog, and the water snake, where the trunks
of pines and hemlocks lay half drowned, half rotting, looking like alligators,
sleeping in the mire.

Tom had long been picking his way cautiously through this treacherous
forest; stepping from tuft to tuft of rushes and roots which afforded precar-
ious footholds among deep sloughs; or pacing carefully, like a cat, along the
prostrate trunks of trees; startled now and then by the sudden screaming of
the bittern, or the quacking of a wild duck, rising on the wing from some
solitary pool. At length he arrived at a piece of firm ground, which ran out
like a peninsula into the deep bosom of the swamp. It had been one of the
strong holds of the Indians during their wars with the first colonists. Here
they had thrown up a kind of fort which they had looked upon as almost
impregnable, and had used as a place of refuge for their squaws and children. Nothing remained of the old Indian fort but a few embankments gradually sinking to the level of the surrounding earth, and already overgrown
in part by oaks and other forest trees, the foliage of which formed a contrast
to the dark pines and hemlocks of the swamp.

It was late in the dusk of evening when Tom Walker reached the old fort,
and he paused there for a while to rest himself. Any one but he would have
felt unwilling to linger in this lonely melancholy place, for the common people had a bad opinion of it from the stories handed down from the time of
the Indian wars; when it was asserted that the savages held incantations here

and made sacrifices to the evil spirit. Tom Walker, however, was not a man to be troubled with any fears of the kind.

He reposed himself for some time on the trunk of a fallen hemlock, listening to the boding cry of the tree toad, and delving with his walking staff into a mound of black mould at his feet. As he turned up the soil unconsciously, his staff struck against something hard. He raked it out of the vegetable mould, and lo! a cloven skull with an Indian tomahawk buried deep in it, lay before him. The rust on the weapon showed the time that had elapsed since this death blow had been given. It was a dreary memento of the fierce struggle that had taken place in this last foothold of the Indian warriors.

"Humph!" said Tom Walker, as he gave the skull a kick to shake the dirt from it.

"Let that skull alone!" said a gruff voice.

Tom lifted up his eyes and beheld a great black man, seated directly opposite him on the stump of a tree. He was exceedingly surprised, having neither seen nor heard any one approach, and he was still more perplexed on observing, as well as the gathering gloom would permit, that the stranger was neither negro nor Indian. It is true, he was dressed in a rude, half Indian garb, and had a red belt or sash swathed round his body, but his face was neither black nor copper colour, but swarthy and dingy and begrimed with soot, as if he had been accustomed to toil among fires and forges. He had a shock of coarse black hair, that stood out from his head in all directions; and bore an axe on his shoulder.

He scowled for a moment at Tom with a pair of great red eyes.

"What are you doing on my grounds?" said the black man, with a hoarse growling voice.

"Your grounds?" said Tom, with a sneer; "no more your grounds than mine: they belong to Deacon Peabody."

"Deacon Peabody be d——d," said the stranger, "as I flatter myself he will be, if he does not look more to his own sins and less to those of his neighbours. Look yonder, and see how Deacon Peabody is faring."

Tom looked in the direction that the stranger pointed, and beheld one of the great trees, fair and flourishing without, but rotten at the core, and saw that it had been nearly hewn through, so that the first high wind was likely to blow it down. On the bark of the tree was scored the name of Deacon Peabody, an eminent man, who had waxed wealthy by driving shrewd bargains with the Indians. He now looked round and found most of the tall trees marked with the name of some great man of the colony, and all more or less scored by the axe. The one on which he had been seated, and which had evidently just been hewn down, bore the name of Crowninshield; and he recollected a mighty rich man of that name, who made a vulgar display of wealth, which it was whispered he had acquired by buccaneering.

"He's just ready for burning!" said the black man, with a growl of triumph. "You see I am likely to have a good stock of firewood for winter."

"But what right have you," said Tom, "to cut down Deacon Peabody's timber?"

"The right of prior claim," said the other. "This woodland belonged to me long before one of your white faced race put foot upon the soil."

"And pray, who are you, if I may be so bold?" said Tom.

"Oh, I go by various names. I am the Wild Huntsman in some countries; the Black Miner in others. In this neighbourhood I am known by the name of the Black Woodsman. I am he to whom the red men consecrated this spot, and in honour of whom they now and then roasted a white man by way of sweet smelling sacrifice. Since the red men have been exterminated by you white savages, I amuse myself by presiding at the persecutions of quakers and anabaptists; I am the great patron and prompter of slave dealers, and the grand master of the Salem witches."

"The upshot of all which is, that, if I mistake not," said Tom, sturdily, "you are he commonly called Old Scratch."

"The same at your service!" replied the black man, with a half civil nod.

Such was the opening of this interview, according to the old story, though it has almost too familiar an air to be credited. One would think that to meet with such a singular personage in this wild lonely place, would have shaken any man's nerves: but Tom was a hard minded fellow, not easily daunted, and he had lived so long with a termagant wife, that he did not even fear the devil.

It is said that after this commencement, they had a long and earnest conversation together, as Tom returned homewards. The black man told him of great sums of money buried by Kidd the pirate, under the oak trees on the high ridge not far from the morass. All these were under his command and protected by his power, so that none could find them but such as propitiated his favour. These he offered to place within Tom Walker's reach, having conceived an especial kindness for him: but they were to be had only on certain conditions. What these conditions were, may easily be surmised, though Tom never disclosed them publicly. They must have been very hard, for he required time to think of them, and he was not a man to stick at trifles where money was in view. When they had reached the edge of the swamp the stranger paused.

"What proof have I that all you have been telling me is true?" said Tom.

"There is my signature," said the black man, pressing his finger on Tom's forehead. So saying, he turned off among the thickets of the swamp, and seemed, as Tom said, to go down, down, down, into the earth, until nothing but his head and shoulders could be seen, and so on until he totally disappeared.

When Tom reached home he found the black print of a finger burnt, as it were, into his forehead, which nothing could obliterate.

The first news his wife had to tell him was the sudden death of Absalom Crowninshield the rich buccaneer. It was announced in the papers with the usual flourish, that "a great man had fallen in Israel."

Tom recollected the tree which his black friend had just hewn down, and which was ready for burning. "Let the freebooter roast," said Tom, "who cares!" He now felt convinced that all he had heard and seen was no illusion.

He was not prone to let his wife into his confidence; but as this was an uneasy secret, he willingly shared it with her. All her avarice was awakened at the mention of hidden gold, and she urged her husband to comply with the black man's terms and secure what would make them wealthy for life. However Tom might have felt disposed to sell himself to the devil, he was determined not to do so to oblige his wife; so he flatly refused out of the mere spirit of contradiction. Many and bitter were the quarrels they had on the subject, but the more she talked the more resolute was Tom not to be damned to please her. At length she determined to drive the bargain on her own account, and if she succeeded, to keep all the gain to herself.

Being of the same fearless temper as her husband, she set off for the old Indian fort towards the close of a summer's day. She was many hours absent. When she came back she was reserved and sullen in her replies. She spoke something of a black man whom she had met about twilight, hewing at the root of a tall tree. He was sulky, however, and would not come to terms; she was to go again with a propitiatory offering, but what it was she forbore to say.

The next evening she set off again for the swamp, with her apron heavily laden. Tom waited and waited for her, but in vain: midnight came, but she did not make her appearance; morning, noon, night returned, but still she did not come. Tom now grew uneasy for her safety; especially as he found she had carried off in her apron the silver teapot and spoons and every portable article of value. Another night elapsed, another morning came; but no wife. In a word, she was never heard of more.

What was her real fate nobody knows, in consequence of so many pretending to know. It is one of those facts which have become confounded by a variety of historians. Some asserted that she lost her way among the tangled mazes of the swamp and sank into some pit or slough; others, more uncharitable, hinted that she had eloped with the household booty, and made off to some other province; while others assert that the tempter had decoyed her into a dismal quagmire on top of which her hat was found lying. In confirmation of this, it was said a great black man with an axe on his shoulder was seen late that very evening coming out of the swamp, carrying a bundle tied in a check apron, with an air of surly triumph.

The most current and probable story, however, observes that Tom Walker grew so anxious about the fate of his wife and his property that he set out at length to seek them both at the Indian fort. During a long summer's afternoon he searched about the gloomy place, but no wife was to be seen. He called her name repeatedly, but she was no where to be heard. The bittern alone responded to his voice, as he flew screaming by; or the bull frog croaked dolefully from a neighbouring pool. At length, it is said, just in the brown hour of twilight, when the owls began to hoot and the bats to flit about, his attention was attracted by the clamour of carrion crows hovering about a cypress tree. He looked up and beheld a bundle tied in a check apron and hanging in the branches of the tree; with a great vulture perched hard by, as if keeping watch upon it. He leaped with joy, for he recognized his wife's apron, and supposed it to contain the household valuables.

"Let us get hold of the property," said he, consolingly to himself, "and we will endeavour to do without the woman."

As he scrambled up the tree the vulture spread its wide wings, and sailed off screaming into the deep shadows of the forest. Tom seized the check apron, but, woful sight! found nothing but a heart and liver tied up in it.

Such, according to the most authentic old story, was all that was to be found of Tom's wife. She had probably attempted to deal with the black man as she had been accustomed to deal with her husband; but though a female scold is generally considered a match for the devil, yet in this instance she appears to have had the worst of it. She must have died game however; for it is said Tom noticed many prints of cloven feet deeply stamped about the tree, and found handsful of hair, that looked as if they had been plucked from the coarse black shock of the woodsman. Tom knew his wife's prowess by experience. He shrugged his shoulders as he looked at the signs of a fierce clapper clawing. "Egad," said he to himself, "Old Scratch must have had a tough time of it!"

Tom consoled himself for the loss of his property with the loss of his wife; for he was a man of fortitude. He even felt something like gratitude towards the black woodsman, who he considered had done him a kindness. He sought, therefore, to cultivate a further acquaintance with him, but for some time without success; the old black legs played shy, for whatever people may think, he is not always to be had for calling for; he knows how to play his cards when pretty sure of his game.

At length, it is said, when delay had whetted Tom's eagerness to the quick, and prepared him to agree to any thing rather than not gain the promised treasure, he met the black man one evening in his usual woodman dress, with his axe on his shoulder, sauntering along the edge of the swamp, and humming a tune. He affected to receive Tom's advances with great indifference, made brief replies, and went on humming his tune.

By degrees, however, Tom brought him to business, and they began to

haggle about the terms on which the former was to have the pirate's treasure. There was one condition which need not be mentioned, being generally understood in all cases where the devil grants favours; but there were
others about which, though of less importance, he was inflexibly obstinate.
He insisted that the money found through his means should be employed
in his service. He proposed, therefore, that Tom should employ it in the
black traffick; that is to say, that he should fit out a slave ship. This, however,
Tom resolutely refused; he was bad enough in all conscience; but the devil
himself could not tempt him to turn slave dealer.

Finding Tom so squeamish on this point, he did not insist upon it, but
proposed instead that he should turn usurer; the devil being extremely anxious for the increase of usurers, looking upon them as his peculiar people.

To this no objections were made, for it was just to Tom's taste.

"You shall open a broker's shop in Boston next month," said the black man.

"I'll do it tomorrow, if you wish," said Tom Walker.

"You shall lend money at two per cent. a month."

"Egad, I'll charge four!" replied Tom Walker.

"You shall extort bonds, foreclose mortgages, drive the merchant to bank-
ruptcy——"

"I'll drive him to the d——l," cried Tom Walker, eagerly.

"You are the usurer for my money!" said the black legs, with delight.
"When will you want the rhino?"

"This very night."

"Done!" said the devil.

"Done!" said Tom Walker.—So they shook hands, and struck a bargain.

A few days' time saw Tom Walker seated behind his desk in a counting
house in Boston. His reputation for a ready moneyed man, who would lend
money out for a good consideration, soon spread abroad. Every body remembers the days of Governor Belcher, when money was particularly
scarce. It was a time of paper credit. The country had been deluged with
government bills; the famous Land Bank had been established; there had
been a rage for speculating; the people had run mad with schemes for new
settlements; for building cities in the wilderness; land jobbers went about
with maps of grants, and townships, and Eldorados, lying nobody knew
where, but which every body was ready to purchase. In a word, the great
speculating fever which breaks out every now and then in the country, had
raged to an alarming degree, and every body was dreaming of making sudden fortunes from nothing. As usual the fever had subsided; the dream had
gone off, and the imaginary fortunes with it; the patients were left in doleful
plight, and the whole country resounded with the consequent cry of "hard
times."

At this propitious time of public distress did Tom Walker set up as a usurer
in Boston. His door was soon thronged by customers. The needy and the

adventurous; the gambling speculator; the dreaming land jobber; the thrift-less tradesman; the merchant with cracked credit; in short, every one driven to raise money by desperate means and desperate sacrifices, hurried to Tom Walker.

Thus Tom was the universal friend of the needy, and he acted like a "friend in need;" that is to say, he always exacted good pay and good security. In proportion to the distress of the applicant was the hardness of his terms. He accumulated bonds and mortgages; gradually squeezed his customers closer and closer; and sent them at length, dry as a sponge from his door.

In this way he made money hand over hand; became a rich and mighty man, and exalted his cocked hat upon change. He built himself, as usual, a vast house, out of ostentation; but left the greater part of it unfinished and unfurnished out of parsimony. He even set up a carriage in the fullness of his vain glory, though he nearly starved the horses which drew it; and as the ungreased wheels groaned and screeched on the axle trees, you would have thought you heard the souls of the poor debtors he was squeezing.

As Tom waxed old, however, he grew thoughtful. Having secured the good things of this world, he began to feel anxious about those of the next. He thought with regret on the bargain he had made with his black friend, and set his wits to work to cheat him out of the conditions. He became, therefore, all of a sudden, a violent church goer. He prayed loudly and stren-uously as if heaven were to be taken by force of lungs. Indeed, one might always tell when he had sinned most during the week, by the clamour of his Sunday devotion. The quiet christians who had been modestly and stead-fastly travelling Zionward, were struck with self reproach at seeing them-selves so suddenly outstripped in their career by this new made convert. Tom was as rigid in religious, as in money matters; he was a stern supervisor and censurer of his neighbours, and seemed to think every sin entered up to their account became a credit on his own side of the page. He even talked of the expediency of reviving the persecution of quakers and anabaptists. In a word, Tom's zeal became as notorious as his riches.

Still, in spite of all this strenuous attention to forms, Tom had a lurking dread that the devil, after all, would have his due. That he might not be taken unawares, therefore, it is said he always carried a small bible in his coat pocket. He had also a great folio bible on his counting house desk, and would frequently be found reading it when people called on business; on such occasions he would lay his green spectacles in the book, to mark the place, while he turned round to drive some usurious bargain.

Some say that Tom grew a little crack brained in his old days, and that fancying his end approaching, he had his horse new shod, saddled and bri-dled, and buried with his feet uppermost; because he supposed that at the last day the world would be turned upside down; in which case he should find his horse standing ready for mounting, and he was determined at the worst to give his old friend a run for it. This, however, is probably a mere old wives' fable. If he really did take such a precaution it was totally super-fluous; at least so says the authentic old legend which closes his story in the following manner.

One hot afternoon in the dog days, just as a terrible black thundergust was coming up, Tom sat in his counting house in his white linen cap and India silk morning gown. He was on the point of foreclosing a mortgage, by which he would complete the ruin of an unlucky land speculator for whom he had professed the greatest friendship. The poor land jobber begged him to grant a few months' indulgence. Tom had grown testy and irritated and refused another day.

"My family will be ruined and brought upon the parish," said the land jobber. "Charity begins at home," replied Tom, "I must take care of myself in these hard times."

"You have made so much money out of me," said the speculator.

Tom lost his patience and his piety—"The devil take me," said he, "if I have made a farthing!"

Just then there were three loud knocks at the street door. He stepped out to see who was there. A black man was holding a black horse which neighed and stamped with impatience.

"Tom, you're come for!" said the black fellow, gruffly. Tom shrunk back, but too late. He had left his little bible at the bottom of his coat pocket, and his big bible on the desk buried under the mortgage he was about to fore-close: never was sinner taken more unawares. The black man whisked him like a child into the saddle, gave the horse a lash, and away he galloped, with Tom on his back, in the midst of a thunder storm. The clerks stuck their pens behind their ears and stared after him from the windows. Away went Tom Walker, dashing down the streets; his white cap bobbing up and down; his morning gown fluttering in the wind, and his steed striking fire out of the pavement at every bound. When the clerks turned to look for the black man he had disappeared.

Tom Walker never returned to foreclose the mortgage. A countryman who lived on the border of the swamp, reported that in the height of the thunder gust he had heard a great clattering of hoofs and a howling along the road, and running to the window caught sight of a figure, such as I have described, on a horse that galloped like mad across the fields, over the hills and down into the black hemlock swamp towards the old Indian fort; and that shortly after a thunderbolt falling in that direction seemed to set the whole forest in a blaze.

The good people of Boston shook their heads and shrugged their shoul-ders, but had been so much accustomed to witches and goblins and tricks of the devil in all kinds of shapes from the first settlement of the colony, that they were not so much horror struck as might have been expected. Trustees were appointed to take charge of Tom's effects. There was nothing, however, to administer upon. On searching his coffers all his bonds and mortgages were found reduced to cinders. In place of gold and silver his iron chest was filled with chips and shavings; two skeletons lay in his stable instead of his half starved horses, and the very next day his great house took fire and was burnt to the ground.

Such was the end of Tom Walker and his ill gotten wealth. Let all griping money brokers lay this story to heart. The truth of it is not to be doubted. The very hole under the oak trees, whence he dug Kidd's money is to be seen to this day; and the neighbouring swamp and old Indian fort are often haunted in stormy nights by a figure on horseback, in a morning gown and white cap, which is doubtless the troubled spirit of the usurer. In fact, the story has resolved itself into a proverb, and is the origin of that popular saying, prevalent throughout New England, of "The Devil and Tom Walker."

———

Such, as nearly as I can recollect, was the purport of the tale told by the Cape Cod whaler. There were divers trivial particulars which I have omitted, and which whiled away the morning very pleasantly, until the time of tide favourable for fishing being passed, it was proposed to land, and refresh ourselves under the trees, until the noontide heat should have abated.

We accordingly landed on a delectable part of the island of Mannahatta, in that shady and embowered tract formerly under dominion of the ancient family of the Hardenbrooks. It was a spot well known to me in the course of the aquatic expeditions of my boyhood. Not far from where we landed, was an old Dutch family vault, constructed in the side of a bank, which had been an object of great awe and fable among my school boy associates. We had peeped into it during one of our coasting voyages, and been startled by the sight of mouldering coffins and musty bones within; but what had given it the most fearful interest in our eyes, was its being in some way connected with the pirate wreck which lay rotting among the rocks of Hell Gate. There were also stories of smuggling connected with it, particularly relating to a time when this retired spot was owned by a noted burgher called Ready Money Prevost; a man of whom it was whispered that he had many and mysterious dealings with parts beyond seas. All these things, however, had been jumbled together in our minds in that vague way in which such themes are mingled up in the tales of boyhood.

While I was pondering upon these matters my companions had spread a repast, from the contents of our well stored pannier, under a broad chesnut, on the green sward which swept down to the water's edge. Here we solaced ourselves on the cool grassy carpet during the warm sunny hours of midday.

While lolling on the grass, indulging in that kind of musing reverie of which I am fond, I summoned up the dusky recollections of my boyhood respecting this place, and repeated them like the imperfectly remembered traces of a dream, for the amusement of my companions. When I had finished a worthy old burgher, John Josse Vandermoere, the same who once related to me the adventures of Dolph Heyliger, broke silence and observed, that he recollected a story of money digging which occurred in this very neighbourhood, and might account for some of the traditions which I had heard in my boyhood. As we knew him to be one of the most authentic narrators in the province we begged him to let us have the particulars, and accordingly, while we solaced ourselves with a clean long pipe of Blase Moore's best tobacco, the authentic John Josse Vandermoere related the following tale.

WOLFERT WEBBER, OR GOLDEN DREAMS

In the year of grace one thousand seven hundred and—blank—for I do not remember the precise date; however, it was somewhere in the early part of the last century, there lived in the ancient city of the Manhattoes a worthy burgher, Wolfert Webber by name. He was descended from old Cobus Webber of the Brille in Holland, one of the original settlers, famous for introducing the cultivation of cabbages, and who came over to the province during the protectorship of Oloffe Van Kortlandt, otherwise called the Dreamer.

The field in which Cobus Webber first planted himself and his cabbages had remained ever since in the family, who continued in the same line of husbandry, with that praiseworthy perseverance for which our Dutch burghers are noted. The whole family genius, during several generations, was devoted to the study and development of this one noble vegetable; and to this concentration of intellect may doubtless be ascribed the prodigious size and renown to which the Webber cabbages attained.

The Webber dynasty continued in uninterrupted succession; and never did a line give more unquestionable proofs of legitimacy. The eldest son succeeded to the looks, as well as the territory of his sire; and had the portraits of this line of tranquil potentates been taken, they would have presented a row of heads marvellously resembling in shape and magnitude the vegetables over which they reigned.

The seat of government continued unchanged in the family mansion:—a Dutch built house, with a front, or rather gabel end of yellow brick, tapering to a point, with the customary iron weathercock at the top. Every thing about the building bore the air of long settled ease and security. Flights of martins peopled the little coops nailed against its walls, and swallows built their nests under the eaves; and every one knows that these house loving birds bring good luck to the dwelling where they take up their abode. In a bright sunny morning in early summer, it was delectable to hear their cheerful notes, as they sported about in the pure sweet air, chirping forth, as it were, the greatness and prosperity of the Webbers.

Thus quietly and comfortably did this excellent family vegetate under the shade of a mighty buttonwood tree, which by little and little grew so great as entirely to overshadow their palace. The city gradually spread its suburbs round their domain. Houses sprang up to interrupt their prospects. The rural lanes in the vicinity began to grow into the bustle and populousness of streets; in short, with all the habits of rustic life they began to find themselves the inhabitants of a city. Still, however, they maintained their hereditary character, and hereditary possessions, with all the tenacity of petty German princes in the midst of the Empire. Wolfert was the last of the line, and succeeded to the patriarchal bench at the door, under the family tree, and swayed the sceptre of his fathers, a kind of rural potentate in the midst of a metropolis.

To share the cares and sweets of sovereignty, he had taken unto himself a help mate, one of that excellent kind, called stirring women; that is to say, she was one of those notable little housewives who are always busy when there is nothing to do. Her activity, however, took one particular direction; her whole life seemed devoted to intense knitting; whether at home or abroad; walking, or sitting, her needles were continually in motion, and it is even affirmed that by her unwearied industry she very nearly supplied her household with stockings throughout the year. This worthy couple were blessed with one daughter, who was brought up with great tenderness and care; uncommon pains had been taken with her education, so that she could stitch in every variety of way; make all kinds of pickles and preserves, and mark her own name on a sampler. The influence of her taste was seen also in the family garden, where the ornamental began to mingle with the useful; whole rows of fiery marigolds and splendid hollyhocks bordered the cabbage beds; and gigantic sun flowers lolled their broad jolly faces over the fences, seeming to ogle most affectionately the passers by.

Thus reigned and vegetated Wolfert Webber over his paternal acres, peaceably and contentedly. Not but that, like all other sovereigns, he had his occasional cares and vexations. The growth of his native city sometimes caused him annoyance. His little territory gradually became hemmed in by streets and houses, which intercepted air and sunshine. He was now and then subjected to the irruptions of the border population, that infest the skirts of a metropolis, who would make midnight forays into his dominions, and carry off captive whole platoons of his noblest subjects. Vagrant swine would make a descent, too, now and then, when the gate was left open, and lay all waste before them; and mischievous urchins would decapitate the illustrious sunflowers, the glory of the garden, as they lolled their heads so fondly over the walls. Still all these were petty grievances, which might now and then ruffle the surface of his mind, as a summer breeze will ruffle the surface of a mill pond; but they could not disturb the deep seated quiet of his soul. He would but seize a trusty staff, that stood behind the door, issue suddenly out, and anoint the back of the aggressor, whether pig, or urchin, and then return within doors, marvellously refreshed and tranquillized.

The chief cause of anxiety to honest Wolfert, however, was the growing prosperity of the city. The expenses of living doubled and trebled; but he could not double and treble the magnitude of his cabbages; and the number of competitors prevented the increase of price; thus, therefore, while every one around him grew richer, Wolfert grew poorer, and he could not, for the life of him, perceive how the evil was to be remedied.

This growing care, which increased from day to day, had its gradual effect upon our worthy burgher; insomuch, that it at length implanted two or three wrinkles on his brow; things unknown before in the family of the Webbers; and it seemed to pinch up the corners of his cocked hat into an expression of anxiety, totally opposite to the tranquil, broad brimmed, low crowned beavers of his illustrious progenitors.

Perhaps even this would not have materially disturbed the serenity of his mind had he had only himself and his wife to care for; but there was his daughter gradually growing to maturity; and all the world knows when daughters begin to ripen no fruit or flower requires so much looking after. I have no talent at describing female charms, else fain would I depict the progress of this little Dutch beauty. How her blue eyes grew deeper and deeper, and her cherry lips redder and redder; and how she ripened and ripened, and rounded and rounded in the opening breath of sixteen summers, until, in her seventeenth spring, she seemed ready to burst out of her boddice, like a half blown rosebud.

Ah, well-a-day! could I but show her as she was then, tricked out on a Sunday morning, in the hereditary finery of the old Dutch clothes press, of which her mother had confided to her the key. The wedding dress of her grandmother, modernized for use, with sundry ornaments, handed down as heir looms in the family. Her pale brown hair smoothed with buttermilk in flat waving lines on each side of her fair forehead. The chain of yellow virgin gold, that encircled her neck; the little cross, that just rested at the entrance of a soft valley of happiness, as if it would sanctify the place. The—but pooh!—it is not for an old man like me to be prosing about female beauty: suffice it to say, Amy had attained her seventeenth year. Long since had her sampler exhibited hearts in couples desperately transfixed with arrows, and true lovers' knots worked in deep blue silk; and it was evident she began to languish for some more interesting occupation than the rearing of sunflowers or pickling of cucumbers.

At this critical period of female existence, when the heart within a damsel's bosom, like its emblem, the miniature which hangs without, is apt to be engrossed by a single image, a new visitor began to make his appearance under the roof of Wolfert Webber. This was Dirk Waldron, the only son of a poor widow, but who could boast of more fathers than any lad in the province; for his mother had had four husbands, and this only child, so that though born in her last wedlock, he might fairly claim to be the tardy fruit of a long course of cultivation. This son of four fathers united the merits and the vigour of his sires. If he had not had a great family before him, he seemed likely to have a great one after him; for you had only to look at the fresh bucksome youth, to see that he was formed to be the founder of a mighty race.

This youngster gradually became an intimate visitor of the family. He talked little, but he sat long. He filled the father's pipe when it was empty, gathered up the mother's knitting needle, or ball of worsted when it fell to the ground; stroked the sleek coat of the tortoise shell cat, and replenished the tea pot for the daughter from the bright copper kettle that sang before the fire. All these quiet little offices may seem of trifling import, but when true love is translated into Low Dutch, it is in this way that it eloquently expresses itself. They were not lost upon the Webber family. The winning youngster found marvellous favour in the eyes of the mother; the tortoise shell cat, albeit the most staid and demure of her kind, gave indubitable signs of approbation of his visits, the tea kettle seemed to sing out a cheery note of welcome at his approach, and if the sly glances of the daughter might be rightly read, as she sat bridling and dimpling, and sewing by her mother's side, she was not a whit behind Dame Webber, or grimalkin, or the tea kettle in good will.

Wolfert alone saw nothing of what was going on. Profoundly wrapt up in meditation on the growth of the city and his cabbages, he sat looking in the fire, and puffing his pipe in silence. One night, however, as the gentle Amy, according to custom lighted her lover to the outer door, and he, according to custom, took his parting salute, the smack resounded so vigorously through the long, silent entry, as to startle even the dull ear of Wolfert. He was slowly roused to a new source of anxiety. It had never entered into his head, that this mere child who, as it seemed but the other day, had been climbing about his knees, and playing with dolls and baby houses, could all at once be thinking of lovers and matrimony. He rubbed his eyes, examined into the fact, and really found that while he had been dreaming of other matters, she had actually grown to be a woman, and what was worse, had fallen in love. Here arose new cares for poor Wolfert. He was a kind father, but he was a prudent man. The young man was a lively, stirring lad; but then he had neither money nor land. Wolfert's ideas all ran in one channel, and he saw no alternative in case of a marriage, but to portion off the young couple with a corner of his cabbage garden, the whole of which was barely sufficient for the support of his family.

Like a prudent father, therefore, he determined to nip this passion in the bud, and forbad the youngster the house, though sorely did it go against his fatherly heart, and many a silent tear did it cause in the bright eye of his daughter. She showed herself, however, a pattern of filial piety and obedience. She never pouted and sulked, she never flew in the face of parental authority; she never flew into a passion, nor fell into hysterics, as many romantic novel-read young ladies would do. Not she, indeed! She was none such heroical rebellious trumpery, I'll warrant ye. On the contrary, she acquiesced like an obedient daughter; shut the street door in her lover's face, and if ever she did grant him an interview, it was either out of the kitchen window, or over the garden fence.

Wolfert was deeply cogitating these matters in his mind, and his brow wrinkled with unusual care, as he wended his way one Saturday afternoon to a rural inn, about two miles from the city. It was a favourite resort of the Dutch part of the community from being always held by a Dutch line of landlords, and retaining an air and relish of the good old times. It was a Dutch built house, that had probably been a country seat of some opulent burgher in the early time of the settlement. It stood near a point of land, called Corlear's Hook, which stretches out into the Sound, and against which the tide, at its flux and reflux, sets with extraordinary rapidity. The venerable and somewhat crazy mansion was distinguished from afar, by a grove of elms and sycamores that seemed to wave a hospitable invitation, while a few weeping willows with their dank, drooping foliage, resembling falling waters, gave an idea of coolness, that rendered it an attractive spot during the heats of summer.

Here, therefore, as I said, resorted many of the old inhabitants of the Manhattoes, where, while some played at the shuffle board and quoits and ninepins, others smoked a deliberate pipe, and talked over public affairs.

It was on a blustering autumnal afternoon that Wolfert made his visit to the inn. The grove of elms and willows was stripped of its leaves, which whirled in rustling eddies about the fields. The ninepin alley was deserted, for the premature chilliness of the day had driven the company within doors. As it was Saturday afternoon, the habitual club was in session, composed principally of regular Dutch burghers, though mingled occasionally with persons of various character and country, as is natural in a place of such motley population.

Beside the fire place, in a huge leather bottomed arm chair, sat the dictator of this little world, the venerable Rem, or, as it was pronounced, Ramm Rapelye. He was a man of Walloon race, and illustrious for the antiquity of his line, his great grandmother having been the first white child born in the province. But he was still more illustrious for his wealth and dignity: he had long filled the noble office of alderman, and was a man to whom the governor himself took off his hat. He had maintained possession of the leathern bottomed chair from time immemorial; and had gradually waxed in bulk as he sat in this seat of government, until in the course of years he filled its whole magnitude. His word was decisive with his subjects; for he was so rich a man, that he was never expected to support any opinion by argument. The landlord waited on him with peculiar officiousness; not that he paid better than his neighbours, but then the coin of a rich man seems always to be so much more acceptable. The landlord had ever a pleasant word and a joke, to insinuate in the ear of the august Ramm. It is true, Ramm never laughed, and indeed, maintained a mastiff-like gravity, and even surliness of aspect, yet he now and then rewarded mine host with a token of approbation; which, though nothing more nor less than a kind of grunt, yet delighted the landlord more than a broad laugh from a poorer man.

"This will be a rough night for the money diggers," said mine host, as a gust of wind howled round the house, and rattled at the windows.

"What, are they at their works again?" said an English half-pay captain, with one eye, who was a frequent attendant at the inn.

"Aye, are they," said the landlord, "and well may they be. They've had luck of late. They say a great pot of money has been dug up in the field, just behind Stuyvesant's orchard. Folks think it must have been buried there in old times, by Peter Stuyvesant, the Dutch Governor."

"Fudge!" said the one eyed man of war, as he added a small portion of water to a bottom of brandy.

"Well, you may believe, or not, as you please," said mine host, somewhat nettled; "but every body knows that the old governor buried a great deal of his money at the time of the Dutch troubles, when the English red coats seized on the province. They say, too, the old gentleman walks; aye, and in the very same dress that he wears in the picture which hangs up in the family house."

"Fudge!" said the half-pay officer.

"Fudge, if you please!—But didn't Corney Van Zandt see him at midnight, stalking about in the meadow with his wooden leg, and a drawn sword in his hand, that flashed like fire? And what can he be walking for, but because people have been troubling the place where he buried his money in old times?"

Here the landlord was interrupted by several guttural sounds from Ramm Rapelye, betokening that he was labouring with the unusual production of an idea. As he was too great a man to be slighted by a prudent publican, mine host respectfully paused until he should deliver himself. The corpulent frame of this mighty burgher now gave all the symptoms of a volcanic moun-

tain on the point of an eruption. First, there was a certain heaving of the
abdomen, not unlike an earthquake; then was emitted a cloud of tobacco
smoke from that crater, his mouth; then there was a kind of rattle in the
throat, as if the idea were working its way up through a region of phlegm;
then there were several disjointed members of a sentence thrown out, ending in a cough; at length his voice forced its way in the slow, but absolute
tone of a man who feels the weight of his purse, if not of his ideas; every
portion of his speech being marked by a testy puff of tobacco smoke.

"Who talks of old Peter Stuyvesant's walking?—puff—Have people no respect for persons?—puff—puff—Peter Stuyvesant knew better what to do
with his money than to bury it—puff—I know the Stuyvesant family—puff—
every one of them—puff—not a more respectable family in the province—
puff—old standers—puff—warm householders—puff—none of your up-
starts—puff—puff—puff.—Don't talk to me of Peter Stuyvesant's walking—
puff—puff—puff—puff."

Here the redoubtable Ramm contracted his brow, clasped up his mouth,
till it wrinkled at each corner, and redoubled his smoking with such vehemence, that the cloudy volumes soon wreathed round his head, as the smoke
envellops the awful summit of Mount Etna.

A general silence followed the sudden rebuke of this very rich man. The
subject, however, was too interesting to be readily abandoned. The conversation soon broke forth again from the lips of Peechy Prauw Van Hook, the
chronicler of the club, one of those prosy, narrative old men who seem to
be troubled with an incontinence of words, as they grow old.

Peechy could at any time tell as many stories in an evening as his hearers
could digest in a month. He now resumed the conversation, by affirming
that, to his knowledge, money had at different times been digged up in
various parts of the island. The lucky persons who had discovered them had
always dreamt of them three times before hand, and what was worthy of
remark, these treasures had never been found but by some descendant of
the good old Dutch families, which clearly proved that they had been buried
by Dutchmen in the olden time.

"Fiddle stick with your Dutchmen!" cried the half-pay officer. "The Dutch
had nothing to do with them. They were all buried by Kidd, the pirate, and
his crew."

Here a key note was touched which roused the whole company. The name
of Captain Kidd was like a talisman in those times, and was associated with
a thousand marvellous stories.

The half-pay officer took the lead, and in his narrations fathered upon
Kidd all the plunderings and exploits of Morgan, Blackbeard, and the whole
list of bloody buccaneers.

The officer was a man of great weight among the peaceable members of
the club, by reason of his warlike character and gunpowder tales. All his

golden stories of Kidd, however, and of the booty he had buried, were obstinately rivalled by the tales of Peechy Prauw, who, rather than suffer his Dutch progenitors to be eclipsed by a foreign freebooter, enriched every field and shore in the neighbourhood with the hidden wealth of Peter Stuyvesant and his contemporaries.

Not a word of this conversation was lost upon Wolfert Webber. He returned pensively home, full of magnificent ideas. The soil of his native island seemed to be turned into gold dust; and every field to teem with treasure. His head almost reeled at the thought how often he must have heedlessly rambled over places where countless sums lay, scarcely covered by the turf beneath his feet. His mind was in an uproar with this whirl of new ideas. As he came in sight of the venerable mansion of his forefathers, and the little realm where the Webbers had so long, and so contentedly flourished, his gorge rose at the narrowness of his destiny.

"Unlucky Wolfert!" exclaimed he; "others can go to bed and dream themselves into whole mines of wealth; they have but to seize a spade in the morning, and turn up doubloons like potatoes; but thou must dream of hardship, and rise to poverty—must dig thy field from year's end to year's end, and—and yet raise nothing but cabbages!"

Wolfert Webber went to bed with a heavy heart; and it was long before the golden visions that disturbed his brain, permitted him to sink into repose. The same visions, however, extended into his sleeping thoughts, and assumed a more definite form. He dreamt that he had discovered an immense treasure in the centre of his garden. At every stroke of the spade he laid bare a golden ingot; diamond crosses sparkled out of the dust; bags of money turned up their bellies, corpulent with pieces of eight, or venerable doubloons; and chests, wedged close with moidores, ducats, and pistareens, yawned before his ravished eyes, and vomited forth their glittering contents.

Wolfert awoke a poorer man than ever. He had no heart to go about his daily concerns, which appeared so paltry and profitless; but sat all day long in the chimney corner, picturing to himself ingots and heaps of gold in the fire. The next night his dream was repeated. He was again in his garden, digging, and laying open stores of hidden wealth. There was something very singular in this repetition. He passed another day of reverie, and though it was cleaning day, and the house, as usual in Dutch households, completely topsy turvy, yet he sat unmoved amidst the general uproar.

The third night he went to bed with a palpitating heart. He put on his red nightcap, wrong side outwards for good luck. It was deep midnight before his anxious mind could settle itself into sleep. Again the golden dream was repeated, and again he saw his garden teeming with ingots and money bags.

Wolfert rose the next morning in complete bewilderment. A dream three times repeated was never known to lie; and if so, his fortune was made.

In his agitation he put on his waistcoat with the hind part before, and this was a corroboration of good luck. He no longer doubted that a huge store of money lay buried somewhere in his cabbage field, coyly waiting to be sought for, and he repined at having so long been scratching about the surface of the soil, instead of digging to the centre.

He took his seat at the breakfast table full of these speculations; asked his daughter to put a lump of gold into his tea, and on handing his wife a plate of slap jacks, begged her to help herself to a doubloon.

His grand care now was how to secure this immense treasure without its being known. Instead of working regularly in his grounds in the day time, he now stole from his bed at night, and with spade and pickaxe, went to work to rip up and dig about his paternal acres, from one end to the other. In a little time the whole garden, which had presented such a goodly and regular appearance, with its phalanx of cabbages, like a vegetable army in battle array, was reduced to a scene of devastation, while the relentless Wolfert, with nightcap on head, and lantern and spade in hand, stalked through the slaughtered ranks, the destroying angel of his own vegetable world.

Every morning bore testimony to the ravages of the preceding night in cabbages of all ages and conditions, from the tender sprout to the full grown head, piteously rooted from their quiet beds like worthless weeds, and left to wither in the sunshine. In vain Wolfert's wife remonstrated; in vain his darling daughter wept over the destruction of some favourite marygold. "Thou shalt have gold of another guess sort," he would cry, chucking her under the chin; "thou shalt have a string of crooked ducats for thy wedding necklace, my child." His family began really to fear that the poor man's wits were diseased. He muttered in his sleep at night about mines of wealth, about pearls and diamonds and bars of gold. In the day time he was moody and abstracted, and walked about as if in a trance. Dame Webber held frequent councils with all the old women of the neighbourhood. Scarce an hour in the day but a knot of them might be seen wagging their white caps together round her door, while the poor woman made some piteous recital. The daughter too was fain to seek for more frequent consolation from the stolen interviews of her favoured swain Dirk Waldron. The delectable little Dutch songs with which she used to dulcify the house grew less and less frequent, and she would forget her sewing and look wistfully in her father's face as he sat pondering by the fire side. Wolfert caught her eye one day fixed on him thus anxiously, and for a moment was roused from his golden reveries.—"Cheer up my girl," said he, exultingly, "why dost thou droop— thou shalt hold up thy head one day with the Brinkerhoffs and the Schermerhorns, the Van Hornes, and the Van Dams—By St. Nicholas, but the patroon himself shall be glad to get thee for his son!"

Amy shook her head at this vain glorious boast, and was more than ever in doubt of the soundness of the good man's intellect.

In the mean time Wolfert went on digging and digging, but the field was extensive, and as his dream had indicated no precise spot, he had to dig at random. The winter set in before one tenth of the scene of promise had been explored. The ground became frozen hard, and the nights too cold for the labours of the spade. No sooner, however, did the returning warmth of spring loosen the soil, and the small frogs begin to pipe in the meadows, but Wolfert resumed his labours with renovated zeal. Still, however, the hours of industry were reversed. Instead of working cheerily all day, planting and setting out his vegetables, he remained thoughtfully idle, until the shades of night summoned him to his secret labours. In this way he continued to dig from night to night, and week to week, and month to month, but not a stiver did he find. On the contrary, the more he digged, the poorer he grew. The rich soil of his garden was digged away, and the sand and gravel from beneath were thrown to the surface, until the whole field presented an aspect of sandy barrenness.

In the mean time the seasons gradually rolled on. The little frogs which had piped in the meadows in early spring, croaked as bull frogs during the summer heats, and then sank into silence. The peach tree budded, blossomed, and bore its fruit. The swallows and martins came, twittered about the roof, built their nests, reared their young, held their congress along the eaves, and then winged their flight in search of another spring. The caterpillar spun its winding sheet, dangled in it from the great buttonwood tree before the house; turned into a moth, fluttered with the last sunshine of summer, and disappeared; and finally the leaves of the buttonwood tree turned yellow, then brown, then rustled one by one to the ground, and whirling about in little eddies of wind and dust, whispered that winter was at hand.

Wolfert gradually woke from his dream of wealth as the year declined. He had reared no crop for the supply of his household during the sterility of winter. The season was long and severe, and for the first time the family was really straightened in its comforts. By degrees a revulsion of thought took place in Wolfert's mind, common to those whose golden dreams have been disturbed by pinching realities. The idea gradually stole upon him that he should come to want. He already considered himself one of the most unfortunate men in the province, having lost such an incalculable amount of undiscovered treasure, and now, when thousands of pounds had eluded his search, to be perplexed for shillings and pence was cruel in the extreme.

Haggard care gathered about his brow; he went about with a money seeking air, his eyes bent downwards into the dust, and carrying his hands in his pockets, as men are apt to do when they have nothing else to put into them. He could not even pass the city almshouse without giving it a rueful glance, as if destined to be his future abode.

The strangeness of his conduct and of his looks occasioned much speculation and remark. For a long time he was suspected of being crazy, and then every body pitied him; at length it began to be suspected that he was poor, and then every body avoided him.

The rich old burghers of his acquaintance met him outside of the door when he called, entertained him hospitably on the threshold, pressed him warmly by the hand on parting, shook their heads as he walked away, with the kind hearted expression of "poor Wolfert," and turned a corner nimbly, if by chance they saw him approaching as they walked the streets. Even the barber and cobbler of the neighbourhood, and a tattered tailor in an alley hard by, three of the poorest and merriest rogues in the world, eyed him with that abundant sympathy which usually attends a lack of means; and there is not a doubt but their pockets would have been at his command, only that they happened to be empty.

Thus every body deserted the Webber mansion, as if poverty were contagious, like the plague; every body but honest Dirk Waldron, who still kept up his stolen visits to the daughter, and indeed seemed to wax more affectionate as the fortunes of his mistress were in the wane.

Many months had elapsed since Wolfert had frequented his old resort, the rural inn. He was taking a long lonely walk one Saturday afternoon, musing over his wants and disappointments, when his feet took instinctively their wonted direction, and on awaking out of a reverie, he found himself before the door of the inn. For some moments he hesitated whether to enter, but his heart yearned for companionship; and where can a ruined man find better companionship than at a tavern, where there is neither sober example nor sober advice to put him out of countenance?

Wolfert found several of the old frequenters of the tavern at their usual posts, and seated in their usual places, but one was missing, the great Ramm Rapelye, who for many years had filled the leather bottomed chair of state. His place was supplied by a stranger, who seemed, however, completely at home in the chair and the tavern. He was rather under size, but deep chested, square and muscular. His broad shoulders, double joints, and bow knees, gave tokens of prodigious strength. His face was dark and weather beaten; a deep scar, as if from the slash of a cutlass had almost divided his nose, and made a gash in his upper lip, through which his teeth shone like a bull dog's. A mop of iron grey hair gave a grizzly finish to his hard favoured visage. His dress was of an amphibious character. He wore an old hat edged with tarnished lace, and cocked in martial style, on one side of his head; a rusty blue military coat with brass buttons, and a wide pair of short petticoat trowsers, or rather breeches, for they were gathered up at the knees. He ordered every body about him, with an authoritative air; talked in a brattling voice, that sounded like the crackling of thorns under a pot; damned the landlord and servants with perfect impunity, and was waited upon with greater obsequiousness than had ever been shown to the mighty Ramm himself.

Wolfert's curiosity was awakened to know who and what was this stranger who had thus usurped absolute sway in this ancient domain. Peechy Prauw took him aside, into a remote corner of the hall, and there in an under voice, and with great caution, imparted to him all that he knew on the subject. The inn had been aroused several months before, on a dark stormy night, by repeated long shouts, that seemed like the howlings of a wolf. They came from the water side; and at length were distinguished to be hailing the house in the seafaring manner. "House-a-hoy!" The landlord turned out with his head waiter, tapster, hostler and errand boy—that is to say, with his old negro Cuff. On approaching the place whence the voice proceeded, they found this amphibious looking personage at the water's edge, quite alone, and seated on a great oaken sea chest. How he came there, whether he had been set on shore from some boat, or had floated to land on his chest, nobody could tell, for he did not seem disposed to answer questions, and there was something in his looks and manners that put a stop to all questioning. Suffice it to say, he took possession of a corner room of the inn, to which his chest was removed with great difficulty. Here he had remained ever since, keeping about the inn and its vicinity. Sometimes, it is true, he disappeared for one, two, or three days at a time, going and returning without giving any notice or account of his movements. He always appeared to have plenty of money, though often of very strange outlandish coinage; and he regularly paid his bill every evening before turning in.

He had fitted up his room to his own fancy, having slung a hammock from the ceiling instead of a bed, and decorated the walls with rusty pistols and cutlasses of foreign workmanship. A great part of his time was passed in this room, seated by the window, which commanded a wide view of the Sound, a short old fashioned pipe in his mouth, a glass of rum toddy at his elbow, and a pocket telescope in his hand, with which he reconnoitred every boat that moved upon the water. Large square rigged vessels seemed to excite but little attention; but the moment he descried any thing with a shoulder of mutton sail, or that a barge, or yawl, or jolly boat hove in sight, up went the telescope, and he examined it with the most scrupulous attention.

All this might have passed without much notice, for in those times the province was so much the resort of adventurers of all characters and climes that any oddity in dress or behaviour attracted but small attention. In a little while, however, this strange sea monster, thus strangely cast up on dry land, began to encroach upon the long established customs and customers of the place, and to interfere in a dictatorial manner in the affairs of the ninepin alley and the bar room, until in the end he usurped an absolute command over the whole inn. It was all in vain to attempt to withstand his authority. He was not exactly quarrelsome, but boisterous and peremptory, like one accustomed to tyrannize on a quarter deck; and there was a dare devil air about every thing he said and did, that inspired a wariness in all bystanders.

Even the half-pay officer, so long the hero of the club, was soon silenced by him; and the quiet burghers stared with wonder at seeing their inflammable man of war so readily and quietly extinguished.

And then the tales that he would tell were enough to make a peaceable man's hair stand on end. There was not a sea fight, or marauding, or free-booting adventure that had happened within the last twenty years but he seemed perfectly versed in it. He delighted to talk of the exploits of the buccaneers in the West Indies and on the Spanish Main. How his eyes would glisten as he described the waylaying of treasure ships, the desperate fights, yard arm and yard arm—broadside and broadside—the boarding and cap-turing of huge Spanish galleons! with what chuckling relish would he de-scribe the descent upon some rich Spanish colony; the rifling of a church; the sacking of a convent! You would have thought you heard some gorman-dizer dilating upon the roasting of a savory goose at Michaelmas as he de-scribed the roasting of some Spanish Don to make him discover his treasure—a detail given with a minuteness that made every rich old burgher present turn uncomfortably in his chair. All this would be told with infinite glee, as if he considered it an excellent joke; and then he would give such a tyrannical leer in the face of his next neighbour, that the poor man would be fain to laugh out of sheer faint heartedness. If any one, however, pre-tended to contradict him in any of his stories he was on fire in an instant. His very cocked hat assumed a momentary fierceness, and seemed to resent the contradiction.—"How the devil should you know as well as I! I tell you it was as I say!" and he would at the same time let slip a broadside of thun-dering oaths and tremendous sea phrases, such as had never been heard before within those peaceful walls.

Indeed, the worthy burghers began to surmise that he knew more of these stories than mere hearsay. Day after day their conjectures concerning him grew more and more wild and fearful. The strangeness of his arrival, the strangeness of his manners, the mystery that surrounded him, all made him something incomprehensible in their eyes. He was a kind of monster of the deep to them—he was a merman—he was behemoth—he was leviathan—in short they knew not what he was.

The domineering spirit of this boisterous sea urchin at length grew quite intolerable. He was no respecter of persons; he contradicted the richest burghers without hesitation; he took possession of the sacred elbow chair, which time out of mind had been the seat of sovereignty of the illustrious Ramm Rapelye. Nay, he even went so far in one of his rough jocular moods, as to slap that mighty burgher on the back, drink his toddy and wink in his face, a thing scarcely to be believed. From this time Ramm Rapelye ap-peared no more at the inn; his example was followed by several of the most eminent customers, who were too rich to tolerate being bullied out of their opinions, or being obliged to laugh at another man's jokes. The landlord was almost in despair, but he knew not how to get rid of this sea monster and his sea chest, which seemed both to have grown like fixtures, or excrescences on his establishment.

Such was the account whispered cautiously in Wolfert's ear, by the narrator, Peechy Prauw, as he held him by the button in a corner of the hall, casting a wary glance now and then towards the door of the bar room, lest he should be overheard by the terrible hero of his tale.

Wolfert took his seat in a remote part of the room in silence; impressed with profound awe of this unknown, so versed in freebooting history. It was to him a wonderful instance of the revolutions of mighty empires, to find the venerable Ramm Rapelye thus ousted from the throne, and a rugged tarpaulin dictating from his elbow chair, hectoring the patriarchs, and filling this tranquil little realm with brawl and bravado.

The stranger was on this evening in a more than usually communicative mood, and was narrating a number of astounding stories of plunderings and burnings upon the high seas. He dwelt upon them with peculiar relish, heightening the frightful particulars in proportion to their effect on his peaceful auditors. He gave a swaggering detail of the capture of a Spanish merchantman. She was lying becalmed during a long summer's day, just off from an island which was one of the lurking places of the pirates. They had reconnoitred her with their spy glasses from the shore, and ascertained her character and force. At night a picked crew of daring fellows set off for her in a whale boat. They approached with muffled oars, as she lay rocking idly with the undulations of the sea and her sails flapping against the masts. They were close under her stern before the guard on deck was aware of their approach. The alarm was given; the pirates threw hand grenades on deck and sprang up the main chains sword in hand.

The crew flew to arms, but in great confusion; some were shot down, others took refuge in the tops; others were driven overboard and drowned, while others fought hand to hand from the main deck to the quarter deck, disputing gallantly every inch of ground. There were three Spanish gentlemen on board with their ladies, who made the most desperate resistance. They defended the companion way, cut down several of their assailants, and fought like very devils, for they were maddened by the shrieks of the ladies from the cabin. One of the Dons was old and soon despatched. The other two kept their ground vigourously, even though the captain of the pirates was among their assailants. Just then there was a shout of victory from the main deck. "The ship is ours!" cried the pirates.

One of the Dons immediately dropped his sword and surrendered; the other, who was a hot headed youngster, and just married, gave the captain a slash in the face that laid all open. The captain just made out to articulate the words "no quarter."

"And what did they do with their prisoners?" said Peechy Prauw, eagerly.

"Threw them all overboard!" was the answer.

A dead pause followed this reply. Peechy Prauw shrunk quietly back like a man who had unwarily stolen upon the lair of a sleeping lion. The honest burghers cast fearful glances at the deep scar slashed across the visage of the stranger, and moved their chairs a little farther off. The seaman, however, smoked on without moving a muscle, as though he either did not perceive or did not regard the unfavourable effect he had produced upon his hearers.

The half-pay officer was the first to break the silence; for he was continually tempted to make ineffectual head against this tyrant of the seas, and to regain his lost consequence in the eyes of his ancient companions. He now tried to match the gunpowder tales of the stranger by others equally tremendous. Kidd, as usual, was his hero, concerning whom he seemed to have picked up many of the floating traditions of the province. The seaman had always evinced a settled pique against the one eyed warrior. On this occasion he listened with peculiar impatience. He sat with one arm akimbo, the other elbow on a table, the hand holding on to the small pipe he was pettishly puffing, his legs crossed, drumming with one foot on the ground and casting every now and then the side glance of a basilisk at the prosing captain. At length the latter spoke of Kidd's having ascended the Hudson with some of his crew, to land his plunder in secresy.

"Kidd up the Hudson!" burst forth the seaman, with a tremendous oath; "Kidd never was up the Hudson!"

"I tell you he was," said the other. "Aye, and they say he buried a quantity of treasure on the little flat that runs out into the river, called the Devil's Dans Kammer."

"The Devil's Dans Kammer in your teeth!" cried the seaman. "I tell you, Kidd never was up the Hudson—what a plague do you know of Kidd and his haunts?"

"What do I know?" echoed the half-pay officer; "why, I was in London at the time of his trial, aye, and I had the pleasure of seeing him hanged at Execution Dock."

"Then, sir, let me tell you that you saw as pretty a fellow hanged as ever trod shoe leather. Aye!" putting his face nearer to that of the officer, "and there was many a land lubber looked on, that might much better have swung in his stead."

The half-pay officer was silenced; but the indignation thus pent up in his bosom glowed with intense vehemence in his single eye, which kindled like a coal.

Peechy Prauw, who never could remain silent, observed that the gentleman certainly was in the right. Kidd never did bury money up the Hudson, nor indeed in any of those parts, though many affirmed such to be the fact. It was Bradish and others of the buccaneers who had buried money, some said in Turtle Bay, others on Long Island, others in the neighbourhood of

Hell Gate. Indeed, added he, I recollect an adventure of Sam, the negro fisherman, many years ago, which some think had something to do with the buccaneers. As we are all friends here, and as it will go no farther, I'll tell it to you.

"Upon a dark night many years ago, as Black Sam was returning from fishing in Hell Gate——"

Here the story was nipped in the bud by a sudden movement from the unknown, who laying his iron fist on the table, knuckles downward, with a quiet force that indented the very boards, and looking grimly over his shoulder, with the grin of an angry bear. "Heark'ee, neighbour," said he, with significant nodding of the head, "you'd better let the buccaneers and their money alone—they're not for old men and old women to meddle with. They fought hard for their money, they gave body and soul for it, and wherever it lies buried, depend upon it he must have a tug with the devil who gets it."

This sudden explosion was succeeded by a blank silence throughout the room. Peechy Prauw shrunk within himself, and even the one eyed officer turned pale. Wolfert, who from a dark corner of the room, had listened with intense eagerness to all this talk about buried treasure, looked with mingled awe and reverence on this bold buccaneer, for such he really suspected him to be. There was a chinking of gold and a sparkling of jewels in all his stories about the Spanish Main that gave a value to every period, and Wolfert would have given any thing for the rummaging of the ponderous sea chest, which his imagination crammed full of golden chalices and crucifixes and jolly round bags of doubloons.

The dead stillness that had fallen upon the company was at length interrupted by the stranger, who pulled out a prodigious watch of curious and ancient workmanship, and which in Wolfert's eyes had a decidedly Spanish look. On touching a spring it struck ten o'clock; upon which the sailor called for his reckoning, and having paid it out of a handful of outlandish coin, he drank off the remainder of his beverage, and without taking leave of any one, rolled out of the room, muttering to himself, as he stumped up stairs to his chamber.

It was some time before the company could recover from the silence into which they had been thrown. The very footsteps of the stranger which were heard now and then as he traversed his chamber, inspired awe.

Still the conversation in which they had been engaged was too interesting not to be resumed. A heavy thunder gust had gathered up unnoticed while they were lost in talk, and the torrents of rain that fell forbade all thoughts of setting off for home until the storm should subside. They drew nearer together, therefore, and entreated the worthy Peechy Prauw to continue the tale which had been so discourteously interrupted. He readily complied, whispering, however, in a tone scarcely above his breath, and drowned occasionally by the rolling of the thunder; and he would pause every now and then, and listen with evident awe, as he heard the heavy footsteps of the stranger pacing over head.

The following is the purport of his story.

THE ADVENTURE OF THE BLACK FISHERMAN

Every body knows Black Sam, the old negro fisherman, or, as he is commonly called, Mud Sam, who has fished about the Sound for the last half century. It is now many, many years since Sam, who was then as active a young negro as any in the province, and worked on the farm of Killian Suydam on Long Island, having finished his day's work at an early hour, was fishing, one still summer evening, just about the neighbourhood of Hell Gate. He was in a light skiff, and being well acquainted with the currents and eddies, had shifted his station according to the shifting of the tide, from the Hen and Chickens to the Hog's Back, from the Hog's Back to the Pot, and from the Pot to the Frying Pan; but in the eagerness of his sport he did not see that the tide was rapidly ebbing; until the roaring of the whirlpools and eddies warned him of his danger, and he had some difficulty in shooting his skiff from among the rocks and breakers, and getting to the point of Blackwell's Island. Here he cast anchor for some time, waiting the turn of the tide to enable him to return homewards. As the night set in it grew blustering and gusty. Dark clouds came bundling up in the west; and now and then a growl of thunder or a flash of lightning told that a summer storm was at hand. Sam pulled over, therefore, under the lee of Manhattan Island, and coasting along came to a snug nook, just under a steep beetling rock, where he fastened his skiff to the root of a tree that shot out from a cleft and spread its broad branches like a canopy over the water. The gust came scouring along; the wind threw up the river in white surges; the rain rattled among the leaves, the thunder bellowed worse than that which is now bellowing, the lightning seemed to lick up the surges of the stream; but Sam, snugly sheltered under rock and tree, lay crouching in his skiff, rocking upon the billows until he fell asleep. When he woke all was quiet. The gust had passed away, and only now and then a faint gleam of lightning in the east showed which way it had gone. The night was dark and moonless; and from the state of the tide Sam concluded it was near midnight. He was on the point of making loose his skiff to return homewards, when he saw a light gleaming along the water from a distance, which seemed rapidly approaching. As it drew near he perceived it came from a lanthorn in the bow of a boat gliding along under shadow of the land. It pulled up in a small cove, close to where he was. A man jumped on shore, and searching about with the lanthorn exclaimed, "This is the place—here's the Iron ring." The boat was then made fast, and the man returning on board, assisted his comrades in conveying something heavy on shore. As the light gleamed among them, Sam saw that they were five stout desperate looking fellows, in red woollen caps, with a leader in a three cornered hat, and that some of them were armed with dirks, or long knives and pistols. They talked low to one another, and occasionally in some outlandish tongue which he could not understand.

On landing they made their way among the bushes, taking turns to relieve each other in lugging their burthen up the rocky bank. Sam's curiosity was now fully aroused, so leaving his skiff he clambered silently up a ridge that overlooked their path. They had stopped to rest for a moment, and the leader was looking about among the bushes with his lanthorn. "Have you brought the spades?" said one. "They are here," replied another, who had them on his shoulder. "We must dig deep, where there will be no risk of discovery," said a third.

A cold chill ran through Sam's veins. He fancied he saw before him a gang of murderers, about to bury their victim. His knees smote together. In his agitation he shook the branch of a tree with which he was supporting himself as he looked over the edge of the cliff.

"What's that?" cried one of the gang. "Some one stirs among the bushes!"

The lanthorn was held up in the direction of the noise. One of the red caps cocked a pistol, and pointed it towards the very place where Sam was standing. He stood motionless—breathless; expecting the next moment to be his last. Fortunately his dingy complexion was in his favour, and made no glare among the leaves.

"'Tis no one," said the man with the lanthorn. "What a plague! you would not fire off your pistol and alarm the country."

The pistol was uncocked; the burthen was resumed, and the party slowly toiled along the bank. Sam watched them as they went; the light sending back fitful gleams through the dripping bushes, and it was not till they were fairly out of sight that he ventured to draw breath freely. He now thought of getting back to his boat, and making his escape out of the reach of such dangerous neighbours; but curiosity was all powerful. He hesitated and lingered and listened. By and bye he heard the strokes of spades.

"They are digging the grave!" said he to himself; and the cold sweat started upon his forehead. Every stroke of a spade, as it sounded through the silent groves, went to his heart; it was evident there was as little noise made as possible; every thing had an air of terrible mystery and secresy. Sam had a great relish for the horrible,—a tale of murder was a treat for him; and he was a constant attendant at executions. He could not resist an impulse, in spite of every danger, to steal nearer to the scene of mystery, and overlook the midnight fellows at their work. He crawled along cautiously, therefore, inch by inch; stepping with the utmost care among the dry leaves, lest their rustling should betray him. He came at length to where a steep rock intervened between him and the gang; for he saw the light of their lanthorn shining up against the branches of the trees on the other side. Sam slowly and silently clambered up the surface of the rock, and raising his head above its naked edge, beheld the villains immediately below him, and so near that though he dreaded discovery he dared not withdraw lest the least movement should be heard. In this way he remained, with his round black face peering above the edge of the rock, like the sun just emerging above the edge of the horizon, or the round cheeked moon on the dial of a clock.

The red caps had nearly finished their work; the grave was filled up, and they were carefully replacing the turf. This done, they scattered dry leaves over the place. "And now," said the leader, "I defy the devil himself to find it out."

"The murderers!" exclaimed Sam, involuntarily.

The whole gang started, and looking up beheld the round black head of Sam just above them. His white eyes strained half out of their orbits; his white teeth chattering, and his whole visage shining with cold perspiration.

"We're discovered!" cried one.

"Down with him!" cried another.

Sam heard the cocking of a pistol, but did not pause for the report. He scrambled over rock and stone, through bush and briar, rolled down banks like a hedge hog; scrambled up others like a catamount. In every direction he heard some one or other of the gang hemming him in. At length he reached the rocky ridge along the river; one of the red caps was hard behind him. A steep rock like a wall rose directly in his way; it seemed to cut off all retreat, when fortunately he espied the strong cord-like branch of a grape vine, reaching half way down it. He sprang at it with the force of a desperate man, seized it with both hands, and being young and agile, succeeded in swinging himself to the summit of the cliff. Here he stood in full relief against the sky, when the red cap cocked his pistol and fired. The ball whistled by Sam's head. With the lucky thought of a man in an emergency, he uttered a yell, fell to the ground, and detached at the same time a fragment of the rock, which tumbled with a loud splash into the river.

"I've done his business," said the red cap, to one or two of his comrades as they arrived panting. "He'll tell no tales, except to the fishes in the river."

His pursuers now turned off to meet their companions. Sam sliding silently down the surface of the rock, let himself quietly into his skiff, cast loose the fastening, and abandoned himself to the rapid current, which in that place runs like a mill stream and soon swept him off from the neighbourhood. It was not, however, until he had drifted a great distance that he ventured to ply his oars; when he made his skiff dart like an arrow through

the strait of Hell Gate, never heeding the danger of Pot, Frying Pan, or
Hog's Back itself; nor did he feel himself thoroughly secure until safely nestled in bed in the cockloft of the ancient farm house of the Suydams.

Here the worthy Peechy Prauw paused to take breath and to take a sip of
the gossip tankard that stood at his elbow. His auditors remained with open
mouths and outstretched necks, gaping like a nest of swallows for an additional mouthful.

"And is that all?" exclaimed the half-pay officer.

"That's all that belongs to the story," said Peechy Prauw.

"And did Sam never find out what was buried by the red caps?" said Wolfert, eagerly; whose mind was haunted by nothing but ingots and doubloons.

"Not that I know of," said Peechy; "he had no time to spare from his work,
and to tell the truth he did not like to run the risk of another race among
the rocks. Besides, how should he recollect the spot where the grave had
been digged? every thing would look so different by daylight. And then,
where was the use of looking for a dead body, when there was no chance of
hanging the murderers?"

"Aye, but are you sure it was a dead body they buried?" said Wolfert.

"To be sure," cried Peechy Prauw, exultingly. "Does it not haunt in the
neighbourhood to this very day?"

"Haunts!" exclaimed several of the party, opening their eyes still wider
and edging their chairs still closer.

"Aye, haunts," repeated Peechy, "has none of you heard of father red cap
that haunts the old burnt farm house in the woods, on the border of the
Sound, near Hell Gate?"

"Oh, to be sure, I've heard tell of something of the kind, but then I took
it for some old wives' fable."

"Old wives' fable or not," said Peechy Prauw, "that farm house stands hard
by the very spot. It's been unoccupied time out of mind, and stands in a
lonely part of the coast; but those who fish in the neighbourhood have often
heard strange noises there; and lights have been seen about the wood at
night; and an old fellow in a red cap has been seen at the windows more
than once, which people take to be the ghost of the body buried there. Once
upon a time three soldiers took shelter in the building for the night, and
rummaged it from top to bottom, when they found old father red cap astride
of a cider barrel in the cellar, with a jug in one hand and a goblet in the
other. He offered them a drink out of his goblet, but just as one of the
soldiers was putting it to his mouth—Whew! a flash of fire blazed through
the cellar, blinded every mother's son of them for several minutes, and when
they recovered their eye sight, jug, goblet, and red cap had vanished, and
nothing but the empty cider barrel remained."

Here the half-pay officer, who was growing very muzzy and sleepy, and nodding over his liquor, with half extinguished eye, suddenly gleamed up like an expiring rushlight.

"That's all fudge!" said he, as Peechy finished his last story.

"Well, I don't vouch for the truth of it myself," said Peechy Prauw, "though all the world knows that there's something strange about that house and grounds; but as to the story of Mud Sam, I believe it just as well as if it had happened to myself."

The deep interest taken in this conversation by the company, had made them unconscious of the uproar abroad among the elements, when suddenly they were electrified by a tremendous clap of thunder. A lumbering crash followed instantaneously shaking the building to its very foundation. All started from their seats, imagining it the shock of an earthquake, or that old father red cap was coming among them in all his terrors. They listened for a moment but only heard the rain pelting against the windows, and the wind howling among the trees. The explosion was soon explained by the apparition of an old negro's bald head thrust in at the door, his white goggle eyes contrasting with his jetty poll, which was wet with rain and shone like a bottle. In a jargon but half intelligible he announced that the kitchen chimney had been struck with lightning.

A sullen pause of the storm, which now rose and sunk in gusts, produced a momentary stillness. In this interval the report of a musket was heard, and a long shout, almost like a yell, resounded from the shore. Every one crowded to the window; another musket shot was heard, and another long shout, mingled wildly with a rising blast of wind. It seemed as if the cry came up from the bosom of the waters; for though incessant flashes of lightning spread a light about the shore, no one was to be seen.

Suddenly the window of the room overhead was opened, and a loud halloo uttered by the mysterious stranger. Several hailings passed from one party to the other, but in a language which none of the company in the bar room could understand; and presently they heard the window closed, and a great noise over head as if all the furniture were pulled and hauled about the room. The negro servant was summoned, and shortly afterwards was seen assisting the veteran to lug the ponderous sea chest down stairs.

The landlord was in amazement. "What, you are not going on the water in such a storm?"

"Storm!" said the other, scornfully, "do you call such a sputter of weather a storm?"

"You'll get drenched to the skin—You'll catch your death!" said Peechy Prauw, affectionately.

"Thunder and lightning!" exclaimed the merman, "don't preach about weather to a man that has cruised in whirlwinds and tornadoes."

The obsequious Peechy was again struck dumb. The voice from the water was heard once more in a tone of impatience; the bystanders stared with redoubled awe at this man of storms, who seemed to have come up out of the deep and to be summoned back to it again. As, with the assistance of the negro, he slowly bore his ponderous sea chest towards the shore, they eyed it with a superstitious feeling; half doubting whether he were not really about to embark upon it and launch forth upon the wild waves. They followed him at a distance with a lanthorn.

"Dowse the light!" roared the hoarse voice from the water. "No one wants lights here!"

"Thunder and lightning!" exclaimed the veteran, turning short upon them; "back to the house with you!"

Wolfert and his companions shrunk back in dismay. Still their curiosity would not allow them entirely to withdraw. A long sheet of lightning now flickered across the waves, and discovered a boat, filled with men, just under a rocky point, rising and sinking with the heaving surges, and swashing the water at every heave. It was with difficulty held to the rocks by a boat hook, for the current rushed furiously round the point. The veteran hoisted one end of the lumbering sea chest on the gunwale of the boat, and seized the handle at the other end to lift it in, when the motion propelled the boat from the shore; the chest slipped off from the gunwale, and, sinking into the waves, pulled the veteran headlong after it. A loud shriek was uttered by all on shore, and a volley of execrations by those on board; but boat and man were hurried away by the rushing swiftness of the tide. A pitchy darkness succeeded; Wolfert Webber indeed fancied that he distinguished a cry for help, and that he beheld the drowning man beckoning for assistance; but when the lightning again gleamed along the water all was void. Neither man nor boat was to be seen; nothing but the dashing and weltering of the waves as they hurried past.

The company returned to the tavern to await the subsiding of the storm. They resumed their seats and gazed on each other with dismay. The whole transaction had not occupied five minutes, and not a dozen words had been spoken. When they looked at the oaken chair they could scarcely realize the fact that the strange being who had so lately tenanted it, full of life and Herculean vigour, should already be a corpse. There was the very glass he had just drunk from; there lay the ashes from the pipe which he had smoked as it were with his last breath. As the worthy burghers pondered on these things, they felt a terrible conviction of the uncertainty of existence, and each felt as if the ground on which he stood was rendered less stable by this awful example.

As, however, the most of the company were possessed of that valuable philosophy which enables a man to bear up with fortitude against the misfortunes of his neighbours, they soon managed to console themselves for the tragic end of the veteran. The landlord was particularly happy that the poor dear man had paid his reckoning before he went; and made a kind of farewell speech on the occasion.

"He came," said he, "in a storm, and he went in a storm; he came in the night, and he went in the night; he came nobody knows whence, and he has gone nobody knows where. For aught I know he has gone to sea once more on his chest and may land to bother some people on the other side of the world! Though it's a thousand pities," added he, "if he has gone to Davy Jones' locker, that he had not left his own locker behind him."

"His locker! St. Nicholas preserve us!" cried Peechy Prauw. "I'd not have had that sea chest in the house for any money; I'll warrant he'd come rack eting after it at nights, and making a haunted house of the inn. And as to his going to sea on his chest I recollect what happened to Skipper Onderdonk's ship on his voyage from Amsterdam.

"The boatswain died during a storm, so they wrapped him up in a sheet, and put him in his own sea chest, and threw him overboard; but they neglected in their hurry skurry to say prayers over him—and the storm raged and roared louder than ever, and they saw the dead man seated in his chest, with his shroud for a sail, coming hard after the ship; and the sea breaking before him in great sprays like fire, and there they kept scudding day after day and night after night, expecting every moment to go to wreck; and every night they saw the dead boatswain in his sea chest trying to get up with them, and they heard his whistle above the blasts of wind, and he seemed to send great seas mountain high after them, that would have swamped the ship if they had not put up the dead lights. And so it went on till they lost sight of him in the fogs of Newfoundland, and supposed he had veered ship and stood for Dead Man's Isle. So much for burying a man at sea without saying prayers over him."

The thundergust which had hitherto detained the company was now at an end. The cuckoo clock in the hall told midnight; every one pressed to depart, for seldom was such a late hour of the night trespassed on by these quiet burghers. As they sallied forth they found the heavens once more serene. The storm which had lately obscured them had rolled away, and lay piled up in fleecy masses on the horizon, lighted up by the bright crescent of the moon, which looked like a little silver lamp hung up in a palace of clouds.

The dismal occurrence of the night, and the dismal narrations they had made, had left a superstitious feeling in every mind. They cast a fearful glance at the spot where the buccaneer had disappeared, almost expecting to see him sailing on his chest in the cool moonshine. The trembling rays glittered along the waters, but all was placid; and the current dimpled over the spot where he had gone down. The party huddled together in a little crowd as they repaired homewards; particularly when they passed a lonely field where a man had been murdered; and even the sexton, who had to complete his journey alone, though accustomed, one would think, to ghosts and goblins, yet went a long way round, rather than pass by his own churchyard.

Wolfert Webber had now carried home a fresh stock of stories and notions to ruminate upon. These accounts of pots of money and Spanish treasures, buried here and there and every where, about the rocks and bays of these wild shores made him almost dizzy.

"Blessed St. Nicholas!" ejaculated he half aloud, "is it not possible to come upon one of these golden hoards, and so make one's self rich in a twinkling. How hard that I must go on, delving and delving, day in and day out, merely to make a morsel of bread, when one lucky stroke of a spade might enable me to ride in my carriage for the rest of my life!"

As he turned over in his thoughts all that had been told of the singular adventure of the negro fisherman, his imagination gave a totally different complexion to the tale. He saw in the gang of red caps nothing but a crew of pirates burying their spoils, and his cupidity was once more awakened by the possibility of at length getting on the traces of some of this lurking wealth. Indeed, his infected fancy tinged every thing with gold. He felt like the greedy inhabitant of Bagdad, when his eye had been greased with the magic ointment of the dervise, that gave him to see all the treasures of the earth. Caskets of buried jewels, chests of ingots, and barrels of outlandish coins, seemed to court him from their concealments, and supplicate him to relieve them from their untimely graves.

On making private inquiries about the grounds said to be haunted by Father red cap, he was more and more confirmed in his surmise. He learned that the place had several times been visited by experienced money diggers, who had heard Black Sam's story, though none of them had met with success. On the contrary, they had always been dogged with ill luck of some kind or other, in consequence, as Wolfert concluded, of not going to work at the proper time, and with the proper ceremonials. The last attempt had been made by Cobus Quackenbos, who dug for a whole night and met with incredible difficulty, for as fast as he threw one shovel full of earth out of the hole, two were thrown in by invisible hands. He succeeded so far, however, as to uncover an iron chest, when there was a terrible roaring, and ramping, and raging, of uncouth figures about the hole, and at length a shower of blows, dealt by invisible cudgels, fairly belaboured him off of the forbidden ground. This Cobus Quackenbos had declared on his death bed, so that there could not be any doubt of it. He was a man that had devoted many years of his life to money digging, and it was thought would have ultimately succeeded, had he not died recently of a brain fever in the alms house.

Wolfert Webber was now in a worry of trepidation and impatience; fearful lest some rival adventurer should get a scent of the buried gold. He determined privately to seek out the black fisherman and get him to serve as

guide to the place where he had witnessed the mysterious scene of inter-
ment. Sam was easily found; for he was one of those old habitual beings that
live about a neighbourhood until they wear themselves a place in the public
mind, and become, in a manner, public characters. There was not an unlucky urchin about town that did not know Sam the fisherman, and think
that he had a right to play his tricks upon the old negro. Sam had led an
amphibious life for more than half a century, about the shores of the bay,
and the fishing grounds of the Sound. He passed the greater part of his time
on and in the water, particularly about Hell Gate; and might have been
taken, in bad weather, for one of the hobgoblins that used to haunt that
strait. There would he be seen, at all times, and in all weathers; sometimes
in his skiff, anchored among the eddies, or prowling, like a shark about some
wreck, where the fish are supposed to be most abundant. Sometimes seated
on a rock from hour to hour, looking, in the mist and drizzle, like a solitary
heron watching for its prey. He was well acquainted with every hole and
corner of the Sound; from the Wallabout to Hell Gate, and from Hell Gate
even unto the Devil's Stepping Stones; and it was even affirmed that he
knew all the fish in the river by their christian names.

Wolfert found him at his cabin, which was not much larger than a tolerable
dog house. It was rudely constructed of fragments of wrecks and drift wood,
and built on the rocky shore, at the foot of the old fort, just about what at
present forms the point of the Battery. A "most ancient and fish-like smell"
pervaded the place. Oars, paddles, and fishing rods were leaning against the
wall of the fort; a net was spread on the sands to dry; a skiff was drawn up
on the beach, and at the door of his cabin was Mud Sam himself, indulging
in the true negro luxury of sleeping in the sunshine.

Many years had passed away since the time of Sam's youthful adventure,
and the snows of many a winter had grizzled the knotty wool upon his head.
He perfectly recollected the circumstances, however, for he had often been
called upon to relate them, though in his version of the story he differed in
many points from Peechy Prauw; as is not unfrequently the case with authentic historians. As to the subsequent researches of money diggers, Sam
knew nothing about them; they were matters quite out of his line; neither
did the cautious Wolfert care to disturb his thoughts on that point. His only
wish was to secure the old fisherman as a pilot to the spot, and this was
readily effected. The long time that had intervened since his nocturnal adventure had effacéd all Sam's awe of the place, and the promise of a trifling
reward roused him at once from his sleep and his sunshine.

The tide was adverse to making the expedition by water, and Wolfert was
too impatient to get to the land of promise, to wait for its turning; they set
off, therefore, by land. A walk of four or five miles brought them to the edge
of a wood, which at that time covered the greater part of the eastern side of
the island. It was just beyond the pleasant region of Bloomen-dael. Here

they struck into a long lane, straggling among trees and bushes, very much overgrown with weeds and mullein stalks as if but seldom used, and so completely overshadowed as to enjoy but a kind of twilight. Wild vines entangled the trees and flaunted in their faces; brambles and briars caught their clothes as they passed; the garter snake glided across their path; the spotted toad hopped and waddled before them, and the restless cat-bird mewed at them from every thicket. Had Wolfert Webber been deeply read in romantic legend he might have fancied himself entering upon forbidden enchanted ground; or that these were some of the guardians set to keep a watch upon buried treasure. As it was, the loneliness of the place, and the wild stories connected with it, had their effect upon his mind.

On reaching the lower end of the lane they found themselves near the shore of the Sound in a kind of amphitheatre, surrounded by forest trees. The area had once been a grass plot, but was now shagged with briars and rank weeds. At one end, and just on the river bank, was a ruined building, little better than a heap of rubbish, with a stack of chimneys rising like a solitary tower out of the centre. The current of the Sound rushed along just below it; with wildly grown trees drooping their branches into its waves.

Wolfert had not a doubt that this was the haunted house of Father red cap, and called to mind the story of Peechy Prauw. The evening was approaching and the light falling dubiously among these woody places, gave a melancholy tone to the scene, well calculated to foster any lurking feeling of awe or superstition. The night hawk, wheeling about in the highest regions of the air, emitted his peevish, boding cry. The woodpecker gave a lonely tap now and then on some hollow tree, and the fire bird* streamed by them with his deep red plumage.

They now came to an enclosure that had once been a garden. It extended along the foot of a rocky ridge, but was little better than a wilderness of weeds, with here and there a matted rose bush, or a peach or plum tree grown wild and ragged, and covered with moss. At the lower end of the garden they passed a kind of vault in the side of a bank, facing the water. It had the look of a root house. The door, though decayed, was still strong, and appeared to have been recently patched up. Wolfert pushed it open. It gave a harsh grating upon its hinges, and striking against something like a box, a rattling sound ensued, and a skull rolled on the floor. Wolfert drew back shuddering, but was reassured on being informed by the negro that this was a family vault belonging to one of the old Dutch families that owned this estate; an assertion corroborated by the sight of coffins of various sizes piled within. Sam had been familiar with all these scenes when a boy, and now knew that he could not be far from the place of which they were in quest.

*Orchard Oreole.

They now made their way to the water's edge, scrambling along ledges of rocks that overhung the waves, and obliged often to hold by shrubs and grape vines to avoid slipping into the deep and hurried stream. At length they came to a small cove, or rather indent of the shore. It was protected by steep rocks and overshadowed by a thick copse of oaks and chestnuts, so as to be sheltered and almost concealed. The beach shelved gradually within the cove, but the current swept deep and black and rapid along its jutting points. The negro paused; raised his remnant of a hat, and scratching his grizzled poll for a moment, as he regarded this nook: then suddenly clapping his hands, he stepped exultingly forward and pointed to a large iron ring, stapled firmly in the rock, just where a broad shelve of stone furnished a commodious landing place. It was the very spot where the red caps had landed. Years had changed the more perishable features of the scene; but rock and iron yield slowly to the influence of time. On looking more closely, Wolfert remarked three crosses cut in the rock just above the ring, which had no doubt some mysterious signification. Old Sam now readily recognized the overhanging rock under which his skiff had been sheltered during the thundergust. To follow up the course which the midnight gang had taken, however, was a harder task. His mind had been so much taken up on that eventful occasion by the persons of the drama, as to pay but little attention to the scenes; and these places look so different by night and day. After wandering about for some time, however, they came to an opening among the trees which Sam thought resembled the place. There was a ledge of rock of moderate height like a wall on one side, which he thought might be the very ridge whence he had overlooked the diggers. Wolfert examined it narrowly, and at length discovered three crosses similar to those above the iron ring, cut deeply into the face of the rock, but nearly obliterated by the moss that had grown over them. His heart leaped with joy, for he doubted not they were the private marks of the buccaneers. All now that remained was to ascertain the precise spot where the treasure lay buried, for otherwise he might dig at random in the neighbourhood of the crosses without coming upon the spoils, and he had already had enough of such profitless labour. Here, however, the old negro was perfectly at a loss, and indeed perplexed him by a variety of opinions; for his recollections were all confused. Sometimes he declared it must have been at the foot of a mulberry tree hard by; then beside a great white stone; then under a small green knoll, a short distance from the ledge of rock; until at length Wolfert became as bewildered as himself.

The shadows of evening were now spreading themselves over the woods, and rock and tree began to mingle together. It was evidently too late to attempt any thing farther at present; and, indeed, Wolfert had come unprovided with implements to prosecute his researches. Satisfied, therefore, with having ascertained the place, he took note of all its landmarks, that he might recognize it again, and set out on his return homewards, resolved to prosecute this golden enterprise without delay.

The leading anxiety which had hitherto absorbed every feeling being now in some measure appeased, fancy began to wander, and to conjure up a thousand shapes and chimeras as he returned through this haunted region. Pirates hanging in chains seemed to swing from every tree, and he almost expected to see some Spanish Don, with his throat cut from ear to ear, rising slowly out of the ground, and shaking the ghost of a money bag.

Their way back lay through the desolate garden, and Wolfert's nerves had arrived at so sensitive a state that the flitting of a bird, the rustling of a leaf, or the falling of a nut was enough to startle him. As they entered the confines of the garden, they caught sight of a figure at a distance advancing slowly up one of the walks and bending under the weight of a burthen. They paused and regarded him attentively. He wore what appeared to be a woollen cap, and still more alarming, of a most sanguinary red. The figure moved slowly on, ascended the bank, and stopped at the very door of the sepulchral vault. Just before entering it he looked around. What was the affright of Wolfert when he recognized the grisly visage of the drowned buccaneer. He uttered an ejaculation of horror. The figure slowly raised his iron fist and shook it with a terrible menace. Wolfert did not pause to see any more, but hurried off as fast as his legs could carry him, nor was Sam slow in following at his heels, having all his ancient terrors revived. Away, then, did they scramble, through bush and brake, horribly frightened at every bramble that tugged at their skirts, nor did they pause to breathe, until they had blundered their way through this perilous wood and fairly reached the high road to the city.

Several days elapsed before Wolfert could summon courage enough to prosecute the enterprise, so much had he been dismayed by the apparition, whether living or dead, of the grisly buccaneer. In the mean time, what a conflict of mind did he suffer! He neglected all his concerns, was moody and restless all day, lost his appetite; wandered in his thoughts and words, and committed a thousand blunders. His rest was broken; and when he fell asleep the nightmare in shape of a huge money bag sat squatted upon his breast. He babbled about incalculable sums; fancied himself engaged in money digging; threw the bed clothes right and left, in the idea that he was shovelling away the dirt, groped under the bed in quest of the treasure, and lugged forth, as he supposed, an inestimable pot of gold.

Dame Webber and her daughter were in despair at what they conceived a returning touch of insanity. There are two family oracles, one or other of which Dutch house wives consult in all cases of great doubt and perplexity: the dominie and the doctor. In the present instance they repaired to the doctor. There was at that time a little dark mouldy man of medicine famous among the old wives of the Manhattoes for his skill not only in the healing art, but in all matters of strange and mysterious nature. His name was Dr. Knipperhausen, but he was more commonly known by the appellation of the High German doctor.* To him did the poor women repair for council and assistance touching the mental vagaries of Wolfert Webber.

They found the doctor seated in his little study, clad in his dark camblet robe of knowledge, with his black velvet cap, after the manner of Boerhaave, Van Helmont and other medical sages: a pair of green spectacles set in black horn upon his clubbed nose, and poring over a German folio that reflected back the darkness of his physiognomy. The doctor listened to their statement of the symptoms of Wolfert's malady with profound attention; but when they came to mention his raving about buried money, the little man pricked up his ears. Alas, poor women! they little knew the aid they had called in.

Dr. Knipperhausen had been half his life engaged in seeking the short cuts to fortune, in quest of which so many a long life time is wasted. He had passed some years of his youth among the Harz mountains of Germany, and had derived much valuable instruction from the miners, touching the mode of seeking treasure buried in the earth. He had prosecuted his studies also under a travelling sage who united the mysteries of medicine with magic and legerdemain. His mind therefore had become stored with all kinds of mystic lore: he had dabbled a little in astrology, alchemy, and divination; knew how to detect stolen money, and to tell where springs of water lay hidden; in a word, by the dark nature of his knowledge he had acquired the name of the High German doctor, which is pretty nearly equivalent to that of necromancer. The doctor had often heard rumours of treasure being buried in various parts of the island, and had long been anxious to get on the traces of it. No sooner were Wolfert's waking and sleeping vagaries confided to him, than he beheld in them the confirmed symptoms of a case of money digging, and lost no time in probing it to the bottom. Wolfert had long been sorely oppressed in mind by the golden secret, and as a family physician is a kind of father confessor, he was glad of an opportunity of unburthening himself. So far from curing, the doctor caught the malady from his patient. The circumstances unfolded to him awakened all his cupidity; he had not a doubt of money being buried somewhere in the neighbourhood of the mysterious crosses, and offered to join Wolfert in the search. He informed him that much secresy and caution must be observed in enterprises of the kind; that money is only to be digged for at night; with certain forms and ceremonies; the burning of drugs; the repeating of mystic words, and above all, that the seekers must first be provided with a divining rod, which had the wonderful property of pointing to the very spot on the surface of the earth under which treasure lay hidden. As the doctor had given much of his mind to these matters, he charged himself with all the necessary preparations,

*The same, no doubt, of whom mention is made in the history of Dolph Heyliger.

and, as the quarter of the moon was propitious, he undertook to have the divining rod ready by a certain night.*

Wolfert's heart leaped with joy at having met with so learned and able a coadjutor. Every thing went on secretly, but swimmingly. The doctor had many consultations with his patient, and the good women of the household lauded the comforting effect of his visits. In the mean time the wonderful divining rod, that great key to nature's secrets, was duly prepared. The doctor had thumbed over all his books of knowledge for the occasion; and the black fisherman was engaged to take them in his skiff to the scene of enterprise; to work with spade and pickaxe in unearthing the treasure; and to freight his bark with the weighty spoils they were certain of finding.

At length the appointed night arrived for this perilous undertaking. Before Wolfert left his home he counselled his wife and daughter to go to bed, and feel no alarm if he should not return during the night. Like reasonable women, on being told not to feel alarm they fell immediately into a panic. They saw at once by his manner that something unusual was in agitation; all their fears about the unsettled state of his mind were revived with tenfold force: they hung about him entreating him not to expose himself to the night air, but all in vain. When once Wolfert was mounted on his hobby, it was no easy matter to get him out of the saddle. It was a clear starlight night, when

*The following note was found appended to this passage in the hand writing of Mr. Knickerbocker. "There has been much written against the divining rod by those light minds who are ever ready to scoff at the mysteries of nature, but I fully join with Dr. Knipperhausen in giving it my faith. I shall not insist upon its efficacy in discovering the concealment of stolen goods, the boundary stones of fields, the traces of robbers and murderers, or even the existence of subterraneous springs and streams of water: albeit, I think these properties not to be readily discredited; but of its potency in discovering veins of precious metal, and hidden sums of money and jewels I have not the least doubt. Some said that the rod turned only in the hands of persons who had been born in particular months of the year; hence astrologers had recourse to planetary influence when they would procure a talisman. Others declared that the properties of the rod were either an effect of chance, or the fraud of the holder, or the work of the devil. Thus sayeth the reverend father Gaspard Schott in his Treatise on Magic. 'Propter hæc et similia argumenta audacter ego pronuncio vim conversivam virgulæ bifurcatæ nequaquam naturalem esse, sed vel casu vel fraude virgulam tractantis vel ope diaboli,' &c.

"Georgius Agricola also was of opinion that it was a mere delusion of the devil to inveigle the avaricious and unwary into his clutches, and in his treatise 'de re Metallica,' lays particular stress on the mysterious words pronounced by those persons who employed the divining rod during his time. But I make not a doubt that the divining rod is one of those secrets of natural magic, the mystery of which is to be explained by the sympathies existing between physical things operated upon by the planets, and rendered efficacious by the strong faith of the individual. Let the divining rod be properly gathered at the proper time of the moon, cut into the proper form, used with the necessary ceremonies, and with a perfect faith in its efficacy, and I can confidently recommend it to my fellow citizens as an infallible means of discovering the various places on the Island of the Manhattoes where treasure hath been buried in the olden time.

D.K."

he issued out of the portal of the Webber palace. He wore a large flapped hat tied under the chin with a handkerchief of his daughter's, to secure him from the night damp, while Dame Webber threw her long red cloak about his shoulders, and fastened it round his neck.

The doctor had been no less carefully armed and accoutred by his house-keeper, the vigilant Frau Ilsy; and sallied forth in his camblet robe by way of surtout; his black velvet cap under his cocked hat, a thick clasped book under his arm, a basket of drugs and dried herbs in one hand, and in the other the miraculous rod of divination.

The great church clock struck ten as Wolfert and the doctor passed by the church yard, and the watchman bawled in hoarse voice a long and doleful "all's well!" A deep sleep had already fallen upon this primitive little burgh: nothing disturbed this awful silence, excepting now and then the bark of some profligate night walking dog, or the serenade of some romantic cat. It is true, Wolfert fancied more than once that he heard the sound of a stealthy footfall at a distance behind them; but it might have been merely the echo of their own steps along the quiet streets. He thought also at one time that he saw a tall figure skulking after them—stopping when they stopped, and moving on as they proceeded; but the dim and uncertain lamp light threw such vague gleams and shadows, that this might all have been mere fancy.

They found the old fisherman waiting for them, smoking his pipe in the stern of his skiff, which was moored just in front of his little cabin. A pickaxe and spade were lying in the bottom of the boat, with a dark lanthorn, and a stone bottle of good Dutch courage in which honest Sam no doubt put even more faith than Dr. Knipperhausen in his drugs.

Thus then did these three worthies embark in their cockle shell of a skiff upon this nocturnal expedition, with a wisdom and valour equalled only by the three wise men of Gotham, who adventured to sea in a bowl. The tide was rising and running rapidly up the Sound. The current bore them along, almost without the aid of an oar. The profile of the town lay all in shadow. Here and there a light feebly glimmered from some sick chamber, or from the cabin window of some vessel at anchor in the stream. Not a cloud obscured the deep starry firmament, the lights of which wavered on the surface of the placid river; and a shooting meteor, streaking its pale course in the very direction they were taking, was interpreted by the doctor into a most propitious omen.

In a little while they glided by the point of Corlear's Hook with the rural inn which had been the scene of such night adventures. The family had retired to rest, and the house was dark and still. Wolfert felt a chill pass over him as they passed the point where the buccaneer had disappeared. He pointed it out to Dr. Knipperhausen. While regarding it they thought they saw a boat actually lurking at the very place; but the shore cast such a shadow over the border of the water that they could discern nothing distinctly.

They had not proceeded far when they heard the low sounds of distant oars, as if cautiously pulled. Sam plied his oars with redoubled vigour, and knowing all the eddies and currents of the stream soon left their followers, if such they were, far astern. In a little while they stretched across Turtle Bay and Kip's Bay, then shrouded themselves in the deep shadows of the Manhattan shore, and glided swiftly along, secure from observation. At length the negro shot his skiff into a little cove, darkly embowered by trees, and made it fast to the well known iron ring. They now landed, and lighting the lanthorn, gathered their various implements and proceeded slowly through the bushes. Every sound startled them, even that of their own footsteps among the dry leaves; and the hooting of a screech owl, from the shattered chimney of the neighbouring ruin, made their blood run cold.

In spite of all Wolfert's caution in taking note of the landmarks, it was some time before they could find the open place among the trees, where the treasure was supposed to be buried. At length they came to the ledge of rock; and on examining its surface by the aid of the lanthorn, Wolfert recognized the three mystic crosses. Their hearts beat quick, for the momentous trial was at hand that was to determine their hopes.

The lanthorn was now held by Wolfert Webber, while the doctor produced the divining rod. It was a forked twig, one end of which was grasped firmly in each hand, while the centre, forming the stem, pointed perpendicularly upwards. The doctor moved this wand about, within a certain distance of the earth, from place to place, but for some time without any effect, while Wolfert kept the light of the lanthorn turned full upon it, and watched it with the most breathless interest. At length the rod began slowly to turn. The doctor grasped it with greater earnestness, his hands trembling with the agitation of his mind. The wand continued to turn gradually, until at length the stem had reversed its position, and pointed perpendicularly downward; and remained pointing to one spot as fixedly as the needle to the pole.

"This is the spot!" said the doctor in an almost inaudible tone.

Wolfert's heart was in his throat.

"Shall I dig?" said the negro, grasping the spade.

"*Pots tausends*, no!" replied the little doctor, hastily. He now ordered his companions to keep close by him and to maintain the most inflexible silence. That certain precautions must be taken and ceremonies used to prevent the evil spirits which keep about buried treasure from doing them any harm. He then drew a circle round the place, enough to include the whole party. He next gathered dry twigs and leaves, and made a fire, upon which he threw certain drugs and dried herbs which he had brought in his basket. A thick smoke rose, diffusing a potent odour, savouring marvellously of brimstone and assafœtida, which, however grateful it might be to the olfactory nerves of spirits, nearly strangled poor Wolfert, and produced a fit of cough-

ing and wheezing that made the whole grove resound. Doctor Knipperhausen then unclasped the volume which he had brought under his arm, which
was printed in red and black characters in German text. While Wolfert held
the lanthorn, the doctor, by the aid of his spectacles, read off several forms
of conjuration in Latin and German. He then ordered Sam to seize the pickaxe and proceed to work. The close bound soil gave obstinate signs of not
having been disturbed for many a year. After having picked his way through
the surface, Sam came to a bed of sand and gravel which he threw briskly
to right and left with the spade.

"Hark!" said Wolfert, who fancied he heard a trampling among the dry
leaves, and a rustling through the bushes. Sam paused for a moment, and
they listened.—No footstep was near. The bat flitted by them in silence; a
bird roused from its roost by the light which glared up among the trees, flew
circling about the flame. In the profound stillness of the woodland, they
could distinguish the current rippling along the rocky shore, and the distant
murmuring and roaring of Hell Gate.

The negro continued his labours, and had already digged a considerable
hole. The doctor stood on the edge, reading formulæ every now and then
from his black letter volume, or throwing more drugs and herbs upon the
fire; while Wolfert bent anxiously over the pit, watching every stroke of the
spade. Any one witnessing the scene thus lighted up by fire, lanthorn, and
the reflection of Wolfert's red mantle, might have mistaken the little doctor
for some foul magician, busied in his incantations, and the grizzly headed
negro for some swart goblin, obedient to his commands.

At length the spade of the old fisherman struck upon something that
sounded hollow. The sound vibrated to Wolfert's heart. He struck his spade
again.

"'Tis a chest," said Sam.

"Full of gold, I'll warrant it!" cried Wolfert, clasping his hands with
rapture.

Scarcely had he uttered the words when a sound from above caught his
ear. He cast up his eyes, and lo! by the expiring light of the fire he beheld,
just over the disk of the rock, what appeared to be the grim visage of the
drowned buccaneer, grinning hideously down upon him.

Wolfert gave a loud cry, and let fall the lanthorn. His panic communicated
itself to his companions. The negro leaped out of the hole, the doctor
dropped his book and basket and began to pray in German. All was horror
and confusion. The fire was scattered about, the lanthorn extinguished. In
their hurry skurry they ran against and confounded one another. They fancied a legion of hobgoblins let loose upon them, and that they saw by the
fitful gleams of the scattered embers, strange figures in red caps gibbering
and ramping around them. The doctor ran one way, the negro another, and
Wolfert made for the water side. As he plunged struggling onwards through

bush and brake, he heard the tread of some one in pursuit. He scrambled frantically forward. The footsteps gained upon him. He felt himself grasped by his cloak, when suddenly his pursuer was attacked in turn: a fierce fight and struggle ensued—a pistol was discharged that lit up rock and bush for a second, and showed two figures grappling together—all was then darker than ever. The contest continued—the combatants clenched each other, and panted and groaned, and rolled among the rocks. There was snarling and growling as of a cur, mingled with curses in which Wolfert fancied he could recognize the voice of the buccaneer. He would fain have fled, but he was on the brink of a precipice and could go no farther.

Again the parties were on their feet; again there was a tugging and struggling, as if strength alone could decide the combat, until one was precipitated from the brow of the cliff and sent headlong into the deep stream that whirled below. Wolfert heard the plunge, and a kind of strangling bubbling murmur, but the darkness of the night hid every thing from him, and the swiftness of the current swept every thing instantly out of hearing. One of the combatants was disposed of, but whether friend or foe Wolfert could not tell, nor whether they might not both be foes. He heard the survivor approach, and his terror revived. He saw, where the profile of the rocks rose against the horizon, a human form advancing. He could not be mistaken: it must be the buccaneer. Whither should he fly! a precipice was on one side; a murderer on the other. The enemy approached: he was close at hand. Wolfert attempted to let himself down the face of the cliff. His cloak caught in a thorn that grew on the edge. He was jerked from off his feet, and held dangling in the air, half choked by the string with which his careful wife had fastened the garment round his neck. Wolfert thought his last moment was arrived; already had he committed his soul to St. Nicholas, when the string broke, and he tumbled down the bank, bumping from rock to rock and bush to bush, and leaving the red cloak fluttering like a bloody banner in the air.

It was a long while before Wolfert came to himself. When he opened his eyes, the ruddy streaks of morning were already shooting up the sky. He found himself grievously battered, and lying in the bottom of a boat. He attempted to sit up, but was too sore and stiff to move. A voice requested him in friendly accents to lie still. He turned his eyes towards the speaker: it was Dirk Waldron. He had dogged the party, at the earnest request of Dame Webber and her daughter, who with the laudable curiosity of their sex had pried into the secret consultations of Wolfert and the doctor. Dirk had been completely distanced in following the light skiff of the fisherman, and had just come in time to rescue the poor money digger from his pursuer.

Thus ended this perilous enterprise. The doctor and Black Sam severally found their way back to the Manhattoes, each having some dreadful tale of peril to relate. As to poor Wolfert, instead of returning in triumph laden with bags of gold, he was borne home on a shutter, followed by a rabble rout of curious urchins. His wife and daughter saw the dismal pageant from a distance, and alarmed the neighbourhood with their cries: they thought the poor man had suddenly settled the great debt of nature in one of his way-ward moods. Finding him, however, still living, they had him speedily to bed, and a jury of old matrons of the neighbourhood assembled to determine how he should be doctored. The whole town was in a buzz with the story of the money diggers. Many repaired to the scene of the previous night's adventures: but though they found the very place of the digging, they discovered nothing that compensated them for their trouble. Some say they found the fragments of an oaken chest, and an iron pot lid which savoured strongly of hidden money; and that in the old family vault there were traces of bales and boxes, but this is all very dubious.

In fact, the secret of all this story has never to this day been discovered: whether any treasure was ever actually buried at that place; whether, if so, it was carried off at night by those who had buried it; or whether it still remains there under the guardianship of gnomes and spirits until it shall be properly sought for, is all matter of conjecture. For my part I incline to the latter opinion; and make no doubt that great sums lie buried, both there and in many other parts of this island and its neighbourhood, ever since the times of the buccaneers and the Dutch colonists; and I would earnestly recommend the search after them to such of my fellow citizens as are not engaged in any other speculations.

There were many conjectures formed, also, as to who and what was the strange man of the seas who had domineered over the little fraternity at Corlear's Hook for a time; disappeared so strangely, and reappeared so fearfully. Some supposed him a smuggler stationed at that place to assist his comrades in landing their goods among the rocky coves of the island. Others that he was one of the ancient comrades of Kidd or Bradish, returned to convey away treasures formerly hidden in the vicinity. The only circumstance that throws any thing like a vague light over this mysterious matter is a report which prevailed of a strange foreign built shallop, with much the look of a piccaroon, having been seen hovering about the Sound for several days without landing or reporting herself, though boats were seen going to and from her at night: and that she was seen standing out of the mouth of the harbour, in the grey of the dawn after the catastrophe of the money diggers.

I must not omit to mention another report, also, which I confess is rather apocryphal, of the buccaneer, who was supposed to have been drowned, being seen before daybreak, with a lanthorn in his hand, seated astride his great sea chest and sailing through Hell Gate, which just then began to roar and bellow with redoubled fury.

While all the gossip world was thus filled with talk and rumour, poor Wolfert lay sick and sorrowful in his bed, bruised in body and sorely beaten down in mind. His wife and daughter did all they could to bind up his wounds both corporal and spiritual. The good old dame never stirred from his bed side, where she sat knitting from morning till night; while his daughter busied herself about him with the fondest care. Nor did they lack assistance from abroad. Whatever may be said of the desertions of friends in distress, they had no complaint of the kind to make. Not an old wife of the neighbourhood but abandoned her work to crowd to the mansion of Wolfert Webber, inquire after his health and the particulars of his story. Not one came moreover without her little pipkin of pennyroyal, sage, balm, or other herb tea, delighted at an opportunity of signalizing her kindness and her doctorship. What drenchings did not the poor Wolfert undergo, and all in vain. It was a moving sight to behold him wasting away day by day; growing thinner and thinner and ghastlier and ghastlier, and staring with rueful visage from under an old patchwork counterpane upon the jury of matrons kindly assembled to sigh and groan and look unhappy around him.

Dirk Waldron was the only being that seemed to shed a ray of sunshine into this house of mourning. He came in with cheery look and manly spirit, and tried to reanimate the expiring heart of the poor money digger, but it was all in vain. Wolfert was completely done over.—If any thing was wanting to complete his despair, it was a notice served upon him in the midst of his distress, that the corporation were about to run a new street through the very centre of his cabbage garden. He now saw nothing before him but poverty and ruin; his last reliance, the garden of his forefathers, was to be laid waste, and what then was to become of his poor wife and child.

His eyes filled with tears as they followed the dutiful Amy out of the room one morning. Dirk Waldron was seated beside him; Wolfert grasped his hand, pointed after his daughter, and for the first time since his illness broke the silence he had maintained.

"I am going!" said he, shaking his head feebly, "and when I am gone—my poor daughter——"

"Leave her to me, father!" said Dirk, manfully—"I'll take care of her!"

Wolfert looked up in the face of the cheery strapping youngster, and saw there was none better able to take care of a woman.

"Enough," said he—"she is yours!—and now fetch me a lawyer—let me make my will and die."

The lawyer was brought—a dapper, bustling, round headed little man, Roorback (or Rollebuck as it was pronounced) by name. At the sight of him the women broke into loud lamentations, for they looked upon the signing of a will as the signing of a death warrant. Wolfert made a feeble motion for them to be silent. Poor Amy buried her face and her grief in the bed curtain. Dame Webber resumed her knitting to hide her distress, which betrayed itself, however, in a pellucid tear, which trickled silently down and hung at the end of her peaked nose; while the cat, the only unconcerned member of the family, played with the good dame's ball of worsted, as it rolled about the floor.

Wolfert lay on his back, his nightcap drawn over his forehead; his eyes closed; his whole visage the picture of death. He begged the lawyer to be brief, for he felt his end approaching, and that he had no time to lose. The lawyer nibbed his pen, spread out his paper, and prepared to write.

"I give and bequeath," said Wolfert, faintly, "my small farm——"

"What—all!" exclaimed the lawyer.

Wolfert half opened his eyes and looked upon the lawyer.

"Yes—all," said he.

"What! all that great patch of land with cabbages and sunflowers, which the corporation is just going to run a main street through?"

"The same," said Wolfert, with a heavy sigh, and sinking back upon his pillow.

"I wish him joy that inherits it!" said the little lawyer, chuckling and rubbing his hands involuntarily.

"What do you mean?" said Wolfert, again opening his eyes.

"That he'll be one of the richest men in the place!" cried little Rollebuck.

The expiring Wolfert seemed to step back from the threshold of existence: his eyes again lighted up; he raised himself in his bed, shoved back his red worsted nightcap, and stared broadly at the lawyer.

"You don't say so!" exclaimed he.

"Faith, but I do!" rejoined the other. "Why, when that great field and that huge meadow come to be laid out in streets, and cut up into snug building lots—why, whoever owns them need not pull off his hat to the patroon!"

"Say you so?" cried Wolfert, half thrusting one leg out of bed, "why, then I think I'll not make my will yet!"

To the surprise of every body the dying man actually recovered. The vital spark which had glimmered faintly in the socket, received fresh fuel from the oil of gladness, which the little lawyer poured into his soul. It once more burnt up into a flame.

Give physic to the heart, ye who would revive the body of a spirit broken man! In a few days Wolfert left his room; in a few days more his table was covered with deeds, plans of streets and building lots. Little Rollebuck was constantly with him, his right hand man and adviser, and instead of making his will, assisted in the more agreeable task of making his fortune. In fact, Wolfert Webber was one of those many worthy Dutch burghers of the Man-hattoes whose fortunes have been made, in a manner, in spite of themselves. Who have tenaciously held on to their hereditary acres, raising turnips and cabbages about the skirts of the city, hardly able to make both ends meet, until the corporation has cruelly driven streets through their abodes, and they have suddenly awakened out of a lethargy, and, to their astonishment, found themselves rich men.

Before many months had elapsed a great bustling street passed through the very centre of the Webber garden, just where Wolfert had dreamed of finding a treasure. His golden dream was accomplished; he did indeed find an unlooked for source of wealth; for, when his paternal lands were distributed into building lots, and rented out to safe tenants, instead of producing a paltry crop of cabbages, they returned him an abundant crop of rents; insomuch that on quarter day, it was a goodly sight to see his tenants knocking at his door, from morning to night, each with a little round bellied bag of money, the golden produce of the soil.

The ancient mansion of his forefathers was still kept up, but instead of being a little yellow fronted Dutch house in a garden, it now stood boldly in the midst of a street, the grand house of the neighbourhood; for Wolfert enlarged it with a wing on each side, and a cupola or tea room on top, where he might climb up and smoke his pipe in hot weather; and in the course of time the whole mansion was overrun by the chubby faced progeny of Amy Webber and Dirk Waldron.

As Wolfert waxed old and rich and corpulent, he also set up a great gingerbread coloured carriage drawn by a pair of black Flanders mares with tails that swept the ground; and to commemorate the origin of his greatness he had for his crest a full blown cabbage painted on the pannels, with the pithy motto **Alles Kopf:** that is to say, ALL HEAD; meaning thereby that he had risen by sheer head work.

To fill the measure of his greatness, in the fullness of time the renowned Ramm Rapelye slept with his fathers, and Wolfert Webber succeeded to the leathern bottomed arm chair in the inn parlour at Corlear's Hook; where he long reigned greatly honoured and respected, insomuch that he was never known to tell a story without its being believed, nor to utter a joke without its being laughed at.

EDITORIAL APPENDIX

Textual Commentary,
Discussions, and Lists by
Judith Giblin Haig

LIST OF ABBREVIATIONS

The following abbreviations are used throughout the editorial apparatus to refer to relevant texts of *Tales of a Traveller*.

MS	Author's manuscript of Part II, used as printer's copy for the first American edition
1A	First American edition, Carey & Lea, 1824
2A	Second American edition of Part I, Carey & Lea, 1825
3A	"Second American Edition," Van Winkle, 1825
ARE	"Author's Revised Edition," Putnam, 1849
1F	First French edition, Baudry, 1824
1E	First English edition, Murray, 1824
2E	Second English edition, Murray, 1825
T	Twayne edition

Variant states of an edition are designated by lower case letters added to the abbreviation, as in 1Ea and 1Eb. Inclusive entries reflect genetic rather than chronological order. For example, 2A–1F, includes all editions derived from the 1E proofs: 2A, 3A, ARE, 1F.

EXPLANATORY NOTES

Page and line numbers for each entry locate the subject of the note in this edition. Only typographical rules or spaces and running heads are omitted from the line count. The quotation from the text, to the left of the bracket, is the matter under discussion.

1.4–6 I am neither your minotaure . . . . BEN JONSON] *Cynthia's Revels*, I, iii.

1.5 babion] Baboon.

3.8 Mentz] Mainz or, in French, Mayence. Irving stayed at the Hotel de Darmstadt there for several weeks in August and September 1822, taking vapour baths to relieve a skin inflammation. "To the Reader" was not written until July 1824 in London.

3.10–12 Prussian drum . . . Austrian military band] Mainz was occupied by German confederate troops of several different nations, including Prussia, Austria, and Russia.

3.17 Katrine] Irving wrote his sister from "Mayence" on September 2, 1822, that he had "daily lessons in French and German" from "la belle Katrina, a pretty little girl of sixteen who has been educated in a convent." She was the daughter of the hotel keeper Johann Adnot. See *Letters*, vol. 1, *1802–1823*, ed. Ralph M. Aderman, Herbert L. Kleinfield, and Jenifer S. Banks (Boston: Twayne, 1978), p. 703.

4.20–23 an anecdote . . . in print] Thomas Moore related the anecdote which Irving embellished in "The Adventure of the German Student." On its antecedents, see Walter A. Reichart, *Washington Irving and Germany* (Ann Arbor: Univ. of Michigan Press, 1957), p. 149.

4.25 vague recollections of anecdotes] Hartley Coleridge alleged his father was Irving's source for "The Adventure of the Mysterious Picture" and the related stories which follow it; see *Specimens of the Table Talk of the Late Samuel Taylor Coleridge*, 2 vols. (London: Murray, 1835), I, 42n. For other attributions, see Reichart's *Washington Irving and Germany*, pp. 150–51, and Stanley T. Williams, *The Life of Washington Irving*, 2 vols. (New York: Oxford Univ. Press, 1935), II, 288–89.

4.27–28 authentic narrative in manuscript] Reichart has identified Irving's source as an account of the kidnapping of Swiss painter Friedrich Salathe published in the journal *Überlieferungen zur Geschicte unsrer Zeit* (Aarau, 1820). See *Washington Irving and Germany*, pp. 154–55.

7.4–11 I'll tell you more . . . . FLETCHER'S WIFE FOR A MONTH] II, i.

7.7 letters of mart] Letters of marque: commissions authorizing attacks on merchant ships of an enemy power.

9.1 THE GREAT UNKNOWN] Sir Walter Scott.

9.10 Peveril of the Peak] Irving refers to the compliment Scott pays him in his prefatory letter to *Peveril of the Peak* (1823). Scott playfully preserves his anonymity by identifying himself with Irving's elusive Stout Gentleman, "who offered such subject of varying speculation to our most amusing and elegant Utopian traveller, Master Geoffrey Crayon."

10.12 Nimrod] Genesis 10:8–9.

12.10 Milesian] Descended from the legendary Spanish King Milesius, whose sons reputedly conquered and repeopled Ireland.

14.25 wars of the League] Civil wars between Roman Catholics and protestant Huguenots. Catholics under the leadership of Henry, Duke de Guise, formed the Holy League in 1576 to prevent the accession of the protestant Henry of Navarre, Henry IV.

15.6 which was unto him like a weaver's beam] 1 Samuel 17:7.

15.13 the sad tenth of August] In 1792, when a revolutionary mob massacred loyal courtiers, servants, and the Swiss Guard defending Louis XVI at the Tuileries.

15.15 *sans culottes*] Term applied to extreme republicans who despised knee breeches (culottes) worn by the rich, nobles and bourgeois alike.

15.16 poissarde] One of the Parisian marketwomen who rioted during the revolution.

15.27–29 John Baliol . . . his rival, Robert the Bruce, at the Battle of Bannockburn] Baliol (1249–1315) succeeded in his claim to the Scottish throne against the grandfather of the Robert the Bruce (1274–1329) who defeated England's Edward II at Bannockburn in 1314. Baliol died in Normandy, where he was exiled in 1296, having lost the throne in his defeat by Edward I at Dunbar.

15.30 Duke de Guise] Either Francis (1519–1563) or his son Henry (1550–1588), leaders of the Catholic faction in wars against the Huguenots. (See note at 14.25.)

16.37 Dolly's chop house in London] Popular establishment in Queen's Head Passage, Paternoster Row, built in the reign of Queen Anne and demolished in 1883.

18.27–29 Duchess de Longueville] The Duchess (1619–1679), with her husband and her brothers, the Princes Condé and Conti, was an intriguer in the rebellion against royal power during the minority of Louis XIV, a period presided over by Cardinal Mazarin, successor to Richelieu.

18.33 civil war of the Fronde] A series of uprisings, 1648–1653, against the power and policies of Cardinal Mazarin. The term "Fronde," or "sling," was applied derisively to the unsuccessful efforts of the rebels.

18.34 Turenne] Henri, Vicomte de Turenne (1611–1675), famous general induced by the Duchess de Longueville to fight with the Fronde; he switched allegiance in 1651 and went on to crush the rebels at the Battle of Saint-Antoine in 1652.

18.35 Coligni] Maurice, Comte de Coligny (1618–1643), died of wounds from a duel fought for the honor of the Duchess de Longueville. He was a descendant of Gaspard de Coligny (1519–1572), famous admiral and Huguenot leader.

18.35 Mazarin] Jules Mazarin (1602–1661), Roman Catholic Cardinal and chief minister during the minority of Louis XIV, inflamed the nobility and court bureaucrats by his financial policies; he triumphed over the leaders of the Fronde.

18.36 affairs of the Barricadoes] The Days of the Barricades, August 26–28, 1648, a popular uprising protesting the arrest of a leader of the Parlement de Paris; the beginning of the Fronde.

18.36 chivalry of the Port Cocheres] *La Cavalerie des Portes Cocheres*, an army raised by requiring householders to furnish a man and a horse for each porte cochere, or carriage gate.

18.40–41 Duke de Longueville . . . chateau of Vincennes] Imprisoned by Mazarin in January 1651. Condé was the principal leader of the final phase of the Fronde.

19.34–35 she arrived at this chateau] This part of the story is Irving's invention. The Duchess spent the night of her ordeal, February 9, 1651, at the house of a parish priest in the hamlet of Pourville.

20.10–11 Her father, Henry de Bourbon, Prince of Condé] The Duchess was born Anne Geneviève de Bourbon in 1619 in the castle of Vincennes, where her father (1588–1646) had been imprisoned by Louis XIII.

20.40 *canaille*] The rabble.

24.29 Knight of the Post] A ruffian so called from his familiarity with the pillory or whipping post.

24.30 marauding Tarquin] One of a line of legendary kings of early Rome banished after the rape of Lucrece c. 509 B.C., the traditional date of the beginning of the Roman Republic.

25.7 Botany Bay] English penal colony in Australia, 1788–1841.

25.32–34 uncle Toby . . . doctrine Corporal Trim mentions] *Tristram Shandy*, Volume III, Chapter 11, and Volume V, Chapters 35–40.

26.22 ya vrouws] Unmarried women; Irving's version of Dutch *juffrouws*; as in "Die duyvel!" at 35.18, more faithful to sound than to conventional spelling.

27.1 HEER VERKOOPT MAN GOEDEN DRANK] "One buys good drink here."

27.9 Geneva] Gin.

28.11 ghosts . . . Red Sea] An old superstition had it that ghosts, when laid, were exiled to the Red Sea.

28.21 Ally Croaker] The wooing of Ally Croker is the subject of an Irish ballad popular in the mid- to late-eighteenth century. See Discussions of Adopted Readings at 28.21.

28.25 proper] Handsome.

30.7–8 a gambol . . . enough to astonish St. Anthony] Anthony of Egypt (251–356), first Christian monk, frequently represented in art and legend as resisting the temptations of diabolical apparitions.

30.37–38 strike up "Paddy O'Rafferty,"] Early ballad celebrating "Irish divorce" or murder.

31.27 St. Vitus's dance] Sydenham's chorea, characterized by spasmodic movement. St. Vitus was the patron of sufferers from nervous diseases and by transference from St. Vitus's dance, the patron of dancers and actors.

32.16 Swedenborg] Emanuel Swedenborg (1688–1772), Swedish scientist and mystic.

33.18–19 Hôtel de Ville] Town hall.

34.20 the statue of Henry the Fourth] Torn down in 1792, but restored in 1818.

37.19 the merry thought] The wishbone.

37.38–39 the basilisk] Fabled serpent capable of killing with its gaze.

40.3 besom] Broom.

40.13 humming ale] Ale strong enough to cause the drinker's head to hum.

43.4–5 zendaletto] Gondola; see Discussions of Adopted Readings at 43.4–5.

44.9 Salvator Rosa] (1615–1673), Italian painter known for his romantic landscapes.

44.10 Raphael, Titian and Correggio] Italian painters of the Renaissance.

52.24 moles] Breakwaters.

56.34 Pharo] Lighthouse (also spelled "Faro" at 62.23).

62.43 Metastasio] Pietro Metastasio (1698–1782), Italian poet and librettist.

69.3–7 This world . . . . LINES FROM AN INN WINDOW] Thomas Moore quotes a version of these lines in his journal for July 1845 but claims not to remember their source. See *Memoirs, Journal, and Correspondence of Thomas Moore*, 8 vols., ed. Lord John Russell (London: Longmans, 1853–1856), VIII, 6–7. For Irving's comments on the genre, see "The Stout Gentleman," in *Bracebridge Hall*, ed. Herbert F. Smith (Boston: Twayne, 1977), p. 51.

72.4 Frenchmen in disguise] The influence of French critical ideals on English writers in the era of Dryden and Pope.

72.11–12 'cut and come again,'] An invitation to have a second helping.

72.29 Shadrach, Meshach and Abed-nego] Daniel 3:12–30. The allusion puns on the multiple partners of London publisher Thomas Norton Longman. Thomas Moore's account of such a dinner inspired the sketch. See *Memoirs . . . Moore*, III, 252–53.

73.13 Addison's idea] See *Spectator*, No. 529.

74.4 seated below the salt] According to medieval custom, at the lower or inferior end of the table.

75.34 Hogarth's pencil] William Hogarth (1697–1764), "the moralist and philosopher of the pencil," according to Irving. See *Oliver Goldsmith: A Biography*, ed. Elsie Lee West (Boston: Twayne, 1978), p. 88.

77.19–20 Green Arbour Court] From 1758 to 1760, Goldsmith lived at No. 12 Green Arbour Court, then located between the Old Bailey and Fleet Market but destroyed to make way for the Holburn viaduct. Irving's description of Goldsmith's garret and his own visit to the place occurs in *Oliver Goldsmith: A Biography*, pp. 65–67. *The Vicar of Wakefield* was probably not written there.

78.17–18 honey of Hybla] Mountain region in Sicily famed for its honey.

78.20 circumstance of Mrs. Tibbs] In Letter LV of Goldsmith's *Citizen of the World*.

79.8 blues] Bluestockings.

79.21 Mrs. Montagu] Perhaps a conflation of Lady Mary Wortley Montagu (1689–1762), letter writer, and Elizabeth Robinson Montagu (1720–1800), associated with bluestocking society.

79.31 The Pleasures of Imagination] By Mark Akenside (1744), the first of a series of "Pleasures" poems, including Thomas Warton's *The Pleasures of Melancholy* (1747).

79.31 the Pleasures of Hope] By Thomas Campbell (1799).

79.31–32 the Pleasures of Memory] By Samuel Rogers (1792).

80.17–18 Paternoster Row, and Angel Court, and Ave Maria Lane . . . Amen Corner] Once the locale of London booksellers; the street names derive from proximity to St. Paul's cathedral.

80.35 Minerva] Roman goddess of wisdom. The Minerva Press was a well known purveyor of sentimental and Gothic fiction in the 1790s.

80.37 Bernard Lintot] (1675–1736), Pope's publisher and target of his satire, *Dunciad*, ii, 63.

82.38 Canonbury Castle] For a fuller account of these lodgings and Irving's visit to them, see his *Goldsmith*, pp. 123–24. Goldsmith probably did not write *The Deserted Village* there.

84.9 Crackscull Common] Unlocated. Perhaps a term for any area, such as Hampstead Heath, where robberies were frequent. Goldsmith uses it in *She Stoops to Conquer*, I,ii, and V, ii.

84.11–12 Hither poor Steele had retreated] To a cottage on Haverstock Hill, no longer standing, where Sir Richard Steele resided in summer 1712.

84.40 Gnomes in the "dark gold mine."] Unidentified. Probably an allusion to German folk legend, as in the *Nibelungenlied*.

84.41 Cockney pastorals] The poetry of Leigh Hunt and his "'Ampstead circle" attacked by John Gibson Lockhart in *Blackwood's Edinburgh Magazine* (October 1817) as the Cockney School of Poetry.

85.2 the steeple of Hampstead] Atop St. John's Church, erected in 1745.

85.3 learned height of Harrow] Harrow-on-the-Hill, site of the famous preparatory school.

85.20 Jack Straw's Castle] The establishment still stands at the highest point of Hampstead Heath, having been rebuilt in 1964. Jack Straw was a leader with Wat Tyler of the Peasants' Revolt of 1381. Their "council of war" was held at Blackheath rather than Hampstead.

86.32 merry crew of Sherwood Forest] Robin Hood and his band of outlaws.

86.33 'under the greenwood tree.'] *As You Like It*, II, v; a phrase common in English balladry.

86.35 Clym of the Clough, and Sir William of Cloudeslie] Like Robin Hood, legendary outlaws celebrated in popular literature. They were noted for their skill as archers and said to inhabit Englewood Forest.

86.41 Turpin] Dick Turpin (1705–1739), son of a Hampstead innkeeper, became a notorious highwayman and was hanged as a horse thief.

87.10 Knights of the Post] See entry at 24.29.

87.33 Galloon] Galleon.

87.33 yellow boys] Gold pieces.

88.6 The Newgate Kalender] Biographical record of famous criminals confined in London's Newgate prison.

90.25–26 Lalla Rookh] Poem by Thomas Moore (1817).

90.41 Pegasus] In Greek mythology, synonymous with poetic inspiration.

91.11 "Shall a man fill his belly with the east wind?"] Job 15:2.

91.37 Bow Street Office] Principal London police court.

94.24 the "sweet uses" of adversity] *As You Like It*, II, i.

95.12–17 I care not . . . by living streams at eve——] James Thomson's *The Castle of Indolence* (1748), Canto II.

97.35 Sacharissa] Name by which Edmund Waller addressed Lady Dorothy Sidney in a series of love poems.

98.8 horsing] Flogging.

98.25 Dr. Johnson's Lives] *Lives of the English Poets*, first published 1779–1781.

100.1 Orson] Savage youngster suckled by a bear in the ancient romance *Valentine and Orson*.

100.38–39 "stayed with flaggons . . . sick of love."] Song of Solomon 2:5.

104.23 "never before stood I in such a presence."] Unidentified.

104.27 Jupiter Tonans] Jupiter the Thunderer.

105.10 Simon Snug's part of the Lion] Snug the joiner in *A Midsummer Night's Dream*, V, i.

105.38–39 Prince Hal . . . among his graceless associates] *1 Henry IV*.

108.21–22 "a little more than kin but less than kind"] *Hamlet*, I, ii.

108.31 Belvidera . . . her Jaffier] In Thomas Otway's *Venice Preserved* (1682).

108.36 the melancholy of a gibed cat] *1 Henry IV*, I, ii: "as melancholy as a gib cat." A gibbed cat is one that has been castrated.

111.12 he was . . . "putting my head into Chancery,"] Executing a headlock as difficult to get out of as a lawsuit in the Court of Chancery.

111.32–33 the Santissima Trinidada] Man-of-war captured by Nelson in the Battle of Trafalgar, 1805.

112.10–11 "preying upon her damask cheek."] *Twelfth Night*, II, iv: "Feed on her damask cheek."

112.15–16 "had the world before us, where to choose."] Echoes the final lines of *Paradise Lost*: "The world was all before them, where to choose."

112.39 Jack Straw's Castle] See note at 85.20.

112.41–42 where Whittington of yore heard the Bow bells] At Highgate; according to the popular legend, the runaway apprentice was there restrained by hearing a message in the bells of St. Mary le Bow: "Turn again Whittington, / thrice Lord Mayor of London." The actual Sir Richard Whittington (d. 1423) was thrice Lord Mayor.

115.26 the Isis] At Oxford and upstream, a name given to the Thames.

117.23 "come what come might,"] *Macbeth*, I, iii: "Come what come may."

117.24 dulcinea] Sweetheart, from Don Quixote's Dulcinea del Toboso.

118.28 the figure of Peeping Tom at Coventry] A wooden figure located at the corner of Hertford and Smithford streets. Tom the Tailor was struck blind for peeking at Lady Godiva, according to one version of the legend.

118.42–43 Sporting Magazine, and Racing Calendar] *The Sporting Magazine or Monthly Calendar of the Transactions of the Turf, the Chace, etc.* (London, 1793–1870), and *The Racing Calendar; containing an account of the Plates, Matches, and Sweepstakes, run for in Great Britain and Ireland* (London, 1773–).

119.36–37 "like Niobe all tears;"] *Hamlet*, I, ii.

120.29 gentlemen of the fancy] Sporting enthusiasts, particularly of boxing.

120.30 the Fives Court] A handball court or—as "fives" is slang for "fist"—a boxing ring.

122.27 Elegant Extracts] *Elegant Extracts: Or Useful and Entertaining Pieces of Poetry*, popular anthology by Vicesimus Knox, first published c. 1787 and frequently reprinted in the nineteenth century.

132.24 Caliban] *The Tempest*. His mother is the witch Sycorax.

136.11 the Lord Townly cut] Unidentified. May refer to the character in John Vanbrugh and Colly Cibber's *The Provoked Husband* (1728).

136.27 a brimstone] A virago.

136.30 "Upon this hint, I spake"] *Othello*, I, iii.

136.32–33 "The funeral baked meats did coldly furnish forth the marriage table," as Hamlet says.] *Hamlet*, I, ii.

136.41 Bartlemy Fair] Bartholomew Fair, held annually at Smithfield from the twelfth century to the middle of the nineteenth.

136.41–42 Astley's troop] Philip Astley (1742–1814), famous circus owner and horse tamer.

136.42 the Irish giant] Several eight-foot Irishmen were exhibited at fairs in England in the eighteenth and nineteenth centuries. Charles Byrne (1761–1783), known as O'Brien, the Irish giant, was a popular attraction in London. He was succeeded by Patrick Cotter (1761–1806), also known as O'Brien and last exhibited in 1804, closer to the time of Irving's story.

137.17 "to very rags" as Hamlet says] *Hamlet*, III, ii.

137.31 spouse] Juno.

137.40–41 "the high top gallant of my joy," as Romeo says] *Romeo and Juliet*, II, iv.

138.5 bloods] Dandies.

138.34 the breeches of Rosalind] *As You Like It*, II, iv.

139.2 Bond Street] Between Oxford Street and Piccadilly in London, a fashionable promenade in the eighteenth and nineteenth centuries.

139.29 "debateable lands"] The phrase typically refers to the border between England and Scotland.

140.36 Mr. Walker's Eidouranion] John Walker (1732–1807), lecturer on the Eidouranion, or orrery, a clockwork model of the solar system.

140.37 poor Pillgarlick!] Derived from "peeled garlic," or bald; a pitiful creature.

140.42–43 "a beggarly account of empty boxes."] *Romeo and Juliet*, V, i.

141.25 "one fell swoop,"] *Macbeth*, IV, iii.

141.27 the "be all and the end all"] *Macbeth*, I, vii.

141.31 "the bell then beating one,"] *Hamlet*, I, i.

141.34 the "end of all my greatness."] Compare with Cardinal Wolsey's farewell, *Henry VIII*, III, ii.

141.43–142.1 that part where Richard cries for "a horse! a horse!"] *Richard III*, V, iv.

142.4–5 the taunt at Richmond, "Richard is *hoarse* with calling thee to arms,"] *2 Henry VI*, V, ii: "Warwick is hoarse with calling thee to arms."

142.33 *ore rotundo*] Full voice.

144.8 Alexander the Coppersmith] 2 Timothy 4:14.

144.11–12 Banquo's shadowy line] *Macbeth*, IV, i.

149.15 rosolio] A liquer or cordial.

149.17 "San Gennaro!"] St. Januarius, patron of Naples.

149.40 *Corpo di Bacco!*] Body of Bacchus, an oath.

150.1–2 the Pontine marshes] In Irving's time, a malarial region between Velletri and Terracina.

150.5–6 the ruins of the castle of Theodoric the Goth] Since an excavation in 1894, no longer so regarded. Theodoric, king of the Ostrogoths, ruled Italy A.D. 493–526.

150.10 felucca] A small, narrow ship propelled by oars or lateen sails.

151.21–22 *in cuerpo*] Naked.

154.32 Harvey sauce] Made from Harvey apples.

155.6 John Bull's crustiness] Since Dr. Arbuthnot's *Law Is a Bottomless Pit, or the History of John Bull* (1712), the name has personified the English character. See Irving's "John Bull" in *The Sketch Book*, ed. Haskell Springer (Boston: Twayne, 1978), pp. 248–56.

155.38–39 "San Gennaro, quanto sono singolari questi Inglesi."] St. Januarius, how peculiar these Englishmen are.

156.19 *O Sicuro*] Certainly.

158.16 Roman Consulars] Coins of the Roman Republic, before the rule of the emperors.

158.16 a Roman As] A heavy brass coin of early Rome, c. 550 B.C.

158.16 Punics] Coins from the time of the Punic Wars in the second and third centuries B.C.

158.19 Samnite, struck after the Social War] That is, after 88 B.C., after Samnium and other Italian states had fought a three-year war to gain Roman citizenship.

158.19–20 a Philistis, a queen that never existed] Queen of Syracuse conjectured to have been the wife of Hieron II (275–215 B.C.), known only from silver coins which bear her name.

158.26–27 the ancient cities of the Pelasgi] Irving's footnote aptly summarizes early nineteenth-century speculation about the Pelasgi, a prehistoric people about whom only legendary accounts exist.

162.8 Cardinal Gonsalvi] Ercole Consalvi (1757–1824), secretary of state to Pope Pius VII.

162.20–21 the time of your late abortive revolution] July 1820, Neapolitan revolution against the Bourbon king Ferdinand I; the Austrian army intervened to reestablish the monarchy in March 1821.

162.21 carbonari] Members of a secret society, instigators of the Neapolitan revolution.

169.14 Loretto] Site of the Santa Casa, holy house of the Virgin Mary believed to have been transported by angels from Nazareth in the thirteenth century. Irving visited the shrine in 1805.

169.17 cockleshell] Token of a pilgrimage, usually associated with the shrine of St. James of Compostella in Spain.

171.16 Cospetto!] Oath; from *al cospetto di Dio*, in the presence of God.

175.21 treasury of the Santa Casa] See note at 169.14.

175.29 Throgmorton Street] In London's financial district, the location of the stock exchange.

176.25 principessa Popkins] Irving claims to have made "unintentional use of [the] picturesque name" of an actual person. See Barbara D. Simison, ed., "Some Autobiographical Notes of Washington Irving," *Yale University Library Gazette*, 38 (July 1963), 6–7.

176.36 Mrs. Radcliffe's romances] The Gothic novels of Ann Radcliffe (1764–1823), perhaps most especially *The Italian* (1797), which Irving appears to have read on his European tour in 1804; see *Journals and Notebooks*, vol. 1, *1803–1806*, ed. Nathalia Wright (Madison: Univ. of Wisconsin Press, 1969), pp. 489, 505.

176.39 the "Loves of the Angels;"] Poem by Thomas Moore (1823).

179.36 ancient Tusculum] Town near Frascati, supposedly established by Telegonus; it was destroyed in 1191.

179.36 Cicero] Marcus Tullius Cicero (106–43 B.C.). The location of his villa, where he wrote *Tusculanes Disputationes*, is disputed.

179.37 Sylla] Lucius Cornelius Sulla (c. 138–78 B.C.), dictator of Rome.

179.37 Lucullus] Lucius Licinius Lucullus (c. 117–56 B.C.), nobleman and politician in the service of Sulla.

179.37 Rufinus] Probably Publius Cornelius Rufinus, twice consul (290 and 277 B.C.) and ancestor of Sulla.

180.5 Mæcenas] Gaius Mæcenas (d. 8 B.C.), statesman and patron of Horace and Virgil.

180.28 Barbone] Unidentified. Colloquial Italian for a tramp.

182.18 the road of La Molara] Between the Castle of Molara and the town of Rocca Priori.

186.2 Prossedi] Ancient mountain village on the road to Frosinone.

186.4 Sbirri] The police, a pejorative term.

187.8 Civita Vecchia] Seaport of Rome.

189.4–5 Salvator Rosa] See note at 44.9.

192.26 Teniers] David Teniers the Younger (1610–1690), Flemish painter, especially of peasant life.

203.17–18 "Quanto sono insensibili questi Inglesi."] How insensitive these Englishmen are.

204.42 "Scampa via!"] (Find) a means of escape.

209.5–9 Now I remember . . . . MARLOW'S JEW OF MALTA] II, i. Irving substitutes "youth" where Marlowe has "wealth" in the second line.

211.23–24 the famous squadron of Oloffe the Dreamer] Made famous by Irving's *A History of New York*, ed. Michael L. Black and Nancy B. Black (Boston: Twayne, 1984), Book II, Chapter IV, pp. 68–74.

211.25 Hellegat] In the East River. Irving explores its vexed etymology in *A History of New York*, p. 74.

211.29 St. Nicholas] Patron of New Netherland.

211.36–37 Scylla and Charybdis] Ancient hazards, a rock and a whirlpool opposite each other in the Straits of Messina.

212.13 straits of Pylorus] At Pelorus, now known as Cape Faro, on the Sicilian coast. The straits are a mile-wide channel, once very treacherous, between Italy and Sicily.

212.25 the Devil's Stepping Stones] At Throg's Neck, and, depending on the version of the story, either traversed or hurled by the devil when Indians ran him out of Connecticut.

212.32 old Governor Stuyvesant] Peter Stuyvesant (1592–1672), last Dutch governor of New Netherland.

212.35 Frogs Neck] Corruption of Throg's Neck. See note at 212.25.

212.41–42 the valuable memoir . . . by his friend, an eminent jurist of the place] Egbert Benson (1746–1833). The memoir was read in 1816 and published the next year; it is reprinted in *Collections of the New-York Historical Society*, 2nd ser. (New York: Bartlett and Welford, 1848), II, 28–148.

213.5–6 their High Mightinesses the Lords States General of Holland] Members of the legislative assembly, from the Dutch *Hoogmogenden*.

213.6 King Charles the Second] Took possession of the Dutch colony in 1664 and gave it to his brother James, Duke of York; hence, New York.

214.2 Captain Kidd] William Kidd (c. 1645–1701).

214.6 musquito built vessel] That is, built light and fast.

214.8 a Mother Cary's chicken] The stormy petrel in sailors' argot. Mother Cary derives from *mater cara*, the Virgin Mary.

214.19 Quedah] Kedah.

214.27 Lord Bellamont] Richard Coote, 1st Earl of Bellamont (1636–1701), appointed colonial governor of New England in 1695.

214.41–42 Execution Dock in London] At Wapping on the Thames.

216.27 Adrian Block] Discovered Block Island, now New Shoreham, Rhode Island, in 1614. The Dutch explorer and fur trader is also credited with naming Hellegat.

216.36 'My name is Robert Kidd . . . . As I sailed.'] "A Dialogue Between the Ghost of Captain Kidd and the Napper in the Strand." A false Christian name is given in some versions of the ballad because Kidd died in disgrace.

217.35 savin trees] Red cedars.

223.22 rhino] Money; the derivation of the term is uncertain.

223.29 the days of Governor Belcher] Jonathan Belcher (1681–1757) governor of Massachusetts and New Hampshire, 1730–1741.

223.31 Land Bank] A means of issuing paper currency as notes of credit on land mortgages.

226.22–23 the ancient family of the Hardenbrooks] That is, of Irving's largely fictional Abraham Hardenbroeck, one of the discoverers of Manhattan in *A History of New York*, Book II, Chapter III, pp. 65–66.

226.32–33 a noted burgher called Ready Money Prevost] A smuggler, according to Irving in *Biography of the Late Margaret Miller Davidson*, ed. Elsie Lee West (Boston: Twayne, 1978), p. 272.

227.5–6 John Josse Vandermoere . . . related to me the adventures of Dolph Heyliger] In *Bracebridge Hall* (1822). The narrator derives his name from a Belgian servant who briefly accompanied Irving on his European tour in 1805. See *Letters*, I, 182.

227.11–12 Blase Moore's best tobacco] Unidentified.

227.18 the Brille in Holland] A town on the Meuse River.

227.20–21 Oloffe Van Kortlandt, otherwise called the Dreamer] See note at 211.23.

231.23 Corlear's Hook] Or Corlear's Point, on the East River, on land formerly owned by Jacob Corlear.

231.43 Walloon race] A Belgic people who arrived in 1623, preceding the Dutch colonists. Tradition has it that Sarah D'Rapelje, a Walloon, was the first white child born in the province.

232.24 Peter Stuyvesant, the Dutch Governor] See note at 212.32.

233.40 Morgan] Sir Henry Morgan (c. 1635–1688), Welsh buccaneer, later knighted and appointed governor of Jamaica by Charles II.

233.40 Blackbeard] Edward Teach (d. 1718), English privateer turned pirate.

234.27 moidores . . . pistareens] Moidores were gold coins of Portugal; pistareens were silver Spanish coins. Ducats bore the likenesses of dukes and circulated in several European countries.

235.22 another guess sort] Of quite another kind; corruption of "another-gates," another way.

236.11 stiver] Formerly a small Dutch coin.

237.40 like the crackling of thorns under a pot] Ecclesiastes 7:6—"For as the crackling of thorns under a pot, so is the laughter of the fool" (KJV).

239.8 Spanish Main] The northeast coast of South America bordering on the Caribbean.

241.18 side glance of a basilisk] See note at 37.38.

241.24–25 the Devil's Dans Kammer] The Devil's Dance Chamber, on the Hudson River near Newburgh.

241.42 Bradish] Joseph Bradish (1672–1700), American-born buccaneer.

243.14–15 the Hen and Chickens . . . the Hog's Back . . . the Pot . . . the Frying Pan] The Pot is a whirlpool; the rest are rocks or reefs in the channel known as Hell Gate.

243.19 Blackwell's Island] In the East River, now called Roosevelt Island.

249.24 dead lights] Covers or shutters to prevent water from entering portholes.

249.26 Dead Man's Isle] One of the Magdalene Islands in the Gulf of St. Lawrence.

250.19 the greedy inhabitant of Bagdad] "The Blind Baba-Abdalla" in *The Arabian Nights*.

251.16 the Wallabout] Wallabout Bay, on the Brooklyn side of the East River, opposite Corlear's Point.

251.17 the Devil's Stepping Stones] See note at 212.25.

251.22 A "most ancient and fish-like smell"] *The Tempest*, II, ii.

251.43 Bloomen-dael] Valley of flowers, early settlement in the vicinity of 100th Street on Manhattan's West Side.

255.6 Boerhaave] Hermann Boerhaave (1668–1738), Dutch scholar and physician.

255.7 Van Helmont] Jean Baptiste Van Helmont (1577–1644), Belgian physician and chemist.

255.42 *The same . . . history of Dolph Heyliger.] In *Bracebridge Hall* (1822).

256.32–33 Gaspard Schott in his Treatise on Magic] *Magia Universalis*, 4 vols. (1657–1659). Schott (1606–1666) was a German scientist.

256.33–35 'Propter hæc . . . diaboli,'] Translated in a previous sentence, 256.30–32.

256.36 Gregorius Agricola] (1490–1555), German mineralogist.

256.37 'de re Metallica,'] Published in 1530.

257.24 Dutch courage] Gin.

257.28 the three wise men of Gotham . . . to sea in a bowl] From the nursery rhyme. Gotham, a village in England, was proverbial for the stupidity of its citizens. Irving appropriated the name for New York in *Salmagundi* (1807).

258.4–5 Turtle Bay and Kip's Bay] Along the East River, respectively, north and south of 42nd Street.

258.34 *Pots tausends*] Good God!

259.19 black letter volume] One printed in heavy Gothic type.

TEXTUAL COMMENTARY

The text of *Tales of a Traveller* presented here is a critical, unmodernized edition prepared according to the guidelines of the CEAA *Statement of Editorial Principles and Procedures* and the standards of *The Complete Works of Washington Irving*.[1] The text is historical in its attempt to reconstruct Washington Irving's intentions for the work insofar as surviving bibliographical and textual evidence permits and to report such evidence so as to enable the interested reader to understand the development of the work through each of its identifiable authorial stages. As a critical edition, it is not a reprint of any other version but rather a composite or eclectic text which, by synthesis of available evidence, restores *Tales of a Traveller* to a form more consonant with Irving's intentions and characteristic practices than any previous edition.

The intricate textual history of the work dictates the choice of multiple copy-texts: existing holograph manuscript, and the first American edition where manuscript does not survive, both supplemented by the first English edition. The following sections describe all relevant forms of the work and discuss the choice of copy-texts and the principles by which they are emended.

THE MANUSCRIPT

Approximately one-fourth of Irving's holograph manuscript survives: 184 leaves corresponding to pp. 69.2, 71.28–92.15, and 95.24–146 7 of Part II in this edition.[2] Now owned by the Henry E. Huntington Library, the man-

---

1. Center for Editions of American Authors, *Statement of Editorial Principles and Procedures: A Working Manual for Editing Nineteenth-Century American Texts*, rev. ed. (New York: Modern Language Association, 1972). The Center for Scholarly Editions, successor to the CEAA, allows editions in *The Complete Works of Washington Irving* to continue to request the CEAA seal.

2. Three manuscript fragments listed by H.L. Kleinfield in his "A Census of Washington Irving Manuscripts" (*Bulletin of the New York Public Library*, 68 [January 1964]; rpt. in William R. Langfeld, *Washington Irving: A Bibliography* [Port Washington, NY: Kennikat Press, 1968], p. 27) are not part of the original holograph. One is an itemized series of notes Irving made in 1850 while preparing a memorandum for John Murray III to support the publisher's law suit against Henry George Bohn for violation of the firm's British copyright to Irving's works (Yale, 1 leaf). The second is Irving's handwritten copy of two paragraphs from "A Practical Philosopher," addressed as a gift or courtesy to H.E. Parker in Hampton, NH (Virginia). The third (NYPL, 1 page) is a fragment from *The Alhambra*, mistakenly identified as part of *Tales of a Traveller*.

uscript was acquired from the St. Louis collector William K. Bixby, who preserved it in an album which bears his bookplate, a folio volume bound in three-quarters blue morocco. Gilt letters on the banded spine identify the contents as "TALES / OF A TRAVELLER / BUCKTHORNE / AND HIS FRIENDS / WASHINGTON IRVING / ORIGINAL / MANUSCRIPT." Except for the first manuscript leaf, pasted only at the left corner to permit reading of a note to the printer on the verso, all pages, numbered by Irving 4–186, are pasted flat onto rectos and versos of the album leaves within box rules, hand-drawn in blue ink. The first three manuscript pages of "Literary Life" (71.7–28 in this edition) are missing.

The text appears on the rectos of manuscript leaves, with canceled false starts or titles occasionally on the versos. Because the leaves are pasted into the album, verso cancellations cannot be recovered in every instance without jeopardy to the manuscript. Pasting also impedes an exact identification of the paper. Irving used at least five kinds of wove paper, each of a similar utilitarian grade, in varying shades of tan, from creme to dark beige. Two leaves show the partial watermark J WH[ATMAN]. The two darkest shades of paper are the most prevalent and were probably inscribed latest in the process of composing, copying, and reordering, but patterns in the use of particular kinds of paper at any point are too slight to provide reliable clues to the order of composition or original sequence. Irving used black ink, now faded to varying shades of brown.

Brackets in a darker ink accompanied by signature notations corresponding in every instance to the first American edition identify the manuscript as typesetting copy for that edition. Random smudges and inky fingerprints testify to its handling in the print shop, as do compositorial step marks and stint signatures: "JCannon," fifteen times; "Davy," five times; "office," three times; "William," twice; and "Collins" and "Dowling," once each.

Although Irving submitted the manuscript to his American publishers as a fair copy, it was not thoroughly perfected. Only six pages are free of alterations. All others show varying degrees of cancellation and interpolation, often so extensive as to constitute revision rather than Irving's characteristic "retouching." Forty-eight of the leaves (fully twenty-six percent of the total) are composed of two or more fragmentary slips cut and pasted together; twelve consist of as many as three or four joined fragments. The shortest such composite page measures 6 x 4⅝ inches and the longest, 11⅞6 x 4⅝ inches. Irving folded the overlong pages from the bottom before stitching the manuscript together; they remain folded in the album. The typical size of non-composite leaves is 7⅟₁₆ x 4⅟₁₆ inches, the range being from 7 x 4½ to 7⅞ x 4¹⁵⁄₁₆ inches.

Irving customarily began writing half an inch or less from the top edge, leaving just room enough for the page number. His text ordinarily stops three-eighths to one-half inch from the bottom, but many times runs completely to the end. He averaged twenty-six lines per non-composite page, each line typically extending the full distance to the right edge. He maintained a left margin of three-eighths of an inch to permit room for stitching.

The presence of a third threadhole in nine non-sequential leaves of "Buckthorne" indicates that some sections of that story were sewn together at an earlier time and perhaps in a different way from the present arrangement. Numerous repagings in both pencil and ink show the extensive reworking and reordering Irving accomplished before sending the manuscript to his brother Ebenezer for publication in America. Most leaves, in fact, show evidence of an earlier paging, and twenty percent, a total of thirty-seven leaves, have been renumbered as many as four or five times. The majority of these occur in the last half of "Buckthorne." An editor is compelled by such circumstances to seek understanding of how this particular story developed from 1818 to 1824 and was shaped by Irving's altered conceptions of it—from its planned inclusion in *Bracebridge Hall*, to brief consideration of its possibilities as a novel, through its reworking for *Tales*. Unfortunately, so thorough has been the cutting and pasting that no certain patterns are recoverable. Much of the evidence, however, is preserved in the transcription of the manuscript and on an annotated photocopy of it deposited with other materials for this edition in the library of the University of North Carolina at Chapel Hill.

One additional feature of the manuscript bears on its history, condition, and authority—evidence of Peter Irving's role as his brother's assistant and adviser. The two were together in Paris during the preparation of the manuscript, and, on at least one occasion, Irving noted in his journal that the work had the benefit of "corrections from Peter."[3] It is Peter, writing in ink, who directs the printer to observe the double angle-brackets which signal the start of new paragraphs in the manuscript, Peter who inscribes the epigraph and titles to four of the tales, and Peter who on five occasions recopies lines or phrases to make them more intelligible to a printer. In addition to his help with the physical details of preparing the manuscript for the press, Peter read over it, pencil in hand, with the eye of an astute copy-editor and fond brother, adding punctuation or suggesting changes in wording or commenting marginally on larger passages. Irving later made changes according to some of the suggestions, ignored others, and either erased the penciled comments or, in some cases, neglected to do so.

Not every penciled notation in the manuscript, however, can be attributed to Peter. We know from Irving's journal that he also went over his

3. *Journals and Notebooks*, vol. 3, *1819–1827*, ed. Walter A. Reichart (Madison: Univ. of Wisconsin Press, 1970), p. 333.

manuscripts with pencil. The difficulty of separating Irving's work from Peter's is compounded by the familial similarity of their handwriting and the difficulty of judging a penciled hand. In fact, so alike are the two hands in the individual conformation of specific letters that only the slant and characteristic waver in Peter's handwriting of the period, identified from his letters in the Irving family papers at the New York Public Library, show with any certainty that Peter is responsible for those specific inked changes or additions or recopyings noted before. Penciled notations, many of them smudged, erased, or otherwise recoverable only under ultraviolet light, are more difficult to assign, but context occasionally makes attribution easier. Some we would expect only from a commentator. Irving restored a canceled sentence alongside which Peter had urged, "preserve this" (MS 65), but he ignored the note, "It is a pity to omit this," beside six canceled lines on the next page; in the first instance Irving canceled Peter's words with ink, and in the second he erased them. Moreover, some notations are so out of keeping with Irving's typical practice that they are easily assigned to Peter. The only correct spellings of "recollect" and "recollected" occur in penciled interpolations, over the first of which Irving, with his characteristic doubling of the medial "c," wrote in ink, "reccollect." The other he inked over correctly.

In one noteworthy instance, the brothers' hands are distinct, and their words suggest that the question of where the story "Buckthorne" should begin may have been decided collaboratively. At the top of MS 54, Irving wrote in pencil, "I think the title should / be[?] on this page / Buckthorne / or the young man of great Expectations"; the sentence is partially erased. Written over it in pencil in Peter's hand is a direction to the printer: "This page follows The history of The / Poor Devil author—and presedes / that of Bucthorne—or the Young Man / of Great expectations." Pasted onto the next leaf is a short slip of paper on which Irving inscribed the title in ink: "BUCKTHORNE / or the Young Man of Great Expectations." But the fate of this transitional page between "The Poor Devil Author" and "Buckthorne" was not determined with any finality while the brothers were together in Paris.

Despite Irving's assurance to Peter in a letter from London, "I am rejoiced that I got my work ready before coming here,"[4] he expressed his intention elsewhere in words and more demonstrably in deeds to expand and polish the work while he was in England, "to write upon it while there & . . . while it is printing."[5] In this process of revision and expansion, the transitional page became the kernel from which grew two additional sketches, "Notori-

---

4. *Letters*, vol. 2, *1823–1838*, ed. Ralph M. Aderman, Herbert L. Kleinfield, and Jenifer S. Banks (Boston: Twayne, 1979), p.50.

5. Ibid., II, 42.

ety" and "A Practical Philosopher." Irving also wrote a preface and two new stories and enlarged or otherwise altered many others, adding a total of about 20,000 words. The work Irving did in London in the summer of 1824 accounts for the significant differences among the various early editions and their descendants.

THE EDITIONS

Here, as in the apparatus, the editions are listed in genetic rather than chronological order.

First American Edition (1A)

The first American edition was set from Irving's holograph MS, which he sent in sections to his brother Ebenezer in New York, the parcel containing Part IV being shipped June 22, 1824.[6] It was printed by C.S. Van Winkle in New York and issued in four parts by H.C. Carey & I. Lea of Philadelphia on August 24, September 7, September 25, and October 9, 1824.[7] A variant imprint of Part I lists New York as the place of publication and substitutes "Printed by C.S. Van Winkle" for the imprimatur of Carey & Lea on the title page. Some copies of Carey & Lea's Part IV bear paper wrappers printed on the verso of salvaged wrappers for Part I which have the imprint of C.S. Van Winkle.

The exact nature of the relationship among Ebenezer Irving, C.S. Van Winkle, and Carey & Lea is not known. Carey & Lea, however, were clearly not Irving's "publishers" in the conventional sense of that term or in the comprehensive way in which John Murray II was his publisher in London. More likely the Philadelphia partners served as distributors of the work, the arrangements for manufacture and sale being handled by Ebenezer, perhaps

---

6. *Journals*, III, 353.

7. These are the dates of publication given by Irving in his memorandum to John Murray III on the publication history of *Tales* (see note 2 above); quoted by Ben Harris McClary, ed., *Washington Irving and the House of Murray: Geoffrey Crayon Charms the British, 1817–1856* (Knoxville: Univ. of Tennessee Press, 1969), pp. 198–99. Newspaper advertisements suggest publication dates one day earlier for Part I and two or three days later for Part IV; see Edwin T. Bowden's comprehensive bibliography of Irving editions, the final volume in *The Complete Works of Washington Irving* (in press). C.S. Van Winkle deposited the title pages with the clerk of the Southern District of New York on July 22 and August 14 for Parts I and II respectively and on August 30 for Parts III and IV.

through the agency of Van Winkle and by an agreement in which Van Winkle, and possibly others, shared in distribution rights.[8] This complex arrangement in which Irving, through his brother, was technically his own publisher in America existed until 1829, when the firm of Carey, Lea & Carey began to purchase his copyrights directly.[9]

Several stop-press corrections were made as Parts I and II were printed, resulting in two states of these parts. The A state of Part I can be identified by the error "counteuance" at 43.13, which the B state corrects to "countenance." The variant Van Winkle imprint for Part I appears on a copy which is state B in this respect. In Part II, the A state is recognizable by "at housand" at 99.13, which "B" corrects to "a thousand." Where 1A serves as copytext it is specifically the Huntington Library copy (37931), state A in these particulars and others.

Because it was set from the manuscript Irving "completed" in Paris, 1A does not contain the revisions and enlargements, including the preface, "To the Reader," and the four stories—"The Adventure of the German Student," "Notoriety," "A Practical Philosopher," and "The Belated Travellers"—Irving provided for the first English edition. He was, however, scrupulous to forward duplicate proof sheets from that edition to Ebenezer in New York, beginning on July 8, only three days after he received the first proofs from Murray.[10] These duplicate proof sheets were used in preparing the second and third American editions.

Second American Edition of Part I (2A)

The preface and four new tales first appeared in America in a second edition of Part I printed by C.S. Van Winkle and issued by H.C. Carey & I.

8. For example, advertisements in the *New-York American* for September 24 and October 9, 1824, list Charles Wiley, once a partner of Van Winkle and an associate of H.C. Carey, as "publisher" of the forthcoming Parts III and IV. No copies have been located with his imprint, however.

9. See William Charvat, *Literary Publishing in America, 1790–1850*(Philadelphia: Univ. of Pennsylvania Press, 1959), pp. 38–60. Henry Carey had been trying to interest Irving in such a relationship since the summer of 1825 when Carey and his wife, the sister of Irving's friend Charles R. Leslie, met Irving socially in Paris (*Journals*, III, 508). Later negotiations with Carey are recorded in Irving's letters to him and to Ebenezer Irving (*Letters*, II, 332 and 342). See also David Kaser, *Messrs. Carey & Lea of Philadelphia: A Study in the History of the Booktrade* (Philadelphia: Univ. of Pennsylvania Press, 1957), p. 39.

10. *Journals*, III, 359. Irving forwarded the proofs to Ebenezer via the London bookseller John Miller, who served as an agent for Henry Carey and his successors from 1817 to 1861 (Kaser, pp. 18–19). Miller was also a friend of Irving and the first British publisher of *The Sketch Book*.

Lea early in 1825.[11] "To the Reader" and "The Adventure of the German Student" appear in their proper places in the first series of stories. (The Table of Contents, however, omits the first and lists the second simply as "The German Student.") The three other tales are appended to the end of Part I with notes designating the assigned place of each in Parts II and III.

Proof sheets forwarded to Ebenezer served as copy for setting these additions and as the model for selective resettings in stories which had originated in Part I of 1A. In some instances standing type was altered, and in many others pages were entirely reset to incorporate new readings. Nearly 700 changes were made in existing stories, creating in the process more than two dozen substantive errors, or words which occur in this but no other edition. Such changes in existing stories appear to have been made cursorily, perhaps merely as discrepancies between 1A and the English proofs were noticed in a hasty comparison, with the result that 2A, for these stories, still resembles 1A more than it does the third American edition, which was newly and entirely set from the proofs.

Only four copies of 2A have been located, all of them bound with 1A Parts II–IV. Such sets offered by Carey & Lea would have been in direct competition with the third American edition, published soon thereafter.

Third American Edition (3A)

The third American edition was published in two volumes by C.S. Van Winkle in New York in the spring of 1825. Technically the first full new edition, 3A is designated "Second American Edition" on its title page.[12] Although Van Winkle could have acquired a copy of the first English edition in time to use it as setting copy for 3A or for his printing a few months earlier of 2A, it is clear that he did not. Collation reveals that 3A was set from a relatively early state of the English proofs, or more accurately, from mixed states, many of them early. They were late enough to incorporate the preface and four new pieces and many, but not all, of the enlargements and alterations. The chronology of the proofs from which 3A was set is important. In at least one instance, the case of the story "The Strolling Manager," the proof sheets forwarded for 3A may be said to represent Irving's final intentions for

11. Carey & Lea advertised the work as "in press" in the *United States Literary Gazette* on January 1 and January 15, 1825.

12. Date of publication is uncertain. A "Quarterly List of New Publications" in the *North American Review* for April 1825 lists a second edition of *Tales*, without publisher's name or place of publication. Because 3A is designated "Second American Edition," the notice probably refers to Van Winkle's edition rather than Carey & Lea's 2A.

the story, those which evolved to completion before William Gifford's objections to the Fantadlin section required Irving to alter the story under duress. Two paragraphs deleted from all subsequent versions remain in 3A and its descendants.

Fourth American Edition (4A)

The fourth American edition was published in two volumes in Philadelphia by Carey & Lea in 1832. The title page designates it as "Third American Edition." It was reprinted in 1835 (twice), 1836, 1837, 1838, 1840, and 1841. The impressions of 1835 to 1838 carry the imprimatur of Carey, Lea, & Blanchard; in 1840 and 1841 the publishers are listed as Lea & Blanchard. From the second impression of 1835 until the stereotyped plates were destroyed, all copies proclaim "A New Edition"; machine collations reveal, however, that the setting was the same. Textually, 4A descends from 3A, but its house styling Americanizes spelling and more thoroughly regularizes punctuation. Although Irving returned to the United States in early summer of 1832, there is no evidence, internal or external, that he supervised the publication of 4A or requested any of its numerous small changes. Because it lacks any degree of authority, 4A is not represented in the apparatus.

"Author's Revised Edition" (ARE)

Collation reveals that the George P. Putnam edition, stereotyped by Leavitt, Trow & Co. in New York and published in March of 1849 as volume seven of Irving's collected works in a format labeled the "Author's Revised Edition," was set from a copy of 3A. Irving either made minor alterations to the copy before he submitted it or made small changes in proof, or both. The extent of Irving's role in revising ARE is conjectural. No proof sheets survive from this process. Many of the changes, the variants of ARE from 3A, appear to be authorial in that they correspond to the kinds of revisions Irving was known to have made throughout his career in retouching works for the press, and they correspond as well to the alterations Irving made on proof sheets for Putnam's editions of *A History of New York* (1848) and *Oliver Goldsmith: A Biography* (1849), forty-four of which survive.

Why Irving chose 3A as printer's copy for ARE is a question without a definite answer. We know that for other Putnam volumes he chose setting texts without immediate significance or authority and perhaps on the basis of what was closest at hand. Whether he had any more reason for the choice of 3A for *Tales* than for the choice of non-authoritative editions of *The Sketch Book* and *Bracebridge Hall*, to name but two others, is not clear. But the possibility remains that he might have purposely chosen 3A if he recalled that, in one instance, it preserved readings that he had been forced to change. By his choice, however, Irving perpetuated in his "sanctioned" text more than sixty errors in wording peculiar to 3A, which he did not notice or correct in the preparation of ARE.

The Putnam edition went through more than a dozen impressions in Irving's lifetime and was reset in a variety of formats. No evidence suggests Irving contributed to any but the original 1849 printing. It has been the basis for twentieth-century reprints of the work and the edition most often cited by scholars.

First French Edition (1F)

The first French edition was printed in English by Jules Didot, Senior, and published by L. Baudry in Paris late in October 1824. The same setting was used for copies issued, perhaps simultaneously, with the imprint of A. and W. Galignani, a firm which often served as Irving's agents or publishers and frequently collaborated with Louis Claude Baudry.[13] Proof sheets for the first English edition provided printer's copy for 1F. Irving recorded in a journal entry for August 11, 1824, his concern over "getting proof sheets to the Galignanis."[14] This late date and the testimony of internal evidence suggest that, if multiple proof states existed for any or all of *Tales*, 1F had the benefit of proofs later than those from which 2A and 3A derive. The late revisions to "The Strolling Manager," for example, appear in 1F.

Although Irving was in Paris from August 16 to October 12, 1824, and could well have supervised the printing of 1F, there is no evidence, either internal or external, to suggest that he did.

First English Edition (1E)

The first English edition, printed by Thomas Davison and published in London by John Murray II in two volumes on August 25, 1824, was set from

13. See Giles Barber, "Galignani's and the Publication of English Books in France from 1800 to 1852," *The Library*, 5th ser., 16 (1961), 277. Baudry's collaboration with the Galignani brothers, as the 1824 imprints demonstrate, began earlier than 1831, the date Barber provides.

14. *Journals*, III, 379.

a scribal copy of Irving's holograph manuscript plus additional holograph manuscript provided by Irving for the preface and four new pieces and enlargements to existing stories.[15] Irving oversaw the printing and clearly intended to revise and alter while the work was in press.

Two states of 1E have been identified. State A is defined by the presence of a notice at the end of volume 2 warning the reader against "Several spurious Works . . . alleged to be by the AUTHOR OF THE SKETCH BOOK." State B, clearly the later, is marked by the absence of the notice and 181 verbal changes, the result of extensive resetting. Fully 241 pages, roughly thirty percent of the edition, were reset, either to repair type damage, to improve spacing, or to effect refinements in the text. Some of the 181 variants are errors introduced in the course of resetting for other motives. Motivated changes occur principally for two reasons—to correct errors in "A" or to bring isolated inconsistencies in that state into conformity with house style. In virtually every instance, the A reading corresponds to a textually earlier version (MS, 1A, 3A, or 1F), and the B reading corresponds to the second English edition. No change is of a character necessarily authorial.

The following are representative of changes made to correct error. (Page and line numbers in the Twayne edition appear in parentheses.)

			A	B
Volume 1:	3.12	(9.9)	Waverly	Waverley
	12.1	(11.41)	hatched	hatchet
	189.4	(74.15)	"Gad,∧	"Gad,"
	194.11	(76.10)	booksellers	bookseller's
Volume 2:	39.3	(139.36)	doctors'	doctor's
	39.4	(139.36)	lawyers'	lawyer's
	120.7	(169.43)	Gaspar	Caspar
	150.7	(179.37)	Scilla	Sylla
	264.14	(221.26)	sat	set
	338.15	(246.1)	neve	never
			rheeding	heeding

15. Portions of the original holograph manuscript were copied by an amanuensis in Paris before Irving left for London. The remainder was copied by John Howard Payne and by others at his direction in London in June 1824. See *Journals*, III, 333, 341–45; *Letters*, II, 52–54.

The following are representative of changes made for consistency with house style.

			A	B
Volume 1:	5.7	(9.32)	stage coaches	stage-coaches
	63.8	(29.22)	feather beds	feather-beds
	78.15	(34.30)	old fashioned	old-fashioned
	91.10	(39.1)	clothes' press	clothes-press
	139.9	(54.33)	Saint	saint
	196.20	(77.3)	thread-bare	threadbare
	197.13	(77.13)	poor devil	poor-devil
	285.23	(106.20)	Harlequin	harlequin
Volume 2:	13.6	(131.14)	church-yard	churchyard
	93.17	(161.1)	gallies	galleys
	152.14	(180.26)	strong hold	strong-hold
	241.5	(213.16)	Buccaneers	buccaneers
	253.1	(217.20)	land-marks	landmarks
	317.20	(239.10)	yard arm	yard-arm

In addition to dropped words and the introduction of extraneous words, the resettings introduced errors such as the following.

			A	B
Volume 1:	65.1	(30.7)	gentlemen	gentleman
	204.7	(79.16)	doggerel	doggrel
	204.14	(79.33)	Montagu	Montague
	268.6	(100.24)	these	those
Volume 2:	59.4	(149.3)	estafette	estafatte

Some elaboration of the priority of the two states is necessary because standard bibliographies have reversed them. Implicit in Jacob Blanck's designations and explicit in the conjectured order given by William R. Langfeld is an assumption about the notice at the end of volume 2 in state A but absent from state B: "Since its subject matter is such that, once having appeared, it would remain, copies containing the notice would seem to be the *second state* of the first edition."[16] It is precisely the "subject matter" of the notice that provides a clue to its disappearance in the later state.

Although the notice, undoubtedly written by Irving, warns in a general way against "spurious Works . . . published without his knowledge or approbation," its specific target is *"an* incorrect Edition of SALMAGUNDI" (emphasis added).[17] Irving responded here to a pirated edition of that work published by Thomas Tegg in December 1823, but dated 1824, and hoped to avert a second edition by Tegg which he knew to be in press simultaneously with *Tales,* and in the same printing house. Thomas Davison, the printer for both, told Irving on July 5 that he had intervened with Tegg on Irving's behalf to prevent a second edition of *Salmagundi.*[18] But a month later, on August 7, Irving caught the pirates red-handed. He recorded the incident in his journal: "After breakfast, go down to Mr Davidsons. Find a man there whom I suspect to be Tegg—who was busy with Davidson about a book which I see to be Salmagundi—Takes up the book in confusion[.]"[19] The notice written to contend with Tegg was in all likelihood removed when Tegg subsequently issued his second edition, incorporating some of the revisions Irving had made for a French edition earlier in 1824 and advertising it on the title page as a "NEW EDITION / CORRECTED AND REVISED BY THE AUTHOR."[20]

16. William R. Langfeld, *Washington Irving: A Bibliography,* p. 26. Jacob Blanck, in *Bibliography of American Literature,* (New Haven: Yale Univ. Press, 1969), V, 25, follows Langfeld in designating "A" as the later, or "B," state; however, he cautions that the sequence has not been determined.

17. Because it is omitted from the Twayne edition, the text of the notice in its entirety is included here:

NOTICE.

SEVERAL spurious Works have issued from the / press, alleged to be by the AUTHOR OF THE SKETCH / BOOK, but published without his knowledge or appro- / bation. Among these is an incorrect Edition of / SALMAGUNDI, a work in which he was but partially / concerned, and at a juvenile age. An edition of this / work, revised and corrected, with several papers / originally intended for it, but never published, is / about to appear in America. The Author hopes he / may be judged by such works as appear under his / own sanction, and not by incorrect and adulterated / editions, or by works with which he has had no con- / cern.

18. *Journals,* III, 357. Although he refers to it as "a 2d. Vol," he surely means second edition.

19. Ibid., III, 378.

20. Not all copies contain the claim for authorial sanction. Three versions of the title page—one without a claim, the second labeled only "NEW EDITION," and the third appearing as "NEW EDITION / CORRECTED AND REVISED BY THE AUTHOR"—suggest Tegg's evolving strategy, by which the notice in *Tales* was ultimately made pointless and so abandoned. Irving almost certainly collaborated in the publication. An agreement with John Murray to publish a corrected and enlarged edition of *Salmagundi* (*Letters,* II, 63)

When 1E serves as copy-text, state A is used, specifically a copy owned by the University of Wisconsin (Rare Books CA 218a&b/copy 2).

Second English Edition (2E)

Irving wrote to John Murray on August 14, 1824, the day of his departure from England, requesting a copy of 1E which he might correct for a second edition.[21] That edition, printed by Davison and published in two volumes by Murray in 1825, was set from a copy of the B state of 1E, from which it differs in forty-eight substantives. Most of the variant readings can be attributed to error or copy-editing. Some, however, appear to be authorial, particularly those which restore earlier readings found in MS, 1A, or the 1E proofs. No letters survive to prove that Irving ordered such changes. However, his library at Sunnyside preserves a copy of 1E containing twenty penciled alterations, fourteen of which correspond to changes made in 2E—a much higher ratio of correspondence than with any other edition.[22] Although

---

was apparently abandoned as a result. Reference in the notice to a "revised and corrected" edition "about to appear in America" may have been entirely fictional. No record of plans for such an edition has been found, and the next American edition of *Salmagundi* did not appear until 1835, when James Kirke Paulding released it as part of the Harper edition of his works.

21. *Letters*, II, 73.

22. The leather-bound volumes are 1E, state A. They contain the following penciled alterations (page and line numbers of 1E are followed by corresponding numbers in the Twayne text). At I.xi.3 (4.14) "tale" is inserted after "ghost": "a ghost tale or a love story"; no edition contains this reading. At I.57.3 (27.15) "Der" is canceled and "Die" inserted: "Die duyvel!"; 2E agrees with 2A, 3A, and 1F in this reading. At I.66.10 (30.28) "limb" is substituted for "leg"; 2E, 2A, 3A, ARE, and 1F agree in this reading. At I.68.5 (31.12–13) "arrived at" is substituted for "hurried to"; 2E is unchanged, but 2A, 3A, ARE, and 1F agree. At I.83.12–14 (36.12) the footnote at the end of "The Adventure of the German Student" is canceled; 2E, 2A, 3A, ARE, and 1F omit the note. At I.90.10 (38.29) "peeping" is changed to "peering"; 2E agrees with 1A and 2A in this. At I.107.18 (44.16) "San Georgia" is corrected to "San Georgio"; only 2E and 1A have this spelling. At I.108.6 (44.23) "by" is substituted for "from" in the phrase "from dread of assassination"; 2E alone reads "by." At I.181.4 (71.28) "If ever he speaks" is changed to "If ever he should speak"; only 2E reads "should speak." At I.208.6 (80.31) "e" is substituted for the "o" in "penetrator"; the spelling is unchanged in 2E; only MS, 3A, ARE, and 1F have "penetrater." At I.232.19 (88.41) "full" is emended to "fell"; MS, 2E, and all other editions agree. At I.259.6 (97.22) "squire's" is changed to "squire"; only 2E corresponds to the change. At I.268.4 (100.23) "was" is replaced by "should be"; only 2E agrees. At I.268.11 (100.27) "was" is replaced by "remained"; only 2E agrees. At I.271.1 (101.21) "uncle's" is changed to "uncle"; no edition corresponds. At I.280.4 (104.23) "a" is inserted in the phrase "in such a presence"; MS and all editions except 1E and 2E have this reading. At I.354.17 (124.25) "room: by" is altered to "room. By"; MS and all editions except 1E and 2E agree. At II.55.20 (145.39) "for" is replaced by

both volumes of the Sunnyside copy of 1E bear bookplates of his nephew, Pierre P. Irving, and the handwriting cannot be identified with certainty as Irving's, the annotated 1E must be weighed as evidence supporting the authority of the corresponding variants in 2E. For this reason, all substantive differences between 2E and 1E are reported in the apparatus, and those which restore earlier readings are adopted as emendations.

COLLATIONS

Internal evidence for these descriptions is drawn from extensive collations of relevant forms of the text, performed by numerous individuals working alone or in teams at three universities—the University of Wisconsin at Madison, the University of California at Davis, and the University of North Carolina at Chapel Hill—over a period of fifteen years. Much duplication of effort occurred in the process—a phenomenon which may be the bane of efficiency experts but is unadulterated blessing to the textual editor. Duplicate collations help assure accuracy, and each has been checked, one against the others, toward this end.

Machine Collations
(1) 1Ea^1 vs. 1Ea^2
(2) 1Ea^2 vs. 1Eb
(3) 4A1832^1 vs. 4A1832^2
(4) 4A1835 vs. 4A1836^1
(5) 4A1832^1 vs. 4A1836^1
(6) 4A1836^1 vs. 4A1836^2
(7) ARE1849^1 vs. ARE1849^2
(8) ARE1849^1 vs. ARE1850

The following individual copies were used: 1Ea^1 = U. of Wisconsin Rare Books CA218a&b/copy 1; 1Ea^2 = U. of Wisconsin Rare Books CA218a&b/copy 2; 1Eb = Huntington Library 22800 (xerox); 4A1832^1 = U. of Wisconsin PS2070/.A1/1832; 4A1832^2 = U. of Chicago PS2070/1832 (xerox); 4A1835 = Duke U. 817.24/Ir72/5w (xerox); 4A1836^1 = U. of Wisconsin Rare Books C23540 and C23541; 4A1836^2 = U. of Illinois 813/Ir8t/1836; ARE1849^1 = U. of Wisconsin PS2070/.A1/1849; ARE1849^2 = Library of Congress PS2050/.E49/v.7/copy 2 (xerox); ARE1850 = Ralph M. Aderman Copy, inscribed "R.E. Livingston."

"to" in the phrase "secret attachment to him"; only 2E has this reading. At II.61.23 (149.40) "di" is substituted for "del" to read "Corpo di Bacco!"; 2E, 3A, ARE, and 1F agree. At II.66.13 (151.21) "same" is canceled in the phrase "At the same time"; only 2E and 1A agree in omitting "same."

Sight Collations (Individual)
(1)   MSh vs. MSx (twice)
(2)   MSh vs. MSt (three times)
(3)   MSt vs. MSx (three times)
(4)   MSt vs. 1Aa (twice)
(5)   MSt vs. 3A^1
(6)   MSt vs. ARE^1
(7)   MSt vs. 1F (twice)
(8)   MSt vs. 1Ea
(9)   1Aa vs. 1Ab
(10) 1Ea vs. 1Eb
(11) 1Eb vs. MSt
(12) 1Eb vs. 1Aa
(13) 1Eb vs. 1F, Part II
(14) 1Eb vs. 3A^2
(15) 1Eb vs. 2E
(16) 1Eb vs. ARE^1
(17) 1F vs. 1Aa, Part III
(18) 1F vs. ARE^1
(19) 3A^1 vs. ARE^1
(20) 3A^2 vs. ARE^2
(21) ARE^1 vs. 1Aa
(22) 4A1836 vs. ARE^1, Part I

The following specific copies were used: MSh = Holograph MS of Part II, Huntington Library HM3183; MSx = Xeroxed copy of MSh, deposited U. of N. Carolina; MSt = Typescript of MSh, deposited U. of N. Carolina; 1Aa = Huntington Library 37931 (xerox); 1Ab = U. of N. Carolina microfilm 1 18 (xerox); 1Ea = Washington U. in St. Louis Spec./PS2070/.A1/1824c; 1Eb = Huntington Library 22800 (xerox); 3A^1 = Huntington Library 85819 (xerox); 3A^2 = U. Wisconsin Rare Books C23618 and C23619; 1F = Duke U. 817.24/I72/WG (xerox); ARE^1 = Library of Congress PS2050/.E49/v.7/copy 2 (xerox); ARE^2 = U. of Wisconsin PS2070/.A1/1849; 2E = Wesleyan U. I72tb (xerox); 4A1836 = U. of Illinois 813/Ir8t/1836/v.1.

Sight Collations (Team)
    Team collations were performed by a group of readers, each responsible for a single text.
Part I:
"To the Reader"
(1)   2A vs. 1E^1 vs. 3A vs. ARE vs. 1F
"The Great Unknown"

(2)   1Aa vs. 2A vs. 1E^1 vs. 3A vs. ARE vs. 1F
(3)   1Ab vs. 1E^2 vs. 3A vs. ARE (twice)
"The Hunting Dinner"
(4)   1Aa vs. 2A vs. 1E^2 vs. 3A vs. ARE vs. 1F
(5)   1Ab vs. 1E^1 vs. 3A vs. ARE (twice)
"The Adventure of My Uncle"
(6)   1Aa vs. 2A vs. 1E^2 vs. 3A vs. ARE vs. 1F
(7)   1Ab vs. 1E^2 vs. 3A vs. ARE (twice)
"The Adventure of My Aunt"
(8)   1Aa vs. 2A vs. 1E^2 vs. 3A vs. ARE vs. 1F
(9)   1Ab vs. 1E^2 vs. 3A vs. ARE (twice)
"The Bold Dragoon"
(10) 1Aa vs. 2A vs. 3A vs. ARE vs. 1F vs. 1E^1 vs. 2E
(11) 1Ab vs. 1E^2 vs. 3A vs. ARE
"The Adventure of the German Student"
(12) 2A vs. 1E^1 vs. 3A vs. ARE vs. 1F
(13) 1E^2 vs. 3A vs. ARE
"The Adventure of the Mysterious Picture"
(14) 1Aa vs. 2A vs. 3A vs. ARE vs. 1F vs. 1E^1
(15) 1Ab vs. 1E^2 vs. 3A vs. ARE (twice)
"The Adventure of the Mysterious Stranger"
(16) 1Aa vs. 2A vs. 3A vs. ARE vs. 1F vs. 1E^2 vs. 2E
(17) 1E^2 vs. 1Ab vs. 3A vs. ARE
"The Story of the Young Italian"
(18) 1Aa vs. 2A vs. 3A vs. ARE vs. 1F vs. 1E^1
(19) 1Ab vs. 1E^2 vs. 3A vs. ARE

Part II:
"The Club of Queer Fellows"
(20) 1Ab vs. MSx vs. 1E^2 vs. 3A vs. ARE
(21) 1E^2 vs. MSx vs. 1Ab vs. 3A vs. ARE
"The Poor Devil Author"
(22) MSx vs. 1Ab vs. 1E^2 vs. 3A vs. ARE
(23) 1Ab vs. MSx vs. 1E^2 vs. 3A vs. ARE
"Notoriety"
(24) 2A vs. 1E^1 vs. 3A vs. ARE vs. 1F
(25) 1E^2 vs. 3A vs. ARE
"A Practical Philosopher"
(26) 2A vs. 1E^1 vs. 3A vs. ARE vs. 1F
(27) 1E^2 vs. 3A vs. ARE (twice)
"Buckthorne, or the Young Man of Great Expectations"
(28) 1Ab vs. MSx vs. 1E^2 vs. 3A vs. ARE
"Grave Reflections of a Disappointed Man"

(29) MSx vs. 1Ab vs. 1E^2 vs. 3A vs. ARE
(30) 1Ab vs. MSx vs. 1E^2 vs. 3A vs. ARE
(31) 1E^2 vs. MSx vs. 1Ab vs. 3A vs. ARE
"The Booby Squire"
(32) 1Ab vs. MSx vs. 1E^2 vs. 3A vs. ARE (twice)
(33) 1E^2 vs. MSx vs. 1Ab vs. 3A vs. ARE (twice)
"The Strolling Manager"
(34) 1Ab vs. MSx vs. 1E^2 vs. 3A vs. ARE (twice)
(35) 1E^2 vs. MSx vs. 1Ab vs. 3A vs. ARE

Part III:
"The Inn at Terracina"
(36) 1Ab vs. 1E^2 vs. 3A vs. ARE vs. 1F (twice)
"The Adventure of the Little Antiquary"
(37) 1Aa vs. 3A vs. ARE vs. 1F vs. 1E^1
(38) 1E^2 vs. 1Ab vs. 3A vs. ARE
"The Belated Travellers"
(39) 2A vs. 1E^1 vs. 3A vs. ARE vs. 1F
(40) 1F^2 vs. 3A vs. ARE (twice)
"The Adventure of the Popkins Family"
(41) 1Ab vs. 1E$^?$ vs. 3A vs. ARE vs. 1F
"The Painter's Adventure"
(42) 1Ab vs. 1E^2 vs. 3A vs. ARE vs. 1F (twice)
"The Story of the Bandit Chieftain"
(43) 1Ab vs. 1E ^{2} vs. 3A vs. ARE vs. 1F (twice)
"The Story of the Young Robber"
(44) 1Aa vs. 3A vs. ARE vs. 1F vs. 1E^2
(45) 1Ab vs. 1E^2 vs. 3A vs. ARE (twice)
"The Adventure of the Englishman"
(46) 1Ab vs. 1E^u vs. 3A vs. ARE vs. 1F

Part IV:
"Hell Gate"
(47) 1Aa vs. 3A vs. ARE vs. 1F vs. 1E^2
(48) 1Ab vs. 1E^2 vs. 3A vs. ARE (twice)
"Kidd the Pirate"
(49) 1Aa vs. 3A vs. ARE vs. 1F vs. 1E^2
(50) 1Ab vs. 1E^2 vs. 3A vs. ARE (twice)
"The Devil and Tom Walker"
(51) 1Ab vs. 1E^2 vs. 3A vs. ARE vs. 1F (twice)
"Wolfert Webber, or Golden Dreams"
(52) 1Aa vs. 3A vs. ARE vs. 1F vs. 1E^2
(53) 1Ab vs. 1E^2 vs. 3A vs. ARE (twice)

"The Adventure of the Black Fisherman"
(54) 1Aa vs. 3A vs. ARE vs. 1F vs. $1E^2$
(58) 1Ab vs. $1E^2$ vs. 3A vs. ARE (twice)

The following specific copies were used: 1Aa = Huntington Library 37931 (xerox); 1Ab = U. of N. Carolina Microfilm 1–18 (xerox); 2A = Houghton Library 80–655 (xerox); 3A = Huntington Library 85819 (xerox); ARE = Library of Congress PS2050/.E49/v.7/copy 2 (xerox); 1F = Duke U. 817.24/ I72/WG (xerox); $1E^1$ = State B, Huntington Library 22800 (xerox); $1E^2$ = State B (with mixed sheets from state A), U. of N. Carolina Rare Books PS2070/.A1/1824a (xerox); 2E = Wesleyan U. I72tb (xerox); MSx = Xeroxed copy of holograph MS of Part II, Huntington Library HM3183, deposited U. of N. Carolina.

CHOICE OF COPY-TEXTS

This edition follows the seminal proposals of W.W. Greg that copy-text be chosen for its fidelity in preserving the characteristic spelling, punctuation, capitalization, word division, and paragraphing of the author's manuscript— those features most subject to non-authorial change as a work passes from author to compositor to printer's reader and publisher's reader and into print from one edition to another.[23] When fair-copy manuscript exists, it serves as copy-text. In its absence, the edition set from the manuscript is chosen as more likely than later editions to preserve the texture of the author's "accidentals." Subsequent authorial revisions to "substantives," or the words themselves, are incorporated in the copy-text as emendations.[24]

To recover Irving's accidentals most faithfully, three copy-texts are required for *Tales*. Holograph MS serves as copy-text for eight of the ten tales of Part II. For twenty other stories in Parts I, III, and IV, the edition set from Irving's MS, 1A, is copy-text. For the four stories and preface for which

---

23. The theory was advanced by Greg in "The Rationale of Copy-Text," *Studies in Bibliography*, 3 (1950–1951), 19–36, and adopted for editions of nineteenth-century works in the CEAA *Statement of Editorial Principles and Procedures* (1967; rev. 1972). Copy-text is "the text which the editor follows at all points except those where he believes emendation to be justified" (*Statement*, p. 4).

24. The words "substantives" and "accidentals" are "strangely medieval" and often misleading terms, as Morse Peckham has protested ("Reflections on the Foundations of Modern Textual Editing," *Proof 1* [1971], 125). They are used here for the sake of convention and convenience, although the term "accidentals" may be particularly unfortunate in its connotation and often restrictive as it is applied. Meaning is always affected, even if only in subtle ways, by changes in punctuation, spelling, and the like. But in some cases the effect is more immediate than in others. When change in punctuation—as, for instance, in the

Irving furnished new manuscript in England, 1E is copy-text.[25] Editions which descend from a scribal copy of Irving's manuscript through proofs of 1E—2A, 3A, ARE, 1F—are not candidates for copy-text because they lie at two or more removes from MS.

These choices affirm that the original texture of Irving's accidentals—unconventional and idiosyncratic as it may often be—is worth preserving as an important feature of his style (an attribute for which his writing was and continues to be valued) and is preferable to the house styles inevitably imposed by his printers. This proposition runs counter to the view that because Irving read or revised proofs of his work, as he did for 1E and probably did for ARE, he gave his tacit approval to the printers' styling of those editions.

Nearly two decades of work with Irving manuscripts and editions in the preparation of *The Complete Works* has demonstrated that Irving's natural style of punctuating, capitalizing, spelling, and compounding was very different from the styles imposed by his printers and publishers and that his control over accidentals virtually ended when his manuscripts were set in type. Extant proof sheets show that while he made many changes in substantives, he made few changes in accidentals, usually only to correct typographical error. In proof sheets for *Oliver Goldsmith: A Biography* (ARE, 1849), twenty-eight of which survive, he made only four corrections in accidentals.[26] In sixteen surviving proof sheets for *A History of New York* (ARE, 1848), he made only six isolated corrections.[27] In six surviving proof sheets for his *Life of George Washington* (ARE, 1855–1859), he made only

change of "lawyers'" to "lawyer's"—alters our immediate perception of what the word means, it is a substantive change

25. Specifically, the copy-texts are: Title Epigraph (1E); "To the Reader" (1E); Part I Title (1A); "The Great Unknown" (1A); "The Hunting Dinner" (1A); "The Adventure of My Uncle" (1A); "The Adventure of My Aunt" (1A); "The Bold Dragoon" (1A); "The Adventure of the German Student" (1E); "The Adventure of the Mysterious Picture" (1A); "The Adventure of the Mysterious Stranger" (1A); "The Story of the Young Italian" (1A); Part II Title (MS); "Literary Life" (MS); "A Literary Dinner" (MS); "The Club of Queer Fellows" (MS); "The Poor Devil Author" (MS); "Notoriety" (1E); "A Practical Philosopher" (1E); "Buckthorne, or the Young Man of Great Expectations" (MS); "Grave Reflections of a Disappointed Man" (MS); "The Booby Squire" (MS); "The Strolling Manager" (MS); Part III Title (1A); "The Inn at Terracina" (1A); "The Adventure of the Little Antiquary" (1A); "The Belated Travellers" (1E); "The Adventure of the Popkins Family" (1A); "The Painter's Adventure" (1A); "The Story of the Bandit Chieftain" (1A); "The Story of the Young Robber" (1A); "The Adventure of the Englishman" (1A); Part IV Title (1A); "Hell Gate" (1A); "Kidd the Pirate" (1A); "The Devil and Tom Walker" (1A); "Wolfert Webber, or Golden Dreams" (1A); "The Adventure of the Black Fisherman" (1A).

26. Elsie Lee West, ed., *Oliver Goldsmith: A Biography* (Boston: Twayne, 1978), p 433.

27. The proof sheets and several pages of original manuscript are bound in with a copy of Putnam's 1854 printing of the work at the Huntington Library (HM 3131). See also Michael L. Black and Nancy B. Black, ed., *A History of New York* (Boston: Twayne, 1984), p. 365.

one change, in the spelling of a proper name.[28] There are many reasons for his failure to insist on his own style, some of them no doubt temperamental, but others practical.

Printing practices of the time left a large share of the responsibility for spelling, punctuation, capitalization, hyphenation, and paragraphing to the discretion of the compositor and printer's and publisher's readers. So long did these practices persist that a printer's manual published in America in 1844 still quoted a British manual of 1755 to this effect: "By the laws of printing, indeed, a compositor should abide by his copy, and not vary from it, that he may clear himself, in case he should be charged with having made a fault. But this good law is now looked upon as obsolete, and most authors expect the printer to spell, point, and digest their copy, that it may be intelligible and significant to the reader; which is what a compositor and corrector jointly have regard to. . . ." The codification of house style is emphasized: "every corrector ought to fix upon a method to spell ambiguous words and compounds always the same way. And that the compositors may become acquainted with and accustomed to his way of spelling, the best expedient will be to draw out by degrees, a catalogue of such ambiguous words and compounds."[29] Although C.S. Van Winkle's compositors for 1A interfered less than those of other printers with Irving's punctuation, his own manual echoed virtually all other manuals of the period in appropriating authority for accidentals: "Correct pointing," he claimed, "most certainly depends upon printers."[30]

The condition of Irving's manuscripts suggests that he did in fact expect a certain amount of service of this kind from his printers. He relied on them to perform such routine conversions as substituting "and" for his "&"; to correct such frequent and characteristic misspellings as "sacrafice," "reccollect," or "percieve"; to supply apostrophes in contractions and possessives, which he generally omitted except in those instances where he felt a compositor might not make the appropriate choice. He was careful, for example, in the *Tales* MS to place apostrophes correctly in "Tibbs'" (78.23) and "Steele's" (84.21), two instances where mistakes might be likely to occur. Compositors, however, typically exceeded these specific expectations, and though Irving did not intervene to restore manuscript accidentals, he was

28. Allen Guttmann and James A. Sappenfield, ed., *Life of George Washington*, (Boston: Twayne, 1982), I & II, 677.

29. Thomas F. Adams, *Typographia: or the Printer's Instructor*, 2nd ed. (Philadelphia, 1844; rpt. New York and London: Garland, 1981), pp. 106–107 and pp. 176–77. Adams' manual, essentially an abridgement of John Johnson's *Typographia* (London, 1824), quotes in the first instance from John Smith's *The Printer's Grammar* (London, 1755).

30. C.S. Van Winkle, *The Printers' Guide* (New York, 1818; rpt. New York and London: Garland, 1981), p. vi.

not always satisfied with the styling his printers and publishers imposed. Hence his complaint about excessive punctuation in an American edition of *The Sketch Book*: "High pointing is apt to injure the fluency of the style if the reader attends to all the stops."[31] Hence, also, his protest that Webster's *Dictionary*, the unabridged 1848 edition of which served as a model for Putnam's editions of his collected works, did not represent his personal "Standard of Orthography": "I find it almost impossible to have a work printed in this country free from some of his arbitrary modifications; which are pronounced provincialisms by all foreign scholars critical in the English language," he wrote in 1852.[32] Clearly, then, beyond the corrections or routine conversions he expected his printers to make, Irving's acquiescence to other changes cannot be construed as complete endorsement of them.

Just how far Irving's printers exceeded his expectations is demonstrable and supports the theory that MS or the edition closest to MS should provide copy-text. "The Club of Queer Fellows" offers a representative example. Irving's MS for this story requires fifty-six corrections, in which all editions agree, to correct misspelling or supply needed punctuation. When these blanket changes are set aside, we see the effects of house styling. A collation of all editions against MS strikingly displays the relative faithfulness of the 1A compositors to the accidental texture of MS. Apart from the blanket corrections, 1A introduces fifty eight variants in punctuation or spelling. Other editions introduce more than twice that many: 1E, 124; 3A and 1F, which carry the burden of dual house styles (that reflected in the 1E proofs and those introduced by compositors in New York and Paris setting from those proofs), 131 and 132 respectively.[33] ARE follows its setting copy in most of 3A's 131 changes but corrects two 3A punctuation errors, introduces five additional commas, and intervenes eight times to Americanize "-our" spellings to "-or."

Changes in punctuation are the most numerous. The editions often

31. *Letters*, vol. 1, *1802–1823*, ed. Ralph M. Aderman, Herbert L. Kleinfield, and Jenifer S. Banks (Boston: Twayne, 1978), p. 552.

32. *Letters*, vol. 4, *1846–1859*, ed. Ralph M. Aderman, Herbert L. Kleinfield, and Jenifer S. Banks (Boston: Twayne, 1982), p. 298. See also pp. 255–56 for Irving's official protest against an advertisement which misleadingly excerpted from a letter he wrote to G. & C. Merriam an implied endorsement of Webster, which he in fact considered "an unsafe standard for American writers to adopt" and "not a work advisable to be introduced 'by authority' into our schools as a standard of orthography."

33. What is true of the faithfulness of 1A to the accidentals of Irving's MS in this story is true throughout Part II, where MS is available for comparison. The increasing proportions of change from 1E through 3A, ARE, and 1F generally hold true as well. Compositors for 1A introduced only 1,600 changes in the accidentals of Irving's MS, and nearly one-third of these are in the category of expected corrections made by all editions. The remaining variants, which can be attributed to house style or error, are less than half the number imposed on identical passages by the printers of other editions.

changed Irving's commas to semicolons and his semicolons to colons or the reverse and occasionally omitted punctuation which he had supplied. The omissions typically remove commas Irving used to show pause and emphasis. This is true, for example, in a passage in which Dribble, addressing Buckthorne and Crayon, explains why his wit is more in evidence in the club than at the literary dinner. MS reads: "Who, do you think, would laugh at any thing I could say, when I had some of the current wits of the day about me? But, here, though a poor devil, I am among still poorer devils than myself . . ." (76.31–33). All editions remove commas after "Who," "think," and "But," which, though not grammatically necessary, add an intended emphasis in the case of "But, here," and call attention to Dribble's auditors and the dramatic context in the case of "Who, do you think, would laugh." The MS commas are typical of a writer who "is guided less by grammatical rules or syntactical principles than by what seems to be a kind of half-visual, half-oral sense for supplying punctuation wherever this delicate sixth sense suggests the desirability of indicating a pause, placing a shade of emphasis, or supplying a special nuance of meaning whether covered by the rules or not."[34]

When compositors did not accept Irving's punctuation in MS, it was more often their practice to replace it than to delete it, or to add it where Irving had none. The direction of compositorial change is clearly toward heavier pointing. All editions, for example, agree in adding commas after "market," "it," and "steps" in a sentence for which MS reads: "At length we came out upon Fleet market and traversing it turned up a narrow street to the bottom of a long steep flight of stone steps named Break neck Stairs" (77.35). It is typical of Irving not to interrupt the flow of forward movement in such passages. In all, 1E added forty-eight commas where Irving used no punctuation and where no punctuation is necessary for intelligibility; in similar circumstances 1A added twenty-eight.

Also illustrative of the comparative conservatism of 1A and the heavier pointing of the other editions is the inconsistency in hyphenation styles. Irving's "Green Arbour Court" in MS is retained in 1A but becomes in 3A "Green-arbour court" and in ARE "Green-arbor court" but in 1F and 1E "Green-arbour-court" (at 77.19–20 and four more times in the story). Such changes, of course, arise from British conventions in place names. But other instances abound. Irving's "old school times" in MS is reproduced exactly in 1A, 3A, and ARE, but "school times" is hyphenated in 1F and 1E (76.23). Both 1A and 1E follow MS in not hyphenating "out of the way corners,"

---

34. Henry A. Pochmann, ed., *Mahomet and His Successors* (Madison: Univ. of Wisconsin Press, 1970), pp. 580–81. Pochmann's itemized analysis of Irving's habits of punctuation in a forty-three page fragment of the *Mahomet* MS (pp. 573–80) holds true for his practices in the *Tales* MS.

where 3A, ARE, and 1F have "out-of-the-way" (77.38). Similarly, only 3A, ARE, and 1F hyphenate "wash-tub," while 1A and 1E follow MS "washtub" (78.6), but all editions except 1A change MS "soapsuds" to "soap-suds" (78.9–10). 1A introduces only two hyphens; 1E introduces twenty-eight.

That Irving was not responsible for the changes in accidentals made by 1E in this story is suggested both by his habit of ignoring accidentals in correcting proof and by the relatively minor attention he gave this story during his revisions for 1E and ARE. In 1E he introduced only four substantive changes and made only two others for ARE. Typical of his 1E revisions are his lowering the price of admission to the club from a "shilling" to a "sixpence" (75.13) to better accord with the class distinctions he hoped to portray and his substitution of "called" for "named" to achieve greater colloquial precision in the phrase "called Break neck Stairs" (77.35). The two authorial changes in ARE are stylistic in effect: "square of tall . . . houses" became "square surrounded by tall . . . houses" (77.43–78.1) and "frippery that fluttered from every window" became "frippery fluttering from every window" (78.2).

All editions contain some degree of substantive error, changes in wording introduced by compositors, or, in the case of 1E, perhaps by the amanuensis who copied Irving's MS, through inadvertence or by a misreading of Irving's handwriting. Here, too, is borne out the wisdom of choosing as copy-text either MS or in its absence the first edition set from it as embodying the author's "accidentals   and of course the vast majority of the words . . . closest to the author's intent."[35] Even though 1A did not have the benefit of Irving's proofreading, it introduces only three substantive errors, compared to six in 1E, and, by descent from 3A, eight in ARE. A misreading of Irving's handwriting accounts for the 1A errors "quiz" for MS "quip" (75.25) and "puddle" for MS "fuddle" (75.40). All editions err in the reading "tall and miserable houses" because the 1A compositor and the amanuensis for 1E failed to see, or to accept, Irving's canceled ampersand in the MS: "tall [wretched &] miserable houses." Irving quite frequently neglected to put commas between sequential adjectives and so probably intended the reading "tall miserable houses" (77.43–78.1). A similar kind of copying error on the part of the 1E amanuensis may be responsible for several other substantive variants: the misreadings of "perfectly" for MS "profoundly" (77.32); "there" for MS "then" (76.22); "homeward" for MS "homewards" (77.25); and "afterward" for MS "afterwards" (77.30). The latter two errors were corrected, probably by 1E copy-editors, and so exist only in the editions that descend from proofs: 3A, ARE, and 1F.[36] The others were overlooked; they remain

---

35. CEAA *Statement*, p. 4.

36. Words such as "homewards," "afterwards," "towards," and "downwards" are used consistently in MS, but Irving's final "s" after "d" is easy to mistake as merely a loose down

in all editions except 1A. Two substantive variants are the fault of compositorial error or refinement in 3A: the reading "of a" for MS "of" (76.12) and "I am" for MS "I'm" (76.29). They are perpetuated in ARE.

The Twayne edition, which takes MS as copy-text for this story, respects and adopts as emendations the four substantive changes Irving made for 1E and the two additional changes he made for ARE. Beyond this, it follows its copy-text faithfully and so eliminates the three substantive errors introduced by 1A, eight errors in 3A and ARE, and six errors in 1F and 1E. In the matter of accidentals, where a necessary distinction has been drawn between expectation and acquiescence, this edition performs the service Irving expected of his printers by making the fifty-six corrections in which all other editions agree. Otherwise, it follows copy-text exactly and so rejects from the practice of other editions all vestiges of house style which interfere with Irving's preferences in hyphenation and spelling and his characteristically rhetorical, as opposed to syntactical pointing. The following sections explain the editorial principles more fully.

TREATMENT OF SUBSTANTIVES

Substantive variants from the copy-texts in 1E and ARE are adopted in this edition when they are judged to represent Irving's intentions. About large-scale changes, generally, there can be no question. Irving, and no one else, was responsible for nine paragraphs added in 1E to "The Poor Devil Author" and two sentences added to "The Adventure of My Uncle" (19.3–6, 19.7–9), for example. But in judging smaller changes an editor deals in probabilities, not certainties. The best guide in deciding the authority of changes in individual words and phrases is knowledge of Irving's habits in this work and others and understanding of the conditions which foster non-authorial change. In each case where doubt exists, the editor asks two fundamental questions: Is the change typical of Irving; is there a reason, in other words, for him to have made it? Or, is there equal or greater likelihood that a compositor or proofreader introduced it? If the answer to the first question is affirmative, the variant is accepted as an emendation. If the answer to the first is negative and the answer to the second affirmative, the variant is rejected.

Certain categories of change, typical of Irving throughout his career, influence decisions about the authority of substantive variants. His alterations

---

stroke on the "d." The fact that 1F agrees with 3A in dropping the "s" suggests that a misreading rather than an Americanization accounted for these errors. American house style was often responsible, as the apparatus records. Though in his *Printers' Guide* Van Winkle asked, "What occasion is there for continuing the final s in those words?" (p. 78), he apparently did not challenge Irving's MS, for the 1A compositors set the words as written.

in MS reflect these characteristic revisions. (1) He frequently changed "that" to "which" or "who." So pervasive is this tendency that forty such changes are adopted as emendations from 1E and ARE. (2) He often replaced an equivocal phrase with an assertion, as in MS 79 where he substituted "were" for "seemed to be" or in MS 85 where he achieved greater certainty by replacing "many" with "most." This tendency supports such emendations as 1E's "have" for "seemed to have" (12.1) and ARE's "aunt was" for "aunt, herself, seemed to be" (23.5). (3) He frequently revised to avoid repetition of a word, as in MS 96 where he substituted "party" for "number" in the phrase "party of young ladies" because he had used the phrase "among the number" in the next sentence. Similar changes in 1E and ARE are judged authorial, as, for example, the substitutions of "our host" for "mine host" (11.12) and "gentlemen" for "guests" (11.15) when "mine host" and "guests" are repeated nearby. (4) He often substituted a single word for a phrase—as in MS 79, where "quaffing" is substituted for "taking a friendly draught"— as much in search of aptness as economy, or eliminated superfluous words, as in MS 87 where he canceled the first two words in the phrase "which are held." The revisions in ARE are often of this caliber. (5) His search for a better word or more vivid term is reflected in the substitution of "feasting" for "eating" in MS 86 or of "drooping" for "hanging" in MS 98. Such authorial change is everywhere to be found in the 1E and ARE variants. (6) Alongside his search for aptness is a tendency to temper harsh or frankly suggestive passages. His substitution of "fellow" for "dog" in MS 89 is in this category, as is his substitution of "tossed" for "slipped" to show how Buckthorne delivered the purse of gold "into [Columbine's] bosom" in MS 123, or his revision of the passage in which Buckthorne is beaten fore and aft by Harlequin: "assaults on my most honourable territories" was modified to the less explicit "assaults in a manner most degrading to my dignity" in MS 96. It is this occasional fastidiousness that accounts for his excision in "The Bold Dragoon" of references to the hero's "tight pair of buckskins" or an even franker description of his sexual appeal, "his tight jacket setting off his broad shoulders and plump buckskins, and his long sword trailing by his side" (see List of Emendations at 27.28 and 28.23–24). (7) Most troublesome of Irving's characteristic alterations in MS are his substitutions of one preposition for another. More than a dozen such substitutions occur, usually but not always to achieve greater idiomatic precision. Because such change, particularly when only a single letter or two is involved, as in "of"/"on," "upon"/"on," "in"/"on," is also characteristic of compositorial error or refinement, authority is difficult to decide. In such cases the reading of the copy-text is generally retained. (8) The most pervasive tendency reflected in MS is Irving's inclination to substitute one verb for another or to revise the tense, voice, mood, or number of existing verbs, often by way of correction. More than one hundred MS alterations are in this category, making it the largest and most consistent feature of his retouching. A similar proportion is reflected in the emendations adopted for this edition.

Extant manuscript and proof sheets from the period 1848–1849 show the same categories of authorial change as well as one other which was not typical of his alterations in 1824. In the later period, Irving conscientiously restrained his tendency to write "from whence" and "from thence." He canceled "from" in such phrases twice in his 1849 MS of *Oliver Goldsmith: A Biography* and once in proof sheets for *A History of New York* (ARE 1848). Two ARE variants in *Tales* confirm that Irving, rather than a compositor or copy-editor performing routine deletions, desired and made such changes. In the first instance a passage is rearranged to avoid "from thence" (159.28–29), and in the second a sentence is begun anew to omit "From hence" (184.34). Copy-texts are emended ten times from ARE to respect this category of authorial change.

Substantive variants are generally rejected when (1) no rationale exists, either in the context of the passage or in accordance with Irving's habits, for Irving to have made the change, and (2) the change could have resulted from compositorial or scribal error or refinement. Errors of inadvertence or lapse of memory on the part of a compositor are common. Taking a sentence at a time or a portion of a sentence in memory, the compositor turned from his copy to look at his type case. Many categories of non-authorial change occur in this way: duplication of words; omission of words; addition or omission of final letters, making a singular plural or a plural singular; transpositions; anticipations, by which a word later in a passage is introduced earlier; or intrusion of the force of idiom to reconstruct a phrase. Examples of the first three categories are plentiful in the List of Rejected Substantives. (In one noteworthy instance, dropping "the" from a sentence at 190.10 in "The Story of the Bandit Chieftain" leaves the captive "in charge of" rather than "in the charge of" his guard. The faulty reading appears in all editions except 1A.) The final three categories, particularly, require illustration because they often have the look or feel of authorial change. At 28.42 the copy-text (1A) reads "paintings of fruit, and fish, and game"; the 1E transposition— "paintings of fish, and fruit, and game"—is rejected because no reason exists for Irving to have reversed the order and the change is typical of compositorial error. However, a similar transposition at 14.9–10 is judged authorial because Irving had reason to make the change and made another change in the immediate vicinity. Copy-text (1A) reads: "noseless cold looking statues without any clothing"; Irving, in a typical refinement in 1E, deleted "without any clothing" and reversed the order of the adjectives ("cold looking noseless statues") to achieve parallelism with "cold looking formal garden" earlier in the sentence. There are, of course, other possible explanations for how the change came about, but here as elsewhere, where improvement can be construed and the change is not out of keeping with Irving's habits, the variant is judged authorial and adopted as an emendation of the copy-text. Compositorial anticipation is judged responsible for ARE's insertion of "often" before "found" at 5.1, introducing the kind of repetition Irving conscientiously avoided: "I have often found in travelling . . . that it is often a comfort. . . ." And a compositor, through the intrusion of the force of idiom, is probably responsible for the substitution "was his wont" for Irving's more typical "he was wont" at 15.1.

That a great many compositorial errors were overlooked by Irving in reading proofs for 1E and ARE may be attributable to haste and the fact that he probably did not read proof against copy.[37] Yet Irving often did correct compositorial error in proofs. In one illustrative case he was only partially successful in restoring his original intention. The reading of MS and 1A, "whom he held in almost equal awe" (99.5), was, perhaps through memorial error, rendered "of whom he was in almost equal awe" in the proofs from which 3A and 1F were set. An attempt to restore the reading for 1E resulted in the corruption "whom he had in almost equal awe." Whether Irving was thwarted by compositorial error a second time or by his own uncertain memory of the original reading is not clear. The MS reading is retained.

An especially troublesome category of variants results from misreadings of Irving's handwriting by compositors for 1A or the amanuensis for 1E. Where MS exists for comparison, the 1A compositors must be given greater credit for fulfilling Irving's intentions. The following examples are typical of the errors arising from scribal transmission and unnoticed or uncorrected by Irving in his proofreading of the copied manuscript and his proofreading of 1E. Compositors for 1A correctly read Irving's intended phrase "all its fascination" (107.11); in MS he wrote "fascination" above the word "power" but neglected to cancel "power." The amanuensis is no doubt responsible for the reading "all its power of fascination" perpetuated in 1E; ARE, perhaps through compositorial inadvertence, reads "all its powers of fascination." The Twayne edition adopts the 1A reading. Similarly, in MS Irving meant to substitute the phrase "consoled ourselves with" for his original "made up by"; however, he neglected to cancel "made up," though he did cancel "by" at the beginning of the next line. Only 1A reproduces his intention (106.33); the amanuensis for 1E is apparently at fault for the awkward rendering "consoled ourselves and made up with."

In the case of variants in single words, misreadings are usually easy to spot, but determining which edition contains the authorial reading is not always simple. As the previous discussion of "The Club of Queer Fellows"

---

37. Where proof sheets survive, it is clear Irving did not read them against printer's copy. See, for example, Elsie West's analysis in *Goldsmith*, pp. 433, 438–39. Irving wrote Putnam in 1848 that he "need not send the copy with the proof" of the introduction to *The Sketch Book*; see *Letters*, IV, 180.

indicated, the fact that Irving supervised the publication of 1E but had no role in reading proofs of 1A is no guarantee that 1E is more reliable for substantive readings. Each suspected misreading is judged individually in context and with an awareness of Irving's handwriting. By these criteria, 1A's "sullen" is a misreading of "sallow" (20.36), and it is emended from 1E. However, 1E's "fastnesses," which has a particularly Irvingesque appeal to it as an archaic term for "latches," is more probably a scribal misreading of Irving's "fastenings" (23.6), the copy-text reading. Irving wrote "fastenings" twice in his manuscript of "Dolph Heyliger" in *Bracebridge Hall*, and the formation of letters in both instances provides additional reason to believe "fastnesses" is the misreading.

In spite of every effort to distinguish authorial readings from non-authorial intrusion or error, no definitive exactitude or perfection can be claimed for the editorial decisions recorded in the List of Emendations or the List of Rejected Substantives. The Discussions of Adopted Readings elucidate many of the decisions to emend or not to emend. As a general principle, however, the Twayne edition preserves the reading of the copy-text at all points except where probability, in accord with the principles outlined above, suggests an alternative reading is authorial. Irving's supervision of 1E has not been taken as a mandate to incorporate all or even most of its substantive variants. Each is weighed individually and adopted or rejected according to its particular claims as judged against the rationale.

The rationale, however, does not extend to cover the largest category of rejected substantives—those revisions Irving made in Parts II and III to appease William Gifford, John Murray's "elbow critic" and, as influential editor of the *Quarterly Review*, a man whose favor Irving always sought. In making the changes, however willingly, Irving fulfilled Gifford's intentions, not his own. When Irving's original intentions can be recovered and restored, they have been. The result of this decision, the rejection of some 3,600 words Irving added for 1E, is of such magnitude as to require full discussion here.

Late in the preparation of 1E—less than two weeks before Irving's departure for Paris—Gifford wrote Murray his reaction to proofs of the work. He objected, as Irving's reply to Murray will show, specifically to two sections of "Buckthorne"; the portrait of the Fantadlins in "The Strolling Manager"; and the portrait of the English gentleman in Part III, principally in "The Inn at Terracina" and "The Adventure of the Englishman." His motives were to prevent Irving from making "mistakes" in terminology and characterization "which would have done him no credit." He objected to two terms: Irving "talks of little Cathedral towns. Cathedrals make cities; in short he is [all abroad on?] this subject. It is worse when he talks of Prebends—There are no such persons as Prebend is an office—The holder of it is Prebendary." Principally, though, Gifford was offended by what he construed as Irving's "ridicule [of] our provincial clergy," the "false & slanderous" picture of Oxford, and "so revolting a picture of an English nobleman" among the Italians.[38] Much of Gifford's letter, now in the Murray archives, is indecipherable, and an unpreserved letter from Murray, who was asked to disguise Gifford as the source of the critique, intervened in transmitting the objections to Irving. Their specific nature, or at least their nature as Irving understood it, can be inferred from his response to Murray in a letter written, by the evidence of his journal, on August 5. It is worth quoting at some length:

My dear Sir,

I am always thankful for Criticism when in season, and am always eager to profit by it to the most of my abilities. I feel the value of the suggestions of your friend, and only regret that he had not read my work in Manuscript that I might have had more fully the benefit of his good sense & good taste and been more completely able to modify my writings accordingly. If it be Mr Gifford to whom I am indebted I beg you will assure him that I feel honoured by his censorship, as I have heretofore felt flattered and stimulated by his approbation.

I have been at work half the night to make additions & alterations which might obviate the impression some parts of the story has made upon your friend. I have no idea of ridiculing the provincial clergy; the mentions I have casually made of them have been individual sketches from originals which happened to present themselves to me, but I was not aware that I had sketched in such a way as to incur a Suspicion of the kind—There would be nothing more humiliating to me than to be mistaken for one of that loose rabble of writers who are ready to decry every thing orderly & established—my feelings go the contrary way. I have thrown in a sketch therefore of a country clergyman, as one of a valuable class, which I hope may meet with the approbation of your friend. It shall be my care in any future writings, more effectually to do justice to this body of men, & in so doing to do justice to my own way of thinking of them:

The picture of the cathedral city I will modify, & obliterate any thing that might be considered satirical on the clergy. The picture of the cathedral circle, however, which your friend thinks is 'of the time of the Spectator' was drawn from actual observation, and the lamentations of the young ladies about the dullness of their own & the gaiety of the inferior circle, &c &c were really made to me to greater extent than I have set them down. However, I shall be cautious not to venture too

38. Quoted by McClary, pp. 58–59n; portions of the letter are also quoted in Samuel Smiles, *A Publisher and His Friends: Memoir and Correspondence of the Late John Murray*, 2 vols. (New York: Charles Scribner's Sons, 1891), II, 158–59.

far even when I have fact on my side, lest I should be considered as levelling impertinencies at Reverend persons & Reverend establishments.

The Oxford anecdotes are founded on real characters & circumstances, & the picture of a students room drawn from observation; but I am aware of the general description of college life being applicable only to the times of "town & gown" & had meant to alter it; but in the hurry of various subjects & of printing, it had escaped me. I will attend to it.

The picture of an Englishman at Terracina is not meant for that of an English *Nobleman* specifically; but as one of the general Run of English travelling gentlemen; also appear in the light I have presented this one, in the eyes of foreigners. I have drawn him with the coldness, reserve and abruptness with which English are characterized abroad; but it will be seen that I have done it with a proper motive: as I make him, in the end, when a real call is made upon his better feelings, come out generous, disinterested, brave, and truly gallant. I have drawn the character to exhibit to foreigners what are the real qualities of an Englishman; and how little he is to be judged by this external crust, which is to them so revolting. For this purpose I must make my contrasts a little strong between his character at rest & his character in action. I shall look over the scenes however, with an eye to the objections made; but if I were to make the Englishman a fine polished fellow in the first instance, his chivalry would follow as a matter of course & I should lose my object viz that of indicating the generosity of John Bull, with all his apparent phlegm & that peculiar reserve & testiness which he has when travelling.

The Fantadlins are drawn from life; they may be over charged. I will do the best I can with them, but to dismiss them entirely would make a chasm in my story which I could not readily supply. . . .

I have made these observations both to satisfy you, and to be communicated to the friend who has thought my writings worthy of his critical perusal. I beg you will make him my acknowledgements, and assure him, that if I do not purify my page as thoroughly as he could wish, it will not be from a want of defference to his opinion or diffidence of my own, but because circumstances may prevent my being able, at this state of the publication, thoroughly to remodell whole portions of the work. I will, however, go to work diligently to prune & retouch. . . .

Believe me my dear Sir—

> Ever very sincerely & gratefully
> Your friend
> Washington Irving

Mount St./Thursday morng.
P S. I beg you will not refrain from looking over the remaining sheets as they are struck off—While I am on the spot I am ready to do every thing in my power to improve the work, and I shall always feel obliged to you for the frank communication of any ideas that may arise in your mind. By the suggestions of last evening you saved me, just in time from suffering pages to pass through the press which I could not after-wards have recalled & might have forever regretted.[39]

Despite the apparent sincerity of his desire to please Murray and Gifford, Irving resented the changes demanded of him and did not, in private, con-sider them improvements. His frustration is recorded in a journal entry on August 9: "Work all the morng at alterations in Buckthorne—Marring the story in compliance with critique of Gifford. Come to a conclusion per force."[40] Since he had "thrown in a sketch . . . of a country clergyman" five days earlier,[41] Irving presumably was protesting either his changes in sec-tions on Oxford or the cathedral circle or both. Most readers would probably share his sense that he was damaging "Buckthorne" in those sections as well as in all others where he promised alterations.

Although the sketch of the clergyman who takes Buckthorne under his tutelage has been called "saccharine" and "almost cloying,"[42] it is the only one of the required revisions that has anything to recommend it. It is red-olent of Irving's special mix of sentiment and humor, though rather more heavily endowed with the former; and it has the attraction of providing a view of teaching as the gentle guidance of a flock which effectively contrasts the herding and flogging Buckthorne encounters from his other schoolmas-ter. Moreover the transitional sketch with which it is allied, that of the local parson's three daughters, which repetitiously expands an earlier brief section of the story, contains a valuable comic portrait of the superficial amusements typical of the education of young women. These attractions, however, are largely offset by the damage caused to the story as a whole. Buckthorne's father, a believer in the benefits of flogging, is consistently portrayed as a man who "had bad maxims in education" (101.15); his characterization is

39. *Letters*, II, 67–69.

40. *Journals*, III, 378.

41. Ibid., III, 377.

42. McClary, p. 59n; *Letters*, II, 69n. This sketch was praised in a review essay in Mur-ray's *Quarterly Review*, 31 (March 1825), 485: "the portrait of the good clergyman, Buck-thorne's private tutor, is drawn with a flow of persuasive moral eloquence, which would be broken by quoting any particular part." Interestingly, the review, written by Canon Thomas Hughes of St. Paul's Cathedral and "drastically revised" by Gifford, the *Review*'s departing editor (according to McClary, p. 67), makes passing reference to "scenes in the cathedral town," a locution Gifford insisted was in error.

disrupted by the decision to send his son to the worthy pastor. Moreover, the story emphasizes the making of Buckthorne "a practical philosopher"— one who has learned his lessons the hard way, literally in many instances through hard knocks and painful experience of the world. The idyllic respite in the care of the good shepherd introduces an inconsistency which, try though he did, Irving could not successfully integrate in the context of the story's original movement.

The other mandated revisions are less successful. Despite Irving's claim that he "had meant to alter" his description of Oxford life, his additions and excisions constitute an unctuous concession. Buckthorne's reverence in the revised version for "this most august of cities," whose spires are "the points of a diadem which the nation had placed upon the brows of science" (see Rejected Substantives at 115.15–17), makes his later reversion to type strained and disconcerting. The alterations to the cathedral circle section are equally unfortunate. Irving's attempt to comply with strictures against the term "cathedral town" often results in the lame substitution "place" or "this reverend little place." His attempt to "obliterate any thing that might be considered satirical on the clergy" disrupts not only his characterization of Buckthorne but also the originally intended point of the episode, the pretentious class distinctions and petty amusements that make Buckthorne a prized contrast to the clerics.

The excision of two paragraphs to temper the satire on provincial gentry in the Fantadlin section of "The Strolling Manager" is less damaging in its effect than the changes in "Buckthorne," but it just as clearly violates Irving's original intentions. In Part III, Irving softened the Englishman's curses and made more than a dozen small additions or excisions designed to eliminate or give motive for the character's rudeness to the Italians and his fellow travellers. Like his other changes, these too are concessive, gratuitous, and uncompelling.

The argument for rejecting these alterations, however, does not rest on aesthetic grounds. Discussion of their effect within the stories shows merely that the work is not harmed by dismissing them. The rationale invoked here is that Irving's acquiescence to censorship is analogous to his acquiescence in the matter of the printer's control over accidentals. Acquiescence does not constitute approval. And, because evidence exists that, despite his professed gratitude to Murray and Gifford, Irving felt his work violated by their intrusion, the editor is compelled to carry out those original intentions which Irving at the time was not himself at liberty to effect and which, when confronted with the opportunity twenty-five years later, he had not time or energy to restore. In each case, Irving's original passages are allowed to stand and the last-minute alterations dictated by Gifford are reported in the apparatus.

TREATMENT OF ACCIDENTALS

Because of the choice of multiple copy-texts, two sets of standards are necessary in the treatment of accidentals: one for MS and another for the printed editions, 1A and 1E.

The Manuscript

As the relative accuracy of the 1A compositors suggests, Irving's MS presents little difficulty in transcription, once the characteristics of his handwriting are mastered. There are, however, exceptions. Discrimination of
capital and lower case forms of some letters is particularly difficult.[43] Careful
examination of the formation of letters or their relative height does not always resolve the difficulty. Similarly, Irving occasionally failed to lift his pen
soon enough to permit distinction of an intended period from a short dash.
Relative length or position on or above the line in some instances provide
no clues. In such cases of equally defensible transcriptions, the letter or
mark of punctuation is rendered in accord with the demands of context or
convention.

By a similar principle, when Irving's cancellation of a word or phrase or
clause does not extend far enough to include punctuation specifically allied
with or dependent upon the words canceled, the punctuation is considered
canceled and is not transcribed. Penciled alterations are accepted when they
are inked over. Penciled words or marks of punctuation not confirmed by
ink are ignored in the transcription.

As copy-text, MS requires other categories of decision. Like other extant
manuscripts, this one reflects Irving's inconsistencies in spelling and capitalization, his neglect of hyphenation, his erratic use of the apostrophe, and
his punctuation by natural or emphatic pauses rather than by grammatical
rules. Most of these traits are preserved in the Twayne edition in an attempt
to present the characteristic Irving, freed insofar as possible from the im-
position of house style or the intervention of copy-editors. Corrections of
MS are made only when necessary and with the certainty that Irving expected them. When terminal punctuation is missing at the end of a sentence
or end of a paragraph; when only one of an intended pair of punctuation
marks, such as quotation marks or parentheses, exists; when a truncated line
signals the end of a paragraph, but the next line is not clearly indented—in
all such instances MS is emended to reflect what Irving intended but did
not execute. Similarly corrected are all obvious errors or examples of inad-

---

43. The specific difficulties are efficiently discussed by Nathalia Wright, ed., *Journals
and Notebooks*, vol. 1, *1803–1806* (Madison: Univ. of Wisconsin Press, 1969), p. xxi.

vertence—the repetition or omission of words caused by eyeskip or careless cutting and pasting, for example. Ampersands are changed to "and"; periods are supplied after abbreviations (in such cases as "Dr.," "Mr.," "Mrs."); apostrophes to denote possession or contraction are added when Irving omitted them. His neglect of the hyphen is judged characteristic of his style and not in the category of expected correction. No hyphens are added to compounds or possible compounds which Irving consistently wrote as separate or single words.

Irving's eccentric capitalization is retained when there can be no doubt the letter is in fact a capital and when there seems any possibility that a special nuance may have been intended. However, in instances where such intent seems unlikely, as in the capitalization of "Hares" in the phrase "Hares and pheasants" (99.1), the capital letter is emended to lower case.

Unusual spellings—"sopha," "gallopped," "lanthorn," "taylor," "frolicks," to single out but a few—are generally retained unless dictionaries of the early nineteenth century and the record of the *Oxford English Dictionary* show them to be errors rather than reflections of Irving's preference for old-style picturesqueness or indications of the unfixed state of orthography in the period of Irving's youth or at the time of the composition of *Tales*.[44]

Some normalization of MS inconsistencies is called for, both as an aid to the reader and as a fulfillment of Irving's dominant intentions. For instance, he customarily capitalized street or place names, as in "Covent Garden," "Drury Lane," "Green Arbour Court." When he neglected to do so (see, for example, the emendation of "Drury lane" at 102.24), MS is emended to reflect his majority preference. The same is true in the emendation of "gayety" (104.12). It is spelled with a "y" only once in MS; all five other occurrences are "gaiety." Editorial intervention also normalizes MS "neighbor" and "favor" and their various permutations ("neighborhood," "neighboring," "favorite," etc.) to Irving's predominant British spelling.

The Editions

In the absence of MS, a printed copy-text chosen for its genetic closeness to MS is generally followed in accidentals since separating authorial from compositorial variation is in most cases manifestly impossible. However, in addition to correcting obvious error, an editor is obliged to act when he has reasonable grounds for believing the accidentals of the copy-text differ from the author's habits and he has some certainty of what the author's preference would have been in any particular instance. Because of Irving's inconsist-

44. Irving had access to many contemporary dictionaries, several of which are still in his library at Sunnyside, but there is no evidence he relied on any single dictionary as a standard of orthography at any point in his career. See Pochmann, *Mahomet*, pp. 607–609.

encies such instances are rare. There are only two categories of emendation which a knowledge of Irving's habits makes necessary and desirable. One is to restore spellings for which he demonstrated a strong preference. The other is to restore his characteristic treatment of compound or possible compound words. A careful analysis of his habits and preferences in extant MS for *Tales* serves as the most decisive but not the sole basis for emending accidentals in the printed editions. Also weighed in these decisions is evidence from a survey of Irving's practices in sample sections of other manuscripts, both contemporaneous and later: specifically *The Sketch Book* (1819), *Bracebridge Hall* (1822), his letters for 1823–1824, *Astoria* (1836), and *Oliver Goldsmith* (1849).

We cannot know in every instance whether a compositor altered Irving's spelling. We can suppose, as evidence from the manuscripts suggests, that he wrote "surprize" as often as "surprise" and "enterprize" slightly more often than "enterprise." But in such cases where Irving's usage vacillated, no emendation has been hazarded. The editor does however intervene to emend copy-text if another edition offers a spelling judged more consistent with Irving's typical practice, as in "briars" for "briers" at 92.24 and "conveniencies" for "conveniences" at 151.30. Likewise, when house style appears to account for a spelling inconsistent with Irving's habits, as it must in 1A's frequent use of "visiter" where Irving wrote "visitor" in MS and most certainly does in 1A's following Van Winkle's preference for "farther" when Irving customarily wrote "further,"[45] emendation is warranted. Only a handful of blanket emendations are made to bring spelling in the printed copy-texts in line with Irving's demonstrable preferences. Three prominent examples are "grey," "holyday," and "gaiety"; the first two Irving used consistently in his manuscripts for *Tales* and *Bracebridge Hall*; the third he used pervasively, almost without exception.

In the treatment of compound or possible compound words, the Twayne edition restores Irving's characteristically sparse use of hyphens. Extant MS for Part II contains only a dozen hyphenated compounds, but Irving's printers for 1E, and less often those for 1A, supplied hundreds of hyphens in phrases where Irving had none. A wider survey of Irving manuscripts confirms his tendency to write possible compounds as separate words or, less often, to join them into a single word. In a sample of over 1,700 compounds or possible compounds, Irving hyphenated only thirty-two, or less than two percent. While such a sample cannot tell us what Irving would have done in every instance, it provides a reliable basis for judging his preferences for many specific cases and for inferring his practice by analogy in many others.

45. Of "further," Van Winkle asks in his *Printers' Guide* (p. 78): "Why is this anomaly suffered to remain, when we have the regular degrees of comparison in—Far, farther, farthest?"

We can establish, for example, that he was five times as likely to write "now adays" as any other form (such as "now a days" or "nowadays") and, by available evidence, never hyphenated it. We can infer from nearly fifty occurrences of possible compounds with "well" (out of which only one is hyphenated and another written as a single word) that Irving preferred two words, as in "well known," "well made," "well received." In the same way we can establish his preferences for "old fashioned," "strong hold," "ale house," "fire place," "church yard," "tea kettle," and the like and for whole categories of possible compounds which he typically wrote as two words: those beginning with "half," with "ill," with "long," or ending with "looking."

It might be argued that whether to hyphenate in such instances was a decision Irving expected his printers to make, just as he expected them to supply apostrophes where needed. But the two are not analogous. The hyphen is in a different category precisely because there was little consistency or agreement on conventional usage in Irving's time. His printers overwhelmingly agreed on placing periods after abbreviations and apostrophes in contractions and possessives when Irving omitted them; conventional usage was strong and consistent on these points. There was no such agreement on the treatment of compound or possible compound words, as the discussion of "The Club of Queer Fellows" has demonstrated. Dictionaries, grammars, and printer's manuals from Irving's time until well into the twentieth century reflect widely divergent and unsystematic practices.[46] Even turn-of-the-century printer's manuals evince confusion: "When to set up two meeting words as two words, when to consolidate them in one word, when to connect them with a hyphen, are problems that the compositor has to decide almost every hour. He finds it very difficult to get authoritative instruction. There are not many authors who compound words uniformly, and the dictionaries differ, and sometimes are not consistent in rendering words or phrases of similar class. *Arm chair, arm-chair, armchair*, are suitable illustrations."[47] When it is possible, therefore, to know that Irving customarily wrote "arm chair," while 1E and occasionally 1A hyphenated it, Irving's practice is restored (as at 167.16 and 264.28).

As a practical matter, restoring Irving's known practice results in hundreds

46. Alice Morton Ball provides an instructive survey in her *Compounding in the English Language* (New York: H.W. Wilson, 1941), pp. 1–52. Her assessment is summarized in the Introduction: "Judging from the repeated statements of grammarians and lexicographers, there is probably no phase of English literature which has caused greater uncertainty of mind or resulted in greater inconsistency of practice than the compounding of words" (p. 1). According to Ball, the first attempt to bring system and method to bear on the "prevailing chaos" was F. Horace Teall's *The Compounding of English Words: When and Why Joining or Separation Is Preferable* (New York: John Ireland, 1891).

47. Theodore Low De Vinne, *The Practice of Typography: Correct Composition* (1901), quoted by Ball, pp. 32–33.

of such emendations in the copy-texts. Hyphens uncharacteristic of Irving are permitted to remain only when their removal would impede the reader's ease of understanding, as in the case of a string of adjectives otherwise unpunctuated: "a worthy fox-hunting old Baronet" (10.2). The decision to remove the majority of hyphens undoubtedly introduces some error, but it eliminates much more. And "even if the editorial choice in a specific case might be wrong, the hypothetical error is well within the limits of Irving's own practice, and is not the deliberate perpetuation of mere house style outside those limits."[48]

All departures from the copy-texts in both substantives and accidentals are recorded in the List of Emendations. Only one category of change, that made to the so-called appurtenances of the text, is not reported. No attempt is made to reproduce from the copy-texts the typographical arrangement of title and half-title pages, table of contents, story titles, display capitals and capitalized text letters at the beginning of stories, running heads, or footnote symbols. These matters are standardized for consistency with other volumes in *The Complete Works of Washington Irving*.

The text produced by the procedures and principles outlined above provides a version of the work different from any published before; it is a text closer in every respect to what Washington Irving actually wrote. The apparatus is designed to enable the reader to understand (and, perhaps, to reconsider) all editorial decisions. But more important to the needs of scholarship, the apparatus permits the reader to reconstruct the copy-texts and to trace as thoroughly as the evidence and his own inclinations permit the growth of *Tales of a Traveller* and its history of authorial change.

48. Haskell Springer, ed., *The Sketch Book of Geoffrey Crayon, Gent.* (Boston: Twayne, 1978), p. 379. Springer adopts much the same policy in his edition, based on a slightly different argument.

DISCUSSIONS OF ADOPTED READINGS

These entries discuss the rationale for emending or not emending the copy-text. To the left of the bracket are the page and line numbers and the reading of this edition; the commentary follows to the right. An *E* or *RS* following an entry directs the reader to the List of Emendations or the List of Rejected Substantives. The relevant texts are cited by the abbreviations listed on page 267.

3.13 well known] Irving consistently omitted the hyphen from this phrase and other adjective phrases with "well." See Textual Commentary, pp. 315–16, for a discussion of this and other instances where authorial preference accounts for blanket emendations. *E*

3.28 now adays] Emendation reflects Irving's dominant MS practice, which is adopted as a typical and intentional archaism. *E*

3.29 book making] When Irving's preference for the form of a specific compound or possible compound cannot be established on the basis of extant MS for this volume, the judgment is made by analogy or in conformity with his manuscript practice elsewhere. (See Textual Commentary, p. 315.) *E*

3.34 chair bottoms] The occurrence of the unhyphenated form in 2A serves merely as a precedent for an emendation which would have been made in any case on the basis of MS practice or by analogy with it. *E*

4.17 whence] ARE often reads "whence" or "thence" when other editions read "from whence" or "from thence." Because the deletion of "from" accords with Irving's known practice, copy-texts are emended here and in nine other instances: at 9.18, 84.14, 159.28–29, 184.34, 215.1, 226.9, 238.10, 249.4, and 253.25. (See Textual Commentary, p. 306.) *E*

10.25 which] The change from "that" to "which" (or "that" to "who") is typical of Irving's alterations in his MS and in his revisions on extant proof sheets. (See Textual Commentary, p. 305.) *E*

11.40 church yard] When another edition provides a single-word alternative equally characteristic of Irving as a two-word phrase, it is adopted, as at 12.23, where ARE's "wobegone" is substituted for 1A's "wo-begone." However, when Irving's use of two words is very consistent, as it is for "church yard," the single-word alternative (in this instance "churchyard" in 3A–1E) is ignored. *E*

12.15 to know] Evidence of authorial revision to emphasize the Irishman's dialect later in this paragraph increases the probability that Irving is responsible for adding the preposition and changing "upon" to "on" in the next line. *E*

12.23 wobegone] See DAR at 11.40. *E*

13.23 grey] Emendation restores Irving's distinct preference for this spelling in extant manuscripts from 1822–1824. *E*

13.28 ——,"] The comma separating quoted dialogue from the dialogue tag is added as a correction. Emendations to correct the accidentals of a printed copy-text are made sparingly and only when standard usage and the otherwise consistent practice of that text warrant them. *E*

14.9–10 cold looking noseless] Irving reordered the phrase for 1E, but 2A is cited as the source of the emendation since it best preserves the unhyphenated phrase of the copy-text. (See Textual Commentary, p. 306.) *E*

14.21 the house] Substitution in ARE of "the" for "his" is typical of Irving's retouching to avoid repetition. Note "his country" and "his old family" later in this sentence and in the next. *E*

15.12 Tuilleries] No emendation is made to correct 1A and 1E readings which undoubtedly reproduce Irving's spelling in MS. Although he occasionally spelled it as "Tuileries" (see *Letters*, I, 195), his more typical practice was to double the "l" as he does consistently in the sketch "The Tuilleries and Windsor Castle" in *Wolfert's Roost*, ed. Roberta Rosenberg (Boston: Twayne, 1979), pp. 128–30.

16.40 roused] Irving's stylistic refinements often reflect an attempt to distinguish between "rouse" and "arouse." Such variants are adopted as authorial here and at 45.40 and 174.7. *E*

17.23 towards] Irving consistently wrote "towards" in MS; however, his final "s" after a "d" is often easy to overlook. (See Textual Commentary, p. 303.) Copy-texts are emended here and twice more, at 21.17 and 35.13. This rationale also accounts for the emendation "homewards" at 254.2. *E*

17.39 visitor] Compositors for 1A consistently changed MS "visitor" to "visiter." This feature of 1A's house style is emended in every occurrence. *E*

21.24 further] Compositors for 1A changed MS "further" to "farther" six times in Part II, undoubtedly as a matter of house style. (See Textual Commentary, p. 315n.) Irving, however, almost always made a distinction between these two words, using "further" predominantly to denote time or degree and reserving "farther" to denote distance in space. *E*

23.6 fastenings] The alternative "fastnesses" is rejected as a misreading of Irving's handwriting. (See Textual Commentary, p. 308.) *RS*

24.29 Knight of the Post] Irving capitalized "Knights of the Post" in MS. (See "Poor Devil Author" at 87.10.) The capitals are adopted from 1E as probably authorial. *E*

27.15 Die duyvel] "Die" is accepted as a change Irving ordered for 2E. (See Textual Commentary, p. 293.) Irving was customarily alert to the sounds of dialect, and sound, more than accurate Dutch usage, may be what he sought to capture in this instance. *E*

28.21 Ally Croaker] Irving used the identical spelling for this heroine of Irish song in a letter to James Renwick in 1811. (See *Letters*, I, 329.) All editions except 1A have "Alley."

29.22–23 sandwich] All editions agree with the copy-text in this unusual but not unprecedented reading.

30.28 limb] Irving had reason to prefer "limb," both to accord in tone with "supernumerary" and to avoid repetition of "leg" with "legged" earlier in the sentence. He is judged responsible for the change reflected in 2E and adopted here. *E*

30.32–33 in one corner, like a dowager,] Irving is no doubt responsible for reversing the order of phrases, but the 1E reading, "in a corner . . .," was probably introduced by a compositor in resetting the line. For this reason 2A is the source of the emendation, since it best preserves Irving's intention. *E*

31.12–13 arrived at] Here and in a few other instances substantive readings originating in proof stages of 1E (i.e., present in 2A, 3A, 1F—editions set from 1E proofs) are adopted as authorial. Such cases are always discussed. "Arrived at" avoids the repetition of "hurried" and, more significantly, reinforces the insinuations elsewhere in the story of the true nature of the hotblooded Irishman's activities during the night. Moreover, the adopted reading appears as a penciled change in the Sunnyside copy of 1E believed to reflect changes Irving contemplated for 2E (see Textual Commentary, p. 293), though 2E agrees with 1E and 1A in "hurried to." *E*

31.42 gentleman with the haunted head] The preposition is adopted from 2A–1F as a correction. It is more in keeping with Irving's customary description of this character than 1E's "in"; see, for instance, at 41.20. *E*

33.20 shrank] Irving's manuscripts show that he vacillated in his choice of past tense forms for such verbs as "shrank"/"shrunk"; "sank"/"sunk"; "sang"/"sung"; "rang"/"rung." The emendation of "shrunk" to "shrank" is supported by evidence in his revisions for *A History of New York* (ARE 1848), where he changed "sunk" to "sank" and "rung" to "rang." *E*

35.16 Reason] Irving often formed "R" by enlarging and slightly elevating a lower case "r" above surrounding letters. His intention is easy to mistake. This fact and context of personification encourage the adoption of a capital letter here. *E*

36.12 Paris."] The footnote which follows in 1E was probably furnished with the original manuscript for the story Irving sent to John Murray on June 24, 1824. It was superseded by a virtually identical sentence in Irving's preface (4.19–23), written early in July 1824. The note is omitted here, as it is in all other editions. *E*

36.28 tonight] Although Irving's practice varied, he preferred the unhyphenated form, as he did for "today" and "tomorrow." *E*

36.33 So, gentlemen,] Irving occasionally neglected to set off direct address with commas, so 1A probably reproduces MS. The correction, however, is judged necessary and in keeping with Irving's and 1A's typical practice. *E*

37.27 mantle piece] Irving consistently preferred "mantle" to "mantel," as 1A reflects earlier at 27.34. As both spellings were acceptable in this period, copy-text is emended to respect Irving's preference. *E*

39.38 sopha] Copy-text reading is retained, despite its inconsistency with "sofa" at 40.4 and many times subsequently. 1A probably reproduces MS incongruities. Though Irving wrote "sopha" predominantly in his letters of this period, his spelling in manuscripts vacillated.

43.4–5 zendaletto] The variety of spellings among the printed editions suggests confusion on Irving's part or, more probably, the difficulty of others in reading his handwriting. T adopts the conventional spelling for the term which refers to a Venetian shawl and, by analogy with the shawl-like cloth extending off the hood of a gondola, came to signify the gondola itself. (See *OED.*) *E*

43.11 groupe] Copy-text undoubtedly preserves MS spelling. Irving spelled the word with an "e" as often as he spelled it more conventionally. No correction is warranted.

43.12 seats] Editorial intervention seems necessary to supply what Irving must have intended. If MS had "seat" (as 1A does), either the amanuensis or compositor for 1E was probably responsible for the reading "their seat," in an attempt to improve the sense of the passage. *E*

43.41 self occupied] All instances of possible compounds with "self" are written as two words in MS. In the survey of other Irving manuscripts described in the Textual Commentary (p. 315), a hyphenated form appears only once. MS practice is restored here and in other occurrences of "self" + word. *E*

44.20 gaiety] MS shows a consistent preference for this spelling. (See Textual Commentary, p. 314.) *E*

47.33–34 inclosed] Irving used this spelling and the "enclosed" of all other editions interchangeably, just as he did for "inquire"/"enquire"; "increase"/"encrease"; "imbitter"/"embitter." No emendation is warranted.

49.4 regarded] The reading is probably authorial. It originated in the proofs of 1E, as its presence in both 3A and 1F attests. Although Irving may have been responsible for changing the word to "considered" in 1E, he probably would not have done so if he recognized it would be repeated by "considered" in the next sentence. Since he seems to have wanted a replacement for 1A's "deemed," "regarded" is adopted as best serving the demands of context and Irving's habitual care to avoid repetition. *E*

54.12 by her mother] The phrase is adopted because Irving is no doubt responsible for adding it, perhaps to introduce a chaperone, but he created some confusion in doing so. The story makes no further mention of Bianca's mother, and, on the death of her father, she is portrayed as an orphan. Surely it is Bianca's father Irving had in mind when he wrote that her subsequent meeting with Ottavio is made painful because she remembers "in whose company she had been accustomed to behold" him. *E*

59.26–27 light form beaming forth in virgin white] The copy-text reading is retained to preserve Irving's original intention, which was thwarted by an error in 1E (the substitution of "light" for "white"), which in turn forced him in ARE to delete "light" in the first instance but keep it in the second. *RS*

71.28 the productions] MS for this story begins with these words at the top of a page numbered 4.

72.1 phraze] Irving often spelled this word with a "z." As it is impossible to know whether he consciously adopted it here or in any other instance for its archaic or exotic qualities or simply spelled it by sound rather than by convention, no emendation has been made.

72.26 Buckthorne] The name is written above an earlier designation, "Littlepage."

72.31 Buckthorne] The amanuensis for 1E may have overlooked the canceled "Mr" in MS. The line which cancels "Mr Littlepage" does not completely cross out the "M." *RS*

72.35 favourites] Emended here and in all other occurrences to accord with Irving's dominant preference for "-our" spellings. *E*

73.5 me;] The end of the clause occurs at the end of a line in MS, a location which apparently represented a pause for Irving. He frequently neglected to supply needed punctuation after phrases, clauses, and sentences which stop at the end of a line in MS. *E*

73.6 *Paragraph* "Not] Although he did not clearly indent this line, Irving intended to start a new paragraph, as the truncated line above indicates. MS is emended here and in nine subsequent instances in Part II where a new paragraph was intended but not executed: at 76.8, 81.6, 88.5, 105.20, 121.22, 122.36, 131.16, 132.39, and 134.40. *E*

76.16–17 way, my name is Thomas Dribble,] Irving left unusually wide spaces after "way" and "Dribble" in MS. The commas supplied by all editions are adopted to signify intended pauses. *E*

76.41 may.] The last two lines of MS 16 are partially eaten away, eliminating two words and parts of four others. All editions agree on the missing words and letters adopted here and at 76.42. *E*

77.3 threadbare] In all other occurrences in MS, "threadbare" appears as one word, as it does throughout other manuscripts surveyed. Copy-text is emended to reflect this preference. *E*

77.43 tall] Irving canceled both the word "wretched" and an ampersand after "tall." Compositors for 1A and, presumably, the amanuensis for 1E did not see or accept the cancellation of "&." *RS*

78.31 he] Oversight on Irving's part, probably as he was copying from another page, accounts for the omission of this necessary pronoun in MS. *E*

81.36 overstocked] On three occasions Irving lifted his pen after "over" but wrote the next word so close as to suggest he intended a single word, his preference in this and other manuscripts for participial compounds with "over." *E*

82.9 meantime] Irving wrote "mean time" and "meantime" in almost equal numbers in this and other manuscripts. His preference for the single word in this instance is indicated by the hyphens he supplied where it divided at the end of a line ("mean-/-time"). Only ARE has the single word; all other editions read "mean time."

83.6 hot heads] Irving's "t" occasionally resembles "t-"; in this instance, however, the MS hyphen after "hot" appears distinct. It has been removed by analogy with the immediately preceding "hot hearts," as it was in all other editions. *E*

83.25 shewn] Irving vacillated in his spelling of "shewn" and "shown," while his printers invariably set "shown." A journal entry suggests that on one occasion Irving ordered "shewn" changed to "showed" in a passage in *Bracebridge Hall* (*Journals*, III, 183). This evidence is too slight to warrant a conclusion about Irving's preference, so MS spellings are retained.

84.7 Hampstead] Irving consistently wrote "Hempstead" in MS, which English compositors corrected in every instance to "Hampstead," the conventional spelling both in Irving's time and at the time in which the story is set. *E*

84.13 free spirited] Although the words are joined in MS, Irving customarily wrote them separately, the practice adopted here. *E*

85.39 strongly] This and three other words, on which all editions agree, are absent from MS 42, whose upper right corner has been torn or eaten away. *E*

87.12 now adays] Irving wrote "now a days" only on this one occasion. Emendation reflects his otherwise consistent preference in MS for "now adays." (See DAR at 3.28.) *E*

92.18 Break neck Stairs] Emended on the model of MS practice at 77.35. *E*

92.24 briars] Emended to reflect Irving's customary spelling. *E*

94.5 anecdotes I had heard] Irving expanded two transitional paragraphs between "The Poor Devil Author" and "Buckthorne" for 1E's "A Practical Philosopher." MS is copy-text only for the first and last paragraphs of this sketch.

96.31 spire. Before] Irving canceled "and" after "spire;" and rewrote "Before" with a capital letter, though he neglected to replace the semicolon after "spire" with a period. 1A read his intention correctly and is the source of the emended punctuation. *E*

98.2 schoolmaster;] Irving put a period after "schoolmaster" but canceled the beginning of a new sentence ("They were very"), deciding instead to resume the sequential clauses of the previous sentence. He neglected to alter the punctuation. *E*

99.24 bull's] Irving substituted "Bulls" for "cows" in MS, a change which makes sense in context, the likening of Iron John's wig to "cow's tail" and his leathery face to "bull's hide." It is possible that 1E's "cow's hide" results from scribal error or from Irving's having altered the passage in MS after it had been copied. *RS & E*

101.13–18 attractive . . . . subject] The four sentences adopted from 1E represent a revision judged to have occurred before William Gifford's critique caused Irving to alter other sections of this story. Gifford, in fact, commented to Murray, "All that Buckthorne says of his mother is beautiful—all that he says of his father, his uncle, his cousin is also very good indeed" (quoted by McClary, p. 58n). *E*

101.22 almost seventeen] The slight change in Buckthorne's age is no doubt authorial. It does, however, create an inconsistency with the portrayal of him at 112.5 as "a stripling of little more than sixteen." *E*

101.27 on] Irving wrote "on" above "of" in MS, but neglected to cancel "of." *E*

102.13 holyday] This single occurrence of MS "holiday" is emended to Irving's otherwise consistent preference and his original spelling. The "i" is substituted in a darker ink over the original "y" in MS. *E*

104.11 turned] Irving canceled "to be" but failed to cancel the accompanying "seemed" on the line above. *E*

105.1 of] Irving wrote "of" over "in" as he substituted "of a sudden" for "in a twinkling." The amanuensis for 1E is very probably responsible for the conflated misreading "on." *RS*

106.21 schoolmaster.] The intended period occurs in MS in pencil. Irving changed "but" to "But" immediately afterwards but neglected to ink over the necessary change in punctuation. *E*

106.33 consoled ourselves with] Irving neglected to cancel "made up" after he had substituted "consoled ourselves with" above it. Only 1A adequately reproduces his intention. (See Textual Commentary, p. 307.) *E*

107.11 fascination] Irving neglected to cancel "power" after he had substituted "fascination" above it. (See Textual Commentary, p. 307.) *E*

107.22 life] In MS, "which" is canceled in pencil after "life"; 1A ignored the cancellation, but it is accepted here as typical of Irving's alterations. *E*

109.1 saddle.] Irving neglected to cancel "them" in the otherwise canceled phrase after "saddle": "and for the other to throw them out." *E*

110.31 was a party] MS has "were" in pencil above "was" and "party" substituted in ink above "number." Apparently Irving chose to change the noun rather than the verb, probably motivated to prevent the repetition with "number" in the next sentence. This may have been a late change unrecorded by the amanuensis for 1E. *RS*

110.37 whispering her companions] Such constructions are common in the eighteenth-century literature Irving admired. MS reading is retained, and 1E's "whispering to" rejected as compositorial. *RS*

112.21 playing and] The omission of "playing and" in 1E probably stems from scribal error in mistaking Irving's "and fluttering," inserted above "playing," as a substitution rather than an addition; the ampersand is small and easy to overlook. *RS*

113.37 sewing] MS spelling is retained in the possibility that Irving intended to suggest the form of pronunciation. *RS*

114.17 overrun] See DAR at 81.36. *E*

114.33 spirit, however,] Irving set off "however" in its original position in the sentence but neglected to add commas when he changed its place and inserted it above the line after "spirit." *E*

115.15–17 dirt . . . . seat.] Sixteen paragraphs "thrown in" to placate William Gifford, who had censured Irving for "ridiculing the provincial clergy," are rejected here. (See Textual Commentary, pp. 308–12.) *RS*

115.18–22 I had . . . . fell] In his revisions to satisfy William Gifford, Irving reversed the order of two paragraphs and expanded the second to include a disclaimer about the latter-day Oxford's freedom from the "feuds of Town and Gown.'" The clause rejected at this point actually follows in 3A–1E the entry in the List of Rejected Substantives at 116.1–7. *RS*

115.27 fenced, . . . hunted] The expanded series is adopted from 1E as a revision not motivated by Gifford's censorship and probably made before August 4, 1824, while Irving was retouching and expanding the story to suit his own goals. *E*

115.27 rooms] Irving initially wrote "room," then substituted "chambers" above it; "chambers" was subsequently canceled in pencil and "rooms" penciled in. The substitution is judged authorial and so adopted. *E*

116.1–7 I . . . . hours.] See DAR at 115.18–22. *RS*

116.14 idler?] The question mark appears in pencil in MS over an ink period. *E*

118.4 our plans] Irving earlier canceled a reference to "a ladder of ropes" but did not detect a parallel inconsistency in Buckthorne's manner of entry until he substituted "our plans" for "the ladder of ropes" in the 1E proofs. *E*

118.16 ill spelled] The words are joined in MS, but Irving left sufficient distance between the "l" and the "s" to warrant the supposition he intended two words. *E*

118.38 home, and found] Alterations in this section about Buckthorne's father are judged to have occurred before Irving learned of William Gifford's objections to the story. See DAR at 101.13–18. *E*

120.25 good humouredly] Irving inadvertently connected the words in MS; he customarily wrote them separately. *E*

123.3 a cathedral town] The lengthy section rejected here represents Irving's attempt to satisfy William Gifford's objections. (See Textual Commentary, pp. 308–12.) Here, as elsewhere, from 122.4 to 125.7, MS readings are retained to preserve Irving's original uninfluenced intent. *RS*

124.12–13 I . . . evening] See DAR at 123.3. The portrait of Buckthorne's clerical critic, rejected here in favor of MS, bears no small resemblance to William Gifford and may carry some of the frustration Irving felt when "marring the story in compliance with [his] critique" (see Textual Commentary, p. 311). *RS*

126.21–22 My presence, however,] Irving apparently went back to add commas to set off "however" but inadvertently misplaced them around "presence." *E*

132.11 on many points on which] MS reading is retained. The 3A–1E substitution "in many" probably results from a scribal misreading, an error which in turn forced the successive refinements, "points wherein" and "points where." *RS*

133.31 welcome."] Irving often set off indirect quotations with quotation marks. In this case he neglected to close the quotation marks he opened at "step" earlier in the sentence. *E*

134.39 table—] Irving appears to have converted a period into a dash. The mark, however, is smudged and transcription uncertain. All other editions have a period.

135.22 gentlemanlike] Irving typically combined the two words; they are written so close together in this instance as to suggest he intended to join them. *E*

136.30 I stepped] Flimsey becomes the narrator at this point, making MS and 1E quotation marks before "I" superfluous. 1E drops them after seven paragraphs; 2E drops them here, as all other editions do. *E*

138.1 sir] Although Flimsey has two auditors, the singular form of address is used here and for the remainder of the story. 1E "corrects" only this one occurrence; no emendation is warranted. *RS*

139.1 overrun] See DAR at 81.36. *E*

140.16 theatre;] Authorial revisions in this sentence and the next three paragraphs (140.22–141.8) occurred after the proofs of 1E had been sent to America for preparation of 3A. They are rejected as part of the alterations Irving made to satisfy William Gifford. (See Textual Commentary, pp. 287–88 and 308–12.) *RS*

142.25 Shakespeare] Spelling is emended to reflect Irving's consistent preference in MS. *E*

143.20 former] The 1A variant "famous" comes from an error in Peter Irving's recopying of this passage on a separate slip of paper tipped in over his brother's heavily interlined version at the top of MS 181. Compositors for 1A also followed Peter's copy in omitting the word "familiar" in the next sentence. *RS*

144.10 tail.] The prepositional phrase added in 1E after "tail" is canceled in MS. *RS*

144.24 slip-slop] Irving hyphenated the phrase in two subsequent occurrences in this paragraph. Emendation reflects this preference. *E*

144.25 actors] Either through oversight or a change in his intentions midsentence, Irving wrote "patrons" first and did not cancel it. The word "actor" was written above it in ink and later canceled; "actors"—the appropriate subject of the sentence—appears in pencil, probably in Peter Irving's handwriting, below "patrons." *E*

150.36–37 ribbands] Emendation reflects Irving's consistent spelling of this word. Compare 1A's "ribbands" in the original passage at 157.37 in the List of Emendations. *E*

151.18 serve] This is one of several instances in Part III where editions descending from the 1E proofs contain superior and possibly authorial readings not reflected in 1E. Because Irving revised Part III late in the publishing process, haste to bring out both volumes on August 25 may have caused 1E compositors to overlook or ignore some of Irving's last-minute stylistic changes. However, because Irving could have been responsible for rescinding such changes, these variants are treated cautiously, adopted sparingly, and always explained. In this instance, "serve" is adopted from 3A–1F as a correction more suited to the demands of the sentence for present tense than 1E's "served." *E*

152.32 gruff] The revisions Irving undertook to satisfy Gifford's objections to the portrait of the Englishman begin with the alterations in this sentence, such as the substitution of "bluff" for 1A's "gruff." Such modifications are rejected. (See Textual Commentary, pp. 308–12.) *RS*

156.11 kinds] The plural is accepted as an emendation from ARE because it restores the reading of the original passage in 1A; see List of Emendations at 156.40–42. *E*

157.24 improvvisatore] Emendation substitutes the spelling used consistently in 1A. *E*

167.40 court yard] Irving consistently wrote two words, the form adopted here as preferable to 1E's "court-yard" and ARE's alternative "courtyard." *E*

171.5 were] The plural verb is adopted as a correction to agree with "apartments." *E*

175.25 linen draper and a green grocer] Emended on the model of an identical passage in 1A, which Irving deleted from "The Adventure of the Little Antiquary." See List of Emendations at 163.36–164.14. *E*

180.16 pursuits] Irving's habitual care to avoid repetition increases the likelihood that he wished to substitute "pursuits" for "occupation," which repeats "occupations" in the previous sentence. See DAR at 151.18. *E*

194.18 THE STORY] 1E's "STORY" is rejected as an anomaly. Its Table of Contents reads "THE STORY." *RS*

200.28 anxious] Irving probably intended to substitute "anxious" for "uneasy," which is repeated early in the next sentence. See DAR at 180.16. *E*

202.17–25 The Englishman . . . . are!"] The four paragraphs rejected from
1E which temper "the fair Venetian's" pique at the Englishman and provide a husbandly check to undercut the force of her accusation are rejected as revisions to satisfy Gifford. Irving's changes tend to divert the
emphasis from the Englishman's behavior to her perception of it. *RS*

202.26 THE ADVENTURE OF THE ENGLISHMAN] The title is adopted
from 1E. The Table of Contents for 1A and its running heads call this
section "The Route to Fondi," but no separate title precedes the tale. *E*

206.6–14 He . . . . charge.] Additions in this section are adopted from 1E
because they carry out Irving's original intentions for this story as he described them to Murray. (See Textual Commentary, p. 310.) *E*

212.11 sculls] Irving was inconsistent in his spelling of this word, so no attempt has been made to normalize 1E's "sculls" with 1A's generally consistent "skull"/"skulls."

212.13 Pylorus] The editions set from proofs for 1E and, later, 2E correct
the spelling to "Pelorus." However, 1E's "Pylorus" undoubtedly preserves
Irving's spelling. Compare his journal entry in 1810, "Pylorus" (*Journals*,
II, 22), and his reference in a letter in 1804 to "the Promontory of Pylorus
or Pelorus" (*Letters*, I, 153). Note also "Pylorus" in a passage deleted from
1A: List of Emendations at 212.25. *RS*

216.36 Robert Kidd] A false Christian name is given in some versions of the
ballad because William Kidd died in disgrace. The substitution of "Captain" for "Robert" in 3A–1E may have been a compositorial or editorial
"correction." *RS*

221.26 set] Although it is not likely Irving was directly responsible for this
variant adopted from 1Eb, it is accepted because it accords with parallel
changes at 221.19 and 222.2 for which Irving is credited. *E*

229.31 half blown rosebud] Irving probably wrote "rose bud," which all editions hyphenated. Because he occasionally combined the two words, that
form is adopted here as more characteristic of the author than a hyphenated compound and because some compromise of the sort is desirable to
facilitate reading. *E*

230.26 sly] The copy-text reading is retained, despite 1E's substitution,
"shy." Its sense in context depends on whether Amy's "bridling" is construed as restraint or flirtation. Given her "stolen" interviews with Dirk
Waldron subsequently, Irving may have originally written and intended
"sly." *RS*

237.34 grizzly] Other manuscripts show that Irving wrote "grizly" (1A's reading) for both "grizzly" and "grisly." A distinction is required. ARE's "grisly"
is rejected as less suited to the context than 1E's "grizzly." *E & RS*

240.32–33 resistance. They] The punctuation is adopted from 3A–1E as a
correction. *E*

243.29 Sam,] The adopted punctuation prevents a misreading. *E*

251.43 Bloomen-dael] In editions of *A History of New York* this place name is spelled "Bloemen-dael" and "Bloemen Dael." However, as 1A–1E concur in "Bloomen-dael," no emendation has been made.

254.19 grisly] MS probably read "grizly"; see DAR at 237.34. 1A converted it to "grizzly" and 1E to "grisly," the meaning most suited to the context. It is emended again at 254.29. *E*

LIST OF EMENDATIONS

This list records all changes in the copy-texts, substantive and accidental. The numbers before each entry indicate page and line in this edition. Only typographical rules or spaces and running heads are omitted from the line count. The reading to the left of the bracket is the reading of this text, an emendation of the copy-text. The source of the emendation is identified by symbol after the bracket and is followed by symbols for all relevant texts which duplicate the source. The reading after the semicolon is the rejected reading of the copy-text. The symbol for the copy-text is followed by symbols for any other texts in which that reading appears. When a reading in more than one edition serves as a precedent for an emendation which would have been made in any case to correct error or to reflect manuscript practice, the designation before the semicolon is inclusive—e.g., 2A–1E. (The symbols used are explained in the List of Abbreviations, p. 267.) In some instances, differences in accidentals among texts agreeing substantively are not recorded. The entry at 52.26–28, for example, records a sentence adopted from 1E in which 2A–1F agree substantively. The emendation follows the accidentals of 1E, so no attempt has been made to indicate that 2A, 3A, and ARE omit one of the sentence's three commas.

The swung (wavy) dash ~ is used when a word is repeated after the bracket; the caret ∧ indicates that a mark of punctuation is omitted. T signifies that an emendation has been made on the authority of the editor, without precedent in other editions. Many of these emendations, as well as other decisions to emend or not to emend, are treated in the Discussions of Adopted Readings. An asterisk preceding the page and line numbers refers the reader to explanation in that section.

TO THE READER

*3.13	well known] T; ~-~ 1E, 2A–1F
*3.28	now adays] T; nowadays 1E; now-a-days 2A–1F
*3.29	book making] T; ~-~ 1E, 2A–1F
*3.34	chair bottoms] 2A; ~-~ 1E, 3A–1F
3.40	story telling] T; ~-~ 1E, 2A–1F
3.40	story reading] T; ~-~ 1E, 2A–1F
*4.17	whence] ARE; from ~ 1E, 2A–1F
4.34	ill packed] T; ~-~ 1E, 2A–1F
4.34	travelling trunk] 2A–ARE; ~-~ 1E, 1F

THE GREAT UNKNOWN

9.1   THE GREAT UNKNOWN] 1E, 2A–1F; *omitted* 1A

9.2   ∧The] 1E, 2A–1F; [~ 1A

9.9   Waverley] 1Eb, 3A–1F; Waverly 1A, 2A, 1Ea

9.9   novel] 1E, 2A–1F; romance 1A

9.18   whence] ARE; from ~ 1A, 2A–1E

9.18   comes.] 1E, 2A–1F; ~. He who keeps up such a wonderful and whimsical incognito: whom nobody knows, and yet whom every body thinks he can swear to. 1A

9.25   Waverley] 1Eb, 3A–1F; Waverly 1A, 2A, 1Ea

9.34   ever.∧] 1E, 2A–1F; ~.] 1A

9.35–36 Having . . . stories.] 1E, 2A–1F; *omitted* 1A

THE HUNTING DINNER

10.1   THE] 1E, 3A–1F; A 1A, 2A

10.12   Nimrod] 1E, 2A–1F; Jehu 1A

10.21   tea kettle] T; ~-~ 1A, 2A–1E

*10.25   which] 1E, 2A–1F; that 1A

10.29   long winded] T; ~-~ 1A, 2A–1E

10.37–38 old fashioned] T; ~-~ 1A, 2A–1E

11.12   our] 1E, 2A–1F; mine 1A

11.15   gentlemen] 1E, 2A–1F; guests 1A

11.17   emergencies; so, after] 1E, 2A–1F; emergencies. After 1A

11.24   rosy faced] T; ~-~ 1A, 2A–1E

11.37   good looking] T; ~ ~ 1A, 2A–1E

11.39   long waisted] T; ~-~ 1A, 2A–1E

*11.40   church yard] T; ~-~ 1A, 2A; churchyard 3A–1E

11.43   during] 1E, 2A–1F; throughout 1A

12.1   have] 1E, 2A–1F; seem to ~ 1A

*12.15   to know] 1E, 2A–1F; know 1A

12.16   on] 1E, 2A–1F; upon 1A

12.17   But i'faith] 1E, 2A–1F; But, egad 1A

12.17   we are] 1E, 3A–1F; we're 1A, 2A

12.18   Pray] 1E, 2A–1F; Faith 1A

12.18   haven't] 1E, 3A–1F; have'nt 1A, 2A

*12.23   wobegone] ARE; wo-begone 1A, 2A–1E

12.40   tell . . . . He] 1E, 2A–1F; tell when I was a boy. But whether as having happened to himself or to another, I cannot recollect. But no matter, it's very likely it happened to himself, for he 1A

12.42   singular."] 1E, 2A–1F; ~. At any rate, we will suppose it happened to himself." 1A

THE ADVENTURE OF MY UNCLE

13.10	some] 1E, 2A–1F; a long 1A
13.10	passed] ARE; had ~ 1A, 2A–1E
13.12	cordially] ARE; ~ together 1A, 2A–1E
13.16	choicer than] ARE; ~ then, ~ 1A, 2A–1E
*13.23	grey] 1E; gray 1A, 2A–1F
*13.28	——,"] 2A–1E; ——∧" 1A
13.32	who] 1E, 2A–1F; that 1A
13.36	well known] T; ~-~ 1A, 2A–1E
13.37	put] 1E, 2A–1F; take 1A
14.1	provincial] 1E, 2A–1F; country 1A
14.6	now adays] T; now-a-days 1A, 2A–1F; nowadays 1E
*14.9–10	cold looking noseless] 2A (~-~ ~ 3A–1E); noseless cold looking 1A
14.10	statues] 1E, 3A–1F; ~ without any clothing 1A, 2A
*14.21	the house] ARE; his ~ 1A, 2A–1E
14.23	which] 1E, 2A–1F; that 1A
14.27	the Fourth] 1E, 3A–1F; IV. 1A, 2A
14.29	bows,] 1E, 2A–1F; ~∧ to show; 1A
14.30	to show,] 1E, 2A–1F; *omitted* 1A
14.30	which] 1E, 2A–1F; that 1A
14.35	shanks, and his] 1E, 3A–1F; shanks; his 1A, 2A
14.36	ear locks] T; ~-~ 1A, 2A–1E
14.37	could] 1E, 2A–1F; would 1A
15.2	stuck] ARE; that were ~ 1A, 2A–1E
15.3	flashed] 1E, 2A–1F; sparkled 1A
15.4	two handled] T; ~-~ 1A, 2A–1E
15.15	*sans culottes*] 3A–1E; ~-~ 1A, 2A
15.21	strong hold] 3A–1E; stronghold 1A, 2A; ~-~ ARE
15.30	it] 1E, 2A–1F; ~ during the wars of the League 1A
15.33	long faced] T; ~-~ 1A, 2A–1E
15.33	long bodied] T; ~-~ 1A, 2A–1E
15.41	ill fitted] T; ~-~ 1A, 2A–1E
16.13	wild looking] T; ~-~ 1A, 2A–1E
16.14	gusty,] 1E, 2A–1F; ~, something like the present, 1A
16.18–19	wide mouthed] T; ~-~ 1A, 2A–1E
16.20	long legged] T; ~-~ 1A, 2A–1E
16.24	thinking] 1E, 2A–1F; chuckling to think 1A
16.25	lodging] 1E, 2A–1F; lodgings 1A
*16.40	roused] ARE; aroused 1A, 2A–1E
16.40	footsteps] ARE; ~ that appeared to be 1A, 2A–1E
16.42	supposing this] ARE; ~ that ~ might be 1A, 2A–1E
17.3	stately] ARE; ~ in person 1A, 2A–1E

17.3	a commanding] ARE; ~ most ~ 1A, 3A–1E; the most ~ 2A
17.4–5	fire place] T; ~-~ 1A, 2A–1E; fireplace ARE
*17.23	towards] 1E, 2A–1F; toward 1A
*17.39	visitor] 2A–1E; visiter 1A, 3A
17.43–18.1	complimentary, . . . it] ARE; ~: *Paragraph* "It 1A, 2A–1E
18.1	*bonnes*] 1E, 2A–1F; *braves* 1A
18.2	Monsieur.ʌ] ARE; ~." 1A, 2A–1E
18.10	which] 1E, 2A–1F; that 1A
18.15	blue eyed] T, ~-~ 1A, 2A–1E
18.21	uncle . . . beholding] 1E, 2A–1F; uncle's eye rested on 1A
18.22	portrait,] ARE; ~, which struck him as being 1A; ~, which seemed to him 2A–1E
18.22	visitor] ARE–1E; visiter 1A, 2A, 3A
18.36	Port Cocheres] 1E, 2A–1F; Pertcocheres 1A
18.43	Castle] 1E, 2A–1F; chateau 1A
18.43	Dieppe.] 1E, 2A–1F; ~, and in imminent danger of falling into their hands. 1A
19.3–6	You . . . Dieppe.] 1E, 2A–1F; *omitted* 1A
19.7–9	The . . . hill.] 1E, 2A–1F; *omitted* 1A
19.14	"The] 3A–1E; ʌ~ 1A, 2A
19.17	which] ARE; that 1A, 2A–1E
19.39	broad shouldered] T; ~-~ 1A, 2A–1E
19.40	visitor] ARE–1E; visiter 1A, 2A, 3A
19.42	weather beaten] T; ~-~ 1A, 2A–1E
19.42	travel stained] T; ~-~ 1A, 2A–1E
20.15	very] 1E, 2A–1F; *omitted* 1A
20.36	sallow] 1E, 2A–1F; sullen 1A
21.10	snuff box] T; ~-~ 1A, 2A–1E
21.10	this] 1E, 2A–1F; it 1A
21.14	snuff box] T; ~-~ 1A, 2A–1E
21.17	towards] 1E, 3A–1F; toward 1A, 2A
21.20	narration] 1E, 2A–1F; narrative 1A
*21.24	further] 1E, 1F; farther 1A, 2A–ARE
21.29	the ghost . . . been] 1E, 2A–1F; it was 1A
21.36	countenance] 1Ab–1E; counteuance 1Aa
21.36	which] ARE; that 1A, 2A–1E
22.2	not] 1E, 2A–1F; ~ quite 1A
22.3	it."] 2A–1E; ~.ʌ 1A, 3A

THE ADVENTURE OF MY AUNT

22.11	prescriptions,] 1E, 2A–1F; ~, *willy nilly*, 1A
22.22	wore] ARE; she ~ 1A, 2A–1E
22.23	had] ARE; she ~ 1A, 2A–1E

22.32	grey] T; gray 1A, 2A–1E
22.35	pagan looking] T; ~-~ 1A, 2A–1E
22.36	servants'] 3A–1E; servant's 1A, 2A
22.37	picked] ARE; they had ~ 1A, 2A–1E
23.1	gloomy,] 1E, 2A–1F; forlorn 1A
23.1	black looking] T; ~-~ 1A, 2A–1E
23.1	lady's] 2A–1E; ladies' 1A
23.3	kind hearted] T; ~-~ 1A, 2A–1E
23.5	aunt was] ARE; aunt, herself, seemed to be 1A, 2A–1E
23.5	going] ARE; she went 1A, 2A–1E
23.12	somewhat] 1E, 2A–1F; a little 1A
23.14	whether] 1E, 2A–1F; if 1A
23.19	hanging] ARE; which had been hung 1A, 2A–1E
23.21	then] 1E, 2A–1F; *omitted* 1A
23.21–22	dress, . . . squire.] 1E, 2A–1F; dress. 1A
23.22–23	long drawn] 3A–1E; ~-~ 1A, 2A, ARE
23.28	head,] 1E, 2A–1F; ~, giving a knowing wink on the sound side of his visage— 1A
23.33	herself] 1E, 2A–1F; ~ cautiously 1A
23.42	an] 1E, 2A–1F; a favourite 1A
24.1	articles, one] T (~∧ ~ 2A–1E); ~∧ leisurely, ~ 1A
24.6	weapons first at] ARE; first weapons that came to 1A; weapons that first came to 2A–1E
24.10	hand.] 2A–1E; ~∧ 1A
24.12–13	maid, . . . brought] 1E, 2A–1F; maid brought 1A
24.13	rear,] 1E, 2A–1F; ~, dreading to stay alone in the servant's hall, 1A
24.19	issued] 1E, 2A–1F; was heard 1A
24.21	footman for support.] 1E, 2A–1F; footman. 1A
24.24	round shouldered] T; ~-~ 1A, 2A–1E
24.24	black bearded] T; ~-~ 1A, 2A–1E
*24.29	Knight] 1E, 2A–1F; knight 1A
24.29	Post] 1E, 3A–1F; post 1A, 2A
24.40	beetle browed] T; ~-~ 1A, 2A–1E
25.13	nodding] 1E, 2A–1F; ~ his head 1A
25.23	given] 1E, 2A–1F; been giving 1A
25.24	chapter] 1E, 2A–1F; ~ too, 1A

THE BOLD DRAGOON, OR
THE ADVENTURE OF MY GRANDFATHER

| 26.9 | same.] 1Ab–1E; ~∧ 1Aa |
| 26.10 | old fashioned] T; ~-~ 1A, 2A–1E |

26.36	long legged] T; ~-~ 1A, 2A–1E
27.10	bottle nosed] T; ~-~ 1A, 2A–1E
*27.15	Die] 2E, 2A–1F; Dcr 1A, 1E; De ARE
27.17	at all] ARE; ~ ~, at all, 1A, 2A; ~ ~, at all 1Ea; ~ ~ at all 3A–1Eb
27.17	did not] ARE; ~ ~ himself 1A, 2A–1E
27.26	akimbo—] 2A (~,— ARE; a-kimbo, 3A–1E); ~, slapped his broad thigh with the other hand— 1A
27.28	As . . . emphasis] 1E, 2A–1F; My grandfather had on a tight pair of buckskins 1A
27.33	and] 1E, 2A–1F; *omitted* 1A
27.34	mantle piece] T; ~-~ 1A, 2A, 3A; mantel-~ ARE–1E
27.35	tea pots] T; ~-~ 1A, 2A; teapots 3A–1E
27.42	further] 1E, 2A–1F; farther 1A
28.11	Sea] 3A–1E; sea 1A, 2A
28.14	good humoured] 2A; ~-~ 1A, 3A–1E
28.20	landlord] 1E, 2A–1F; men 1A
28.20	shoulder] 1E, 2A–1F; shoulders 1A
28.20	romped . . . maid] 1E, 2A–1F; tickled the women under the ribs 1A
28.20	bar maid] 2A; ~-~ 1E, 3A–1F
28.23–24	swaggered . . . sword] 1E, 2A–1F; turned his back and swaggered along, his tight jacket setting off his broad shoulders and plump buckskins, and his long sword 1A
28.24–25	looked . . . and] 1E, 2A–1F; *omitted* 1A
28.33	sat] 1E, 2A–1F; had 1A
28.33	a] 1E, 3A–1F; for 1A, 2A
28.36	a] 2A–1E; ~ a 1A
28.40	large] 1E, 2A–1F; huge 1A
29.2	old fashioned] T; ~-~ 1A, 2A–1E
29.3	old times] T; ~-~ 1A, 2A–1E
29.25	time] 1E, 2A–1F; while 1A
29.29	bull frogs] T; ~-~ 1A, 2A, ARE; bullfrogs 3A–1E
29.40	sure—or] 1E, 3A–1F; ~," replied the other, "~ 1A, 2A
30.2	heard] 2A–1E; heared 1A
30.3	were] 1E, 2A–1F; was 1A
30.6	open] 1E, 3A–1F; ajar 1A, 2A
30.8	Anthony himself] 1E, 2A–1F; Anthony 1A
30.16	instrument] 1E, 2A–1F; instruments 1A
30.18	long backed] T; ~-~ 1A, 2A–1E
30.18	bandy legged] T; ~-~ 1A, 2A–1E
30.26	long bodied] T; ~-~ 1A, 2A–1E
30.27	three legged] T; ~-~ 1A, 2A–1E

*30.28   limb] 2E, 2A–1F; leg 1A, 1E
30.30   motion] 1E, 2A–1F; ~, capering about 1A
*30.32–33   in one . . . dowager,] 2A (in a . . . dowager, 3A–1E); like a
                 dowager, in one corner, 1A
30.39   whirr] 1E, 2A–1F; whizz 1A
31.11   below] 1E, 2A–1F; just ~ 1A
*31.12–13   arrived at] 2A–1F; hurried to 1A, 1E
31.16   laid] ARE; lain 1A, 2A–1E
31.17   deuce] 1E, 2A–1F; devil 1A
31.19   broken . . . press] 1E, 2A–1F; prostrate clothes press, and
                 the broken handles, 1A
31.19   clothes press] T; ~-~ 1E, 2A–1F
31.37   which] 1E, 3A–1F; that 1A, 2A
31.41–32.3   There . . . . nature.”] 1E, 2A–1F; *omitted* 1A
*31.42   with] 2A–1F; in 1E

THE ADVENTURE OF THE GERMAN STUDENT

32.22   malady] ARE; ~ that was 1E, 2A–1F
32.35   charnel house] T; ~-~ 1E, 2A–1F
33.6–7   a dream produced] ARE; he had ~ ~ which ~ 1E, 2A–1F
33.8   made] ARE; it ~ 1E, 2A–1F
*33.20   shrank] ARE; shrunk 1E, 2A–1F
34.39   approaching] ARE; that approached 1E, 2A–1F
35.13   towards] ARE; toward 1E, 2A–1F
*35.16   Reason] 2A–1F; reason 1E
35.31   sank] ARE; sunk 1E, 2A–1F
36.12   Paris.”] 2E, 2A–1F; ~.” *Paragraph* *The latter part of the
                 above story is founded on an anecdote related to me, and
                 said to exist in print in French. I have not met with it in
                 print. 1E

THE ADVENTURE OF THE MYSTERIOUS PICTURE

36.15   subject] 1E, 2A–1F; topic 1A
36.16   strange] 1E, 3A–1F; ghost 1A, 2A
36.17   fox hunter] T; ~-~ 1A, 2A–1E
36.19   long drawn] T; ~-~ 1A, 2A–1E
36.26   ghost.”] 2A–1E; ~.∧ 1A
*36.28   tonight] T; to-night 1A, 2A–1E
*36.33   So, gentlemen,] 2A–1E; ~∧ ~∧ 1A
37.10   old fashioned] T; ~-~ 1A, 2A–1E
37.22   which] ARE; that 1A, 2A–1E
37.23   which] ARE; that 1A, 2A–1E

*37.27	mantle piece] T; mantel ~ 1A, 2A; mantel-~ 3A–1E
37.32	staring] ARE; that appeared to be ~ 1A, 2A–1E
37.32	with] ARE; and ~ 1A, 2A–1E
37.41	the illusion] 1E, 3A–1F; this allusion 1A, 2A
37.42	and blood] 1E, 2A–1F; *omitted* 1A
38.31	in] ARE; from 1A, 2A–1E
38.43	quaint] 1E, 2A–1F; ~ old 1A
38.43	more] 1E, 3A–1F; *omitted* 1A, 2A
39.10	in] 1E, 3A–1F; ~ my 1A, 2A
39.14	that] 1E, 2A–1F; this 1A
39.15	gloom] 1E, 2A–1F; darkness 1A
39.16	magnify] 1E, 2A–1F; give it additional power, and to mul-tiply 1A
39.16	hanging] 1E, 2A–1F; hovering 1A
39.18	There] ARE; And there 1A, 2A–1E
39.23	in a] 1E, 2A–1F; ~ such ~ 1A
39.27	me.] 1Ab–1E; ~∧ 1Aa
39.31	ill] 1E, 2A–1F; *omitted* 1A
39.34	wobegone] ARE; wo-begone 1A, 2A–1E
40.7	further] 1E, 3A–1F; farther 1A, 2A
40.28	joke] 1E, 2A–1F; jokes 1A
40.41	the] 1E, 2A–1F; all ~ 1A
40.43	fox hunters] T; ~-~ 1A, 2A–1E
41.1	on the subject] 1E, 2A–1F; at my expense 1A
41.2	nettled.] 1Ab–1E; ~∧ 1Aa
41.8	smile,] 3A–1E; ~∧ 1A, 2A
41.8	there's] 1E, 2A–1F; there is 1A
41.21	nose] 1E, 2A–1F; waggish ~ 1A
41.38	in my house] 1E, 3A–1F; *omitted* 1A, 2A
42.5	to see] 1E, 2A–1F; *omitted* 1A
42.12	denied] 1E, 2A–1F; precluded 1A
42.13	towards] 1E, 2A–1F; beside 1A

THE ADVENTURE OF THE MYSTERIOUS STRANGER

42.19	appears] 1E, 2A–1F; ~ to be 1A
42.20	nine tenths] T; ~-~ 1A, 2A–1E
42.23	prevalent] ARE; that prevailed 1A, 2A–1E
*43.4–5	zendaletto] T; zenduletto 1A; zendaletta 1E; zendeletta 2A–1F
43.7	us] 1E, 2A–1F; me 1A
*43.12	seats] T; seat 1A; their seat 2A–1E
43.26	met] ARE; had ~ 1A, 2A–1E

43.28   recovered from] 1E, 3A–1F; got over 1A, 2A
43.33   of] 1E, 2A–1F; at 1A
43.38   moon beams] T; ~-~ 1A, 2A–1E; moonbeams ARE
*43.41   self occupied] T; ~-~ 1A, 2A–1E
44.1   which] 1E, 3A–1F; that 1A, 2A
44.2   walk] 1E, 2A–1F; walks 1A
44.4–5   mind, and] ARE; mind. There was something in his ap-
               pearance that 1A, 2A–1E
44.5   afterwards] ARE; after 1A, 2A–1E
44.10   Correggio] 3A–1E; Corregio 1A, 2A
44.14   met] ARE; had ~ 1A, 2A–1E
*44.20   gaiety] 2A–1E; gayety 1A, 3A, ARE
44.27   which] 1E, 2A–1F; that 1A
44.28   him,] ARE; ~∧ in my eyes, which was 1A, 2A–1E
44.30   men] 1E, 2A–1F; man 1A
44.31   awkwardness] ARE; ~ of address 1A, 2A–1E
44.31   but] ARE; ~ I subdued it, and 1A, 2A–1E
44.32   I] ARE; omitted 1A, 2A–1E
44.37   Mark] 1E, 2A–1F; Marks 1A
44.37   or] ARE; ~ he 1A, 2A–1E
44.38   apartments] 1E, 3A–1F; apartment 1A, 2A
45.10   panted] 1E, 2A–1F; almost ~ 1A
45.11   of red] 1E, 2A–1F; omitted 1A
45.18   that,"] 2A–1E; ~∧" 1A
45.23   all] 1E, 2A–1F; omitted 1A
45.23   come,"] 3A–1E; ~∧" 1A, 2A
45.34   sake,"] 2A–1E; ~∧∧ 1A
45.35   he,∧] 2A–1E; ~," 1A
45.35   voice] 1E, 2A–1F; agony of ~ 1A
45.35   "never] 2A–1E; ∧~ 1A
45.35   ∧let] T (∧Let 2A–1E); "~ 1A
45.40   roused] 1E, 2A–1F; aroused 1A
46.3   he] ARE; that ~ 1A, 2A–1E
46.4   indulgence,] ARE; ~; he 1A, 2A–1E
46.4   toleration, but] ARE; toleration. He 1A, 2A–1E
46.12   which] ARE; that 1A, 2A–1E
46.13   penetrated] ARE; had ~ 1A, 2A–1E
46.13   open handed] T; ~-~ 1A, 2A–1E
46.15   humiliate] 1E, 2A–1F; often ~ 1A
46.18   self abasement] T; ~-~ 1A, 2A–1E
46.19   He, . . . himself] 1E, 2A–1F; He humbled himself, in a
               manner, 1A
46.22   hoped] ARE; had ~ that 1A; ~ that 2A–1E
46.22   then presented] ARE; which ~ ~ themselves 1A, 2A–1E

46.30	time] 1E, 3A–1F; season 1A, 2A
46.36	kindle] 1E, 2A–1F; ~ up 1A
46.39	sank] ARE; sunk 1A, 2A–1E
46.42–43	circumstance, and let] 1E, 2A–1F; circumstance. I let 1A
47.18	sank] ARE; sunk 1A, 2A–1E
47.21	"But] 2A–1E; ∧~ 1A
47.21	again,"] 2A–1F; ~,∧ 1A
47.30	"And] 2A–1E; ∧~ 1A
47.30	picture?"] 2A–1E; ~?∧ 1A
47.32	that] 1E, 2A–1F; this 1A
47.32	crack brained] T; ~-~ 1A, 2A–1E
47.33	"but] 2A–1E; ∧~ 1A
47.39	long."] 2A–1E; ~.∧ 1A

THE STORY OF THE YOUNG ITALIAN

48.4	on] 1E, 2A–1F; in 1A
48.25	such a] ARE; such 1A, 2A–1E
48.27	can] 1F, 2A–1F; am 1A
48.32	which] ARE; that 1A, 2A–1E
48.34	daunted] ARE; had ~ 1A, 2A–1E
48.34	young] 1E, 2A–1F; strong 1A
*49.4	regarded] 3A–1F; deemed 1A; considered 1E
49.4	self denial] T; ~-~ 1A, 2A–1E
49.21	executed] 1F, 3A–1F; exercised 1A, 2A
49.41	ill directed] T; ~-~ 1A, 2A–1E
50.24	spring time] T (~-~ ARE); spring 1A, 2A–1E
50.27	gaiety] 1F, 1E; gayety 1A, 2A–ARE
50.37	lack lustre] T; ~-~ 1A, 2A–1E
51.3	an] 1E, 2A–1F; my 1A
51.16–17	fondness] 1E, 2A–1F; kindness 1A
51.17	parent:] 1E, 2A–1F; ~. He 1A
52.3	summoning] ARE; he summoned 1A, 2A–1E
52.15	between] 2A–1E; betwen 1A
52.33	Verde] 3A–1E; Verdi 1A; Verda 2A
53.22	and fiction] 1E, 3A–1F; or ~ 1A, 2A
53.26	enchantment.] 1E, 2A–1F; ~. I became devotedly attached to him. 1A
53.27	solicitations] 1E, 2A–1F; solicitation 1A
53.28	works] ARE; ~ he had undertaken 1A, 2A–1E
53.34	of] 1E, 2A–1F; or 1A
53.36	through] 1E, 2A–1F; by 1A
53.37	expressions] 1E, 3A–1F; expression 1A, 2A
53.41	as yet] ARE; who ~ ~ was 1A, 2A–1E

*54.12   by her mother;] 1E, 3A–1F (~ my ~, 2A); and encourage-
                   ment, 1A
54.13   think] ARE; ~ that there was 1A, 2A–1E
54.14   inspired] ARE; that ~ 1A, 2A–1E
54.27   in] 1E, 3A–1F; on 1A, 2A
54.38   I] ARE; Indeed, ~ 1A, 2A–1E
55.9   at] 1E, 2A–1F; in 1A
55.11   di Ponente] 2A–1F; de Ponenti 1A; de Ponente 1E
55.17   repose] 1E, 3A–1F; ~ itself 1A, 2A
55.24   scenery] 1E, 3A–1F; beautiful ~ 1A, 2A
55.24   surrounded] 2A–1E; sur-/ ounded 1A
55.25   villa] 1E, 2A–1F; ~ stood in the midst of ornamented
                   grounds, finely decorated with statues and fountains, and
                   laid out into groves and alleys and shady bowers. It 1A
55.26–28   It . . . lawns.] 1E, 2A–1F; omitted 1A
55.31   which] 1E, 2A–1F; that 1A
55.34   the daughter] 1E, 2A–1F; a ~ 1A, ARE
55.34   relative] 1E, 2A–1F; relation 1A
56.19   unworthiness.] 2A–1E; ~∧ 1A
56.32   along] 1E, 2A–1F; over 1A
56.36–39   How . . . song!] 1E, 2A–1F; omitted 1A
56.40   tenderness] 1E, 2A–1F; love 1A
57.9   walls.] 1Ab–1E; ~∧ 1Aa
58.8   all] 1E, 2A–1F; omitted 1A
58.8   great] 1E, 2A–1F; greatest 1A
58.9   beheld] 1E, 2A–1F; saw 1A
58.10   visions] 1E, 3A–1F; the ~ 1A, 2A
58.11   glory,] 1E, 2A–1F; ~, which seemed breaking upon her,
                   1A
58.28   however,] 3A–1E; ~∧ 1A, 2A
59.1   he] 1E, 2A–1F; the Count 1A
59.15   to be] 1E, 3A–1F; omitted 1A, 2A
59.16   might] 1E, 2A–1F; were to 1A
59.26   which] ARE; that 1A, 2A–1E
59.30   eye] 1E, 3A–1F; eyes 1A, 2A
59.31   discovered] 1E, 2A–1F; discerned 1A
59.38   long withheld] T; ~-~ 1A, 2A–1E
60.14   visitor] ARE–1E; visiter 1A, 2A, 3A
60.15   sank] ARE; sunk 1A, 2A–1E
60.27   childlike] ARE; child-like 1A, 2A–1E
61.6   acquaintances] 1E, 3A–1F; acquaintance 1A, 2A
61.8   them] 1E, 3A–1F; those 1A, 2A
61.9   administer] 1E, 3A–1F; and ~ 1A, 2A
61.11   image] ARE; ~ that was 1A, 2A–1E

61.15	any] ARE; ~ more than a child-like 1A, 2A–1E
61.23	piety] 1E, 2A–1F; feeling 1A
61.25	two years] 1E, 2A–1F; eighteen months 1A
61.39	rolling] 2A–1E; rollling 1A
61.40	creation] 1E, 2A–1F; sweet ~ 1A
61.42	well known] T; ~-~ 1A, 2A–1E
62.9	which] ARE; that 1A, 2A–1E
62.17	soul] 1E, 3A–1F; whole ~ 1A, 2A
62.18	once more] 1E, 2A–1F; *omitted* 1A
62.25	fearful] 2A–1E; fearfu 1A
62.32	gusts] 1E, 3A–1F; these ~ 1A, 2A
62.36–37	Bianca . . . nightingale; the] 1E, 2A–1F; Bianca; the 1A
62.39	thing] 1E, 2A–1F; ~ around 1A
62.41	arbour] 1E, 2A–1F; bower 1A
62.43	Metastasio] 3A–1E; Metestasio 1A, 2A
63.1	with rapture] 1E, 2A–1F; *omitted* 1A
63.1	I,] 1E, 2A–1F; ~, with rapture, 1A
63.10	so] 1E, 2A–1F; *omitted* 1A
63.23	my] 1E, 3A–1F; ~ own 1A, 2A
64.6	"could] 2A–1E; ∧~ 1A
64.34	render . . . all] 1E, 2A–1F; account to me for 1A
64.39	me,"] 3A–1E; ·-∧" 1A, 2A
65.13	spoke] ARE; spake 1A, 2A–1E
65.15–16	blood thirsty] T; ~-~ 1A, 2A–1E
65.30	ears] 1E, 3A–1F; ear 1A, 2A
65.43	Whenever] 1E, 3A–1F; Whenever 1A, 2A
66.2	be] 1E, 2A–1F; is 1A
66.13	thought] 1E, 2A–1F; thoughts 1A
66.15	never dying] T; ~-~ 1A, 2A–1E
66.19	long enduring] T; ~-~ 1A, 2A–1E
66.25	church,] 1E, 2A–1F; performance of the Miserere; 1A
66.30	Tomorrow] T; To-morrow 1A, 2A–1E
66.35	a] 1E, 3A–1F; an 1A, 2A
67.5	which] 1E, 3A–1F; that 1A, 2A

PART II, TITLE

69.2	BUCKTHORNE . . . FRIENDS] 1A, 3A–1E; Buckthorne & his Friends MS
69.3	This . . . best] 1E, 3A–1F; "'Tis a very good world MS, 1A
69.5	man's] 1A–1E; mans MS. *Apostrophe added also at* 72.1, 74.11, 78.36, 81.3, 97.16, 99.11, 110.2, 117.35, 118.7, 132.17.
69.6	known.] 1A–1E; ~∧ MS

LITERARY LIFE

71.2–13   Among . . . . immortality."] 1E, 3A–1F; *missing* MS;
             Among the great variety of characters which fall in a trav-
             eller's way, I became acquainted during my sojourn in
             London, .with an eccentric personage of the name of
             Buckthorne. He was a literary man, had lived much in
             the metropolis, and had acquired a great deal of curious,
             though unprofitable knowledge concerning it. He was a
             great observer of character, and could give the natural
             history of every odd animal that presented itself in this
             great wilderness of men. Finding me very curious about
             literary life and literary characters, he took much pains
             to gratify my curiosity. *Paragraph* "The literary world of
             England," said he to me one day, "is made up of a num-
             ber of little fraternities, each existing merely for itself,
             and thinking the rest of the world created only to look on
             and admire. It may be resembled to the firmament, con-
             sisting of a number of systems, each composed of its own
             central sun with its revolving train of moons and satel-
             lites, all acting in the most harmonious concord; but the
             comparison fails in part, inasmuch as the literary world
             has no general concord. Each system acts independently
             of the rest, and indeed considers all other stars as mere
             exhalations and transient meteors, beaming for a while
             with false fires, but doomed soon to fall and be forgotten;
             while its own luminaries are the lights of the universe,
             destined to increase in splendour and to shine steadily
             on to immortality." 1A

71.2   subjects] 2E, 3A–1F; objects 1E
71.14–28   "And . . . . favourably of] 1A, 3A–1E; *missing* MS
71.14–15   those . . . speak] 1E, 3A–1F; one of these systems you talk
             1A
71.20   once] 1E, 3A–1F; *omitted* 1A
71.21   do,] 1E, 3A–1F; ~∧ when I first cultivated the society of
             men of letters, 1A
71.21   into literary society] 1E, 3A–1F; to a blue stocking coterie
             1A
71.22   before hand. The] T (beforehand; the 3A–1E); ~ ~∧ as dil-
             igently as an actor. ~ 1A
71.24–25   No, . . . good] ARE (~, sir, there is no character that . . .
             ~ 3A–1E); From thenceforth I became a most assiduous
             1A
71.25   you are] 1E, 3A–1F; I were 1A

71.25–26	let . . . when] 1E, 3A–1F; it was 1A
71.26	and then] 1E, 3A–1F; *omitted* 1A
71.28	speaks] 1E, 3A–1F; spoke 1A; should speak 2E
71.28	a] 1E, 3A–1F; some MS, 1A
71.29–31	friend, . . . authors,] 1E, 3A–1F; ~∧ I ventured boldly to dissent from him, and to prove that his friend was a blockhead, and much as people say of the pertinacity and irritability of ~∧ MS, 1A
71.31	such] 1E, 3A–1F; my MS, 1A
71.33	"Indeed] 1A–1E; ∧~ MS
71.33	would . . . be] 1E, 3A–1F; was MS, 1A
71.33	remarks] 1E, 3A–1F; my ~ MS, 1A
71.35–38	day." . . . . be] 1E, 3A–1F; day. I never ventured to praise an author that had not been dead at least half a century; and even then I was MS, 1A
71.41	discussion] 1E, 3A–1F; prejudice and dispute, MS, 1A
72.1	critical] 1E, 3A–1F; *omitted* MS, 1A
72.3	declared] 1E, 3A–1F; ~ to be MS, 1A
72.4	Frenchmen] 1A–1E; frenchmen MS
72.8	Oh,"] 1A (~!" 3A–1E); ~·∧" MS
72.8	which] 1E, 3A–1F; that MS, 1A
72.9	literary] 1E, 3A–1F, ~· world MS, 1A
72.9	amicably, and] 1E, 3A 1F; amicably; lay down their weapons and even MS, 1A
72.10	the excess of their] 1E, 3A–1F; their excess of MS, 1A
72.11	random] 1E, 3A–1F; a venture MS, 1A
72.11–12	'cut . . . again,'] 1A, 1E; "~ . . . ~," MS, 3A–1F
72.15	flavour.∧] 1A–1E; ~." MS
72.19	all] 1E, 3A–1F; *omitted* MS, 1A

A LITERARY DINNER

72.26	Mr.] 1A–1E; ~∧ MS. *Period added also at* 76.23, 76.25, 78.32, 81.43, 83.32, 108.17, 128.2, 140.36.
*72.26	Buckthorne,] 1A–1E; ~∧ MS
*72.35	favourites] 1A–1E; favorites MS, ARE. *Emended also at* 138.16 *and "favourite" at* 85.22, 114.39.
72.36	their] 1A–1E; thier MS
72.36	or] 1E, 3A–1F; and MS, 1A
73.1	author's] 1A–1E; authors MS
73.3	and] 1A; & MS. *Ampersands replaced also at* 73.26 (gay and), 76.28, 77.26, 77.31, 78.17, 80.15, 82.1, 83.15 (and sip), 83.31, 85.11 (and murder), 85.12 (and gaiters), 87.20, 88.11, 95.33, 96.29, 97.11 (and left), 97.15 (*twice*),

99.1 (hares and), 99.10, 99.39 (bow and), 99.42, 100.5, 100.9, 100.16 (damp and), 100.38, 100.41, 101.25, 101.34, 102.30 (knit and), 103.34, 103.35, 104.6 (and burlesque), 104.6 (descriptions and), 104.9, 105.6, 105.29, 105.30 (life and), 105.41, 106.42 (crowd and), 109.16, 109.17, 110.43, 111.19, 112.21, 112.22, 114.23 (and wild), 115.3, 115.7, 115.15, 115.29, 115.37 (professors and), 115.38, 115.40, 115.42, 117.9, 117.21 (and then), 117.32, 118.4, 118.16, 118.42, 119.5, 119.43; 122.2, 123.2 (family and), 123.26, 123.32 (*thrice*), 124.28, 124.37, 124.40, 125.28, 126.4 (and thrust), 126.9, 126.38, 127.14, 127.35 (*twice*), 129.24, 132.34 (youth and), 132.35, 134.31 (and tankards), 140.18 (*twice*), 140.29, 140.33 (lady and), 142.19, 143.20.

73.4	pray,"] 1A–1E; ~∧" MS
*73.5	me;] 1A–1E; ~∧ MS
*73.6	*Paragraph* "Not] 1A–1E; *No Paragraph* "~ MS
73.13	Addison's] 1A–1E; addisons MS
73.22	notoriety] 1E, 3A–1F; notice MS, 1A
73.28	however,] 1A–1E; ~∧ MS
73.34	jokes."] 1A–1E; ~∧" MS
73.43	think] ARE; seem to ~ MS, 1A–1E
74.1	neighbour] 1A–1E; neighbor MS, ARE. *Emended also at* 75.39 *and* "*neighbouring*" *at* 102.5, 129.6, 129.10, 132.1, 132.21, 136.20, 137.34; "*neighbourhood*" *at* 82.40, 84.23, 86.38, 98.25, 99.21, 114.2, 132.4, 133.27, 140.3.
74.3	author's] 1A–1E; authors MS
74.15	Gad,"] 1A–1E; ~∧" MS
74.16	recollect] 1A–1E; reccollect MS. *Emended also at* 76.20, 76.21, 137.3; "*recollected*" *at* 78.30, 110.36; "*recollection(s)*" *at* 76.16, 78.37, 84.31, 85.16, 101.11, 110.17, 119.12, 119.41, 126.37.
74.24	devoted] 1E, 3A–1F; very ~ MS, 1A
74.25–34	Some . . . . life.] 1E, 3A–1F; *omitted* MS, 1A
74.30	drawing room] 3A; ~-~ 1E, ARE, 1F
74.34	in vain] 1E, 3A–1F; *omitted* MS, 1A
74.34	author∧] 1A–1E; ~, MS
74.35	coat; he] 1E, 3A–1F; coat and magnificent frill, but he MS, 1A
74.37	soon after] 1E, 3A–1F; as soon as MS, 1A

THE CLUB OF QUEER FELLOWS

75.11–12	'club . . . fellows,'] T ('Club . . . Fellows.' 1A); "~ . . . ~," MS; ∧~ . . . ~,∧ 3A–1E

75.13	sixpence] 1E, 3A–1F; shilling MS, 1A
75.20	Booksellers'] T (booksellers' 1A–1F); ~∧ MS; bookseller's 1E
75.31	even] 1E, 3A–1F; *omitted* MS, 1A
75.34	Hogarth's] 1A–1E; Hogarths MS
75.38	won't] 1A–1E; wont MS
76.8	*Paragraph* My] 1A–1E; *No Paragraph* ~ MS
76.10	Booksellers'.] T (booksellers'. 1A, ARE, 1F); ~∧∧ MS; booksellers. 1Ea, 3A; bookseller's. 1Eb
76.11	way,"] 1A–1E; ~∧" MS
76.11	he, "it] 1A–1E; ~∧ "It MS
76.12	that] 1E, 3A–1F; the face MS, 1A
76.14	likely,"] 1A–1E; ~·∧" MS
*76.16	way,] 1A–1E; ~∧ MS
*76.17	Dribble,] 1A–1E; ~∧ MS
76.17	service."] 1A–1E; ~·∧ MS
76.18	Birchell's] 1A–1E; Birchells MS
76.18	Warwickshire—"] T (~?" 1A–1E); ~—∧ MS
76.19	same,"] 1A–1E; ~·∧" MS
76.20	it's] 1A–1E; its MS
76.20	don't] 1A–1E; dont MS. *Apostrophe added also at* 76.21, 82.5, 86.13, 86.14, 86.39, 113.14, 143.6.
76.24	"that] 1A–1E; "That MS
76.25	Faith,] 1A–1E; ~∧ MS
76.26	dinner.] 1A–1E; ~∧ MS
76.29	it's] 1A–1E; its MS
76.36	sir,"] 1A–1E; ~,∧ MS
76.36	"I] 1A–1E; ∧~ MS
*76.41	may.] 1A–1E; m[ ] MS
76.42	nonsense as he pleases, and] 1A–1E; nons[ ]leases, a[ ]d MS
*77.3	threadbare] 3A–1Eb; thread bare MS; thread-bare 1A, 1Ea
77.3	coat.∧] 1A; ~." MS, 3A–1E
77.5	there's] 1A–1E; theres MS
77.18	schoolmate's] 1A–1E; schoolmates MS
77.21	ground,] 1A–1E; ~∧ MS
77.23	haunts—"] T (~." 1A–1E); ~—∧ MS
77.33	Market] 1A; market MS, 3A–1E
77.35	called] 1E, 3A–1F; named MS, 1A
77.43	surrounded by] ARE; of MS, 1A–1E
78.2	fluttering] ARE; that fluttered MS, 1A–1E
78.3	washerwomen,] 1A–1E; ~∧ MS
78.5	viragos] 3A–1E; virago's MS, 1A
78.20	Mrs.] 1A–1E; ~∧ MS. *Period added also at* 79.21, 79.33, 140.14, 140.21.

78.20	husband's] 1A–1E; husbands MS
78.21	neighbour's] 1A–1E; neighbours MS
78.25	Dribble's] 1A–1E; Dribbles MS
78.28	us,] 1A–1E; ~∧ MS
78.29	irresistible] 1A–1E; irrisistible MS. *Emended also at* 116.40, 117.8, 132.30.
78.31	swagger,] 1A–1E; ~∧ MS
*78.31	he] 1A, 3A–1E; *omitted* MS

THE POOR DEVIL AUTHOR

79.4	intended] ARE; ~ that MS, 1A–1E
79.9	There was] 1E, 3A–1F; We had MS, 1A
79.10	of us] 1E, 3A–1F; *omitted* MS, 1A
79.12	philos] 1A–1E; philo's MS
79.15	Dr.] 1A–1E; ~∧ MS
79.16	jokes,] 1A–1E; ~∧ MS
79.38	sacrifice] 1A–1E; sacrafice MS
80.12	St. Paul's] 1A; S'Pauls MS; St. Paul 3A–1E
80.14	Pleasures of] 1A–1E; ~ ~ of MS
80.16	printers'] 1A–1E; ~∧ MS
80.17	Court] 1A; court MS, 3A–1E
80.17	Lane] 1A; lane MS, 3A–1E
80.18	Corner] T; corner MS, 1A–1E
80.28	publisher's] 1A–1E; publishers MS
80.31	Greek] 1A–1E; greek MS
81.1	port] ARE; ~ that MS, 1A–1E
81.4	hand] ARE; his ~ MS, 1A–1E
81.5	apparition.] 1A–1E; ~∧ MS
81.6	*Paragraph* I] 1A–1E; *No Paragraph* ~ MS
*81.36	overstocked] 1A–1E; over stocked MS
81.43	himself.] 1A–1E; ~∧ MS
81.43	really,] 1A–1E; ~∧ MS
82.1	he,] 1A–1E; ~∧ MS
82.1	really, sir,] 1A–1E; ~∧ Sir, MS
82.6	morning,] 1A–1E; ~∧ MS
82.7	way—"; so] T; ~—" ~ MS; ~"—~ 1A; ~." So 3A–1E
82.8	short,] 1A–1E; ~∧ MS
82.11	let] 1A–1E; ~ let MS
82.16	bookseller's] 1A–1E; booksellers MS
82.17	printer's] 1A–1E; printers MS
82.21	made] 1A–1E; mad MS
82.24	would call on] 1E, 3A–1F; came to MS, 1A

82.25	recommending] 1A–1E; reccommending MS. *Emended also at* 104.36 (recommendation), *and* 127.38 (recommended).
82.26	to] 1E, 3A–1F; ~ the house of MS, 1A
82.36	broth."] 1A–1E; ~∧" MS
82.43	Deserted Village] 1A–1E; deserted village MS
*83.6	hot heads] 1A–1E; ~-~ MS
83.6	no doubt] 1E, 3A–1F; *omitted* MS, 1A
83.12	new] 1E, 3A–1F; a ~ MS, 1A
83.20	Canonbury] 1A–1E; Cannonbury MS
83.32	Goldsmith's] 1A–1E; Goldsmiths MS
83.33	author's] 1A–1E; authors MS
83.35	room's] 3A–1E; rooms MS, 1A
84.1	With] 3A–1E; with MS, 1A
*84.7	Hampstead] 3A–1E; Hempstead MS, 1A. *Emended also at* 84.33, 85.2, 85.19, 86 41, 88.11, 112.26, 112.38, 113.31, 119.31, 119.33, 120.1
84.7	Farm] 3A–1E; farm MS, 1A
84.8	Camden Town] 3A–1E; Cambden town MS, 1A
84.8	Red Cap] 1A–1E; red cap MS
84.9	Black Cap] 1A–1E; black cap MS
84.9	Common] 3A–1E; common MS, 1A
84.10	was] 1E, 3A–1F; is MS, 1A
84.12	perdu] 3A–1F (perdù 1E); perdue MS, 1A
*84.13	free spirited] 1A; freespirited MS; ~-~ 3A–1E
84.14	hence] ARE; from ~ MS, 1A–1E
84.21	time] 1E, 3A–1F; ~ or not MS, 1A
84.28	St. Paul's] 1A–1E; S'Pauls MS
84.30	fields,] 1A–1E; ~∧ MS
84.33	Shepherd's] 1A–1E; Shepherds MS
84.33	Fields] 3A–1E; field MS; Field 1A
84.43	West End] 3A–1E; westend MS; Westend 1A
85.10	conceive] 1A–1E; concieve MS
85.20	Jack Straw's] 1A–1E; Jackstraws MS
85.29	search] ARE; researches MS, 1A–1E
85.32	moment's] 1A–1E; moments MS
85.32	days'] 3A–1E; ~∧ MS, 1A
85.36	there] 1E, 3A–1F; taking a meal ~, MS, 1A
85.36	rather a] 1E, 3A–1F; a rather MS, 1A
*85.39	strongly] 1A–1E; *missing* MS
85.39	romantic] 1A–1E; *missing* MS
85.39	of a] 1A–1E; *missing* MS
86.10	author's] 1A–1E; authors MS

86.17	them's] 1A–1E; thems MS
86.18	sentiment] 1E, 3A–1F; sentiments MS, 1A
86.18	it is] 1E, 3A–1F; They are MS, 1A
86.22	Archipelagos] 3A–1E; Archipelago's MS, 1A
86.24–25	Stick . . . sentiments.—] 1E, 3A–1F; *omitted* MS, 1A
86.26	perfectly."] 1A–1E; ~.∧ MS
86.27	I;] 1A–1E; ~∧ MS
86.32	Forest] 1A, ARE; forest MS, 3A–1E
86.33	'under . . . tree.'] 3A–1E; "~ . . . ~." MS, 1A
86.38–39	Blackheath] 3A–1E; Black heath MS; Black Heath 1A
86.39	drink."] 1A–1E; ~.∧ MS
86.40	I,] 1A–1E; ~∧ MS
86.40	glass,] 3A–1E; ~. MS; ~— 1A
87.3	I,] 1A–1E; ~∧ MS
87.3	Chingford] 3A–1E; Chinkford MS, 1A
87.5	Forest] 1A–1E; forest MS
*87.12	now adays] T; now a days MS; now-a-days 1A–1F; nowadays 1E
87.12	King's] 1A–1E; Kings MS
87.16	*Paragraph* "We] 1A; *Paragraph* ∧~ MS; *No Paragraph* ∧~ 3A–1E
87.26	sir] 1A–1E; Sir MS
87.28	that, sir,] 1A–1E; ~∧ ~∧ MS
87.40	sir] 1A–1E; Sir MS
87.40	You're] 1A–1E; Youre MS
87.41	acquaintances] 1E, 3A–1F; ~ in general MS, 1A
87.42	be] 1E, 3A–1F; stand MS, 1A
88.1	Them's] 1A–1E; Thems MS
88.1–2	sentiments, sir] 1A–1E; ~∧ Sir MS
88.2	sir] 1A–1E; Sir MS
88.2	here's] 1A–1E; heres MS
88.2	Straw's] 1A–1E; Straws MS
88.4	heart,"] 1A–1E; ~∧" MS
88.4	Turpin's] 1A–1E; Turpins MS
88.5	*Paragraph* "Ah] 1A–1E; *No Paragraph* "~ MS
88.5	sir] 1A–1E; Sir MS
88.5	"those] 3A–1E; ∧~ MS, 1A
88.6	The Newgate] 1A–1E; ~ New gate MS
88.6	Kalender, sir] T (kalendar, ~ 1A); Kalender∧ Sir MS; Calendar, ~ 3A–1E
88.7	There's] 1A–1E; Theres MS
88.18	that's] 1A–1E; thats MS
88.18	that's] 1A–1E; thats MS
88.18	Damme,] 1A–1E; ~∧ MS

88.25	Camden Town] 3A–1F (~-town 1E); Cambden town MS, 1A
88.26	Common] 1A–1E; common MS
88.26	poem.] 1A–1E; ~∧ MS
89.5	Straw's] 1A–1E; Straws MS
89.6	Common] 1A–1E; common MS
89.6	summer's] 1A–1E; summers MS
89.10	Steele's] 1A–1E; Steeles MS
89.12–90.38	I . . . . literature.] 1E, 3A–1F; *omitted* MS, 1A
89.42	first rate] T; ~-~ 1E, 3A–1F
90.30	drunk] ARE; drank 1E, 3A, 1F
90.39–40	so . . . career. I] 1E, 3A–1F; so I MS, 1A
90.40	a detail] 1E, 3A–1F; any more MS, 1A
90.40	various] 1E, 3A–1F; luckless MS, 1A
90.41–91.1	Pegasus; . . . . me.] 1E, 3A–1F; Pegasus. MS, 1A
91.2	prevail upon myself] 1E, 3A–1F; consent MS, 1A
91.2	nor] 1E, 3A–1F; and MS, 1A
91.6	existence] 1A–1E; existance MS
91.7–12	I . . . . poetry.] 1E, 3A–1F; *omitted* MS, 1A
91.14	o'clock] 1A–1E; O'clock MS
91.15	kitchen] 1A–1E; Kitchen MS
91.17	felt] 1E, 3A–1F; have ~ MS, 1A
91.18	kitchens] 1A–1E; Kitchens MS
91.19	Apollo] 1A–1E; apollo MS
91.22	kitchen] 1A–1E; Kitchen MS
91.29	who] 1E, 3A–1F; that MS, 1A
91.30	little,] 1E, 3A–1F; ~∧ however, MS, 1A
91.33	Creeper.∧] T (creeper.∧ 1A–1E); ~." MS
91.34	"Creeper! and] 1E, 3A–1F; "~," interrupted I, "~ MS, 1A
91.34	said I.] 1E, 3A–1F; *omitted* MS, 1A
91.34	sir] 1A–1E; Sir MS
91.36	who] 1E, 3A–1F; that MS, 1A
91.37	Office] 3A–1E; office MS, 1A
91.40	day's] 1A–1E; days MS
92.4	literature."] 3A–1E; ~.∧ MS, 1A
92.5	I,] 1A–1E; ~∧ MS
92.15	reputation."] 3A–1E; ~.∧ MS, 1A

NOTORIETY

*92.18	Break neck Stairs] T; ~-~-stairs 1E, 2A–1F
92.19	Fleet Market] T; ~-market 1E, 2A–1F
*92.24	briars] 2A–1F; briers 1E, ARE
93.17	fire eater] T; ~-~ 1E, 2A–1F

A PRACTICAL PHILOSOPHER

*94.5	anecdotes . . . heard] 1E, 2A–1F; preceding anecdotes MS, 1A
94.5	Buckthorne's] 1A–1E; Buckthornes MS
94.5	together with] 1E, 2A–1F; and MS, 1A
94.7–12	I . . . . alone.] 1E, 2A–1F; *omitted* MS, 1A
94.13	careless dash of] 1E, 2A–1F; dash of careless MS, 1A
94.13	which] 1E, 2A–1F; that MS, 1A
94.14	an odd] 1E, 2A–1F; a whimsical MS, 1A
94.14	mingled with] 1E, 2A–1F; ran through MS, 1A
94.14	and] 1E, 2A–1F; that MS, 1A
94.15	zest] 1E, 2A–1F; relish MS, 1A
94.15–19	He . . . . frail.] 1E, 2A–1F; *omitted* MS, 1A
94.17	ill tempered] T; ~-~ 1E, 2A–1F
94.18	fellow man] T; ~-~ 1E, 2A–1F
94.21	more . . . flavour] 1E, 2A–1F; sweeter, MS, 1A
94.22	and] 1E, 2A–1F; or MS, 1A
94.26	good humouredly] T; ~-~ 1E, 2A–1F
95.1	yellow cups] 1Eb; ~-~ 1Ea, 2A–1F
95.26	rest."] 2A–1E; ~.∧ MS, 1A

BUCKTHORNE, OR THE YOUNG MAN
OF GREAT EXPECTATIONS

95.29	BUCKTHORNE,] 1A; ~∧ MS; ~: 3A, ARE; ~; 1F, 1E
95.32	fortunes] ARE; ~ that MS, 1A–1E
95.36	mother's] 1A–1E; mothers MS. *Apostrophe added also at* 96.15, 97.34, 100.24, 119.7, 119.12, 126.42, 128.38, 129.43, 130.11, 130.19 (*twice*), 131.7.
96.6	father,] 1A–1E; ~∧ MS
96.15	sent∧] 3A–1E; ~, MS, 1A
96.19	lessons.] 1A–1E; ~∧ MS
96.30	Gothic] 1A–1E; gothic MS
*96.31	spire. Before] 1A; ~; Before MS; ~; before 3A–1E
96.32	bounding] ARE; that bounded MS, 1A–1E
96.37	flagellation] 3A–1E; flaggellation MS, 1A
97.1	his] 1E, 3A–1F; ~ own MS, 1A
97.1	theory,] 1A–1E; ~∧ MS
97.7	Deity] 1A–1E; deity MS
97.9	unto] 1E, 3A–1F; into MS, 1A
97.18	pew,"] 1A–1E; ~∧" MS
97.22	squire's] 1A–1E; squires MS
97.23	squire's] 1A–1E; squires MS
97.24	lurk] ARE; would ~ MS, 1A–1E

97.26	nor] 1E, 3A–1F; or MS, 1A
97.28	Ovid's] 1A–1E; Ovids MS
97.29	pursuit.] 1A–1E; ~∧ MS
97.32	I carried] 1E, 3A–1F; I now began to read poetry, ~ ~ MS, 1A
97.35	Sacharissa.] 1A–1E; ~∧ MS
98.1	poetry,] 1A–1E; ~∧ MS
*98.2	schoolmaster;] 1A–1E; ~. MS
98.4	Parnassus] 1A–1E; parnassus MS
98.21	parson's] 1A–1E; parsons MS
98.22	parson's] 1A–1E; parsons MS
98.25	Dr. Johnson's] 1A–1E; ~∧ Johnsons MS
98.25	Lives] 3A 1E; lives MS, 1A
98.39	porter's] 1A–1E; porters MS
98.40	permitted] 1A–1E; ~ permitted MS
99.1	hares] 1A–1E; Hares MS
99.9	stranger's] 1A–1E; strangers MS
99.10	uncle's] 1A–1E; uncles MS. *Apostrophe added also at* 99.33, 100.11, 100.12, 101.21, 114.37, 119.21, 126.33, 126.37, 126.43, 132.43, 134.22, 135.14.
99.11	before] 1E, 3A–1F; have ~ MS, 1A
99.15	jogged] 1E, 3A 1F; seemed to jog MS, 1A
99.17	my] 1E, 3A 1F; ~ gun and MS, 1A
99.18	from] 1E, 3A–1F; ~ the park and MS, 1A
99.23	cow's] 1A 1E; cows MS
*99.24	bull's] 1A; Bulls MS
99.36	hares] 1A–1E; Hares MS
100.6	stalls;] 1A–1E; ~: MS
100.16	wandered] 1E, 3A–1F; sauntered MS, 1A
100.24	had] ARE; was the same that ~ MS, 1A–1E
100.39	love."] 1A–1E; ~.∧ MS
100.39	spectacles] 1E, 3A 1F; spectacle MS, 1A
100.40	Hebrew] 1A–1E; hebrew MS
100.42	Pilgrim's] 1A–1E; pilgrims MS
100.42	Progress,"] T (~;" 1A–1E); ~∧" MS
*101.13–18	attractive . . . . subject.] 1E, 3A–1F; attractive, for my father was harsh, as I have before said, and had never treated me with kindness. Not that he exerted any unusual severity towards me, but it was his way. I do not complain of him. In fact, I have never been much of a complaining disposition. I seem born to be buffetted by friends and fortune, and nature has made me a careless endurer of buffettings. MS, 1A
101.19	therefore] 1E, 3A–1F; however MS, 1A

*101.22   almost seventeen,] 1E, 3A–1F; turned of sixteen; MS, 1A
101.27   sit] 1E, 3A–1F; set MS, 1A
*101.27   on] 1A–1E; ~ of MS
101.27   summer's] 1A–1E; summers MS
102.1   purse,] 1A–1E; ~∧ MS
*102.13   holyday] 1A; holiday MS, 3A–1E
102.13   absent] 1E, 3A–1F; ~ from the school MS, 1A
102.16   heart's] 1A–1E; hearts MS
102.16   set] 1E, 3A–1F; sat MS, 1A
102.22   tragedy,] 1A–1E; ~∧ MS
102.24   Lane] 1A–1E; lane MS
102.25   the course of] 1E, 3A–1F; *omitted* MS, 1A
102.25   evening.] 1A–1E; ~∧ MS
102.30   knit] 1A–1E; Knit MS
102.35   white handkerchief] 1E, 3A–1F; pocket ~ MS, 1A
103.7   Punch] 1A–1E; punch MS
103.10   perceiving] 1A–1E; percieving MS
103.13   seized] 1A–1E; siezed MS
103.17   night's] 1A–1E; nights MS
103.34   tragedy,] 1A–1E; ~∧ MS
103.39   humoured] 1A–1E; humored MS, ARE
103.42   tyranny] 1A–1E; tyrrany MS
*104.11   turned] 1A–1E; seemed ~ MS
104.12   gaiety] 1F, 1E; gayety MS, 1A–ARE
104.15   stole] 1E, 3A–1F; crept MS, 1A
104.15   crept] 1E, 3A–1F; scrambled MS, 1A
104.20   judgment] 1A–1E; judjement MS
104.27   Tonans] 3A–1E; tonans MS, 1A
104.36   gentleman's] 1A–1E; gentlemans MS
105.3   dramas] 1A–1E; drama's MS
105.10   Snug's] 1A–1E; Snugs MS; Smug's ARE
105.12   situation.] 1A–1E; ~∧ MS
105.20   *Paragraph* It] 1A–1E; *No Paragraph* ~ MS
105.24   vulgar, and had] ARE; ~; ~ I have always ~ MS, 1A–1E
105.24   whether] 1A–1E; whither MS
105.39   humour.] 1A–1E; ~∧ MS
106.7   father's] 1A–1E; fathers MS. *Apostrophe added also at*
                 114.14, 117.26, 118.42.
*106.21   schoolmaster.] 1A–1E; ~; MS
106.22   which] 1E, 3A–1F; that MS, 1A
106.31   houses,] 3A–1E (~; 1A); ~∧ MS
*106.33   consoled ourselves with] 1A; ~ ~ made up ~ MS; ~ ~,
                 and made up ~ 3A–1E

106.34	day's] 1A–1E; days MS
107.7	Park] 3A–1E; park MS, 1A
107.7	Corner] 3A–1F; corner MS, 1A, 1E
*107.11	fascination] 1A; power ~ MS; power of ~ 3A–1E; powers of ~ ARE
107.12	"beauty] 1A–1E; ∧~ MS
107.15	which] 1E, 3A–1F; that MS, 1A
107.18	before] ARE; that passed ~ MS, 1A–1E
107.19	conceived] 1A–1E; concieved MS
107.19	shrank] ARE; shrunk MS, 1A–1E
*107.22	life] 1E, 3A–1F; ~ which MS, 1A
108.10	gradually faded] 1E, 3A–1F; began to fade MS, 1A
108.10	began to find] 1E, 3A–1F; discovered MS, 1A
108.12	other's] 1A–1E; others MS
108.18	fellow,] 1A–1E; ~∧ MS
108.30	other's] 1A–1E; others MS
*109.1	saddle] 1A–1E; ~ them MS
109.10	consequence,] 1A–1E; ~∧ MS
109.11	manager's] 1A–1E; managers MS
109.19	Harlequin's] 1A–1E; Harlequins MS
109.23	Park] 1A–1E; park MS
109.23	Forest] 1A–1E; forest MS
109.43	still] 1A–1E; Still MS
110.3	is] ARE; it ~ MS, 1A–1E
110.9	Alas!] 1A–1F; ~∧ MS
110.12	Pantaloon] 1A, ARE; pantaloon MS, 3A–1E
110.13	rival's] 1A–1E; rivals MS
110.28	End] 1A–1E; end MS
110.41	Pantaloon] 1A, ARE; pantaloon MS, 3A–1E
111.12	boxing] 1E, 3A–1F; vulgar MS, 1A
111.16	interposed] 1E, 3A–1F; interfered MS, 1A
111.25	among] ARE; that had been made ~ MS, 1A–1E
111.40	incontestable] 3A–1E; incontestible MS, 1A
111.41	woman's] 1A–1E; womans MS
112.7	West End] 1A–1E; west end MS
112.14	sacrificed] 1A–1E; sacraficed MS
112.15	Eve,] 1A–1E; ~∧ MS
112.21	the] 1A–1E; ~ the MS
112.22	nor] 1E, 3A–1F; or MS, 1A
112.25	which] 1E, 3A–1F; that MS, 1A
112.26	hautboy] 1A–1E; Hautboy MS
112.29	Lane] T; lane MS, 1A–1E
112.38	Nursery Tale] 1E, 3A–1F; nursery chronicle MS, 1A

112.39   Straw's] 1A–1E; Straws MS
113.1   wrap itself] 1E, 3A–1F; ~ ~ up MS, 1A
113.5   her?] 1E, 3A–1F; ~? I had never contemplated such a di-
              lemma; and I now felt that even a fortunate lover may be
              embarrassed by his good fortune. I really knew not what
              was to become of me; for I had still the boyish fear of
              returning home; standing in awe of the stern temper of
              my father, and dreading the ready arm of the pedagogue.
              And even if I were to venture home, what was I to do
              with Columbine? MS, 1A
113.5–6   return to my father,] 1E, 3A–1F; *omitted* MS, 1A
113.6   throw] 1E, 3A–1F; and ~ MS, 1A
113.14   "don't] 1A–1E; ∧dont MS
113.15   Come,] 1A (~; 3A–1E); ~∧ MS
113.15   it's] 1A–1E; its MS
113.17   fallen . . . men] 1E, 3A–1F; a couple of Bow street officers
              hold of me MS, 1A
113.20   inserted . . . papers] 1E, 3A–1F; forwarded to the police
              office in town MS, 1A
113.23   In vain] ARE; It was in vain that MS, 1A–1E
113.23–24   In vain] ARE; It was in vain that MS, 1A–1E
113.38   dine] 1E, 3A–1F; ~ with him MS, 1A
114.11   willing] ARE; was ~ MS, 1A–1E
*114.17   overrun] 1A–1E; over run MS
*114.33   spirit, however,] 1A–1E; ~∧ ~∧ MS
114.34   park,] 1A–1E; ~∧ MS
114.35   him,] 1A (~; 3A–1E); ~∧ MS
114.36   untameable.] 1A–1E; ~∧ MS
114.39   him,] 1A–1E; ~∧ MS
115.5   which] 1E, 3A–1F; that MS, 1A
*115.27   fenced, . . . hunted] 1E, 3A–1F; and fenced. I was a keen
              huntsman MS, 1A
*115.27   rooms] 1E, 3A–1F; chambers MS, 1A
115.28   fowling pieces, fishing rods,] T (~-~, ~-~, 3A–1E); *omit-
              ted* MS, 1A
116.5   Addison's Walk] 1A–1E; Addisons walk MS
*116.14   idler?] 1A; ~. MS
116.16   enamoured of] 1E, 3A–1F; smitten with MS, 1A
116.16   shopkeeper's] 1A–1E; shopkeepers MS
116.16   High] 3A–1E; high MS, 1A
116.23   all] 1E, 3A–1F; *omitted* MS, 1A
116.30   arm,] 1E, 3A–1F; ~, and his ivory headed cane in his hand,
              MS, 1A

116.31	vigilance] 1A–1E; vigilence MS
116.41	truth,] 1A–1E; ~∧ MS
116.43	so potent] 1E, 3A–1F; irrisistible MS; irresistible 1A
117.4	grant] 1E, 3A–1F; ~ me MS, 1A
117.4	this] 1E, 3A–1F; it MS, 1A
117.9	All] 1A–1E; all MS
117.9	girl's] 1A–1E; girls MS
117.20	shopkeeper's] 1A–1E; shopkeepers MS
117.20	What] 1A–1E; what MS
117.20	her?"] 1A–1E; ~?∧ MS
117.36	an] 1A–1E; a ~ MS
117.40	seized] 1A–1E; siezed MS
*118.4	our plans] 1E, 3A–1F; the ladder of ropes MS, 1A
118.14	weeks'] ARE–1E; ~∧ MS, 1A, 3A
118.15	Consolations] 1A–1E; consolations MS
*118.16	ill spelled] T (~-~ 1A–1E); illspelled MS
118.29	Oxford] 1A–1E; oxford MS
118.35	year.] 1A–1E; ~∧ MS
118.36	much] 1E, 3A–1F; omitted MS, 1A
118.37	felt] 1E, 3A–1F; ~ myself MS, 1A
*118.38	home, and] 1E, 3A–1F; home to act as chief mourner at his funeral. It was attended by many of the sportsmen of the county, for he was an important member of their fraternity. According to his request his favourite hunter was led after the hearse. The red nosed fox hunter, who had taken a little too much wine at the house, made a maudlin eulogy of the deceased, and wished to give the view Halloo over the grave; but he was rebuked by the rest of the company. They all shook me kindly by the hand, said many consolotary things to me, and invited me to become a member of the Hunt in my fathers place. *Paragraph* When I MS, 1A
118.38	the solitary . . . the] 1E, 3A–1F; alone in my MS, 1A
118.39	mansion. A] 1E, 3A–1F; home, a MS, 1A
118.40	sobered] 1E, 3A–1F; seemed to sober MS, 1A
118.40	brought] 1E, 3A–1F; bring MS, 1A
118.41	melancholy.] 1E, 3A–1F; ~; the furniture displaced about the room; the chairs in groups, as their departed occupants had sat, either in whispering tete a tetes, or gossipping clusters; the bottles & decanters and wine glasses, half emptied, [and scattered 1A (scattered MS, *in pencil*)] about the tables—all dreary traces of a funeral festival. MS, 1A

118.42–43	place; . . . . His] 1E, 3A–1F; ~, and his MS, 1A
118.42–43	Stud Book] T (~-~ ARE); ~-book 1E, 3A–1F
119.1	spaniel] 1E, 3A–1F; pointer MS, 1A
119.1	lay] 1E, 3A–1F; lying MS, 1A
119.1–2	animal, . . . came] 1E, 3A–1F; animal came MS, 1A
119.2	licked] 1E, 3A–1F; and ~ MS, 1A
119.2	hand,] 1E, 3A–1F; ~, though he had never before noticed me; and MS, 1A
119.2	looked] 1E, 3A–1F; he ~ MS, 1A
119.3	whined] 1E, 3A–1F; and ~ MS, 1A
119.3	wagged] 1E, 3A–1F; and ~ MS, 1A
119.5	we'll] 1A; well MS; will 3A–1E
119.16	property,] 1A–1E; ~∧ MS
119.25	Away] 1E, 3A–1F; Well Sir, away MS, 1A
119.25	London, therefore,] 1E, 3A–1F; London MS, 1A
119.31	End] 1A–1E; end MS
119.33	Straw's] 1A–1E; Straws MS
119.33	Castle,] 3A–1E (castle, 1A); castle∧ MS
119.35	had looked] 1E, 3A–1F; looked MS, 1A
119.36	hill's] 1A–1E; hills MS
120.8	recollected] ARE; recognized MS, 1A–1E
120.13	the] 1E, 3A–1F; their former comrade, ~ MS, 1A
120.18	horses] 1A–1E; Horses MS
*120.25	good humouredly] 1A (~-~ 3A–1E); goodhumouredly MS
120.26	fashionable,] 3A–1E; ~∧ MS, 1A
120.26– 121.17	I gained . . . . ladies.] 1E, 3A–1F; *omitted* MS, 1A
120.32	knight errant] T; ~-~ 1E, 3A–1F
121.1	bull dog] T; ~-~ 1E, 3A–1F
121.2	bull dogs] T; ~-~ 1E, 3A–1F
121.5	bully ruffian] T; ~-~ 1E, 3A–1F
121.8	uninitiated] 3A–1F; unitiated 1E
121.8	boxing match] 3A–1F; ~-~ 1E
121.22	*Paragraph* I] 1A; *No Paragraph* ~ MS, 3A–1E
121.41	life, however,] 1E, 3A–1F; life MS, 1A
122.5	Latin] 1A–1E; latin MS
122.5–12	The . . . . advances.] 1E, 3A–1F; *omitted* MS, 1A
122.13	I . . . favourably] 1E, 3A–1F; I payed my court to her, and was favourably MS, 1A
122.13	by . . . lady] 1E, 3A–1F; both by her MS, 1A
122.13–14	It . . . . A] 1E, 3A–1F; Nay I had a MS, 1A
122.15	was immediately] 1E, 3A–1F; *omitted* MS, 1A
122.15	two rivals,] 1E, 3A–1F; *omitted* MS, 1A

122.21–22   Both . . . displayed] 1E, 3A–1F; They displayed, however, MS, 1A

122.26   excruciating] ARE; that were ~ MS, 1A–1E

122.26   author's] 1A–1E; authors MS

122.27   Elegant Extracts] 3A–1E; elegant extracts MS, 1A

122.30   lady's] 3A–1E; ladies MS, 1A

122.33   nieces'] 1A–1E; neices' MS

122.34   driving] 1E, 3A–1F; my ~ MS, 1A

122.36   *Paragraph* I] 1A–1E; *No Paragraph* ~ MS

123.19   however,] 1A; ~∧ MS

123.29   other's] 1A; others MS

124.8   Latin] 1A; latin MS

124.12   Adonis] 1A; adonis MS

124.20   exhilarated] 1A–1E; exhiliarated MS

124.40   perceive] 1A–1E; percieve MS

124.41   grown] 1E, 3A–1F; ~ up MS, 1A

125.2   flagellations] 1A–1E; flaggellations MS

125.3   bursting] ARE; that was ~ MS, 1A–1E

125.4   out,] ARE; ~∧ in my bosom; MS, 1A, 1E; ~∧ of my bosom, 3A, 1F

125.10   sunrise,] 1A 1E; ~∧ MS

125.14   spent,] 1A 1E; ~∧ MS

125.19   both,] ARE; ~∧ one and the other; MS, 1A–1E

125.20   economy,] 1A–1E; ~∧ MS

125.33   received] 1A–1E; recieved MS

125.34   heir's] 1A–1E; heirs MS

125.34   receive] 1A–1E; recieve MS

125.38   received] 1A–1E; recieved MS

126.2   underneath] 1A–1E; Underneath MS

126.14   "why] 1E, 3A–1F; "~ would you not let me love you?— why MS, 1A

*126.21–22   My presence, however,] 1A–1E; ~, ~, ~∧ MS

126.24   appeared] 1E, 3A–1F; seemed MS, 1A

126.25   sank] ARE; sunk MS, 1A–1E

126.36   apartment] 1A–1E; appartment MS

126.41   should] 1E, 3A–1F; would MS, 1A

126.43   knew that] ARE; knew there was MS, 1A–1E

126.43   respected] ARE; that ~ MS, 1A–1E

127.1   determined] ARE; ~ that MS, 1A–1E

127.2   funeral] 1E, 3A–1F; ~ wines MS, 1A

127.5   most] 1E, 3A–1F; the ~ MS, 1A

127.10   house] 1A–1E; House MS

127.12   breakfast] 1A–1E; Breakfast MS

127.17   Despair!∧] 1A–1E; ~!" MS
127.21   smile,] 1A–1E; ~∧ MS
127.25   mistake,"] 1A–1E; ~∧" MS
127.26   ∧creaking] 1A–1E; "~ MS
127.31   witnessed and] 1E, 3A–1F; witnessed— MS; witnessed; 1A
127.33   astonishment,] 1A–1E; ~∧ MS
127.36   inheritance.] 1A–1E; ~∧ MS

GRAVE REFLECTIONS OF A DISAPPOINTED MAN

128.3   he said,] 1A–1E; ~, ~∧ MS
128.8   naked] 1A–1E; neked MS
128.17   philosophers'] 1A (philosopher's 3A–1E); ~∧ MS
128.24   some,] 1A (~; 3A–1E); ~∧ MS
128.30   loose] 1A–1E; lose MS
128.31   little] 1E, 3A–1F; omitted MS, 1A
129.8   hills] 1A–1E; Hills MS
129.37   towards] 1E, 3A–1F; to MS, 1A
130.6   vain;] 1A–1E; ~, MS
130.10   mother.] 3A–1E (~, 1A); ~∧ MS
130.14   meet with] ARE; find MS, 1A–1E
130.20   mother!"] 1A–1E; ~!∧ MS
130.20   I,] 1A–1E; ~∧ MS
130.20   ∧burying] 1A–1E; "~ MS
131.1   sprang] ARE; sprung MS, 1A–1E
131.1–2   "I have] 1A–1E; ∧~ ~ MS
131.8   I,] 1A–1E; ~∧ MS
131.11   compunctious] 1A–1E; compunctuous MS
131.16   Paragraph Here] 1A–1E; No Paragraph ~ MS
131.20   "No,"] 1A–1E; "~∧" MS
131.27   history,] 1A–1E; ~∧ MS
131.29   communicate."] 1A–1E; ~.∧ MS

THE BOOBY SQUIRE

132.8   servants,] 1A–1E; ~∧ MS
132.39   Paragraph It] 1A–1E; No Paragraph ~ MS
132.39   o'clock] 1A–1E; oclock MS
132.41   porter's] 1A–1E; porters MS
133.8   driven] 1E, 3A–1F; drove MS, 1A
*133.31   welcome."] 1A; ~.∧ MS, 3A–1E
134.13   Exciseman,] T (exciseman, 1A–1E); ~∧ MS
134.16   crossing] 1E, 3A–1F; managing MS, 1A
134.30   tumult] 1E, 3A–1F; scene of ~ MS, 1A

134.30	succeeded.] 1A (~: 3A–1E); ~∧ MS
134.30	Bottles,] 1A (bottles, 3A–1E); ~∧ MS
134.32	any] 1E, 3A–1F; *omitted* MS, 1A
134.40	*Paragraph* "Stop] 1A; *No Paragraph* "~ MS, 3A–1E
134.42	thought] 1E, 3A–1F; reflected MS, 1A
135.1	"that's] 1A–1E; "thats MS
135.1	that's] 1A–1E; thats MS
135.5	he,] 1A–1E; ~∧ MS
135.10	his] 1E, 3A–1F; all ~ MS, 1A
135.11	two heinous] 1E, 3A–1F; *omitted* MS, 1A

THE STROLLING MANAGER

*135.22	gentlemanlike] 3A–1F; gentleman like MS, 1A; gentleman-like 1E
135.24	"These,"] 3A–1E; "~∧∧ MS; ∧~,∧ 1A
135.24	he,] 1A–1E; ~∧ MS
135.24	"are] 3A–1E; ∧~ MS, 1A
135.32	"Nothing] T; ∧~ MS, 1A–1E
135.37	room."] 3A–1E; ~.∧ MS, 1A
136.1	reconnoitering] ARE (reconnoitring 1A–1E); recconnoitering MS
136.5	"There's] 1A ARE ("There 1F, 1F); ∧~ MS
136.6	extremely] ARE; that is ~ MS, 1A–1E
136.7	mistaken, that] ARE; ~," added he, "~ MS, 1A–1E
136.12	intimacy,] 1A–1E; ~∧ MS
136.20	Jack."] 1A–1E; ~∧" MS
136.23	heroes] 1A–1E; heroe's MS
136.27	manager's] 1A–1E; managers MS
136.28	for a woman] 1E, 3A–1F; *omitted* MS, 1A
*136.30	∧I stepped] 1A–1F, 2E; "~ ~ MS, 1E
136.31	week's] 1A–1E; weeks MS
136.36	molestation.] 1A–1E; ~∧ MS
136.38	attractive,] 1A–1E; ~∧ MS
136.41	Astley's] 1A–1E; Astleys MS
137.16	reduce] 1E, 3A–1F; to ~ MS, 1A
137.16	tatters,] 1A–1E; ~∧ MS
137.24	there's] 1A–1E; theres MS
137.41	says.] 1A–1E; ~" MS
137.43	Lane] 1A–1F; lane MS, 1E
*139.1	overrun] 1A–1E; over run MS
139.2	counterfeits] 1A–1E; counterfiets MS
139.9	'Sblood, sir,] 1E, 3A–1F; Sir∧ MS; Sir, 1A

139.19   town's] 3A–1E; towns MS, 1A
139.30   which] 1E, 3A–1F; that MS, 1A
139.34   manufacturer's] 1A–1E; manufacturers MS
139.35   shopkeeper's] 1A–1E; shopkeepers MS
139.36   Doctor's] T (doctor's 1A–1Eb); Doctors MS; doctors' 1Ea
139.36   Lawyer's] T (lawyer's 1A–1Eb); Lawyers MS; lawyers' 1Ea
139.40   claimed to be] 1E, 3A–1F; was MS, 1A
139.40   all.] 1E, 3A–1F; ~. She had been exiled from the great
                 world, but here she ruled absolute. MS, 1A
140.1   all,] 1A–1E; ~∧ MS
140.1   her . . . and] 1E, 3A–1F; omitted MS, 1A
140.3   virtue] 1E, 3A–1F; reputations MS, 1A
140.20   theatre's] 1A–1E; theatres MS
140.21   Honourable] 1A–1E; Honorable MS, ARE
140.22   Banker's] T (banker's 1A–ARE); Bankers MS
140.23   grievously] 1A–ARE; grieviously MS
140.26–28   Presume . . . . forsooth!] 1E, 3A–1F; omitted MS, 1A
140.27   "The Honourable!"] 1F; '~ ~!' 3A–1E
140.30   assumption.] 1E, 3A–1F; ~.—Presume to patronize the
                 theatre!—insufferable! MS, 1A
140.31   banker's] 1A–ARE; bankers MS
140.32   were] 1E, 3A–1F; ~, therefore, MS, 1A
140.33   Doctor's] T (doctor's 1A–1E); Doctors MS
140.33   Lawyer's] T (lawyer's 1A–1E); Lawyers MS
140.33   Manufacturer's] T (manufacturer's 1A–1E); Manufacturers
                 MS
140.34   Shopkeeper's] T (shopkeeper's 1A–1E); Shopkeepers MS
140.34   Banker's] T (banker's 1A–1E); Bankers MS
140.36   Walker's] 1A–1E; Walkers MS
140.37   mischief] 1A–ARE; mischeif MS
141.5   Banker's] T (banker's 1A–ARE); Bankers MS
141.5   lady's] 1A–ARE; ladys MS
141.8   afterwards.] 1A–ARE; ~∧ MS
141.10   family.] 1E, 3A–1F; ~. It became the vogue to abuse the
                 theatre and declare the performers shocking. An eques-
                 trian troop opened a circus in the town about the same
                 time, and rose on my ruins. MS, 1A
141.14–18   I . . . . affairs.] 1E, 3A–1F; omitted MS, 1A
141.19   My] 1E, 3A–1F; The MS, 1A
141.19   became] 1E, 3A–1F; now ~ MS, 1A
141.28   Egad,] 1A–1E; ~∧ MS
141.28   I,] 1A–1E; ~∧ MS
141.28   I'll] 1A–1E; Ill MS

141.30	hero's] 1A–1E; heroes MS
141.34	Such,] 1A–1E; ~∧ MS
141.36	actor's] 1A–1E; actors MS
141.40	Third] 1A–1E; third MS
141.40–43	and . . . much.] 1E, 3A–1F; and absolutely "outheroding herod." MS, 1A
141.43– 142.14	There . . . . day.] 1E, 3A–1F; *omitted* MS, 1A
142.15	He] 1E, 3A–1F; An agent of one of the great London Theatres was present. ~ MS, 1A
142.15	now] 1E, 3A–1F; *omitted* MS, 1A
142.15	a foraging . . . quest of] 1E, 3A–1F; the look out for MS, 1A
142.17–18	had . . . and had] 1E, 3A–1F; *omitted* MS, 1A
142.19–20	gait; . . . so the] 1E, 3A–1F; gait, and having taken to drink a little during my troubles, my voice was somewhat cracked; so that it seemed like two voices run into one. The MS, 1A
142.22	When he] 1E, 3A–1F; He waited upon me the next morning and MS, 1A
142.22	plan∧] 1E, 3A–1F; ~. MS, 1A
142.23–24	doubted . . . undertaking] 1F, 3A–1F; felt myself unworthy of such praise MS, 1A
142.25– 143.5	I hinted . . . . praise.] 1E, 3A–1F; *omitted* MS, 1A
*142.25	Shakespeare] T; Shakspeare 1E, 3A–1F
142.30	Shakespeare] T; Shakspeare 1E, 3A–1F
143.2	common place] T; ~-~ 1E, 3A, 1F; commonplace ARE
143.6	'Sblood] 1A–1E; ∧~ MS
143.6	cried] 1E, 3A–1F; said MS, 1A
143.6	I] 1E, 3A–1F; that I MS, 1A
143.7	a wonder] 1E, 3A–1F; all this MS, 1A
143.8	prodigy.] 1E, 3A–1F; ~. You need not try to act well. You must only act furiously. No matter what you do or how you act, so that it be but odd and strange. MS, 1A
143.8–16	Common . . . . avenue.] 1E, 3A–1F; *omitted* MS, 1A
143.16–19	The pit . . . . action.] 1E, 3A–1F; We will have all the pit packed and the newspapers hired. MS, 1A
143.19–20	Wherever I differed] 1E, 3A–1F; Whatever you do different MS, 1A
143.20	was to be maintained] 1E, 3A–1F; shall be insisted MS, 1A
143.20	I was] 1E, 3A–1F; you are MS, 1A
143.21	I ranted,] 1E, 3A–1F; you rant∧ MS, 1A

143.21	was to be] 1E, 3A–1F; shall be MS, 1A
143.21	I were] 1E, 3A–1F; you are MS, 1A
143.21	vulgar,] 1A–1E; ~∧ MS
143.21–22	was to be pronounced] 1E, 3A–1F; shall be MS, 1A
143.22–28	nature; . . . . strange.] 1E, 3A–1F; nature. Every one shall be prepared to fall into raptures, and shout & yell, at certain points which you shall make. MS, 1A
143.31	in . . . author,] 1E, 3A–1F; *omitted* MS, 1A
143.32	plans and new] 1E, 3A–1F; *omitted* MS, 1A
143.39	of] 1A–1E; off MS
143.39	Saqui's] 1A–1E; Saquis MS
143.42–144.4	When . . . . studies.] 1E, 3A–1F; *omitted* MS, 1A
144.5–7	theatre . . . corps] 1E, 3A–1F; manager was in honour bound to provide for me he kept his word MS, 1A
144.11–17	those . . . . men"] 1E, 3A–1F; who, let me tell you, MS, 1A
144.17	You] ARE; No, no, you 1E, 3A, 1F
144.19	critic's] 1A–1E; critics MS
*144.24	slip-slop] 1A, ARE, 1Eb; ~∧ ~ MS; slipslop 3A–1Ea, 2E
*144.25	actors] 1A–1E; patrons MS
144.30	brethren] 1A–1E; bretheren MS
144.31	experience] 1E, 3A–1F; know MS; knew 1A
144.35	smile] 1E, 3A–1F; smile too, MS, 1A
144.38	and trouble] 1A–1E; and ~ ~ MS
145.3	essence] 1E, 3A–1F; very ~ MS, 1A
145.5–19	It . . . . public.] 1E, 3A–1F; *omitted* MS, 1A
145.20	*Paragraph* A] 1E, 3A–1F; *No Paragraph* ~ MS, 1A
145.20	hearing] ARE; our ~ MS, 1A–1E
145.20–21	I . . . Buckthorne] 1E, 3A–1F; he bounced into my room MS, 1A
145.21–22	He . . . travelling.] 1E, 3A–1F; *omitted* MS, 1A
145.23	he,] 1A–1E; ~∧ MS
145.25	gazed] 1E, 3A–1F; stared MS, 1A
145.26	"may] 1A–1E; ∧~ MS
145.32	"Come] 1A–1E; ∧~ MS
145.32	Castle] 1A–1E; castle MS
145.33	I'll] 1A–1E; Ill MS
145.36	lately] 1E, 3A–1F; a short time since, MS, 1A
146.1	"I find,"] 1A–1E; ∧~ ~∧∧ MS
146.1	"you] 1A–1E; ∧~ MS
146.3	Castle] 1A–1E; castle MS
146.4	I'll] 1A–1E; Ill MS

THE INN AT TERRACINA

149.5	came] 1E, 3A–1F; ~ as usual 1A
149.5	according to custom] 1E, 3A–1F; *omitted* 1A
149.6	short handled] T; ~-~ 1A, 3A–1E
149.8	usual] 1E, 3A–1F; customary 1A
149.16	*per l'amor di Dio,*] 1E, 3A–1F; *omitted* 1A
149.17	Gennaro] 3A–1E; Genaro 1A
149.40	*di*] T (di 3A–1F, 2E); *del* 1A; del 1E
150.4	which . . . speaking] 1E, 3A–1F; Terracina 1A
150.4–9	Terracina. . . . it—] 1E, 3A–1F; the old town of that name, on the frontiers of the Roman territory. A little, lazy, Italian town, the inhabitants of which, apparently heedless and listless, are said to be little better than the brigands which surround them, and indeed are half of them supposed to be in some way or other connected with the robbers. A vast, rocky height rises perpendicularly above it, with the ruins of the castle of Theodoric the Goth, crowning its summit; before it spreads the wide bosom of the Mediterranean, 1A
150.9	reflux.] 1E, 3A–1F; ~. There seems an idle pause in every thing about this place. 1A
150.11	or codfish,] ARE; *omitted* 1A, 3A–1E
150.12–16	The . . . . them.] 1E, 3A–1F; *omitted* 1A
150.16–17	solitary] 1E, 3A–1F; naked 1A
150.17	erected] 1E, 3A–1F; rising 1A
150.19	up] 1E, 3A–1F; *omitted* 1A
150.23	has several winding] 1E, 3A–1F; winds among rocky 1A
150.25	at] 1E, 3A–1F; ~ the 1A
150.27–151.20	The . . . . bandit.] 1E, 3A–1F; *omitted* 1A
*150.36–37	ribbands] T; ribands 1E, 3A–1F
151.4	good will] T; ~-~ 1E, 3A–1F
151.15	*gens d'armes*] T; ~-~ 1E, 3A–1F
151.16	road side] 1Eb; ~-~ 1Ea, 3A–1F
*151.18	serve] 3A–1F; served 1E
151.21–22	*in cuerpo*] 1E, 3A–1F; in *cuerpo* 1A
151.22	as . . . mentioned,] 1E, 3A–1F; *omitted* 1A
151.23–26	had laid . . . they] 1E, 3A–1F; *omitted* 1A
151.27	inn] 1E, 3A–1F; osteria 1A
151.27	along . . . roads,] 1E, 3A–1F; *omitted* 1A
151.28	travellers.] 1E, 3A–1F; ~. They did not scruple to send messages into the country towns and villas, demanding

certain sums of money, or articles of dress and luxury; with menaces of vengeance in case of refusal. 1A

151.30–31   into their hands] 1E, 3A–1F; in their power 1A

151.32–34   Such . . . Terracina.] 1E, 3A–1F; The police exerted its rigour in vain. The brigands were too numerous and powerful for a weak police. They were countenanced and cherished by several of the villages; and though now and then the limbs of malefactors hung blackening in the trees near which they had committed some atrocity; or their heads stuck upon posts in iron cages made some dreary part of the road still more dreary, still they seemed to strike dismay into no bosom but that of the traveller. 1A

151.34   *No Paragraph* The] 1E, 3A–1F; *Paragraph* ∼ 1A

151.35   incidentally] 1E, 3A–1F; whom I have 1A

151.38   bride's] 1E; young lady's 1A; bride 3A–1F, 2E

152.15   so] 1E, 3A–1F; *omitted* 1A

152.22   we will] 1E, 3A–1F; we'll 1A

152.25   direction of] 1E, 3A–1F; road across 1A

152.26   rate] 1E, 3A–1F; pace 1A

152.30   well arranged] 2E; ∼-∼ 1A, 3A–1E

152.30   conveniencies] 1E; conveniences 1A, 3A–1F

152.32   gruff looking] T; ∼-∼ 1A

152.34   Horses] 1E, 3A–1F; Fresh horses 1A

152.36   Eccellenza] 1F, 1E; Excellenza 1A, 3A, ARE

152.37   Fondi!"] T (∼." 3A–1E); ∼!' 1A

152.40   Eccellenza] 1F, 1E; Excellenza 1A, 3A, ARE

153.2   postmaster] 3A–1E; post-master 1A

154.11   portfolios] 3A–1E; port-folios 1A

154.11   conveniencies] 1Ea; conveniences 1A, 3A–1Eb

154.13   dirt coloured] T; ∼-∼ 1A, 3A–1E

154.18   "Milor's"] T (*Milor's* 3A, ARE); "Milors" 1A; *milor's* 1F, 1E

154.29   field] 1E, 3A–1F; earth 1A

155.6   Nothing] ARE; There is nothing 1A, 3A–1E

155.6   conquers] ARE; that ∼ 1A, 3A–1E

155.12–13   usual . . . reports] 1E, 3A–1F; tales 1A

155.14   Venetian.] 1E, 3A–1F; ∼, were brought into discussion. 1A

155.14–15   dipped . . . and] 1E, 3A–1F; *omitted* 1A

155.15–16   so . . . tales] 1E, 3A–1F; such a number of them 1A

155.17–24   The . . . . ransom.] 1E, 3A–1F; Among these was the story of the school of Terracina, still fresh in every mind, where the students were carried up the mountains by the banditti, in hopes of ransom, and one of them massacred, to bring the parents to terms for the others. There was a story also of a gentleman of Rome, who delayed remitting the ransom demanded for his son, detained by the banditti, and received one of his son's ears in a letter, with information that the other would be remitted to him soon, if the money were not forthcoming, and that in this way he would receive the boy by instalments until he came to terms. 1A

155.18	technically] ARE; that is ~ 1E, 3A, 1F
155.19	well known] T; ~-~ 1F, 3A–1F
155.20	scholars] ARE; students 1E, 3A, 1F
155.26	narrator of the terrible] 1E, 3A–1F; story teller 1A
155.29	travellers'] 3A–1E; traveller's 1A
155.30	ignorant] 1E, 3A–1F; omitted 1A
155.30	designing] 1E, 3A–1F; omitted 1A
155.32	cited, . . . terrible.] 1E, 3A–1F; cited half a dozen stories still more terrible, to corroborate those he had already told. 1A
155.34	have] 1E, 3A–1F; had 1A
155.36	are] 1E, 3A–1F; were 1A
155.38–39	Gennaro] 3A–1E; Genaro 1A
155.39	quanto] 1E, 3A–1F; come 1A
155.42	hoofs] 1E, 3A–1F; horses' ~ 1A
156.1	caravan] 1E, 3A–1F; ~ of merchandise, 1A
156.1	which] 1E, 3A–1F; that 1A
156.1	certain] 1F, 3A–1F; stated 1A
156.1–2	days . . . with] 1E, 3A–1F; days, under 1A
156.3	its protection] 1E, 3A–1F; the occasion 1A
156.3	a long file of] 1E, 3A–1F; many 1A
156.4	generally] 1E, 3A–1F; omitted 1A
156.4	it] 1E, 3A–1F; the procaccio 1A
156.4	A . . . elapsed] 1E, 3A–1F; It was a long time 1A
156.5–7	hither . . . accession of] 1E, 3A–1F; away by the tempest of new 1A
156.7	reappeared] ARE (re-appeared 3A–1E); appeared 1A
156.8	cleared] 1E, 3A–1F; ~ away 1A
156.11	Why] 1E, 3A–1F; Oh 1A
156.11	has] 1E, 3A–1F; has arrived, and ~ 1A
156.15	exultingly] 1E, 3A–1F; emphatically 1A
156.18	Popkins] 1E, 3A–1F; Popkin 1A
156.19	who] 1E, 3A–1F; that 1A
156.19–20	mi ladi] 1E, 3A–1F; Milady 1A
156.20	her] 1E, 3A–1F; omitted 1A

156.23   principessa] T (Principessa 3A–1E); principezza 1A
156.23–24   signorine] T (Signorine 3A–1E); signorina 1A
156.24–25   now . . . been] 1E, 3A–1F; would now have entered into a
              full detail, but was 1A
156.26   neither] 1E, 3A–1F; not 1A
156.26   nor] 1E, 3A–1F; or 1A
156.27   stories, . . . table.] 1E, 3A–1F; stories. 1A
156.29   wag] 1E, 3A–1F; run on 1A
156.29   reliques] 1E (relics 3A–1F); fragments 1A
156.31   iteration] 1E, 3A–1F; constant recurrence 1A
156.34   walked] 1E, 3A–1F; ~ out 1A
156.35   up and down] 1E, 3A–1F; into 1A
156.35   large] 1E, 3A–1F; great 1A
156.35   ran] 1E, 3A–1F; runs 1A
156.36   building . . . . dirty] 1E, 3A–1F; building; a gloomy, dirty-
              looking apartment 1A
156.37   parts] 1E, 3A–1F; ~ of it 1A
156.37   groups . . . seated;] 1E, 3A–1F; some of the travellers were
              seated in groups, 1A
156.38   about, waiting] 1E, 3A–1F; about 1A
156.40–42   *Paragraph* It . . . . together] 1E, 3A–1F; *No Paragraph* As
              the procaccio was a kind of caravan of travellers, there
              were people of every class and country, who had come
              in all kinds of vehicles; and though they kept in some
              measure in separate parties, yet the being united 1A
*156.41   kinds] ARE; kind 1E, 3A–1F
156.43   a certain degree of] 1E, 3A–1F; *omitted* 1A
156.43–   road: . . . inns.] 1E, 3A–1F; road. 1A
    157.3
157.3   of the procaccio∧] ARE (~ ~ ~, 3A–1E); that accompanied
              them, 1A
157.4   banditti] 1E, 3A–1F; the ~ 1A
157.4   party of travellers] 1E, 3A–1F; carriage 1A
157.5   carriage] 1E, 3A–1F; *omitted* 1A
157.5–6   its budget . . . . seen] 1E, 3A–1F; the recital. Not one but
              had seen groups of robbers 1A
157.7   carbines . . . gleaming] 1E, 3A–1F; or their guns peeping
              out 1A
157.7   bushes;] 1E, 3A–1F; ~, or had been reconnoitred by some
              1A
157.8–9   fellows . . . had] 1E, 3A–1F; fellow with scowling eye, who
              1A
157.10   avidity] 1E, 3A–1F; eager curiosity 1A
157.11   always] 1E, 3A–1F; seek to 1A

157.12	common topic] 1E, 3A–1F; subject 1A
157.13	mere] 1E, 3A–1F; these ~ 1A
157.15	Italian] 1E, 3A–1F; person 1A
157.15	aquiline] 1E, 3A–1F; Roman 1A
157.16	tassel.] 1E, 3A–1F; ~. He was holding forth with all the fluency of a man who talks well and likes to exert his talent. 1A
157.17	something] 1E, 3A–1F; one who was ~ 1A
157.19–25	*Paragraph* In . . . . furnished.] 1E, 3A–1F; *No Paragraph* He soon gave the Englishman abundance of information respecting the banditti. "The fact is," said he, "that many of the people in the villages among the mountains are robbers, or rather the robbers find perfect asylum among them. They range over a vast extent of wild impracticable country, along the chain of Appenines, bordering on different states; they know all the difficult passes, the short cuts and strong holds. They are secure of the good will of the poor and peaceful inhabitants of those regions whom they never disturb, and whom they often enrich. Indeed, they are looked upon as a sort of illegitimate heroes among the mountain villages, and some of the frontier towns, where they dispose of their plunder. From these mountains they keep a look out upon the plains and valleys, and meditate their descents. *Paragraph* "The road to Fondi, which you are about to travel, is one of the places most noted for their exploits. It is overlooked from some distance by little hamlets, perched upon heights. From hence, the brigands, like hawks in their nests, keep on the watch for such travellers as are likely to afford either booty or ransom. The windings of the road enable them to see carriages long before they pass, so that they have time to get to some advantageous lurking place from whence to pounce upon their prey." 1A
*157.24	improvvisatore] T; improvisatore 1E, 3A–1F
157.26	exert itself] 1E, 3A–1F; interfere 1A
157.26	demanded] 1E, 3A–1F; said 1A
157.28	Because the] 1E, 3A–1F; The 1A
157.29	other] 1E, 3A–1F; improvvisatore 1A
157.30	almost] 1E, 3A–1F; *omitted* 1A
157.30	the mountain peasantry and] 1E, 3A–1F; *omitted* 1A
157.31	villages. The] 1E, 3A–1F; villages and the peasantry generally; the 1A
157.32	country round. A] 1E, 3A–1F; people of various conditions

in all parts of the country. They know all that is going on;
a 1A

157.33   scouts . . . who] 1E, 3A–1F; spies and emissaries in every
direction; they 1A

157.34   and inns] 1E, 3A–1F; inns 1A

157.34   and pervade] 1E, 3A–1F; pervade 1A

157.35   surprised if] 1E, 3A–1F; ~," said he, "~ 1A

157.37   pale.] 1E, 3A–1F; ~. *Paragraph* "One peculiarity of the
Italian banditti," continued the improvvisatore, "is that
they wear a kind of uniform, or rather costume, which
designates their profession. This is probably done to take
away from its skulking lawless character, and to give it
something of a military air in the eyes of the common
people; or perhaps to catch by outward dash and show
the fancies of the young men of the villages. These dresses or costumes are often rich and fanciful. Some wear
jackets and breeches of bright colours, richly embroidered; broad belts of cloth; or sashes of silk net; broad
high-crowned hats, decorated with feathers or variously
coloured ribbands, and silk nets for the hair. *Paragraph*
"Many of the robbers are peasants who follow ordinary
occupations in the villages for a part of the year, and take
to the mountains for the rest. Some only go out for a
season, as it were, on a hunting expedition, and then resume the dress and habits of common life. Many of the
young men of the villages take to this kind of life occasionally from a mere love of adventure, the wild wandering spirit of youth and the contagion of bad example; but
it is remarked that they can never after brook a long con-
tinuance in settled life. They get fond of the unbounded
freedom and rude license they enjoy; and there is something in this wild mountain life checquered by adventure
and peril, that is wonderfully fascinating, independent of
the gratification of cupidity by the plunder of the wealthy
traveller." 1A

157.39   "By . . . little] 1E, 3A–1F; "Your mention of the younger
robbers∧" said he, "puts me in mind of an 1A

157.40–42   neighbourhood; . . . town."] 1E, 3A–1F; neighbourhood.∧
1A

158.1   excepting] 1E, 3A–1F; except 1A

THE ADVENTURE OF THE LITTLE ANTIQUARY

158.9   cheese,—] 3A–1E; ~, 1A

158.10	suited] 1E, 3A–1F; was to 1A
158.13	palaces] 1E, 3A–1F; edifice 1A
158.14–25	He . . . . breeches.] 1F, 3A–1F; *omitted* 1A
158.26	The . . . taken] 1E, 3A–1F; He had taken a maggot 1A
158.26	was] 1E, 3A–1F; at one time 1A
158.28	about . . . prevails.*] 1E, 3A–1F; the condition of which is strangely unknown to antiquaries. 1A
158.28	prevails.*] 3A, ARE; ~*. 1E; ~.¹ 1F
158.28–159.1	He . . . recorded] 1E, 3A–1F; It is said that he had made 1A
158.29–159.43	*Footnote* *Among . . . . Italy!] 1E, 3A–1F; *omitted* 1A
158.31	richly wooded] T; ~-~ 1E, 3A–1F
158.32	fairy land] 3A–1F; ~-~ 1E
159.2–3	in . . . book,] 1E, 3A–1F; *omitted* 1A
159.4	through fear lest] 1E, 3A–1F; because he feared 1A
159.4	document should] 1E, 3A–1F; documents might 1A
159.5–6	in . . . tome] 1E, 3A–1F; behind, in which he carried them 1A
159.8–9	Thus . . . sojourn] 1E, 3A–1F; Be this as it may; happening to pass a few days 1A
159.9	mounted one day] 1E, 3A–1F; in the course of his researches, he one day mounted 1A
159.15	carbines] 1E, 3A–1F; fusils 1A
159.16	no] 1E, 3A–1F; in ~ 1A
159.19–20	gold . . . . He] 1E, 3A–1F; money in his pocket; but he 1A
159.20	had, moreover,] 1E, 3A–1F; had 1A
159.20	other] 1E, 3A–1F; *omitted* 1A
159.22	dangling] ARE; that dangled 1A, 3A–1E
159.23	way] 1E, 3A–1F; *omitted* 1A
159.23	knees. All these] 1E, 3A–1F; ~; all which 1A
159.28–29	thence of the Pelasgi] ARE; of the Pelasgi from thence 1E, 3A, 1F
160.1–2	knuckles . . . . But] 1E, 3A–1F; knuckles; but 1A
160.2–3	his . . . relative to] 1E, 3A–1F; the precious treatise on 1A
160.17	guns] 1E, 3A–1F; fusils 1A
160.18	it upon] 1E, 3A–1F; it, with some emphasis on 1A
160.18–19	drew . . . board,] 1E, 3A–1F; *omitted* 1A
160.19	wine,] 1E, 3A–1F; ~; drew benches round the table, 1A
160.21	The worthy man] 1E, 3A–1F; He 1A
160.22	uneasily] 1E, 3A–1F; *omitted* 1A
160.22	chair] 1E, 3A–1F; bench 1A
160.22–23	eyeing . . . stilettos; and] 1E, 3A–1F; *omitted* 1A
160.22	eyeing] 3A–1F; eying 1E

160.23	black muzzled] T; ~-~ 1E, 3A–1F
160.24	liquor.] 1E, 3A–1F; ~; eyeing ruefully the black muzzled pistols, and cold, naked stilettos. 1A
160.24	His . . . however,] 1E, 3A–1F; They 1A
160.25	they sang] 1E, 3A–1F; sang 1A
160.25–26	they laughed] 1E, 3A–1F; laughed 1A
160.26	their] 1E, 3A–1F; *omitted* 1A
160.26–27	mingled . . . jokes;] 1E, 3A–1F; *omitted* 1A
160.27	all their] 1E, 3A–1F; these 1A
160.31	out of the] 1E, 3A–1F; in the mere 1A
160.32	murderous] 1E, 3A–1F; *omitted* 1A
160.35	today] T; to-day 1A, 3A–1E
160.35	tomorrow] T; to-morrow 1A, 3A–1E
161.3	hour] 1E, 3A–1F; fearful ~ 1A
161.9	this] 1E; his 1A, 3A–1F
161.11	drunk] 1E, 3A–1F; drank 1A
161.14	cannot] 1E, 3A–1F; can't 1A
161.16	yourself] 1E, 3A–1F; your mind 1A
161.18–21	ire . . . . intaglio.] 1E, 3A–1F; doctor would have put in a word, for his antiquarian pride was touched. 1A
161.18	doctor] T; Doctor 1E, 3A–1F
161.22	robber] 1E, 3A–1F; other 1A
161.22	we have] 1E, 3A–1F; we've 1A
161.23	you're] 1E, 3A–1F; you are 1A
161.24–25	You shall . . . guest—] 1E, 3A–1F; *omitted* 1A
161.25	upon] 1E, 3A–1F; on 1A
161.27–28	mountains, . . . company."] 1E, 3A–1F; mountains." 1A
161.29	guns] 1E, 3A–1F; fusils 1A
161.29	gaily] 1F, 1E; gayly 1A, 3A, ARE
161.30	left] 1E, 3A–1F; let 1A
161.30	his watch] 1E, 3A–1F; his seal ring, ~ ~ 1A
161.31	his coins,] 1E, 3A–1F; *omitted* 1A
161.31	unmolested] 1E, 3A–1F; escape ~ 1A
161.31	but still indignant] 1E, 3A–1F; though rather nettled 1A
161.32	Venus an imposter] 1E, 3A–1F; veritable intaglio a counterfeit 1A
161.34	hands] 1E, 3A–1F; ~ by a rival story teller 1A
161.35	grievance] 1E, 3A–1F; serious ~ 1A
161.35–36	but . . . be] 1E, 3A–1F; it was also in danger of being 1A
161.35	improvvisatore] T; improvisatore 1E, 3A–1F
161.36	Neapolitan] 1E, 3A–1F; ~, and that 1A
161.37	the inhabitants] 1E, 3A–1F; as the members 1A
161.37	having] 1E, 3A–1F; have 1A
161.37	implacable] 1E, 3A–1F; incessant 1A

162.1	observed before," said] 1E, 3A–1F; was saying," resumed 1A
162.1	prowlings] 1E, 3A–1F; prevalence 1A
162.1	the banditti] 1E, 3A–1F; these ~ 1A
162.1	are] 1E, 3A–1F; is 1A
162.2	they . . . and so] 1E, 3A–1F; their power so combined and 1A
162.3	various] 1E, 3A–1F; other 1A
162.5	has winked] 1E, 3A–1F; winked 1A
162.6	their misdeeds] 1E, 3A–1F; them 1A
162.12	Neapolitan] 1E, 3A–1F; other 1A
162.12	openly said] 1E, 3A–1F; whispered 1A
162.13	mountains] 1E, 3A–1F; mountain 1A
162.14	told, moreover,] 1E, 3A–1F; told 1A
162.14	while] 1E, 3A–1F; when 1A
162.18	observed] 1E, 3A–1F; replied 1A
162.18	improvvisatore] T (improvisatore 3A–1E), Roman 1A
162.20	late] 1E, 3A–1F; omitted 1A
162.22	which] 1E, 3A–1F; that 1A
162.22	such men] 1E, 3A–1F; men like these 1A
162.23	the recesses] 1E, 3A–1F; all ~ ~ 1A
162.24	the] 1E, 3A–1F; all ~ 1A
162.24	who] 1E, 3A–1F; and 1A
162.24–25	every . . . knew] 1E, 3A–1F; omitted 1A
162.26	men as] 1E, 3A–1F; omitted 1A
162.29	them . . . . that] 1E, 3A 1F; them; for it is well known the robbers 1A
162.29	the . . . always] 1E, 3A–1F; are 1A
162.32	Roman] 1E, 3A–1F; improvvisatore 1A
162.32–34	They . . . . hear] 1E, 3A–1F; Scarce one of them but will cross himself and say his prayers when he hears in his mountain fastness 1A
162.35–36	valleys; . . . visit] 1E, 3A–1F; valleys. They will often confess themselves to the village priests, to obtain absolution; and occasionally visit the village churches to pray at 1A
162.37	Frascati] 3A–1F; Frescati 1A, 1E
162.37–38	stands . . . just] 1E, 3A–1F; lies 1A
162.38	Abruzzi mountains] 1E, 3A–1F; mountains of Abruzzi 1A
162.39	is] 1E, 3A–1F; omitted 1A
162.39–40	recreating . . . chatting] 1E, 3A–1F; standing about 1A
162.40–41	square . . . . noticed] 1E, 3A–1F; square, conversing and amusing themselves. I observed 1A
162.41	tall] 1E, 3A–1F; ~, muscular 1A

163.1	dusk] 1E, 3A–1F; dark 1A
163.1	anxious . . . observation] 1E, 3A–1F; avoiding notice 1A
163.1	people drew] 1E, 3A–1F; people, too, seemed to draw 1A
163.15	noon day] 3A; ~-~ 1A; noonday ARE–1E
163.32	watching] 1E, 3A–1F; by 1A
163.32–33	afterwards] 1E, 3A–1F; after 1A
163.36– 164.14	Here . . . . beforehand.] 1E, 3A–1F; The conversation was here taken up by two other travellers, recently arrived, Mr. Hobbs and Mr. Dobbs, a linen draper and a green grocer, just returning from a tour in Greece and the Holy Land: and who were full of the story of Alderman Popkins. They were astonished that the robbers should dare to molest a man of his importance on 'change; he being an eminent dry salter of Throgmorton-street, and a magistrate to boot. *Paragraph* In fact, the story of the Popkins family was but too true; it was attested by too many present to be for a moment doubted; and from the contradictory and concordant testimony of half a score, all eager to relate it, the company were enabled to make out all the particulars. 1A
163.38	improvvisatore] T; improvisatore 1E, 3A–1F
164.10	bystanders] T; by-standers 1E, 3A–1F
164.11	improvvisatori] T; improvisatori 1E, 3A–1F

THE BELATED TRAVELLERS

164.24	grey] T; gray 1E, 2A–1F
164.27	crusty looking] T; ~-~ 1E, 2A–1F
164.32	once of] ARE; which had lived with 1E, 2A–1F
164.32	but] ARE; ~ had been 1E, 2A–1F
165.1	gained] ARE; had ~ 1E, 2A–1F
165.2	broken down] T; ~-~ 1E, 2A–1F
165.3	probable] ARE; ~ that 1E, 2A–1F
165.4	became] ARE; had become 1E, 2A–1F
165.5	sank] ARE; sunk 1E, 2A–1F
165.12	sabre cut] T; ~-~ 1E, 2A–1F
165.26	halting place] T; ~-~ 1E, 2A–1F
165.31	view] ARE; the ~ 1E, 2A–1F
165.31	air] ARE; ~ of these heights, too, 1E, 2A–1F
165.37	pile] ARE; ~ of building 1E, 2A–1F
165.43	wayworn] ARE; way-worn 1E, 2A–1F
165.43	leg weary] 1Eb; ~-~ 1Ea, 2A–1F
166.12	hunting seat] T; ~-~ 1E, 2A–1F

166.13	and] ARE; ~ in its 1E, 2A–1F
166.27	bedrooms] ARE; bed-rooms 1E, 2A–1F
166.28	misshapen] 2A–1F; mishapen 1E
166.34–35	wood, just] ARE; ~∧ had ~ been 1E, 2A–1F
166.35	puffed] ARE; which ~ 1E, 2A–1F
167.4	sullen looking] T; ~-~ 1E, 2A–1F
167.5	servant maid] T; ~-~ 1E, 2A–1F
167.10	servant maid] T; ~-~ 1E, 2A–1F
167.13	good humoured] T; ~-~ 1E, 2A–1F
167.16	arm chair] T; ~-~ 1E, 2A–1F
167.16	fireside] ARE; fire-side 1E, 2A–1F
167.17	rearrange] T; re-arrange 1E, 2A–1F
167.25	servant maid] T; ~-~ 1E, 2A–1F
*167.40	court yard] T; ~-~ 1E, 2A–1F; courtyard ARE
168.5	new comers] 3A; ~-~ 1E, 2A–1F
168.8	gold headed] T; ~-~ 1E, 2A, 1F
168.13	rheumatic looking] T; ~-~ 1E, 2A–1F
168.26	supper table] ARE, 2E; ~-~ 1E, 2A–1F
168.28	new comers] T; ~-~ 1E, 2A–1F
169.3	sank] ARE; sunk 1E, 2A–1F
169.17–18	self denial] T; ~-~ 1E, 2A–1F
169.43	Caspar] 2A–1Eb; Gaspar 1Ea
170.42	window frame] T; ~-~ 1F, 2A–1F
*171.5	were] 2A–1F; was 1E
171.12	servant woman] T; ~-~ 1E, 2A–1F
171.14–15	kind hearted] T; ~-~ 1E, 2A–1F
171.19	calculated] ARE; that was ~ 1E, 2A–1F
172.17	at] ARE; who were ~ 1E, 2A–1F
172.24	court yard] T; ~-~ 1F, 2A–1F; courtyard ARE
172.41–42	chance medley] T; ~-~ 1E, 2A–1F
173.27	court yard] T; ~-~ 1F, 2A–1F; courtyard ARE
173.31	pile:] T (~; ARE); ~∧ of building: 1E, 2A–1F
173.33	inmates were] ARE; house was 1E, 2A–1F
173.40	ill omened] T; ~-~ 1F, 2A–1F
174.1	started] ARE; became restive, ~ 1E, 2A–1F
174.7	roused] ARE; aroused 1E, 2A–1F
174.15	purpose] ARE; sake 1E, 2A–1F
174.21	gens d'armes] T; ~-~ 1E; gendarmes 3A–1F; gensdarmes 2A
174.34–35	gens d'armes] T; ~-~ 1E; gendarmes 2A–1F
175.3	gens d'armes] T; ~-~ 1E; gendarmes 2A–1F
175.4	shot holes] T; ~-~ 1E, 2A–1F
175.4	window frames] T; ~-~ 1E, 2A–1F

175.18   afterwards] ARE; after 1E, 2A–1F
*175.25   linen draper] T; linendraper 1E; ~-~ 2A–1F
175.25   green grocer] 2A; greengrocer 1E; ~-~ 3A–1F
175.28   dry salter] T; ~-~ 1E, 2A–1F
175.29   Throgmorton Street] T; ~-street 1E, 2A–1F

THE ADVENTURE OF THE POPKINS FAMILY

176.4   have remarked] 1E, 3A–1F; know 1A
176.6   about it] 1E, 3A–1F; so 1A
176.6   snug] 1E, 3A–1F; so ~ 1A
176.6   finished] 1E, 3A–1F; so ~ 1A
176.7   turning] 1E, 3A–1F; that roll 1A
176.7   hanging] 1E, 3A–1F; that hangs 1A
176.8   protecting from] 1E, 3A–1F; proof against 1A
176.9   from the] 1E, 3A–1F; out of the 1A
176.11   well dressed] T; ~-~ 1A, 3A–1E
176.18   with] 1E, 3A–1F; ~ all 1A
176.20   a] 1E, 3A–1F; *omitted* 1A
176.25   principessa] T (Principessa 3A–1E); principezza 1A
176.27   signorine] T (Signorine 3A–1E); signorini 1A; Signorines
                    ARE
176.29   swore] 1E, 3A–1F; was sure 1A
176.37   sketches.] 3A–1E; ~∧ 1A
176.39   lost . . . Angels;"] 1E, 3A–1F; reading the last works of Sir
                    Walter Scott and Lord Byron, 1A
177.2   moved] 1E, 3A–1F; toiling 1A
177.8   who] 1E, 3A–1F; that 1A
177.24   beheld] 1E, 3A–1F; saw away down the road 1A
177.27   principessa's] T (Principessa's 3A–1E); principezza's 1A
177.30   ire] 1E, 3A–1F; fury 1A
177.33   seized] 1E, 3A–1F; grasped 1A
177.34   open] 1E, 3A–1F; partly off 1A
177.38   frippery] 1E, 3A–1F; the ~ 1A
178.16   indignantly] 1E, 3A–1F; *omitted* 1A
178.23   obliged] 1E, 3A–1F; requested 1A
178.25   And if] ARE; If 1A, 3A–1E
178.26   "Pish! . . . away.] 1E, 3A–1F; *omitted* 1A
178.27   had been] 1E, 3A–1F; was 1A
178.38   proffered] T; profered 1A
178.40   As . . . beach] 1E, 3A–1F; Not far distant from the inn 1A
178.40   where] 1E, 3A–1F; ~ there was 1A
178.41   were stationed . . . . were] 1E, 3A–1F; on the beach, en-
                    circling and 1A

178.42	sport] 1E, 3A–1F; to ~ 1A
179.1–2	The . . . sports.] 1E, 3A–1F; *omitted* 1A
179.2	is] 1E, 3A–1F; was 1A
179.2	said he] 1E, 3A–1F; the Frenchman observed 1A
179.3	is] 1E, 3A–1F; was 1A
179.3–5	Many . . . . country.] 1E, 3A–1F; *omitted* 1A
179.5–6	the miscreant . . . kind] 1E, 3A–1F; who had 1A
179.6	flies] 1E, 3A–1F; fled 1A
179.6	turns] 1E, 3A–1F; turned 1A
179.6–7	when . . . traitor to] 1E, 3A–1F; by betraying 1A
179.7–8	betrays . . . buys] 1E, 3A–1F; had bought 1A
179.8–9	his . . . happy in] 1E, 3A–1F; punishment, and 1A
179.9	an] 1E, 3A–1F; for ~ 1A
179.10	in this . . . enjoyment.] 1E, 3A–1F; with this wretched crew of miscreants! 1A
179.11	The fair Venetian] 1E, 3A–1F; The remark of the French-man had a strong effect upon the company, particularly upon the Venetian lady, who 1A
179.11	look] 1E, 3A–1F; timid ~ 1A
179.11	the] 1E, 3A–1F; this 1A
179.12	amusement] 1E, 3A–1F; relaxation 1A
179.12–13	serpents writhing] 1E, 3A–1F; ~, wreathing and twisting 1A
179.13–16	And . . . chained.] 1E, 3A–1F; *omitted* 1A
179.17–26	The . . . . existence."] 1E, 3A–1F; The Frenchman now adverted to the stories they had been listening to at the inn, adding, that if they had any farther curiosity on the subject, he could recount an adventure which happened to himself among the robbers, and which might give them some idea of the habits and manners of those beings. 1A
179.19	improvvisatore] T; improvisatore 1E, 3A–1F
179.27	*Paragraph* There] 1E, 3A–1F; *No Paragraph* ~ 1A
179.27	mingled . . . modesty] 1E, 3A–1F; modesty and frankness 1A
179.29–30	eagerly . . . to,] 1E, 3A–1F; gladly accepted his proposi-tion; 1A

THE PAINTER'S ADVENTURE

180.5	vast, deserted,] 1E, 3A–1F; ~∧ ~∧ 1A
180.5	melancholy] 1E, 3A–1F; *omitted* 1A
180.6	winding] 1E, 3A–1F; running 1A

180.8	researches] 1E, 3A–1F; the ~ 1A
*180.16	pursuits] 3A–1F; occupation 1A, 1E
180.22	early] 1E, 3A–1F; first 1A
180.25	might] ARE; that he ~ 1A, 3A–1E
180.25	Not . . . with] 1E, 3A–1F; at 1A
180.26	valley,] 3A–1E; ~∧ 1A
180.27	past] 1E, 3A–1F; *omitted* 1A
181.19	practice] 1E, 3A–1F; execution 1A
181.20	it,] 1E, 3A–1F; ~, just between the mastoides; 1A
181.33	andiamo] 3A–1E; audiamo 1A
181.36	flowed] 1E, 3A–1F; was flowing 1A
181.42	ferocious] 1E, 3A–1F; furious 1A
182.3	threat] 1E, 3A–1F; menace 1A
182.12	"that] 3A–1E; "That 1A
182.18	La] 3A–1E; la 1A
182.21	approached] 1E, 3A–1F; then ~ 1A
182.29	welcome.] 1E, 3A–1F; ~. Many an isolated inn among the lonely parts of the Roman territories, and especially on the skirts of the mountains, have the same dangerous and suspicious character. They are places where the banditti gather information; where they concert their plans, and where the unwary traveller, remote from hearing or assistance, is sometimes betrayed to the stiletto of the midnight murderer. 1A
182.30	further] 1E, 3A–1F; farther 1A
182.34	ground] 1E, 3A–1F; earth 1A
182.37	serve] 1E, 3A–1F; seem 1A
182.41	garments] 1E, 3A–1F; under dresses 1A
182.42	strong marked] 3A, ARE; ~-~ 1A, 1F, 1E
183.3	inkhorn] 3A–1E; ink-horn 1A
183.14	nor] 1E, 3A–1F; or 1A
183.17	set] 1E, 3A–1F; sat 1A
184.4	my] 1E, 3A–1F; *omitted* 1A
184.5	the Abruzzi] ARE; Abruzzi 1A, 3A–1E
184.10	Frascati] 3A–1E; Frescati 1A
184.10	lines] 1E, 3A–1F; line 1A
184.11	towers] 1E, 3A–1F; towns 1A
184.15	of] 1E, 3A–1F; ~ the 1A
184.25–26	look out] T; ~-~ 1A, 3A–1E
184.30	which] 1E, 3A–1F; that 1A
184.32	in] 1E, 3A–1F; on 1A
184.34	They] ARE; From hence they 1A, 3A–1E
185.7	not always] 1E, 3A–1F; often not 1A

185.10	technically] 3A–1E; technially 1A
185.15	him and] ARE; him. I 1A, 3A–1E
185.16	degrees] 3A–1E; degress 1A
185.17	self love] T; ~-~ 1A, 3A–1E
185.18	an artist] 1E, 3A–1F; artist 1A
185.30	"I] 3A–1E; ∧~ 1A
185.32	which] 1E, 3A–1F; that 1A
185.34	them."] 3A–1E; ~.∧ 1A

THE STORY OF THE BANDIT CHIEFTAIN

186.4	Sbirri] 3A–1E; sbirri 1A
186.21	grey] T; gray 1A, 3A–1E
186.26	Sbirri] 3A–1E; sbirri 1A
186.33	flying with precipitation] 1E, 3A–1F; *omitted* 1A
186.34	so] 1E, 3A–1F; flying with precipitation, ~ 1A
188.10	posted] ARE; who had been ~ 1A, 3A–1E
188.11	La] 3A–1E; la 1A
188.11	us] ARE; ~ with precipitation 1A, 3A–1E
188.12	Frascati] 3A–1F; Frescati 1A, 1E
189.3	portfolio] 1F, 1E; port-folio 1A, 3A, ARE
190.8	time] 1E, 3A–1F; *omitted* 1A
190.9	exhausted] 3A–1F; exausted 1A
191.4	self condemnation] T; ~-~ 1A, 3A–1E
191.6	follower] 1E, 3A–1F; followers 1A
191.9	feel,"] 3A–1E, -∧" 1A
191.10	life." As] 3A–1E; ~," as 1A
191.13	miserable] 3A–1E; misirable 1A
191.17	while] 1E, 3A–1F; time 1A
191.20	stillness] 1E, 3A–1F; sultriness 1A
191.20	midday] T; mid-day 1A, 3A–1E
191.28	look out] T; ~-~ 1A, 3A–1E
192.5	had] 1E, 3A–1F; seemed 1A
192.6	sleeping bandit] ARE; bandit that lay sleeping 1A, 3A–1E
192.6	noontide] ARE–1E; noon-tide 1A, 3A
192.10	which] 1E, 3A–1F; that 1A
192.10	the] 1E, 3A–1F; *omitted* 1A
192.11	midday] 1E; mid / day 1A; mid-day 3A–1F, 2E
192.12	which] 1E, 3A–1F; that 1A
192.19	well filled] T; ~-~ 1A, 3A–1E
192.37	three times] 1E, 3A–1F; twice 1A
192.42	was picturesque] 1E, 3A–1F; seemed picture 1A
192.43	noontide] 3A–1E; noon-tide 1A

193.10	oaks] 1E, 3A–1F; oak 1A
193.10	corks] 1E, 3A–1F; cork 1A
193.11	foreground] 3A–1E; fore-ground 1A, 1F
193.11	of the] 1E, 3A–1F; ~ those 1A
193.15	form . . . value] 1E, 3A–1F; inform them of their nature 1A
193.20–21	towns: but as] 1E, 3A–1F; towns. As 1A
193.33	much] 1E, 3A–1F; *omitted* 1A
193.34	them] 1E, 3A–1F; themselves 1A
193.38	it.*] 3A, ARE (~*. 1E); ~.∧ 1A; ~.¹ 1F
193.39–42	*Footnote* *The . . . . him.] 1E, 3A–1F; *omitted* 1A

THE STORY OF THE YOUNG ROBBER

194.27	was] 1E, 3A–1F; *omitted* 1A
194.32	off] 1E, 3A–1F; *omitted* 1A
194.34	gave] 1E, 3A–1F; ~ her 1A
194.35	town,] 3A–1E; ~∧ 1A
195.10	market place] T; ~-~ 1A, 3A–1E
195.17	enrol] 1E, 3A–1F; enlist 1A
196.27	begged] ARE; ~ that 1A, 3A–1E
196.31	shoulder;] 1E, 3A–1F; ~, her mouth was near to mine. 1A
197.11	ought to] 1E, 3A–1F; should 1A
197.35	self will] T; ~-~ 1A, 3A–1E
198.10	reduced] 1E, 3A–1F; recovered 1A
198.20	the woods] 1E, 3A–1F; woods 1A
198.21	over] 1E, 3A–1F; upon 1A
198.40	be] ARE; become 1A, 3A–1E
199.2	Dante] 3A–1E; Danté 1A
199.13	All] 1E, 3A–1F; ~ that 1A
199.14	kindness] ARE; fondness for her 1A, 3A–1E
199.14	though] ARE; but 1A, 3A–1E
199.21	or] 1E, 3A–1F; and 1A
199.25	But my] 1E, 3A–1F; My 1A
200.17	to menace her] 1E, 3A–1F; for menace 1A
200.21	crouching] 1E, 3A–1F; couching 1A
200.24	dared] 1E, 3A–1F; dare 1A
*200.28	anxious] 3A–1F; uneasy 1A, 1E
201.10	further] 1E, 3A–1F; farther 1A
201.11	feel] 1E, 3A–1F; put 1A
201.40	great] ARE; *omitted* 1A, 3A–1E
202.8	Frenchman] 1E, 3A–1F; artist 1A
202.9	shore] 1E, 3A–1F; ~ of Terracina 1A
202.9	story] 1E, 3A–1F; ~ they had heard 1A

202.9	impression] 1E, 3A–1F; ~ on them 1A
202.10	Venetian lady] 1E, 3A–1F; fair Venetian, who had gradually regained her husband's arm 1A
202.10	that] 1E, 3A–1F; the 1A
202.10	which] 1E, 3A–1F; that 1A
202.11	was] 1E, 3A–1F; had been 1A
202.11	closer] 1E, 3A–1F; close 1A
202.12–13	moon beams] T; ~-~ 1A, 3A–1E
202.13	usual] 1E, 3A–1F; ~ with terror 1A
202.14	eyes.] 1E, 3A–1F; ~. "O caro mio!" would she murmur, shuddering at every atrocious circumstance of the story. 1A
202.15	said he] 1E, 3A–1F; was the reply 1A
202.15	as he] 1E, 3A–1F; ~ the husband 1A

THE ADVENTURE OF THE ENGLISHMAN

*202.26	THE ADVENTURE . . . ENGLISHMAN] 1E, 3A–1F; *omitted* 1A
202.28	day break] T; ~-~ 1A, 3A–1E; daybreak ARE
203.7	gingerbread coloured] T; ~-~ 1A
203.17	Quanto] 1E, 3A–1F; come 1A
203.18	insensibili] 1E, 3A–1F; freddi 1A
203.32	eccellenza] 3A–1E; excellenza 1A
203.33	eccellenza] 3A–1E; excellenza 1A
203.35	Gennaro] 3A–1E; Genario 1A
204.18	down] 1E, 3A–1F; over 1A
204.29	forest] 1E, 3A–1F; ~ trees 1A
204.39	discharged] 1E, 3A–1F; had ~ 1A
205.10	mountain] 1E, 3A–1F; mountains 1A
205.15	reports] 1E, 3A–1F; report 1A
205.16	footpath] 3A–1E; foot-path 1A
205.17	rocks] 1E, 3A–1F; rock 1A
205.38	he was] 1E, 3A–1F; and the Englishman saw him 1A
205.38–39	and . . . desperate,] 1E, 3A–1F; *omitted* 1A
205.43	The Englishman] 1E, 3A–1F; His adversary 1A
*206.6–14	He . . . . charge.] 1E, 3A–1F; *omitted* 1A
206.16–22	The . . . . on.] 1E, 3A–1F; The carriage was righted; the baggage hastily replaced; the Venetian, transported with joy and gratitude, took his lovely and senseless burthen in his arms, and the party resumed their route towards Fondi, escorted by the dragoons, leaving the foot soldiers to ferret out the banditti. 1A

206.23	John] 1E, 3A–1F; While on the way ~ 1A
206.23	now] 1E, 3A–1F; *omitted* 1A
206.23–27	serious, ... banditti.] 1E, 3A–1F; serious. 1A
206.26	foot soldiers] T; ~-~ 1E, 3A–1F
206.28	completely] 1E, 3A–1F; *omitted* 1A
206.29–33	swoon . . . . her."] 1E, 3A–1F; swoon, and was made conscious of the mode of her deliverance. 1A
206.34	*Paragraph* Her] 1E, 3A–1F; *No Paragraph* ~ 1A
206.37	arms with] 1E, 3A–1F; arms, and clasped him round the neck with all 1A
206.37–38	nation, . . . gratitude.] 1E, 3A–1F; nation. 1A
206.39	woman.] 1E, 3A–1F; ~. *Paragraph* "My deliverer! my angel!" exclaimed she. 1A
206.41	blood] 1E, 3A–1F; the ~ 1A
207.1	My . . . angel] 1E, 3A–1F; O Dio 1A

HELL GATE

211.2	in] 1E, 3A–1F; and ~ 1A
211.3–4	Long Island] 1E, ARE, 1F; ~-~ 1A, 3A
211.5	perplexed] 1E, 3A–1F; irritated and ~ 1A
211.6	impetuous] 1E, 3A–1F; hasty 1A
211.8	ripples; . . . rapids and] 1E, 3A–1F; ripples and 1A
211.9	wrong headed] T; ~-~ 1A, 3A–1F, 2E; wrongheaded 1E
211.11	humour, however, prevails] 1E, 3A–1F; humour is said to prevail 1A
211.11	certain . . . tide] 1E, 3A–1F; half tides 1A
211.12	water, for instance,] 1E, 3A–1F; water 1A
211.12–13	a stream . . . as] 1E, 3A–1F; as any other stream. As 1A
211.13–14	roars . . . bully] 1E, 3A–1F; rages and roars as if 1A
211.14	drink] 1E, 3A–1F; water 1A
211.15	relapses] 1E, 3A–1F; ~ again 1A
211.15	sleeps] 1E, 3A–1F; seems almost to sleep 1A
211.16	In fact, it] 1E, 3A–1F; It 1A
211.16	a quarrelsome toper] 1E, 3A–1F; an inveterate hard drinker 1A
211.18	who,] 1E, 3A–1F; *omitted* 1A
211.18	over,] 1E, 3A–1F; ~∧ 1A
211.19	blustering, . . . drinking] 1E, 3A–1F; blustering bullying 1A
211.19	hard drinking] T; ~-~ 1E, 3A–1F
211.20	danger and perplexity] 1E, 3A–1F; difficulty and danger 1A
211.21	tub built] T; ~-~ 1A, 3A–1E

211.23–24   reefs, . . . Manhattoes.] 1E, 3A–1F; reefs. 1A
211.25   and] 1E, 3A–1F; (literally Hell Gut) ~ 1A
211.30–31   This . . . boyhood;] 1E, 3A–1F; From this strait to the city
                of the Manhattoes the borders of the Sound are greatly
                diversified: in one part, on the eastern shore of the island
                of Mannahata and opposite Blackwell's Island, being very
                much broken and indented by rocky nooks, overhung
                with trees which give them a wild and romantic look.
                Paragraph The flux and reflux of the tide through this
                part of the Sound is extremely rapid, and the navigation
                troublesome, by reason of the whirling eddies and count-
                er currents. I speak this from experience, 1A
211.30   Hell Gate] T; ~-gate 1E, 3A–1F
211.31   on those] 1E, 3A–1F; of these 1A
211.31   seas] 1E, 3A–1F; ~ in my boyhood 1A
211.33   certain] 1E, 3A–1F; divers 1A
211.33   other] 1E, 3A–1F; the 1A
211.34–37   Indeed . . . yore.] 1E, 3A–1F; *omitted* 1A
211.38   strait] 1E, 3A–1F; perilous ~ 1A
211.39   lay] 1E, 3A–1F; ~ in my boyish days 1A
211.40   a wild] 1E, 3A–1F; some wild 1A
211.40–41   told to us of] 1E, 3A–1F; about 1A
211.41   some] 1E, 3A–1F; of ~ 1A
211.41   tale of] 1E, 3A–1F; *omitted* 1A
211.41   murder] 1E, 3A–1F; ~, connected with it, 1A
211.42–   recollect, . . . cruisings.] 1E, 3A–1F; recollect. 1A
  212.1
212.2   enough] 1E, 3A–1F; sufficient 1A
212.3   notions] 1E, 3A–1F; ~ concerning it 1A
212.3   just] 1E, 3A–1F; *omitted* 1A
212.6   and . . . weeds] 1E, 3A–1F; *omitted* 1A
212.6   sea weeds] T; ~-~ 1E, 3A–1F
212.6   huge] 1E, 3A–1F; *omitted* 1A
212.9   the] 1E, 3A–1F; this 1A
212.9–19   I . . . . myself.] 1E, 3A–1F; *Paragraph* The stories con-
                nected with this wreck made it an object of great awe to
                my boyish fancy; but in truth the whole neighbourhood
                was full of fable and romance for me, abounding with
                traditions about pirates, hobgoblins, and buried money.
                1A
212.10   sailors'] 3A–1F, 2E; sailors, 1E
212.15   Sound] 3A–1F; sound 1E
212.20   *Paragraph* As] 1E, 3A–1F; *No Paragraph* ~ 1A

212.20   diligent research] 1E, 3A–1F; many researches 1A
212.25   unearthed.] 1E, 3A–1F; ~; for the whole course of the
                Sound seemed in my younger days to be like the straits
                of Pylorus of yore, the very region of fiction. 1A
212.26   Long Island] 3A–1E; ~-~ 1A
212.26–27   across the Sound;] 1E, 3A–1F; *omitted* 1A
212.27   seeing] 1E, 3A–1F; ~ that 1A
212.28   historian∧] T (~, 3A–1E); ~* 1A
212.29   thereof.*] 3A, ARE; ~.∧ 1A; ~.¹ 1F; ~*. 1E
212.29   three cornered] T; ~-~ 1A, 3A–1E
212.31   Spuke∧] T (*spuke*∧ 1E, 3A, 1F); ~, 1A; *spuke*, ARE
212.31   (i.e.] 1E, 3A–1F; or 1A
212.32   Ghost),] T [ghost), 1E, 1F]; Ghost, 1A; ghost,) 3A, ARE
212.32–33   and . . . bullet;] 1E, 3A–1F; *omitted* 1A
212.36   say] 1E, 3A–1F; said 1A
212.38–39   pirates and their] 1E, 3A–1F; *omitted* 1A
212.40   and authentic] 1E, 3A–1F; *omitted* 1A
212.41   valuable] 1E, 3A–1F; learned 1A
213.1   is] 1E, 3A–1F; was 1A

KIDD THE PIRATE

213.6   King] 1E, 3A–1F; *omitted* 1A
213.7   great] 1E, 3A–1F; favourite 1A
213.7   random] 1E, 3A–1F; *omitted* 1A
213.7–10   adventurers, ... Buccaneers] 1E, 3A–1F; adventurers of
                all kinds, and particularly of buccaneers 1A
213.9   old fashioned] T; ~-~ 1E, 3A–1F
213.10   rovers] 1E, 3A–1F; piratical ~ 1A
213.10–17   who, ... and] 1E, 3A–1F; who 1A
213.18   merchantmen] 1E, 3A–1F; merchant ships 1A
213.18   The] 1E, 3A–1F; They took advantage of the 1A
213.19–20   the number . . . waters,] 1E, 3A–1F; *omitted* 1A
213.19   hiding places] 3A; ~-~ 1E, ARE, 1F
213.20   and] 1E, 3A–1F; ~ of 1A
213.20   made] 1E, 3A–1F; to make 1A
213.21   great] 1E, 3A–1F; kind of 1A
213.21   of the pirates] 1E, 3A–1F; *omitted* 1A
213.21   booty] 1E, 3A–1F; ill-gotten spoils 1A
213.22–26   As . . . Manhattoes.] 1E, 3A–1F; *omitted* 1A
213.26   therefore,] 1E, 3A–1F; *omitted* 1A
213.27   every] 1E, 3A–1F; *omitted* 1A

213.29	or quarter] 1E, 3A–1F; *omitted* 1A
213.30	prize money] T (~-~ 1E, 3A–1F); gains 1A
213.31–32	midnight] 1E, 3A–1F; sudden 1A
213.33–35	these . . . . and] 1E, 3A–1F; the indignation of government was aroused, and it was determined 1A
213.35	widely extended] T; ~-~ 1E, 3A–1F
213.36	ferret] 1E, 3A–1F; ~ out 1A
213.36	out of] 1E, 3A–1F; from 1A
213.36	colonies.] 1E, 3A–1F; ~. Great consternation took place among the pirates on finding justice in pursuit of them, and their old haunts turned to places of peril. They secreted their money and jewels in lonely out of the way places; buried them about the wild shores of the rivers and sea coast, and dispersed themselves over the face of the country. 1A
214.1	execute this purpose] 1E, 3A–1F; hunt them by sea 1A
214.1	notorious] 1E, 3A–1F; renowned 1A
214.2–4	an equivocal . . . . smuggler] 1E, 3A–1F; a hardy adventurer, a kind of equivocal borderer, half trader, half smuggler 1A
214.4	considerable] 1E, 3A–1F; tolerable 1A
214.5	many years] 1E, 3A–1F; some time 1A
214.5	pirates,] 1E, 3A–1F; ~, lurking about the seas 1A
214.6–8	that . . . . and] 1E, 3A–1F; prying into all kinds of odd places, 1A
214.7	lurking places] T; ~-~ 1E, 3A–1F
214.8	storm] 1E, 3A–1F; gale of wind 1A
214.9	nondescript] 3A–1E; non-descript 1A
214.10	hunt . . . sea,] 1E, 3A–1F; command a vessel fitted out to cruise against the pirates, since he knew all their haunts and lurking places: acting 1A
214.10	good] 1E, 3A–1F; shrewd 1A
214.11–12	rogue;" . . . fish.] 1E, 3A–1F; rogue." 1A
214.11–12	cousins german] T; ~-~ 1E, 3A–1F
214.12–13	for . . . called] 1E, 3A–1F; from New-York in 1A
214.13	Galley] 3A–1E; galley 1A
214.13	well] 1E, 3A–1F; gallantly 1A
214.13–16	commissioned . . . . East.] 1E, 3A–1F; commissioned, and steered his course to the Madeiras, to Bonavista, to Madagascar, and cruised at the entrance of the Red Sea. 1A
214.16	Instead . . . against] 1E, 3A–1F; Instead, however, of making war upon the 1A

214.17–19   steered . . . . merchantman] 1E, 3A–1F; captured friend
                 or foe; enriched himself with the spoils of a wealthy In-
                 diaman 1A
214.20–24   Englishman . . . . Kidd] 1E, 3A–1F; Englishman, and hav-
                 ing disposed of his prize, 1A
214.24   booty] 1E, 3A–1F; wealth 1A
214.25   swaggering companions] 1E, 3A–1F; his comrades 1A
214.26–31   Times . . . . the] 1E, 3A–1F; His fame had preceded him.
                 The 1A
214.31   his] 1E, 3A–1F; the 1A
214.31–35   and measures . . . . this] 1E, 3A–1F; of this cut-purse of
                 the ocean. Measures were taken for his arrest; but he had
                 time 1A
214.34   bull dogs] T; ~-~ 1E, 3A–1F
214.35–36   treasures, . . . Boston.] 1E, 3A–1F; treasures. 1A
214.36   to] 1E, 3A–1F; ~ draw his sword and 1A
214.38   his followers] 1E, 3A–1F; several of ~ ~ 1A
214.38–41   Such . . . . comrades] 1E, 3A–1F; They were carried to
                 England in a frigate, where they 1A
214.41–42   in London] 1E, 3A–1F; omitted 1A
215.1   more] 1E, 3A–1F; omitted 1A
215.1   hence] ARE (from ~ 3A–1E); from whence 1A
215.1–2   came . . . be] 1E, 3A–1F; arose the story of his having been
                 1A
215.4   report] 1E, 3A–1F; circumstance 1A
215.5   before his arrest] 1E, 3A–1F; after returning from his cruis-
                 ing 1A
215.7   of money] 1E, 3A–1F; omitted 1A
215.8   coins] 1E, 3A–1F; trees and rocks bearing mysterious
                 marks, doubtless indicating the spots where treasure lay
                 hidden. Of ~ 1A
215.8   with] 1E, 3A–1F; found ~ 1A
215.8   inscriptions, doubtless] 1E, 3A–1F; characters, 1A
215.9   spoils] 1E, 3A–1F; plunder 1A
215.9   his] 1E, 3A–1F; Kidd's 1A
215.9   prizes] 1E, 3A–1F; prize 1A
215.9–10   looked . . . as] 1E, 3A–1F; took for 1A
215.10–11   magical characters] 1E, 3A–1F; magic inscriptions 1A
215.12   treasure] 1E, 3A–1F; spoils 1A
215.13–15   but . . . were] 1E, 3A–1F; many other parts of the eastern
                 coast, also, and various places in Long-Island Sound,
                 have been 1A

215.15–25   rumours . . . . booty.] 1E, 3A–1F; rumours, and have been
ransacked by adventurous money diggers. 1A

215.16   spread] ARE; had ~ 1E, 3A, 1F

215.17   secreted] ARE; had ~ 1E, 3A, 1F

215.18   out of the way] T; ~-~-~-~ 1E, 3A–1F

215.19   sea coast] T; ~-~ 1E, 3A–1F

215.22   money digger] T; ~-~ 1E, 3A–1F

215.26   which once abounded] 1E, 3A–1F; *omitted* 1A

215.28   solemn] 1E, 3A–1F; bargain or 1A

215.28–29   ever prone] 1E, 3A–1F; sure 1A

215.29   would dig] 1E, 3A–1F; had succeeded 1A

215.30   come to an] 1E, 3A–1F; touch the 1A

215.30   chest] 1E, 3A–1F; ~ which contained the treasure 1A

215.32   frighten] 1E, 3A–1F; throw 1A

215.32   party] 1E, 3A–1F; ~ into a panic and frighten them 1A

215.33   when within] 1E, 3A–1F; from 1A

215.34   revisited] 1E, 3A–1F; visited 1A

215.34   place] 1E, 3A–1F; ~ on 1A

215.34   found] 1E, 3A–1F; seen 1A

215.36   All . . . and] 1E, 3A–1F; Such were the vague rumours
which 1A

215.37   curiosity] 1E, 3A–1F; ~ on the interesting subject of these
pirate traditions 1A

215.38–39   truth, and . . . for.] 1E, 3A–1F; truth. 1A

215.39   all] 1E, 3A–1F; *omitted* 1A

216.1   that] 1E, 3A–1F; *omitted* 1A

216.1   I] 1E, 3A–1F; that ~ 1A

216.4–6   city, . . . page.] 1E, 3A–1F; city. 1A

216.7   frequently] 1E, 3A–1F; had ~ 1A

216.8   were] 1E, 3A–1F; *omitted* 1A

216.17   drop line] T; ~ ~ 1A, 3A–1E

216.22   lain] 1E, 3A–1F; been 1A

216.32   no] 1E, 3A–1F; not a 1A

216.32   it is] 1E, 3A–1F; it's 1A

216.33   times . . . himself?"] 1E, 3A–1F; times." *Paragraph* "Like
enough," said another of the party. "There was Bradish
the pirate, who at the time Lord Bellamont made such a
stir after the buccaneers, buried money and jewels some
where in these parts, or on Long-Island; and then there
was Captain Kidd—" 1A

216.34   resolute fellow] 1E, 3A–1F; daring dog 1A

216.34   cried] 1E, 3A–1F; said 1A

216.34   iron faced] T; ~-~ 1A, 3A–1E
216.38   then] 1E, 3A–1F; *omitted* 1A
216.38   all about] 1E, 3A, 1F; *omitted* 1A
217.3   Odsfish] 1E, 3A–1F; Egad 1A
217.3   I thought] 1E, 3A–1F; *omitted* 1A
217.3   Kidd] 1E, 3A–1F; him 1A
217.3   great] 1E, 3A–1F; some 1A
217.4   for curiosity's sake] 1E, 3A–1F; out of sheer curiosity 1A
217.4–6   By . . . . As] 1E, 3A–1F; Ah, well, there's an odd story I
                have heard about one Tom Walker, who they say dug up
                some of Kidd's buried money; and as 1A
217.6   bite] 1E, 3A–1F; seem to ~ 1A
217.6   just now] 1E, 3A–1F; at present 1A
217.7–8   you, ... narration.] 1E, 3A–1F; you to pass away time."
                1A

                THE DEVIL AND TOM WALKER

217.15   Under] 1E, 3A–1F; It was under 1A
217.16   there . . . pirate] 1E, 3A–1F; that Kidd the pirate buried
                his treasure 1A
217.27   New England] 1F, 1E; ~-~ 1A, 3A, ARE
217.31–32   new laid] T; ~-~ 1A, 3A–1E
217.34   forlorn looking] T; ~-~ 1A, 3A–1E
218.11   shrank] 1E; shrunk 1A, 3A–1F
218.11   clapper clawing] T; ~-~ 1A, 3A–1E
218.18   noonday] 3A–1E; noon-day 1A
218.22   bull frog] T; ~-~ 1A, 3A–1E
218.22   where the] 1E, 3A–1F; and where 1A
218.35   old] 1E, 3A–1F; *omitted* 1A
218.39   when] 1E, 3A–1F; that 1A
219.26   on] 1E, 3A–1F; in 1A
219.31   those of] 1E, 3A–1F; *omitted* 1A
219.32   neighbours] 1E, 3A–1F; neighbour's 1A
219.37–38   Peabody, . . . Indians.] 1E, 3A–1F; Peabody. 1A
219.39   man] 1E, 3A–1F; men 1A
220.6   white faced] T; ~-~ 1A, 3A–1E
220.6   put] 3A–1E; poot 1A
220.10   consecrated] 1E, 3A–1F; devoted 1A
220.11   in . . . they] 1E, 3A–1F; *omitted* 1A
220.22   hard minded] T; ~-~ 1A, 3A–1E
220.27   buried] ARE; which had been ~ 1A, 3A–1E
221.19   set] 1E, 3A–1F; sat 1A

221.24	forbore] 3A–1E; forebore 1A
*221.26	set] 1Eb; sat 1A, 3A–1Ea
221.34	which] 1E, 3A–1F; that 1A
221.36	sank] ARE, 1Eb; sunk 1A, 3A–1Ea
222.2	set] 1E, 3A–1F; sat 1A
222.9	hovering] ARE; that were ~ 1A, 3A–1E
222.10	up] 1E, 3A–1F; omitted 1A
222.23	for] 1E, 3A–1F; from the part that remained unconquered. Indeed, 1A
222.25	found] 1E, 3A–1F; several 1A
222.28	clapper clawing] T; ~-~ 1A, 3A–1E
222.30	with] 1E, 3A–1F; by 1A
222.31	man of fortitude] 1E, 3A–1F; little of a philosopher 1A
222.33	further] 1E, 3A–1F; farther 1A
222.41	advances] 1E, 3A–1F; advance 1A
223.15	tomorrow] T; to-morrow 1A, 3A–1E
224.26	new made] T; ~-~ 1A, 3A–1E
224.35	counting house] T; ~-~ 1A, 3A–1E
224.37	in] 1E, 3A–1F; on 1A
225.2	wives'] 3A–1E; ~∧ 1A
225.5	One] ARE; On one 1A, 3A–1E
225.10	months'] 3A–1E; ~∧ 1A
225.23–24	foreclose] 3A–1E; forclose 1A
225.25	into . . . lash,] 1E, 3A–1F; astride the horse 1A
225.25–26	galloped, . . . back,] 1E, 3A–1F; galloped 1A
225.33	border] 1E, 3A–1F; borders 1A
225.35	running] ARE; that when he ran 1A, 3A–1E
225.35	caught] ARE; he just ~ 1A, 3A–1E
225.38	falling] ARE; fell 1A, 3A–1E
225.38	seemed] ARE; which ~ 1A, 3A–1E
226.9	whence] ARE; from ~ 1A, 3A–1E
226.10	are] 1E, 3A–1F; is 1A
226.14	New England] ARE–1E; ~-~ 1A, 3A
226.16	purport] 1E, 3A–1F; tenor 1A
226.19	proposed] ARE; ~ that we should go 1A, 3A–1E
226.20	noontide] ARE; noon-tide 1A, 3A–1E
226.25	constructed] 1E, 3A–1F; omitted 1A
226.26–28	We . . . sight of] 1E, 3A–1F; There were several 1A
226.27	been] ARE; had ~ 1E, 3A, 1F
226.28	and musty bones] 1E, 3A–1F; omitted 1A
226.28	had given] 1E, 3A–1F; gave 1A
226.29	the most] 1E, 3A–1F; a 1A
226.29	in our eyes] 1E, 3A–1F; with us 1A

226.29	in some way] 1E, 3A–1F; *omitted* 1A
226.29	connected] 1E, 3A–1F; ~ in our minds 1A
226.30	rotting] 1E, 3A–1F; *omitted* 1A
226.31	relating to] 1E, 3A–1F; during 1A
226.32	when] 1E, 3A–1F; that 1A
226.37	pondering] 1E, 3A–1F; musing 1A
226.38	well stored] T; ~-~ 1A, 3A–1E
226.38	under] 1E, 3A–1F; and we solaced ourselves during the warm sunny hours of mid-day under the shade of 1A
226.39	green sward] 1E, 3A–1F; cool grassy carpet 1A
226.39	which] 1E, 3A–1F; that 1A
226.39–40	Here . . . midday.] 1E, 3A–1F; *omitted* 1A
227.1–2	grass, . . . fond,] 1E, 3A–1F; grass 1A
227.4	amusement] 1E, 3A–1F; entertainment 1A
227.7	of] 1E, 3A–1F; about 1A
227.7–9	neighbourhood, . . . boyhood.] 1E, 3A–1F; neighbourhood. 1A
227.9	in] 1E, 3A–1F; of 1A
227.11	solaced] 1E, 3A–1F; refreshed 1A
227.11	best] 1E, 3A–1F; *omitted* 1A

WOLFERT WEBBER, OR GOLDEN DREAMS

227.36	Dutch built] T; ~-~ 1A, 3A–1E
228.1	long settled] 1E; ~-~ 1A, 3A–1F, 2E
228.2	its] 1E, 3A–1F; the 1A
228.3	house loving] T; ~-~ 1A, 3A–1E
228.11	sprang] 1E, ARE, 1F; sprung 1A, 3A
228.14	city.] 3A–1E; ~, 1A
228.33	hollyhocks] 3A–1E; holly-hocks 1A
228.41	subjected] 1E, 3A–1F; subject 1A
228.42	skirts] 1E, 1F; streets 1A, 3A, ARE
228.42	make] ARE; sometimes ~ 1A, 3A–1E
229.2	decapitate] ARE; often ~ 1A, 3A–1E
229.6	mill pond] T; ~-~ 1A, 3A–1E
229.8	anoint] 3A–1E; annoint 1A
229.8	aggressor] 3A–1E; agressor 1A
229.20	broad brimmed] T; ~-~ 1A, 3A–1E
229.20	low crowned] T; ~-~ 1A, 3A–1E
*229.31	rosebud] T; rose-bud 1A, 3A–1E
230.5	visitor] ARE–1E; visiter 1A, 3A
230.11	not had] 1E, 3A–1F; not 1A
230.13	bucksome] 1Ea, 3A–1F; gamesome 1A; buxom 1Eb

230.15	visitor] ARE–1E; visiter 1A, 3A
230.17	knitting needle] 1F, 1E; ~-~ 1A, 3A, ARE
230.18	tortoise shell] T; ~-~ 1A, 3A–1E
230.19	tea pot] T; ~-~ 1A, 3A, 2E; teapot ARE–1E
230.19	sang] 1E, 3A–1F; sung 1A
230.23–24	tortoise shell] T; ~-~ 1A, 3A–1E
230.25	tea kettle] T; ~-~ 1A, 3A–1E; teakettle ARE
230.25	cheery] 1E, 1F; cheering 1A, 3A, ARE
230.28–29	tea kettle] T; ~-~ 1A, 3A–1E; teakettle ARE
230.38	baby houses] T; ~-~ 1A, 3A–1E
230.39	lovers] 1E, 3A–1F; love 1A
230.41	to be] 1E, 3A–1F; into 1A
230.41	worse] 1E, 3A–1F; more 1A
230.42	arose] 1E, 3A–1F; were 1A
230.43	lively,] 1E, 3A–1F; very 1A
231.10	flew] ARE; fell 1A, 3A–1E
231.10	nor] ARE; or 1A, 3A–1E
231.12	I'll] 1E, 3A–1F; I 1A
231.13	street door] 3A, ARE; ~-~ 1A, 1F, 1E
231.16	matters] 1E, 3A–1F; things 1A
231.23	Corlear's] 3A–1E; Corlcars 1A
231.31	shuffle board] T; ~-~ 1A, 3A–1E
231.41	in] 1E, 3A–1F; and ~ 1A
232.11	ever] 1E, 3A–1F; always 1A
232.25	one eyed] T; ~-~ 1A, 3A 1E
232.29	red coats] T; ~-~ 1A, 3A–1E
232.34	didn't] ARE–1E; did'nt 1A, 3A
233.23	chronicler] 3A–1E; cronicler 1A
233.23	prosy,] 1E, 1F; *omitted* 1A
233.24	be . . . incontinence] 1E, 3A–1F; grow incontinent 1A
233.24	old.] 1E, 3A 1F; ~·, until their talk flows from them almost involuntarily. 1A
233.25	Peechy] 1E, 3A–1F; ~, who 1A
233.26	month. He] 1E, 3A–1F; month, 1A
233.27	digged] ARE; dug 1A, 3A–1E
233.36	which] 1E, 1F; that 1A, 3A, ARE
233.39–42	took . . . . officer] 1E, 3A–1F; *omitted* 1A
233.43	warlike] 1E, 3A–1F; military 1A
233.43	character∧] 1E, 3A–1F; ~, 1A
233.43	and] 1E, 3A–1F; ~ of the 1A
233.43	tales] 1E, 3A–1F; scenes which, by his own account, he had witnessed 1A
233.43	*No Paragraph* All his] 1E, 3A–1F; *Paragraph* The 1A

234.1	and . . . buried,] 1E, 3A–1F; *omitted* 1A
234.2	obstinately] 1E, 3A–1F; resolutely 1A
234.4	field and shore] 1E, 3A–1F; spot 1A
234.7	ideas] 1E, 3A–1F; ~ of buried riches 1A
234.8	to teem] 1E, 3A–1F; teemed 1A
234.11	an uproar] 1E, 3A–1F; a vertigo 1A
234.36	topsy turvy] T; ~-~ 1A, 3A–1E
235.3	repined] 1E, 3A–1F; half ~ 1A
235.18	full grown] T; ~-~ 1A, 3A–1E
235.20	In] ARE; It was in 1A, 3A–1E
235.20	in vain] ARE; it was ~ ~ 1A, 3A–1E
235.25	about] 1E, 3A–1F; of 1A
235.26	about] 1E, 3A–1F; of 1A
235.28	neighbourhood. Scarce] 1E, 3A–1F; neighbourhood, not omitting the parish dominie; scarce 1A
235.38	Brinkerhoffs] 1E, 1F; —————— 1A; Brinckerhoffs, 3A, ARE
235.39	By . . . but] 1E, 3A–1F; *omitted* 1A
235.43	and digging] 1E, 3A–1F; *omitted* 1A
236.3	frozen hard] 1E, 3A–1F; too frozen 1A
236.13	presented] 1E, 3A–1F; resented 1A
236.15	which] 1E, 3A–1F; that 1A
236.16	bull frogs] T; ~-~ 1A, 3A–1E
236.16	during] 1E, 3A–1F; in the brooks, ~ 1A
236.17	sank] ARE; sunk 1A, 3A–1E
236.22	before] 1E, 3A–1F; that shaded 1A
236.27	woke] 1E, ARE, 1F; awoke 1A, 3A
236.28	for the supply] 1E, 3A–1F; to supply the wants 1A
237.6	kind hearted] T; ~-~ 1A, 3A–1F, 2E; kindhearted 1E
237.18	Saturday] 3A–1E; saturday 1A
237.27	leather bottomed] T (~-~ 1E, 3A–1F); *omitted* 1A
237.34	mop] 1E, 3A–1F; mass 1A
237.34	grey] 1E; gray 1A, 3A–1F
*237.34	grizzly] 1E, 3A, 1F; grizly 1A
237.34	hard favoured] T; ~-~ 1A, 3A–1E
238.2	domain.] 1E, 3A–1F; ~. He could get nothing, however, but vague information. 1A
238.10	whence] ARE; from ~ 1A, 3A–1E
238.35	small] 1E, 3A–1F; little 1A
238.35	In] 1E, 3A–1F; But in 1A
238.36	while, however,] 1E, 3A–1F; while 1A
238.38	place, and] 1E, 3A–1F; place; 1A
238.40	whole] 1E, 3A–1F; little 1A

238.42	dare devil] T; ~-~ 1A, 3A–1E
239.8	West Indies] ARE–1E; ~-~ 1A, 3A
239.11	huge] 1E, 3A–1F; large 1A
239.14	of] 1E, 3A–1F; *omitted* 1A
239.20	faint heartedness] T; ~-~ 1A, 3A–1E
239.29–30	arrival . . . his] 1E, 3A–1F; *omitted* 1A
240.2	both] 1E, 3A–1F; *omitted* 1A
240.3	excrescences] 3A–1E; excresences 1A
240.6	bar room] T; ~-~ 1A, 3A–1E
240.11	throne, and] 1E, 3A–1F; throne; 1A
240.18	swaggering] ARE; long ~ 1A, 3A–1E
240.19	lying] 1E, 3A–1F; laying 1A
*240.32–33	resistance. They] 3A–1E; ~, they 1A
241.1	was the answer] 1F, 3A–1F; said the merman 1A
241.5	moved] 3A–1E; mooved 1A
241.14	one eyed] T (~-~ 1E, 3A–1F); red-faced 1A
241.15	akimbo] ARE, 1F; a-kimbo 1A, 3A, 1E
241.34	land lubber] T (~-~ 1E, 3A–1F); coward 1A
241.39	observed] 1E, 3A–1F; now took up the word, and in a pacifying tone ~ 1A
241.41	such to be] 1E, 3A–1F; *omitted* 1A
242.1	Sam] 1E, 3A–1F; Mud ~ 1A
242.5	Black] 1E, 3A–1F; *omitted* 1A
242.17	one eyed] T (~-~ 1E, 3A–1F); red-faced 1A
242.32	stumped] 1E, 1F; stamped 1A, 3A, ARE

THE ADVENTURE OF THE BLACK FISHERMAN

243.5	OF] 1E, 3A–1F; ~ SAM, 1A
243.5	FISHERMAN] 1F, 3A–1F; ~, COMMONLY DENOMINATED MUD SAM 1A
243.6	Black] 1F, 3A–1F; Mud 1A
243.6–7	fisherman, . . . Sam,] 1E, 3A–1F; fisherman 1A
243.7–8	half century] 1E, 3A–1F; twenty or thirty years 1A
243.8	It] 1E, 3A–1F; Well, it 1A
243.8	many, many] 1E, 1F; many 1A, 3A, ARE
243.8	since] 1E, 3A–1F; ~ that 1A
243.8–9	as . . . province] 1E, 3A–1F; a young fellow 1A
243.10	day's] 1E, 3A–1F; *omitted* 1A
243.10	at an] 1E, 3A–1F; *omitted* 1A
243.10	hour] 1E, 3A–1F; *omitted* 1A
243.13	had] ARE; he ~ 1A, 3A–1E
243.13	shifted] 1E, 3A–1F; been able to shift 1A

243.13   according to] 1E, 3A–1F; with 1A
243.14   Back] ARE–1E; back 1A, 3A
243.14   from] 1E, 3A–1F; and ~ 1A
243.14   Back] ARE–1E; back, 1A, 3A
243.15   Pan] ARE; pan 1A, 3A–1E
243.15   he] 1E, 3A–1F; Sam 1A
243.17   eddies] 1E, 3A–1F; rapids 1A
*243.29   Sam,] 3A–1E; ~∧ 1A
243.30   crouching] ARE; crouched 1A, 3A–1E
243.31   woke] ARE; awoke 1A, 3A–1E
244.1   gliding] ARE; which was ~ 1A, 3A–1E
244.3   exclaimed,] 3A–1E; ~∧ 1A
244.6   desperate looking] T; ~-~ 1A, 3A–1E
244.7   three cornered] T; ~-~ 1A, 3A–1E
244.12   a] 1E, 3A–1F; the 1A
244.35   powerful] 1E, 3A–1F; ~ with poor Sam 1A
244.40   terrible] 1E, 3A–1F; *omitted* 1A
244.42   not] 1E, 3A–1F; ~, therefore, 1A
244.43   to the . . . mystery] 1E, 3A–1F; *omitted* 1A
245.1   midnight fellows] 1E, 3A–1F; villains 1A
245.4   for] 1E, 3A–1F; *omitted* 1A
245.11   round cheeked] T; ~-~ 1A, 3A–1E
245.28   fortunately] 1E, 3A–1F; *omitted* 1A
246.1   Pan] ARE; pan 1A, 3A–1E
246.2   Hog's Back] 3A–1E; Hogs back 1A
246.3   farm house] T; ~-~ 1A, 3A–1E
246.4   Prauw] 1E, 3A–1F; *omitted* 1A
246.8   half-pay] 3A–1E; ~∧ ~ 1A
246.12   of," . . . "he] 1E, 3A–1F; of; he 1A
246.15   so] 1E, 3A–1F; *omitted* 1A
246.24   farm house] T; ~-~ 1A, 3A–1E
246.25   Gate?"] 3A–1E; ~?∧ 1A
246.28   farm house] T; ~-~ 1A, 3A–1E
246.30   lonely] 1E, 3A–1F; wild ~ 1A
246.33   buried] ARE; that was ~ 1A, 3A–1E
247.3   fudge] 1E, 3A–1F; humbug 1A
247.5   that house] 1E, 3A–1F; the ~ 1A
247.9   abroad] ARE; that prevailed ~ 1A, 3A–1E
247.10   were] ARE; ~ all 1A, 3A–1E
247.11   shaking the building] 1E, 3A–1F; that made the building
                shake 1A
247.11   very] 1E, 3A–1F; *omitted* 1A
247.16   thrust] 3A–1E; thurst 1A

247.24	mingled] ARE; that ~ 1A, 3A–1E
247.29	bar room] T; ~-~ 1A, 3A–1E
247.32	afterwards] ARE; after 1A, 3A–1E
248.1	heard once more] 1E, 3A–1F; again heard 1A
248.3	summoned] 1E, 3A–1F; called 1A
248.10–11	veteran, . . . them;] 1E, 3A–1F; veteran; 1A
248.18	and] ARE; he 1A, 3A–1E
248.20	and, sinking] 1E, 3A–1F; sunk 1A
248.21	pulled] 1E, 3A–1F; and ~ 1A
248.26	void] 1E, 3A–1F; drear and ~ 1A
248.29	tavern . . . storm] 1E, 3A–1F; tavern, for they could not leave it before the storm should subside 1A
248.37	existence] 1E, 3A–1F; human ~ 1A
248.43	particularly] 1E, 3A–1F; *omitted* 1A
249.1–2	went; . . . occasion.] 1E, 3A–1F; went. 1A
249.3	came," . . . "in] 1E, 3A–1F; came in 1A
249.4	whence] ARE; from ~ 1A, 3A–1E
249.7	pities,"] 3A–1E; ~ʌ" 1A
249.7	added he] 1E, 3A–1F; ~ the landlord 1A
249.8	Jones' locker,] 1E, 3A–1F; Jones 1A
249.8	own locker] 1E, 3A–1F; sea chest 1A
249.9	His locker] 1E, 3A–1F; The sea chest 1A
249.9	cried] 1E, 3A–1F; said 1A
249.29	told] 1E, 3A–1F; struck 1A
249.30	of the night] 1E, 3A–1F; *omitted* 1A
249.34	little] 1E, 3A–1F; *omitted* 1A
249.43	even . . . who] 1E, 3A–1F; he who had farthest to go and 1A
250.1	accustomed] 1E, 3A–1F; a veteran sexton, and ~ 1A
250.5	These] 1E, 3A–1F; His mind was all of a whirl with these freebooting tales; and then these 1A
250.6	these] 1E, 3A 1F; this 1A
250.7	shores] 1E, 3A–1F; shore 1A
250.14	negro] 1E, 3A–1F; black 1A
250.21	and barrels] 1E, 3A–1F; bags 1A
250.27	Black] 1E, 3A–1F; Mud 1A
250.29	not] 1E, 3A–1F; their ~ 1A
250.36	fairly] ARE; that ~ 1A, 3A–1E
250.40	recently] 1E, 3A–1F; suddenly 1A
250.43	black] 1E, 3A–1F; negro 1A
251.5	Sam] ARE; Mud ~ 1A, 3A–1E
251.6	had led] 1E, 3A–1F; was 1A
251.7	amphibious life] 1E, 3A–1F; amphibious kind of animal,

something more of a fish than a man; he had led the life
of an otter 1A

251.14	looking, in the] 1E, 3A–1F; looming through 1A
251.25	was] 1E, 3A–1F; lay 1A
251.26	the true] 1E, 3A–1F; a ∼ 1A
251.26	negro luxury of] 1E, 3A–1F; negro's luxury— 1A
252.5	garter snake] 1E; ∼-∼ 1A, 3A–1F
252.14	grass plot] T; ∼-∼ 1A, 3A–1E; grassplot ARE
252.21	woody] 1E, 3A–1F; omitted 1A
252.25	bird*] 1E, ARE (∼,* 3A; ∼¹ 1F); ∼,* as he 1A
252.26	plumage.] 1E, 3A–1F; ∼, seemed like some genius flitting about this region of mystery. 1A
252.36	the negro] 1E, 3A–1F; Sam 1A
252.38	corroborated] ARE; which was ∼ 1A, 3A–1E
253.2	rocks . . . obliged] 1E, 3A–1F; rocks, and having 1A
253.6	shelved] 1E, 3A–1F; sloped 1A
253.8	The negro] 1E, 3A–1F; Sam 1A
253.14	closely] 1E, 3A–1F; narrowly 1A
253.21	these] 1E, 3A–1F; omitted 1A
253.21	so] 1E, 3A–1F; omitted 1A
253.24	he] 1E, 3A–1F; Sam 1A
253.25	whence] ARE; from which 1A; from ∼ 3A–1E
253.25	had] 1E, 3A–1F; omitted 1A
253.26	discovered] 1E, 3A–1F; descried 1A
253.28	over] 1E, 3A–1F; on 1A
253.28	not] 1E, 3A–1F; ∼ but 1A
253.29	buccaneers.] 1E, 3A–1F; ∼, to denote the places where their treasure lay buried. 1A
253.30	spot . . . buried,] 1E, 3A–1F; spot; 1A
253.31	in . . . crosses] 1E, 3A–1F; omitted 1A
253.32	spoils] 1E, 3A–1F; spoil 1A
253.33	the old negro] 1E, 3A–1F; Sam 1A
253.36	beside] ARE; it was just ∼ 1A, 3A–1E
253.36	under] ARE; it must have been ∼ 1A, 3A–1E
253.42	unprovided] 1E, 3A–1F; unprepared 1A
254.2	homewards] 1E, 3A–1F; homeward 1A
254.7	from] 1E, 3A–1F; on 1A
254.18	affright] 1E, 3A–1F; horror 1A
*254.19	grisly] 1E, ARE, 1F; grizzly 1A, 3A
254.21	any] 1E, 3A–1F; omitted 1A
254.24	tugged] 1E, 3A–1F; tagged 1A
254.26	fairly] ARE; had ∼ 1A, 3A–1E
254.29	grisly] 1E, ARE, 1F; grizzly 1A, 3A

254.36	away] 1E, 3A–1F; among 1A
255.6	Boerhaave] 1F, 1E; Boorhaave 1A, 3A, ARE
255.8	reflected] 1E, 3A–1F; seemed to reflect 1A
255.15	among] 1E, 3A–1F; in 1A
255.18	united] 1E, 3A–1F; ~ all 1A
255.29	oppressed] 1E, 3A–1F; depressed 1A
255.30	an] 1E, 3A, 1F; the 1A
255.38	first] 1E, 3A–1F; *omitted* 1A
256.8–9	the black fisherman] 1E, 3A–1F; Mud Sam 1A
256.10	pickaxe] ARE; pick-axe 1A, 3A–1E
256.17	revived] 1E, 3A–1F; roused 1A
256.19	once] 1E, 3A–1F; *omitted* 1A
256.19	mounted] 1E, 3A–1F; once ~ 1A
256.21	passage] 1E, 3A–1F; paper 1A
256.21	Mr.] 3A–1E; ~∧ 1A
256.27	readily] 1E, 3A–1F; easily 1A
256.34	bifurcatæ] 3A–1E; befurcatæ 1A
256.36	Agricola] 3A–1E; Agricula 1A
257.14	night walking] T; ~-~ 1A, 3A–1E
257.17	along] ARE; echoing ~ 1A, 3A–1E
257.21	old] 1E, 3A–1F; negro 1A
257.22	pickaxe] ARE; pick-axe 1A, 3A–1E
257.33	on] 1E, 3A–1F; in 1A
257.37	Corlear's] 1E, 1F; Corlaers 1A; Corlaer's 3A, ARE
258.4	Turtle Bay] 1F, 1E; ~ bay 1A, 3A, ARE
258.5	Kip's Bay] 1F, 1E; ~ bay 1A, 3A, ARE
258.6	the negro] 1E, 3A–1F; Sam 1A
258.10	own] 1E, 3A–1F; *omitted* 1A
258.12	the neighbouring] 1E, 3A–1F; Father red cap's 1A
258.26	hands] 1E, 3A–1F; hand 1A
258.27	to turn gradually] 1E, 3A–1F; slowly to turn 1A
258.33	the negro] 1E, 3A–1F, Sam 1A
258.38	He] 1E, 3A–1F; The doctor 1A
259.5–6	pickaxe] ARE; pick-axe 1A, 3A–1E
259.6	close bound] T; ~-~ 1A, 3A–1E
259.12	by] 1E, 3A–1F; about 1A
259.13	roost] 1E, 3A–1F; nest 1A
259.17	The negro] 1E, 3A–1F; Sam 1A
259.19	his] 1E, 3A–1F; the 1A
259.21	lighted] 1E, 3A–1F; strangely ~ 1A
259.23	grizzly headed] T (~-~ 1E, 3A–1F); grizzled-~ 1A
259.24	negro] 1E, 3A–1F; Sam 1A
259.24	for] 1E, 3A–1F; as 1A

259.25	old] 1E, 1F; *omitted* 1A, 3A, ARE
259.31	above] 1E, 3A–1F; over head 1A
259.42	the negro] 1E, 3A–1F; Mud Sam 1A
260.5	second] 1E, 3A–1F; period 1A
260.15	him] 1E, 3A–1F; view 1A
260.27	was] 1E, 3A–1F; had 1A
260.32	morning] 1E, 3A–1F; the ~ 1A
260.33	grievously battered, and] ARE; *omitted* 1A, 3A–1E
260.33	boat.] ARE; ~, grievously battered. 1A, 3A–1E
260.41	Black] 1E, 3A–1F; Mud 1A
261.5	speedily] 1E, 3A–1F; conveyed ~ 1A
261.10	them] 1E, 3A–1F; *omitted* 1A
261.11	pot lid] T; ~-~ 1A, 3A, ARE; potlid 1F, 1E
261.26	Corlear's] 1E, 1F; Corlaers 1A; Corlaer's 3A, ARE
261.29	was] 1E, 3A–1F; ~ a buccaneer; 1A
261.29	comrades] ARE; ~ either 1A, 3A–1E
261.32	much] 1E, 3A–1F; *omitted* 1A
261.36	grey] 3A; gray 1A, ARE–1E
262.35	yours] ARE–1E; your's 1A, 3A
262.37	round headed] T; ~-~ 1A, 3A–1E
263.1	which] 1E, 3A–1F; that 1A
263.26	huge] 1E, 3A–1F; piece of 1A
263.34	spirit broken] T; ~-~ 1A, 3A–1E
263.39	many] 1E, 1F; *omitted* 1A, 3A, ARE
264.10	knocking] 1E, 3A–1F; rapping 1A
264.23	his] 1E, 3A–1F; a 1A
264.28	arm chair] T; ~-~ 1A, 3A–1E
264.28	Corlear's] 1E, 1F; Corlaers 1A; Corlaer's 3A, ARE

LIST OF REJECTED SUBSTANTIVES

This list records substantive variants in all relevant texts which were not adopted for the critical edition. Page and line numbers locate the reading in this edition. Only typographical rules or spaces and running heads are omitted from the count. The reading to the left of the bracket is the substantive reading of the Twayne text; its source and all other editions in which it occurs are designated by symbols to the right of the bracket. Following the semicolon are the rejected reading and the symbol for the edition or editions in which it appears. The List of Abbreviations, p. 267, explains the symbols used. A swung dash ~ signifies the repetition of a word after the bracket. An asterisk preceding an entry directs the reader to the Discussions of Adopted Readings.

Except in a few instances, accidental differences among texts agreeing substantively with the copy-text are not recorded. Likewise, accidental differences among texts containing the same substantive departure from copy-text are usually not recorded.

TO THE READER

3.4	tripped] 1E, 3A–1F; been ~ 2A
3.8	town] 1E, 3A–1F; tour 2A
4.14	or a] 1E, 3A–1F; or 2A
5.1	found] 1E, 2A–1F; often ~ ARE

THE GREAT UNKNOWN

9.10	Gentleman] 1A, 2A–1E; gentlemen 3A

THE HUNTING DINNER

10.5	young] 1A, 2A–1E; younger ARE
10.8	he] 1A, 2A–1E; omitted ARE
10.24	wassail] 1A, 2A; the ~ 3A–1E
11.8	of] 1A, 2A–1E; omitted 3A, ARE
11.10	to] 1A; ~ a 2A–1E
11.37	those] 1A, 2A–1E; these 2E
11.38	of this] 1A, 2A–1Ea; this 1Eb
11.39	these] 1A; those 2A–1E
12.3–4	could never] 1A; never could 2A–1E
12.11	wails] 1A, 2A; waits 3A–1E
12.13	and] 1A; ~ with 2A–1E
12.37	a] 1A, 2A, ARE, 1Eb; an 3A–1Ea

12.43   of] 1A; ~ a 2A–1E
13.3   this] 1A; that 2A–1E
13.6   our] 1A, 2A–1Ea; your 1Eb

THE ADVENTURE OF MY UNCLE

13.18   at] 1A; in 2A–1E
13.32   knew] 1A, 1E; ~ well 2A–1F
14.15   the dove] 1A, 2A–1E; a ~ ARE
14.30   jerkins] 1A, 3A–1E; jerking 2A
15.1   he was] 1A, 2A–1E; was his ARE
15.9   uncle's] 1A; uncle 2A–1E
15.14   flourished] 1A, 2A–1E; flourishing 3A, ARE
15.15   sa-sa] 1A, 2A; ça-ça 3A–1E
15.31   upon] 1A; on 2A–1E
16.18   sent] 1A, 3A–1E; set 2A
16.21   on top] 1A; ~ the ~ 2A–1E
17.12   nor] 1A, ARE; or 2A–1E
18.9   family] 1A; *omitted* 2A–1E
18.18   hoop] 1A; hooped 2A–1E
19.1   with] 1A, 2A–1E; from 3A, ARE
19.5   rusty little] 1E, 3A–1F; little rusty 2A
19.21   wind] 1A; winds 2A–1E
20.2   while] 1A; ~ the 2A–1E
20.7   refreshments] 1A; refreshment 2A–1E
20.8   little] 1A; *omitted* 2A–1E
22.2   at] 1A, 2A–1E; *omitted* ARE

THE ADVENTURE OF MY AUNT

22.20   his] 1A, 2A–1E; the ARE
*23.6   fastenings] 1A; fastnesses 2A–1E
23.27   towards] 1A, ARE; toward 2A–1E
23.29   towards] 1A, 2A, ARE; toward 3A–1E
23.30   eye] 1A; eyes 2A–1E
24.16   left] 1A, 2A; had ~ 3A–1E
24.18   me] 1A, 2A–1E; *omitted* ARE
24.41   nor] 1A; no 2A–1E
25.2   into] 1A; in 2A–1E
25.11   observe] 1A; ~ that 2A–1E
25.24   e'en] 1A, 2A; even 3A–1E

THE BOLD DRAGOON, OR
THE ADVENTURE OF MY GRANDFATHER

25.27	it's] 1A, 2A–1F, 2E; its 1E
25.28	upon] 1A; on 2A–1E
26.5	at] 1A; from 2A–1E
26.14	the time] 1A; at ~ ~ 2A–1E
26.21	on] 1A, 2A–1E; in 3A, ARE
26.22	ya vrouws] 1A, 2A; yafrows 3A–1E
26.24	their] 1A; the 2A–1E
26.28	rackety] 1A, 2A–1E; rickety ARE
26.39	a brewery—] 1A; *omitted* 2A–1E
26.42	altogether have] 1A, 2A; have altogether 3A–1E
27.23	eyed] 1A, 2A; eying 3A, 1E; eyeing ARE, 1F
27.26	hat] 1A, 2A; head 3A–1E
28.7	for some time been] 1A, 2A; been for some time 3A–1E
28.8	you're] 1A, 2A; you are 3A–1E
28.42	fruit, and fish] 1A; fish, and fruit 2A–1E
29.5	diseased] 1A, 3A–1E; deceased 2A
29.5	and] 1A, 2A; or 3A–1E
29.6	have been] 1A, 2A; be 3A–1E
29.26	fever] 1A, 2A; a ~ 3A–1E
30.5	room's] 1A, 2A; room 3A–1E
30.7	gentlemen] 1A, 2A–1Fa, 2E; gentleman 1Eb
30.33	either] 1A; rather 2A–1E
30.37	calling] 1A; called 2A–1E
30.38	two] 1A, 2A 1E; the ~ ARE
31.8	suppose] 1A, 2A; ~ that 3A–1E
31.27	no doubt had] 1A, 2A; had no doubt 3A–1E

THE ADVENTURE OF THE GERMAN STUDENT

34.1	conflicting] 1E, 3A–1F; contradictory 2A
34.32	which] 1E, 3A–1F; that 2A
35.12	even] 1E, 3A–1F; ever 2A

THE ADVENTURE OF THE MYSTERIOUS PICTURE

36.20	a] 1A, 2A, ARE; an 3A–1E
36.28	a] 1A; the 2A–1E
36.30	cried] 1A; said 2A 1E
37.6	its] 1A, 2A, ARE; the 3A–1E
38.4	visage] 1A, 3A–1E; image 2A

38.6	black] 1A, 2A; back 3A–1E
38.16	and] 1A, 2A; *omitted* 3A–1E
38.19	tried] 1A; and ~ 2A–1E
38.20	and howling] 1A, 2A–1E; ~ a ~ ARE
38.28	now] 1A, 2A–1E; *omitted* 3A, ARE
38.29	peering] 1A, 2A, 2E; peeping 3A–1E
38.30	insufferable] 1A; insupportable 2A–1E
39.20	this] 1A, 1E; the 2A–1F
39.31	consequence] 1A, 2A–1E; consequences 3A, ARE
40.9	toilette] 1A, 2A; toilet 3A–1E
40.12	were] 1A, 2A; *omitted* 3A–1E
40.36	in] 1A, 2A–1E; with 3A
40.38	thou'rt] 1A, 2A, 1E; thou art 3A–1F
41.9–10	gentlemen] 1A, 3A–1E; gentleman 2A
41.17	with] 1A, 2A; and ~ 3A–1E
41.20	gentleman] 1A, 3A–1E; gentlemen 2A
41.24	both] 1A, 2A–1E; ~ of ARE
41.42	it produces] 1A, 2A; which ~ ~ 3A–1E
42.9	strongly] 1A; strangely 2A–1E

THE ADVENTURE OF THE MYSTERIOUS STRANGER

49.19	hopes] 1A, 2A–1E; ~ that 3A, ARE
42.22	the place] 1A, 1E; that ~ 2A–1F
42.27	purpose] 1A, 1E; purposes 2A–1F
42.27	Indeed,] 1A; *omitted* 2A–1E
43.30	refreshments] 1A; refreshment 2A–1E
44.16	Georgio] 1A, 2E; Georgia 2A–1E
44.20	or] 1A, 1E; ~ the 2A–1F
44.23	from] 1A, 2A–1E; by 2E
44.32	Cassino] 1A, 2A–1E; cassinos ARE
44.35	found] 1A; ~ that 2A–1E
44.36	upon] 1A, 2A; on 3A–1E
45.8	a soft] 1A, 3A–1E; soft 2A
45.15	and] 1A, 2A–1E; *omitted* 3A, ARE
45.22	is] 1A, 2A–1E; was 3A, ARE
45.25	upon] 1A, 2A; on 3A–1E
45.30	gave involuntarily] 1A; involuntarily gave 2A–1E
46.1	or] 1A, ARE; nor 2A–1E
46.13	this] 1A, 2A–1E; his 3A, ARE
46.26	had] 1A; have 2A–1E
46.26	returned] 1A, 2A–1E; rereturned 3A
47.19	this] 1A; the 2A–1E

THE STORY OF THE YOUNG ITALIAN

48.13	relatives] 1A, 2A; relations 3A–1E
50.37	the music of] 1A, 2A–1E; *omitted* 3A, ARE
52.5	felt I] 1A, 1E; ~ that ~ 2A–1F
52.37	distress] 1A, 3A, ARE; distresses 2A–1E
52.41	pensively] 1A, 2A; pennyless 3A–1E
54.12	her] 1E, 3A–1F; my 2A
55.4	an] 1A, 2A–1Ea; *omitted* 1Eb
55.20	an] 1A, 2A; *omitted* 3A–1E
55.20	manner] 1A, 2A; manners 3A–1E
55.25	and] 1A, 2A; ~ of 3A–1E
55.31	blending] 1A, 3A–1E; blended 2A
55.38	central] 1A, 3A–1E; centre 2A
56.20	mortality's] 1A, 3A–1E; morality's 2A
57.1	prospects] 1A, 2A; prospect 3A–1E
57.14	mere] 1A, 2A, 1E; the ~ 3A–1F
57.25	relatives] 1A, 2A; relations 3A–1E
58.19	notice] 1A, 2A; *omitted* 3A–1E
59.5	compunctious] 1A, 2A–1E; compunctions ARE
59.6	having ever] 1A, 2A–1E; ever having ARE
59.20	me] 1A, 2A–1E; *omitted* 3A, ARE
*59.26–27	light . . . white] 1A, 2A; light . . . light 3A–1E; *omitted* . . . light ARE
60.13	ravage] 1A, 2A–1E; ravages ARE
60.14	the] 1A, 2A; that a 3A–1E
60.15	that] 1A, 2A; *omitted* 3A–1E
60.17	knees] 1A, 2A–1E; knee ARE
60.18	stifled] 1A, 2A–1E; filled ARE
60.25	powers] 1A, 2A–1E; power 3A, ARE
60.35	to] 1A, 2A–1E; *omitted* 3A, ARE
60.38	of assurances] 1A, 2A–1E; assurances ARE
62.13	sprung] 1A, 2A; sprang 3A–1E
62.19	that] 1A, 3A–1E; the 2A
62.39	still] 1A, 3A–1E; *omitted* 2A
62.42	a glove] 1A, 2A–1E; glove ARE
63.28	and] 1A, 2A–1E; ~ and ARE
64.1	the] 1A, 3A–1E; her 2A
64.1	at] 1A; for 2A–1E
64.26	been] 1A, 2A–1E; beed ARE
64.32	with] 1A, 3A–1E; by 2A
65.13	word] 1A, 2A–1E; work ARE
65.15	sprang] 1A, 2A, ARE; sprung 3A–1E

66.2   of] 1A, 3A, ARE; to 2A–1E
66.33   when] 1A, 2A, 1E; that ~ 3A–1F
67.12   and I] 1A, 2A–1E; and 3A, ARE

LITERARY LIFE

71.22   I] 1A; that ~ 3A–1E
71.34   excepting] MS, 1A, 1E; except 3A–1F
71.40   complete] MS, 1A; completely 3A–1E
72.2   any] MS, 1A; ~ of the 3A–1E
72.5   then] MS, 1A; *omitted* 3A–1E
72.5   to] MS, 1A; then ~ 3A–1E
72.7   lines] MS, 1A; line 3A–1E
72.10   is] MS, 1A, 1E; ~ in 3A–1F

A LITERARY DINNER

72.29   even] MS, 1A; *omitted* 3A–1E
*72.31   Buckthorne] MS, 1A; Mr. ~ 3A–1E
73.2   but] MS, 1A; and 3A–1E
73.3   and] MS, 1A; or 3A–1E
73.7   one, two] MS, 1A, 1E; one or two 3A–1F
73.13   idea] MS, 3A–1E; ideas 1A
73.16   which] MS, 1A; that 3A–1E
73.19   volume] MS, 1A–1E; volumed 3A, ARE
74.13   Garretteer] MS (garreteer 3A–1E); gazeteer 1A
74.37   further] MS, 3A–1E; farther 1A
74.38   poet] MS, 3A–1E; port 1A
74.39   gentleman] MS, 3A–1E; gentlemen 1A

THE CLUB OF QUEER FELLOWS

75.2   but] MS, 1A; *omitted* 3A–1E
75.17   taste] MS, 1A; tastes 3A–1E
75.18   individual] MS, 1A; individuals 3A–1E
75.25   quip] MS, 3A–1E; quiz 1A
75.28   in] MS, 1A; over 3A–1E
75.40   fuddle] MS, 3A–1E; puddle 1A
76.22   then] MS, 1A; there 3A–1E
76.22   scene of] MS, 1A–1E; ~ ~ a 3A, ARE
76.29   I'm] MS, 1A–1E; I am 3A, ARE
77.19   lodgings] MS, 1A–1E; lodging 2E
77.25   homewards] MS, 1A, 1E; homeward 3A–1F
77.30   afterwards] MS, 1A, 1E; afterward 3A–1F

| 77.32 | profoundly] MS, 1A; perfectly 3A–1E |
| *77.43 | tall] MS; ~ and 1A–1E |

THE POOR DEVIL AUTHOR

79.3	further] MS, 3A–1E; farther 1A
79.21	Montagu] MS, 1A–1Ea; Montague 1Eb
80.26	in wood] MS, 1A; on ~ 3A–1E
80.34	scholar . . . genius] MS, 1A; genius, or a great scholar, 3A–1E
81.24	went] MS, 1A; ~ out 3A–1E
81.25	buried] MS, 3A–1E; busied 1A
81.38	those] MS, 3A–1E; these 1A
82.1	cutting] MS, 1A; casting 3A–1E
82.3	any] MS, 1A–1E; *omitted* 2E
82.3	production] MS, 1A; productions 3A–1E
82.7	he] MS, 1A–1E; be 2E
82.23	career] MS, 3A–1E; course 1A
82.40	pleasures] MS, 1A; pleasure 3A–1E
83.33	thing] MS, 1A, 1E; ~ of 3A–1F
84.3	bade] MS, 1A–1E; bid 3A, ARE
84.22	attempts] MS, 3A–1E; attempt 1A
84.24	would they] MS, 1A; they would 3A–1E
85.29	ever] MS, 1A–1E; never 3A, ARE
86.23	own] MS, 1A–1F; *omitted* 1E
86.30	flinch] MS, 1A; to ~ 3A–1E
86.35	Clym] MS, 1A, 1E, Clymm 3A, 1F; Clymm ARE
86.40	said] MS, 1A–1E; cried ARE
87.7	last] MS, 1A; best 3A–1E
87.8	Knights errants] MS, 1A; knights-errant 3A–1F; knight-er-rants 1E
87.20	dusk] MS, 1A; dark 3A–1E
87.23	Carolina] MS, 1A; Caroline 3A–1E
87.33	Galloon] MS (galloon 3A–1E); galleon 1A, ARE, 2E
88.11	he] MS, 1A; we 3A–1E
88.17	but] MS, 1A, 1E; *omitted* 3A–1F
88.41	fell] MS, 1A–1F, 2E; full 1E
89.2	scapegraces] MS, 1A–1E; scrape-graces 3A, 1F
89.17	in] 1E, ARE; of 3A, 1F
89.25	capacitated to write] 1E; capable of writing 3A–1F
89.26	than a] 1E, 3A, 1F; a than ARE
89.40	slightingly] 1E, ARE; slightly 3A, 1F
90.8	nobleman] 1E, ARE, 1F; noblemen 3A

90.9   who] 1E, 1F; *omitted* 3A, ARE
90.17   sorely] 1E; sore 3A–1F
91.3   ever] MS, 1A; *omitted* 3A–1E
91.22   towards] MS, 1A–1E; toward 1F
91.28   led] MS, 1A; had 3A–1E
91.36   one] MS, 1A–1E; and 3A, ARE
92.10   gives] MS, 1A; ~ me 3A–1E

NOTORIETY

92.16   NOTORIETY] 1E, 3A–1F; ~* *Footnote* *To follow "The
              Poor Devil Author" in Part II. 2A
93.24   routs] 1E, 3A–1F; routes 2A
93.30   to talk] 1E, 2A–1F; talk ARE
93.35   drank] 1E, 2A; drunk 3A–1F

A PRACTICAL PHILOSOPHER
95.7   trilling] 1E, ARE; thrilling 2A–1F
95.20   ever] 1E, 3A–1F; have ~ 2A
95.20   a time] 1E, 2A–1F; time ARE
95.27   further] MS, 2A–1E; farther 1A

BUCKTHORNE, OR THE YOUNG MAN
OF GREAT EXPECTATIONS

96.19   into] MS, 1A–1E; in ARE
97.22   squire's] MS, 1A–1E; squire 2E
97.25   lawns] MS, 1A; lawn 3A–1E
97.31   thrilling] MS, 1A; throbbing 3A–1E
97.39   lines] MS, 1A–1E; rhymes ARE
98.14   others] MS, 1A, 1E; other 3A–1F
98.33   during] MS, 1A–1E; on ARE
98.42   grown] MS, 1A, 1E; were ~ 3A–1F
99.4   whom] MS, 1A–1F; which 1E
99.5   whom he held] MS, 1A; of whom he was 3A–1F; whom he
              had 1E
99.9   this] MS, 1A–1F; the 1E
99.20   for] MS, 1A, 1E; to 3A–1F
*99.24   bull's] MS, 1A; cow's 3A–1E
99.29   to let] MS, 1A–1E; let 2E
99.43   unsocial] MS, 1A–1E; unsociable ARE
100.7   Rooks] MS (rooks 1A–1E); rocks 3A
100.11   when] MS, 1A; where 3A–1E
100.19   rove] MS, 1A; roam 3A–1E

100.23	was] MS, 1A–1E; should be 2E
100.24	these] MS, 1A–1Ea; those 1Eb
100.27	was still] MS, 1A–1E; remained 2E
101.8	until] MS, 1A; till 3A–1E
101.11	wayworn] MS, 1A; wayward 3A–1E
101.15	on] 1E; in 3A–1F
101.21	uncle's] MS, 1A, 1E; ~ house 3A–1F
101.40	attractions] MS, 1A–1E; attraction ARE
103.15	if] MS, 1A–1E; *omitted* 2E
103.36	the] MS, 3A–1E; their 1A
104.23	stood I] MS, 1A–1F; had I stood 1E
104.23	a] MS, 1A–1F; *omitted* 1E
104.32	us] MS, 1A; as 3A–1E
104.38	could] MS, 3A–1E; would 1A
104.40	further] MS, 3A–1E; farther 1A
*105.1	of] MS, 1A; on 3A–1E
105.4	were] MS, 1A; was 3A–1E
105.10	Snug's] MS, 1A–1E; Smug's ARE
105.14	differences] MS, 1A; difference 3A–1E
105.16	now] MS, 1A, 1E; ~ that 3A–1F
105.28	gratification of] MS, 1A; ~ to 3A–1E
105.42	of] MS, 1A–1E; on 2E
106.13	in me] MS, 1A; me in 3A–1E
106.15	vocation] MS, 3A–1E; vocations 1A
107.24	continual] MS, 1A; continued 3A–1E
108.31	of her] MS, 1A 1E; of 2E
109.1	the] MS, 1A–1E; ~ the 3A
109.23	of] MS, 1A–1E; ~ the ARE
109.28	my character] MS, 1A; the ~ 3A–1E
110.17	narration] MS, 1A; narrative 3A–1E
110.29	by] MS, 1A; with 3A–1E
110.30	front] MS, 1A 1E, first ARE
*110.31	was a party] MS, 1A; were a number 3A–1E
*110.37	whispering her] MS, 1A; ~ to ~ 3A–1E
111.10	advantages] MS, 1A; advantage 3A–1E
111.19	fray] MS, 1A–1E; affray 3A, ARE
111.26	further] MS, 3A–1E; farther 1A
111.40	were] MS, 1A–1E; wore ARE
112.17	back] MS, 1A–1E; *omitted* ARE
*112.21	playing and] MS, 1A; *omitted* 3A–1E
112.38	in] MS, 1A, 1E; ~ a 3A–1F
113.6	and his] MS, 1A–1E; and ARE
113.9	on the] MS, 1A–1F; ~ my 1E

113.12   I] MS, 1A–1E; *omitted* ARE
*113.37   sewing] MS, 1A; sowing 3A–1E
113.38   several] MS, 1A; some 3A–1E
114.5   true] MS, 1A; fine 3A–1E
114.22   should] MS, 1A, 1E; would 3A–1F
114.32   in] MS, 1A–1E; into 3A, 1F
115.5   these] MS, 1A; those 3A–1E
115.14   of me] MS, 1A–1E; with ~ ARE
*115.15–17   dirt . . . . sent.] MS, 1A; dirt: so I found myself getting in
                [into 3A–1F] disgrace with all the world, and would have
                got heartily out of humour with myself, had I not been
                kept in tolerable self-conceit by the parson's three daugh-
                ters. *Paragraph* They were the same who had admired
                my poetry on a former occasion, when it had brought me
                into disgrace at school, and I had ever since retained an
                exalted idea of their judgment. Indeed, they were young
                ladies not merely of taste but [but of ARE] science. Their
                education had been superintended by their mother, who
                was a blue stocking. They knew enough of botany to tell
                the technical names of all the flowers in the garden, and
                all their secret concerns into the bargain. They knew mu-
                sic too, not mere common-place music, but Rossini and
                Mozart, and they sang Moore's Irish Melodies to perfec-
                tion. They had pretty little work-tables, covered with all
                kind [kinds ARE] of objects of taste; specimens of lava,
                and painted eggs, and work-boxes, painted and var-
                nished by themselves. They excelled in knotting and net-
                ting, and painted in water-colours; and made feather
                fans, and fire-screens, and worked in silks and worsteds;
                and talked French and Italian, and knew Shakspeare by
                heart. They even knew something of geology and min-
                eralogy; and went about the neighbourhood knocking
                stones to pieces, to the great admiration and perplexity
                of the country folk. *Paragraph* I am a little too minute,
                perhaps, in detailing their accomplishments, but I wish
                to let you see that these were not common-place young
                ladies, but had pretensions quite above the ordinary run.
                It was some consolation to me, therefore, to find favour
                in such eyes. Indeed, they had always marked me out for
                a genius, and considered my late vagrant freak as fresh
                proof of the fact. They observed that Shakspeare himself
                had been a mere Pickle in his youth; that he had stolen
                deer, [a deer, ARE] as every one knew; and kept loose

company, and consorted with actors: so I comforted myself marvellously with the idea of having so decided a Shakspearean trait in my character. *Paragraph* The youngest of the three, however, was my grand consolation. She was a pale, sentimental girl, with long "hyacinthine" ringlets hanging about her face. She wrote poetry herself, and we kept up a poetical correspondence. She had a taste for the drama too, and I taught her how to act several of the scenes in Romeo and Juliet. I used to rehearse the garden scene under her lattice, which looked out from among woodbine and honeysuckles into the churchyard. I began to think her amazingly pretty as well as clever, and I believe I should have finished by falling in love with her, had not her father discovered our theatrical studies. He was a studious, abstracted man, generally too much absorbed in his learned and religious labours to notice the little foibles of his daughters, and, perhaps, blinded by a father's fondness; but he unexpectedly put his head out of his study window one day in the midst of a scene, and put a stop to our rehearsals. He had a vast deal of that prosaic good sense which I for ever found a stumblingblock in my poetical path. My rambling freak had not struck the good man as poetically as it had his daughters. He drew his comparison from a different manual. He looked upon me as a prodigal son, and doubted whether I should ever arrive at the happy catastrophe of the fatted calf. *Paragraph* I fancy some intimation was given to my father of this new breaking out of my poetical temperament, for he suddenly intimated that it was high time I should prepare for the university. I dreaded a return to the school from whence [school whence ARE] I had eloped: the ridicule of my fellow-scholars, and the glances [glance ARE] from the squire's pew, would have been worse than death to me. I was fortunately spared the humiliation. My father sent me to board with a country clergyman, who had three or four other boys [four boys ARE] under his care. I went to him joyfully, for I had often heard my mother mention him with esteem. In fact, he had been an admirer of hers in his younger days, though too humble in fortune and modest in pretensions to aspire to her hand; but he had ever retained a tender regard for her. He was a good man; a worthy specimen of that valuable body of our

country clergy who silently and unostentatiously do a
vast deal of good; who are, as it were, woven into the
whole system of rural life, and operate upon it with the
steady yet unobtrusive influence of temperate piety and
learned good sense. He lived in a small village not far
from Warwick, one of those little communities where the
scanty flock is, in a manner, folded into the bosom of the
pastor. The venerable church, in its grass-grown ceme-
tery, was one of those rural temples which are scattered
[temples scattered ARE] about our country as if to sanctify the land. *Paragraph* I have the worthy pastor before
my mind's eye at this moment, with his mild benevolent
countenance, rendered still more venerable by his silver
hairs. I have him before me, as I saw him on my arrival,
seated in the embowered porch of his small parsonage,
with a flower-garden before it, and his pupils gathered
round him like his children. I shall never forget his reception of me, for I believe he thought of my poor mother at the time, and his heart yearned towards her child.
His eye glistened when he received me at the door, and
he took me into his arms as the adopted child of his affections. Never had I been so fortunately placed. He was
one of those excellent members of our church, who help
out their narrow salaries by instructing a few gentlemen's
sons. I am convinced those little seminaries are among
the best nurseries of talent and virtue in the land. Both
heart and mind are cultivated and improved. The preceptor is the companion and the friend of his pupils. His
sacred character gives him dignity in their eyes, and his
solemn functions produce that elevation of mind and so-
briety of conduct necessary to those who are to teach
youth to think and act worthily. *Paragraph* I speak from
my own random observation and experience, but I think
I speak correctly. At any rate, I can trace much of what
is good in my own heterogeneous compound to the short
time I was under the instruction of that good man. He
entered into the cares and occupations and amusements
of his pupils; and won his way into our confidence, and
studied our hearts and minds more intently than we did
our books. *Paragraph* He soon sounded the depth of my
character. I had become, as I have already hinted, a little
liberal in my notions, and apt to philosophise on both
politics and religion; having seen something of men and

things, and learnt, from my fellow-philosophers, the
strollers, to despise all vulgar prejudices. He did not attempt to cast down my vain glory, nor to question my
right view of things; he merely instilled into my mind a
little information on these topics; though in a quiet, unobtrusive way, that never ruffled a feather of my self-con-
ceit. I was astonished to find what a change a little
knowledge makes in one's mode of viewing matters; and
how very different [how different 3A, ARE] a subject is
when one thinks or when one only talks about it. I conceived a vast deference for my teacher, and was ambitious of his [his his 3A] good opinion. In my zeal to make
a favourable impression, I presented him with a whole
ream of my poetry. He read it attentively, smiled, and
pressed my hand when he returned it to me, but said
nothing. The next day he set me at mathematics. *Paragraph* Somehow or other the process of teaching seemed
robbed by him of all its austerity. I was not conscious that
he thwarted an inclination or opposed a wish, but I felt
that, for the time, my inclinations were entirely changed.
I became fond of study, and zealous to improve myself. I
made tolerable advances in studies which I had before
considered as unattainable, and I wondered at my own
proficiency. I thought, too, I astonished my preceptor,
for I often caught his eyes fixed upon me with a peculiar
expression; I suspect, since, that he was pensively tracing in my countenance the early lineaments of my mother. *Paragraph* Education was not apportioned by him
into tasks and enjoined as a labour, to be abandoned with
joy the moment the hour of study was expired. We had,
it is true, our allotted hours of occupation, to give us habits of method, and of the distribution of time; but they
were made pleasant to us, and our feelings were enlisted
in the cause. When they were over, education still went
on. It pervaded all our relaxations and amusements.
There was a steady march of improvement. Much of his
instruction was given during pleasant rambles, or when
seated on the margin of the Avon; and information received in that way often makes a deeper impression than
when acquired by poring over books. I have many of the
pure and eloquent precepts which [that 3A–1F] flowed
from his lips associated in my mind with lovely scenes in
nature, which make the recollection of them indescrib-

ably delightful. *Paragraph* I do not pretend to say that any miracle was effected with me. After all said and done, I was but a weak disciple. My poetical temperament still wrought within me and wrestled hard with wisdom, and, I fear, maintained the mastery. I found mathematics an intolerable task in fine weather. I would be prone to forget my problems to watch the birds hopping about the windows, or the bees humming about the honeysuckles; and whenever I could steal away, I would wander about the grassy borders of the Avon, and excuse this truant propensity to myself with the idea that I was treading classic ground, over which Shakspeare had wandered. What luxurious idleness have I indulged as I lay under the trees and watched the silver waves rippling through the arches of the broken bridge, and laving the rocky bases of old Warwick Castle; and how often have I thought of sweet Shakspeare, and in my boyish enthusiasm have kissed the waves which had washed his native village. *Paragraph* My good preceptor would often accompany me in these desultory rambles. He sought to get hold of this vagrant mood of mind and turn it to some account. He endeavoured to teach me to mingle thought with mere sensation; to moralize on the scenes around; and to make the beauties of nature administer to the understanding and the heart. He endeavoured to direct my imagination to high and noble objects, and to fill it with lofty images. In a word, he did all he could to make the best of a poetical temperament, and to counteract the mischief which had been done to me by my great expectations. *Paragraph* Had I been earlier put under the care of the good pastor, or remained with him a longer time, I really believe he would have made something of me. He had already brought a great deal of what had been flogged into me into tolerable order, and had weeded out much of the unprofitable wisdom which had sprung up in my vagabondizing. I already began to find that with all my genius a little study would be no disadvantage to me; and, in spite of my vagrant freaks, I began to doubt my being a second Shakspeare. *Paragraph* Just as I was making these precious discoveries, the good parson died. It was a melancholy day throughout the neighbourhood. He had his little flock of scholars, his children as he used to call us, gathered round him in his dying moments; and

he gave us the parting advice of a father, now that he had
to leave us, and we were to be separated from each other
and scattered about in the world. He took me by the
hand, and talked with me earnestly and affectionately,
and called to mind my mother, and used her name to
enforce his dying exhortations, for I rather think he considered me the most erring and heedless of his flock. He
held my hand in his, long after he had done speaking,
and kept his eyes [eye 3A–1F] fixed on me tenderly and
almost piteously: his lips moved as if he were silently
praying for me; and he died away, still holding me by the
hand. *Paragraph* There was not a dry eye in the church
when the funeral service was read from the pulpit from
which he had so often preached. When the body was
committed to the earth, our little band gathered round
it, and watched the coffin as it was lowered into the
grave. The parishioners looked at us with sympathy; for
we were mourners not merely in dress but in heart. We
lingered about the grave, and clung to one another for a
time, weeping and speechless, and then parted, like a
band of brothers parting from the paternal hearth, never
to assemble there again. *Paragraph* How had the gentle
spirit of that good man sweetened our natures and linked
our young hearts together by the kindest ties! I have always had a throb of pleasure at meeting with an old
school-mate, even though one of my truant associates;
but whenever, in the course of my life, I have encountered one of that little flock with which I was folded on
the banks of the Avon, it has been with a gush of affection, and a glow of virtue, that for the moment have
made me a better man. *Paragraph* I was now sent to
Oxford, and was wonderfully impressed on first entering
it as a student. Learning here puts on all its majesty; it
is lodged in palaces; it is sanctified by the sacred ceremonies of religion; it has a pomp and circumstance which
powerfully affect the imagination. Such, at least, it had
in my eyes, thoughtless as I was. My previous studies
with the worthy pastor had prepared me to regard it with
deference and awe. He had been educated here, and always spoke of the University with filial fondness and classic veneration. When I beheld the clustering spires and
pinnacles of this most august of cities rising from the
plain, I hailed them in my enthusiasm as the points of a

diadem which the nation had placed upon the brows of
science. 3A–1E

*115.18–22   I had . . . . fell] MS, 1A; I felt ashamed to play the owl
among such gay birds 3A–1E

115.25   fellow students] MS, 1A; companions 3A–1E

115.25   sports] MS, 1A, 1E; sport 3A–1F

115.32–35   I . . . . love] MS, 1A; For a time old Oxford was full of
enjoyment for me. There was a charm about its monastic
buildings; its great Gothic quadrangles; its solemn halls,
and shadowy cloisters. I delighted, in the evenings, 3A–
1E

115.37   to . . . twilight, and] MS, 1A; omitted 3A–1E

115.38   caps] MS, 1A; antiquated ~ 3A–1E

115.38–39   There . . . scene.] MS, 1A; omitted 3A–1E

115.39   It . . . me] MS, 1A; I seemed for a time to be transported
3A–1E

115.40   edifices] MS, 1A; people 3A–1E

115.40   the people] MS, 1A; edifices 3A–1E

115.40   old] MS, 1A; the ~ 3A–1E

115.40   It . . . attend] MS, 1A; I was a frequent attendant, also, of
3A–1E

115.41   Chapel] MS, 1A; Hall 3A–1E

115.41   and] MS, 1A; omitted 3A–1E

115.42–43   painting and] MS, 1A; painting, 3A–1E

115.43   seem . . . effects] MS, 1A; are in such admirable unison
3A–1E

*116.1–7   I . . . . hours.] MS, 1A; A favourite haunt, too, was the
beautiful walk bordered by lofty elms along the river, behind the gray walls of Magdalen College, which goes by
the name of Addison's Walk, from being his favourite resort when an Oxford student. I became also a lounger in
the Bodleian library, and a great dipper into books,
though I cannot say that I studied them; in fact, being no
longer under direction nor [or 3A–1F] control, I was
gradually relapsing into mere indulgence of the fancy.
Still this would have been pleasant and harmless enough,
and I might have awakened from mere literary dreaming
to something better. The chances were in my favour, for
the riotous times of the University were past. The days
of hard drinking were at an end. The old feuds of "Town
and Gown," like the civil wars of the White and Red
Rose, had died away, and student and citizen slept in
peace and whole skins, without risk of being summoned

in the night to bloody brawl. It had become the fashion to study at the University, and the odds were always in favour of my following the fashion. Unluckily, however, I fell in company with a special knot of young fellows, of lively parts and ready wit, who had lived occasionally upon town, and become initiated into the Fancy. They voted study to be the toil of dull minds, by which they slowly crept up the hill, while genius arrived at it at a bound. 3A–1E

116.8	came] MS, 1A–1E; come 3A
116.8	college] MS, 1A; ~ when I was in the height of my career 3A–1E
116.10	sporting] MS, 1A; various ~ 3A–1E
116.10	apparatus] MS, 1A; ~ with a curious eye 3A–1E
116.12	this reading] MS, 1A; their studying 3A–1E
116.12	was rather] MS, 1A; must be 3A–1E
116.12–14	Such . . . idler?] MS, 1A; We had a day's shooting together: I delighted him with my skill, and astonished him by my learned disquisitions on horse-flesh, and on Manton's guns; so, upon the whole, he departed highly satisfied with my improvement at college. 3A–1E
116.16	I became] MS, 1A; I had not been a very long time a man of spirit, therefore, before ~ ~ 3A–1E
116.23	sociable] MS, 1A–1E; social 1F
116.23	with] MS, 1A–1E; omitted 3A
117.21	her] MS, 1A; the 3A–1E
117.35	and] MS, 1A; ~ the 3A–1E
117.40	from] MS, 1A; of 3A–1E
118.12	abroad] MS, 1A; about 3A–1E
118.18	misfortunes] MS, 1A–1E; misfortune ARE
118.24	or] MS, 1A–1E; nor ARE
118.31–32	People . . . university.] MS, 1A; omitted 3A–1E
118.34	a] MS, 1A; omitted 3A–1E
119.5	we'll] MS, 1A; will 3A–1E
119.10	My . . . seared] MS, 1A; I was a careless dog, it is true, hardened a little, perhaps, 3A–1E
119.19	further] MS, 3A–1E; farther 1A
119.20	not I] MS, 1A–1E; I not ARE
119.29	in the] MS, 1A, 1E; the 3A–1F
119.35	upon] MS, 1A; on 3A–1E
120.10	the change of] MS, 1A, 1E; ~ ~ in 3A–1F
121.32	of it] MS, 1A–1E; it 2E
122.4	town] MS, 1A; city 3A–1E

122.4   prebendaries] MS, 1A; poets of the place 3A–1E
122.36   town] MS, 1A; place 3A–1E
122.40   It . . . buzz.] MS, 1A; *omitted* 3A–1E
122.41   pew of] MS, 1A; same pew with 3A–1E
122.42–43   All . . . . stalls;] MS, 1A; *omitted* 3A–1E
123.3   pleased] MS, 1A; much struck 3A–1E
*123.3   a cathedral town,] MS, 1A; this reverend little place. A ca-
                 thedral, with its dependencies and regulations, presents
                 a picture of other times, and of a different order of things.
                 It is a rich relique of a more poetical age. There still lin-
                 ger about it the silence and solemnity of the cloister. In
                 the present instance especially, where the cathedral was
                 large, and the town was small, [town small, ARE] its in-
                 fluence was the more apparent. The solemn pomp of the
                 service, performed twice a day, with the grand intona-
                 tions of the organ, and the voices of the choir swelling
                 through the magnificent pile, diffused, as it were, a per-
                 petual sabbath over the place. This routine of solemn
                 ceremony continually going on, independent as it were
                 of the world; this daily offering of melody and praise as-
                 cending like incense from the altar, had a powerful effect
                 upon my imagination. *Paragraph* The aunt introduced
                 me to her coterie, formed of families connected with the
                 cathedral, and others of moderate fortune, but high re-
                 spectability, who had nestled themselves under the
                 wings of the cathedral to enjoy good society at moderate
                 expense. It was a highly aristocratical little circle; scru-
                 pulous in its intercourse with others, and jealously cau-
                 tious about admitting any thing common or unclean.
                 Paragraph It seemed as if the courtesies of the old school
                 had taken refuge here. 3A–1E
123.3–29   where . . . . evening.] MS, 1A; *omitted* 3A–1E
123.29–31   The . . . to house] MS, 1A; There were continual inter-
                 changes of civilities, and of small presents of fruits and
                 delicacies, and of complimentary crow-quill billets 3A–
                 1E
123.31   tranquil] MS, 1A; quiet, well-bred 3A–1E
123.32   and having little to do,] MS, 1A; *omitted* 3A–1E
123.32   little civilities . . . amusements] MS, 1A; little amuse-
                 ments, and little civilities 3A–1E
123.33   smiled] MS, 1A; seen 3A–1E
123.33–34   as . . . cathedral,] MS, 1A; *omitted* 3A–1E
123.34   middle . . . see] MS, 1A; midst of a warm day, 3A–1E

123.35	in . . . carrying] MS, 1A; issuing from the iron gateway of a stately mansion, and traversing the little place with an air of mighty import, bearing 3A–1E
123.36–37	A . . . Prebend.] MS, 1A; *omitted* 3A–1E
123.38–40	Nothing . . . . two] MS, 1A; Their evening amusements were sober and primitive. They assembled at a moderate hour; the young ladies played music and the old ladies whist; and at an early hour they dispersed. There was no parade on these social occasions. Two 3A–1E
123.39	hands] MS; hand 1A
123.40–41	that . . . place;] MS, 1A; were in constant activity, 3A–1E
123.41	or] MS, 1A; and 3A–1E
123.43	at . . . night] MS, 1A; long before midnight 3A–1E; before midnight 1E
123.43– 124.1	the gleam . . . jack lanthorns] MS, 1A; gleam of lanterns 3A–1E
124.1	here and there] MS, 1A; *omitted* 3A–1E
124.1	town] MS, 1A; place 3A–1E
124.1	gave notice,] MS, 1A; told 3A–1E
124.2	cathedral card party] MS, 1A; evening party 3A–1E
124.2–3	dissolved, . . . homes.] MS, 1A; dissolved. 3A–1E
124.4–11	To . . . . muse.] MS, 1A; *omitted* 3A–1E
*124.12–13	I was thus . . . evening] MS, 1A; Still I did not feel myself altogether so much at my ease as I had anticipated, considering the smallness of the place. I found it very different from other country places, and that it was not so easy to make a dash there. Sinner that I was! the very dignity and decorum of the little community was rebuking to me. I feared my past idleness and folly would rise in judgment against me. I stood in awe of the dignitaries of the cathedral, whom I saw mingling familiarly in society. I became nervous on this point. The creak of a prebendary's shoes, sounding from one end of a quiet street to the other, was appalling to me; and the sight of a shovel hat was sufficient at any time to check me in the midst of my boldest poetical soarings. *Paragraph* And then the good aunt could not be quiet, but would cry me up for a genius, and extol my poetry to every one. So long as she confined this to the ladies it did well enough, because they were able to feel and appreciate poetry of the new romantic school. Nothing would content the good lady, however, but she must read my verses to a prebendary, who had long been the undoubted critic of the place. He

was a thin, delicate old gentleman, of mild, polished manners, steeped to the lips in classic lore, and not easily put in a heat by any hot-blooded poetry of the day. He listened to my most fervid thoughts and fervid words without a glow; shook his head with a smile, and condemned them as not being according to Horace, as not being legitimate poetry. *Paragraph* Several old ladies, who had heretofore been my admirers, shook their heads at hearing this; they could not think of praising any poetry that was not according to Horace; and as to any thing illegitimate, it was not to be countenanced in good society. Thanks to my stars, however, I had youth and novelty on my side: so the young ladies persisted in admiring my poetry, in despite of Horace and illegitimacy. *Paragraph* I consoled myself with the good opinion of the young ladies, whom I had always found to be the best judges of poetry. As to these old scholars, said I, they are apt to be chilled by being steeped in the cold fountains of the classics. Still I felt that I was losing ground, and that it was necessary to bring matters to a point. Just at this time 3A–1E

124.13–14	which . . . likewise] MS, 1A; attended by the best society of the place, and 3A–1E
124.16	batter] MS, 1A; battle 3A–1E
124.30	a] MS, 1A–1E; the 2E
125.7	my poetic rival] MS, 1A; Sacharissa 3A–1E
125.8	up] MS, 1A; ~, as I imagined, 3A–1E
125.19	against both] MS, 1A–1E; both against 2E
126.7	himself] MS, 1A; to ~ 3A–1E
126.14	would] MS, 1A–1E; should 3A, ARE
126.30	his smile] MS, 1A, 1E; the ~ 3A–1F
127.7	of the] MS, 1A; ~ his 3A–1E
127.19	lost] MS, 1A; so ~ 3A–1E
127.30	perfect] MS, 1A–1E; prefect 3A
127.31	he] MS, 1A, 1E; the deceased 3A–1F

GRAVE REFLECTIONS OF A DISAPPOINTED MAN

128.6	domains] MS, 1A; remains 3A–1E
128.18	other] MS, 1A; otherwise 3A–1E
128.33	But] MS, 1A, 1E; yet 3A–1F
129.9	beyond] MS, 1A–1E; yond 2E
129.13	ever I] MS, 1A, ARE; I ever 3A–1E

129.21	getting] MS; in ~ 1A–1E
129.26	up] MS, 1A; *omitted* 3A–1E
129.30	this] MS, 1A; his 3A–1E
129.34	until] MS, 1A; till 3A–1E
129.39	these] MS, 1A; them 3A–1E
130.8	sank] MS, 1A, ARE; sunk 3A–1E
130.15	is] MS, 1A; ~ that 3A–1E
130.25	griefs] MS, 1A; grief 3A–1E
130.40	were] MS, 1A–1E; was 3A, ARE
130.42	towers] MS, 3A–1E; towns 1A
131.7	her] MS, 1A–1E; the ARE
131.10	such] MS, 1A; ~ a 3A–1E
131.11	in] MS, 1A–1E; with ARE
131.14	spirits] MS, 1A–1E; spirit 3A, ARE
131.22	adventured] MS, 1A; ventured 3A–1E
131.28	further] MS, 1F; farther 1A–1E

THE BOOBY SQUIRE

131.34	into] MS, 1A; to 3A–1E
132.3	such] MS, 1A–1E; ~ a 3A, ARE
132.8	in their turns] MS, 1A; in turn 3A–1F, in turns 1E
132.9	this] MS, 1A; his 3A–1E
132.11	on many] MS, 1A; in ~ 3A–1E
*132.11	on which] MS, 1A; wherein 3A–1F; where 1E
132.13	on the] MS, 1A; ~ his 3A–1E
132.15	strong] MS, 1A–1E; were ~ ARE
132.21	a] MS, 1A; the 3A–1E
132.25	servant] MS, 1A; a ~ 3A–1E
132.26	mistress] MS, 1A–1E; a ~ 3A, ARE
133.5	or] MS, 1A–1E; of 3A
133.6	had had] MS, 1A; had 3A–1E
133.8	had] MS, 1A–1E; *omitted* ARE
133.14	old] MS, 1A–1E; *omitted* 2E
133.15	ancient] MS, 1A–1E; old 2E
133.26	told] MS, 1A–1E; ~ that ARE
133.29	at his] MS, 1A, 1E; in ~ 3A–1F
133.31	would] MS, 1A–1F; could 1E
134.5	muzzy] MS, 3A–1E; muggy 1A
134.32	further] MS, ARE, 1F; farther 1A, 3A, 1E
135.1	clean] MS, 3A–1E; clear 1A
135.7	damme] MS, 1A; damn me 3A–1E

THE STROLLING MANAGER

136.5	There's] MS, 1A–ARE; There is 1F, 1E
136.11	Townly] MS, 1A, 1E; Townley 3A–1F
136.30	spake] MS, 3A–1E; spoke 1A, ARE
136.41	Bartlemy] MS, 1A–1E; Batlemy 3A, ARE
137.25	sirs] MS, 1A, 1E; sir 3A–1F
137.41	Romeo] MS, 3A–1E; Thomas 1A
137.41	the] MS, 1A; a 3A–1E
137.43	cousin] MS, 1A; cousins 3A–1E
*138.1	sir] MS, 1A–1F; sirs 1E
138.13	were ever] MS, 1A; ever were 3A–1E
138.16	with] MS, 1A; of 3A–1E
138.18	know] MS, 3A–1E; knew 1A
138.20	confounded] MS, 1A; *omitted* 3A–1E
138.29	upon] MS, 1A; about 3A–1E
138.35	stalk] MS, 1A; to ∼ 3A–1E
138.36	manager's] MS, 3A–1E; managers' 1A
138.43	on] MS, 1A; in 3A–1E
139.6	to] MS, 1A; at 3A–1E
139.10	or] MS, 1A; on 3A–1E
139.29	on] MS, 1A; in 3A–1E
139.34	drawings] MS, 1A–1Ea; drawing 1Eb
140.5	had] MS, 3A–1E; and ∼ 1A
*140.16	theatre;] MS, 1A–ARE; ∼; that her daughters entered like a tempest with a flutter of red shawls and feathers; 1F, 1E
140.17	and talked] MS, 1A–ARE; talked 1F, 1E
140.17	loudest] MS, 1A–ARE; *omitted* 1F, 1E
140.18–19	then . . . and] MS, 1A–ARE; *omitted* 1F, 1E
140.20	flaring] MS, 1A; staring 3A–1E
140.21	under] MS, 1A; as ∼ 3A–1E
140.22–26	The . . . . before.] MS, 1A–ARE; *omitted* 1F, 1E
140.29	a] MS, 1A–1F; *omitted* 1E
140.30–32	Those . . . acquaintance.] MS, 1A–ARE; *omitted* 1F, 1E
140.36	Eidouranion] MS, 3A–1E; Eidonianeon 1A
140.37–141.8	Alas . . . . afterwards.] MS, 1A–ARE; *omitted* 1F, 1E
140.37	little knew] MS, 1A; knew little 3A, ARE
141.12	county] MS, 1A; country 3A–1E
141.20	course] MS, 1A–1E; coarse 3A
142.16	as] MS, 1A; for 3A–1E
143.7	so easy] MS, 1A; is ∼ ∼ 3A–1E

143.7	gulling] MS, 1A; to gull 3A–1E
*143.20	former] MS, 3A–1E; famous 1A
143.22	familiar] MS, 3A–1E; *omitted* 1A
143.32	restorer] MS; the ~ 1A–1E
143.39	flame] MS, 1A; flesh 3A–1E
144.7	up] MS, 1A; *omitted* 3A–1E
*144.10	tail] MS, 1A; ~ of it 3A–1E
144.34	petted] MS, 1A; patted 3A–1E
145.30	or] MS, 1A–1E; nor ARE
145.30	know] MS, 3A–1E; knew 1A
145.32	fingers] MS, 1A–1E; finger ARE
145.37	into] MS, 1A–1E; in ARE
145.39	for] MS, 1A–1E; to 2E

THE INN AT TERRACINA

149.25	a] 1A, 3A–1E; the ARE
150.6	Theodoric] 1E, 1F; Theodric 3A, ARE
150.18	which] 1A; that 3A–1E
151.21	time] 1A, 3A–1F, 2E; same ~ 1E
151.21	this] 1A; the 1E; his 3A–1F
151.27–28	quality and movements] 1A; movements and quality 3A–1E
151.32	amount] 1E, 3A, 1F; account ARE
152.14	that] 1A, 3A–1E; the ARE
152.27	or the] 1A; ~ of ~ 3A–1E
152.31	and upper benjamins] 1A; *omitted* 3A–1E
152.31	and the] 1A; the 3A–1E
*152.32	gruff] 1A; bluff 3A–1E
152.32	face] 1A; ~ of the master 3A–1E
152.32	window,] 1A; ~; and the ruddy, round-headed servant, in close-cropped hair, short coat, drab breeches, and long gaiters, all 3A–1E
152.32	it] 1A; this 3A–1E
152.36	refreshment] 1A, 3A–1E; refreshments ARE
152.39	case] 1A; way 3A–1E
153.4–7	He . . . him.] 1A; *omitted* 3A–1E
153.17	on."] 1A; ~." Perhaps too he was a little sore from having been fleeced at every stage of his journey [of his journey *omitted* 3A–1F]. 3A–1E
153.18–19	as sour . . . master] 1A; a look of some perplexity 3A–1E
154.3–4	an . . . civil] 1A; a polite 3A–1E
154.7	the best] 1A; an 3A–1E

154.15   And the] 1A, 1E; The 3A–1F
154.17   toilette] 1A; toilet 3A–1E
154.23   formal] 1A; civil 3A–1E
154.24–25   which no . . . seat] 1A; in the unprofessing English way,
                which the fair Venetian, accustomed to the complimen-
                tary salutations of the continent, considered extremely
                cold 3A–1E
154.34–35   Every . . . execrable.] 1A; Indeed the repast was one of
                those Italian farragoes which require a little qualifying.
                3A–1E
154.37   meagre winged animal] 1A, 3A–1F; ~-~ ~ 1E
154.37–38   was . . . it] 1A; omitted 3A–1E
154.39–41   flesh, ... palate but] 1A; ~. There was what appeared to
                be 3A–1E
154.41   he] 1A; the Englishman 3A–1E
155.1–6   In . . . . him.] 1A; omitted 3A–1E
155.6   John Bull's crustiness] 1A; a traveller's spleen 3A–1E
155.14   the waiter] 1A; waiter 3A–1E
155.25   tales. The] 1A, 1E; ~; and the 3A–1F
155.28   testily] 1A; omitted 3A–1E
155.29   mere] 1A; to be ~ 3A–1E
155.41   clamours] 1A; of ~ 3A–1E
156.12   signor] 1A; omitted 3A–1E
156.21   un] 1A; an 3A–1E
157.3   Their] 1A; The 3A–1E
157.12   gaining] 1A; getting 3A–1E
157.13–14   He . . . round] 1A; Conquering, therefore, that shyness
                which is prone to keep an Englishman solitary in crowds,
                he approached one of the talking groups, the oracle of
                which was 3A–1E
157.42   Theodoric's] 1E, 1F; Theodric's 3A, ARE

THE ADVENTURE OF THE LITTLE ANTIQUARY

159.10   Theodoric] 1A, 3A–1E; Theodric ARE
159.10   these] 1A; the 3A–1E
160.17   in a] 1A, 1E; ~ the 3A–1F
160.41   which] 1A, 1E; that 3A–1F
161.6   of] 1A; omitted 3A–1E
161.18   arose] 1E, 3A, 1F; rose ARE
162.3   various] 1Ea, 3A–1F; the ~ 1Eb
162.5   these] 1A; those 3A–1E
162.16   these] 1A; those 3A–1E

162.24	knew] 1A, 3A–1E; know 2E
162.26	in the] 1A, 1F, 1E; ~ a 3A, ARE
162.37	hills] 1E; a hill 3A–1F
163.6	numbers] 1A, 1E; number 3A–1F
163.19	devotions] 1A; devotion 3A–1E
163.28	charactered] 1A; characterised 1F, 1E; characterized 3A, ARE
163.34	his mountain] 1A; the mountains 3A–1E
163.34	with] 1A; ~ a 3A–1F

THE BELATED TRAVELLERS

164.15	TRAVELLERS] 1E, 3A–1F; ~ *Footnote* *To follow "The Little Antiquary" in Part III. 2A
164.20	ancient] 1E, 3A–1F; an ~ 2A
164.29	mustachios] 1E, 2A–1F; mustaches ARE
165.19	in] 1E, 2A, 1F; at 3A, ARE
165.21	edge] 1E, 2A, 1F; edges 3A, ARE
166.10	palazza] 1E; palace 2A–1F
166.12	for] 1E; of 2A–1F
166.26	distinctness] 1E, 2A–1F; distinction ARE
166.33	there] 1E, 2A–1F; *omitted* ARE
167.3	were] 1E; felt 2A–1F
167.8	mustachios] 1E, 2A–1F; mustaches ARE
167.11	expression] 1E, 3A–1F; expressions 2A
167.15	make] 1E, 2A–1F; made 2E
167.21	a] 1E, 2A–1F; *omitted* 3A
167.42	the] 1E, 2A, 1F; a 3A, ARE
168.7	and a] 1E, 2A, 1F; and 3A, ARE
168.8	gold] 1E, 2A, 1F; golden 3A, ARE
169.10	liqueurs] 1E, 2A–1F; liquors ARE
170.9	made] 1E; has ~ 2A–1F
170.18	and] 1E, 3A–1F; *omitted* 2A
170.33	scarce] 1E; scarcely 2A–1F
171.5	apartments] 1E, 2A–1F; apartment 2E
171.18	further] 1E, 3A–1F; farther 2A
171.26	her] 1E, 3A–1F; the 2A
171.42	warning] 1E, 2A–1F; warnings ARE
172.6	barricado] 1F, 2A–1F; barricade ARE
172.7	were] 1E; are 2A–1F
172.16	a] 1E; *omitted* 2A–1F
173.30	an] 1E; *omitted* 2A–1F
173.32	dusty] 1F, 2A, 1F; dusky 3A, ARE

173.38   where] 1E, 2A–1F; were 3A
174.29   barricadooed] 1E, 2A–1F; barricaded ARE

THE ADVENTURE OF THE POPKINS FAMILY

176.11   dickcys] 1A, 3A–1F; dickey's 1E
176.17   riches] 1A, 3A–1E; richness ARE
176.34   Misses] 1A, ARE, 2E; Miss 3A–1E
176.34   Popkins] 1A, 3A–1F, 2E; Popkins' 1E
177.5   rock] 1A, 3A–1E; a ~ ARE
177.6   route] 1A, 3A–1E; road ARE; rout 2E
177.16   rose] 1A, 3A–1E; arose ARE
177.28   Misses] 1A, ARE; Miss 3A–1E
177.28   Popkins] 1A, 3A–1Eb; Popkins' 1Ea
177.40   lamb's] 1A; lambs' 3A–1F; lambs 1E
178.1   soldiery] 1A, 3A–1E; soldiers ARE
178.9   Misses] 1A, ARE; Miss 3A–1E
178.32   toward] 1A, 1F, 1E; towards 3A, ARE
178.32–39   The . . . . delinquent.] 1A; *omitted* 3A–1E
178.40   beach] 1E, 3A, ARE; beech 1F
178.40   body] 1A, 1E; party 3A–1F
179.30   circumstance] 1E, 1F; circumstances 3A, ARE

THE PAINTER'S ADVENTURE

179.33   an] 1A, 1E, ARE; a 3A, 1F
179.37   Sylla] 1A, 1Eb; Scilla 1Ea, 1F; Scylla 3A, ARE
180.12   its] 1A, 3A–1F; his 1E
180.20   first] 1A; at ~ 3A–1E
181.26   more] 1A, 1E; *omitted* 3A–1F
181.31   effects] 1A; effect 3A–1E
184.1   those] 1A; these 3A–1E
185.25   ensure] 1A, 1E; assure 3A–1F

THE STORY OF THE BANDIT CHIEFTAIN

186.13   on] 1A; in 3A–1E
186.15   my] 1A; the 3A–1E
187.23   who] 1A, 1E; whom 3A–1F
188.1   these] 1A; the 3A–1E
188.4   those] 1A; these 3A–1E
188.24   which] 1A, 1E; from ~ 3A–1F
188.25   most] 1A, 3A–1E; the ~ ARE
188.25   from] 1A, 1E; *omitted* 3A–1F

188.33	or] 1A; a 3A–1E
188.36	towards] 1A, ARE, 1E; toward 3A, 1F
188.41	such] 1A, 3A–1E; ~ a ARE
189.9	I] 1A, 3A–1E; *omitted* ARE
189.13	hung] 1A, 1E; hanging 3A–1F
189.18	wide] 1A, 3A–1E; wild 2E
189.26	whomever] 1A; whomsoever 3A–1E
190.6	of] 1A; about 3A–1E
190.10	the] 1A; *omitted* 3A–1E
190.28	staffs] 1A, 1E; staves 3A–1F
190.38	traits] 1A; traces 3A–1E
191.3	every] 1A; any 3A–1E
191.11	deep] 1A, 1E; a ~ 3A–1F
191.25	But two] 1A, 1E; Two only 3A–1F
192.1	certain] 1A, 1E; confident 3A–1F
192.16	the] 1A; his 3A–1E
192.29	his] 1A, 1F, 1E; with ~ 3A, ARE
193.5	summits] 1A, 1E; summit 3A–1F
193.24	which] 1A, 1E; whom 3A–1F
194.11	kind of] 1A, 3A–1E; kind ARE
194.13	an] 1A; any 3A–1E
194.15	but] 1A, 1E; when 3A–1F

THE STORY OF THE YOUNG ROBBER

*194.18	THE STORY] 1A, 3A, ARE; STORY 1F, 1E
194.19	born at] 1A, 1E; ~ in 3A–1F
194.23	occasions] 1A; occasion 3A–1E
194.25	prince's] 1A, 1E; prince 3A–1F, 2E
194.29	whom] 1A, 3A–1F; which 1E
195.40	It is about] 1A, 1E; About 3A–1F
195.41	in hopes] 1A, 1E; suggesting the chance 3A–1F
197.11	for] 1A, 1E; to 3A–1F
197.21	a] 1A, 3A–1E; the ARE
198.15	of all] 1A; at ~ 3A–1E
198.38	knew] 1A, 1E; ~ that 3A–1F
199.6	some] 1A; to ~ 3A–1E
199.19	seize] 1A; ~ upon 3A–1E
200.17	fly] 1A, 3A–1F, 2E; flee 1E
200.37	evidences] 1A, 1E; evidence 3A–1F
200.40	mountains] 1A; mountain 3A–1E
201.15	procure] 1A; ~ for 3A–1E
201.15	for] 1A, 1E; to 3A–1F

201.19   robber's mantle] 1A; robber-mantle 3A–1E; robber mantle
                 2E
202.7   towards] 1A, 1E; toward 3A–1F
202.12   if] 1A; *omitted* 3A–1E
*202.17–25   The Englishman . . . . are!"] 1A; The party now returned
                 to the inn, and separated for the night. The fair Venetian,
                 though of the sweetest temperament, was half out of hu-
                 mour with the Englishman for a certain slowness of faith
                 which he had evinced throughout the whole evening.
                 She could not understand this dislike to "humbug," as he
                 termed it, which held a kind of sway over him, and
                 seemed to control his opinions and his very actions.
                 Paragraph "I'll warrant," said she to her husband, as
                 they retired for the night, "I'll warrant, with all his af-
                 fected indifference, this Englishman's heart would quake
                 at the very sight of a bandit." *Paragraph* Her husband
                 gently, and good-humouredly, checked her. *Paragraph*
                 "I have no patience with these Englishmen," said she, as
                 she got into bed—"they are so cold and insensible!" 3A–
                 1E

THE ADVENTURE OF THE ENGLISHMAN

203.3–5   from . . . exempt;] 1A; *omitted* 3A–1E
203.6–7   in . . . . He] 1A; *omitted* 3A–1E
203.16   not . . . such] 1A; a little piqued at what she supposed 3A–
                 1E
203.20   carriages] 1A; carriage 3A–1E
203.28   the cursed] 1A; he had not a doubt that the 3A–1E
203.31   contortions] 1A, ARE, 2E; contortion 3A–1E
203.38   d——d] 1A; vile 3A–1E
204.1   D—n] 1A; Curse 3A–1E
204.20   Hang . . . carriage] 1A; Pish 3A–1E
204.20   crustily] 1A; testily 3A–1E
204.21   strangers] 1A; the concerns of ∼ 3A–1E
204.23   in] 1A; on 3A–1E
204.29   and] 1A, 3A–1E; of ARE
204.33   sprang] 1A, ARE, 1E; sprung 3A, 1F
204.36   deliberate] 1A; a ∼ 3A–1E
204.38   in] 1A, 1E; into 3A–1F
205.33   art] 1A, 3A–1F; arts 1E
206.15–16   a retreating] 1A, 3A–1E; are treating 1F
207.3   looking] 1A; with a good-humoured tone, but ∼ 3A–1E

207.4   nonsense."] 1A; humbug." *Paragraph* The fair Venetian,
               however, has never since accused the English of insen-
               sibility. 3A–1E

PART IV, TITLE

209.5   women's] 1A, 3A–1F; woman's 1E
209.7   spirits] 1A, 1E; sprites 3A–1F

HELL GATE

211.14   bully] 1E, 3A, 1F; bull ARE
212.1   this] 1A; the 3A–1E
*212.13   Pylorus] 1E; Pelorus 3A–1F, 2E
212.14   strait] 1E, ARE, 1F; straight 3A
212.24   which] 1A, 1E; that 3A–1F
212.25   that] 1A; the 3A–1E
212.35   Conklin] 1A; Conklen 3A–1E
212.37   farther] 1A, 3A–1F; further 1E

KIDD THE PIRATE

213.16   who] 1E, 3A, 1F; that ARE
214.26   had] 1E; were 3A–1F
215.25   pirates'] 1E, 1F; pirate's 3A, ARE
215.32   and sometimes] 1A, 1E; sometimes 3A–1F
215.41   myself] 1A; ~ that 3A–1E
216.10   Mannahata] 1A; Manhatta 3A–1E
216.13   dry] 1A, 3A–1E; high ARE
216.20   find] 1A; ~ it 3A–1E
216.33   Kidd] 1E, 3A–1F; Kid 2E
216.34   an] 1A, old 3A–1E
*216.36   Robert] 1A; Captain 3A–1E
216.38   all] 1E, 3A, 1F; *omitted* ARE

THE DEVIL AND TOM WALKER

217.14   grow] 1A, 3A–1F; grew 1E
217.26   when] 1A; that 3A–1E
218.6   inmates] 1A, 3A–1Eb; intimates 1Ea
218.15   homewards] 1A, 1E; homeward 3A–1F
218.40   there for a while] 1A; therefore awhile 3A–1E; there awhile
               ARE
219.12   the skull] 1A, 1E; it 3A–1F

219.17   seen nor heard] 1A; heard nor seen 3A–1E
220.5   prior] 1A; a ~ 3A–1E
220.26   homewards] 1A, 1E; homeward 3A–1F
221.38   assert] 1A, 1E; surmised 3A–1F
221.39   top] 1A, 1E; the ~ 3A–1F
222.25   handsful] 1A, 3A, 1F; handfuls 1E, ARE
222.26   woodsman] 1A; woodman 3A–1E
222.32   woodsman] 1A; woodman 3A–1E
222.39   woodman] 1A; woodman's 3A–1E
222.40   edge of the] 1A, 1F, 1E; *omitted* 3A, ARE
223.9   dealer] 1A, 1F, 1E; trader 3A, ARE
223.20   eagerly] 1A, 1E; *omitted* 3A–1F
223.29   days] 1A; time 3A–1E
223.33   cities] 1A, ARE–1E; cites 3A
223.34   Eldorados] 1A, 3A, ARE; El Dorados 1F, 1E
223.42   a] 1A, 3A–1E; *omitted* ARE
223.43   the] 1A, 1F, 1E; *omitted* 3A, ARE
224.5   he] 1A, 1F, 1E; *omitted* 3A, ARE
224.11   change] 1A; 'Change 3A–1E
224.15   wheels] 1A, ARE–1E; the ~ 3A
225.16   devil] 1A, 3A, ARE; d—l 1F, 1E
225.25   a lash] 1E, 1F; the ~ 3A, ARE
225.26   a] 1A; the 3A–1E
225.42   kinds] 1A; kind 3A–1E
226.11   in a] 1A; in 3A–1E
226.19   for] 1A; to 3A–1E
226.20   until] 1A, 1E; till 3A–1F
226.21   Mannahatta] 1A, 3A, ARE; Mannahata 1F, 1E
226.22   dominion] 1A; the ~ 3A–1E
226.24   was] 1A; there ~ 3A–1E
226.25   in] 1A, 3A–1E; on 2E
226.31   also stories] 1A; stories, also, 3A–1E
226.33   Prevost] 1A; Provost 3A–1E
227.11   Blase] 1A, 3A–1E; Blasc ARE

WOLFERT WEBBER, OR GOLDEN DREAMS

227.27–28   size and] 1A, 3A–1E; *omitted* ARE
228.37   peaceably] 1A; peacefully 3A–1E
229.18   on] 1A; in 3A–1E
229.24   knows] 1A, 1E; ~ that 3A–1F
229.25   or] 1A; nor 3A–1E
230.11   his] 1A, 1E; all ~ 3A–1F

*230.26	sly] 1A, 3A, ARE; shy 1F, 1E
230.40	he] 1A, 3A–1E; she 1F
230.42	poor] 1A, 3A–1E; *omitted* ARE
231.12	ye] 1A, 3A, ARE; you 1F, 1E
231.27	falling] 1A, 3A–1E; fallen ARE
231.31	Manhattoes] 1A; Manhattan 3A–1E; Manahattoes ARE
231.31	the] 1A; *omitted* 3A–1E
231.42	Rem] 1A, 3A, ARE; Ramm 1E; Remm 1F
231.43	Walloon] 1A, 3A–1F; Wallon 1E
232.4	leathern] 1A; leather 3A–1E
232.6	this] 1A, 1F, 1E; his 3A, ARE
232.13	maintained] 1A, 1E; ever ~ 3A–1F
232.15	yet] 1A, 1E; still 3A–1F
232.20	frequent] 1A, 1E; very ~ 3A–1F
232.22	field] 1A, 1F, 1E; fields 3A, ARE
232.27	believe] 1A, 3A–1E; ~ it ARE
232.31	which] 1A, 1E; that 3A–1F
232.34	Corney] 1A, 3A, ARE; Corny 1F, 1E
233.13	standers] 1A, 1F, 1E; standards 3A, ARE
233.23	prosy] 1E, 1F; prosing 3A, ARE
233.30	these] 1A; those 3A–1E
234.18	hardship] 1A, 1F, 1E; hardships 3A, ARE
234.18	field] 1A, 3A, ARE; fields 1F, 1E
234.19	and—and] 1A; and 3A–1E
235.39	St.] 1E, 1F; Saint 3A, ARE
236.10	a] 1A, ARE–1E; ~ a 3A
237.5	on] 1A, 1E; at 3A–1F
237.14	Dirk] 1A, 3A–1F; Dick 1E
237.25	tavern] 1A, 1E; inn 3A–1F
*237.34	grizzly] 1E, 3A, 1F; grisly ARE
237.40	damned] 1A; d——d 3A–1E
238.21	very] 1A, 3A–1E; a ~ ARE
238.27	old] 1A, 3A, ARE; odd 1F, 1E
238.30	descried] 1A, ARE–1E; described 3A
238.31	or yawl] 1A, 3A, ARE; yawl 1F, 1E
238.36	up on] 1A; upon 3A–1E
239.5	or marauding] 1A, 3A–1E; nor ~ ARE
239.5	or freebooting] 1A, 3A–1E; nor ~ ARE
239.26	those] 1A; these 3A–1E
239.27	these] 1A, 1F, 1E; those 3A, ARE
239.32	behemoth] 1A (Behemoth 1F, 1E); a ~ 3A, ARE
239.32	leviathan] 1A (Leviathan 1F, 1E); a ~ 3A, ARE
239.41	his] 1A, 3A, ARE; and ~ 1F, 1E

240.2	which] 1A; who 3A–1E
240.16	upon the] 1A, 1E; on ~ 3A–1F
240.43	their] 1A, 3A, ARE; the 1F, 1E
241.2	this] 1A, 3A–1E; the ARE
241.2	shrunk] 1A, 3A–1E; sunk ARE
241.7	upon] 1A, 3A, ARE; on 1F, 1E
242.3	farther] 1A, 3A–1F; further 1E
242.18	of] 1A, 3A, ARE; in 1F, 1E
242.20	on] 1A; at 3A–1E
242.24	and crucifixes] 1A; crucifixes 3A–1E
242.42	He readily] 1A, 3A–1E; Her eadily 1F

THE ADVENTURE OF THE BLACK FISHERMAN

243.21	bundling] 1A, 3A–1F, 2E; brindling 1E
243.25	cleft] 1A, ARE; ~ in the rock 3A–1E
245.23	bush] 1A, 3A–1E; brush ARE
245.38	off] 1A, 3A–1E; *omitted* ARE
246.1	or] 1A, 3A–1E; nor ARE
246.23	has] 1A; have 3A–1E
246.24	that] 1A, 1E; who 3A–1F
247.1	over] 1A, 3A–1E; ever ARE
247.6	grounds] 1A, 3A, ARE; ground 1F, 1E
247.22	shore] 1A, 1F, 1E; shores 3A, ARE
248.27	was] 1A, 3A, ARE; were 1F, 1E
248.35	drunk] 1A, 3A–1F; drank 1E
249.12	on] 1A; in 3A–1E
249.25	fogs of] 1A, 1E; ~ off 3A–1F
249.28	now] 1A, 3A, ARE; *omitted* 1F, 1E
250.2	yet] 1A, 3A–1E; *omitted* ARE
250.9	so] 1A; to 3A–1E
250.9	one's self] 1A, 3A–1F; oneself 1E
250.19	eye] 1A, 1F, 1E; eyes 3A, ARE
250.34	and ramping] 1A; a ramping 1E; ramping 3A–1F
252.9	a] 1A, 3A–1E; *omitted* ARE
252.35	sound] 1A, 3A–1E; *omitted* 2E
253.2	obliged] 1E, 3A–1F; ~ them 2E
253.27	the moss] 1A, 3A–1E; moss ARE
253.37	rock] 1A, 3A–1E; rocks ARE
253.41	farther] 1A, 3A–1E; further 1F
254.12	him] 1A, 3A, ARE; them 1F, 1E
255.3	council] 1A, 3A, 1E; counsel 1F, ARE
255.20	and] 1A; *omitted* 3A–1E

255.24	rumours] 1A, 3A, ARE; the ~ 1F, 1E
255.25	on] 1A, ARE; in 3A–1E
255.30	an] 1E, 3A, 1F; any ARE
256.5	women] 1A; woman 3A–1E
256.9	them] 1A, 3A, ARE; him 1F, 1E
256.32	Schott] 1A; Sebett 3A–1E
256.33	pronuncio] 1A; promisero 3A–1E
257.4	it] 1A, 3A–1E; *omitted* 1F
257.7	surtout] 1A; surcoat 3A–1E
258.1	sounds] 1A, 3A, ARE; sound 1F, 1E
258.34	*Pots tausends*] 1A, 3A, ARE; Potstansends 1E; Potstausends 1F, 2E
258.37	keep] 1A; kept 3A–1E
258.38	round] 1A, 1E; about 3A–1F
258.41	rose] 1A, 3A–1E; arose 1F
259.1	Doctor] 1A, 3A, ARE; Dr. 1F, 1E
259.26	to] 1A, 3A–1E; on 2E
260.1	bush] 1A, 3A–1E; brush ARE
260.10	farther] 1A, 3A–1F; further 1E
260.18	nor] 1A, 3A, ARE; or 1F, 1E
261.15	was] 1A, 1E; were 3A–1F
261.16	was] 1A, 1F; were 3A–1F
261.20	many] 1A, 3A–1E; *omitted* ARE
261.24	were] 1A, 3A–1F; are 1E
261.31	over] 1A; on 3A–1F
261.40	astride] 1A, 1F, 1E; aside 3A; ~ of ARE
262.3	corporal] 1A, 3A–1E; corporeal 2E
262.6	desertions] 1A, 3A; desertion ARE–1E
262.38	Roorback] 1A, 3A–1E; Roorbach 1F
263.22–23	red worsted] 1A, 2E; worsted red 3A–1F
263.27	them] 1A; it 3A–1E
264.2	a] 1A, 1F; their 3A–1F
264.11	to] 1A, 1E; till 3A–1F
264.12	the golden] 1A, 1F, 1E; a ~ 3A, ARE
264.25	sheer] 1A, 3A–1F, 2E; their 1E
264.28	leathern] 1A; leather 3A–1E

COMPOUND WORDS HYPHENATED AT
THE ENDS OF LINES

The first list records all compound or possible compound words hyphenated at the end of a line in the copy-texts which required a decision about whether a single word or a hyphenated word was intended. The second list records all words hyphenated at the ends of lines in the Twayne text whose intended form may be uncertain. They are listed as they would appear had they occurred mid-line.

LIST I

3.37	portfolio	74.28	forte-piano
3.10	barefaced	82.9	meantime
19.43	careworn	99.43	twopence
21.34	afterpart	108.14	headdress
26.9	nightfall	115.26	oarsmen
27.25	browbeaten	133.1	overgrown
29.4	superannuated	133.5	horseback
36.8	madhouse	141.23	wardrobe
37.21	nightmare	160.27–28	cut-throat
57.40	offcast	167.12	eyebrows
58.28	overpowered	194.29	sunburnt
58.33	outcast	213.25	freebooters
66.12	footsteps	233.40	Blackbeard
71.23	excommunicated	254.33	nightmare

LIST II

78.9–10	soapsuds	136.14–15	waistcoat
86.38–39	Blackheath	160.27–28	cut-throat
88.25–26	Crackscull	189.1–2	knapsack
113.33–34	good-for-nothing	239.5–6	freebooting
135.12–13	ill-will	259.5–6	pickaxe